Bonded Souls

Coral McCallum

The characters, names, places, brands, media and events are either the product of the author's imagination or are used fictitiously. Any similarity to real persons, living or deceased, is coincidental and not intended by the author.

The author acknowledges the trademarked status and trademark owners of the various products referenced within this work of fiction, which have been used without permission. The publication/use of these trademarks is not authorised, associated with or sponsored by these trademark owners.

Thank you for respecting the hard work of this author.

Well, here we are again for the third time in as many years. Still all feels surreal.

This time round, I've arrived at this point slightly later than originally planned.

"Book Baby 3" aka Bonded Souls proved to be a difficult child right from the outset. Mid-way through 2016 I paused to reflect on where the storyline was heading, then made the gut-wrenching decision to scrap almost half of what I'd written (some 45 000 words). It wasn't an easy decision, nor one I took lightly, but it proved to be the right one as "Book Baby 3" then settled down and has been a golden child ever since.

For those of you who are already Silver Lake fans, thank you for your patience and for your ongoing love and loyal support.

If you've not yet met Jake and Lori and the rest of the Silver Lake family, welcome to the fold.

Like the first two books in the series, Bonded Souls is written in UK English. Yes, I know it's set in the USA but I was taught UK English in school (a long time ago!). If the S's instead of Z's and the British terminology offend then I humbly apologise.

Again my "infamous five" have been an incredible source of love, support and, when I needed it most, motivation. This one really has been a long, hard labour of love and I seriously couldn't have completed it without your encouragement. I can't put into words how much your unwavering support means to me. Big hugs and much love to each of you.

Huge thanks also to my "cavalry", my beta readers. Your words of encouragement and your belief in me helped to make this dream a reality. Big love to you both.

My writer "fairy godmother" again stepped in and saved the day. With one "stroke", she made all my Photoshop woes disappear! Thank you!

I'd also like to thank my long-suffering family for their love and patience throughout the writing of this tale.

And, finally, a heartfelt thank you to YOU for picking up this copy of "Book Baby 3". Happy reading!

Hugs and much love to each and every one of you.

Coral McCallum   19th March 2017

Coral McCallum

2

As Lori drove out of the Lincoln Tunnel into the mayhem of the Manhattan traffic, she felt a flurry of nerves mixed with excitement flutter through her. Wedding lists and plans had been ticking over in her mind as she had driven up from the beach and, now that she was actually heading towards her apartment, the reality of it hit her. In four short days, she would be married to Jake; only four short days to go until she could reveal her final secret to him. While she had toured Europe with Jake and the rest of Silver Lake, the wedding plans had had to take a back seat. As she had waited around back stage and on the bus, Lori had busied herself with emails back and forth to Lucy and to David, doing her best to keep on top of things from several thousand miles away.

In her mind, she had pictured their wedding day as being clear and sunny with crisp, white snow on the ground. In reality, as she headed through the traffic, the weather was grey and wet, reminding her of the December weather of two years previously. Despite the warmth in the Mercedes, a chill ran through her. With a sigh of relief, Lori finally turned into the basement car park below her apartment block. Parking in her nominated spot, Bay 16, she spotted David's car parked in one of the guest spaces. Knowing he was already there made her smile. At least she wasn't arriving to an empty house. Having exchanged pleasantries with the garage attendant, she took the elevator up to the foyer where she was greeted warmly by Charles, the duty concierge.

"Thank you, Charles," said Lori warmly. "It's lovely to be home. Could you please bring my bags upstairs for me? They're all in the trunk of my car."

"Of course, Miss Hyde," he replied, accepting the key fob from her. "I'll bring them right up."

"Thanks."

Noting the large red and gold Christmas tree in the lobby, Lori headed past it towards the open elevator. When the doors opened again, Lori discovered that her own private lobby was also decorated with a matching tree and that a festive red and gold runner had been laid on the marble floor.

Opening the front door, she called out, "David?"

"In the lounge, Lori," came the reply.

When she entered her lounge room, Lori found him sitting with two smartly dressed young women. He quickly explained that they were the wedding coordinators and recapped on the plans that had been discussed so far. Everything was booked and arranged but there were still a few final last minute things to be put in place.

"When will the Christmas decorations go up in here?" asked Lori as she removed her coat, tossing it onto the couch. "I thought they'd be done by now."

"First thing tomorrow, Miss Hyde. We'll start with the hallway and lounge then set up the dining room. The caterer is meeting us here tomorrow afternoon at three to finalise the menu. We've arranged for the celebrant to come over on Saturday morning to meet you and Mr Power at eleven."

"That works out OK," agreed Lori. "Jake gets back today from Europe and will arrive here on Friday afternoon. David, have you sorted out accommodation for Jake's family and the other guests?"

"Of course, Lori," he assured her with a fatherly smile. "There are two apartments vacant on the fifth floor just now so I've made arrangements to use those. There's plenty of beds for everyone."

"Perfect."

It took another half an hour to run through the wedding planners' checklists. After a few minor amendments at Lori's request, they said their farewells and left her alone with David. Hugging her, he declared that she was looking fantastic.

"I don't feel it," she joked as she headed through to the kitchen to fetch them a drink. "I only arrived back on Tuesday, so I'm still feeling a bit jet lagged."

"How's did the tour go?" asked David, following her through to the dining room.

4

"Really well. They played their last European show on Wednesday night in Rome."

"So where did you fly home from?"

"Munich," replied Lori, filling the water reservoir of the coffee machine. "I stayed longer than I originally meant to. I met them in Edinburgh and intended to fly from Paris on December 11th, but Jake convinced me to stay a few extra days."

"All that travelling wouldn't suit me," laughed David. "But then I'm not as young as I once was."

"Nonsense," corrected Lori with a giggle. "Now, how are you feeling about walking me down the aisle on Sunday?"

"Honoured," replied the older man without hesitation.

Shortly before seven, Lori put the finishing touches to her make-up, picked up a folio folder from the hallway then headed out for the evening. While she had been on tour with Silver Lake, she had finalised the designs for her latest jewellery collection and had arranged to meet Lin, her designer friend from college, for dinner at a nearby Thai restaurant to go over the designs. In need of some fresh air, she abandoned her plan to hail a cab and, instead, decided to walk the short distance, drinking in the sounds of the city around her. The rain had stopped, the sky had cleared and it was shaping up to be a cold, frosty night. When she arrived, Lin was already seated at their table.

"You look fabulous, darling!" gushed the oriental designer as she hugged her friend tightly. "Any pre-wedding nerves yet?"

"Not yet," giggled Lori as she sat down. "I still don't believe it's actually happening."

"Well, you'd better believe it's happening, girl!" laughed Lin loudly. "I've even bought new Louis Vuitton's for the occasion."

"You and your shoe fetish."

"My one major weakness, I know," agreed the designer. "Now I see a folio. Have you brought me something special?"

"As promised," said Lori, passing her the folder. "Twelve new designs. Four pairs of earrings. Four pendants. Two bangles and two bracelets."

Opening the folder, the designer admired the twelve designs inside. As they ate their meal, both girls discussed the finer details of each of the designs, with Lori making a few tweaks under Lin's expert direction. With the work aspect of the evening out of the way, their conversation naturally drifted onto the tour and then the wedding. They talked flowers, dresses, menus and, finally, Lin asked about the music for the event.

"Jake's taking care of that," answered Lori. "I don't know what he has planned."

"When does he get here?" asked Lin, sipping her wine.

"The boys flew in from Italy today. Jake's coming up tomorrow with his sister and her family. He's staying with them tonight."

"And the whole band's coming?"

Lori nodded, "Yes. The others are arriving at some point tomorrow."

"I can't wait to see the twins," confessed Lin. "It's been months since I saw Maddy."

"Oh, they're adorable! They've been so good while the boys have been on tour. Maddy hired a nanny to watch them during the shows, but they found their way to the side of the stage a couple of times."

"Rock babies!" giggled Lin, the wine beginning take effect. "I can just imagine them as little mini-rock stars!"

"Well, they've got voices to rival Jake's!" declared Lori, remembering several sleepless nights on the tour bus as the twins screamed in harmony with each other. They had both been teething as the band had toured the length of the UK.

"I assume David's giving you away?"

Lori nodded, her mouth full of dessert.

"Who's your bridesmaid?"

"Grey's little girl, Becky," replied Lori, wiping her mouth with her napkin. "She's adorable. Wait till you see her."

"And the best man?"

"Men," corrected Lori softly. "Jake couldn't choose so all three of the guys from the band are best man."

Despite all the touring and travelling, Jake lay wide awake in the strange bed in his sister's guest room. A glance at his phone informed him it was after midnight; his internal body clock had long since surrendered and given up trying to determine the time of day. He could hear one of his nephew's snoring in the room next door. Reaching for his phone, Jake re-read his last message from

Lori. "Sweet dreams, rock star. Love you L x"

With a smile, he laid the phone back down on the night stand. Only a few short hours until he would be reunited with her. After having Lori with him for two full weeks on tour, the last couple of days had felt empty without her presence. The final two shows of the tour had been incredible. In Zurich, the Swiss fans had filled the concert hall, but seemed more reserved than the other European fans had been. When they had reached Rome the following day for the final show, the Italian fans' passion had blown the band away. All of them agreed that they had never heard such a loud crowd. The atmosphere in the venue had been amazing and Jake was genuinely sorry that Lori had missed it and the end of tour party that had followed.

His mind wandered to thoughts of the wedding and he ran through the music he had in mind plus his plans for a romantic dinner on Saturday evening. He had already booked a table at Lori's favourite Italian restaurant and requested that her favourite champagne be waiting on them.

"The ring!" he suddenly thought. Where had he put it? Just as panic was about to sweep in, he remembered that Lori had both their rings.

Earlier in the day he had received messages from both of his brothers and his dad promising to be in New York on Saturday. Knowing that his family were going to be there made him feel more than a little anxious. Although he had gone a long way to restoring relations with them, Jake still felt stressed at the thought of them all being together. He also felt guilty, knowing that Lori had no immediate family to invite.

With his mind still racing and no sign of sleep in sight, Jake slipped out of bed and crept quietly down to the kitchen to fetch himself a warm drink. His mother had always sworn that warm milk helped you to sleep. Trying not to make too much noise, Jake filled a mug with milk and popped it into the microwave to heat through. As the timer "pinged" a few seconds later, he heard the kitchen door open behind him and turned around to see Lucy standing there in her fleecy Pooh Bear pyjamas.

"Oh, it's you," she mumbled sleepily. "I thought it was one of the boys prowling."

"Sorry," apologised Jake, taking the mug from the microwave.

"I didn't mean to wake you."

"Warm milk?"

He nodded as he took a seat at the table. "Can't sleep and Mom always swore by it."

"Yeah, she did," sighed Lucy, fetching herself a clean mug from the dishwasher. "Mind if I join you?"

"Not at all," replied Jake, sipping his milk. "Feels kind of weird being here. It's like I've stepped into another life."

"Not enough partying?" teased Lucy as she sat down opposite him. "I would've thought after the last month that you'd be glad to be able to relax for a while."

"I am," began Jake. "But it takes a few days to adjust after a tour. Plus, I've a wedding on my mind."

"Nervous, big brother?"

"A bit," he confessed, sounding almost shy. "I was lying in bed thinking about everything. Thinking about family. Stressing a bit."

"And wishing mom was here to keep those guys under control," finished Lucy quietly.

Silently, Jake nodded.

They sat drinking their milk for a few minutes, both of them lost in their own memories.

"I wish she'd met Lori," said Jake, staring down into his empty mug. "Wish she'd seen the band come together. Wish she'd seen us play a show. Seen me get my act together."

Reaching out to touch his hand, Lucy said, "I like to think she's keeping an eye on us all. Sometimes I can hear her in my head. Hear her approval or disapproval. I know in my heart that she would be proud of you. Mom would've adored Lori. In a lot of ways, they are very alike."

With a wistful smile, Jake said, "I still hear her too. Usually it's when I'm writing late at night. I can almost smell her Chanel perfume as I hear her say to keep working on it. Hear her tell me when it's time to call it a day and get to bed."

"Speaking of bed," yawned Lucy, getting to her feet. "I'm going back to mine. We need to be up early to get everything packed in the car. I've no idea where we are putting all your gear!"

"Sweet dreams," said Jake with a yawn as he watched her head out the door and down the hall.

Organised chaos reigned over the apartment when Jake finally arrived mid-afternoon. The drive up from Philadelphia had taken twice as long as planned due to emergency roadworks along a two-mile section of the highway. Traffic had been backed up for miles following an earlier accident in the midst of the roadworks. Once they had cleared the traffic chaos, both of his nephews started protesting that they were hungry and needed the bathroom. It had taken them five hours to make the drive and his head was now pounding and his temper somewhat frayed.

Dumping his bags and guitar cases in the hallway, Jake was greeted by several people busily decorating the hall and lounge. There seemed to be people everywhere! Gazing round, he could see through the mayhem that it was all starting to come together just as he had visualised it.

"Lori!" he called out as he entered the lounge.

"In the dining room," came the sharp reply, his fiancée's voice sounding harassed and stressed.

Excusing himself past two young decorators carrying silver garlands, Jake headed into the dining room. He found Lori sitting at the table with the caterers.

"Hi, li'l lady," greeted Jake, coming over to take a seat at the table beside her.

"Hi yourself, rock star," she replied with a warm smile. "We're just finalising the menu and wine list for Sunday. Any special requests?"

"No pizza," joked Jake, draping his arm around her shoulders, his mood instantly lightening.

"Guaranteed no pizza, sir," reassured the caterer as he closed over his folder. "If you've nothing else to add, Miss Hyde, I'll leave you to it."

"Everything looks fine," agreed Lori, gathering together the paperwork in front of her. "What time will your team be here on Sunday?"

"We'll be here by eleven thirty."

"Fine. If I want to make any last minute adjustments, I'll call you by lunchtime tomorrow."

"Perfect."

Once alone in the dining room, Jake reached out and took Lori into his arms, kissing her tenderly. Burying his face in her long golden blonde hair, he whispered, "God, I've missed you, li'l lady."

"Missed you too, rock star," she purred as she ran her fingers through his hair. "How's the jet lag?"

"So, so," he replied softly. "Now, how about filling me in on what's going on around here?"

"Don't ask!" sighed Lori, sounding exasperated. "There was a delay with the decorations. Everything was scheduled to be done on Wednesday. They only arrived today and have been working on them all day. The catering is all sorted. The celebrant is coming to meet us tomorrow morning. That leaves the music. Do you have that under control?"

"Of course," declared Jake, feigning indignance. "Don't stress. This will all be perfect."

"Oh!" squealed Lori suddenly, giving him a start. "Where's Lucy?"

Laughing, Jake replied, "I wondered when you'd remember about her. I left them all getting settled downstairs. Nice apartment, by the way. She said to tell you she'd run up to see you later."

"And the others?"

"Grey and Becky will be here tonight. Rich and Linsey said they'd arrive tomorrow afternoon sometime. My brothers and my dad are arriving tomorrow afternoon," rhymed off Jake before adding, "Maddy and Paul are already at her apartment. They drove up last night. Maddy had a meeting today with Jason about the west coast tour in January."

"What about Todd and Kate?"

"They'll be here late tomorrow night. Kate's got to work tomorrow, but Todd's picking her up straight from work and bringing her here. Did you reserve a parking bay for him?"

Lori nodded.

"Don't stress, li'l lady. Everyone will be here in plenty time," promised Jake, as he got to his feet. "I'm going to take my gear down to the bedroom. Is that ok? There's nothing hanging up that I shouldn't see?"

"Nothing," replied Lori. "Then do you fancy going for a walk?"

"I'd rather not," admitted Jake. "I could use a little time to work on something for Sunday. I'll hide out in one of the bedrooms."

"Ok, I'll stay here until the decorators need in."

With his holdall and large wheeled suitcase deposited in the bedroom, Jake took his laptop out of his beaten up, leather book bag, grabbed his notebook and his guitar case then retreated to the sanctuary of the smallest of the three guest bedrooms. He set up his laptop on the dressing table with his notebook of lyrics beside it, then settled himself with his acoustic guitar on the low dressing table stool. After playing in concert halls all over Europe, it felt strange to be playing in the bedroom, resurrecting old memories from his teenage years of practicing at home. Smiling at the memory, he began to play. During the quieter moments on tour and on the bus, Jake had begun work on a new piece of music. Initially, he had intended to play it as an instrumental during the wedding service, but over the last few days, lyrics had begun to run through his head. Since his return, he hadn't had the opportunity to pull it all together. In the notebook, he had scribbled down a few phrases and the skeleton outline of the chorus. Within minutes, he was lost in the song as he worked the emotion that he wanted to convey into the lyrics.

"Jake!"

Lori calling his name startled him back to reality. A quick glance at his watch told him he had been closeted away for over three hours.

"Jake?" called Lori again.

"Just coming," he called back, quickly reaching to shut down his laptop. He had only just closed over the notebook with the lyrics when Lori opened the door.

"Are you ready for dinner, rock star?" she asked, sticking her head round the door. "Lucy is expecting us to join them downstairs."

"Give me five minutes," replied Jake, suddenly realising he was starving. "Any word from Grey?"

"They arrived an hour ago. He's already headed downstairs with Becky."

When Jake and Lori entered the fifth floor apartment a few minutes later, they collided with Jake's nephews, who were chasing Becky through the hallway. Grabbing Josh under the shoulders,

Jake swung the boy into his arms.

"No running in the house, young man," he cautioned sternly. "You almost knocked Lori over."

"Sorry," replied Josh looking guilty.

Setting him down on his feet, Jake suggested they go and watch TV quietly.

"Jake! Lori!" squealed Lucy from the kitchen. "You made it! Food's just arrived."

"What did you order?" asked Jake curiously. "I'm starving."

"The boys wanted pizza."

Jake groaned as Lori began to giggle at his side.

"What's wrong with pizza?" asked Lucy as she headed into the lounge carrying three huge flat boxes.

"Nothing at all," he sighed resignedly. "It's just I've seen enough of it to last me a lifetime."

"Do you want to send out for something else?" suggested Lori as they followed Lucy into the lounge.

"It's ok," said Jake with a smile. "I can eat pizza if I have to."

Soon they were all sitting around eating large slices of the best pizza Jake had ever tasted. His forward-thinking brother-in-law had packed a cooler full of beer and it was washing the pepperoni down nicely. After running through all the movie channels, Lucy had found a kid's Christmas film and the three children were sitting quietly eating, totally engrossed in the movie. This left the adults free to chat undisturbed. Prompted by the movie, their conversation centred around Christmas, making it a pleasant diversion from wedding chat for Lori. With all the planning and organising for the wedding, she had all but forgotten about Christmas. Jake's gift had been arranged months before and had been discretely delivered a few hours earlier, while he was ensconced in the guest room. As far as the day itself went though, she hadn't made any definite arrangements.

"We'll head home early on Christmas Eve," said Lucy in between mouthfuls of pepperoni.

"We promised the boys some ice skating on Monday," added Robb before continuing. "And someone wants to go shopping."

"What about you guys?" asked Grey curiously. "Any plans you care to share?"

Exchanging glances, Jake said, "None. We planned to stay here until the start of January but I hadn't really given Christmas much thought yet."

"Me neither," confessed Lori, looking slightly embarrassed.

"You can be forgiven just this once," teased Lucy. "You've both had other priorities."

And with that, the conversation returned to all things wedding related. After a few more minutes, Lori let out a squeal, startling them all, "Scott!"

"What about Scott?" asked Jake, his tone sharper than he'd intended. "He's taking the photos for us."

"Yes, but where's he staying? I've not included him in the sleeping plan," exclaimed Lori anxiously.

"Don't panic, li'l lady," laughed her fiancé. "He's staying with Maddy and Paul. He's flying back to London to spend Christmas was his family. Paul's taking him to the airport on Monday night so it made sense for him to stay with them. Not that he'll get much sleep with the meatballs still teething and screaming all night."

"And you?" continued Lori, staring intently at Jake. "Where are you sleeping tomorrow night?"

"With you," he replied innocently.

"No!" scolded Lucy, looking horrified. "It's bad luck to see your bride before the wedding. You'll need to stay down here with us or next door with Dad and your brothers."

"Think I'd rather take my chances with the teething meatballs," he muttered under his breath.

"You can stay here with us," offered Lucy, hugging her brother. "I've put the boys in one room so there's a spare bedroom. Grey, Becky can stay here on Sunday night if it makes it easier for you and Kola."

Immediately catching her meaning, the bass player blushed, before graciously accepting the offer.

"So, is everyone accounted for?" asked Lori, running through a mental list in her head.

"Yes," promised Jake warmly. "Now. It's getting late. I'm done in. Time to call it a night."

Pale, wintery sunlight was visible round the edges of the drapes when Jake wakened on Saturday morning. A glance at the clock told him they had both overslept. With her head resting on his chest, Lori was still sound asleep. When they had returned to the apartment the previous evening, they had gone straight to bed, leaving Grey and Becky to watch yet another Christmas movie upstairs in the lounge. It had been late, but Grey had relented and allowed his little girl to persuade him to let her stay up late. Once down in the bedroom, Jake had slowly and teasingly undressed Lori. She, in turn, had stripped him expertly. Leaving two crumpled piles of clothing discarded on the floor, they had snuggled under the thick feather duvet and lingered over their lovemaking, both of them conscious that this was their last night together before the wedding. Now, with Lori still slumbering beside him, Jake didn't want it to end.

Gently, he fingered a strand of her long, golden blonde hair, marvelling for the hundredth time at all the different shades to it. She stirred beside him, then slowly opened her eyes.

"Morning, li'l lady," he whispered, kissing the top of her head. "We've overslept."

"Morning," she yawned. "What time is it?"

"Almost ten," replied Jake, knowing as soon he told her she would break the "duvet spell".

"Shit," she muttered, but never moved.

"What time's the celebrant due here?"

"Shit!" she swore again "Eleven!"

Before Jake could say anything else, she had rolled over and thrown back the duvet.

"I'll go and check on our house guests," said Jake, getting up at a more leisurely pace. "Coffee will be waiting for you."

"Thanks," answered Lori, already in the bathroom.

They were still finishing off their late breakfast when the celebrant arrived. Ever discrete, Grey had taken Becky out earlier, promising her a trip to the American Girl store. Jake was pleasantly surprised when he opened the door to discover the celebrant was a woman. In his head, he had assumed it would be a man, an old man at that, but had never thought to ask. Over a cup of coffee, she walked them through the service and the vows, confirmed there would be readings and music and double checked the time.

"Any questions?" she asked as she closed over her notebook.

"I can't think of anything," said Lori, glancing over at Jake.

"Can you?"

"No," he agreed. "It seems quite straight forward."

"Well, if you've no questions for me, I'll take my leave," she said warmly. "I'll be here by one thirty. If you do think of anything, you have my cell number. I've two weddings this afternoon, but I'll pick up my messages between five and six."

"Thanks," said Jake, getting to his feet to walk her out.

At that moment, there was a knock at the door. When Jake and the celebrant reached the front door, they found Rich and Linsey in the hallway. Politely, the celebrant excused herself, allowing Jake to welcome his fellow band member and former colleague into the apartment. Hearing their voices, Lori came rushing out into the hall to join them. After more hugging and kissing, she showed them both downstairs to their room. While the guitarist and his girlfriend got themselves settled, Lori despatched Jake to her favourite deli to pick up some sandwiches for lunch.

"This place looks magical," declared Linsey when she entered the lounge a few minutes later. "A real Narnia setting."

"All we need is some snow," joked Lori, guiding her through to the dining room. "The decorators have done an amazing job though. It's exactly what I had pictured in my head."

"It's not too late to change your mind, Lori," teased Rich with a mischievous grin.

"And why would she want to do that, Ricardo?" asked Jake as he walked in carrying a bag from the deli.

Their relaxed, good humour lasted throughout their leisurely lunch. In almost a replay of the dinner conversation from the night before, they idly chatted about their plans for Christmas before returning to discuss the wedding.

"Speaking of which," began Jake. "Do you have plans for this afternoon, Rich? I need your help with something."

"Well, we were going to go shopping."

"Lori and I can go," suggested Linsey swiftly. "I need to pick up a couple of last minute gifts."

"Fine by me," agreed Lori. "What do you need to get?"

"I'll tell you on the way," replied the art teacher with a wink.

"Be back before six," cautioned Jake softly. "I'm taking my fiancée out to dinner. Table's booked for seven."

Warmth and the buzz of conversation welcomed Jake and Lori as they entered Amarone a few minutes after seven. Spotting them almost instantly, Marco, the maître d', was at their side showing them to a discrete, candlelit corner table and offering to take their coats. He helped Lori to slip her wool jacket from her shoulders, then turned to take Jake's leather jacket. Politely Jake declined the offer, hanging his jacket over the back of the chair instead. Beside the table, as requested, sat an ice bucket with a bottle of Lori's favourite champagne chilling inside. Both of them were relieved to note that none of the other diners had given them a second glance.

Having hung Lori's jacket up, Marco returned with the menus and offered to open the champagne. Suppressing a giggle, Lori watched as he struggled with the cork before it finally came loose with a resounding POP.

"Can we keep that one, please?" asked Jake, his question surprising both the maître d' and his fiancée.

"But of course, Mr Power," replied Marco, handing the cork to him.

Lori looked at him quizzically.

"Call me old fashioned," began Jake, after they had been left alone with their champagne. "My mom always used to keep the cork from any special bottles. She said it brought luck if you put a silver coin in the cork."

Rummaging in his pocket, Jake produced a dime and rammed it hard into the swollen damp cork base.

"A gift from me to you to wish you luck for tomorrow," he said warmly, passing the cork to Lori.

Giggling, she accepted it graciously, turning it over in her hand a few times before putting it carefully into her small purse.

"Thank you," she whispered, suddenly feeling very emotional.

Raising his glass, Jake smiled at her, "Here's to us, li'l lady."

"To us," echoed Lori, mirroring his smile before taking a small sip from the glass.

Amidst more nervous laughter, they both opted for their favourite dishes from the menu, realising that they almost always chose the same thing when they dined there. As ever, the meal was delicious, both of them relishing in the company of the other. Completely relaxed, they chatted animatedly about their hopes and fears about the wedding, both of them confessing to being more than a little nervous about being the centre of attention for the day.

"That's rich coming from you," laughed Lori. "You can stand on that stage and sing to thousands of fans, but you're scared of facing our closest friends and family in the lounge room!"

Blushing, Jake nodded silently.

"I love you, rock star," she said, reaching across the table to take his hand.

"I love you too, Mz Hyde," he declared formally. "And to show it, I have a gift, well two actually, for you."

Jake reached into the inside pocket of his leather jacket and brought out two small, silver, cloth bags with a blue cord fastening each of them.

"I wasn't sure when was the right moment to give you these," he said, feeling like a tongue-tied teenager on a first date.

Accepting the two small bags, Lori carefully untied the bows and lifted out two silver bangles. The two silver bangles Jake had purchased in London when they visited the British Museum. Looking puzzled, Lori turned them over in her hand.

"They're perfect, Jake," she breathed. "Thank you."

Both bangles were an identical Mobius strip design; both had a different verse engraved into them. Silently, she read the first one, "May all beings be peaceful. May all beings be happy. May all beings be safe. May all beings awaken to the light of their true nature. May all beings be true."

"It's a Metta prayer," explained Jake shyly. "A Buddhist meditation."

"And the other one?" asked Lori, admiring it.

"It's an extract from a Shakespearean sonnet. Sonnet 116 to be exact," he replied. Clearing his throat, Jake began to recite the entire verse, that he had memorised for just this moment,

"Let me not to the marriage of true minds
Admit impediments. Love is not love
Which alters when it alteration finds,
Or bends with the remover to remove:
O no; it is an ever-fixed mark,
That looks on tempests, and is never shaken;
It is the star to every wandering bark,
Whose worth's unknown, although his height be taken.
Love's not Time's fool, though rosy lips and cheeks

Within his bending sickle's compass come;
Love alters not with his brief hours and weeks,
But bears it out even to the edge of doom.
If this be error and upon me proved,
I never writ, nor no man ever loved."

"Beautiful," sighed Lori, feeling her emotions threatening to overcome her again. "Thank you. I feel guilty now. I didn't bring you a gift."

"No need," assured her fiancé with a smile. "Will you wear these tomorrow?"

"Of course," she promised, slipping them back into their little bags. "They are absolutely perfect."

"That's what I thought when I saw them in London."

"London?" she echoed.

"I've had these since our trip to the British Museum back in October," confessed Jake. "I couldn't choose between them so thought "what the hell" and bought them both."

"And here I thought you only had your mind on the ancient Egyptians when you were in the gift store," giggled Lori, remembering their afternoon in the museum fondly.

Sitting at her dressing table, Lori stared at her reflection in the mirror. She had shunned all offers of help with her hair and her make-up, preferring to do it herself. The apartment was surprisingly quiet with less than an hour to go before the ceremony. As she brushed her hair, Lori could hear Lucy talking to Becky and her boys in the spare room. She had offered to get them ready to leave Lori more time to focus on herself.

Lori's wedding dress hung on the outside of the closet, the crystal beads casting small rainbows of light on the floor.

"Show time," thought Lori as she got to her feet.

Her hands were shaking with nerves as she lifted down the white silk dress. Just as she was about to call to Lucy to come and help her, there was a soft knock at the door and Maddy stepped in.

"Need a hand?" she asked with a smile.

"Perfect timing," giggled Lori nervously. "Can you help me with my dress?"

"I'd be honoured," declared Maddy proudly. "How're your nerves?"

"Almost under control," said Lori as she carefully stepped into the dress.

Gently, Maddy helped her to pull it up and, once Lori was happy with the way it was sitting, Maddy began to fasten the tiny buttons that ran down the back of the bodice. It was a stunning dress – strapless with a sweetheart neckline, crystal beaded bodice and flowing A-line skirt with a small train, the edge of which was decorated with an intricate beaded design of music notes and two treble clefs.

"Oh, Lori!" sighed Maddy, when she stepped back to look at her friend. "You look beautiful, darling."

"Thanks," replied Lori blushing. "Better than I did two years ago today?"

"Much," agreed Maddy, shuddering at the memory of seeing Lori lying in the hospital after her accident. "You look radiant!"

A pair of silver ballet pumps sat beside the dressing table. Lori carefully walked over and slipped her slender feet into them. Her jewellery lay out on the dressing table. She had chosen to wear the silver set that Silver Lake had given her for her thirtieth birthday. The charm bracelet and pendant matched her dress perfectly. Beside them lay the two bangles that Jake had given her the night before. Carefully, she began to put her jewellery on under Maddy's watchful gaze.

"Cane or no cane?" asked Maddy, noting a silver cane with a crystal handle propped up in the corner.

"I'm ok just now," Lori assured her, "But maybe later."

"Don't overdo things," cautioned her friend, showing a rare soft streak. "You looked so pale and tired on tour. I was beginning to worry about you."

"I'm fine."

"If you're sure. Now, is there anything else I can do to help?" asked Maddy, glancing at her watch. "I'd better get back to Paul to help him. He's stressing with the kids and his lines."

"On you go. I'll be fine here till David arrives."

A short while later, Lori heard the first of their guests arriving. She also heard Jake's voice as he greeted them. Knowing he was upstairs helped to calm her growing nerves. In the room next door, she could hear Lucy losing the battle to keep the kids quiet. Carefully gathering up her skirts, Lori crept out of the master bedroom and knocked on the other bedroom door.

"Come in if you dare!" called Lucy brightly as Lori opened the door.

"Lori!" cried Becky excitedly. "You look like a fairy princess!"

The little girl looked wonderful in her midnight blue dress with silver sash. Her blonde hair has been coaxed into long ringlets and they danced as she jumped up and down with excitement. Both Sam and Josh looked very grown up in their black trousers, white shirts and blue and silver brocade waistcoats. Josh was to carry the wedding rings during the ceremony and his older brother was to perform a reading.

"Lori, Becky's right," breathed Lucy, tears glistening in her eyes. "You look stunning."

"Thanks," said Lori, blushing again. "I was getting nervous waiting next door on my own."

"Not long to wait," Lucy said, looking at the clock. "It's almost two."

Behind them they could hear footsteps on the oak staircase and a moment later David appeared. He stopped in his tracks when he saw Lori standing before him.

"Oh, if only your father could see his little girl now," he sighed wistfully. "You look beautiful, Lori."

"Oh, David," began Lori, going over to take his hand, "He'd be having a fit at all this fuss."

"True," agreed the older man with a sad smile. "The celebrant sent me to see if you are nearly ready. All of your guests are seated in the lounge."

"Ready as I'll ever be," she confessed.

"I'll leave you two to gather your thoughts," suggested Lucy as she herded the three children up the stairs. "We'll be waiting for you at the top of the stairs."

"We'll be two minutes," promised David as he guided Lori back into the master bedroom.

Upstairs in the lounge, Jake was anxiously pacing up and down in front of the fireplace. All of their guests were already seated around the room, including his two brothers and father in their air force dress uniforms. Beside him, his three band mates were standing casually chatting. All three of them were dressed the same – black shirt and pants with a silver waistcoat. Jake fiddled nervously with a loose thread at the button of his own blue and silver brocade waistcoat. He too was wearing black pants, but had opted for a white shirt. A leather cord held his long hair neatly at the nape of his neck. He glanced over at the corner where two of his acoustic guitars sat beside Rich's ready for later.

"Relax," said Grey, putting a hand on his shoulder. "She'll be here in a minute. Look, the kids are already out in the hall."

Forcing a smile, Jake looked up and saw his nephews standing beside Becky in the doorway. The little girl gave him a shy smile; he blew her a kiss.

Downstairs, Lori ran the brush through her hair one final time, then turned to face David, who was hovering anxiously in the doorway.

"Show time," she said softly.

"Show time" echoed the older man, his voice catching with emotion. "Your dad and your mom would be so proud of you today, Lori."

"I know. I'm wearing mom's wedding ring on my right hand. I'm sure they're watching this circus," replied Lori with a sad smile.

"Why did you choose today? I've been meaning to ask."

"It seemed the best way to put the spectre of the accident behind me once and for all," she began. "And it fitted well with everyone's busy schedules."

"It's the perfect date," he agreed, giving her a hug. "I don't want to remember that accident any more than you do. I was so scared we were going to lose you that Christmas."

"No such luck," joked Lori in a feeble attempt to lighten the mood.

"Well, it's an honour to give your safe keeping over to Jake," said David. "Now, let's not keep him waiting any longer."

Slowly, they made their way up the wide oak staircase, Lori taking extra care not to tread on the hem of her gown. When they reached the top, Lucy signalled to them to stay out of sight. She spoke quietly to the three children, passed Becky her small posy of white roses, then gave Lori the larger bouquet of roses. Without a word, she entered the lounge and took her seat between her husband and her father. This was the cue for the bridal music to start – All I Ask of You from Phantom of the Opera.

With a deep breath, Lori took David's arm and together they walked slowly into the lounge with her three small attendants following in single file behind. Ahead of her, Lori saw Jake standing facing the fireplace, trembling slightly. As she was almost level with him, he turned to face her. His whole face lit up as he smiled at her, melting away the last of her nerves.

Having fulfilled his duties, David discretely moved to sit beside his wife.

"Ladies and gentlemen, friends and family," began the celebrant warmly. "We are here to celebrate the marriage today of Lori Hyde to Jacob, sorry, Jake Power. If anyone knows of any reason why we cannot now proceed, please speak up or forever remain silent."

She paused for a few seconds before continuing. Her words

were a blur to both Jake and Lori, who stood gazing at each other. Before they exchanged their wedding vows, the celebrant called Sam forward to perform his reading. It had been too much for him to memorise so Lucy had typed it up, mounted it on silver card and tied it in a scroll with a blue ribbon.

Theatrically, he unfurled the scroll, looked around the room and in a clear, confident and well- rehearsed voice began, "Guess How Much I Love You by Sam McBratney."

He paused to smile at Lori and Jake then continued, "Little Nutbrown Hare, who was going to bed, held on tight to Big Nutbrown Hare's very long ears. He wanted to be sure Big Nutbrown Hare was listening. "Guess how much I love you," he said."

Everyone in the room listened, entranced, as the young boy told the story of the two hares. As he reached the end of the tale, Sam began to roll up the scroll. "Then he lay down close by and whispered with a smile, "I love you right up to the moon and back.""

"Thank you, Sam," said the celebrant. "I'm sure everyone will agree that that was beautifully read."

As Sam stepped back, Josh stepped forward carrying the small, square, blue, velvet cushion with silver braided edges. The two wedding bands lay in the centre. He stood shyly beside the celebrant.

"Jake, will you please take Lori by the left hand and repeat after me," began the celebrant formally. "I, Jacob Power, take you, Lori Hyde…"

I, Jake Power, take you, Lori Hyde, to be my beloved wife, to have and to hold you, to honour and treasure you, to be at your side in sorrow and in joy, in good times and in bad, and to love and cherish you always. I promise you this from my heart for all the days of my life."

With a deep breath, Jake lifted Lori's tiny white gold band and slipped it onto her finger.

"Lori," prompted the celebrant softly.

"I, Lori Hyde, take you, Jake Power, to be my beloved husband, to have and to hold you, to honour and to treasure you, to be at your side in sorrow and joy, in the good times and in the bad, and to love and cherish you always. I promise you this from my heart, for all the days of my life."

Her hand trembling, Lori lifted Jake's titanium band and slipped it onto his finger.

"I'd like to welcome forward the best men to bless this marriage," said the celebrant, signalling for the three members of Silver Lake to step forward.

Rich was first to speak, "A traditional Apache blessing for you both. Now you will feel no rain, for each of you will be the shelter for the other. Now you will feel no cold, for each of you will be warmth to the other. Now there will be no loneliness, for each of you will be companion to the other."

Next it was Paul's turn to continue the blessing, "Now you are two persons, but there is only one life before you. May beauty surround you both in the journey ahead and through all the years. May happiness be your companion and your days together be good and long upon the earth."

Last to speak was Grey, who had his words neatly written on a prompt card. He was visibly shaking as he began, "Treat yourselves and each other with respect and remind yourselves often of what brought you together. Give the highest priority to the tenderness, gentleness and kindness that your connection deserves. When frustration, difficulties and fear assail your relationship, as they threaten all relationships at one time or another, remember to focus on what is right between you, not only the part which seems wrong. In this way, you can ride out the storms when clouds hide the face of the sun in your lives – remembering that even if you lose sight of it for a moment the sun is still there. And, if each of you takes responsibility for the quality of your life together, it will be marked by abundance and delight."

"Thank you, gentlemen," said the celebrant. "Now all that is left for me to say is that I declare you to be husband and wife. Jake, you may kiss your bride."

Needing no second invitation, Jake drew Lori into his arms and kissed her tenderly to a round of applause and cheers from their gathered friends and family. Reluctantly, the newlyweds broke their embrace, Jake keeping a protective arm around Lori's waist.

"Ladies and gentlemen, to draw this ceremony to a close, I'd like to invite the groom to come forward."

Pausing to brush another kiss on Lori's cheek, Jake stepped forward towards the guitars set up in the corner. Taking his cue,

Rich followed him, both of them quickly getting settled to play. Without a word, both the musicians began to play the familiar introduction to Simple Man.

As Lori stood with Grey and Paul behind her, Jake started to sing, his voice husky with the emotions of the occasion, "Mama told me when I was young. Come sit beside me, my only son...."

Tears sparkled unshed in Lori's eyes as he sang the song with more love and deep felt emotion than she had ever heard him pour into it. She was oblivious to the gathering of friends and family while she stood spellbound by Jake's performance. Rich's playing was soft and subtle, allowing the groom to shine. By the time Jake had reached the final chorus, a single tear of happiness slid down Lori's cheek.

Having placed his guitar back on its stand, Jake moved swiftly over to stand beside Lori again. Taking his hand, she squeezed it gently and whispered, "That was perfect."

"Ladies and gentlemen," announced the celebrant. "It gives me great pleasure to introduce you to Mr and Mrs Jake Power!"

The lounge echoed with the sound of their guests cheering and clapping. Soon the newlyweds were swamped by people congratulating them. There were tears, hugs and kisses a plenty. Right on cue, the hostesses who had been waiting unseen in the dining room, began to circulate with trays of champagne and canapés. In the midst of it all, Scott was trying to get to the happy couple to invite them out into the hall to take some formal photographs. Eventually, he caught up with Jake, who promised he would fetch his wife and meet the photographer in the hallway.

While their guests mingled in the lounge, Scott gathered the wedding party together. After almost an hour, he suggested that he take a few outdoor shots of Jake and Lori. He had already captured every combination of family and attendants, but sensed that the happy couple needed some quiet space for a few minutes.

Despite the presence of several patio heaters, the roof terrace was chilly. It had snowed overnight, dusting the city in a layer of white. It was now a cloudless, crisp winter's day; Lori's dream day.

"I'd love to take you over to the park," commented Scott casually as Jake stood with his arm protectively around Lori's waist.

"Too public," replied Jake bluntly. "But I know what you

mean."

"We could sneak over," said Lori, warming to the idea. "It would look stunning in the photos. Sun and snow and just us."

"I guess," relented Jake, sensing he was losing the battle. "Won't you be cold?"

"I've a wrap that will keep me warm enough," countered Lori with a mischievous smile.

"OK, I surrender!" laughed Jake, hugging her. "Lead the way, Mrs Power."

Once back indoors, it took them a few minutes to get organised. Simon agreed to drive them over to Central Park. While Lori went downstairs to fetch her wrap, Jake lifted a glass of champagne, sipping it patiently as he waited for her to return.

Luck was on their side when Simon stopped the car near the Natural History Museum. Within a few yards of entering the park, they found an ideal spot for their photographs. The snow was still largely untouched, creating the perfect festive background. Apart from a couple of dog walkers, this small corner of the park was deserted. Deciding to brave the cold, Lori removed her silver wrap, passing it to Scott and posed with Jake for a few quick shots, before the winter chill got the better of her. Feeling her shivering by his side, Jake called a halt. He fetched her wrap, gently placing it over her bare shoulders.

"Too cold for this, li'l lady wife," he said, holding her close. "Let's head back."

"You're right," she sighed with a satisfied smile. "Scott, could you give us a minute alone, please?"

"Sure. I'll head back to the car."

Taking Jake's hand, Lori led him down a side path towards one of the park's many small bridges.

"You ok?" asked Jake when she stopped halfway across the bridge.

"Couldn't be better. I just wanted you to myself for a minute," she replied, taking both his hands in hers. "I've got something to tell you."

"You have?"

Lori nodded. Gazing up into his hazel eyes, she said softly, "I'm pregnant."

He stared at her in stunned disbelief as the news slowly filtered through to him.

"You're going to be a daddy, rock star."

Wrapping his arms around her, Jake held her tight, tears escaping down his cheeks.

"Oh, Lori," he whispered, when he was able to speak. "You're sure? When?"

"I'm sure. The baby's due late June," she said with a smile. "I'm about twelve weeks, I think."

"Why didn't you say before? You were out on the road. I never suspected a thing," he blurted out, then he added, "A dad? I'm going to be a dad?"

"Yes," she repeated with a giggle. "I didn't want to worry you or distract you when you were so focused on the tour. I've been lucky. No morning sickness so it was easier to hide things. The few mornings I did feel rough, I passed it off as too much wine or lack of sleep."

"Have you seen a doctor?" he asked, still not believing what he was hearing.

"I've an appointment for the first week in January when we get home. Are you pleased?"

"Thrilled to bits! I just want to tell the whole world!" laughed Jake grinning broadly.

"Well, let's start by telling our friends and family," suggested Lori. "Not a word on the way back to the house though."

"Let's save the news for dinner," suggested Jake. "I know we said no speeches, but we never ruled out announcements. I still can't believe you kept this a secret from all of us. Did you tell Maddy?"

"Not a soul until I could tell you," she confessed as they turned to go back to the car.

Dinner was served at five o'clock sharp with all twenty-five of their guests seated at the one table, including two high chairs for Wren and Hayden. Before the waitresses began to serve, Jake got to his feet.

"Folks, I know we said no speeches today, but I want to say a few words," he began nervously. "Thank you all for being here today. For making it the perfect day. I didn't think it could get any more perfect until Lori told me something while we were over at the park."

Every eye in the room was on him.

"My wife and I would like to announce that we're having a baby!"

This unexpected announcement prompted squeals and shrieks of delight. Both Maddy and Lucy were the first to rush round the table, from opposite sides, to hug and congratulate them both. Eventually, Grey stood up and clinked his glass to get everyone's attention, "Guys, I'd like to propose a toast. To the new Mr and Mrs Power and to new life."

"To Jake and Lori!" echoed Rich and Paul, standing beside him.

As the catering staff served the soup course, Maddy was the first to ask when the baby was due.

"June," replied Lori, relieved that her secret was finally out in the open. "Late June, I think."

"That means you must have been pregnant the whole time you were on tour with us," said Maddy, quickly doing the mental maths. "How in God's name did you keep that to yourself, girl?"

This triggered a ripple of laughter around the table before Lori replied, "It wasn't easy. Fortunately, I've not had any real morning sickness. You were all so caught up in the tour schedule you never really noticed when I did feel a bit rough."

"Now that you mention it," admitted Grey. "There were a few days when you were a bit green about the gills. A bit quiet. I just assumed you were hungover!"

"Never assume, Grey," teased Lori playfully. "This "hangover" has feet."

Once the wedding feast was over, their guests drifted back through to the lounge, some of them venturing out onto the terrace for some air. Both Jake and Lori made a conscious effort to speak to everyone. The strain of being on her feet for so long was beginning to take its toll on Lori and she quietly asked Becky to fetch her cane from the bedroom. Leaning heavily on it a few minutes later, she went over to talk to Jake's father and brothers. They had lingered in the dining room, enjoying a second cup of coffee.

"Are you coming through to the lounge?" Lori asked. "The boys are going to play a few songs and we'll see where that takes this party."

"Wouldn't miss it," declared Ben Power. "This is a beautiful place you have here, Lori."

"Thank you," she said, taking a seat at the table for a moment. "Did you get settled in the apartment downstairs ok?"

"It's perfect," said Simon warmly. "You didn't need to go to all that hassle for us. We could've got a hotel room."

"The perks of owning the building," joked Lori, noticing the three Power men exchanging glances.

"You what?" said Peter, his eyes wide.

"Well, Hyde Properties to be more accurate," she corrected. "Those apartments were empty, so I had them prepared for this weekend. They'll be up for lease again in January if you're interested."

"Nice little earner," mused Ben Power softly.

"It pays the bills," laughed Lori, getting to her feet. "I'm going to head back through to find Jake. Come through when you're ready."

As she made her way down the hall, Lori met David and his wife preparing to leave.

"Do you have to leave so early?" she asked as David hugged her.

"I'm sorry, my dear. We've an early morning flight to catch," apologised Olivia calmly. "And, much as we love Jake, that music gives me a headache."

"Where are you flying to?"

"Las Vegas," revealed David. "We've always said we'd like to spend the holidays there one year. This is the year."

"Sounds like fun."

"Thank you for a wonderful day, Mrs Power," said David warmly. "And congratulations again about the baby."

"Thank you for everything. I couldn't have done it without you," said Lori, hugging him tight.

Through in the lounge someone had rearranged the furniture back into its usual position. Rich and Jake were organising themselves to play a few songs to kick start the evening's entertainment. Two of the chairs had been brought through from the dining room and placed in front of the fireplace. Some of the guests were out on the terrace enjoying the view of the city all lit up for the night. Out in the hallway, the three children were playing quietly at the top of the stairs.

When he saw Lori walk back into the room and take a seat on the couch, Jake took that as his cue to play. Nudging Rich to come and join him, he took his seat and settled himself with his guitar. Just as they had rehearsed the previous afternoon, the two musicians played three classic rock tracks that he knew were favourites of Lori's. By the time they had finished the third song, all of the guests were gathered in the living room. Even the three children had crept into the back of the room.

"Folks, I'd like to play something special," began Jake, suddenly feeling very self-conscious in front of his friends and family. "I wrote this recently just for today. I had planned to play it earlier during the ceremony as an instrumental, but changed my mind and added some lyrics. This is," he paused and laughed nervously, "without a title as yet!"

Jake reached round to the back of his neck and loosened his ponytail, allowing his hair to fall forward in an attempt to hide his embarrassment at having no title for his new song. He sighed deeply, then with a nod to Rich, began to pick out a gentle country rock melody. Within a few bars, Rich had joined in with a simple accompaniment. When Jake started to sing, his tone was husky and warm. He sang about the changes in his life; he sang about the highs and the lows. The lyrics painted a clear picture for his captive audience of the influence Lori had had on him and of how grateful he was to have her in his life. As the last notes faded out through the room, he bowed his head, allowing his hair to fall over his face once more to hide his emotions. While their guests called for more, Jake sat silently trying to regain some self-control. Eventually, Lori called for calm and asked if the boys would play Guns N Roses Sweet Child o' Mine for her.

"Ask for an easy one, Mrs Power," teased Rich with an impish grin.

Lori's request started the requests flowing from their friends. Some chose Silver Lake songs; some asked for other well-known favourites. After an hour, Jake called Todd forward to take over from Rich then two songs later he beckoned Kate to join him. Initially, she tried to refuse, but, after some gentle cajoling, she was tempted out of her seat. She had a quick whispered conversation with Jake then agreed to sing Rod Stewart's Handbags And Gladrags. It had been a long time since Lori had heard the girl sing and she was amazed anew by the calibre of her voice. Beside her, Maddy whispered, "That girl's incredible. I need to speak to her."

"She's got so much talent," agreed Lori. "But she's committed to her studies for now."

"Colleges get plenty of vacation time," countered Maddy with a conspiratorial wink.

Midnight had long since passed and the musicians had laid down their guitars for the night, allowing Jake's iPod to provide the background music as the last of the wedding guests sat chatting quietly. Noticing how tired Lori was beginning to look, Jake came over to kneel in front of her.

"Time for bed, li'l lady wife," he said softly, taking her hand

"But we've still got guests," Lori began, before a yawn swallowed up the rest of her protest.

"Guests who are all staying the night," he reminded her as he helped her to her feet. "Come on, beautiful wife. You look worn out."

"I guess," she sighed with a weary smile

"Night, folks," called Jake as he led Lori towards the door. "Whoever is up first, remember to make a pot of coffee."

"Night," called back Grey as he cuddled in closer to Kola on the couch.

Once down in the bedroom, Lori took a seat at her dressing table while Jake began to get undressed. He removed his waistcoat and his shirt, then came over to assist her. As she stood up to allow him to unbutton her dress, Lori swayed slightly with fatigue. Clumsily, Jake fumbled the tiny buttons undone.

"You looked incredible today," he said softly as the dress cascaded down around her feet.

"You didn't look so bad yourself, rock star," she replied. Chivalrously, Jake held her hand to steady her as she carefully stepped out of the sea of silk at her feet.

Slowly, he slid down her lacy hooped underskirt and was about to remove her underwear when she turned away out of his reach. With a tired but mischievous smile, Lori stepped forward and began to unfasten his trousers. Soon they were both standing facing each other in their underwear. Expertly, Jake reached round and unhooked her bra. It fell slowly to the floor, revealing her smooth breasts, already beginning to swell with maternal fullness. Within a few seconds, they were both standing in the middle of the room naked. Tentatively, Jake reached out and ran his warm hand across her slightly rounded belly.

"I can't believe I never noticed. Never guessed," he whispered, bending to kiss her tummy. "Our baby's really growing in there?"

"Yes," breathed Lori, running her fingers through his long, thick hair.

"Is it safe to make love to you? I won't hurt you?" he asked, his voice husky with emotion.

"Perfectly safe," she promised him as she led him by the hand over to their bed.

As they lay on their sides facing each other, Jake delivered light feathery kisses to his new bride's neck and shoulders. Gently, he rolled her over onto her back and sensually kissed her breasts, teasingly licking each erect nipple. Kneeling astride her, he kissed her stomach, murmuring softly to the baby. His words were muffled and quiet and Lori couldn't make out what he was saying to their unborn child. Ever so gently, he parted her legs, then finding her wet and ready to receive him, entered her slowly. He began to move with long, leisurely, tender strokes. Understanding that he was being deliberately careful, Lori tried to hold back her orgasm. The slower Jake moved inside her, the quicker it built. In a moment of naughtiness, she bit him on the shoulder.

"Patience, li'l lady wife," he whispered as he quickened his movements.

He thrust hard and fast, feeling her respond as their bodies came to an overwhelming climax in unison. They lay entwined in each other's arms for a few minutes, with Jake nuzzling her neck. Just as she was beginning to drift off to sleep, Lori felt him harden again inside her, felt her own body respond. This time the sex was urgent and intense, a complete contrast to their earlier lovemaking. Satiated and spent, Jake rolled off her and lay propped up on one elbow watching her.

"Today really has been perfect," he sighed as he ran his hand over her stomach again.

"It has," purred Lori, snuggling closer to him. "And I'm glad my secret is out in the open at last."

"I still can't believe you kept that news to yourself. How long have you known?"

"Six weeks," she confessed with a sleepy giggle.

"You knew the whole time you were with us?"

"I found out the day before the New York show."

"You really are quite something, Mrs Power," he said, kissing her slowly.

Beside him, she giggled.

"What's so funny?"

"Mrs Power," she laughed. "It sounds strange."

"Better get used to it, li'l lady wife."

The newlyweds slept late the next morning, left undisturbed by their houseguests. Despite the late night, Grey and Kola had been up early and had crept out of the apartment before eight to join Lucy and her family for breakfast down on the fifth floor. The noise of them climbing the stairs had wakened Rich and Linsey, who were the first upstairs and into the kitchen. Without being asked, while Linsey made a pot of coffee, Rich gathered up all the dirty glasses and party debris from the lounge and dining room. Together, they washed off the glassware by hand, not wanting the noise from the dishwasher to disturb everyone. They had just sat down to a breakfast of coffee and leftover canapés when Todd and Kate walked in. All former teacher/student barriers had long since melted and the four of them sat in the dining room debating what they were going to do for the day.

Kate had just made a fresh pot of coffee when a freshly showered Jake wandered in. Dressed in a worn pair of jeans and thick checked shirt with a white T-shirt underneath, he looked more relaxed than he had in his formal wedding outfit.

"Ah, the real Jake Power's back!" teased Linsey. "Good morning!"

"Morning," he replied as he headed through to the kitchen to fetch some juice. "Is everyone ok today?"

"Fine, now I've had some caffeine," answered Rich, his voice sounding hoarse. "Awesome wedding yesterday."

"It was an amazing day," agreed Jake. "So, what's everyone's plans for today?"

"We've tentatively arranged to meet the others at the Rockefeller Plaza at one," explained Linsey, pouring Jake a coffee as he sat down at the table. "Your sister has ice skating booked for one thirty. We thought it would be fun to tag along."

"I've not skated in at least fifteen years," admitted Jake, adding half and half to his coffee. "Could be fun."

"What could be fun?" asked Lori from the doorway.

"Ice skating with Lucy and the kids," replied Jake with a grin.

"My ice skating days are long gone," she declared. "But I'm happy to watch you slither about like Bambi."

After a few hurried phone calls to round up the rest of Silver Lake and Jake's family, they had extra ice skating passes booked for the one thirty session. While Jake had been organising that, Lori had called the gourmet burger restaurant near Rockefeller Plaza and secured tables for them for a late lunch at two thirty. As they were finishing off their breakfast, Jake's brothers and father came up to say their goodbyes. There were hugs and kisses and promises to keep in touch more often. At last the past seemed to have been laid to rest and Jake looked genuinely disappointed that they couldn't stay any longer. He walked them out into the lobby and waited with them until the elevator arrived. With a final hug from his father, Jake watched as the doors closed and they were gone.

In his head, as he turned back to re-enter the apartment, Jake could hear his mother saying, "Now that wasn't so hard, was it, Jake?"

Still smiling, he closed the front door behind him.

Rockefeller Plaza was crowded as they made their way towards the ice rink. The surrounding restaurants were filled with a mix of city workers enjoying an office pre-Christmas lunch and of last minute shoppers grabbing a quick bite to eat before heading back to the crowded stores. Accepting Jake's phone from him for safe keeping, Lori gave him a hug and made him promise to be careful. As he loped off to join his nephews, she spotted Maddy and Paul approaching with the twins in a double stroller. With a wave towards her, Paul darted off after Jake like an over grown, over excited teenager.

"Afternoon, Mrs Power," greeted Maddy as she reached her friend.

Giggling at the use of her new married name, Lori said, "Afternoon," then looked around before adding, "Where's Scott?"

"Down at the side of the ice rink with his camera," explained Maddy, reaching into the pram to check on her sleeping babies. "He's going to try to get some shots for Lucy to use on the fan page and maybe even some video footage."

"I just hope the four of them are careful out there," muttered Lori as they found a place at the railing to spectate from. "With the tour so close, they can't afford any injuries."

"Very true," agreed Maddy, "But it's Christmas and they've earned a bit of down time to have some fun."

Within a few minutes, the two friends spotted the first of the group to take to the ice. Grey and Kola, with a rather scared looking Becky between them, were the first to skate past. They were soon joined by Todd, Kate, Rich and Linsey, who all looked more than a little anxious. At the far side of the crowded rink, Lucy and Rob were helping their young sons to find their balance. Just as Lori was about to ask where Jake and Paul were, the two musicians skated expertly across, weaving their way through the other skaters.

"So much for being like Bambi," muttered Lori as she watched in amazement.

Beside her Maddy laughed. "Didn't he tell you he could skate?"

"No!"

"Paul told me on the way over," she said, watching her partner proudly. "They were both hockey players in high school."

"I never knew," laughed Lori as Jake waved up to her. "And here I thought all the secrets were out in the open!"

Silently, the two girls watched their friends down on the ice rink. After a few minutes, Jake had Becky by the hand was and was teaching her how to skate, leaving Grey and Kola to circle the ice hand in hand. Jake's nephews had found their balance and were soon whizzing over to join their uncle, closely followed by their dad. Meanwhile, Lucy stayed at the side, holding onto the rail, her face a picture of fear. A few flurries of snow began to fall, creating the perfect relaxed Christmas atmosphere. Subconsciously, Lori's hand moved to her stomach, a movement that didn't go unnoticed by the ever watchful Maddy at her side.

"Christmas is looking pretty good this year, isn't it?" said Maddy softly.

"Much better than it did a couple of years ago," agreed Lori with a smile.

Rosy cheeked and a little weary, the Silver Lake party piled into the restaurant shortly after two thirty. All of them had survived the ice rink unscathed and the three children were chattering excitedly, musing about whether Santa Claus would bring them ice skates on Christmas morning. The twins had wakened from their nap, but seemed content to sit in their stroller with a cup of juice and a bread stick each to chew on. With the three youngsters seated at the far end of the table, each with a kid's activity pack, the adults ordered lunch, then began to relive memories of the wedding. All of them relaxed and forgot about Scott and his ever present camera. Avoiding photographing the children, he managed to shoot plenty of off-duty footage of the band. Enough, he hoped, to keep Lucy happy for a few months. As the afternoon wore on, he nudged Maddy and reminded her that he had a flight to catch. With some help from Jake, she wrestled the twins back into their snowsuits and they said their Christmas farewells.

"When will you be back from the UK?" asked Grey curiously.

"I'll be back on 15th January. Just in time to get some shots of you guys in pre-tour rehearsals. Lord Jason's orders," replied Scott, hefting his bag of camera equipment onto his shoulder. "Lori, I'll email the wedding proofs to you over Christmas and you can let me know which ones you want for your album. Jason wants an official photo to release to the media tomorrow though. I'll email you a couple for approval from the airport."

"Perfect," agreed Lori, getting up to hug him. "Thank you for everything. Have a wonderful Christmas."

"I'll try," he promised with a wave as he followed Maddy and Paul out of the restaurant.

After a quick debate about their plans for the remainder of the afternoon, the rest of the group split up and went their separate ways, promising to meet up later back at Lori's apartment. Once outside the restaurant, Todd announced that they wanted to walk back through the park. Snow was falling quite heavily so Jake and Lori declined to join them. While the two youngsters headed off into the snow, the newlyweds walked out towards Fifth Ave to hail a cab to take them home.

"I can hardly believe tomorrow's Christmas Eve," sighed Lori as she watched the snowflakes melt down the windows of the cab.

"What is the plan for Christmas?" asked Jake, draping his arm around her shoulder.

"No plans," she admitted sheepishly. "I think part of me was too scared to plan too far ahead. Didn't want to tempt fate. I guess we'll have to sort something out food wise tomorrow."

"How would you feel about going away for a few days? Just you and me?"

"Where to?"

"A log cabin in the Poconos. It's a wedding present from Jethro. We're booked in for three nights," explained Jake hopefully. "It's only a couple of hours drive away and we can still be back here to celebrate New Year."

With a relaxed smile spreading across her face, Lori nodded. She had been disappointed when the band's manager and her long-time friend couldn't be at the wedding. Hearing about his wedding gift brought back memories of a Christmas spent with him and Maddy in the past.

"I bet it has a hot tub," she giggled and then remembering her pregnancy added, "Although I'm not sure it would be good for the baby."

"Yes, it has a hot tub. Jethro also gave me a black bikini for you," commented Jake with a wicked grin. "Care to explain that, li'l lady wife."

Blushing profusely, Lori said hurriedly, "What happened in that particular hot tub stays there. It was a long time ago!"

"According to Jethro, your bikini didn't stay long," teased Jake playfully.

"Jake!" she shrieked, now completely mortified and aware that the cab driver was trying hard not to laugh. "Wait till I get my hands on that old trouble maker!"

"So, you're up for a few days in the mountains?"

"Sounds perfect to me."

Magically, Jake managed to arrange to rent a 4x4 for the journey by the time they were due to leave. He had thought better of taking Lori's car, especially since he wasn't too sure how far off the beaten track their cabin was. In his email, Jethro had given him directions to the cabin, confirmation of the booking details and the code numbers for the keypad entry and alarm systems. Another couple of phone calls took care of their food supplies for the next three days. The groceries were delivered first thing on Christmas Eve to the apartment. The unexpected trip posed a challenge for Lori regarding how to hide Jake's Christmas gift. How do you hide a guitar case from a musician? Try as she might, she failed to come up with a solution until Jake said he was taking his guitars and his small practice amp with him. Seizing her chance while he was in the shower, Lori switched the guitar in his old battered case and prayed that he wouldn't open it until the following day. In the circumstances, it was the best plan she could devise.

By lunchtime on Christmas Eve, they were packed and ready to go. There had been tearful farewells to Lucy and her family and to the remaining guests over breakfast. Once clear of the city traffic, Jake relaxed and turned the volume up on the stereo. The radio station played Christmas hit after Christmas hit as they headed along the highway, both of them singing along, teasing each other about knowing all the words. As they headed further away from New York, the snow got deeper and deeper at the side of the road and, by the time Jake turned off I-80 almost three hours later, it lay several feet thick. He navigated his way through one small town, noting with relief the gas station, supermarket and pharmacy, then followed Jethro's map up a single track road. This stretch hadn't been ploughed but someone had driven up it since the last heavy snowfall giving him a set of tyre tracks to follow.

"This is a real winter wonderland," sighed Lori as they bounced along the snowy track. "Look, there's two deer!"

Jake slowed the jeep to a crawl as they paused to watch two deer saunter across the road in front of them.

"Wonder if Santa Claus knows they've escaped?" he joked as they watched them disappear into the trees at the side of the road.

A couple of miles further on, the track forked and their map indicated that their cabin lay at the end of the right hand track. Sure enough, a few hundred yards later, the track opened out into a wide yard in front of a snow-capped log lodge.

"So much for quaint log cabin!" laughed Jake, pulling up at the front door. "This looks like the log cabin to end all log cabins! It's fucking huge!"

"It's stunning," sighed Lori as she admired their home for the next three days.

Whoever had left the tyre tracks on the road for them had ploughed the area in front of the cabin as well as clearing the surrounding paths and front steps. Jumping down from the jeep,

Jake came round to help Lori out. Before she could protest, he scooped her up into his arms and carried her up the front steps. Adjusting her weight in his arms, Jake managed to enter the code numbers into the door entry and alarm systems. The door opened into the cabin's luxurious lounge, where a log fire burned welcomingly in the fireplace.

"Home Sweet Home, Mrs Power," he joked, kissing her on the cheek. "Well, for the holidays at least."

Giggling, Lori hugged him tight before declaring him to be a romantic fool. Carefully, he set her down on her feet, then together they explored the house. Inside, it seemed even bigger than it had from the outside. An open plan lounge, dining and kitchen area dominated the ground floor with a large open tread staircase leading up to the upper galleried level. Behind the three closed doors downstairs, they found a bathroom, a games room complete with a play station and two arcade style games machines and a second games room complete with pool table and a fully stocked bar. Through a glass pane in the back door, they could see the decking that led out to the hot tub. Upstairs, there were no less than six bedrooms, two of which were en suite plus a huge main bathroom. Every room was finished and furnished to an exceptionally high standard. Once back downstairs, Lori noticed that the landlord had even gone to the bother of supplying them with a Christmas tree and two boxes of decorations. This last touch made her smile.

"What do you want to do first?" asked Jake, taking her into his arms. "Go for a short walk to stretch our legs or decorate that tree?"

"Let's explore a little while it's still light," suggested Lori. "Although I'm not sure where we can go or how I'll cope on snow."

"You'll be fine," promised Jake warmly. "I'm here to look after you. Both of you."

Once back outside, they found a path that led away from the house towards a stand of trees. An information board at the side of the path indicated that it led down to a lake and the private jetty that belonged to the cabin. The trees overhanging the path had prevented too much snow from landing and they slowly made their way along it in search of the lake. All around them was silent, the only noise was the soft scrunch of their boots on the snow. Occasionally, they heard a twig snap in the trees or the dull thud of snow falling from a branch. All too soon the path reached a wide wooden jetty that jutted out into the most beautiful lake either of them had ever seen. Ice was crusted round the edges and the watery, late afternoon sun was glinting off the still surface.

Together they stood gazing out across the lake as the sun began to turn sunset red.

"Time to go back," said Jake, his voice barely more than a whisper. "I don't want to get stuck out here in the dark."

Reluctantly, they turned and re-traced their steps back to the cabin, promising to explore further the next day when they had more daylight left. In their absence, the log fire had burned low so, while Lori unpacked their food supplies into the refrigerator and the cupboards, Jake fetched more logs from outside and soon had the flames crackling again. When she opened the refrigerator, Lori found a bottle of her favourite champagne inside with a small card taped to the bottle. Opening the card, she found a note from Jethro, "Congratulations and Merry Christmas, Mr and Mrs Power. See you in the new year." It was signed rather formally, Jethro Steele.

With the fire burning brightly and two mugs of hot chocolate sitting on the coffee table, Jake and Lori set about decorating the little Christmas tree. It was a small tree, barely five feet high and it stood in a large red ceramic pot. As they began to string the lights round its delicate branches, Jake commented that it looked as though it was a real living tree and not one that had been chopped down for the season. A subtle aroma of pine resin wafted from its needles as they carefully hung red and gold glass baubles on its branches. At the bottom of the box Lori found both an angel and a star.

"Which one?" she asked, holding them both up for Jake to inspect.

"The angel," he replied almost instantly. "We always had a star on the tree when I was a kid and I always wanted an angel up there instead."

"Same here," giggled Lori, remembering the large antique star that used to adorn their tree every year. It had been handed down several generations on her mother's side of the family, but she had no idea what had eventually happened to it.

"You put her on top," said Jake softly.

Carefully Lori reached up and settled the white angel with

sparkling silver wings on the top of the tree.

"Perfect," she sighed, stepping back to admire their handiwork. "Pity we've no presents for underneath it."

Whether it was the clean mountain air or life in general catching up, but by ten o'clock both of them were struggling to stay awake. Stretched out together on one of the couches, they lay watching the flames burn down in the hearth. As Lori yawned again, Jake declared it was time for bed if she wanted Santa Claus to come to visit. Giggling, she asked if they should leave out milk and cookies. Humouring her inner child, Jake poured a small glass of milk and set it beside the hearth with a plate of chocolate chip cookies.

"Bedtime, li'l lady wife," he said with a smile.

With a protective arm around her waist, he guided her up the stairs up to bed.

Sun streaming into the unfamiliar bedroom, woke Lori next morning. Beside her, Jake was still asleep, lying on his side with his hair covering most of his face. His tattooed shoulder was exposed and she smiled as she watched him. Watching him and listening to his deep breathing, she noticed that he hadn't shaved for a few days and that the blonde stubble was only enhancing his good looks. Trying not to disturb him, she slipped out of the bed and crept into the bathroom. One thing she had discovered about pregnancy was that she needed to pee more often. A quick search of the internet a couple of weeks before had reassured her that it was perfectly normal and would ease off as the baby developed. When she tiptoed back into the bedroom a few minutes later, she found Jake awake.

"Merry Christmas," he said, his voice husky with the last remnants of sleep.

"Merry Christmas, rock star," said Lori, sitting down on top of the thick patchwork quilt.

"So, what's the plan for our first Power family Christmas?" asked Jake, sitting up and reaching out to take her hand.

"Breakfast would be a good start," suggested Lori, wriggling closer to him. "I'm starving."

"I thought pregnant women were meant to feel sick in the mornings?" he teased as he pulled her down to lie beside him.

"I did a little for the first couple of weeks but it passed. Now, I'm hungry," she giggled.

"Well," he began, gently lifting her pyjama top and exposing her stomach. "If baby is hungry then I guess I'd better get up and feed my family breakfast." Tenderly he kissed her firm stomach, then laid his hand on it, smiling.

"When is it you go to the hospital?" asked Jake.

"I have an appointment for January 7th," replied Lori. "And, yes, I want you there. And, yes, we should get an ultrasound done and get to see our baby."

"Now that's all the Christmas present I need," sighed Jake contentedly.

"Depending on the dates, I might be getting this little one as a birthday present," laughed Lori, rubbing her stomach. "If my calculations are right, I should be due round about then."

"When do you think it happened?" asked Jake curiously.

Lori looked at him, a little confused by the question.

"Do you have any idea what night we may have created this little miracle?"

"Ah!" she said, realising what he was getting at. "I'm not sure, but I think it might have been the night of the MMR Awards ceremony. We weren't too careful that night as I remember."

"No, we weren't," agreed Jake with an impish grin. "But it was fun."

"The hangover the next day wasn't," muttered Lori, remembering how awful she had felt when she had wakened up on the living room floor, still in her black dress from the night before.

"What would you like for breakfast?" asked Jake.

"Surprise me."

"Come on then," said Jake, climbing of bed. As he pulled a T-shirt over his head, he added, "Let's see if Santa Claus has been, li'l lady."

Giggling, Lori took his hand and allowed him to lead her out of the bedroom. When they reached the top of the stairs, she gasped at the sight below. The lounge room was lit up by the Christmas tree and underneath the tree was a pile of beautifully wrapped gifts. Across the dark oak floor she could see footprints leading from the fireplace to the tree and back again. Feeling like a child all over again, Lori glanced up at Jake, who smiled knowingly at her.

"What? How?" she asked as they made their way down the stairs into the lounge.

"Magic?" suggested Jake with a wink.

Soon they were both seated on the floor beside the tree. A wave of guilt washed through Lori as she realised Jake's gifts were still in her holdall upstairs and that his main present wasn't even properly wrapped. His guitar case, hiding its secret, was now lying on the couch beside them.

"Breakfast or presents first?" asked Jake, smiling at her.

"Presents," replied Lori softly. "But I need to go back upstairs to fetch yours."

"The one's you hid in the grey holdall?"

"Yes!" she exclaimed.

"They're under the tree," said Jake, looking a little sheepish. "I kind of guessed that's where you would hide things if you'd brought me a gift. I brought them down while you were sleeping last night. When I set all of this up for you."

"Raiding the closet looking for your presents," teased Lori with a laugh. "You're a naughty boy, rock star.

"Plenty of practice as a kid," he confessed with a mischievous grin.

Sure enough, the six small parcels that she had brought were among the others under the tree. Before she could ask where he wanted to start, Jake handed her a small, square, gold wrapped box with a neat, red bow.

"Merry Christmas," he said, kissing her on the forehead.

Carefully, she undid the red bow, then removed the paper to reveal a dark red, leather box. Her hands trembled as she opened it to reveal a white gold pendant. It was the Silver Lake Celtic knot that she had gifted to Jake and that the band all had tattooed after Gary's tragic death.

"It's perfect!" she sighed as she held it up. "Thank you!"

"I know you didn't want to get the tattoo done so I had Lin make this especially for you."

"I love it!"

Both of them had obviously been in a similar frame of mind when they had picked their other gifts out. The colourful parcels revealed simple things like a new wallet for Jake, a handbag for Lori, silly character pyjamas for each other, a sketchbook and pencils, a leather bound journal to replace Jake's full lyrics book. Each of them had bought the other the same book that they'd talked about a few weeks before.

Sheets of torn up coloured paper and ribbons littered the room by the time all the gifts were unwrapped.

"Breakfast," declared Jake after the last gift had been unwrapped.

"Not so fast," cautioned Lori. "There's one more gift for you."

"There is?"

"Yes, but I couldn't wrap it," she confessed, trying to keep a serious look on her face. "I've hidden it."

"Hidden it?" echoed Jake, looking confused. "Where?"

"Open your guitar case," she instructed.

"My guitar case?" he asked, clambering to his feet.

He laid the battered case flat on the couch and flipped the catches open. As he lifted the lid, Jake gasped. Inside lay his custom made signature model guitar, but instead of the black and grey design he had discussed with the company, this one had a different custom paint job. With trembling hands, he lifted the guitar out and silently marvelled at the intricate design. All of his own tattoos were incorporated into the artwork, as was the Silver Lake knot and the imp. The colours blended perfectly as they worked through a spectrum of greens, blues and greys.

"Oh, Lori!" he said as he laid it back in the velvet lined case. "That's incredible! How did you find the time to create that masterpiece?"

"Do you like it?" she asked anxiously. "The original design that you requested is at home if you prefer it. I had them deliver both just in case."

"Like it? I love it!" he cried, hardly able to take his eyes off the unique instrument.

"I had a little help getting it done," she confessed. "Jethro helped me to stall the company and to get them to make both versions. They delivered this one to me blank and I transferred my design onto it."

"It's beautiful!" he said, coming back over to sit beside her on the floor. "I don't know what to say. Who did the paintwork?"

"Someone at the factory finished it off," she replied. "I did the initial paint job and shipped it back to the company to add the finishing touches."

"I can't wait to play it," Jake declared, sounding like a little boy desperate to play with his new toys.

"There's another part to it," teased Lori. "It should be in the storage compartment in the case."

Sliding across the floor to the couch, Jake reached into the open case and brought out a small, round, black tin with the guitar maker's logo on it. Inside were six guitar picks, all with different designs on one side and his signature on the reverse. Each design reflected a small part of the guitar's artwork.

"And now I've something to play it with," he laughed. "These are awesome!"

"Well, you can thank Jethro and Maddy for suggesting those. They're getting some made for the tour for you. The fans will love them."

"And I love you," he said, kissing her softly. "Now, breakfast, li'l lady wife."

At Jake's insistence, Lori sat on one of the high cocktail bar style chairs at the breakfast bar in the kitchen while he rustled up some scrambled eggs and bacon. Sipping her orange juice, she watched as he moved expertly around the kitchen in his Marvel comic book lounge pants and a Ramones T-shirt. The normality of the scene was a million miles away from the on-tour rock star lifestyle he had been leading for the past couple of months. It made her smile to see her husband so relaxed after the stress of the tour and the wedding.

After both of them had eaten their fill, Lori announced that she was going to shower and dress, leaving Jake sitting at the breakfast bar enjoying his second mug of coffee. When she came out of the en suite bathroom half an hour later, it didn't surprise her to hear him playing with his new toy downstairs. The familiar strains of Dragon Song rang out through the cabin, followed by Engine Room as Jake put the instrument through its paces. By the time she had dressed in her jeans and a loose checked shirt and made her way to the top of the stairs, he was retuning the guitar in preparation for playing some more.

"Having fun?" she called out as she descended the stairs.

"Just a bit," replied Jake as he adjusted one of the machine heads. "This really is an awesome guitar."

"Are you going to play all day?" she teased as reached the bottom step.

"No," he promised. "Let me finish tuning it, then I'll jump in a shower. What do you feel like doing today? What are we supposed to do on Christmas Day?"

"We could go for a walk in the snow," she suggested. "Unless you've a better idea."

"A walk sounds like a good place to start. We could head back to the lake and see if there's a path round it."

"Deal," agreed Lori. "Now, go and get cleaned up, rock star."

The crisp, cold air nipped at their cheeks as they walked slowly along the path through the trees. They drank in the silence around them, both of them relishing in the isolation of their surroundings. After an extended period of having so many people around them all day every day, it was nice to just have the world to themselves. As the lake came into sight, a movement off to the left caught Jake's eye and he motioned to Lori to stop and turn round. Three deer were sauntering through the trees parallel to the path. One of them paused to stare at them, then picking up on their human scent, all three bounded off into the woods and out of sight.

"I guess Santa Claus let the boys have the day off," joked Jake as the deer disappeared.

When they reached the edge of the lake, they found a narrow path that ran along the edge. It was badly rutted and there were low hanging branches, making progress impossible. Not wanting to take any risks, they agreed to turn and head back to the cabin. When they reached the jetty, they walked out to the end of it and stood watching the lake. A few birds were soaring high above it. They watched in fascination as one suddenly made a dive for the surface of the lake before soaring again with a fish grasped in its talons.

"Eagles," commented Lori as she watched the majestic bird fly across the lake, leaving the water below rippling.

"Nature at her best," agreed Jake, putting his arm around her waist. "Let's head back and figure out how we are cooking this Christmas dinner."

Candlelight and the flames from the fireplace cast shadows around the room as they lay together on the couch. Behind them in the kitchen lay the piles of dishes from their Christmas dinner. Together, they had prepared a veritable feast from the hamper Lori had ordered from her favourite deli They had opened the bottle of champagne that Jethro had left for them and it sat half drunk on the floor beside them, two empty glasses beside it. In the background, Jake's iPod was playing a mellow, country rock playlist, contrasting entirely with Silver Lake's usual genre.

"Today's been perfect," he murmured softly, running his

fingers through Lori's hair.

"Magical," sighed Lori, snuggling into his chest. "And we've Jethro to thank for it. He's quite the old romantic."

"That he is," agreed Jake. "With a soft spot for you, Mz Hyde."

"Perhaps," she admitted, her mind drifting back to memories of partying with Maddy and Jethro in the past. "A long time ago."

"I wasn't sure of him at first, but he's been good for the band. He was just what we needed after Gary," reflected Jake slowly. He paused then whispered, "I hate the thought of being away from you again so soon."

"You're not away for nearly four weeks yet," countered Lori, wriggling round to face him, "It's what you do, rock star. It's the day job."

"I know. The dream day job at that," he agreed. "But how many shows are you coming to this tour?"

"A few," she assured him. "And you're only away for about six weeks.

"Will you be ok to fly?" he asked, resting his hand on her stomach.

"For a few more months, yes," replied Lori, putting her own hand on top of Jake's. "But you're not the only one with the day job and commitments. I've work to do too."

"I guess," he sighed, turning his gaze to the flames.

"Get Maddy to send me the dates and I'll fit in at least two weeks with you," she promised.

Rain was lashing down as Jake drove through the late afternoon Manhattan traffic. The closer they got to the city, the less snow there was outside. Now, there were only large puddles instead of snow drifts. It was dark before he finally pulled into the guest parking bay under the apartment block. Beside him, Lori had dozed off in the passenger seat. The sudden stop wakened her and, with a yawn, she asked where they were.

"Home, li'l lady," replied Jake, removing the key from the ignition. "Let's get you upstairs, then I'll come back for the bags."

"Sorry, I must have drifted off."

"Yes, you did" he laughed. "An hour ago."

Both of them were tired after the long drive and, having unpacked, neither of them could face going out for dinner. They debated the choices before Jake volunteered to run out to the nearest food store for essentials and to pick up something for dinner on his way back. Pulling his leather jacket and stripy beanie on, he left, promising not to be too long.

Outside the rain had stopped, but an icy wind was whistling up the city blocks. Stuffing his hands in his pockets, head down, he walked briskly towards the nearby corner market. In his pocket, he felt his phone vibrating.

"Hello," he said, catching the call just before it went to voice mail.

"Jake!" came Maddy's shrill voice. "Are you guys back in the city yet?"

"Yeah. We arrived home about an hour ago."

"What are your plans for New Year's Eve?"

From her tone of voice, Jake sensed the band's manager was plotting something.

"We don't have any," he heard himself reply, almost against his better judgement "Why?"

"We've decided to throw a party," Maddy replied. "I was hoping you'd both come along and that you'd bring your guitar."

He had almost reached the food market so he stepped to the side and stopped in a doorway.

"Maddison, what are you plotting now?"

"Me? Plotting? I'm insulted, Mr Power!"

"Why don't I believe you?" he muttered. "Let me ask Lori if she feels up to a party. If she says yes, then we'll be there."

"And you'll bring along a guitar or two?"

"If you're good, I might," he teased her. "I'll talk to Lori and get her to call you tomorrow."

Over dinner, Lori explained to Jake that Maddy used to be infamous for her New Year's Eve parties. Regardless of where she was in the world, she always threw a party.

"Even the year you were in the hospital?" he asked, immediately regretting the question.

Lori nodded, "But I believe she came to see me first. I was pretty heavily sedated still. I don't remember much until a few days after New Year." She paused before continuing, "The hot tub with the black bikini was a New Year party near the Canadian border. She's hired out a bar in Las Vegas before too. It's been a while since she's hosted one in the house."

"Are we going?" asked Jake.

"We will never be forgiven if we don't," stated Lori bluntly. "It's more than our lives are worth to not be there. Don't worry. It'll be fun."

As they stepped out of the cab, Lori and Jake could hear Maddy's party at street level. Their instructions had been to be there for nine, but as usual Jake had been running behind schedule and they were almost an hour late. Muttering about having to bring two guitars with him, Jake followed Lori into the narrow, brick fronted building. It was the first time he had been in the East Village area of the city and the contrast in architecture surprised him. The elevator had an "out of order" sign on the door when they entered the small lobby.

"What floor are we headed to?" he asked, anxious that a lengthy climb would wear Lori out.

"Second," replied Lori, opening the door to the stairwell. "And the elevator never works. Another reason I've not been here for a long time."

As they reached the apartment, the music was rattling the windows in the hallway. The apartment's front door was wedged open and the hallway was a sea of people. Excusing themselves past them, Lori led Jake inside in search of their hosts. Every room was crammed full of party guests. In the vast brick walled lounge, they found the only clear space. A small corner in front of the window had been set up as a mock stage. Three stools and mics were in position with two small stacks of speakers and amps behind them.

"I'd leave your gear over there," suggested Lori, spotting two other guitar cases resting against the wall.

"Wonder who the other two seats are for?" mused Jake, glancing round the crowded room.

"Time will tell," said Lori with a wink. "Oh, there's Maddy!"

Her friend, wearing a tight fitting black dress with purple corset bodice, made her way across the room to greet them. There was no sign of the "Mommy Maddy" or the "Manager Maddy." The vision before them was most definitely the party vampire that Lori knew of old.

"You finally made it!" she shrieked to be heard over the music. "I was getting worried."

"My fault, Maddison," apologised Jake, flashing her one of his most dazzling smiles. "You are looking incredible tonight, boss!"

"Thank you," she said with a wicked smile. "I'll forgive your lateness if you'll play and sing for me later."

"I could be persuaded, I guess," answered Jake. "Who else is playing though? I see three spots over there."

"You'll see," teased the Goth. "Go fetch yourselves a drink in the kitchen."

And with that she disappeared back into the crowd to mingle with her guests.

Taking Jake by the arm, Lori led him through to the long galley style kitchen. It was slightly less crowded and decidedly less noisy in the kitchen. Over by the sink, Paul was standing chatting to two familiar figures, who had their backs to the room. When he spotted Lori, he said something to the two guys in front of him, who promptly turned around. It was Mikey from Weigh Station and another of Jake's heroes, Garrett Court.

"Mr Power!" cried out Mikey loudly. "And the beautiful, Mz Hyde!"

"Hi, Mikey," said Lori warmly, hugging the musician. "And its Mrs Power now."

"So I heard. Congratulations, princess."

"Yes, congratulations, darling," said Garrett, hugging her warmly. He then turned to Jake and shook his hand, saying, "You're a lucky man, sir."

"Thanks," mumbled Jake, feeling suddenly tongue tied in front of the older musical icon.

Apart from Weigh Station, his other musical heroes while he had been growing up had been another English band called Royal Court. The sudden departure of the lead singer, Andrew Royal, had signalled the end of the road for the band. Occasionally, Garrett Court appeared as a guest artist but he had been reclusive for a long time. Standing in Maddy's kitchen, Jake was seeing his idol in the flesh for the first time.

"Garrett," began Lori, sensing Jake's emotion. "What brings you out of hiding?"

"The lure of a good party," he replied. "And, of course, the chance to meet you again, darling."

"Behave!" scolded Lori playfully. "I'm a pregnant, married woman now."

"And still beautiful, Lori."

Regaining a little of his composure, Jake asked, "You two know each other?"

Lori nodded. "I've done some work for Garrett in the past. Sourced a few pieces for him too."

Passing Jake a beer, Mikey enquired, "You up for playing a few numbers to see in the New Year, young man?"

"Sure," agreed Jake, accepting the beer. "I've already promised the boss."

Kissing him gently on the cheek, Lori said, "I'll leave you guys to work out what you're going to play."

Without a backwards glance, she left the kitchen and returned to the lounge. Smiling as she surveyed the room, Lori felt as though she had stepped back in time by about five years. Familiar, if slightly older, faces from the past were everywhere. Friends of Maddy's from college were gathered in one corner, sharing a joint.

Over by the window, she recognised two other band managers deep in conversation with two well-known rock photographers. Some of Silver Lake's stage crew were loitering near the doorway, looking a little out of place.

"You ok, honey?" asked Maddy, appearing with a sleepy Hayden in her arms.

"Fine," replied Lori, taking the baby's outstretched hand. "This is some party. A bit like a step into the past."

"Oh, just the usual crowd plus a few extras," dismissed Maddy with a laugh. "Same crowd, different year."

"I suppose," agreed Lori. "Where's Wren? Is she asleep?"

"Is she hell!" exclaimed Maddy sharply. "She's in the kitchen wrapped round her Uncle Jake."

"Well, give Hayden to me and I'll try to settle him while you circulate," offered Lori, reaching to take the baby into her arms.

"Why don't I carry him back through to the nursery?" suggested Maddy. "He's getting too heavy for you to hold one handed."

Half an hour later, when Jake came looking for her, he found Lori in the twins' nursery gently rocking back and fro in an old pine rocking chair. On her lap, Hayden was almost asleep. A sleeping Wren was nestled in Jake's arms, her thumb firmly secured between her tiny rosebud lips. Gently, Jake laid her down in her crib and pulled the blankets up round her. She stirred slightly but he spoke softly to her until she settled back into a sound sleep,

"Paul said I'd find you in here," whispered Jake, kneeling on the floor beside his wife. "You ok?"

"Fine. I've read this little guy a story and sang him a song or two. We've had our own private party," replied Lori, keeping her voice soft. "It's been really peaceful considering the party raging out there."

"I'll bet," said Jake, almost jealous that she had managed to enjoy some quiet time. "Are you ready to come back through? We're about to play for a while."

Lori nodded and allowed him to lift the baby boy from her arms. Taking care not to disturb him, Jake settled Hayden into his crib and tucked him in with his favourite rabbit. Instinctively the baby grabbed the rabbit's ear and began to suck on it.

"Hope our little one is as peaceful," commented Lori with a wistful smile.

The party was in full swing when they walked into the lounge room and even more guests appeared to be crammed into the space. Having made sure Lori had a seat in full view of the "stage", Jake joined his two fellow musicians over by the window. From her seat on the couch, Lori watched as they prepared to play. With their guitars plugged in and the amps turned on, Mikey gave Paul the nod to turn off the music.

"Good evening!" called out Jake loudly. Everyone turned to face the three musicians. "Welcome to the world premiere performance of Maddison's All Stars."

A ripple of laughter ran through the room.

"This first song is for our hosts for this evening," continued Jake, adjusting the position of his guitar. "Unrehearsed, we give you House Of The Rising Sun."

At his feet, Jake had a hastily written set list scrawled onto the back of a paper plate. The three musicians had picked three classic rock tracks plus one from each of their own standard set lists. Everyone in the room soaked up the impromptu performance, seemingly oblivious to the fact that this musical interlude had been hurriedly planned in the kitchen less than an hour before. Pausing to take a mouthful of beer, Jake said, "Folks, this is our last one for this year. We'll leave you with one of our Weigh Station favourites. This is Broken Bottle Empty Glass."

It was the first time he had performed the song since the London show to celebrate the band's twenty fifth anniversary and Dan's life. It was a struggle to keep his emotions in check, but Jake sang with his usual dedication and passion, praying that he would get through it without a hitch.

They finished the number with a couple of minutes to spare before midnight. As they laid down their instruments, Maddy came over to take the mic.

"Let's give a huge cheer for Garrett, Mikey and Jake! My All Stars!"

As the applause and cheers died down, she glanced at the clock.

"Ok, people!" she yelled. "It's time for the countdown!"

Every guest joined in the count down from ten to one as the

clock ticked towards midnight. As she reached one, Mikey snatched the microphone from her and roared, "Happy New Year!"

While the party wound its way into the first hours of the new year, the guests slowly began to drift off into the night, either heading home or to their next party. Eventually, shortly before three, there were only a handful of partygoers left and they were all gathered in the kitchen. With a tired smile, Lori noted that Jake had lost the star struck look in his eyes and was deep in conversation with Garrett Court. Leaning heavily on her cane, she approached them, putting her arm around Jake's waist with a gentle squeeze.

"Definitely an idea worth exploring," said Jake, nodding approvingly in Garrett's direction.

"What is?" asked Lori, stifling a yawn.

"A charity fundraiser in memory of Dan," said Garrett, slurring his words slightly. "I've a meeting set up for Friday. Will you both come?"

"I'll be there," promised Jake without hesitation. "Lori, are you up for joining us?"

"Sure," she replied, curious to know what they had planned. "I'm not sure what I can bring to the table, but I'm happy to support it if I can."

"You, my darling, Lori," purred Garrett. "You are the lynchpin in this project. All will be revealed on Friday."

"Garrett, you're drunk!" stated Lori, suppressing a giggle. "Call me when you're sober and tell me where and when we've to meet you."

Beside her, she felt Jake flinch at her boldness, but he remained silent.

"Jake," said Lori, resting her head on his chest. "I need to get home. I've called a cab. It should be here any minute."

"I hear you, li'l lady," replied Jake. "Let me grab my gear."

On their way to the front door, they stopped to say goodnight to Paul who was doing shots with two of the band's lighting crew. He raised a glass to them, downed the shot of tequila, then slumped over on the couch. Shaking his head at the drunken state of his band mate, Jake led them to the door.

True to his word, Garrett called Lori late on Thursday afternoon to advise her of the time and place for the mystery meeting. Despite her best efforts, the reclusive musician wouldn't be drawn into further conversation about his proposals, promising to reveal all when they met. The meeting was scheduled for four o'clock at a well-known music store near the studio where Silver Lake had first met Weigh Station. When Jake asked her why they were meeting there, Lori laughed.

"Garrett owns that place," she revealed with a smile. "And lives above the shop."

"He lives in an apartment over a shop?" queried Jake, looking surprised.

"You'll see," replied Lori cryptically.

A bell tinkled as Jake opened the music store door for Lori and a blast of heat hit them from the fan above the door. Unusually for Jake, they were early and while Lori went over to the counter to ask the assistant to let Garrett know they'd arrived, Jake began to browse through the guitars on display. For a small shop, they carried a vast selection. He was lovingly admiring a vintage resonator when Garrett appeared beside them.

"Nice choice, young man," he commented, reaching up to lift the guitar down. "Here, give it a try. Plays well."

Not needing a second invite, Jake accepted the dark green instrument from his fellow musician then, lacking a stool or a chair to sit on, he sat cross legged on the floor. With an impish grin up at Lori, he began to play a blues style piece that he had taught in the past. The older musician had been right, the guitar did play well and had a beautiful tone to it. One glance at the price tag and he decided that perhaps the guitar wasn't for him.

"Well?" enquired Garrett as Jake passed the resonator back to him.

"Awesome but I don't think it has my name on it today," replied Jake, reluctant to let the guitar return to the rack.

"Try this one," suggested the older man, passing him a different, but not dis-similar model.

Again, Jake played the same blues piece, but didn't instantly feel the same love for the guitar. Its tone was more muffled and the neck was too wide for his liking.

"Preferred the first one," commented Jake, handing it back.

"Humour me. Try this," teased Garrett, looking round for a

particular model. Spotting it behind him, he lifted it down. He handed the battered looking grey resonator to Jake then stood back beside Lori whispering, "Watch this and look out your wallet, darling."

As soon as he began to play, Jake began to smile. He played through the short blues piece twice, then lovingly ran his hand over the body of the guitar. "This is without doubt, the most perfect instrument of its kind that I've ever played. I think I'm in love."

"Told you," said Garrett to Lori. "It's a gift I've perfected. A bit of a game I play with my clients. Each instrument will eventually find its natural musician. Your young man just found a musical mate for life."

"Not at that price I haven't," stated Jake as he continued to play a gentle blues melody.

"What year is it?" asked Lori, eyeing up the guitar.

"A 1932, my dear. The perfect vintage for Mr Power."

"Throw in a case, a couple of sets of spare strings and take fifteen hundred off that tag and you have a deal," stated Lori plainly.

"I'll take five hundred off," countered Garrett with a mischievous grin.

"Twelve hundred off."

"I'll compromise at seven fifty."

"No deal," said Lori, ignoring the angry looks she was getting from her husband, who was still sitting on the floor playing the guitar under debate.

"Eight hundred and only because it's you, Mz Hyde," offered Garrett extending her his hand in the hope of shaking on the deal.

"A thousand off, but that's as far as I'm prepared to come up," Lori answered. She too extended her hand towards the older musician.

"You drive a hard bargain," said Garrett, shaking her hand. "One thousand dollars off the tag price, its original case in mint condition and two sets of strings. I'll even throw in a couple of slides."

"Pleasure doing business with you, Garrett."

"Likewise, darling."

While Garrett took the vintage guitar over to the counter, Jake got to his feet ready to scold Lori for agreeing to buy it. Before he could say anything, she led him over to another rack of guitars, ran her hand over a few then pointed one out.

"Lift that one down carefully and try it out," she instructed firmly.

"Lori," he began to protest.

"Not another word, rock star," she interrupted.

As instructed Jake carefully slid a Gibson Les Paul out, then, realising what he was holding in his hands, said, "No. I'm not playing it. No way!"

"Please," she said softly. "Just humour me. There's an amp over there."

Knowing it was pointless to argue with her, Jake took the guitar over to the practice corner, plugged it in and settled himself on a wooden chair to play. He tried a few chords and the intro to Dragon Song then looked up at her with a grin.

"Do you share the same magic as Garrett, li'l lady?"

"Perhaps," she replied with a wink. "Like it?"

"I do, indeed," he admitted. "It's almost as beautiful as the National you just haggled for."

"No haggling on this one," commented Garrett, re-appearing beside them. "Tag price or nothing on this particular one. I don't own it. I'm selling it for a friend."

"I thought I recognised it," said Lori, stepping closer to inspect the headstock. "Hmm, he never repaired the scratch."

She fingered the tag, acknowledging the price, then said simply, "Add it to the bill. I assume you have its original case?"

"But of course," replied Garrett, accepting the guitar form Jake. "1959 was a good year, You've got yourself a bargain there, Mz Hyde."

"I know," she agreed, adjusting her grip on her cane. "That's ten thousand less than I sold it to him for."

As they followed Garrett to the counter, Jake asked her quietly who she had been referring to. All she replied was "later." Still feeling somewhat left out, he stood back while she paid for the two guitars. With the transaction completed, Garrett handed Jake the two guitar cases and requested that they both follow him. He led them back through the shop then opened a plain white door and ushered them through.

Instantly the world around them changed, both of them feeling as if they had stepped back in time. They were in a narrow, dark passageway that was lit by several mock flaming wall sconces. At the end of the corridor, Garrett opened an ornate dark wooden door to reveal a small carpeted elevator. Once they were all safely inside, he pulled over the door and they glided up two floors. This time the door opened out into a large hallway with a black and white chequerboard marble floor. In front of them were intricately carved dark wooden doors.

"Mikey arrived earlier," said Garrett, reaching to open the door. "Leo couldn't make it unfortunately. He's in Asia somewhere on tour."

He showed them into a large, Gothic lounge room lined with black wooden carved panels, tall bookcases and gilt framed paintings. A huge candelabra hung down from a beautifully carved ceiling rose. Every occasional table in the large room boasted a smaller matching candelabra style candlestick, all of which were lit with red candles. Over at the windows, which were hung with rich, dark red velvet drapes, Mikey stood sipping a glass of red wine. On one of the dark red leather chesterfields sat a stick thin man with waist length, gleaming black hair. He looked up as they entered.

"Jake, let me introduce you to my partner," said Garrett, his voice suddenly filled with warmth. "This is Salazar Mendes."

The vampire-like man looked up and smiled before getting to his feet. He towered over Jake by a good three inches causing Lori to giggle a little.

"Pleasure," he said, his voice a surprisingly deep bass tone. "And the exquisite Mz Hyde. An unexpected pleasure, my dear."

He bent down to hug Lori as Jake stood open mouthed. Salazar Mendes was a legendary blues guitarist who had disappeared into retirement almost a decade before. The blues piece that Jake had played downstairs in the shop had been written and performed by Salazar. Never in his wildest dreams had he ever thought he would meet the man. The penny suddenly dropped as he thought back to the conversation downstairs. It was the legendary guitarist's Les Paul that Lori had just bought.

"Let me fetch you both a drink," said Garett, bringing Jake back to reality. "Wine?"

Jake nodded, but Lori asked for something non-alcoholic.

"Are congratulations in order?" enquired Salazar, raising one thick dark eyebrow and fixing her with an intense stare.

"Yes," replied Lori, taking a seat beside him. "Now, what is this secret meeting all about, Sal?"

"Music," stated Mikey, coming over to join them. "Is there anything else?"

"Any music in particular?" asked Jake, taking a seat on a dark red leather wing-backed chair.

"Patience, dear boy," chastised Garrett, returning with their drinks. Having handed them both a goblet shaped glass, he took a seat to the right of Salazar.

Before he could say anything else, the lounge doors opened again and Dr Marrs strode into the room, apologising profusely for being late and saying he only had half an hour to spare. The producer declined Garrett's offer of a drink.

"As we are short of time for Dr Marrs here," began their host. "I'll cut to the chase. Sal and I have been talking to Mikey and a few others and we want to do something to celebrate Dan's legacy. We are hoping to produce a record of Dan's music to raise money for charity. I spoke to Dan's daughters just before Christmas and they loved the idea."

"When were you thinking of doing this?" asked Dr Marrs, checking the calendar on his phone. "I'm fully booked for the next three months. It would need to be April or May."

"I'm out on tour until the start of March with Silver Lake," added Jake. "But count me in for the project."

"When's JJL free, Jim?" asked Lori, her mind already visualising the project coming together.

"Late April, early May I think," replied the producer. "I'd need to check the exact dates."

Nodding, Lori said, "How about using JJL to record this record? Free of charge, of course. Let me know what artwork you want and consider it done."

"Thank you, darling," purred Salazar, flashing her a dazzling smile.

"Dare I ask," began Jake, slowly realising how huge this project could become "Are you planning to play, Salazar?"

"Yes, I will, if you will sing," replied Salazar quietly. "I would prefer to keep my involvement quiet for as long as possible though."

Jake sat back, stunned into star struck silence.

By the time Jake and Lori bade their farewells, it was late, but a rough plan had been worked out. After he had returned to the studio, Dr Marrs had phoned Lori to confirm the dates that JJL was available. None of them were sure exactly how long this whole process would take so Lori suggested he block it out from April 14th through until May 23rd thereby giving them a generous six week window to work to. This idea met with approval and tied in with the schedules of all present. With email addresses and cell numbers exchanged, they agreed to keep in touch, with Garrett being nominated as the person in charge and Mikey with overseeing the list of tracks to be recorded.

During the cab ride back up town, Jake and Lori sat with the two guitar cases between them. The hard shells put up a barrier to conversation, but Lori smiled silently to herself as she noted how Jake kept running his hands over the cases. Seeing him initially star struck back at the Gothic palace, but then relax and hold his own in the discussion had filled her with pride. It was easy for her to forget that he was still unaccustomed to socialising with his fellow rock stars as an equal. While they were stuck in traffic, Lori called her favourite Italian restaurant and placed an order for dinner, asking that it be delivered in an hour. The hour was almost up by the time the cab pulled up outside her building. With the fare paid, they both made their way upstairs, pausing to chat briefly with Charles, the concierge.

Once upstairs, Jake took the two guitars straight into the lounge, leaving them lying on the couch. In the background, he could hear Lori going downstairs, her cane clicking on the wooden treads. Running his hands through his hair, Jake gazed down at the two guitar cases, reflecting on the surreal afternoon he had just spent. In fact, life had been pretty surreal since they had returned from the mountains. Meeting Garrett at the New Year's Eve party and being asked to play with him and Mikey had been the most incredible experience. Being treated as an equal among "rock giants" had been a huge compliment, but now having met and agreed to record with Salazar Mendes took things to a whole new level. How, in the space of one short year, had his life soared to such heights?

Opening the resonator's case, he carefully lifted the guitar out, fished in his pocket for a pick and a slide then sat down to play. As he played one of his favourite blues pieces, he reflected on the instrument's history. Who else had sat and played it just as he was doing now? He knew he had to have words with Lori for investing so much money in the two guitars. It had been an expensive afternoon for her, but, for now, he wanted to enjoy the music.

The buzz of the phone to announce the arrival of their meal jolted Jake back to reality. He laid the guitar back in its case and went down to the lobby to collect the food delivery from a rather shy, gawky teenager. The boy thanked him for the generous tip, then disappeared back out into the street. Bidding the concierge goodnight, Jake took the elevator back up to the apartment. In the few short minutes that he had been downstairs, Lori had set two places at one end of the dining room table and poured him a large glass of red wine.

In between mouthfuls of pasta, they discussed the tentative plans for the charity record and how it would slot into their schedules. The Silver Lake tour was scheduled to end at the start of March and the band had discussed getting together to write and record the next album over the summer before playing a few of the late summer rock festivals. Add in the arrival of the baby in late June, for Jake, it was all actually piecing together beautifully.

"So, li'l lady," began Jake as he set his cutlery down on his empty plate. "Care to tell me how you come to know Salazar Mendes?"

"Through Garrett," she replied, before swallowing the last bite of her linguine. "I met Garrett through Maddy not long after college. I've no idea how she met him. Our paths have crossed a few times. I've sourced a few guitars for him. Bought and sold a few for my own collection too."

"And the Les Paul? What's the story there?"

"It was one of the last guitars I tracked down before my accident," said Lori quietly. "I brought it back from London and sold it to Sal. Made a nice profit on it too, but he didn't like playing it. I think Garrett had hoped he would fall in love with it and be lured out of retirement but it wasn't meant to be. Maddy told me at the party that it was up for sale again."

"How can you not love that guitar?" questioned Jake in

complete disbelief. "It's beautiful to play."

"Apparently, Sal didn't share your love for it. Maybe Garrett's right and it's found its true owner at last."

"I should be angry with you, li'l lady," stated Jake, trying not to smile. "You spent a small fortune this afternoon."

"Do you want me to return them?" teased Lori, a mischievous look dancing in her blue eyes.

"No!"

"Call them a late wedding present, husband," she said warmly. "Now, if we're heading home tomorrow, I need to start packing. I have no idea how we are squeezing everything into the car this time."

A watery, wintery sun hung low in the sky over the Delaware coast as the Rehoboth Beach water tower came into sight. Almost home.

Reaching over to touch Lori's hand, Jake flashed her a smile. At the first hint of ocean salt in the air, she had felt him relax and his mood lighten. It had been almost eight weeks since he had last been home and she knew he was desperate to see the ocean after being cooped up in cities, planes and buses. When he pulled into the driveway, Jake let out a long sigh, "Home Sweet Home, li'l lady wife."

"It's good to be back," she admitted, realising that she too had missed the place over the last two weeks.

Slowly, she opened the car door and stepped out onto the driveway. Before she could take more than a couple of steps towards the front door, Jake rushed round and scooped her effortlessly into his arms. Kissing her on the end of the nose, he said, "Time to do this properly."

"Romantic fool," giggled Lori as he carried her up to the front door.

It took a bit of balancing and team effort to get the door open, but finally they managed it and Jake carried her through the house to the sun room.

"Welcome home, Mrs Power," he said, kissing her again as he sat her down on the footstool. "I've missed this place. This room."

"You are in a sentimental mood today, rock star," she teased softly.

"A bit," he conceded, his cheeks colouring slightly with embarrassment. "I'm going back out for the bags before you embarrass me any further."

His sentimental mood did not last long once he had emptied the Mercedes and brought in his guitar cases. The lure of the music and the comfort of the basement proved to be too strong to resist. While

Lori disappeared down to the bedroom to unpack her bags, Jake took his guitars, including the three new ones, downstairs. When he had played the National back in New York and mused over its history, a blues influenced melody had begun to nibble away at his creative conscience. Now, he settled himself down to play and develop the melody, content to be back in his own environment.

Upstairs in the bedroom, Lori heard him begin to play and smiled. Jake was right – it was good to be home. As she unpacked her two suitcases, she listened to the unfamiliar blues tune echoing up from the studio. Knowing that Jake was playing the vintage guitar warmed her heart. True, both instruments had cost a tidy sum, but neither of them was meant to live in their velvet lined coffins. She had invested in them with the full intention that Jake play them. Hearing him tease new music from the resonator made every cent of the investment worth it.

As she opened the closet to hang up some of her clean clothes that she had brought home, Lori caught sight of her reflection in her full length mirror. Her stomach was taking on a definite rounded shape and her breasts looked fuller. Smiling, she ran her hand gently over her firm belly.

Filled with nervous anticipation, Jake and Lori sat holding hands in the waiting room at the maternity unit at Beebe Medical Center on Tuesday morning. Around them, the other seats were almost all occupied by women at various stages of their pregnancy. There was only one other male in the waiting room and he looked to be a boy of about eighteen, sitting beside an equally young girl with a hugely swollen belly. Upon their arrival, Lori had been handed a sheaf of forms to complete. Together, they had filled in all the details, then laid the forms down on the low table in front of them. The receptionist had asked Lori how much fluid she had had to drink that morning, then, upon hearing the answer, directed her to the water fountain, advising her to drink at least four cups.

"You ok, li'l lady?" asked Jake softly as she fidgeted in her seat.

"I need to pee," she confessed with some embarrassment. "If they don't call us soon, I'm going to have to go."

Trying not to laugh, Jake assured her that they would be called through soon.

"Mrs Power!" called a small nurse several long minutes later.

"Here," replied Lori, getting swiftly to her feet. Jake lifted the forms from the table and followed her from the waiting room.

They were shown into a small room across the corridor and invited to take a seat while the nurse checked the paperwork.

"Excuse me," said Lori, interrupting her halfway through the second form. "I really need to visit the ladies' room."

"Not advisable until we complete the ultrasound scan" replied the nurse, her voice warm and reassuring. "Let's do it first though, so you can get yourself comfortable, honey."

"Thank you," sighed Lori, relief written all over her face.

"Can you lie up on the bed, please? Pull your jeans down to the top of your thighs, then lift your top up to your bra-line," instructed the nurse. "Sir, you can come over too."

Soon Lori was lying in position on the narrow medical exam table, clutching Jake's hand nervously. Both of them watched as the nurse keyed Lori's details into the pc then she turned her attention back to them. Lifting a tube of gel, she said, "This is going to feel cold, honey."

Lori shivered as the nurse smeared a liberal amount of the cold gel over her stomach.

"Ready?" asked the nurse, lifting the transducer from its cradle.

With a glance up at Jake, Lori nodded.

"Keep your eyes on the screen, folks," said the nurse as she pressed the ultrasonic sensor firmly down on Lori's gel covered skin.

Both of them watched in fascination as the tiny image of their baby appeared on the screen. They could clearly see its head and profile. Its little arms were waving and its legs were kicking furiously.

"I don't think Junior likes that," commented Jake with a proud grin.

"Totally normal movement pattern, Mr Power," replied the nurse as she zoomed the screen in a little closer. "Give me a minute or two to capture some measurements and details then I'll talk you through what you're seeing."

There were tears glistening in Lori's eyes as she watched their baby wriggling on the screen beside her. When she glanced up at Jake, his eyes were wide with wonder.

"Well?" asked Lori softly, squeezing his hand.

"That's our baby," he whispered. "It even looks like a baby. A tiny baby."

"And," added the nurse. "I'm sure you're both relieved to know there's only one."

"Just a bit," giggled Lori nervously. "Our friends have twins. I don't think I could cope with that."

"You'd be surprised," smiled the nurse. "But you are definitely just having one baby, honey"

"What size is it?" asked Jake curiously.

"Just now, I'd reckon you're about the thirteen or fourteen week mark. I need to double check your dates with the scan details to be sure. Baby's about the size of a plum."

"That's tiny!" exclaimed Lori. "So tiny to look so human!"

"Incredible," breathed Jake as he watched their little person roll away from the sensor, turning its back on them. "Oh, Junior's camera shy!"

"Don't make me laugh, Jake," scolded Lori. "It makes me need to wee even more."

"There's a restroom over in the corner," advised the nurse as she wiped the gel from Lori's stomach. "Go and get comfortable while I print out your first photos for you."

"Thank you," sighed Lori as Jake helped her down. Without pausing to lift her cane, she limped quickly towards the toilet.

When she came back into the room a few minutes later, Jake was sitting chatting to the nurse, staring at two screenshots of the ultrasound. As Lori took a seat beside him, he passed her the pictures. Fresh tears welled up in her eyes as she stared at them; stared at their baby's first photographs.

"Here you go, honey," said the nurse, passing her a box of Kleenex. "You look like you'll need those."

"Thank you," replied Lori as a tear of relieved joy slid down her cheek.

It took them another twenty minutes to finish going over all the paperwork, to take some blood samples and then the discussion moved on to thoughts about the actual birth.

"That bit scares me," confessed Lori, keeping her eyes cast down at the photos.

"That's perfectly normal."

"It's not the thought of the pain," added Lori quietly. "I'm scared my pelvis won't cope. If this is a big baby, I could be in trouble. I was warned about that after my accident."

"We'd need to check with your ortho consultant, but you should be fine to have a natural delivery, if that's what you want. Or we can book you in for a planned C-section. Plenty of time to work that out, but you do need to give it some thought," reassured the nurse calmly. "Now, from my calculations and the dates you've given me, I would expect you to give birth around June 30th to July 4th."

"How accurate are those dates?" asked Jake, trying to visualise the band's schedule.

"It's an indication, Mr Power. Baby will arrive when he or she decides the time's right," replied the nurse. "Unless of course you decide to go down the elective C-section route."

"Any date's fine with me," said Lori, squeezing Jake's hand. "As long as he or she arrives safely."

After they left the maternity unit, Jake suggested that they go over to book an appointment with John Brent, Lori's orthopaedic consultant. He was thankful when she didn't instantly disagree with the idea. Hand in hand, they made their way through the medical centre. When they reached Dr Brent's office, his secretary apologised that he was off ill, but booked Lori in for an appointment at the end of the month.

"Guess you're not coming to Reno," observed Jake as they walked back out the car. "I'm pretty sure that's where I am on January 28th."

"I can change the appointment if you want," offered Lori. "There's no desperate rush to see John."

"No, don't cancel it. There's plenty other shows for you to make it to."

"As long as you're sure, rock star."

"I'm sure," he said with a smile. "Now let's go and get something to eat."

"Can we head over to the outlets? I need to go shopping," asked Lori. "We can grab some lunch over there."

"Shopping?"

Lori nodded, "I need to buy some looser clothes. Things are getting a little tight. I just need to run into a couple of stores. Promise."

"Alright, li'l lady. Shopping then lunch."

Her shopping took slightly longer than planned, but Lori managed to find everything she was looking for eventually. Declaring that he was starving to death, Jake insisted that they head to the iHop for Philly Cheese Steaks for lunch. As he bit into the thick sandwich, Lori asked what his plans were for the rest of the week.

"Rehearsals for the tour start on Thursday. I need to catch up with the guys before then," replied Jake in between bites. "Apart from that, I want to tidy up the basement and I've a couple of guitars that need a bit of time spent on them. What about you?"

"I've a couple of pieces to finish off then new projects to start."

"Have you got much lined up?"

"When I checked my mail, there were two big commissions on offer and a couple of smaller projects. I've not accepted them yet, but I intend to," she replied, pinching an onion ring from her husband's plate. "All going to plan, these should take me up to the start of May. If I've to do the Dan tribute piece too, then that's more than enough. Lin was asking for another LH collection too."

"Busy lady," he mused. "Just don't overload yourself. I know what you're like, li'l lady."

"I'll be sensible. I promise," she said softly. "And, yes, I'll fit in two weeks out with you guys. I'll talk to Maddy and firm up some dates."

"Plenty to choose from. Twenty four shows at the last count and Jethro was hoping to add to that."

"Why don't we invite everyone over on Friday night?" suggested Lori as she ate the last bite of her sandwich. "We haven't really seen them all since the wedding. It'll be good to catch up."

"Sounds like a plan to me," he agreed.

Plans for Friday became plans for Saturday once the band started to try to agree a time to get together. Eventually, after a flurry of calls and messages, they arranged to meet up at the beach house for a rehearsal around three. In preparation for the afternoon, Jake spent most of Friday down in the basement. The rehearsal space had become cluttered and untidy over the months and the addition of his new guitars brought home to him the fact that he needed to sort the place out. After a trip out to Lowe's and the music store, Jake spent several hours constructing a new storage space for his guitar collection. He also invested in some shelving and storage boxes to tidy up the spare leads and pedals that were littered around the place. As he tidied up the pile of cables and assorted clutter from the couch, he found the lyrics folder that Weigh Station has given him back in London. Idly, he flicked through the pages, hearing Dan's voice in his head at every turn. With a smile, he sat the folder down on the desk.

Mid-afternoon next day, Jake was still messing about down in the basement when he heard the door open and the thunder of footsteps on the creaky, wooden stairs.

"Afternoon," called Grey, the first to appear. "What happened down here? It's all neat!"

"Very funny," said Jake, looking round. "There's a box over there that's yours."

"There is?"

"Yup. Full of bass gear."

Both Rich and Paul had arrived at the same time, nodding approvingly at the improvements Jake had made to their favourite rehearsal space. Almost instantly, Rich spied the resonator and the Les Paul in the new rack.

"Is that Les Paul what I think it is?" he asked, raising one eyebrow.

"It sure is. One of Mz Hyde's investments," replied Jake, grinning proudly. "Lift it down. It's beautiful to play."

Needing no second invitation, the Silver Lake guitarist lifted the guitar down, caressing it adoringly. Within seconds he had plugged it into Jake's practice amp and begun to play. He played his solo from Engine Room, smiling all the way through it.

"Sweet," declared Rich when he was finished. "Very sweet."

"You're surely not taking that out with us?" commented Grey as he lifted his bass from its case.

"Wasn't planning to," Jake acknowledged. "I got two other new models for Christmas."

Turning to the rack, he lifted down the custom signature model that Lori had given him.

"I was planning to bring this one out with us."

His fellow band members admired the custom paint job, each of them spotting different highlights to the design.

"Right, let's get to work," declared Paul after a few minutes. "What's the plan here, guys? New set? Old set?"

"Good question," nodded Rich, putting the Les Paul back on the rack. "Personally, I don't think we need to change it about too much for these shows."

"I agree," said Jake, plugging his guitar in and rummaging in his pocket for a pick. "Let's just play for the hell of it today though. Run through some of the easier stuff."

"Works for me," agreed Grey with a slow nod of his head.

"Right," stated Paul with a solid thump from his bass drum. "Out of the Shadows first!"

A couple of hours later, Jake called a halt to the rehearsal. They had played through most of their set, stopping and starting a few times to change bits and to write down a proposed new set list for their West Coast tour. It had been a productive session and had felt good to be playing together again after their Christmas and New Year break.

"Beer o'clock," announced Grey with a glance at his watch.

"Is Becky not with you?" asked Jake.

The bass player shook his head, "I dropped her off at a friend's for a sleepover."

"Then beer o'clock it is," agreed Rich, putting his guitar down on a stand. "Is Maddy coming over, Paul?"

"She should be here in about an hour," replied the drummer as he followed Jake up the stairs. "She was in the city for a meeting at the record company. Pre-tour stuff. My sister's watching the meatballs."

Beers in hand the four members of Silver Lake spilled into the sunroom where Lori was sitting reading her book. Closing the book over as the boys found a seat, she said, "Maddy called a few minutes ago. She'll be here in half an hour. She's bringing extra guests with her."

"Who?" asked Jake curiously.

"She said it was a surprise," replied Lori. "All she would say was that she was bringing three extra over."

"Hope you've cooked enough food, Mrs Power," teased Paul with a mischievous grin.

"So do I!" laughed Lori. "If we run out, we can always send out for pizza."

"Over my dead body," growled Jake.

Lori was in the kitchen checking the fillet of beef was almost ready when she heard her friend's car in the driveway. She could hear muffled voices then a distinctive laugh as the new arrivals made their way around the side of the house. Just as she was putting the tray of roast potatoes into the oven, the back door opened.

"Hi," called out Maddy shrilly. "Sorry we're late. Traffic was backed up out on the highway."

"Don't panic," replied Lori, turning to greet her friend. When she saw who the "three guests" were, she smiled warmly and added, "Welcome, gentlemen."

Beside Maddy stood Dr Marrs, Garrett and Salazar.

"Thank you for inviting us, darling," said Garrett, giving her a hug.

"I hope we're not imposing," added Salazar shyly. "We could have just stayed out at the studio, but Maddison insisted we come over."

"I'm glad you did," said Lori. "Can I fetch you a drink?"

"Beer for me, Lori," requested Jim Marrs.

"In the refrigerator behind you," she replied. "Help yourself. Gentlemen?"

"Red wine, if you have any."

"Go on through to the sunroom. I'll bring it through."

Silver Lake were in the midst of a debate about football when Maddy waltzed into the room, closely followed by the two musicians and Dr Marrs.

"I brought some friends over," she announced casually as she flopped down onto the couch beside Paul.

"Humble apologies for imposing," said Salazar awkwardly.

"No need for apologies," said Jake, getting up to greet the new arrivals. "Great to see you. What brings you down here?"

"Business," replied Garrett, shaking Jake's hand. "We came down for a few days to check out JJL."

"Any plans to record?" asked Jake hopefully.

"Perhaps," said Salazar softly. "We just wanted to give the place the once over. See the facilities for ourselves."

"You won't be disappointed," promised Dr Marrs as he sat down beside Rich.

"No, you won't," agreed Jake then remembering his manners, said, "Garrett, Salazar, allow me to introduce you to the other members of Silver Lake. In the corner, we have Grey Cooper and on the couch Rich Santiago. I think you already know Paul."

"Pleasure," purred Salazar as Lori came through with the wine. "Now, what were you saying about the Eagles, Mr Santiago? Not a fan, I gather?"

Flushing scarlet, Rich mumbled something about not really following the NFL.

"Shame," sighed Garrett as he sat down on the smaller of the two couches, indicating Salazar should sit too. "We love a good game."

"Well, the Eagles are playing ok I guess," replied Grey in an attempt to rescue the moment "I'm a 49ers fan myself."

"Give me the Eagles over the 49ers any day," commented Jake.

And with that, the football debate continued.

By the time Lori called them all through to the dining room for dinner, the football debate was long over and their conversation had progressed to the planned charity Weigh Station album. As they took their seats at the table, Jim Marrs was waxing lyrical about the JJL facilities much to Lori's amusement.

"Jim," she said as she passed round the dish of vegetables, "Let them judge for themselves."

"But it's the top facility in the state!"

"We know," said Grey and Rich in unison before Rich added, "When do you have space for us?"

"For Silver Lake?" echoed the producer, glancing over at Maddy. "Did you have dates in mind?"

Maddy looked round the table before saying, "Personally, I'd be looking at July through August. Maybe a little earlier. Aiming for a release date in late October."

"Was that what your meeting was about earlier?" asked Jake, helping himself to two slices of roast beef.

"Partly," she replied evasively. "We can discuss it next week."

In an attempt to steer the conversation onto safer ground, Lori asked Garrett how long they planned to stay in town.

"Only till Wednesday," he replied with a glance at his partner. "We might be back later this month. We need to check out some rental properties and a few other essentials."

"We both have commitments in New York later in the week," added Salazar. "This visit was a spur of the moment trip."

"Mr Power," began Garrett, staring intently down the table at Jake. "Are you free for a few hours on Monday?"

"I could be," replied Jake, curious to learn what the older musician was planning.

"Bring yourself and your guitar out to JJL for say four o'clock," Garrett instructed. "In fact, bring that resonator."

"And the Les Paul too," added Salazar, his bass voice sounding like melted chocolate.

"Yes, sir," agreed Jake without question.

Several hours later, after their guests were long gone, Jake lay in bed beside Lori, staring up at the ceiling. His mind was racing with thoughts of being in the studio with two of his idols. Logic told him it was most likely to be an impromptu jam session. Playing alongside Garrett at New Year had been a dream come true. He couldn't imagine how it would feel to play with Salazar Mendes. Beside him, Lori rolled over to face him.

"Penny for them, rock star," she said softly as she ran a finger round the edges of the Silver Lake knot tattoo on his chest.

"I was just daydreaming," he admitted, rolling over to face her. "Wondering what it will be like to play with Salazar."

"Difficult I'd imagine," she replied, trying not to dampen his enthusiasm. "I believe he can be quite temperamental to work with."

"Did you pick up any clues as to what they are planning?"

"No," she said honestly. "Over the years Garrett has tried several times to get Sal into the studio again. He's always failed. Maybe this time will be different."

"Why?

"Because Sal obviously likes you," she observed simply.

Her words were echoing in his head as he pulled into a parking space in front of JJL late on Monday afternoon. It had been almost six months since he had last visited the studio. The place looked different in the dying light of the afternoon. With a wistful smile, he noticed that the old, wooden rocking chair still sat in the middle of grass in front of the JJL house. Memories of sitting there after the accident and Gary's death flooded back. The band had come a long way since then. It had been a tough six months.

Reaching into the back of the truck to fetch his guitar cases, Jake wondered for the hundredth time just what awaited him inside the studio.

A blast of warm air hit him as he stepped into the reception area, contrasting sharply with his summer memories. Taking a deep breath and carrying the ghosts deep in his heart, Jake walked through to the control room. Almost silently, he opened the door, his ears picking up on the gentle strains of an unfamiliar blues melody. As he stepped into the room, Dr Marrs, who was sitting at the desk, signalled to him to be quiet. Through in the live room, there in front of him, sat Salazar Mendes playing with his head bowed and his long, black hair shielding him like a cloak. On the couch, in the corner of the live room, Garrett sat watching with an anxious look on his face.

Fearful of making a noise and breaking the spell, Jake stood completely mesmerized, still holding onto his guitar cases. It had been a long time since he had been held as captivated by a performance. The hairs on the back of his neck stood on end as Salazar reached the climax of the piece then slowly brought it to an end.

"Beautiful," declared Dr Marrs into the microphone.

Lifting his head, Salazar stared straight at the producer. The expression on his face was blank, showing no hint of emotion.

"I see we have company," he said, his rich bass tone voice echoing round the studio. "Come and join us, Jake."

Without hesitation, Jake opened the door and walked through to the live room.

"Afternoon," he said, suddenly feeling a little out of his depth and well out of his comfort zone.

"Are you ready to play?" enquired Salazar bluntly. "And sing?"

"Yes," replied Jake, taking his thick winter jacket off and tossing it onto the floor beside the couch. "I'll need to warm up a bit before I sing though."

"How long will that take you?"

"Ideally an hour."

"Too long," dismissed the blues guitarist. "Just play for now."

"Sal," interrupted Garrett calmly. "You'll need to tell Jake what you want him to play. He's not a mind reader."

"I beg to differ," snapped Salazar sharply. "Make that Les Paul sing and follow my lead. When I give you the nod, improvise, but keep playing."

"I'll give it my best shot," promised Jake as he unfastened the guitar case.

The blues guitarist gave him instructions about tuning and watched intently while Jake retuned the guitar.

"Ready?"

"As I'll ever be," replied Jake unable to suppress his grin. Another dream was about to become a reality. He was actually about to sit down and play with the legendary Salazar Mendes.

"Dr Marrs?" asked Salazar, staring at the control room window.

"Ready and waiting," acknowledged the producer.

Bowing his head, Salazar began to play. His fingers danced over the frets as he played with a precise passion that took Jake's breath away. Keeping his eyes focussed on the older musician, Jake watched for his cue. Eventually, Salazar lifted his head and nodded slowly in Jake's direction. Trembling slightly with nerves, Jake began to play an accompanying melody to the blues piece. With a nod and a smile of approval, Salazar continued to play. After another couple of minutes, he finished the piece with a flourish.

"Beautifully played," praised Salazar, his deep voice barely above a whisper. "Again, if you please. You start."

This time the vampiric blues maestro sat back watching Jake play and then carefully chose his moment to come in. Together, they played this tag game for more than two hours. Occasionally

Salazar would offer some constructive criticism or request that Jake change tuning or change guitar. Like the apprentice following the master's instructions, Jake did as he was asked without question.

All the while Garrett sat silently on the battered couch, watching and listening.

"I see you brought the National with you. Are you ready to play some true Delta blues on her, Jake?" asked Salazar, setting his own guitar down on a nearby stand. "Rett, if you please."

Almost as if it were some secret code that was passing between them, Garrett opened an ancient, tattered, brown leather guitar case and handed his partner the twin of Jake's resonator.

After a brief discussion about tuning, Salazar requested that Jake watch for his cue and to pick up where he would leave off. Grinning like a star struck teenager, Jake soaked up every note his idol played. When his turn came, he played the same blues piece back to Salazar, adding in his own improvisations. They continued to play like this for a further hour, then the older man stopped playing. Without a word, he handed his guitar to Garrett and left, not even pausing to speak to Dr Marrs.

"Did I do something wrong?" asked Jake, looking bemused.

"Not at all," assured Garrett as he packed his partner's guitars away. "In fact, I'd say you did a hell of a lot right."

"I don't understand," began Jake.

"Stepping in here today was a big deal for Sal. He's not made it into the studio in over five years. The fact that he managed to play at all is testament to how highly he regards your talent, Jake," explained Garrett, his voice tinged with sadness. "Sal suffers from crippling panic and anxiety attacks. My guess is that he left before his medication wore off."

"Is he alright?"

"I hope so," sighed the older man. "Today has been a huge leap forward for him."

"So what now?" asked Jake.

"I go and check on him. Calm him down," replied Garrett. "Same as I do every time he leaves the house. And you, Mr Power, go home to your beautiful wife."

Before Jake could say another word, Garrett picked up the two guitar cases belonging to Salazar and left, pausing to say a brief goodbye to Dr Marrs on the way out.

At a loss as to what to do next, Jake began to play a slow, sultry blues number. With his head bowed over the resonator, he poured his heart and soul into the music. It had been written many years before by Salazar and had always been one of his favourite blues pieces to play and to teach. In a sad way, it seemed a fitting way to draw the session to a close. He had been the student all afternoon.

"Incredible, Jake," called Jim Marrs from the booth when he finished. "Great choice."

"Thanks," said Jake with a sad sigh. "Felt like the right thing to play."

"Well, it's now recorded for posterity."

"Pardon?"

"My orders were to record every note played in this studio until all three of you left."

"Yeah, well, whatever," acknowledged Jake as he got to his feet. "Time I went home."

"I'll tidy these up tomorrow and give you a copy when you come out later in the week," said the producer. "Salazar didn't say I couldn't share the session with you."

"Thanks. Appreciate it," replied Jake before adding. "Later in the week? I thought we were rehearsing at the beach house?"

"Not according to my records. Maddison booked you into the rehearsal room out back. You boys will be the first to use it officially. It was only completed mid-December."

"Fine. Guess I'll see you Thursday then."

With Jake out of the house for a few hours, Lori had seized the opportunity to liaise with Maddy and Jethro to determine which shows she could travel to on the Silver Lake tour. Emails had flown back and forth all afternoon as they tried to agree on her travel dates. Conscious that she had promised her husband that she would be there for two weeks, Lori opted to split it into two separate trips and try to link in with as many of the band's free days as possible. Eventually the two managers reached an agreement with her and the flights were arranged.

By the time everything was in place, Lori's desk was littered with Post-it notes with flight times and venue names scrawled on them. In total she would be with the band for seven shows and six days when they were off duty. Carefully, she plotted the dates into her calendar, satisfied that nothing clashed with her own work deadlines. Once it was all down on paper, it looked quite simple and she marvelled at the length of time it had taken to agree it all. Quickly, she calculated how many weeks pregnant, she would be by the time she flew home from Kansas City and sighed with relief when she counted it as twenty weeks.

"Not too huge," she thought as she placed her hands on her rounded stomach. "I hope you love your daddy's music as much as I do, little one."

A glance at the time prompted Lori to shut down her laptop and head into the kitchen to start dinner. As she chopped up the two plump chicken breasts she planned to pan fry, she heard Jake's truck pull into the driveway. The cab door slammed and, a few moments later, the back door opened. Followed by a blast of icy ocean air, Jake clattered his way into the kitchen, weighed down by his guitar cases.

"Evening, li'l lady," he greeted with a huge smile. "What's cooking?"

"Nothing yet, but it will be oriental chicken shortly," she replied, relieved to see him smiling. "How was your afternoon?"

"Incredible!" proclaimed Jake enthusiastically. "Surreal. Bizarre. Wonderful. Let me put these in the basement and I'll fill you in."

As he headed down the narrow staircase to the basement studio, Jake felt his phone vibrate in his jeans pocket. Leaving the guitar cases on the floor in front of the rack, he pulled out the handset. There was a text message from an unknown number.

"Thank you for today, Jake. Heading back to NYC. Will see you at JJL in April. Will be in touch about the output from today. Salazar."

"Thank you, Meister," replied Jake, his hands trembling slightly as he typed the words.

Rain was lashing off the windshield as he turned into JJL on Thursday morning. Driving past the main studio, he followed the driveway round to the right towards the new refurbished rehearsal studio. There were several vehicles already parked outside and a glance at the time confirmed his suspicions. He was late!

With his hood pulled up in an effort to shield himself from the rain, he sprinted into the building.

"Sorry," he called as he walked into the large rehearsal space.

"You know the rules, Mr Power," said Grey bluntly. "Another twenty in the pot."

"I've got it here," declared Jake, waving a twenty dollar bill above his head.

"Thank you," acknowledged Rich, plucking the note from his friend's grasp. Passing it to the bass player, he asked, "How much is in that pot now?"

"Must be about a thousand bucks," mused Grey, pocketing the money. "Maybe more. I've never counted it."

"Yeah, and most of it mine," muttered Jake sourly. "My gear's out in the truck. Can someone give me some help with it?"

"I'll help," offered a familiar voice from behind him.

"Todd!" he exclaimed as he turned round to face his young protégé. "What're you doing here? Shouldn't you be in school?"

"Student placement. Work experience," Todd replied with a mischievous grin. "Looks like you're stuck with me for the next six or eight weeks, thanks to Maddy and Jethro."

"Glad to hear it," said Jake warmly. "Saves me kicking a new guitar tech into shape. Right, let's grab this gear and get this rehearsal started. I've new toys for you to play with, young man."

"So I heard."

It took them another hour to get everything set up before the rehearsal could start. While Paul and his drum tech had been setting his kit up, Jake had introduced Todd to his new custom made guitars. When he saw the Mz Hyde designed model, Todd nodded approvingly.

"Stunning," he murmured as he lifted the guitar out of its case. "Does it play as well as it looks?"

"Sure does. Try it," suggested Jake, trusting his former student implicitly.

A little hesitantly, Todd plugged the guitar into the nearest amp, checked it was in tune and began to play. Like the master supervising the apprentice, Jake watched and listened as the young musician ran through a few practice exercises then played part of At The Beach, the instrumental piece Jake had written in Gary's memory. Hearing it again stirred up emotions that he thought he had buried deep, causing Jake to step in and halt Todd.

"Sorry," apologised the younger musician. "I love that solo. You should be proud of it."

"I am," admitted Jake, accepting his guitar back from the boy. "But this isn't a good time to play it, Todd. Too many ghosts around today."

"I hear you."

Before either of them got to say another word, Rich yelled over, "When you boys are finished playing with your fancy toys..."

"Just coming," replied Jake, adjusting the guitar's position as he put the strap over his head. "Where'd you want to start?"

"Set opener?" suggested Grey, glancing at the draft set list that was taped on the floor in front of him.

"How about a move away from Dragon Song?" commented Jake as he took his position on the low practice stage. "Let's mix it up a bit and open with Engine Room."

"That's a huge song to start with," mused Rich as he picked idly at his guitar strings. "But it might just work."

"And what do we add into the set in its slot?" called out Paul from behind the drums. "Dragon Song would sit well as an encore opener. Dragon Song then Flyin' High."

"Works for me," agreed Jake as he read over the set list that was taped down beside his mic stand. "Let's try Fall And Winter now and see how it sounds. We've not done it live yet."

"Engine Room first, then Fall And Winter," stated Grey gruffly.

"Let's do this," agreed Rich grinning.

For over an hour Silver Lake played, steadily working their way through the first half of the draft set list. There were a few stops and starts as they debated the running order and, after they had run through Out Of The Shadows, Rich asked Jake if he wanted to play through the acoustic interlude. Before he could change guitar, the door opened and Jethro, closely followed by Scott came in calling out, "Happy New Year, boys!"

"And a Happy New Year to you," laughed Jake. "You're almost three weeks late though"

"True," agreed the white haired tour manager with a smile. "How's married life?"

"Pretty damn good," answered Jake before turning his attention to Scott, "I didn't know you were back."

"Yeah, I got back last week," said the young photographer. "Meant to call, but I got caught up with a few things."

"Few things, my ass," teased Jethro, slapping Scott on the back. "I saw who was in your apartment, young man."

Blushing, Scott muttered something about them being friends.

"And just who are you being friends with?" enquired Jake. "As your landlord, I have a right to know who's staying in that apartment with you."

"Ellen," revealed Scott, his cheeks still scarlet. "I covered their New Year's Eve show and it just kind of happened."

"The witchy singer from After Life?" called out Rich, remembering the girl from London.

"Yes."

"Pretty girl," agreed Jethro, winking at Scott. "But I don't want her distracting you on tour, boy!"

"She won't."

"Leave the kid alone," said Grey, trying not to laugh as the young British photographer squirmed under Jethro's stern gaze. "He deserves some fun."

"Hmph," muttered the manager, glancing down at one of the set lists. "Where are you boys up to?"

"Just about to do Stronger Within and Lady Butterfly," answered Jake as he switched guitars. "Then we were going to break for something to eat. Todd's agreed to do a burger run."

"Sounds like we arrived at the perfect moment," declared Jethro, checking his cell phone for messages. "Make mine a veggie burger and fries. I've a call to make but I'll be back in a bit."

As the door slammed shut behind their manager, Jake turned back to Scott, "Are you armed and dangerous?"

Laughing as he opened his camera bag, the young photographer said, "Soon will be. Ignore me though, and carry on with rehearsals. I've orders to be here for the next two days."

"Whose orders?" snarled Grey, really not relishing the prospect of being videoed and photographed.

"Jethro and Maddy's," replied Scott. "And I'm not about to argue with either of them. I'll keep out of the way as much as I can."

"Good," muttered the bass player sourly.

Ignoring their banter, Jake settled himself on a stool with his acoustic guitar and quietly began to play the intro to Stronger Within. Out of the corner of his eye, he saw Scott was taking a few test shots. Trying not to smile, Jake bowed his head a little lower than usual, so his hair fell forwards, hiding his face completely from the camera. Focussing on the song, he began the vocal without raising his head. Every time he sang it, especially in rehearsal, he was mentally transported back to the night he first played it for Lori. Out of all the songs he had written over the years, Stronger Within held a special place in his heart.

When the song ended, he raised his gaze and with a flick of his head, he threw his hair back over his shoulder. As he did so, he heard the distinct whir of Scott's camera.

"Beautiful, Jake," declared the photographer with a wink.

With a grin, Jake began to play Lady Butterfly while the photographer fired off shot after shot. From their vantage point at the far side of the room, Jake could hear Rich and Grey joking about how hard he was trying not to look at Scott's camera. Eventually, he stopped playing midway through the last verse and burst out laughing.

"Ok, enough," he said, pointing at Scott. "You're distracting me. Go and sit over there with Paul."

"Can I shoot from over there?"

"Yes, as long as it's not more shots of me!"

At the second attempt, Jake played through the acoustic ballad note and word perfect, earning him a round of applause from his fellow band members.

While they waited for Todd returning with their food order, Jake continued to play. Unaware that the others were listening, he began to play a new piece he had been working on. It was unfinished and he hadn't written any lyrics yet, but the melody caught the attention of the others. The song had more of a blues vibe to it than most of his other material, perhaps subconsciously influenced by meeting Salazar.

"That's sweet," said Rich when he was done. "I like that."

"Thanks," replied Jake as he set his guitar down on a nearby stand. "Still a work in progress. It's got potential."

"Yeah," nodded his fellow guitarist. "You got any lyrics to go with it?"

"Not yet. Just been playing around with it for a few days."

"I might have something to go with it. I've a bridge and a solo looking for a melody and a chorus," Rich explained, lifting his own acoustic. "Here, see what you think."

While Rich played through the pieces he had written, Jake nodded approvingly. He asked his friend to run through it again with him and together they merged their ideas. Intrigued by what he was hearing, Grey came over and joined in with a subtle bass riff that helped to gel the song together. Without a word, the three of them ran through the new song again from the start. It was the first time they had collaborated so spontaneously and, by the time Todd returned with their food, they were satisfied with their progress.

"Let's record this and we can work on it from there," said Rich, bringing out his cell phone.

"Fine," agreed Jake, doing the same.

"One of you send it to me," muttered the bass player. "My phone's in the truck."

While Todd unpacked their lunch order and sorted out drinks for everyone, the three musicians made a rough recording of the new Silver Lake song.

"First track for the new album in the bag!" joked Rich, slipping his phone back into his pocket.

"Could be," acknowledged Jake with a nod. "I'll work on the lyrics. I've a couple of ideas for it."

As the band devoured their late lunch, Jethro came striding back into the rehearsal room, still chatting on the phone. Their eccentric manager ended his call, unwrapped his burger then announced, "Change of plan for next week, boys."

Suspicious, Grey enquired, "What kind of change?"

"We need to ship out two days early. Flights have all been moved to Tuesday," he said bluntly. "Jason's got one of the TV music channels interested in the band. You are booked to do a six song studio set in LA on January 22nd. We can fly to Seattle on the 23rd from LAX and start the tour as planned."

"A bit more notice would've been good," commented Grey as he tried to hide his anger at the change. "I've Becky to think about here."

"Can't your mom take her two days early?" asked Rich as he tossed the wrapper from his burger into the trash can.

"Perhaps. I'll need to call her," replied the bass player. "Becky's already upset that I need to be away so long this time. How do I tell her?"

A subdued silence filled the studio as the bass player calmly walked out to make his phone call.

"He's got a point, Jethro," said Jake, breaking the silence. "Yeah, it's great that we get extra exposure, but we all have families to think of."

"I'll be honest, boys," conceded Jethro, idly twisting the end of his long braid. "I forgot about his little girl. I knew Maddison was ok about the changes. She was on the call."

"Lesson learned," said Paul quietly. "Consult us all in future before making changes, Jethro. What do we do if Grey can't change his plans?"

"Annie'll take Becky," commented Rich with a shrug of his shoulders. "I guess."

"If she can't then I'm sure Lori will step in," added Jake, then changing the subject, added, "Tell us more about this studio set. What's it for? Is it in front of an audience?"

"It's a half hour slot in front of an invited audience," explained Jethro as he bit into his burger. "They want four electric tracks and two acoustic. There may be a short Q&A slot too."

"So it's a half hour of performing, fifteen minutes of Q&A, maybe twenty. Add in the commercials and they have a one hour TV show," stated Rich with a hint of cynicism.

"That's about the size of it," acknowledged Jethro. "However, it pays well, boys."

None of them could argue with that.

Rehearsal had resumed by the time Grey returned. The two guitarists were standing back, watching Paul rehearse a drum solo that they had discussed slotting into the encore. It was something they had talked about incorporating into the set on and off over the last few months, but previously the idea had never got off the ground. By shifting the set around, they had created a natural opportunity for Paul to be centre stage for a few minutes. From the look of glee on the drummer's face, it was an opportunity he intended to relish.

"Quite something, young man," declared Grey when Paul was

finished.

"Spectacular display," agreed Jethro before turning to face Grey. "Did you manage to get something sorted out for your daughter?"

"Yes," he replied coldly. "Took a few calls, but it's all good. Lori is taking her for one night, then her best friend's mom will take her the next night so she can go to my mom's as planned on the 23rd."

"Sincere apologies for causing you this trouble, Grey," said Jethro warmly. "I'll be honest, I never considered your family circumstances. I won't be so remiss in future. It won't happen again."

"Too damn right it won't," growled Grey. "Now, I need to go. I'll see you guys back here tomorrow."

Without a backward glance, the bass player left the room.

"Let's call it a day," suggested Jake, all enthusiasm for rehearsing gone.

Artistic progress at the beach house had been slow all afternoon. During the morning, Lori had reviewed her work schedule, then, after a brief break for lunch, had settled herself down at her drawing board to start her latest commission. While she had been eating lunch, she had listened to the three tracks that had been shared with her to support the project. The band was a young up and coming Japanese heavy metal band, but one that did try to incorporate some of the more traditional elements of Japanese culture. She had studied the biography that had been emailed to her, homing in on the various Japanese folk tales and legends that were woven into the band's music. Even their name, Watatsumi, came from a mythological creature that represented a sea god often referred to as the Dragon God. An hour of research on the internet drew her towards one Zen legend that was encapsulated in the music. As legend told, carp who successfully swam up a waterfall known as Dragon Gate at the head of China's Yellow River, were rewarded for their courage and perseverance by being transformed into dragons. It sparked an idea. After a quick refresher on Manga styles, Lori set up a fresh sheet of paper and began to sketch, creating Manga caricatures of the five band members.

She was so engrossed in the task that she never heard Jake's truck pull up outside nor did she hear him enter the house.

"Hey, li'l lady," he called from the doorway.

At the sound of his voice, she let out a squeal.

"Jesus, where did you spring from?"

"Sorry. Didn't mean to scare you," he apologised.

"Don't creep up on me like that," she chastised. "You scared me half to death."

"Sorry."

"No real harm done," replied Lori with a smile. "How was rehearsal?"

"So, so. We made progress until Jethro wound Grey up. It all fell apart after that."

"He was pretty angry when he called here," admitted Lori, putting the lid back on the pen she had been using.

"I'll bet," nodded Jake, knowing full well how angry his friend had been. "Thanks for agreeing to have Becky overnight. You've helped to save the day."

"Not a problem. I love that little girl. She's good company."

"Yeah, she's a lot of fun," agreed Jake then glancing at his watch, added, "I've some work to do. It should take me a couple of hours. Do you feel like going out to dinner later? Saves either of us are cooking."

"Sounds good," Lori said, picking her pen up again. "I've plenty to get on with here."

"Fine. If I'm not back up here in two hours come down and fetch me," he instructed as he headed for the door down to the basement.

Soon Lori was engrossed in her drawing, swiftly losing all track of time. The cartoon versions of the five musicians were beginning to take shape. In the background, she was aware of Jake playing and repeating one section of music. With a smile, Lori guessed she wasn't the only one in a creative mood. She had just begun work on the Dragon Gate for the cover when she heard the door from the basement creak open.

"Are you ready to go to dinner?" called out Jake. "I'm starving."

"Give me five minutes," she replied without looking up.

"Five minutes. No longer. It's after eight."

"Five minutes," promised Lori.

True to her word, she put the lids back on her pens a few minutes later and got stiffly to her feet. Her leg was aching a little more than usual and sitting in one position for so long hadn't helped. Limping heavily, Lori made her way down to the bedroom to get changed before going out.

"Ready," she called a short while later as she lifted her cane and her purse.

When Jake noticed her leaning so heavily on her cane, his eyes filled with concern. Before he could voice his feelings, Lori said, "I'm fine. A combination of this cold, damp weather and the fact that I've been sitting for the last four hours straight have left me sore. No big deal."

"As long as you're sure, li'l lady," he said softly.

"I'm sure. Now, baby and I are hungry. Where are we going?"

"Sushi or steakhouse?"

"Steakhouse," said Lori without hesitation. "Or we could try the new steakhouse over towards Dewey Beach that Rich was telling us about."

"Fine by me. It's probably closer," agreed Jake, fishing his truck keys out of his pocket.

There were several cars parked outside the restaurant when Jake pulled into the parking lot. Choosing a well-lit spot near the front door, he switched off the engine then came round to help Lori down from the cab. As he took her hand, he noticed that her baby bump was showing. Smiling, he waited until she was steady on her feet before placing a hand on her taut rounded stomach.

"And what does Junior want for dinner?"

"Anything," giggled Lori, putting her smaller hand over his. "We're starving."

As they walked towards the entrance, Lori said, "I'm not going to be able to disguise this bump much longer, am I?"

"No," admitted Jake. "But it makes you look even more beautiful than ever, li'l lady."

"You're biased," she stated with a giggle as he opened the door for her.

"Perhaps," conceded Jake with a smile.

Soon they had been seated at a quiet table and their server for the evening had brought their drinks order. Having listened to the high speed, lengthy run down of the day's specials, they both opted for a simple rib eye steak with fries and a side order of onion rings.

"Would you like a salad bowl and some bread sticks to start with, Mr Power," asked the young waiter.

Raising an eyebrow at the use of his name, Jake replied, "Yes, please."

"Coming right up," promised the waiter before adding, "I loved your last record. I wish you were playing nearer here on the next tour."

"Thank you," he acknowledged, suddenly feeling a little shy. "Hopefully we'll play a few east coast shows in the fall."

"I'll look forward to it."

When the young fan was out of earshot, Lori commented, "It's a shame that there's no local shows in the pipeline."

"Yeah. Rich and I were saying the same thing to Maddy the other day," agreed Jake, fingering his cutlery nervously. "She suggested we could do some acoustic slots when we are recording the tribute record in the spring. I'm not sure what she has in mind, but you can be sure she's scheming."

"Planning a mini super group?"

"Lord knows," said Jake trying not to laugh. "Wouldn't it be something if we could pull that off? It would be incredible if Garrett and Salazar would play with us."

"Well, you never know," replied Lori. "If anyone can make that happen its Maddy."

"You're not wrong there," he agreed with a sigh. "I can't believe this tour's so close. We're going to be tight on rehearsal time now that Jethro's pulled it all forward."

"You'll be fine," she assured him warmly. "You've still got a few days left to rehearse before you leave."

Their conversation was interrupted by the arrival of their salad. As he dished up the green leaves onto his plate, Jake asked his wife if she had finalised her own plans to join them.

"Yes," she replied, nibbling on a piece of breadstick. "I'll meet you in Las Vegas on February 3rd and stay with you for a week. I'm not coming to Canada, but I'll catch up with you in Minneapolis on Valentine's Day then fly home after the Kansas City show. I believe you're staying on in Kansas City for two days before you head back to Canada."

"How many shows will you be at? Six?"

"Seven," she corrected. "If I feel alright, I might come out to St Louis for the last show, but I don't want to plan too far ahead."

"When's your next medical appointment?"

"I see John Brent on January 28th and my next pre-natal check is February 26th, I think."

"Damn, we're in Chicago then, aren't we?"

Lori nodded, "You don't need to come to them all. There will be others."

"I guess."

It was late when they finally returned to the beach house. While Jake went through to watch the news in the sunroom, Lori said she was going to have a bath to see if a soak in the tub would help to ease her aching leg.

Turning on the taps, Lori added some luxury bubble bath that she had received for Christmas then watched the large bath tub turn into a sea of scented, iridescent bubbles. Leisurely, she undressed, tossing her clothes into the large wicker laundry hamper. As she turned back towards the bath, she caught sight of herself in the mirror. Lightly, she ran her hand over her baby bump, marvelling silently at the thought of a little person growing in there. The scars on her thigh caught her attention and she ran a hand over them, still feeling a wave of revulsion wash through her. No matter how often she saw them, she still loathed them. After two years, they had faded considerably, but the longest one remained a thick, angry, purple highway down her thigh. With a sigh, she turned off the taps and tested the water temperature. It was perfect. Taking care not to slip, she stepped into the tub, allowing herself to sink into the cloud of aromatic bubbles. As she felt the heat begin to seep into her weary body, she lay back and closed her eyes.

She must have dosed off for a few minutes because the next thing Lori was aware of was the bathroom door opening and Jake coming in.

"Can I join you?" he asked, his voice soft and husky.

With a smile, she nodded, then watched while he stripped off his shirt, jeans and underwear.

Jake stepped into the large bathtub and lowered himself into the water so that he sat facing her. His long legs were still bent and he looked so uncomfortable that Lori began to giggle.

"Move round," she suggested. "And let me lean back against you."

Amid more giggling and a few slops of watery bubbles over the rim, Jake repositioned himself so that Lori sat between his well-muscled thighs, reclining against him. Wrapping his arms around her, he hugged her close. Feeling his body warm and strong beneath her, Lori relaxed onto his chest with a contented sigh.

"Has the hot water helped?"

"A bit," she replied.

"I wish I could take the pain away," he whispered as he fingered her long, blonde hair. "It kills me to see you in pain."

"It's not so bad, honestly," she said, taking his hand and moving it so that it rested on the firm swell of her stomach. "I can't take any pain meds in case it harms this little one. When I see John, I'll ask him what I can take to help."

"Promise?"

"Promise."

As the water cooled around them, Jake reached out with his foot and turned the dial to raise the plug.

"Li'l lady," he murmured nuzzling her neck. "I'm going to wrap you in a towel, carry you to bed and make love to you."

"Sounds like a fine idea to me," purred Lori.

As the last of the water drained away, Jake lifted her out and wrapped a huge, warm, white, fluffy bath sheet round her. Tenderly, he dried her off, then carried her through to the bedroom. Having laid her down in the centre of the bed, Jake knelt astride her and slowly peeled away the towel. Pregnancy only enhanced her beauty, he thought as he bent forward to deliver soft kisses to her swelling belly.

"Close your eyes and ears little one," he whispered almost silently. "I need to spend time with your mommy."

It wasn't only Lori's stomach that was swelling. As he cupped her breasts, Jake realised that they too were heavier and more voluptuous than before. Teasingly, he licked their curvaceous circumference, then blew cold air onto her nipples, causing them to harden instantly. Beneath him, Lori let out a soft, almost purr-like moan.

"Patience, li'l lady," he cautioned softly as he allowed his long, slender fingers to explore between her thighs.

Obligingly, she spread her legs a little wider, allowing Jake to feel her feminine, moist warmth. His own erection betrayed his needs. In one graceful move, he had slipped his manhood deep inside her, eliciting another louder moan of pleasure from his wife. Whispering in her ear, Jake asked, "And you're a thousand percent sure this won't harm baby?"

"A thousand percent," she said, arching her pelvis to encourage him to penetrate deeper inside her.

With long, gentle strokes, Jake teased them both to the precipice of orgasmic ecstasy. Feeling her climax around him, he came hard and fast inside her then lay gasping on top of her.

"God, how much I love you," he breathed as he rolled off her, scared in case his weight harmed her.

"Love you too, rock star," whispered Lori, her whole body glowing with sexual satisfaction.

Propping himself up on one elbow, Jake bent forward to kiss her on the cheek. Before his lips reached her, Lori moved and kissed him full on the lips. He felt the tip of her tongue forcing his lips apart, then she teasingly licked the inner edge of his lips. Sensing his loins stirring again, Jake murmured, "Hungry again already, li'l lady wife?"

"Ravenous," she said with a mischievous giggle as he pulled her closer to him.

As was becoming tradition, Maddy had arranged a full band dinner for the evening before they were due to depart for LA. Instead of booking a restaurant, she invited them all out to the farmhouse for dinner, claiming that it would be a more relaxed and family friendly. When Jake and Lori pulled up in front of the farmhouse, they found that yet again they were the last to arrive.

"Grey's going to fine you again," teased Lori as she climbed out of the car.

"So what's new there?" declared Jake with a laugh. "We left in plenty of time. It's not my fault we hit traffic in town."

"Heard that excuse before," called the bass player from the porch. "Twenty bucks in the pot, Mr Power."

"Yeah. Yeah," growled Jake as he walked towards the front door, hand in hand with his wife.

When they reached the top step, the bass player stepped forward to hug Lori.

"Looking radiant, Mrs Power," he complimented with a smile. "Pregnancy suits you."

"Thanks, Grey," she replied softly, feeling her cheeks redden at the compliment.

"We'd better get inside before the boss yells at us," suggested Jake, hearing voices and the clatter of crockery coming from the house.

"Oh, she's in a fiery mood today," warned Grey as he followed them down the hallway. "Lack of sleep, I believe."

"Thanks for the warning."

As they reached the kitchen door, they were met by little Wren, who had crawled out of the lounge room. When she saw Jake, her little face lit up and she squealed in delight. Unable to resist her smiles, he bent down and scooped her up into his arms.

"And where are you escaping to, little princess?" he asked as she pulled his hair.

"Mom," stated the baby girl, pointing into the kitchen. "Mom."

"You wanting your mommy?"

"Mom," repeated Wren clearly.

At nine months old, the twins were becoming more mobile and more vocal. In the background, they could hear Paul warning Hayden to put something down. Taking them on tour this time was going to prove more of a challenge, but Maddy refused to even consider leaving them at home.

"Mom!" wailed Wren shrilly as she wriggled furiously in Jake's arms. "Mom!"

"Maddison!" called out Jake as he carried the squirming baby into the kitchen. "Your daughter wants you."

"Oh, you made it!" declared Maddy, accepting the baby girl into her arms. "Help yourselves to a drink. It's a bit chaotic around here today."

"Do you need a hand?" offered Lori, laying her jacket over the back of one of the pine kitchen chairs.

"Please," sighed Maddy, looking and sounding more than a little defeated.

"What can we do to help, boss?" asked Jake, flashing her one of his irresistible Power smiles.

"Oh, where to start!" replied the band's manager as she struggled to hold her wriggling daughter in her arms. "Lori, could you be a dear and finish laying the table in the dining room? All the cutlery is in the middle of the table. I'd made a start. And Jake, can you help me in here?"

"Your wish is our command," answered Jake warmly.

The farmhouse's large dining room was at the front of the house. It was dominated by a large oval dining table that had fourteen chairs placed around it plus the twins' highchairs. A large pile of mixed cutlery lay in the centre on top of the crisp, white linen tablecloth. Taking her time to ensure the cutlery matched, she laid out the fourteen place settings. Just as she was placing the last spoon on the table, her thoughts were interrupted by the throaty growl of an approaching motorbike. A shiver ran down her spine at the memories the noise stirred. Glancing out of the window, she watched Kola park her Harley Davidson at the front of the house. Just as she was about to go and open the door, Lori heard footsteps in the hall.

"Maddy," she heard Grey shout. "Kola's here."

When Lori went back through to the kitchen, she found Jake standing at the stove, stirring a pot of pasta sauce with Wren snuggled into his shoulder, half asleep. At the table, Maddy was slicing some garlic bread and arranging the slices into two large baskets.

"Will I take these through?" offered Lori.

"Oh, please, honey," said Maddy as she added the last slices to the baskets. "Hey, you've no cane today!"

"One of my better days," answered Lori with a faint smile, as she lifted both baskets of warm bread.

"And you're showing!" squealed Maddy excitedly. "Oh, what a cute, little baby bump!"

"Can't hide it forever," joked Lori. "I hid it long enough before the wedding."

"You sure did!"

Dinner proved to be a noisy affair and reminded Lori of a scene from the TV series, The Waltons, as they all took their seats then passed the serving dishes up and down the table. When everyone had trooped through from the family room, she had been delighted to see Todd among the guests. It was the first time she had seen him since the wedding and was keen to catch up on his progress at college. She had already heard all about his work experience placement with the band for the duration of the tour and was secretly pleased that he would be there with Jake. When the band's resident photographer and film maker wandered in, she was pleasantly surprised to see Ellen, the lead singer from After Life, follow him into the room. Off stage and away from the limelight, there was an air of fragility about the girl. Gone was the "witch" persona and, instead, there was a young woman with her hair pulled up into a messy ponytail, a loose sweater with the sleeve altered to disguise her disability and a pair of glasses with the right lens blacked out. Once they were all settled round the table, Lori discovered she was seated across from her.

"How are you enjoying your trip so far?" asked Lori as she offered Ellen some bread.

"It's been great. We've not done much, but I love what I've seen so far," replied the shy Englishwoman. "Scott's been showing me around town and we drove up to Philadelphia the other day to play tourist. Beautiful city."

"When are the rest of your band arriving?"

"The boys arrived in LA last weekend. I think they've partied ever since!"

"Easily done in LA," acknowledged Jake with a grin. "Are you looking forward to touring with us?"

"Of course!" responded Ellen almost instantly. "I'm a little anxious. It's our first trip to America. The single has been doing well over here, but I'm not sure how the audiences will react."

"When's the album due out?" asked Jethro, joining in the conversation from further down the table.

"Beginning of April," said Ellen, before turning to Lori and adding, "I love the outline you sent through for the cover artwork. It's fantastic!"

"Thanks," said Lori blushing. "The title made it easier to work out a theme and hearing the songs live in London helped. I'll have the finished piece to you guys by the end of the month."

"Did I hear right that you're coming to do some of the vocals on the Weigh Station project?" Jethro enquired with a glance at Dr Marrs, who was seated at the other end of the table.

"I've been invited to sing on one track," revealed Ellen, suddenly sounding a little shy. "If the band's schedule allows, I'll do it."

"Which track?" asked Jake, curious to learn more.

"The email said Download but it also said that could be subject to change."

"Yeah," nodded Jake. "I've not heard much, but I don't think anything is finalised yet. Jim, you got any updates on it all?"

"No, Mr Power," called out the producer. "I'm waiting on a track list from either Mikey or Garrett."

"Any other names been added to the list?" asked Jake.

"One or two, but nothing definite," replied Dr Marrs. "Kola, I believe your dad's been invited to play on it."

Looking up from her plate, Kola said softly, "He won't be."

An awkward silence descended on the table. Grey put his hand on Kola's and whispered something quietly to her. As ever, Maddy was quick to rescue things by proposing a toast to the success of the upcoming tour. Amidst the clinking of glasses, the party atmosphere was restored.

As they finished off a delicious dessert from a local Italian bakery, Becky called down the table to Lori, "Are you picking me up from school tomorrow?"

"I believe I am, honey," replied Lori. "Grey, can you give me the address of the school again, please?"

"Sure," called back the bass player. "I'll message you the details later. I've told her class teacher that you'll be fetching her."

"Do you know something," began Lori with a smile at Becky, "I don't think I've ever picked someone up from school before. Well, apart from Jake!"

"It's easy, Lori," replied the little girl seriously. "Just stand by the front gate with the other mommies. They'll show you what to do."

This caused a ripple of laughter round the table.

"What time are we getting picked up, boss?" asked Jake as he rose to begin clearing away the empty plates.

"The car will be for you about nine thirty," answered Maddy as she wrestled Hayden out of his high chair. "We're driving up in our car so we'll meet you at the airport."

"Who's travelling with us?"

"The car will get you first, then Grey and Rich before picking Jethro up at JJL," she replied.

"What about us?" asked Scott. "Any space for two more?"

"I thought you were making your own travel arrangements?"

"I've got them sorted," interrupted Jethro calmly. "A car will fetch you both at ten. You're booked on the same flight as us. I confirmed it all before I came over here. Don't panic, young man. Todd, you're with Scott and Ellen too."

"Have we forgotten anyone?" asked Jake, glancing round the table. "Kola, are you coming?"

"No," she said with a shake of her head. "I'm down here to work at JJL for a few months. Doctor's orders."

"Very funny," muttered Dr Marrs.

"Looks like we're organised," declared Jethro. "Time to get this rock show on the road again!"

It was almost ten thirty before Jake and Lori returned to the beach house. While Lori went down to the bedroom to get ready for bed, Jake made his way down to the basement to finish packing. It didn't take him long to store his favourite guitars in their cases. Gone were the days of throwing a couple of electric guitars and his acoustic in the back of the truck and heading out. Instead, he had a list from Jethro detailing which instruments he was to bring with him.

Soon he had eight guitar cases piled up in the middle of the room ready to be taken upstairs to join the growing pile of luggage in the lounge room. Clicking the catches shut on the case of his treasured acoustic, Jake looked round the basement, smiling wistfully. The empty spaces on the rack and the empty guitar stands made the place seem bare.

This time the band would be gone for six weeks. It was their longest tour so far. Every time they met with the management to discuss schedules, the tours seemed to get longer. Silently, he wondered how long it would be before they were counting tours in months instead of weeks. Long gone were the days of working week to week with their gigs in the local bars and clubs.

With everything packed up and ticked off Jethro's list, Jake took them up to the lounge, then headed down the hall to the bedroom to finish packing his suitcase. Under Lori's expert packing guidance, he had invested in a large, hard shell, wheeled case. It lay on the small couch in the bedroom half-packed. When he wandered into the softly lit room, Lori was just getting into bed.

"Have you much left to put in there?" she asked, trying to stifle a yawn.

"A few bits and pieces. The case with the stage gear is done. It's just my real clothes that I need to pack and my wash bag," replied Jake opening the closet. "I'm tempted not to take too much. I always seem to end up buying stuff and needing an extra bag."

"Just take enough for a week," suggested Lori. "You can always get your clothes laundered. You're not going to the middle of nowhere. If there's anything you really desperately need, you can buy it or I can bring it out when I fly out to join you."

"I guess," he agreed as he began to fold some T-shirts and lay them in the case.

Midnight had come and gone before Jake climbed into bed beside Lori. She had fallen asleep while he'd been packing. Lying facing her, propped up on one elbow, Jake watched her sleep. The thought of not seeing her for almost two weeks filled him with dread. Gently, he reached over and put a hand on her gently swelling belly, feeling it surprisingly firm under his fingers. His wife stirred slightly in her sleep. It still amazed him that their baby was growing inside her and that by the summer he would be a father. He wondered how long it would be before Lori would feel the baby moving and how long he would have to wait until he could feel its kicks under his hand.

"Take care of your mommy, little one," he whispered before rolling over onto his other side to get to sleep.

As she stood outside the school gates waiting for the bell to ring, Lori felt more than a little out of place. There were a handful of other mothers gathered nearby, who were all deep in conversation. From the occasional glances in her direction, Lori realised they were talking about her, apparently wondering who she was.

"Excuse me," said one of them after a few minutes. "Are you new in town? I haven't seen you here before."

"No," replied Lori calmly. "I'm picking up a friend's daughter. She's staying with me tonight while her dad's at work."

"Oh, that's sweet of you. Does her teacher know? They need parental permission if someone new is collecting a student. Can't be too careful these days."

"Grey cleared it with the school," stated Lori, feeling slightly embarrassed at being quizzed but at the same time understanding the need for caution.

"Grey Cooper? The musician guy?"

"Yes."

At that the bell rang and within seconds the school yard was full of children either rushing towards the row of yellow school buses or towards the gates.

"Lori!" squealed Becky from halfway across the yard.

Smiling and glad to see a friendly face, Lori waved and watched as the little girl came running over. She was carrying her backpack and lunch bag, but was also pulling her small, wheeled suitcase behind her.

"You've almost as many bags as Jake left with," teased Lori as the little girl reached her. "Do you want a hand to carry something?"

"I can manage," stated Becky firmly. She paused, then added, "But I do need help with my homework though."

"I'm sure I can manage that," said Lori warmly. "The car's parked just over here. You can tell me all about the homework in the car."

As she led the little girl over to the car, Lori could feel the eyes of the other mothers following her.

Once back at the house, she sent Becky down to the bedroom with her bags while she made her little house guest a snack. Lori had just poured some apple juice into Becky's favourite Elmo glass when the little girl returned carrying her backpack.

"Lori," she said. "Will you help me with my numbers?"

"Of course, honey," promised Lori. "Let me fetch a coffee, then we'll make a start."

Much to her surprise, Lori enjoyed helping the little girl with the simple addition and subtraction questions. Seeing Becky work so studiously on her assignment brought home to her just how fast the little girl was growing up. With her maths finished, Becky sat quietly and completed the sentences she was to write from her vocabulary words. As she put her books back in her bag, she said, "Lori, could we do some painting? There's a competition at school and Mrs Glass said we've to bring in a drawing or a painting by Friday."

"What have you to draw?" asked Lori. "Is there a theme?"

"Things that make you happy," revealed Becky. "I wanted to draw Daddy and Silver Lake but the teacher said to pick something easier to draw."

"Well, what else makes you happy?" enquired Lori, quietly agreeing with the teacher that to draw Silver Lake was perhaps too big a challenge for a seven year old.

"Ice cream and sprinkles!"

"Anything else?"

"Playing in the ocean."

"Hm..that might be difficult to draw."

The little girl thought for a moment or two, then said, "Watching the butterflies on Grammy's butterfly bush beside her pond. I love the colours. I love the big yellow ones."

"Do you want me to show you a fun way to paint butterflies?" suggested Lori with a smile.

"Could you?"

"Sure," agreed Lori. "Give me fifteen minutes to tidy up and find paper and some paints. Why don't you go and watch TV while I get set up in here?"

"OK," called Becky as she scampered towards the sunroom.

Half an hour later, Lori called her back through to the kitchen. She had covered the table with newspaper, laid out two large sheets of drawing paper and an array of paints. One of Jake's old T-shirts lay across the back of one of the chairs. Lifting it, Lori said, "Slip this on, missy. This is going to get messy."

"Messy?"

"Very," said Lori with a wink. "Now, what colour of butterfly do you want to create?"

"Yellow with blue bits on its wings," replied Becky with no hesitation. "But, I'm not good at drawing butterfly shapes."

"That's where the magic comes in," promised Lori, picking up a paintbrush. "Turn both your hands over. Palms up."

The little girl did as she was asked and watched with fascination while Lori painted both her hands with a thick layer of yellow paint. She then quickly changed brush and painted the little girl's fingertips blue. Praying that she had used enough paint, Lori showed Becky how to place her hands on the paper to print the top half of the butterfly's wings. The handprints were perfect. Turning the page upside down, Lori helped the little girl to line up the position of her hands to print the lower half of the wings. Again, luck was on their side and the prints were perfect.

"Wow!" exclaimed Becky as she looked at the page. "That's magic."

"Let's leave the paint to dry and we can finish it off after dinner," suggested Lori, swirling the two paint brushes in a jar of water to clean them. "Do you want to do a second one for your Grammy while the paints are out?"

"Can I?"

"Sure. What colour would she like?"

"Purple and pink," stated Becky. "They're her favourite colours."

"Well, go over to the sink and wash your hands and we'll make a pink and purple one."

After dinner, once the two handprint butterflies were dry, Lori helped Becky to outline them, add in the bodies and the antennae. Both paintings turned out really well and, when they were finished, the little girl threw her arms around Lori's neck.

"Thank you, Lori!" she squealed as she hugged her tightly. "You're the best."

"You did all the hard work," replied Lori, hugging her back. "Now, it's time for bed, young lady. You've school in the morning. Go and get your pjs on and brush your teeth."

"Will you read me a story?"

"Yes, if you go and get ready right now," promised Lori with a smile.

Much to Lori's surprise, Becky had packed a storybook in her suitcase. The little girl explained that her daddy had been reading it to her before he left. The book was "Charlie and the Chocolate Factory" by Roald Dahl and had been a favourite of Lori's when she was a little girl. Reading the chapter where the children arrive at the factory with their golden tickets brought back memories of her own mother reading the story to her. After they had read one chapter, Becky pleaded for a second.

"Just this once," said Lori softly. "Then I need to go to bed too. I'm tired."

"Is your leg sore?" asked Becky with a worried look on her face.

"A bit but it's being pregnant that's making me feel more tired than usual. Also, I was up extra early this morning. Your Uncle Jake set his alarm for five thirty."

"That's early!" agreed Becky before asking, "When will your baby be born?"

"Not until about the 4th of July. A long time to go yet."

"And will it grow in your tummy all that time?"

"Yes," replied Lori, a little concerned about where the conversation was heading. "Just like the twins did in Maddy's tummy."

"She had a big tummy!"

Laughing, Lori had to agree. By the time the twins had been due, Maddy had been enormously pregnant.

"I'm only having one baby," explained Lori, resting her hand on her stomach. "So, I won't be as big as that... I hope!"

"One little Power Pack," giggled Becky mischievously, "A little battery."

"Very funny, young lady. Now it's time you were asleep."

Temperatures were rising in the TV studio as Silver Lake rehearsed, then recorded the short six song set that they had pulled together for the music show. The studio's air conditioning had failed, but, as time was tight, they had no choice but to continue under the full heat of the studio lighting. At the last minute, the show's producer had changed the plan and they weren't required to play in front of an invited audience. Instead, though, they were to be interviewed up on the studio's roof terrace once the set had been recorded.

Sweat was pouring off all four members of the band by the time they began to play their final number. Instead of ending the set with their standard set closer, they had opted to end with Engine Room.

"Fabulous, guys!" declared the show's producer when the song ended. "Grab a drink and we'll set up for the interview. Ready to go to camera in fifteen."

"No way!" challenged Jake as he opened a bottle of water. "I need a shower before I'm going in front of any camera."

"We don't have….," began the producer sharply.

"No showers, no interview," intervened Maddy sharply. "These guys need to rehydrate after melting their asses off under those lights. They'll be ready in an hour."

"But the light will be wrong outside," protested the producer.

"It'll be early evening sun. It'll be perfect," countered Jethro, checking the time.

"One hour. Not a minute longer."

When Silver Lake walked out onto the roof terrace, exactly one hour later, the sun was just sinking behind the skyline. Compared to the January chill on the East Coast, the balmy California temperatures felt idyllic. A table and five chairs were set up in the middle of the terrace. Off to the side, there was a small hospitality table. Beers in hand, the four musicians took a seat at the table.

"This beats the winter weather back home," sighed Paul as he reclined back in his seat. "I could get used to this."

"It's quite pleasant," agreed Rich, gazing round at the view over the city.

"Evening, guys!" called out a voice from the doorway. "Let me grab a beer and I'll be right with you."

It was the show's presenter, a larger than life gentleman called Zachary. He was dressed in ripped jeans, a white T-shirt with a loud Hawaiian shirt over it. His unruly, black hair cascaded down his back.

"Nice night to shoot this," he acknowledged as he sat down in the last empty seat. "I heard some of your set. Awesome. Fucking amazing!"

"Thank you," said Jake, setting his beer bottle down on the table. "If we'd known the AC was blown, we could've played up here too."

"Now that would've been sweet," agreed Zachary with a grin. "You boys ready to answer a few questions for me?"

"As we'll ever be," replied Grey gruffly.

It took them another few minutes before the producer and the camera crew were ready. Eventually, Zachary was given the nod to begin his introduction.

"I'm delighted to be joined this week by the hottest rock band to come over from the East Coast in recent years. Tonight, my special guests have flown all the way across our great country to join me up here on the roof. It's a pleasure to be sitting out here with Silver Lake."

"Pleasure to be here," responded Rich calmly.

"Now, you played a short set for us a bit earlier and are about to embark on the West Coast leg of your Impossible Depths tour, how are you all feeling about those shows?"

"Nervous," admitted Jake with a smile. "We got our first big break out here supporting Molton so it's nice to be back as the headliners. Albeit the venues are a lot smaller."

"Do you prefer larger venues?"

"Not at all," answered Rich before his fellow band members could jump in. "In a smaller venue, I feel as though we connect better with the fans. It's harder to make that connection in those big arenas."

"Jake, as front man, do you agree?"

"Yes and no," he replied diplomatically. "As long as the crowd are on side, it's fine. I like the intimacy of the smaller venues but I get a kick out of the larger crowds too."

"You played to a rather special, large crowd in London last October when you stepped out with Weigh Station for the anniversary show. How did that feel?"

"That was a pretty emotional show," began Jake, a little hesitantly. "Originally, I was only to play a few numbers with them, but, due to the tragic turn of events, and at Dan's request, I was asked to front the band for the night. It was an incredible honour to play that one."

"And is there any truth to the rumour that you've been invited to stay on as front man for them?"

"We're still talking the logistics of that through," Jake divulged with an anxious glance across the terrace towards Maddy and Jethro. "My Silver Lake commitments will always come first. If I can fit any Weigh Station opportunities around those, then who knows what the future may hold."

Much to Jake's relief, Zachary directed the next half a dozen questions towards the other members of the band. He sat back and listened as the interview wound on. Eventually, Zachary returned his focus to Jake.

"If I've got this right, the tour winds up March 1st in St Louis at The Pageant. What's next for Silver Lake, Jake?"

"A couple of weeks off then we hope to start writing material for our next album," replied Jake, running his hand nervously through his hair. "We're involved in a charity project during April and May then hope to hit the studio and record around July or August time."

"And will that be at JJL with Dr Marrs again?"

"Definitely," he agreed.

"And will Mz Hyde be doing the honours with the artwork?"

"I'd like to hope so, if her schedule allows."

"Surely you can pull in a few favours on that front?" cajoled the interviewer. "Keep it in the family so to speak?"

"Family might be what prevents it," revealed Jake shyly. "We're expecting a baby in early July so I suspect Silver Lake's artwork won't be high on my wife's list of priorities."

"Congratulations!" said Zachary, reaching out to shake Jake's hand. "And I guess that's a good high point to end on, folks. If you want to see Silver Lake play live, they're back in LA on January 31st at the Hollywood House of Blues. Boys, it's been a pleasure. Thanks for dropping by and I wish you all the best for the tour and the new record."

"Thank you," said Jake warmly.

As the cameramen and production team began to pack up, an assistant brought a fresh round of beers over to the table. Both Jethro and Maddy came over to join them and, after a couple of extra chairs had been brought out, they all sat relaxing in the balmy evening air watching the sun set.

"So, what now?" asked Rich with a yawn.

"Dinner then back to the hotel," answered Maddy, checking the time on her phone. "I promised the nanny I'd be back by nine."

"Doesn't mean we have to be," teased Rich, with a conspiratorial wink to his band mates.

"Any shows worth catching?" asked Grey. "Any bands in town?"

"Not that I've heard," replied Jethro. "Let me make a couple of calls and I'll see what we can find. Maddison, did you book somewhere for dinner?"

"No. I thought you had."

"Not for tonight, I didn't," admitted the older man. "But I know a place not far from the hotel. I'll call them just now."

Under the watchful eye of Maddy, Silver Lake had eaten their fill of Mexican food, then been safely escorted back to the hotel by nine o'clock. Leaving them in the foyer, their manager headed back to her room to check on the twins.

"Now what?" asked Rich, eyeing up the signs for the bar.

"Beer?" suggested Grey with a nod towards Jethro.

"Not for me, boys," declared their snowy haired manager. "But don't let me stop you. I'll be fine with a club soda."

"Paul," called out Grey, "You up for a few beers?"

"Lead the way," stated the band's drummer theatrically.

With a quiet smile, Jake followed them across the foyer as Rich led the way to the hotel's bar. His quiet mood continued as they settled themselves at a corner table with a round of drinks. Around him, his fellow band members were talking about movies they wanted to watch on the tour bus over the next few weeks. Half-heartedly, Jake joined in the discussion, commenting that he wouldn't mind watching the Star Wars movies again.

When it was Jake's turn to go up to the bar, Jethro volunteered to accompany him to help carry the drinks.

"You're kind of quiet tonight, son," observed Jethro while they waited to be served. "You ok?"

"Yeah," said Jake, running his hand through his hair. "I was thinking back to that question from earlier on. The one about fronting Weigh Station. It's been preying on my mind for a while."

"Why? Have they contacted you again?"

"No," replied Jake, shaking his head. "It's just the way it was all left with them. The assumption that I'd do it simply because that was what Dan wanted."

"And is it not what you want?"

"Sometimes I think it is," admitted Jake as the bartender approached. "At others, I'm less sure."

He turned and placed the band's drinks order, then turned back to Jethro, "Do you really think that I can front both bands?"

"Yes, I do, Mr Power," answered Jethro confidently. "As long as you keep them separate. Think of it as two different characters that you play. There's Silver Lake Jake then there's Weigh Station Jake. Don't confuse the two. Create it as two different entities."

"Perhaps."

"I wouldn't worry about it for now, son," continued Jethro warmly. "Focus on this tour. Play the Silver Lake Jake role for a while and forget about Weigh Station."

"Sounds like a plan," agreed Jake as the he handed over the money for their drinks. "I'm probably over thinking the whole thing. Worrying about nothing."

All thoughts of Weigh Station were long gone as Silver Lake headed off to Seattle the following day. During the flight, Rich and Jake ran over the set lists again, debating whether to mix them up a bit more. The debate continued the following day while the band were en route to the venue. All of them agreed to leave the set list as it was for the first few shows, but were keen to add in more songs from Impossible Depths as the tour progressed.

During the sound check, Jake suggested they try Page After Page. It was one they hadn't even discussed playing live. There were a few false starts, but they eventually made their way through it.

"Let's work on that for a few more days," muttered Rich as he messed up the guitar solo for the third time. "I don't remember that being as fiddly when we were in the studio."

"Fine by me," agreed Jake, handing his guitar over to Todd to re-tune. "I think it'll go down well live though. Let's aim to add it for Reno."

"We'll see," said Rich. "It might fit in well after Out Of The Shadows. Let me work on that solo."

"Grey, you ok to do the backing vocals on it by Reno?" asked Jake.

"I guess," agreed the bass player. "Nothing ventured and all that."

"Right, Reno it is, guys," stated Jake with a grin. "Now back to business. Engine Room from the top."

Sweat was pouring off Jake as he left the stage a few hours later. The Seattle show had been a sell out and the fans had been on side right from the first notes of Engine Room through to the end of Flyin' High. It was the first full set that Silver Lake had played since December and the pace took its toll on them all.

"Awesome, boys!" praised Maddy as the weary musicians trooped past her, heading towards the dressing room. "Amazing set!"

"Fucking tough set!" muttered Paul, rubbing his chest muscles. "I'm fucked. Who had the bright idea of adding in a drum solo?"

"You!" came the united reply from the others.

"And the fans loved it," stated Jethro, tossing a clean towel to the sweat soaked drummer. "Personally speaking, I feel it could've done with being a bit longer."

"Fuck off!" declared Paul. "That was tough, Jethro."

"I'm messing with you, son," laughed the older man with a wink to the others. "Get cleaned up, boys. Clock's ticking and the silver bullet's waiting outside"

A handful of fans were waiting outside the tour bus when Silver Lake finally left the venue. The four tired musicians spent a few minutes signing autographs and posing for photos before their managers intervened and shepherded them onto the bus. All four of them collapsed onto the long leather sofa and breathed a sigh of relief as they heard the door close and the engine start.

"Home Sweet Home!" announced Grey, stretching out then, glancing round, asked, "Where's the boss? She was here a minute ago."

"She's on the other bus," replied Paul with a yawn. "The nanny and the twins are with the crew tonight. Maddy's riding with them."

"Don't you want to be with them?" asked Rich as the bus lurched forwards.

"Yeah, but we don't need the twins in here tonight. They're teething again."

"No argument there," agreed Grey.

Still to find his "bus legs", Jake staggered slightly as he stood up, "I'm going through the back to call Lori then I'm turning in for the night. I'm beat, guys. That was a tough one tonight."

"We'll not be far behind you," said Rich through a yawn.

Seeking a little privacy in the small back lounge of the tour bus, Jake pulled the door closed behind him. With a weary sigh, he sat down on the small bench-like couch and kicked off his boots. Wriggling his toes, he reached into his pocket and pulled out his phone. As he lay back, he called home.

"Hi, rock star."

Hearing Lori's voice made him smile and forget how tired he was.

"Hi, li'l lady," he replied, his voice still a little husky after the show.

"How was Seattle?"

"Awesome. Tiring. Crowd were amazing," enthused Jake. "I'd forgotten how long that set felt. We're all exhausted."

"I guess the first night's always the toughest," said Lori warmly. "You'll be racing through it all by the time I catch up with you."

"Yeah, we'll be back in our tour routine in a day or two. How was your day?"

"Busy. I was working all day. I've a couple of pieces to finish up before I fly out to meet you."

"Hope you're not working too hard," cautioned Jake. "Make sure you're getting enough rest."

"Well, I was trying to sleep when this rock star guy called me at four in the morning," giggled Lori.

"Oh shit! Sorry. So sorry," exclaimed Jake, glancing at his watch. "I forgot the time difference."

"It's ok, Jake. I'm glad you called."

"Look, get back to sleep. I'll call you in the morning. We're on our way to Portland. I'll call back when we get there."

"Deal," agreed Lori, trying to stifle a yawn. "I'll be home until late afternoon. I'm having dinner with Becky and Annie in Lewes tomorrow. I'll need to leave about five."

"I'll call before then," promised Jake, feeling guilty for

wakening her. "Sweet dreams, li'l lady."

"Night, rock star. Love you."

Laying the phone on the couch beside him, Jake closed his eyes and sighed. Guilt washed over him as he realised how selfish he'd been. How could he have forgotten the three hour time difference? As he visualised Lori in their bed back at the beach house, he smiled then drifted off to sleep.

When Jethro came through the bus looking for him a short while later, he was curled up sound asleep on the couch. Quietly, the band's manager fetched a blanket from one of the empty bunks and draped it over him. With a smile, he switched off the small light and left Jake snoring softly.

The car park at the medical centre was surprisingly quiet when Lori pulled in on Tuesday morning. When she entered the waiting room a few minutes later, it too was virtually empty, with only two other patients waiting. Quickly, she sent Jake a message to say she'd arrived safely for her appointment and promised to call him as soon as she was done.

"Mrs Power," called out the nurse a short while later. "Second door on your right today."

"Thanks," replied Lori with a smile as she made her way along the corridor.

The door was open so she knocked, then entered the office. John Brent had his back to her as she came in and was talking on the phone. He turned slightly, smiled and indicated she should take a seat. Ending his call a moment or two later, he turned his chair round so that he was facing her. Immediately, Lori noticed that his right leg was in a full length brace.

"Been in the wars?" she asked.

"Yes," nodded the doctor, looking a little embarrassed. "I fell getting the Christmas decorations down from the attic at the start of December. My leg went through between the rungs of the ladder as I fell. Snapped my femur clean in half."

"Oh, not nice!" exclaimed Lori, wincing at the thought. "Hope you had a good surgeon?"

"I did. Almost as good as yours," he replied with a smile. "I'm only just back at work this week. Reduced hours for now until I can get this brace off." The doctor paused, then declared, "Enough about me. How are you? How's married life?"

"I'm fine. Married life is quiet. Jake's out on tour until the start of March. He's in Reno today," replied Lori.

"And what brings you here?"

"I'm pregnant."

"Congratulations!" said the doctor warmly, genuinely pleased to hear some good news. "When are you due?"

"Beginning of July," answered Lori, subconsciously running her hand over her small baby bump. "The obstetrician recommended that I come to see you to check if I would be allowed a natural birth or whether the internal fixators in my pelvis would cause any issues."

"Good question," John Brent acknowledged. "Give me a moment until I find the correct image in your file to explain this."

It only took him a few seconds to bring the image up on screen of her pelvic x-ray from shortly after her accident. Turning the monitor towards her, he said, "I think you'll be ok, Lori. The internal fixation is on the iliac wings of your pelvis. There was no damage to the pubis or the pubic symphysis at the time. As your pregnancy progresses and your pelvis prepares to deliver the baby, there's no hardware there to cause any issues."

"Oh, that's good news," sighed Lori, looking relieved. "If I can avoid any form of surgery here, I will. I don't want a C-section. I've enough scars!"

Nodding, the doctor said, "I understand completely. However, we may need to keep an eye on your lower back, Lori."

"Why?"

"Your sacrum was cracked in the accident and may still be a little weaker than normal. Also, the previous trauma to the sacroiliac joints may have weakened them. It's not a show-stopper, but just something to be mindful of as you get bigger."

"I understand. What about my leg? Will it be ok with the extra weight that I'll gain?"

"It'll be fine," promised John with a smile. "Nothing's going to break, if that's what's worrying you. We may need to review whether you revert back to crutches for the last few weeks. Your balance may be a bit off as the baby grows bigger. Crutches will give you extra stability. Plenty of pregnant women end up using them as their pelvis softens in readiness for the birth."

Lori nodded slowly and sighed. "But that's worst case scenario, right?"

"Well, worst case scenario is enforced bed rest, but I'm sure it won't come to that so don't panic."

"Thanks, John."

As he turned the screen back to its usual position, the doctor asked, "How much travelling are you planning between now and

July?"

"Not much," replied Lori with a giggle. "I'm flying out to meet Jake and the band on February 3rd in Vegas then home about a week later from Dallas. I join them again in Minneapolis on the 13th and fly back from Kansas City on the 18th. Nothing too extreme."

"No overseas trips?"

"None," said Lori. "They're more or less here from March through until the end of August as far as I know."

"Glad to hear it."

"They're planning to write and record a new album over the summer," explained Lori. "The dates have all worked out quite nicely for once."

"Sounds like everything is working out well," agreed John. "I'm pleased for you both."

"Thanks."

"OK, Mrs Power," began the doctor. "Make an appointment for eight weeks' time and we'll reassess things then. If you have any concerns before then just call me."

Lori nodded. "Thanks, John. I will. And you take care of yourself too."

"I'll try, Lori."

Having checked the time, Lori decided not to call Jake until she got back to the house. She guessed it would still be too early in Reno, especially as the band had been planning to enjoy their night off the day before. As she drove down the highway, she swithered about stopping off at the outlets, but decided against it on the grounds it was too cold outside. The grey, damp, winter weather was starting to wear her down and Lori was longing for some sunshine. Hopefully, she would see the sun in Las Vegas.

Only a few tables were occupied in the hotel dining room when Jake wandered in, scanning the restaurant searching for his fellow band mates. He wasn't surprised to discover that none of them were there. Both Rich and Grey had decided to spend a late night in the casino. Both of them had been on a winning streak when he'd left them around one thirty. Casinos had never really been Jake's thing, but he had entered into the spirit of the evening, quitting while he was ahead. With his thousand dollar winnings in his pocket, he had bade them all goodnight and gone back to the hotel.

A familiar face at a corner table caught his attention. It was Ellen from After Life.

"Morning," greeted Jake warmly as he approached her table "Mind if I join you?"

"Hi," she said, looking up from her coffee cup. "Please, feel free. You just missed your manager and the drummer guy with their babies."

"Where's the rest of your band?" asked Jake, taking a seat. "And Scott?"

"The boys are still upstairs. Scott left before dawn. He's gone on a helicopter ride to photograph sunrise in the mountains," Ellen explained. "I declined to get up at three AM to go with him."

"I'm not surprised," agreed Jake smiling at her. "Way too early for me too."

"I'm sure it would be spectacular, but I wanted some sleep. I've not slept too great on our bus," confessed the young songstress.

"Me neither," admitted Jake. "It takes a while to get used to those bunks. How are you finding the tour so far? Have the crowds been kind to you?"

"It's been fantastic! Those first three shows have been amazing."

"I'm hoping to watch your set tonight," said Jake, causing her to blush bright red. "Jethro was waxing lyrical about it for hours after we left Portland the other night."

"No pressure on me tonight, then," she said with a nervous laugh. "I'll confess, I only saw a few minutes of you guys in Boise. I need to try to catch the rest of it soon."

"Any time," replied Jake, flashing her one of his "Power" smiles. "Maybe we could work out a duet? How would you feel about joining us on stage for a few shows?"

"Me?"

"Yes, you. How about it?"

"I'd be honoured to," replied Ellen with a shy smile. "I'd better clear it with the rest of the band first. Politics and all that."

"Likewise," said Jake, spotting his two gambling band mates approaching. "Have a think about what we could duet on. Doesn't need to be one of our songs. I'm open to suggestions."

"Who's suggesting what now?" asked Grey, pulling up a chair

to join them.

"I suggested to Ellen here that she and I should work out a duet and that she could join us for a few shows. Maybe come out for a slot after the acoustic interlude?" explained Jake.

"Not such a bad idea," nodded Rich, with a glance over at the young British singer. "Could be fun having some female company on stage. Come along to our sound check this afternoon. See what we can work out."

"Ok," agreed Ellen, getting to her feet. "I will. After I've spoken to the guys. I'm pretty sure they'll be fine about it."

The three members of Silver Lake watched as she walked out of the dining room. She had a denim jacket casually draped over her shoulder, discretely disguising her arm. When she reached the doorway, she turned her head and glanced back at the table. With a wave to the three musicians, she disappeared from sight.

"That's one unusual girl," commented Grey as the waiter poured their coffees. "She's so fragile looking off stage, but I caught their sound check in Boise. Boy, can she sing!"

"Yeah, she's got quite some voice," agreed Jake. "It's almost as if she gets into character to step out there every night. It's like watching two totally different people."

"So, what are you planning to duet with her?" asked Rich, stirring his coffee.

"I've no idea," confessed Jake, shrugging his shoulders. "It felt like the right thing to suggest. Feels like the right thing to do. It'd be good to do something different."

Several hours later, sound check was not running smoothly. An electrical storm had knocked out the power in the area for an hour, delaying everything. By the time Silver Lake stepped out on stage, the lighting crew were still assembling the rig and their sound engineer, Cam Joe, was still attempting to get his desk set up.

"Want us to run through the acoustic stuff to give you some more time?" offered Jake.

"No, you're good to go," Cam Joe called over.

Half an hour later, Silver Lake were in full flow, back in control and happy with the sound. They stopped for a short discussion and agreed to move a few songs around on the set list, conscious that this venue was smaller and stage space was tighter. When they read down the revised set, they had only five songs from Impossible Depths on the list.

"We need to add another couple in there," said Rich as he scanned over the list. "How do you feel about adding Fear Of The Sun and Mysteries tonight, Mr Power?"

"Been a few weeks since we played those but let's give it a try."

"You were looking for a song to duet with Witchy Woo on," began Grey. "Why not bring her out on Mysteries?"

"What did you just call her?" laughed Jake with a quizzical look towards the bass player.

"Witchy Woo," he repeated with a grin. "All the cloaks and smoke. All she's missing is a broom and some flying monkeys!"

Amid their laughter, Jake had to agree that Mysteries could be a good choice for the duet, but argued that they didn't have time to work on it before the show.

"Let's aim to go with it in LA or San Diego," Jake suggested. "Gives us a couple of days to work on it. Instead of Mysteries, we could add in Four?"

"Means an extra guitar change," countered Rich, working out in his head the tuning and which instruments they'd need.

"Slot it in after the acoustic tracks. Plenty of time, then move Impossible up the list. It's the same tuning," said Jake.

"Works for me," agreed Paul. "Drumming's easier on me that way. Gives me a bit of a breather before the solo."

"Win all round then, gentlemen," acknowledged Grey with a nod.

"Better tell Todd and the bosses," said Jake, shifting the weight of his guitar off his shoulder for a moment.

As Silver Lake were running through their final checks, Jake spotted Ellen at the side of the stage. Swiftly, he suggested to the band that they spend a few extra minutes trying out Mysteries. Despite mutterings about time being tight, they agreed to give the duet a try.

"Ellen, step out here," called Jake loudly.

Confidently, the young singer walked across the stage to join them.

"We've come up with a suggestion," he began warmly. "Do you know Mysteries from our last record?"

"Love it!" she replied, her eyes lighting up.

"Want to try it with us?" asked Jake. "If you'd rather choose something else that's fine by us, but we are hoping to add Mysteries to the set and figured it would work out ok as a duet."

"Happy to run through it," agreed Ellen. "But you're not planning on us performing it tonight, are you?"

"Don't panic," said Rich calmly. "We were thinking of adding it at the weekend. Either in LA or San Diego."

"Thank Christ for that!" giggled Ellen nervously.

"Let's give it a try and see how it goes," suggested Jake, feeling himself slip back into school teacher mode. "What time's your sound check?"

"Five," she answered. "We've got time."

"Ok. Fifteen minutes," agreed Grey, checking the time on his phone. "Let's get to work."

By the end of the brief fifteen minute rehearsal, they had worked out the division of the song and run through it twice. It still needed some work, but considering how little time they had spent, it sounded not too bad. Behind them, the stage crews were gathering to get the Silver Lake gear covered over and the After Life equipment set up. Eventually, Maddy interrupted them all by announcing that their pre-show meal was waiting for them backstage.

"Let's work in some more time tomorrow," said Jake as he handed his guitar to Todd. "Maddison, is there a VIP session for tomorrow's show?"

"Yes, Mr Power," called back the manager.

"Right, we need to work on this before the VIPs enter the venue. Maddy, can you work the schedule out so we can grab an hour to work on this?"

"Leave it with me," she agreed. "Now, go eat!"

A few hours later, as the house lights dimmed and After Life took to the stage to open the show, both Rich and Jake stood in the wings watching. Gone was the frail Ellen from earlier in the day. Instead, they were watching Rock Witch Ellen. Her pale denims and white shirt had been replaced with a skin tight, black leather cat suit with a plunging neckline and a black cloak with a purple satin lining. As before, she was wearing her Eye of Horus eye patch and playing her role to perfection. Down in the pit, they could see

Scott photographing the set and noted the occasional glances in his direction by his songstress girlfriend. Just as After Life began their second last song, Jethro appeared at the side of the stage between the two musicians.

"Time to break the spell, boys," he said, putting a hand on their shoulders. "Boss is waiting for you both."

Silently, they slipped away and headed back to the dressing room to prepare for their own set.

Shortly before nine, Silver Lake were back at the side of the stage. The house lights were down and the capacity crowd were chanting, "Silver Lake! Silver Lake! Silver Lake, Lake, Lake!" Anxious to get out on stage, Paul was bouncing up and down on the balls of his feet, twirling his drumsticks through his fingers. As usual, Grey was pacing backwards and forwards while Rich and Jake were chatting quietly to each other.

"Show time, boys," declared Maddy.

Their intro tape played and, as the lights came up, Silver Lake ran out on stage and began the show with the pounding, driving rhythm of Engine Room. The fans cheered wildly as Jake stepped up to the mic. He loved the power of the vocal on the song and couldn't help but grin as he stepped back to the drum riser when Rich came forward for the short mid-song solo. Already Jake could sense it was going to be a fun show.

"Good evening, Reno!" he roared to the crowd a few minutes in.

In front of him, the fans roared back.

"Ok, I heard that!" laughed Jake. "We're going to play something new for you now. First time we've played this one live. This is Fear Of The Sun."

Compared to most of their music, Fear Of The Sun had a definite 1950's rock-n-roll/Chuck Berry flavour to it. At sound check they hadn't had time to work out a routine for it, but, as Jake sang the first chorus, he could just see Rich and Grey duck walking behind him. He only just managed to swallow his laughter before the second verse began. Including the new song had added just the right element of fun to the set.

Half an hour later, as Todd passed him his acoustic guitar, Jake decided to abandon his usual wooden stool and to sit on the edge of the stage to play the acoustic slot. As soon as he sat down, two security personnel moved to stand close by, just in case any of the fans became a little over zealous. Jake had chosen his position carefully though. He had recognised a group of fans down to the left of centre stage. He was almost sure it included some of the fans, he had met in London.

"Still with us?" he asked, gently finger picking a melody on his guitar. "Reno, are you ready to sing for me?"

The crowd's response left him in no doubt that they were ready.

"If you know the words, feel free to sing along," invited Jake as he began Stronger Within.

In front of him, the crowd lit up with lighters and cell phones. No matter how often he saw that sight, it always made him smile.

"Beautiful, folks," he commented in between verses. "Just beautiful."

Down in the pit, he caught sight of Scott crouched down with his camera in position. There was someone else crouched down beside the photographer, wearing dark glasses and a Silver Lake beanie. It took him a moment or two to register who it was, then smiled as he recognised Ellen.

As he sang Lady Butterfly, Jake kept glancing down at them and at the end of the song, couldn't resist giving them both a wink accompanied by one of his "Power" smiles.

Having scrambled to his feet, Jake accepted his custom made electric guitar from Todd and returned to his position centre stage.

"Thank you, guys. You've stolen my heart, Reno!"

His heartfelt comment earned the band a raucous roar from the fans.

"Time for another treat. Another venture into the unknown. Another new song," announced Jake with a glance over at Rich. "When we were recording Impossible Depths, we struggled to come up with titles for all the songs we had marked up on the board. This one never got beyond its number. No hidden meaning to the title. It's simply Four."

Despite their lack of rehearsal for the new addition to the set, Silver Lake carried the song off almost to perfection. There was one section of the middle verse that Jake forgot the lyrics on but he filled in the forgotten lines by repeating the section from the first verse. One glance over at Grey nearly made him laugh out loud mid-song as the bass player shook his head at him with a look of despair. If the fans noticed his *faux pas*, they never let on. Their reaction to the premiere performance of Four was overwhelming.

All too soon, Silver Lake found themselves playing Flyin' High and the best show of the tour so far came to a thunderous end.

As the band made their way off stage, sweat pouring from them all, Scott was waiting in the narrow corridor to capture the moment. Still in her shades and beanie disguise, Ellen stood quietly nearby while he coerced the tired musicians into sparing him a few moments.

"Enough!" growled a rather tired Grey. "I need a beer right fucking now."

Obligingly, the photographer stepped aside and allowed them to troop into the dressing room. The last to pass by was Jake. Rubbing the sweat from his face with a towel, he stopped beside Ellen.

"Neat way to see the show," he complimented with a cheeky grin. "You got lucky that you weren't recognised."

"It was worth it to see you guys from out front," she confessed. "Fantastic set. Learned a lot from watching you."

"Probably all you learned was how to cover up forgotten lyrics!"

"And you did it so well."

In the background, Maddy was demanding to know where he was.

"Boss is hollering. I'd better scoot. I'll see you at sound check tomorrow."

With Jake away, life at the beach house was quiet. A storm had blown in and settled over the Delaware coast, bringing driving rain and icy cold temperatures. As the rain lashed off the patio doors for the third day in a row, Lori began to wish she had booked an earlier flight to Las Vegas. After three days of being cooped up alone, she was like a caged lioness. The inclement weather had been good for her productivity though, as she had little else to occupy her time. Both of her major projects were nearing completion, almost three weeks ahead of schedule. Wind howling round the house was making sleep nigh on impossible, so Lori had spent her sleepless nights at her drawing board.

Normally, she was content with her own company, but, as the days passed, Lori could feel herself growing more and more restless. With no one else in the house to talk to, she found herself talking to the baby while she worked. It was comforting to know she had someone's undivided attention.

By late Saturday afternoon, the storm had finally blown itself out and the rain had stopped.

"Ok, little Power Pack," declared Lori, rubbing her bump. "Time for some emergency shopping. Mommy's clothes are getting tight."

When she pulled off the highway an hour later, the parking lot at the Seaside Outlets was busy. It looked as though everyone for miles had had the same urge to shop the minute the weather improved. She parked as close to the stores as she could, then carefully got out of the car. Her leg was stiff after so many hours spent sitting over the past few days and Lori was acutely aware that she was limping more than normal. Wishing she had taken some pain medication before she left, Lori made her way to the maternity wear store.

A blast of welcome warmth enveloped her as she stepped into the store. Suddenly, Lori felt self-conscious and shy at being there.

Several of her fellow shoppers had much larger and more prominent baby bumps, causing her to feel a little embarrassed at looking for looser clothes so soon.

"Can I help you, ma'am?" asked a petite assistant with a bright, welcoming smile.

"I hope so," sighed Lori, sounding a little nervous. "I'm looking for some maternity clothes that will be comfortable for travelling in and that won't crush easily."

"Formal or casual wear?"

"A mix of both, but nothing too fancy," replied Lori. "I was thinking leggings with perhaps a couple of dresses or smart pants."

"I'm sure we can find what you're looking for," assured the assistant. "Are you going somewhere nice?"

"I fly to Vegas on Monday to meet my husband then we're touring about for a week and I fly home from Dallas," answered Lori as she followed the girl across the store to a display of jeans and leggings.

"Oh, I love Vegas!" exclaimed the sales assistant enthusiastically. "Wish it was me! Here's our range of bottoms. Have a look through these. Our tops are over at your left and the more formal dresses and skirts are at the rear of the store. If you want to try anything on, the changing rooms are over there." She pointed towards the sign, then, almost as an afterthought added, "Remember to shop for your usual size."

"Thank you."

Taking her time, Lori browsed through the selection of clothes, trying to work out a suitable "wardrobe". While she didn't want to buy too much, she also wanted to have a variety to choose from. After two trips to the changing rooms, Lori had assembled her capsule wardrobe and took her purchases over to the cash desk. She had opted for a largely black and white theme, reasoning that her choices could be dressed up with accessories.

With her new clothes bought and paid for, Lori headed towards the jeans outlet to check if they had Jake's favourite jeans in stock. He had called the day before from LA and had been bemoaning the fact that his jeans weren't going to survive the tour. While she was on her way through the store to pay for the jeans she had picked up, Lori treated herself to two checked shirts to compliment her maternity wardrobe.

"Ok, little bump," she whispered to herself as she stepped back out into the cold air. "Time to go home and pack."

Having made a quick stop at the food store, Lori headed home to pack her suitcase. When Jake had called, he had given her a list of things he wanted her to bring with her. Taking those items plus her own clothes into account, she decided to take her large wheeled bag, the zebra print one that Maddy had purchased for her while she had been in the hospital after her accident.

After a light dinner, Lori wandered down to the bedroom to begin packing. She had just gathered up all of the items on Jake's list when the phone rang.

"Hello?"

"Hi. It's Lucy," came the bright, bubbly reply. "How are you?"

"I'm good, thanks," replied Lori, relieved to have someone to talk to for a while. "How are you? And your boys?"

"We're all fine. Rob's away for the weekend at a seminar in Chicago. He'll be back on Tuesday. When do you head off to meet Jake?"

"Monday. I'm flying out to Vegas to spend a week with them. In fact, I'm just packing," replied Lori as she placed some of Jake's T-shirts in the suitcase.

"What time's your fight?" asked Lucy. "If it's an early one, you could stay here tomorrow night if you like?"

"It's around lunchtime but I'd love to come up and stay, if you don't mind," answered Lori, without a second thought. "It's kind of lonely here without Jake and the boys."

"I bet it is. Quiet too, I suspect. No music blasting up from your basement," giggled Lucy.

"Exactly."

"Why don't you drive up tomorrow afternoon and get here in time for dinner?" suggested Lucy. "It won't be anything fancy but you're more than welcome."

"I'll make a deal with you," countered Lori. "I'll drive up in the afternoon, but I'm taking you and the boys out for dinner. My treat. No arguments."

"You don't have to!" protested Lucy.

"I want to," insisted Lori firmly. "Let the boys choose where we go."

"We can work it out when you get here," relented her sister-in-law resignedly.

"Perfect. If I leave here around two I should be with you just after four."

"We'll watch out for you."

"Thanks, Lucy. I'll see you tomorrow."

"Looking forward to it."

It didn't take Lori long to finish packing the rest of her suitcase, then she turned her attention to her "carry on" bag. Having added the essentials from the bedroom, Lori went through to the study to fetch her laptop and some art basics. Her work space was cluttered and disorganised after her three days of intense creative activity. Laying the things to be packed to one side, she sat down and began to restore law and order to the area. Beside her, her cell phone gave a loud cricket chirp, signalling the arrival of a message. With a smile, she saw it was from Jake.

"Tonight's the night. Duet with Witchy Woo on Mysteries. Wish you were here. Love you. J x"

"Who? Love you too. L x" she typed quickly.

"Ellen. Grey calls her Witchy Woo. Suits her. J x"

Giggling, Lori replied, "It does. Let me know how it goes. Wish I was there too. Going to Lucy's tomorrow. See you on Monday in Vegas. L x"

"Counting the hours. J x"

Still smiling, she laid her phone down on the desk and continued to rearrange her workspace.

Silver Lake were almost finished their sound check when Jake spotted Ellen standing out in the venue. All around, the various technicians and lighting crew were still working to finalise the set up for the show. Traffic and time weren't being kind to any of them this tour and tempers were already slightly frayed one week in. Up on stage, Jake nudged Rich and pointed to Ellen.

"Get your ass up here, Witchy Woo!" hollered Grey from the back of the stage.

Looking like a startled deer in the headlights, Ellen approached the stage. Using a discarded transport case as a step, she climbed up and, accepting a steadying hand from Jake, she whispered, "What did Grey just call me?"

Trying not to laugh, Jake said softly, "Witchy Woo. He thinks it's cute."

Much to Jake's surprise, she threw back her head and howled with laughter. With tears in her eyes, she said, "I love it! Perfect coming from old grumpy balls on bass."

This time Jake doubled up, not daring to look at his friend behind him.

"Care to share the joke?" called out Grey, causing both vocalists to giggle helplessly.

"Later, Grey," promised Jake as he fought to compose himself. Turning his attention back to Ellen, he asked if she was ready to run through Mysteries. Wiping tears of mirth from her eyes, she nodded.

Twenty minutes later, they had run through the duet twice and were all happy with the plan for the show. Handing his guitar to Todd, Jake asked Ellen if she planned to join them on stage in "Witchy Woo mode." Giggling, she shrugged, "I hadn't really thought it through. I guess I should change."

"Wear whatever you feel comfortable with," said Jake as they headed off stage. "Just don't come out there naked!"

"No chance of that!"

As Jake began to play Lady Butterfly, he spotted Ellen at the side of the stage waiting for her cue. He smiled over, then returned his attention to the song in hand. The sell-out crowd were singing along passionately and a sea of lighters lit up the hall in front of him. No matter how many times he saw the tiny lights flickering like lightning bugs, it made Jake feel grateful for the opportunity to perform for them and to be living his dream. When he reached the end of the ballad, he sat for a moment with his head bowed, drinking in the emotional response of the audience, then, pushing his hair out of his eyes, he smiled out at them.

"Thank you," said Jake as he stepped down from his perch on the stool.

Instantly, Todd was at his side with his Lori-designed custom signature guitar.

"Thanks, buddy," he whispered to his young guitar tech.

Behind him, the rest of Silver Lake had returned to the stage.

"San Diego, are you ready for a world premiere?" he called out loudly.

Immediately, a roar came back at him.

"Rich, what do you think? Are these guys ready?" teased Jake as he played with the fans.

"I don't know, Mr Power," commented Rich with a cheeky grin. "Ask them again."

"Are you ready for a world premiere, San Diego?" Jake roared with full force.

The crowd's reaction almost lifted the roof off the hall.

"They're ready," stated Rich plainly.

"I believe you're right, Mr Santiago," laughed Jake, adjusting his guitar on his shoulder. "We'd like to welcome a special guest on stage to help us out on this next one. Please give a huge welcome to Ellen from After Life!"

Gone was the witch persona that the crowd had seen earlier as Ellen confidently strode across the stage. Her black leather and cloak look had been replaced by skin tight ripped jeans, Converse, a simple black top and she had a biker style leather jacket slung over her shoulder to disguise her arm. Instead of her eye patch, she had donned dark glasses.

Once she was in position on stage between Jake and Rich, Jake called out, "Mysteries!"

The fans went wild as Jake signalled for silence.

A single spot focussed on Rich as he played the slow, almost eerie guitar intro. With a deep, throaty whisper, Jake came in on the first spoken section of the song before Grey and Paul thundered in with a powerful rhythm. Glancing over at Ellen, Jake nodded as she sang the first full verse. Her own voice was husky and warm, complimenting the throaty tone Jake had used. Their voices came together for the chorus, then Jake led the vocal for the second verse. As the fans joined in, the two vocalists came together for the chorus, then Ellen and Jake traded lines for the final verse after a blistering solo from Rich. Mysteries ended with a spoken section, mirroring the beginning, only this time Ellen was completing the vocal. Gone was her sweet husky voice, replaced instead with a tortured, hissing, evil voice that brought the song to a dark conclusion.

The stage lights dimmed, then two green spots were trained on Jake and Ellen. The crowd erupted in front of them. From the reaction, Silver Lake plus Ellen concluded that Mysteries had been a resounding success. The two vocalists exchanged hugs then still holding Ellen by the hand to prevent her from escaping off stage, Jake called out, "Give it up, San Diego, for the beautiful and talented Ellen!"

Flushing at his compliment, the shy, English songbird kissed him on the cheek as she slid her hand free. Blowing a kiss to the fans, she added, "And give it up for Silver Lake and the silvery tongue of Jake Power, folks!"

As the audience cheered, she took a bow and left the stage without a backwards glance.

All too soon the show was over and the members of Silver Lake found themselves waving goodnight to the fans. It had been hot as hell in the hall and sweat was pouring off all four of them. Towels had been left on the drum riser for them to dry themselves off and as he walked off stage, Jake tossed his sweat soaked towel down to a small group of female fans on the rail and grinned as they fought over possession of it.

A couple of hours later they were all showered and back on the bus. Instead of going out for a late dinner, Jethro had arranged for some Chinese food to be delivered. Accompanied by both managers, Silver Lake sat in the front lounge of the bus opening cartons and passing out plates as the bus pulled out. The back lounge had been declared out of bounds for the night as Maddy had settled the twins down to sleep in two travel cots that had been set up in there earlier.

"Mr Power," she said, pausing to take a mouthful of rice. "That duet was inspired! I've sent a video of it to Jason. He's going to fucking love it!"

"It was fun," agreed Jake with a sleepy smile. "Fans seemed to like it."

"Like it?" echoed Jethro. "They loved it! I think you should get it recorded."

"Aren't we recording one of the shows for a live DVD or album release anyway?" queried Grey as he opened a beer.

"We are indeed," acknowledged Jethro. "The Pageant in St Louis."

"We're also recording the show in Detroit," added Maddison. "Just in case. Contingency."

"My voice is likely to be tired by then, Maddison," commented Jake with a hint of concern. "Twenty four shows is the biggest run we've done so far."

"I know," she nodded. "But that's the way it's all worked out this time round."

"Can we pull it forward? Maybe record in Canada or Kansas City?"

"I'll ask, but it's kind of late in the day to change it. The film company have visited the venues and have this planned like a military expedition. Let me speak to Jason tomorrow and see if he has any contacts in Canada that could help out. No promises."

"Thanks, boss."

An hour or so later, the band began to drift off to their bunks, all of them tired and in need of some privacy. With the tiny reading light on, Jake lay on his back, staring at the photo of Lori he had taped above his bed. He wished he could call her, but it was too early. She would still be asleep. His mind wandered back over the night's show, analysing his performance and mentally noting bits he could've done better. Sleep was eluding him. In an attempt to drift off, he plugged in his iPod and nestled the ear buds into his ears. Despite the gentle strains of some soft, country rock, he was still wide awake.

From further through the bus, he could hear one of the twins whimpering and Maddy's soft voice singing a lullaby. Quietly, Jake climbed down from his bunk and crept through the bus to the back lounge. He opened the door to find Maddison rocking a fractious Wren in her arms. The baby's cheeks were scarlet and her sleepy eyes tear filled.

"Is she ok?" asked Jake softly.

"I think so," replied Maddy, rubbing her daughter's back. "She's just a little out of sorts."

"Here," said Jake. "Give her to me. I'll settle her back down. You go and get some sleep."

"You need rest too, Jake."

"I know, but I can't sleep. I'll be fine, Maddison. Good practice for me."

Handing her daughter over to him, Maddy said, "You missing Lori?"

He nodded.

"She'll be here the day after tomorrow."

"Can't come soon enough," he sighed as Wren snuggled into his shoulder, burying her face in his long hair. She snorted and snuffled for a moment, then wrapped her tiny fist in his hair.

"Sure you're ok here?" confirmed Maddy with a yawn.

"We'll be fine. Get to bed, boss."

"Fetch me if she doesn't settle."

"Bed."

Alone in the small lounge with the twins, Jake gently rubbed Wren's back as he gazed down at her sleeping twin. Her brother was curled up on his side with his thumb in his mouth, sound asleep. With his other hand, he was clutching his rabbit by the ear. Carefully, Jake lifted the blanket from Wren's travel crib and wrapped it around her and over his own shoulder. She snuffled again in his ear, snuggling in even closer to him. Deciding he couldn't stand there all night, Jake settled himself on the couch and lay back with the baby stretched out across his chest. She wriggled for a moment or two until she got herself comfortable with her head resting on his left shoulder. The gentle rhythm of the baby girl's breathing helped to soothe Jake and, as she drifted off to sleep, his own eyelids grew heavy. Not wanting to spend a second night sleeping in the lounge, he started to sit up with every intention of placing Wren back in her travel bed. As soon as he moved, she whimpered and began to stir. Not wanting to disturb her, Jake lay back, telling himself he would give it ten minutes, then try to put her back to bed.

It was early when the bus pulled into the parking lot at the venue in Phoenix. Once the driver switched off the engine, killing the rhythmic thrum, everyone on board soon began to stir. In the back lounge, Jake opened his eyes to find Wren staring up at him, both of them still reclined on the couch under her soft blanket. Before he could move, the door opened and Maddy crept back in.

"Did you stay here all night?" she gasped when she saw Jake sprawled out along the couch.

With a yawn, he nodded, "This little angel was so settled, I hadn't the heart to move her. I guess I fell asleep too. What time is it?"

"Around seven. We've just pulled into Phoenix."

Hearing her mother's voice, the little girl wriggled round and held her arms out, "Mama! Mama!"

With her daughter in her arms, Maddy stepped aside to allow Jake space to stand up. He felt stiff from sleeping twisted all night and his shoulder was aching from the weight of the little girl. Rubbing sleep from his eyes, Jake said, "I'm going to freshen up and make some coffee. I'll leave you to sort these little guys out."

"Thanks for last night, Jake," said Maddison warmly. "Appreciated your help."

With a smile, he wandered off through the bus.

Snow was falling in soft flakes as Lori drove north, but, as she turned onto I-95, it fell thicker and heavier. The road in front of her was changing from grey to white, making her feel more than a little apprehensive. After what felt like an eternity of driving in blizzard conditions, she turned off the highway, safe in the knowledge that there were only a few more miles to go. Fortunately, the roads had been recently ploughed but it was with a huge sigh of relief that she drove slowly up Lucy's long, narrow driveway. The car snaked a little on the untreated surface, but, more than three hours after she had left the beach, she had made it safely.

"Oh, Lori, thank God!" squealed Lucy as she ran down her front steps into the snow. "I've been frantic! When I saw the snow, I didn't know where you were. Didn't know if you were ok. Oh, if anything had happened to you!"

"Calm down, Lucy," said Lori, sounding calmer than she truly felt. "The roads weren't so bad. They've mostly been ploughed."

"I'm just relieved you made it here safely."

"You and me both," agreed Lori as she limped round to open the trunk. "Can you give me a hand with my suitcase please? I didn't want to bring an extra overnight bag so my big bag needs to come in. Sorry."

"Of course," said Lucy, slithering through the snow to lift the zebra print suitcase from the car. "We might need to re-think going out to dinner."

"Let's wait an hour or so and see how it looks," suggested Lori, locking the car and following her sister-in-law indoors.

Within five minutes, they were both sitting in the warmth of the family kitchen with a mug of coffee and a packet of soft baked, chocolate chip cookies. The two boys, having come through to say hello, had disappeared back into the family room to continue playing with their Lego. Both of them had been disappointed that Jake hadn't arrived along with their aunt.

"You'd better let Jake know you got here safely," suggested

Lucy as she slipped a second cookie from the packet. "He'll be worried about you making that drive."

"I spoke to him earlier," replied Lori. "They are all tied up with press and media stuff for a few more hours. If I call him around eight, he should be free to talk for a minute or two. The time difference is making it awkward. He'd usually call after a show but it's been the middle of the night here."

"And I'll bet that hasn't stopped him!" giggled Lucy.

"Only once."

While they chatted and caught up with each other's news, it grew dark and the snow storm stopped. Inevitably, their conversation turned to the Silver Lake fan page that Lucy administered with help from Maddy. The band and Scott had been really generous with fresh stage shots and short video clips but what she was hoping for was some behind the scenes photos to share. It never ceased to amaze Lori how dedicated her sister-in-law was to the social media based fan page, but she drew a line at divulging too many personal photos.

"Mom!" called Sam from the family room. "I'm hungry. When's dinner?"

"Lord, it's after six!" exclaimed Lucy, glancing up at the wall clock above the family notice board. "What do you want to do about dinner? I could run out for pizza or steak sandwiches. I don't feel up to bundling everyone into their snow gear and into the car."

"Whatever the boys want is fine with me."

"Let me go through and ask them," said Lucy, getting up from the table.

While her sister-in-law was out of the room, Lori reached for her purse to fetch her phone. Quickly, she typed a message to Jake to say she was safely at Lucy's. Deliberately, she omitted to mention the blizzard conditions. As she was putting the phone back into her bag, Lucy returned.

"Well, the boys both voted for steak sandwiches and cheese fries," she declared. "Is that ok with you?"

"Perfect," said Lori, reaching for her wallet. "If you let me pay for them."

"No!" protested Lucy as Lori passed her forty dollars. "I'm not taking it, Lori."

"I insist."

"No."

"Ok, how about we split the bill?" offered Lori as a compromise.

"No. My treat," stated Lucy firmly. "It's a sorry day in this house if a guest buys their own cheese fries!"

Her emphatic comment made Lori giggle.

"I surrender," she said between giggles. "But at least let me lay the table for you?"

"Deal. We'll eat in here," replied Lucy as she lifted her car keys from the dish on the counter. "I'll call the order in to the new place up at the mall. Should be ready by the time I get there."

By the time Lucy returned with dinner, Lori had set the table, the boys were seated and she had poured glasses of apple juice for all four of them. After a bit of a hunt, she had located the cupboard where the dinner plates lived and had heated four up in the oven. Soon they were contentedly eating the best steak sandwiches Lori had tasted in a long time. While they ate, the boys plied her with questions about their Uncle Jake, the rest of the band and the tour.

"Mom," began Sam, helping himself to another half of sandwich. "When can we go to another Silver Lake show?"

"I don't know," replied Lucy, glancing over at Lori. "There aren't any shows near here just now."

"Lori," said Sam seriously. "Do you think Uncle Jake could play a show at my school? My friends would love to hear Silver Lake."

"I don't know, honey," answered Lori with a smile. "I'll ask Jake, but the boys are kind of busy just now. Once this tour is over they need to plan for their new album then record it this summer. I believe they are recording it at JJL. Perhaps Jake could take you to the studio to see how they make the record."

"That would be so cool!" exclaimed her nephew, his eyes wide with excitement at the very thought of being in the recording studio.

"No promises, but I think we can make that work," said Lori, lifting another cheese fry from the carton. "But I'll ask if they can play at your school too."

Philadelphia airport was crowded when Lori arrived to check in the following morning. There had been no more snow overnight, but, as a precaution, she had called to confirm the airport was open before she left the house.

Having checked in her luggage, Lori scanned the departures board. Delayed. Cancelled. There were very few flights on time, but, by some miracle, the Las Vegas flight was still showing as "on time." Once clear of security, Lori headed through the airport in search of a sandwich for lunch and some magazines for the flight. There were still two hours to kill until the flight was due to be called. Every food outlet was crowded with weary, delayed travellers so finding a seat proved impossible. Eventually, Lori surrendered and ordered herself a ham salad sandwich to take out. She paid the extra two dollars to add juice and a cookie to the meal deal then left the sandwich bar in search of a seat near her departure gate. Halfway along the concourse she paused to check one of the departures screens. Still "on time." Having made a stop at the newsstand to pick up some reading material, she finally made her way through the crowds to her departure gate. It too was busy, but there was one seat left facing the window.

With a sigh of relief, she lowered herself onto the hard, plastic chair. The damp snowy weather wasn't agreeing with her and, having walked twice the length of the airport, her leg was throbbing. Just as she bit into her sandwich, her phone began to ring in the depths of her bag. Quickly, she grabbed it, almost spilling her bottle of juice in the process.

"Hi," she answered brightly, smiling at the sight of Jake's contact details on the screen.

"Hi, li'l lady," came the familiar voice of her husband. "You ok?"

"Fine. Just grabbing a sandwich while I wait on them calling my flight."

"Is it on time?" asked Jake, concern echoing in his voice. "We've just pulled into Vegas and the news report on the radio said there had been a major snow storm on the east coast."

"So far, it's on time," replied Lori. "The snow storm stopped around here last night just after I arrived at Lucy's. It was pretty bad when I was on I-95."

"And you're sure you're ok?"

"Stop worrying. I'm absolutely fine. The roads were clear this morning. No issues getting here," assured Lori. "How was Phoenix?"

"Incredible! Amazing crowd. Really neat venue," enthused Jake. "Eight shows in ten days has been hard going."

"I'll bet," agreed Lori warmly. "But you're in good shape, aren't you?"

"Yeah, I'm good, li'l lady," he assured her. "Looking forward to seeing you in a few hours."

"Same here. Who's picking me up?"

"Most likely Jethro. We've some press interviews today. Tomorrow's totally free though, then we've the show on Wednesday," answered Jake.

In the background, Lori could hear voices then one of the twins squealing. She thought she could hear Maddy's shrill voice in the distance. Before she could ask, Jake spoke. "Need to go. Boss' yelling about checking in and grabbing our bags. I'll see you this afternoon."

"See you soon, rock star."

Despite the travel chaos surrounding her, the Las Vegas flight was called on time, wasn't over booked and left on schedule. Lori found herself sitting next to a tiny woman with snowy white hair. When the stewardess came round with the drinks trolley, the old woman ordered two Jack Daniels which she proceeded to drink neat. After a while, she engaged Lori in conversation and explained that she was returning to Las Vegas to play poker. She was the most unlikely looking gambler that Lori had ever met.

"My dear," she began sincerely. "Age works like a charm. No one suspects little ole me is a pro. I've been playing poker for nigh on seventy years. My daddy taught me when I was a little girl. I spend most of my winter in Vegas and then the summer in Atlantic City. Never gone home out of pocket yet."

"Love it!" giggled Lori, before taking a sip of her apple juice. "If you don't mind me asking, how much do you win on average?"

"Per trip?"

Lori nodded.

"In the past five years, I've never gone home without less than twenty five thousand dollars. Every trip's been a good 'un."

"How many trips a year do you take?"

"Oh, I travel at least once a month, honey."

For the remainder of the flight, Lori's magazines lay unopened on the small fold down table while she was kept entertained by her travelling companion. By the time the plane touched down at McCarran International airport, she had heard the woman's entire life story and found none of it boring. As they taxied towards the terminal building, the old woman asked her what brought her to Vegas.

Evasively, Lori replied, "I'm joining my husband on a business trip for a few days."

"A business trip? How dull!" commented her elderly companion. "From the magazines you've bought and not read, I figured you must be here to go to one of those God-awful rock-and-roll shows. A pretty girl like you should have a rock star on her arm."

Lori laughed before saying, "I'll tell my husband you said that!"

"Is he meeting you here?"

"His boss is picking me up, I think."

Towing her case behind her, Lori made her way out of the baggage hall towards the exit. She could feel bubbles of excitement mounting inside her at the thought of seeing Jake at the hotel in less than an hour. Two weeks apart had felt more like two months. When the automatic doors opened, she scanned the arrivals hall in search of Jethro. There was no sign of the band's manager. Slowly, she wandered towards the exit to the outside world, scanning the area for a familiar face or a hint of anyone from the Silver Lake camp. No one. A wave of panic was about to engulf her when a voice behind her said quietly, "Need a ride, li'l lady?"

"Jake!" she squealed, turning to find herself face to face with her husband.

Instantly, she was wrapped in his arms. With a sigh, she breathed in the aroma of his favourite deodorant and rested her cheek against his chest. She could hear his heart pounding.

"God, I've missed you," he whispered into her hair.

"I've missed you too," she replied, her eyes brimming with tears, happy tears. "I thought Jethro was meeting me."

"No," said Jake, shaking his head. "The plan was always that it would be me. I wanted to surprise you. Maddy wasn't too keen on letting me escape."

"I'll bet."

"Come on," said Jake, kissing her gently. "Let's get out of here before anyone recognises us."

As they walked hand in hand out into the cool February sun, Lori's travelling companion dashed past them. With a wave, she called back, "I knew you belonged with a rock star, honey!"

Jake drew his wife a puzzled look.

"I'll explain later," replied Lori with a smile. "You'd love that little old lady. She's quite a character. She's here to play poker."

"Poker?" echoed Jake as he led her towards a waiting minibus.

"Yes," nodded Lori. "She's a professional."

"Grandma the poker player?" laughed Jake, opening the door for her. "I can't wait to hear this story! Do you ever sit next to boring people on a flight, li'l lady?"

With a helping hand from her husband, Lori was soon comfortably seated in the minibus. Closing the door, Jake said, "Lori, this is Grime, our driver and new security detail."

"Hi," said Lori as the burly driver turned round.

"Afternoon, Mrs Power. Good flight?" he asked in a deep Southern drawl.

"Yes, thanks."

As the driver pulled away from the kerb, easing his way out into the traffic, Jake explained that Jethro had hired Grime after the show in Los Angeles. When they had left the venue, a crowd of fans had mobbed them as they tried to board the Silver Bullet. A few of them had been drunk and quite aggressive, causing the band's management to panic. When they had arrived in San Diego, Grime had been waiting for them and had become the latest member of the Silver Lake family.

It only took them fifteen minutes to drive to the hotel. In the chill of winter, it struck Lori as unusual to find herself being driven up a palm tree lined driveway to the front door of their hotel. The band had checked in earlier and, having thanked Grime for driving them, Jake helped Lori down from the bus and guided her into the hotel. Highly polished marble floors and towering pillars dominated the open reception area. With his arm securely around her waist, Jake headed straight for the elevators.

"We're on the eighth floor," he commented as they entered the large empty elevator. "Maddy's booked out a whole section of the floor for the band and crew. Grey's in the room next to us. Maddy and Paul are across the hall and Rich is next door to them."

"What's the plan for the rest of today?" asked Lori curiously. "Did you not say earlier that you had press stuff today?"

"I did my stint before I left to fetch you. Grey and Rich are doing the last couple of interviews on their own," explained Jake, smiling down at her. "We've an hour or so to ourselves before I said we'd meet Maddy, Paul and the meatballs for an early dinner. I guessed you'd be keen to see them."

"Sounds fine to me," agreed Lori, cuddling into him. "Anything's fine as long as we're together. I've missed you, rock star."

Just as Jake moved to kiss her, the elevator stopped and the doors opened. Towing her suitcase, he led her down the corridor to the left. When they reached their room, he slipped the key card out of the back pocket of his jeans, opened the door and allowed Lori to enter first. His bags lay on the floor at the foot of the king-sized bed, their contents already scattered around the large room. The floor to ceiling window afforded them a stunning view of the strip, which was just beginning to light up as the last of the daylight faded.

Laying her cane against the bed, Lori limped over to admire the view. Thoughtfully, she wondered which of the city's many casinos her elderly travelling companion had headed towards. With a smile, she unzipped her jacket, slipped it off, then turned round to lay it on the chair beside the dressing table.

"Wow!" exclaimed Jake, stepping over his bags to reach her. He laid his hand on her baby bump. "There's definitely no hiding this now."

"I know," said Lori with a giggle, placing her hand over his. "So much for hoping for a small bump. I think I'm going to be huge!"

"You look fabulous, li'l lady. Being pregnant suits you."

"Tell me that in a few weeks," she said. "When I can't see my feet and can barely walk."

"You'll still be beautiful," whispered Jake, his voice soft and husky. Lovingly, he bent down to kiss her. Their lips met. As Lori's lips parted, Jake bit her lower lip, then ran his tongue over her teeth. She stepped closer into his embrace, her growing baby belly hard between them, and began to kiss him deeply. Through his jeans, she could feel his erect hunger for her. Running his hand down her back and round to cup one breast, Jake murmured softly, "Hmmm, something else impending motherhood enhances."

Just as he was about to reach to undo her top, a knock at the door interrupted them.

"Shit," muttered Jake, pulling his shirt out of his jeans to hide his straining erection. "If this is Maddison, I'll throttle her."

Laughing, Lori limped over to the door, looked through the spy hole and said, "Be ready to commit murder, rock star," as she opened the door,

Out in the corridor, Maddy stood with Hayden balanced on her hip. The little boy was clutching a wooden toy truck in his hand and waved it at Lori as she opened the door wider.

"You made it!" shrieked Maddy with her distinctive harsh New York accent. "And look at you! You've a real baby belly!"

"Maddison," called Jake from behind Lori, "Your timing is impeccable!"

"Ignore him," laughed Lori, hugging her friend. "It's great to finally be back with you guys."

Before either of them could say another word, Hayden struck Lori on the side of the face with his toy truck.

"Ouch!" squealed Lori, stepping back.

"Naughty boy!" scolded Maddy sharply, snatching the wooden toy from her son. "That's bad, Hayden!"

"You ok?" asked Jake, immediately appearing at his wife's side.

Reaching up, Lori touched her brow then looked down at her fingers. They were covered in blood. Trying to hold back her tears, she replied, "I'll be fine. Stings. Let me go and put something cold on this."

Leaving Maddy disciplining her now tearful son and Jake berating the band's manager over allowing her child to have a dangerous toy, Lori made her way into the bathroom. She let the water run cold for a moment or two before soaking a wash cloth and pressing it to the cut. The gash was nipping. She had been surprised by the amount of blood that had run down her face as she had pressed the wet flannel in place. Pressing firmly, she took a few deep breaths, desperately trying to remain calm. After a couple of minutes, she lifted the cloth off and inspected the wound in the mirror. It was still bleeding freely and looked to be a gash about an inch long just beneath her eyebrow. Common sense told her it needed a couple of sutures. Holding the cloth firmly in place, she went back into the room.

"Are you ok, honey?" asked Maddy, her voice filled with concern.

"I'll be fine," replied Lori, forcing a weak smile. "But I think we may need to find an emergency room. The cut's quite deep. He caught me right on the edge of my eye socket."

"Let me see," said Jake, reaching to carefully remove the wet wash cloth. When he saw the fresh blood running out of the deep wound, he replaced the cloth and said, "Fetch Grime. We're going to the nearest medical centre, Maddison. That needs proper attention now."

Without a word of argument, Maddy rushed from the room in search of the band's driver. A few moments later, Jethro appeared with Grime close on his heel. Quickly, Jake filled them in on what had happened, explaining that it was an accident. When the band's older manager saw the blood on the flannel, he agreed they needed to find a doctor but suggested calling the concierge for advice.

"What a fuss," sighed Lori, taking a seat on the end of the bed. "Poor Hayden didn't mean any harm."

"I know he didn't," agreed Jake sitting beside her. "But that cut's nasty. You need to get someone to take a look at it."

"I know," she admitted. "Great start to my trip!"

A few minutes later, Jethro returned to say that the concierge had given him directions to the best medical centre in town and that Grime had gone to fetch the minibus from the car park. Still with the cloth in place, Lori allowed Jake and Jethro to fuss over her as they escorted her downstairs.

Two hours later, with a supporting arm around Lori's waist, Jake led her back into their hotel room. Between her flight, the time difference and the stress of the unplanned trip to the ER, she was exhausted and hungry. They had been fortunate to be seen quickly at the medical centre and, after an examination by a young doctor, a triage nurse had come in and put three neat sutures in the cut before covering it over with a small dressing. She had cautioned Lori that it would be a little tender for a day or two and that it was likely to bruise.

As soon as she was back in the hotel room, Lori went over to the dressing table to inspect her eye in the mirror.

"Guess I'll need to buy some sunglasses to cover this," she observed with a smile. "People might think you hit me!"

"Never," responded Jake instantly. "I'd never raise my hand to you. Or to any other woman. The shades might be a good move though. Now, what do you want to do about dinner? You must be starving."

"Let's just get room service," suggested Lori with a yawn. "Order me some kind of chicken. Something light but not a salad. I'm going to go and see Maddy for a few minutes."

Leaning heavily on her cane, she made her way across the room, closing the door behind her. Once alone out in the corridor, Lori stood for a moment to gather her thoughts. It had been a whirlwind few hours and she needed a minute or two alone. Taking a deep breath, she went over to knock on Maddy and Paul's door. She could hear one of the twins crying. It was Paul who opened the door.

"Shit, Lori!" he gasped at the sight of the white dressing on her eyebrow. "You ok?"

"I'm fine," she assured him with a warm smile. "It was an accident. I just came to let Maddy know we were back."

"Come on in," said the band's drummer, stepping aside. "She's trying to settle Wren. Little madam is fighting sleep."

"OK, just for a minute," agreed Lori.

The entire hotel room was in a state of chaos. It was an identical room to the one she and Jake had, except for the two travel cribs that were set up under the window. Dimmed lighting illuminated the room and Lori could see that Hayden was already curled up sound asleep. Hearing voices, Maddy turned towards the door and let out a soft squeal when saw the dressing on Lori's eye.

"Oh, Lord, I am so sorry," she said quietly. "Did it need sutured, honey?"

Lori nodded, "Three small sutures. The nurse thought about gluing it, but decided to suture it instead. It's fine though. Nothing to worry about."

"But you'll have a scar," sighed Maddy sadly as she clutched a wriggling, fretful Wren.

"Another one to add to my collection," joked Lori. "Look, let's hear no more about it. I'll buy some sunglasses in the morning to hide it from prying eyes. Can't have the media making up stories about Jake being a wife beater."

"Fuck! I hadn't thought of that!" shrieked Maddy shrilly, startling her daughter into silence.

"Look, I'm going to get some dinner. I'll see you all in the morning," said Lori, trying to stifle a yawn. "It's been a long day."

Midnight had come and gone and Jake was still sitting on the couch that ran the length of the room's magnificent picture window. He had changed into lounge pants and a T-shirt, fully intending to follow Lori to bed and have an early night but sleep refused to come. After an hour of lying staring up at the ceiling, he had slipped out of bed and gone to sit by the window, gazing out at the neon lit strip below. Every few minutes, he glanced over at his sleeping wife and a fresh wave of guilt washed through him when he spotted the dressing over her eye. Her throwaway comment about the press suspecting he'd hit her had sent chills through him. Never would he lift his hand to a woman. The very thought made his blood run cold.

His battered, leather book bag lay on the floor beside him. Reaching down, he pulled out the journal he used to scribble his lyrics in. He still hadn't come up with lyrics to go with the blues based track the band had recorded in rehearsal before they had left for the tour. Now, as he watched Lori sleep, her hand resting protectively across her pregnant belly, words flowed effortlessly through his mind. His acoustic guitar lay in its case in the corner of the room and Jake was itching to play the song over to check that his newly penned words went with the flow of the melody line but that confirmation would need to wait until morning. Instead, he fetched his cell phone and his ear buds and listened to the rough recording they had made in rehearsal. Hearing it again helped as he ran over the words scrawled on the page in front of him. Ever the perfectionist, it took him another two hours to be content with the final wording of his lyrics. In his usual messy hand writing, he scribbled the title last – Baby Eyed Blues.

With a yawn, Jake laid the journal and his phone down on the couch beside him, then lay back looking at the world outside.

"And they say New York is the city that never sleeps," he thought as his eyelids began to feel heavy.

The sound of a TV show wakened Lori not long after dawn. It seemed to be coming from the room above, the theme tune reminding her of one of the shows Becky liked to watch. Beside her, the bed lay empty and looked as though it hadn't been slept in. A wave of panic washed over her. Where was Jake? Through the last foggy haze of sleep, she could hear him snoring. She rolled over then smiled when she saw him spread eagled across the couch. It reminded her of the first night he had fallen asleep at the beach house and Mary, her housekeeper at the time, had found him, half dressed and snoring in the morning. Precious happy memories.

She lay on her side, watching him sleep; watching the gentle rhythm of his breathing as his chest rose and fell. Long strands of his sun-bleached hair fell over his face, occasionally causing his mouth to twitch. Gently, Lori rubbed her baby bump and half whispered, "Your daddy looks so peaceful sleeping over there, little one."

As she moved her hand away, she felt a gentle fluttery feeling in her stomach. Over the past few days she had felt it a few times, but dismissed it as her stomach rumbling through hunger, but was it? Slowly, she massaged her swollen tummy, then lifted her hand off. Again, she felt a flurry of flutters, almost like bubbles popping inside her. With a smile, Lori realised it was the baby! She was feeling their baby moving and seemingly responding to the touch of her hand. The movements were too tiny to be detected from the outside but knowing that the baby was awake and kicking her gently was reassuring.

Over by the window, Jake stirred as he rolled onto his side. With a soft snort and a grunt, he wriggled restlessly, then opened his eyes. When he saw his wife staring at him from the warmth of the bed, he grinned.

"Morning," he whispered huskily. "Wha' time is it?"

"Just gone seven," replied Lori quietly. "Have you been there all night?"

"Looks like it," sighed Jake as he sat up. His back was aching from sleeping at an inclined angle on the firm settee. Stiffly, he walked over to the bed then slid in under the duvet beside her.

"You ok?" he asked, gently fingering the dressing over her eye.

"I'm fine. Don't fuss."

"And what about baby?" asked Jake softly, resting his hand on her bump.

"Awake," she revealed with a smile.

"You can feel it?"

Lori giggled and nodded. "I felt it a few minutes ago. Tiny flutters but definitely our baby moving about."

"And how does it feel?" asked Jake, gently drawing circles on her stomach. "How does it feel to know he or she is wriggling about ready to start their day?"

"Reassuring. Weird in a nice way," replied Lori as she felt another flurry of fluttery movements inside her. "It feels a bit like bubbles popping. Tiny little movements."

"Well, we both know that's not going to last," teased Jake with a grin. "Remember Maddy complaining about the twins kicking her day and night? You could see lumps sticking out of her belly too!"

Giggling, Lori agreed that she wasn't too sure how she would feel when the movements grew stronger.

"What's the plan for today?" she asked, rolling over to face her husband.

"Before or after I make love to you?" countered Jake, reaching down and slipping his hand inside her lacy underwear. He slipped his fingers between her legs, quickly finding the nub of her clitoris. Slowly, he began circling it with his thumb. Beside him, Lori purred softly as she rolled onto her back.

"Definitely after," she whispered as Jake bent to kiss her.

Covering her in tender kisses, Jake helped her to remover her T-shirt and to discard her flimsy hot pink panties on the floor. With a show of impatience, Jake roughly hauled off his own top and lounge pants. He knelt in between her legs and bent forward so that his long hair tickled her bare stomach. With a mischievous glint in his eyes, Jake slowly but firmly licked tiny circles around her firm rounded belly. As she relaxed beneath her husband's caresses, Lori could feel her stomach alive with activity. Carefully, she arched her back, thrusting her hips forward towards her husband. His tongue continued its exploratory journey down towards her pubic bone, then he could hold back no longer. Two weeks without his wife in his bed had put paid to patience. Slowly, he eased his manhood inside her, feeling her moist and ready to receive him. All thoughts of taking it slowly and gently vanished the instant their intimate flesh connected. While Lori wrapped her legs around him, Jake thrust hard and fast, every inch of him craving the intimacy. Beneath him, Lori moved in time with his frenzied rhythm, moaning softly as their bodies soared towards a mutual orgasm.

As Jake climaxed explosively inside her, filling her with a fire that she had craved for days, Lori breathed out his name with a low husky moan and dug her long, manicured nails into his shoulders.

Spent, Jake rolled to the side and lay with one leg draped over her thighs.

"God, I've missed you," he sighed, his hazel eyes still burning with lust for his wife.

"I could tell."

They lay entwined together for another hour, sometimes chatting, sometimes kissing, but mainly just enjoying simply being together again.

Eventually, Lori apologised and said she really had to get up. While she was in the bathroom taking a shower, Jake ordered breakfast from room service and slipped back into his lounge pants, not wanting the bus boy to catch him in a state of undress. When Lori re-entered the bedroom, wrapped in a large, fluffy towelling robe, a trolley full of pastries and cereal had been delivered, along with juice and coffee. Jake had switched on the TV and stumbled across Scooby Doo on one of the cartoon channels. Like two big kids, they sat on the bed, eating their breakfast watching cartoons.

While Jake took a shower, Lori got dressed then called out that she was going down to see if the hotel's shops were open. Feeling self-conscious about her eye injury, she had brushed her hair to the side so that it fell in a cascade over her face, shielding prying eyes from the wound.

Having consulted the resort map in the room, Lori set off in search of the shops that were located between their building and the Luxor Hotel next door. It took her longer than she had expected to find her way through the hotel, then up the escalators to the strip mall. Most of the stores were just opening up to start trading for the day. After a quick check of the store directory, Lori set off again, the tip of her cane squealing slightly on the polished floor. Fortunately, the first store she chose had a good range of sunglasses on display. Having tried on a few pairs, she opted for two pairs in a classic Jackie Onassis style – one in black, one in tortoiseshell and both pairs large enough to cover her wound. Having paid for them, she asked the assistant to remove the tags. Wearing the tortoiseshell pair, Lori made her way back through the complex to their room.

When she stepped out of the elevator, she bumped into Grey and Rich, who had been standing waiting for it to take them downstairs.

"Good morning, Mrs Power," greeted Grey with mock formality. "Travelling incognito this morning?"

"Not exactly," she replied. "Didn't you hear about all the fuss last night?"

"No," said Rich, spotting the edge of the dressing at the side of her sunglasses. "We were in the casino. What happened to you?"

"Hayden hit me with a wooden toy truck. Split my eye," explained Lori, removing her glasses. "Cue mad dash to the ER and, three sutures later, welcome to Vegas!"

"Ouch!" said Grey, squirming at the thought. Coping with the sight of blood had never been one of his strong points and the thought of the cut made him feel nauseous. "You ok?"

"I'm fine, but I thought I better invest in some shades before we venture out. Don't want any journalists thinking Jake did it!"

"Now, there's a point," acknowledged Rich with a nod. "Quick thinking. So, what are your plans for the day?"

"No idea," replied Lori. "I'm just going to see if Jake's decided what he feels like doing. What are your plans?"

"We were going to explore a bit then probably check out the casino," replied Rich. "We could meet for lunch or dinner if you like?"

"Let me check with Jake and one of us will call you later," said Lori, reluctant to commit to anything without speaking to her husband first. "Try not to lose too much money if you are playing with the big boys."

"Won two grand last night," commented Grey with a wink. "Some of my mom's luck must have rubbed off on me."

"Grey, we both know, if Annie had been playing, she would be up at least ten," teased Lori light heartedly. "Have a fun day, boys. I promise we'll catch up with you later."

When she reached the hotel room door, Lori realised she had forgotten to lift a key card to get back into the room. As she stood outside the door, she could hear Jake playing some Delta blues on his guitar. Smiling, she stood listening for a minute or two before reaching out to knock the door. The music stopped and, a few seconds later, she heard the door being unlocked.

"Forget your key, li'l lady?" teased Jake as she stepped inside. "Li'l shady lady."

"Very funny, rock star," laughed Lori, removing her dark glasses. "I feel kind of ridiculous wearing shades in February."

"It's Vegas. Nothing is too ridiculous for this town!"

"True," she agreed, before adding. "I met Rich and Grey by the elevator. They want to meet up later for lunch or dinner. I said one of us would call them. Hope that's ok?"

"I guess," said Jake, crossing the room to lift his guitar. "Jethro called while you were gone. Wanted to know our plans. Maddy and Paul are having a family day with the meatballs. Think Jethro was feeling a bit lost and out of things."

"We can spend the day with Jethro," said Lori without hesitation.

"I hoped you'd say that," confessed Jake with a relieved smile. "We're meeting him for lunch at twelve thirty."

"Perfect. Now, what were you playing when I came to the door, rock star? Blues?"

"Grab a seat and I'll show you."

He settled himself on the couch with his acoustic guitar while Lori sat down in the big armchair in the corner. Bowing his head and closing his eyes for a moment, Jake composed himself before beginning to play. His first guitar teacher had been a blues fan and had taught him to play using several well-known blues songs and practice pieces. Playing again more recently with Salazar had refreshed the technique. With a calm confidence, he played through the song without adding the lyrics.

"Love it," declared Lori, when he was finished. "Different to your usual Silver Lake style, but it works. Any lyrics for it?"

"Yes," he replied a little hesitantly, glancing down at his open journal. "That's what I was doing last night when I fell asleep over here."

Taking a deep breath, Jake began the song for a second time, tapping his toe to a steady blues rhythm. With a slightly more nasal sound to his voice, Jake sang the lyrics he had written; lyrics that described an unborn child's thoughts on the world they were about to enter.

"Clever," nodded Lori when the song was over. "Nice twist on the view of the world."

"Thank you," replied Jake, feeling himself blush at his wife's compliments. "I'll play it for the guys at sound check tomorrow. We worked on the music in rehearsal at JJL. The lyrics only became clear last night."

"They'll love them," promised Lori, watching him place his guitar back into its velvet lined case. "Is that the first track for the new record?"

Jake nodded. "We've been playing with a few bits and pieces at sound checks and on the bus, but that's the first full song."

"Good start. "

"I hope so," he sighed. Glancing at his watch, Jake added, "We've just over an hour until we're due to meet Jethro. Do you want to take a walk? Explore this place a bit?"

"Fine by me."

Deciding to stay indoors, Jake and Lori meandered through the glittering hotel complex, hand in hand. Ultimately, they ended up in one of the casinos and Lori joked that they should check the poker room to see if her elderly travelling companion was at one of the tables. Everywhere was bustling with activity and, as they entered the poker room, Lori nudged Jake, pointing across the room.

"There she is," she whispered, trying to stifle a giggle.

"And that's some pile of chips beside her," commented Jake, shaking his head. "Pity Annie isn't here. They'd make the perfect pair."

"They'd clean up," laughed Lori as they turned to leave.

"Most likely."

With time to kill until lunch, Lori suggested they play some of the machines. Before Jake could stop her, she'd cashed in a hundred dollars and split it with him. They found two adjacent machines that were vacant near to where they had arranged to meet Jethro and spent a fun few minutes battling the odds against the bright, flashing lights of the slot machines. Neither of them were winning much, apart from five or ten dollars here and there.

"Try that one by the door, Lori," suggested Jethro when he arrived. "I've a good feeling in my braids about it."

"You're incorrigible," laughed Lori, switching machines. "Here goes nothing."

As the machine swallowed the last of her gambling stake money, she watched as the symbols lined up. Amid a frenzy of over the top music and flashing lights, the machine paid out a jackpot of five thousand dollars. The win attracted the attention of those nearby. Exactly the attention Lori had been keen to avoid. She excused herself and left Jake to collect her winnings while she hurriedly left the area, heading towards the nearest restaurant.

When Jake and the band's manager caught up with her, she was standing with her back to them, pretending to be engrossed in the menu board.

"You're ok, Lori," assured Jake, putting his arm around her waist. "No one recognised us."

"Oh, thank goodness," she gasped, turning to bury her face in his chest. "I'm so scared the press pick up on my eye injury and get the wrong idea. When all those lights and bells went off, I panicked."

"Relax," soothed Jake warmly. "Now, lunch is definitely on you, Mrs Power. That was a sweet little five thousand dollar bonus."

"I guess it was," she agreed. "Ok, but it's noodles for lunch. I like the sound of this menu."

"Noodles work for us," agreed Jake, leading the way into the restaurant.

The following day, almost exactly twenty four hours later, the band met in the same spot for a pre-show lunch. Between one thing and another, their paths had barely crossed the day before, and, due to various press commitments that had filled the morning, they'd barely had a chance to chat. Now that they were all gathered round the one dining table, they were all talking at once. The twins had been left back at the hotel with the nanny. Just as their meal was served, Scott arrived with his camera bag.

"Christ, can't I even enjoy my lunch in peace without you appearing with that fucking camera?" grumbled Grey as the photographer unpacked his bag.

"Candid shots by the request of the management," stated Scott, glancing over at Maddy for confirmation.

"He's right, Grey," confirmed Maddy firmly. "Relaxed pre-show promo shots so chill a bit."

Before Scott could start, Jethro interrupted, "And be mindful of which angle you shoot Lori from. No baby bump or eye bump pictures, young man."

"Yes, sir," agreed Scott, winking over at Lori. "Message received and understood."

"Thanks, Scott," said Lori with a smile.

"Where's Ellen?" asked Rich, noting that the After Life songstress was absent.

"Packing her suitcase so she's ready to check out later," replied Scott, casually photographing the band.

"Jake," began Lori. "Are you duetting with Ellen tonight? I'm looking forward to hearing Mysteries."

"That's the plan."

"I'd love to watch from out front," commented Lori, almost wistfully. "Soak up some of the atmosphere."

"No way, li'l lady," said Jake. "Not in your delicate condition."

"I'm pregnant, not ill," retorted Lori sharply.

"Not tonight, honey," intervened Maddy calmly. "Wait until you're with us in Minneapolis or, even better, Kansas City. Your eye will be healed up and you'll not need those Jackie O shades."

"Promise?"

"I promise," said Maddy, ignoring the dark look that Jake was drawing her. "But only if Grime goes with you as chaperone."

"Deal," agreed Lori quickly, avoiding Jake's thunderous glare.

"What time do we need to head over to the venue?" asked Grey, in an attempt to diffuse matters.

"As soon as we're through here," answered Jethro. "There's no official fan meet and greet today, but there's a few invited guests coming along. Sound check's at three thirty."

Once the band were in the venue, the Silver Lake machine slipped into motion. Leaving Lori backstage, Jake was the first onto the stage ready for sound check. Deliberately he had sidestepped half a dozen invited guests, wanting to focus on the rehearsal before switching on the "corporate smile." This show was the first in a run of four consecutive nights and he wanted to ensure he was warmed up thoroughly beforehand. When he'd seen the tour schedule, Jake had voiced his concern about doing two stints of four shows in a row. It was a big ask of his voice. The set lists were lying on top of the drum riser, ready to be taped to their positions on the stage. Scanning the proposed list of songs, Jake inwardly debated about whether to change a few around.

"What's up?" asked Rich, appearing on stage beside him. "You wanting to change it?"

"Perhaps," replied Jake without looking up. "Maybe not for tonight though. I think I need to make it easier on me for one night out of the four though. We can talk about moving it about for Oklahoma City or Dallas."

"Four in a row's really worrying you, isn't it?"

"A bit. I'm just being paranoid, but I don't want to damage my voice," admitted Jake honestly. "Don't want to risk anything we don't have to."

"I hear you."

Behind them, they could hear Grey begin to run through his standard warm up riffs.

"Are you two going to whisper all day or are we getting started?" he called over.

"We're getting started," declared Jake, reaching for his own guitar. "Engine Room?"

"Fine by me," agreed Grey. "Then can we run through Far Reaches?"

"Deal."

Backstage, Lori had settled herself in the dressing room with her laptop and her sketchpad. Experience had taught her to stay out of the way while the band were getting set up unless she was specifically invited to watch their sound check. Both Maddy and Jethro had disappeared, both running errands to make sure everything was in place for the show. In the room next door, she could hear After Life chilling before it was time for their sound check. Her laptop powered up swiftly and Lori was soon hooked up to the venue's internet connection. As she browsed through her emails, she spotted that there were four messages from David, her financial advisor, all of which had been sent as high importance, flagged and marked as urgent in the subject heading. She read over them carefully, each of them relating to different aspects of her Hyde Properties business; all of them advising of contracts that needed her signature before close of business on 14th February. Consulting her schedule and travel arrangements, Lori decided to change her plans. Instead of flying back to Philadelphia from Dallas, she would fly to New York, spend a few days at her apartment and travel to Minneapolis to catch up with the tour from there. She had no medical appointments lined up or anything else that couldn't be postponed. A few phone calls later and her flights had been re-arranged. As she heard the thunder of footsteps and the band's voices approaching, she typed up a brief email to David advising him she would arrive in New York on Sunday, depart on Thursday and requesting that he have her apartment stocked and ready for her arrival.

"You've got your Mz Hyde look on," commented Jake as he came over to sit on the table beside her laptop. "You ok?"

"Fine. Just taking care of some business," she replied as she shut down the computer. "I had some urgent emails from David. I need to be in New York for a few days. I'll head there after Dallas and fly back out to meet you in Minneapolis on the 13th."

"And I assume you've already changed your flights?"

Lori nodded. "David needs me to sign some paperwork. It makes sense."

"I guess," he agreed, getting to his feet. "Maddy has a light dinner set up for us next door. Let's go eat before I need to go and warm up."

Over dinner, Lori commented that she would like to watch After Life's set. Before Maddy or Jethro could object, Jake said he wouldn't mind watching some of it too. All too soon their early evening meal was over and the band members each went about their own pre-show rituals. The VIP guests that the record company had invited had arrived and were all contentedly mingling in the backstage area. Several of them were musicians that Lori had done work for in the past and she spent a pleasant enough hour, making polite conversation with them and dodging awkward questions about the cut over her eye. She was relieved when she saw Jake come back into the room. Excusing himself past two record company representatives, he made his way over to join her. Putting his arm around her waist, he apologised to the journalist she was speaking with and led her through the room and back out into the corridor without another word.

"Where are we going?" she asked as she watched Jake put on his hoodie and beanie.

"Sh, li'l lady," he said. "Put this on. Keep your shades on and follow me."

He handed her a Silver Lake beanie that he had begged from the merchandise girls earlier. As he guided her through the venue, Jake put on a pair of dark glasses and double checked that his hair was all tucked up into his hat. They stopped by one of the exits and he advised her to put her hood up.

"Jake, where are you taking me?"

"You wanted to see After Life, didn't you?"

"Yes," replied Lori looking confused.

"Well, I checked and there are a few empty seats on the balcony. We're going to watch the show."

"Did you clear this with Maddy?"

Jake shook his head and grinned, "I won't tell her if you don't, li'l lady."

Lori squeezed his hand and promised to stay silent.

Leading her through to a staircase to the balcony, Jake added, "I'll need to disappear when they start their last number. You stay in your seat though. Grime will be up to join you. It's all sorted."

"I get to watch your set too?"

"That's what you wanted, wasn't it?"

"Yes, but you were so against it earlier," said Lori as they climbed the stairs.

"I was against you being out on the floor in the general access area," countered Jake. "But, if you want to watch from out there, then your wish is my command."

"Thank you."

"You can thank me later," he teased.

The loge level seating was steadily filling up as Jake guided his wife towards their seats. He had secured two end of row seats, just below the disabled access area. Around them, the seats were full of excited Silver Lake fans. Through her tinted lenses, Lori was struggling to see clearly, but Jake whispered that she could take them off once the lights went down.

Trying not to giggle and draw attention to them, Lori sat quietly, holding Jake's hand. Below them, she watched as After Life's roadies finished setting up the stage. Laying out water and towels beside the drum kit. Bang on eight thirty, the house lights dimmed and an expectant cheer rose from the capacity crowd. In a blaze of red light, After Life appeared on stage. Without daring to glance over at her husband, Lori removed her beanie and her sunglasses.

Out on stage, After Life were delivering a first class performance. Ellen, in her witch guise, was wearing a new costume. The English songstress had back combed her platinum blonde hair and the lights enhanced the crazed effect. She was wearing a new hooded, red, velvet cloak and was using its voluminous fabric with dramatic effect.

"That girl has an awesome future," commented Jake after Ellen had delivered a blistering performance of the band's current single. "One more and I need to slip out. Stay here. Grime will be up in a few minutes."

"Do I get to stay for the full Silver Lake set?"

Jake nodded, "Unless Grime tells you to leave before the end. We can't hang about tonight. We've a long drive to Albuquerque ahead of us and press to do before lunch tomorrow."

"I hear you," said Lori quietly as After Life began their penultimate song.

Less than five minutes later, Jake tapped her on the knee, blew her a kiss and slipped silently out of his seat.

When the house lights went up at the end of the support band's forty minute set, Lori glanced round. There was no sign of Grime. To her right sat a woman with her teenage daughter. They were sharing a bag of hard candy.The woman turned and offered some to Lori.

"No, thank you," she replied with a smile.

"You sure, honey?" said the woman, her accent echoing with a hint of a Southern drawl. "Where did your friend go?"

"He had to go into work," replied Lori evasively.

"Pity. He's going to miss an awesome show."

"Yeah," agreed Lori still smiling. "At least he got to see After Life before he got the call to go in."

"Have you seen Silver Lake before?" asked the woman.

"Once or twice."

"I love them!" gushed the older woman, flushing red. "Especially Jake. He's hot! I wish he'd take his shirt off like he did for the Weigh Station shows in London. Oh to have been there!"

Giggling, Lori replied, "Well, it's getting kind of hot in here so you never know."

Before she could continue the conversation, she felt someone move into the seat to her left. Much to her surprise, she turned around to find Jethro beside her.

"Hi," she said quietly. "Where's Grime? I thought he was coming up?"

"Issue with security at the bus. Someone tried to break in. He's staying downstairs to keep an eye on it," explained the band's tour manager. "Jake insisted someone come up and sit with you so here I am."

"Glad to see you," replied Lori with a warm smile at her old friend. "I'll let him know you're here."

She reached into her bag for her cell phone. Quickly she typed a message to Jake. "Jethro here. Fan beside me wants you to take your shirt off! Thanks for this. Love you. L x."

Slipping the phone back into her bag, Lori settled herself back in her seat. Gently, she ran her hand over her bump.

"You ok?" asked Jethro, noticing the movement.

"I'm fine," assured Lori softly. "First time this little Power Pack has been to a show. Well, since they've been big enough to wriggle about."

"I'm sure it'll be at plenty more before they arrive into this world," commented Jethro with a wink. "We're finalising a few contracts for festivals in May. Plenty of opportunity for your little angel to rock out."

"May?" echoed Lori, trying to figure out how many weeks pregnant she would be by then. "As long as I don't need to fly and all goes well, I should be fine for May."

As Jethro began to comment further, the lights dimmed and the almighty roar from the crowd drowned out his reply. Around them in the dark, the chant started, gradually growing louder and louder. "Silver Lake, Silver Lake, Silver Lake, Lake, Lake." Just as Lori didn't think the fans could get any louder, Silver Lake ran out on stage, the lights blazed and the opening segment of Engine Room filled the room. Smiling proudly, she watched Jake and Rich stand back to back, heads pounding in time to the music. With a flick of his hair, Jake looked up and spun round to stand in front of his microphone, his movement timed to perfection.

It was the first time Lori had heard the boys play some of the songs from Impossible Depths on stage. Hearing them live for the first time brought out her inner rock fan and she was soon on her feet, singing and cheering along with the other fans on the balcony.

"Good evening, Vegas!" roared Jake from the stage.

The crowd roared back.

"I can't hear you! Good evening, Las Vegas!" Jake screamed. "How the fuck are you tonight?"

A deafening roar surged back at him as he threw back his head and laughed.

"Are you in fine voice tonight?" He paused until the roar subsided. "Who's got our album Impossible Depths?"

From the thunderous reaction, his question generated, everyone in the room had it.

"Ok. This is a new one for us from the record. First time we've attempted this one live. This is Vortex!"

As soon as she heard Jake's vocal for the song, Lori realised why they had added it. It was his mid-range, no extremes therefore easier to sing. Trying to recall the set list she had seen earlier, she wondered which song had been sacrificed for the evening.

A hush fell over the crowd when one of the stage crew brought out a wooden stool three songs later. It stood alone in a single spotlight for a few moments until Jake re-appeared with his acoustic guitar. With a wave to the fans, he took a moment or two to settle himself, then said, "You still with us?"

The cheer echoing back left him in no doubt.

"I'm going to mix things up a bit tonight, folks. This is another track from the record, but let's do it acoustically tonight. This is

Depths."

From her seat, Lori watched as Jake closed his eyes and began to play the soft, eerie intro to the song. A few bars in, he started to whistle an equally chilling accompaniment. Around her, the crowd were silent, unsure what to expect. On her left, she was aware of Jethro leaning forward, engrossed in the show. Opening his eyes, Jake started to sing, his voice lighter and higher than his usual style. Keeping her eyes focussed on him, Lori watched as her husband poured all his emotions into the song. As the last note faded out, Jake bowed his head and she watched as his shoulders rose and fell a few times as he took a few deep breaths to compose himself.

Raising his head, Jake gazed out at the audience, drinking in their applause. He glanced up towards where Lori and Jethro were seated and flashed them a smile.

"This is Stronger Within," he announced, still looking up towards where Lori was sitting. "Li'l lady wife, this is for you."

The woman on Lori's right nudged her and said, "Oh, his wife must be up here! I wonder where she's sitting?"

"I'm sure she's somewhere he can keep an eye on her," commented Lori as Jake began the familiar intro to Stronger Within.

Half an hour later, as Silver Lake began Flyin' High to bring their encore to an end, Jethro leaned over and said to Lori, "Time to go."

She nodded and got stiffly to her feet. With a quick check that she had lifted all of her things, Lori slowly followed the band's manager out of the row, towards a door marked "Private." Behind her, she could hear Silver Lake reaching the climax of the song and she couldn't resist pausing for a moment to watch.

"Come on, young lady," scolded Jethro with fatherly concern.

Reluctantly, Lori followed the band's manager out into the private stairwell and back through the corridors to the dressing rooms.

It was almost two in the morning by the time Jethro and Grime escorted Silver Lake from the venue and on to the Silver Bullet. Both Paul and Maddy had slipped off quickly after the show, having opted to travel separately with the twins and their nanny and the After Life entourage. Jake and Lori were the last two to board the tour bus. As usual, Jake had mislaid something, prompting a frantic search of the dressing rooms for his wallet and his phone.

"Sorry, folks," apologised Jake as they entered the lounge.

"Did you find your gear?" asked Rich, who was stretched out along the couch.

"Yeah. They were in my jacket pocket," replied Jake sheepishly. "And the jacket was still hanging over the back of a chair."

"Close call, Mr Power," commented Grey as he opened a bottle of beer. "Want one?"

"Not tonight," said Jake. "Warm honey water for me."

"Is your throat ok?" asked Lori, taking a seat next to Grey.

"Fine. Just taking precautions."

With a judder, the bus's engine started and the driver pulled out of the parking lot. Soon they were clear of the city and gliding smoothly along the highway. A noise from the back lounge caught their attention and they all looked up as Todd and Scott came stumbling down past the bunks and into the front lounge.

"Yes, gentlemen?" said Jethro sternly. "What were you two up to back there?"

"Watching a movie," replied Scott without hesitation. "With a few beers."

"Short movie. We've only been on the road for about half an hour," observed Jethro, again playing the fatherly role.

"We skipped a few scenes," confessed Todd. "We only watched the educational sections."

"I'll bet," said Jake, trying not to laugh as his former student squirmed under his gaze.

"Tell me about these "educational sections", Todd," teased Lori innocently.

The young guitar technician flushed scarlet as the rest of them burst out laughing.

"Get to bed, son," suggested Jethro with a grin. "That's where I'm headed. And take some Kleenex with you."

This prompted a further round of hilarity as Rich tossed a box of tissues at Todd.

"I'll leave you to it," declared Lori. "I'm calling it a night. And, Todd, no sound effects from that bunk of yours, please."

"Mz Hyde!" he exclaimed, a scarlet flush rising up from his neck again.

"Did you leave the DVD back there?" enquired Grey casually,

bending to pick up the box of tissues.

"Yeah. It's still in the player," replied Scott, fearing they were in trouble for breaking a bus rule about returning discs to their boxes.

"Then I think I may "educate" myself before bed," said the bass player.

Without a backwards glance, Grey headed for the back lounge.

Life on the road with Silver Lake fell into an easy routine and, within a day, Lori felt as though she'd been with them since the start of the tour. Sleeping on the bus still proved to be a challenge for her and being pregnant wasn't making it any easier to get some sleep. Their schedule didn't allow for hotels until they reached Dallas. Both the shows in Albuquerque and Oklahoma City were sell out successes. The band had tweaked the set list each night, but Jake's duet with Ellen and the acoustic version of Depths made the cut every night. Each night, Lori watched the band's performance from the side of the stage and, while she loved to watch the boys in action, she missed the buzz of being a part of the crowd.

It wasn't long after sunrise when the Silver Bullet pulled up outside the band's chosen hotel in Dallas. None of them had had any sleep during the four hour ride from Oklahoma City. When the bus stopped, they all stumbled wearily down the steps. Efficient as ever, Maddy took Lori inside to start their check in while the boys sorted out their luggage. The band's manager had called on ahead to confirm Silver Lake's dawn check in time and the booking clerk had promised to have everything waiting for them.

When they reached the front desk, it was the same young male clerk who greeted them.

"Morning, Miss Addison. I've got all your room cards ready. We've put you all on the third floor for your stay. All adjacent or facing rooms."

Efficiently, he issued her with the room numbers and agreed she could sign for the group check in rather than delay them all individually. By the time Jake and the others wandered in, Maddy and Lori were waiting to hand out their room details.

"Come on, rock star," said Lori with a yawn. "Let's get some sleep."

Jake nodded and followed her towards the elevators. Both Rich and Grey stepped into the waiting elevator beside them and they all travelled up to the third floor in exhausted silence. With mumbled "good nights", they wandered off in search of their rooms. As Jake's hands were full with his suitcase, guitar case and book bag, Lori led the way and opened the door. A huge bed dominated the room. Dropping his belongings over by the window, Jake drew the drapes, kicked off his shoes and collapsed onto the bed.

"I'm beat," he said, his words almost swallowed up in a yawn.

"Me too," agreed Lori, taking her jacket off. "Get undressed and get into bed, rock star."

With a sleepy but mischievous grin, he replied, "There'll be none of that, Mz Hyde. I need my beauty sleep."

Giggling, Lori began to get undressed. As she slipped under the crisp, fresh bedcovers, she said, "I'll set the alarm for noon. Maddy said to be ready for one."

Stripping off his jeans, Jake sighed, "Great. Five hours sleep if we're lucky."

"Sh," said Lori, snuggling down. "Sleepy time. Night. Night."

Midday came all too quickly. Leaving Jake to enjoy a few extra precious minutes asleep, Lori climbed stiffly out of bed and limped into the bathroom, pausing only to retrieve her washbag from her suitcase. The hot jet of water from the shower helped to ease off her weary body. After three nights sleeping on the bus, every inch of her ached. Inhaling the clean cotton fresh scent of her favourite shower gel, she spent a few extra seconds gently massaging her growing baby bump. Her soft touch was rewarded with a fresh flurry of activity from within that made her smile. Every day the tiny movements were growing stronger.

Wrapped up in one of the hotel robes and having towel dried her hair, Lori went back through to waken Jake. He had rolled over onto his back and was spread eagled across the bed. The room was warm and he'd pushed the covers down, revealing his bare tattooed chest.

"Jake," she said softly, laying her hand on his shoulder. "Shower time."

Opening one sleepy, hazel eye, he asked, "Wha' time is it?"

"Almost twelve thirty. You need to hurry, rock star."

Nodding, he slowly sat up, rubbing his left shoulder, then circling it round to loosen it up.

"You ok?" asked Lori, noticing a grimace of pain shoot across her husband's face.

"Aches a bit," he confessed as he climbed out of bed. "It's never been quite right since I dislocated it last summer."

"Be careful with it," she cautioned warmly.

Jake nodded and staggered off towards the bathroom.

When they stepped out of the elevator and crossed the foyer, hand in hand, Jake noted they were the last to come down. Ahead of them, he could see his fellow band members plus their managers waiting.

"Twenty bucks, Mr Power," stated Grey bluntly. "You're ten minutes late."

"Sorry, guys," apologised Jake, deliberately keeping his voice quiet. Three nights in a row singing a two hour show were beginning to take its toll and he was trying to avoid unnecessary conversation.

"Sh!" scolded Maddy sharply. "We agreed last night. No talking today. No interviews for you either before the show today, Jake."

With a resigned smile, he nodded.

"Ok," began Maddy, consulting the schedule, she held in her hand. "We're going to grab some lunch here, then a minibus will take us over to the House of Blues at two. Rich and Grey, you're doing press at two thirty for half an hour. Sound check is three until four today. Jake, minimal vocals during sound check, please. Dinner's at four thirty until six. Any questions?"

"Are we going out after the show?" asked Rich.

"I've booked us into a restaurant for a late dinner. Tomorrow's schedule is free up until four o'clock. You're due at a local radio station for a show at six. As long as you are here for four, your time's your own."

"I hear you, boss," replied Rich with a wink to Grey.

"Any more questions?" Maddy glanced round the group of tired faces. "Right, lunch!"

During lunch, Jake struggled to remain silent. In his heart, he knew he had to rest his voice, but listening to everyone chatting and joking around him was hard. As soon as he was finished, he whispered to Lori that he was going upstairs and promised to be back down in time to catch the bus. She offered to come with him, but he shook his head and kissed her on the forehead. Without a backwards glance, he walked out of the restaurant towards the elevators.

While he had been silently observing lunch, some lyrics had been forming in his mind and he was keen to scribble them down before he forgot them. It had struck him as he'd listened to Lori chatting to his bandmates that he knew instinctively what she was going to say. His mind was completely tuned into her train of thought. Not in a psychic sense, but almost as though their minds were one; as though they were bonded souls. The phrase stuck in his head.

A glance at his watch informed Jake that time was short. There were only about twenty minutes until he was due back downstairs to travel to the venue. His book bag lay discarded on the floor beside the window and Jake quickly retrieved his lyrics journal and a pen. With a satisfied smile, he noted that the journal was three quarters full already. It had been a creative few weeks since Christmas.

In front of the window there were two soft armchairs. With the journal balanced on the arm of the chair, Jake hastily scribbled down the words. Already he could hear the chorus in his head and, with a grin, guessed that this was "the one" for the next record. With three verses and a chorus scrawled haphazardly across two pages, Jake finished with a minute to spare. Bonded Souls was the working title he chose and those were the final words he noted down before closing over the leather bound book.

His new text alert tone, the R2D2 noise from Star Wars, warbled out from his pocket.

"Ready? L x"

"On my way. J x," he replied. Almost as an afterthought, Jake lifted his book bag, stuffed the journal in then hurried out of the room, mentally wondering if he'd forgotten anything of vital importance.

By six thirty, Jake had had enough of the vow of silence. Not singing much during sound check had felt alien to him and he could feel himself sliding under the dark cloud of a foul mood. When he started to ask a question about the set list during their early dinner, Maddy had barked at him to save his voice. Shooting her a dark look, he had quietly finished his chicken salad, then gone and sat alone at the far side of the room, revising the lyrics he had penned earlier. Rereading them reinforced the gut feeling that Bonded Souls was something a bit special.

"I'm going to warm up," Jake announced loudly. "I'll be right down the hall if anyone's interested."

"Want me to come with you?" offered Lori warmly. She could see that he was struggling and understood that it had been a long, awkward afternoon.

"You're too big a distraction, li'l lady," he teased, his mood lightening somewhat. "Don't want to scare the baby with my caterwauling."

"If you're sure."

"Positive," answered Jake. "I'll be back in an hour."

In the small dressing room at the end of the hallway, Jake worked his way through his usual vocal warm up routine. Focussing on his breathing and on clearing his mind of the clutter of the day, he lost himself in the routine. Once he got started, he was relieved to feel his throat relaxed and less tired than he had anticipated. It had been a long time since he had had to sing four nights in a row, but it seemed that his concerns had been over nothing. Testing the full extent of his vocal range, Jake was happy that the warmth and resonance to his mid-lower range was there and that his top notes were crystal clear. His confidence returned and the last of his earlier fears evaporated.

A scream from further down the hallway stopped him mid-scale.

Quickly, he sprinted back down the short corridor to the main dressing room to find Rich doubled over in agony, clutching his right hand.

"What happened?" asked Jake anxiously, looking round, half expecting his band mate to have punched someone or something.

"Jammed it in the fucking door," growled Rich through gritted teeth. "Hurts like fuck."

"Let me look at it," said Jethro calmly.

Shaking his head, Rich said, "You're not touching it, old man!"

"Get some ice on it," stated Maddy firmly. "Jethro, go and fetch a first aid responder."

There was an ice bucket on the table beside the small refrigerator. Trying not to panic, Maddy wrapped a handful of ice cubes in a napkin and passed it to the injured guitarist. As soon as the cold hit the injury site, he groaned and went pale.

"Boss," he said shakily. "We've got a problem."

"What?

"Look," said Rich, lifting the ice pack off his right hand. His ring and little fingers were both swollen, bruised and out of shape.

"Shit!" muttered Maddy. "Shit! Shit! Shit!"

"Broken?" asked Grey, finally voicing the question they were all scared to ask.

Rich nodded. "Feels that way."

"Right," said Maddy sharply. "Let's get you to the nearest ER. We'll need to cancel, boys."

"Cancel?" echoed Rich. "No way! Tape them together. Get me some pain meds. I'll play."

"No," snapped Maddy,glaring at him. "You are going to get that hand X-rayed."

"After Life are due on stage in twenty minutes," stated the injured musician. "And that hall's full of Silver Lake fans expecting a show tonight. I will not let them down."

"Rich," began Jake, feeling his friend's pain and frustrations. "Maddison's right. Get yourself checked out at the hospital. Boss, can we delay things by an hour? See if Rich can play after he's been seen by a doctor?"

"I don't know."

At that moment, Jethro returned with a first aider who took one look at the guitarist's fingers and stated that he needed to get to the medical centre for a proper assessment. She concurred, though, that both fingers looked to be broken.

"We're not cancelling," stated Rich as he reapplied the ice pack gingerly. "Where's Todd?"

"Checking the gear most likely," replied Jethro. "Why?"

"He can play tonight or at least fill in until we get back here."

"That's a big ask," began Jake, running his hand through his hair. "It might just work though. Let me go and talk to him. See if he's up for it."

"And if he's not?" growled Grey sourly.

"Let me talk to him first and we'll worry about that if he says no," answered Jake, heading towards the door.

As he expected, Jake found Todd at the side of the stage double checking the tuning on Silver Lake's guitars. Beside him, After Life's guitar tech was performing the same chore.

"Boys," started Jake, sounding calmer than he felt. "We've hit a technical issue. I need to ask for some help here."

"What's up, boss?" asked Todd, sensing his former music teacher's anxiety.

"Rich can't play."

"Why?"

"Looks like he's broken two fingers on his right hand. Jammed them in the dressing room door. He's away to the nearest ER to get checked out," explained Jake. "Time to invoke emergency contingency plans, young man."

"What are they?" quizzed Todd, looking bemused.

"How do you feel about standing in for him?"

The question hung in the air as the young guitar technician stared disbelievingly at him.

After Life's tech was glancing anxiously from one of them to the other as the seconds ticked by.

Taking a deep breath and swallowing hard, Todd finally nodded. "I'll do it. I'll give it my best shot."

"Thanks," said Jake, clapping him on the back. "I can't ask any more of you."

"I won't let you down," promised his former student with a nervous smile.

Turning to After Life's technician, Jake said, "Now I need to ask you a huge favour."

"I get it," he said. "You need me to cover for Todd here?"

"Got it in one, Michael," nodded Jake. "I've cleared it with Rocky already. You up for it?"

"Sure."

"We owe you boys big time for this. Thank you," said Jake, looking relieved. "Todd, fill Michael in on the basics for tonight. What needs to come out when. Tuning. No changes to the set list. When you're done, come back and find me. You've got fifteen minutes."

Without waiting for a reply, Jake dashed back to the dressing room to tell Grey and Paul that they were all systems go. His band mates looked up expectantly as he entered the room.

"He'll do it," announced Jake, grinning. "And I've scored us a replacement guitar tech. Michael's going to cover for Todd when he's done with After Life."

"Thank Christ," sighed Grey. "Didn't fancy cancelling a sell-out show."

"Me neither," agreed Jake, taking a seat beside Lori. "Who took Rich to the ER?"

"Maddy went with him," replied Lori. "She said she'd call me as soon as she hears anything."

"What a fucking mess," muttered Paul, opening a bottle of beer. "What if Ricardo can't play the Canadian shows?"

"We'll deal with it," answered Jake calmly. "Now, I need to get changed. If Todd arrives before I'm back, send him down the hall will you."

"Sure," promised Lori, smiling at her husband.

Shortly before nine, Jethro opened the dressing room door, stuck his silver head in and said, "Show time. Move it on out, boys."

"I feel sick," muttered Todd as he followed Jake out into the hallway.

"You'll be fine once you're out there," assured Jake warmly.

"I've never played in front of so many people!"

"Just remember to breathe," said Jake as they reached the side of the stage.

They could see that the house lights were dimmed and the capacity crowd were already chanting, "Silver Lake, Silver Lake, Silver Lake, Lake, Lake."

"Ready, boys?" asked Jethro.

"As we'll ever be," replied Grey.

"Fuck, let's do this!" declared Paul, drumming his sticks gently on Grey's back.

Right on cue, Paul led Silver Lake out onto the stage. As the crowd roared loudly, Todd was the last to head out, with an anxious glance back towards Lori and Jethro.

Watching as the band began Engine Room, Jethro whispered to Lori, "I hope that kid's as good as Jake says he is."

"He is," she replied, without taking her eyes off the stage. "And he idolises Jake. He won't let him down."

Out on stage, Jake was focusing on the job in hand, but kept glancing to his left to check on his young protégé. Concentration was etched into the teenage guitarist's face and, by the end of the third song, sweat was pouring off him. As the song ended, he looked over at Jake and forced a nervous smile. With a wink to him, Jake stepped up to the mic.

"Good evening, Dallas!"

As ever the crowd cheered loudly.

"I never heard that. I said, good evening, Dallas!" bellowed Jake theatrically.

He stepped back as the fans screamed and roared back at him.

"More like it," acknowledged Jake, grinning broadly. "You may have noticed we've had a change of line-up for tonight. Unfortunately, my usual partner in crime, Mr Santiago injured his hand back stage. Our guitar tech, the incredibly talented Todd Denby has joined us. Please give a huge Texan cheer for Todd!"

The crowd cheered wildly and a group of female fans on the barrier in front of Todd whistled shrilly. Even under the huge lighting rig, Jake could tell that the young guitarist had flushed scarlet beside him.

"Ladies and gentlemen, this is from our latest record. This is Vortex!"

The mid-song guitar solo was quite technically challenging and, as it approached, Jake moved closer to Todd, trying to gauge if his former pupil was ready for his first moment in the spotlight. The green spot homed in on Todd. With his head bowed over Rich's Gibson, he executed the solo to perfection. His relieved smile to the crowd as he finished the last few notes said it all. With his nerves beginning to fade, Todd was loving his two hours of Silver Lake fame.

When Ellen walked out to join Silver Lake for Mysteries, Jake noticed that Rich was standing behind Lori at the side of the stage. It was too dark to see his friend's hand, but he guessed that Rich wasn't planning on playing. Turning his attention back to the fans, Jake growled into the microphone, "Dallas, this is Mysteries."

Once again, Todd was in the spotlight as he played the haunted introduction to the song. When Jake began his vocal, he saw the young musician to his left finally begin to relax a little. The duet was becoming one of his favourite points in the set and each night he and Ellen playfully tried to out "creep" each other with their performance. For the Dallas show, Ellen had surprised him by appearing on stage in a long Gothic velvet dress and a hooded cloak. She was wearing very round John Lennon style glasses with filled in sides. As the lights caught the lenses, Jake saw they were emerald green. He stifled a laugh as he stepped back up to the mic. This round for "creepiness" definitely went to Ellen he decided. Both of them moved across the stage to stand either side of Todd as he powered his way through the guitar solo. If their close proximity made the young guitarist nervous, he never let it show and his flawless, dramatic solo was rewarded by a kiss on the cheek from Ellen before she began the eerie, poetic lyric epilogue to the song.

When Silver Lake left the stage at the end of their main set, they crowded around Rich in the wings. They were all relieved to see his fingers were taped up and not in a cast, suggesting that the injury wasn't as severe as they had all feared.

"You coming out for the encore?" asked Jake, breathing heavily. "Those fans would love to see you out there."

Rich shook his head, "I don't think so."

"Your call, buddy," said Jake as he chugged down a bottle of water. "Even step out and take a bow right at the end."

"Maybe," conceded Rich with a tired smile. "Todd!"

"Yes, sir," replied Todd, wiping sweat off his face.

"Awesome job tonight, young man," complimented Rich, clapping him on the back with his good hand. "Now, you lead Silver Lake back out there!"

"Me?"

"Yes. You're the star tonight."

Needing no second invitation, Todd checked the rest of the band were ready before calmly leading them back out onto the stage. The crowd were chanting "Silver Lake, Silver Lake, Silver Lake, Lake, Lake" at full volume.

From her position in the wings, Lori watched as Todd lapped up the attention. Fired up on adrenaline, he flew through Dragon Song without missing a beat.

"Jake's right," said Lori to Rich quietly. "You should be out there for Flyin' High."

"You think?"

Lori nodded and Jethro added, "Get your ass out there, Mr

Santiago."

As Silver Lake began to play their final number, Rich slipped out onto the stage and sat on Paul's drum riser. Spotting him, the fans went wild. When they reached the bridge section mid-song, Jake gave Todd a signal to just keep it going for a minute or two.

"Dallas, the late and slightly broken, Rich Santiago!" roared Jake, beckoning his friend forward.

Displaying his taped up hand to the crowd, Rich waved, then with his good hand grabbed the microphone.

"Folks, give a huge cheer for Mr Denby here. If he hadn't stepped in, tonight wouldn't have gone ahead," he declared, gesturing for Todd to come forward. "Let's hear it one last time for Todd!"

The sell-out crowd cheered the young guitarist then sang their hearts out with Jake as he finished off the night with Flyin' High.

Midnight had come and gone before the band arrived at the city centre restaurant for their late dinner. With their food ordered, Maddy called for quiet around the table. Raising her glass, she said, "Here's to the star of tonight's show. To Todd!"

Blushing profusely, he bowed his head and smiled as they all congratulated him again on a flawless performance.

"Think you're up to repeating it a couple of more times?" asked Rich hopefully.

"Pardon?"

"How do you feel about playing the two Canadian shows?" Rich enquired. "I'm under orders not to play for a week at least."

"Well?" asked Jake, staring at his protégé. "You in?"

Grinning broadly, Todd replied, "Would love to, if you're all sure."

"We're sure, son," confirmed Jethro warmly. "That was quite some performance out there tonight."

"Thank you, sir."

As their meal arrived and the waiters bustled round the table setting down plates, Lori called over, "Rich, if you're not playing in Canada, do you want to come to New York with me?"

"I thought you were going home for a few days?"

"Change of plan," she replied. "I need to go to New York to sign some contracts for Hyde Properties. You're more than welcome to join me. I'm booked on a flight first thing on Monday."

"I'll sleep on it," said Rich, inwardly reluctant to leave the tour even if it was for only a few days.

After a bit of persuading by the band's managers and his fellow band members, Rich reluctantly agreed to travel to New York with Lori. It was Jethro, with some support from Jake, who finally convinced him that it would be a good idea. When Jake confided in him that he didn't like the thought of Lori travelling alone so much while she was pregnant, Rich surrendered and said he would go with her.

On Monday, the Silver Lake contingent left first thing to catch their flight to Vancouver, leaving Rich and Lori to travel together to the airport. With their luggage checked in and the security checks completed, they wandered through the terminal building in search of a coffee shop. Once they were seated at a small bistro table for two, Lori began to giggle.

"What's so funny?" asked Rich, stirring his latte.

"I was just thinking how this would look if the press spot us together," she giggled, keeping her voice deliberately low. "I look like someone punched me. Your hand's damaged. It's mid-tour and you're sitting here with the front man's wife. Imagine the stories they could concoct!"

"I guess it is kind of funny when you look at it that way," he said grinning. "No wonder the boss warned us to keep our heads down."

"We'll be fine. Maddy worries too much."

"So, what's the plan for New York then?" asked Rich casually. "I assume you'll need to get that eye attended to while we're there."

"If I can avoid a trip to the doctor's office, I will," stated Lori, staring down into her coffee cup. "I've an all day meeting with David tomorrow at the office. Lin called and wants to meet up at some point on Wednesday to discuss the next LH jewellery collection then we fly to Minneapolis on Thursday. You're more than welcome to come with me on Wednesday, but I'll need to abandon you for most of tomorrow, I'm afraid."

"Not a problem. I can amuse myself. Play tourist or laze on your couch watching crap TV all day."

"I promise we will go out to dinner tomorrow night. I'll be done at Hyde Properties by late afternoon."

"Only if you let me pay," countered Rich warmly.

"We'll see."

Snow was piled high on the sidewalks as the cab drove them towards the Upper West Side a few hours later. It was already growing dark and the city was lighting up around them. Watching Rich gaze up out of the car windows, searching for famous landmarks, made Lori smile. It was easy for her to forget that Rich and the rest of the band were still relatively unfamiliar with her hometown. Eventually, the cab pulled up outside her building and Lori allowed Rich to help her out of the back seat. She was stiff after travelling all day and the cold, damp city was already eating into her.

"Good afternoon, Mrs Power," greeted Charles, the duty concierge, appearing beside them to assist with the luggage. "Welcome home."

"Hi, Charles. What's with all this snow?" replied Lori as she passed the fare to the cab driver.

"Oh, it's been like this for two weeks," he explained, taking their suitcases. "Forecast is for rain tomorrow through until Saturday."

"As long as it's not for more snow," declared Lori, following him into the warm, brightly lit foyer. "We fly out again on Thursday and can't afford to get stranded here."

"Short visit then?" commented the concierge as he pressed the call button beside the elevator.

"This time," replied Lori as she followed Rich into the elevator. "Thank you for your help, Charles. We'll be sending out for dinner later, so can you please watch for a delivery arriving. I'm also expecting some paperwork to be couriered over shortly."

"I'll bring it up personally when it arrives."

Once upstairs, Rich took their bags down to the bedrooms while Lori went through to the kitchen to make a pot of coffee. While she was waiting for it to filter down into the pot, she sent a text message to Jake to say they had arrived safely. Opening the refrigerator in search of some milk or half'n'half for Rich's coffee, Lori was pleasantly surprised to see David had had it stocked with some of her favourite foods. He knew her so well. Before she poured the coffee, she decided to call him to let him know she had arrived. The call went straight to his voicemail so she left a brief message, then turned her attention back to the coffee pot.

She had just carried the two mugs through to the lounge when there was a knock at the door.

"I'll get it," called Rich from the hallway.

"Thank you," replied Lori, setting the steaming mugs down on the coffee table.

Behind her, Rich entered the room carrying a thick document wallet.

"Your reading material, Mz Hyde," he teased as he presented her with the folder.

"Jesus," sighed Lori, balking at the size of the file. "I'll be up all night reading through this!"

"Good luck," said Rich with a smile as he sat down in the soft armchair opposite her.

"I'll make a start after dinner," she replied, praying that David had included his own summary reports that might prevent her from reading every last word.

"Doesn't David sign off on deals on your behalf?" asked Rich, slightly curious to learn more about Lori's business empire.

"He does up to a financial limit set by the company's board. Discretionary powers to act on my behalf. Anything in excess of that figure requires my personal attention. Usually there's only one or two contracts a year that need me to sign off on them. He's been working on a couple of takeover deals though to build up the property portfolio. Hyde Properties are expanding across into New Jersey and Connecticut," she explained, keeping the details deliberately vague.

"Empire building?"

"Something like that," answered Lori with a smile. "What do you feel like for dinner? I'm actually quite hungry and wouldn't mind eating early."

"Fine by me. Touring messes with your meal schedule. I can pretty much eat anytime," said Rich. "How about we rebel and order pizza?"

Lori burst out laughing. "Suits me. Just don't tell Jake!"

"I won't if you don't," he replied with a conspiratorial wink.

Dispensing with all formalities, Lori broke her own house rules and agreed that they could eat in the lounge in front of the early evening news programme. A huge, flat pizza box sat on the coffee table and between them they were steadily munching their way through the large pepperoni. She had found some beers in the refrigerator for Rich and settled for some apple juice for herself. After the last few hectic days, it was nice to just sit and relax, but she couldn't help but wish Jake was with them. They'd been apart for less than twelve hours and she was missing him already.

A cricket chirp from her phone alerted her to a message. Lori smiled when she saw it was from Jake.

"How was your pizza? J x" it read.

Raising one eyebrow, she looked over at Rich. "Did you tell him?"

"Tell who what?" asked the injured guitarist, looking bemused.

"Jake," replied Lori with a giggle. "He wants to know how the pizza was."

"He knows you too well," laughed Rich as he helped himself to another slice.

Still smiling, she typed her reply, "Not as good as you would make. L x"

Immediately he replied, "My pizza making days are long gone. Miss you. Cold here in Canada. J x"

"Two feet of snow here. Miss you too. L x"

"Will call tomorrow after sound check. If you have time take Rich to Garrett's music store. He will love that place. Hope meeting with David goes well. Love you. J x"

"Love you too. L x"

Minneapolis and Thursday suddenly both seemed a lifetime away.

Having finished their meal, Lori cleared the box away and brought Rich another beer plus a bag of tortilla chips. Lifting the heavy document wallet, she said, "I'm heading downstairs to work my way through this. I'll be leaving early tomorrow to meet David for breakfast before the board meeting. The spare keys are on the hall table and you know the door code, don't you?"

"Yup," agreed Rich, opening the bottle of beer. "I'll keep myself amused. Don't worry about me."

"I won't have time to," replied Lori with a sigh. "I'll call when I know what time I'll be done at. If it's early enough, you can come along and meet me."

"Sounds like a plan," he agreed. "Don't stay up all night reading those contracts."

"No promises on that."

Once downstairs in the master bedroom, Lori dumped the folder on the bed and got changed into her pyjamas. She caught sight of her sutured eye in the mirror and reached up to finger it. There was no way she could attend Hyde Properties with those black, fuzzy stitches still in place! There was also no way she was trailing across town in search of a nurse to remove them. Not even daring to think what Jake would say about her plan, Lori went back upstairs to her small art studio. As she passed through the lounge, Rich looked up from his reclined position on the couch.

"Forgot my highlighters," she lied swiftly as she headed into the deep recess that was her home studio.

As she'd expected, her artist's scalpel and a packet of new blades were in the drawer labelled "craft knives". Closing the drawer and pausing to lift a packet of highlighter pens, Lori limped back out into the hallway and retreated back downstairs.

With a freshly sterilised blade slotted into place and her tweezers handy, using the bright light of the *en suite* vanity mirror, Lori cut through the black sutures. The thread was tougher to cut than she had anticipated, but she soon had the three sutures loosened. Using the tweezers, she pulled them free, dropping the offcuts into the waste basket. With the last thread removed, she inspected the fresh scar. It didn't look as bad as she had feared. Taking care not to damage the freshly healed skin, she smothered the wound in antiseptic cream, then, having disposed of the soiled scalpel blade, Lori returned to the bedroom to begin reading her way through the monumental pile of paperwork.

After six hours in the board room at Hyde Properties' offices, Lori was losing patience. Business negotiations had gone smoothly and agreement had been reached on all three of the deals with only minor amendments to be made. The final agenda item was a presentation of the refurbishment schedule for one of their Lower Manhattan office buildings. Listening to the IT geeks extolling the virtues of various telephony and internet options left her cold. As the senior project manager droned on, she could feel the baby twitching. The flurries of activity were getting longer and stronger. Casually, she rubbed her swollen belly and felt the tiny kicks quicken under her hand.

"Any questions?" asked the IT guru, disturbing her daydream. "Mrs Power, any comments?"

"Cost out options one and four and present them to David by Friday lunchtime. Include the projected rental increase for our tenants to cover the costs of the refurbishment work. If any of these offices are due to be vacated within the next six months, include details of that projected rental decrease, working on the assumption that we can't get them leased again for a further quarter," replied Lori, staring directly at the young man.

"Yes, Mrs Power," he replied.

"Thank you, Jerry," said David firmly. "As there are no other agenda items, I say we draw the meeting to a close."

Stifling a yawn, Lori watched her board of directors troop back out into the hallway. Once the last person had left the room, David got up and closed the door.

"Everything alright, Lori?" he asked warmly.

As her financial advisor and confidante, David could read her like a book.

"Just tired, David," she admitted, resting a hand on her neat baby bump. "It's been a busy week with the band and a late night last night reading through the reports for today."

"Make sure you get an early night tonight, my dear."

"I'll try," promised Lori, rifling through her bag for her cell phone. "I'm going to get Rich to meet me here, then we've one more appointment before dinner."

Half an hour later, Rich arrived at the office block to meet her. Since she had called and asked him to make his way over, Lori had arranged with David to have one of the company cars brought round. Looking slightly disappointed at not getting a tour of the building, Rich followed her out to the waiting BMW.

"Where are we going?" he asked as the driver pulled out into the stream of traffic and headed downtown.

"Surprise," teased Lori playfully. "Jake's idea actually."

"Should I be worried?"

"I don't think so," she assured him with a mischievous smile.

A few minutes later, in the fading afternoon light, the car drew up outside the music store. Eyeing the display in the window, Rich stepped out of the car and crossed the sidewalk to gaze longingly in the window.

"Come on," called Lori. "Let's get inside. It's freezing out here."

The bell tinkled above the door as they entered the shop. Wide eyed, Rich looked around. His childlike fascination made Lori giggle.

"Go and browse," she suggested.

Without a second thought, Rich wandered off towards a rack of acoustic guitars. Leaving him to wander, Lori went over to the counter.

"Well, if it isn't the beautiful, Mz Hyde."

"Afternoon, Garrett," greeted Lori warmly. "I hoped you'd be here. I brought you some fresh blood. He needs cheering up, but not bankrupting. See what you can do."

"And who have you delivered into my domain?" enquired Garrett with a theatrical wave of his hand.

"Rich from Silver Lake," revealed Lori, before going on to explain about his injury and unscheduled break from the tour.

"Most unfortunate," sympathised Garrett sincerely, stepping out from behind the counter. "Let's see what we can do to take his mind off things."

They found Rich running his hand over a beautiful acoustic guitar with stunning Mother of Pearl inlays on the neck.

"Good afternoon, Mr Santiago," said Garrett brightly. "What brings you into my lair?"

"Your lair?" echoed Rich, looking a little bewildered.

"Rich," explained Lori softly. "This is Garrett's store."

"Wow!" sighed the Silver Lake guitarist. "I feel like I've died and gone to heaven in here."

With a laugh, Garrett agreed, "It has that effect on folk."

"I just wish I could play," sighed Rich, indicating his taped up fingers.

"Yes, Mz Hyde explained," said Garrett, lifting down a simple looking acoustic instrument. He passed it to Rich then fished in his pocket for a pick. "Try this."

"I don't know," began Rich with a glance towards Lori.

"Trust him. He's a magician at this," promised Lori, anxious to see what Garrett would select for Rich to potentially own.

Taking care not to aggravate his broken fingers, Rich played a gentle classical piece and nodded.

"No," declared Garrett. "Not for you."

He took the instrument out of Rich's hand before he had a chance to comment and returned it to the rack. Without pausing for further thought, he lifted down another model and passed it over to his fellow musician.

Playing this guitar elicited the same reaction as Jake had had playing the vintage resonator when he had visited the store. Both Lori and Garrett watched as Rich disregarded the pain in his hand and kept playing. When he stopped a few minutes later, he looked up at them grinning like a kid on Christmas morning.

"That looks like the one, Mz Hyde," commented Garrett with a wink. "Do you concur?"

Giggling, Lori nodded. "Let's try an experiment," she suggested with a mischievous twinkle in her blue eyes. "Rich, maybe you better put that one back."

"What? No!" exclaimed the Silver Lake star. "Let's not be hasty here."

Both Lori and Garrett started to laugh.

"Sold," stated Lori simply.

"I believe it is," said Garrett with a smile.

"I do have something else that may interest our friend here. Give me a moment."

A few moments later, he reappeared with a 1957 Les Paul gold top reissue and passed it to Rich. Not daring to look at the price tag, Rich began to play the intro to Dragon Song then attempted part of the solo from Mysteries. Grinning through the pain in his hand, he looked up and asked, "Are you both conspiring to bankrupt me here? This lady is incredible."

"Magic's struck again, Garrett," said Lori as Rich lovingly as caressed the body of the guitar. "Rich, what do you think?"

"I'm thinking you're a devious woman, Mrs Power," replied the guitarist, still grinning. "Garrett, let's talk money for these ladies."

With a price agreed and, with Lori's subtle assistance, a

substantial discount negotiated, Rich finally signed the credit card receipt.

"How long are you in town for?" asked Garrett as he closed the catches on the Gibson's hard case.

"Just until Thursday."

"Pity. We have plans for tomorrow, but I know Sal would like to see you both. He'll be sorry he missed you."

"Do you have plans for tonight?" asked Lori with a glance at Rich. "We were going to go to dinner before heading back to my apartment. You'd be more than welcome to join us."

"That would be too much for Sal," sighed Garrett sadly. "This isn't one of his better weeks."

"Would he feel up to coming over to Lori's for a few drinks later?" suggested Rich as he put his wallet back in his pocket.

"He might," said the older man. "Let me ask him and I'll call you. Let you know what he says."

"Don't stress him," said Lori softly, understanding how emotionally fragile the reclusive Salazar Mendes could be. "We'll be home by nine. If you both feel up to it, come over around then. You know the address, don't you?"

Garrett nodded. "Thank you for understanding."

"Hope to see you both later then," said Rich, lifting the guitar cases, feeling thankful that the acoustic had come with a gig bag with a shoulder strap rather than a handheld case.

"Until later, folks."

While Rich went to put his guitars down in the bedroom, Lori wandered through to the lounge to turn on the lamps and some music. They had enjoyed a lovely meal at a Greek restaurant in Hell's Kitchen after they'd left the music store. Throughout dinner, Rich had talked animatedly about writing material for the new record and about how excited he was to be involved in the Weigh Station charity record. He confessed to feeling more than a little in awe of both Garrett Court and Salazar Mendes but couldn't contain his excitement at the thought of recording with them. Seeing him relaxed and enthusiastic made Lori smile. Ever since the accident that had killed Gary, there had been a sadness cast across Rich's usually passionate personality. It looked as though he was finally putting the tragedy behind him.

Shortly after nine thirty, the duty concierge called up to confirm that Lori was expecting two guests. By the time she reached the front door of the apartment, the elevator doors were opening and the two musicians were stepping out onto the marble floored hallway.

"Darling," purred Salazar, wrapping his arms around her. "You look radiant, my dear."

"Thank you," she replied a little shyly. "How are you? I'm glad you made it over."

"For now, I'm back," commented the reclusive star cryptically.

Putting his comment down to creative eccentricity, Lori led them both through to the lounge. Hearing voices in the hallway, Rich had got to his feet to come and greet his fellow musicians.

"Ah, the injured Mr Santiago," declared Salazar, his deep voice sounding warm and sincere. "How is the hand?"

"Tender," confessed Rich with an air of exasperation. "My own dumb fault though."

"How long are you out of action for?"

"Hopefully only a few more days," replied Rich. "I re-join the tour at the end of the week, but we may need to work around some of my solos. We'll see how it works out when we get to Minneapolis."

"Nice city," mused the tall, skeletal guitarist.

"Can I get you both a drink?" offered Lori warmly.

"I've brought my own medicinal tea," answered Salazar. "But I'm sure Rett won't refuse some wine."

Seeing Rich's beer bottle on the table, Garrett said, "Lori, beer's fine. Don't open wine just for me."

"Are you sure?"

"Positive," replied Garrett with a smile as he took a seat on the couch.

While Lori fetched some beers and a glass for Salazar's tea, the three musicians fell into easy conversation about the forthcoming charity project. Garrett had received an email from Mikey from Weigh Station with a proposed track list. It included all the big Weigh Station hits, plus Broken Bottle Empty Glass that had featured Jake on vocals. There had also been a list of confirmed guest artists and, as she scanned through the list of names, Lori was surprised at a few of them.

"Any idea who's singing and playing on what?" enquired Rich as he nodded approvingly at the lists.

"That's still up for debate as far as I know," replied Garrett. "Mikey is keen for Jake to sing Broken Bottle as the final track. That's about as much as I know."

"I guess we'll find out when we all get to JJL," agreed Rich. "What date are you guys coming down?"

"We've rented a house nearby for six weeks. The last couple of weeks in March and all of April," said Salazar quietly. "A bolt hole from the musical mayhem."

"We've also booked out JJL for a week in March," confided Garrett with a glance towards his partner. "The hope is to build on the earlier recordings we made in January. Perhaps gather enough material for a new record. Keep that to yourselves for now, though."

As the evening wore on, conversation turned to Lori's involvement with the charity project. The four of them discussed ideas for the artwork. Throughout the conversation, Salazar remained quieter than the others, calmly sipping his glass of tea. After a couple of hours, he seemed to grow agitated, fidgeting restlessly in his seat before rising to pace up and down in front of the fireplace.

"Time to go," said Garrett, a look of concern etched into his features. "If we don't see you before, we'll see you next month."

"Keep in touch," said Lori, moving to get to her feet.

"Stay where you are, Mz Hyde," purred Salazar, coming to kneel in front of her.

Before she could stop him, he'd laid his long, pale, slender hands on her swollen stomach.

"And take care of this precious gift of life," he added, gazing straight into her eyes.

"And you take care of yourself, Sal," said Lori, lifting his hands and holding them tight. "Stay strong."

"Until later, darling," he whispered, kissing her hands, then rising gracefully to his feet.

The eccentric musician's actions had unnerved her slightly and she was still sitting on the couch contemplating them when Rich returned from showing their visitors out to the elevator. His face was a mask of fury and, muttering under his breath, he lifted

Salazar's glass from the table and sniffed at the dregs left in the bottom. There was a small amount of the "medicinal tea" left and he took a tiny sip, then spat it back into the glass.

"What's wrong?" asked Lori, looking up at him anxiously.

"That's no "medicinal" tea!" growled Rich angrily. "He's high as a fucking kite on this stuff."

"I did wonder."

"Christ knows what's in this," muttered Rich, screwing up his face at the sour taste the small sip had left in his mouth. "Smells like mushrooms, but I'd put money on the fact there's some kind of opiate in there too."

Before Lori could comment, he took the dirty glasses through to the kitchen. When she came through carrying the empty beer bottles, he was washing the offending glass out in scalding hot water.

Luck wasn't on Lori and Rich's side as they attempted to leave New York to travel to Minneapolis. An unexpected snowstorm blew in on Wednesday night, leaving all flights cancelled until noon the following day. Trying to remain calm, Lori had liaised with Maddy and booked them on a later flight scheduled to leave early on Thursday afternoon. When they arrived at the airport, the schedule was still severely disrupted. After several hours of hanging about, the weary travellers finally boarded a flight at seven o'clock in the evening. There was little or no chance of Rich making it to the venue in time for the show. Throughout the day, he had kept in almost constant phone contact with the band, before resigning himself to making his return to the Silver Lake stage either after the acoustic interlude or for the encore.

During the two and a half hour flight, he sat silently brooding over the situation. It pained Lori to see him so stressed after their relaxed few days away from the tour. As the plane touched down in Minneapolis, she said to him, "You go on through security, grab a cab and get to the venue. I'll wait and collect all the luggage and meet you there."

"You sure?"

She nodded. "I'll get help in the baggage hall and Maddy promised Grime would be waiting for us. You need to get yourself to the show as fast as you can."

"Thanks, Lori," he smiled.

It took Lori an hour to gather all their luggage together, with the help of one of the airport staff. She rarely played on her physical infirmity, but for once she made an exception, explaining the situation and adding that she was pregnant. A helpful young man fetched a luggage trolley for her, lifted the bags from the carousel and collected Rich's two guitars. He insisted on pushing the trolley through to the arrivals' hall for her. As soon as they were through the automatic doors, she spotted Grime towering over the other people who were patiently waiting. With a wave, he came forward to take charge of the luggage.

"You finally made it, Mrs Power," he said with a smile.

"Better late than never," joked Lori as she handed the porter a twenty dollar tip then thanked him for his assistance.

Leading the way towards the exit, Grime explained that Rich had jumped in a cab and, to the best of his knowledge, had arrived at the concert hall. He had a minibus waiting for them and, while Lori settled herself on board, he stowed the luggage at the back. It only took them twenty minutes to reach the venue and, as Lori made her way to the side of the stage,she could hear that Jake and Ellen were midway through Mysteries. She was mildly surprised to find Rich watching from the wings.

"Are you not going out there tonight?" he asked quietly.

"Just for the encore," he replied. "Todd'll stay out too."

"How're the fingers?"

"Agony after trying to play one of my solos in the dressing room," he confessed, sounding rather deflated.

"Take it easy," she said, giving him a hug.

Deliberately, Lori kept to the shadows so that her presence wouldn't distract Jake. Watching her husband, knowing he was unaware that she had arrived, was a rare treat. Seeing him focussed on the fans and the band, without stealing glances into the wings, reinforced just how far the band had come over the last couple of years.

When Silver Lake came off stage at the end of the main set, she stepped forward into the light.

"Thank God you finally made it, li'l lady," sighed Jake, sweeping her into his sweat soaked embrace. "I've missed you."

"Me too,"confessed Lori, kissing him tenderly.

Around them, she was aware of Rich picking up his guitar and chatting with Todd about how the two encore songs were going to go. Keeping his arm around Lori's waist, Jake said, "Wait back here until I call you out, Rich."

"Can't I just come back on with you guys?"

"No," stated Jake firmly. "Let's welcome you back out in style."

Before Rich could argue, Jethro was signalling to them to get back out on stage.

At the sight of Silver Lake returning to the stage, the Minneapolis fans went wild. A group of female fans right down at the front threw their bras up onto the stage, one of them landing at Jake's feet. Not really knowing how to react, he bent and picked it up by the end of the strap and held it aloft.

"Not sure this is my size," he quipped as he draped it on his mic stand. "Minneapolis, you've been incredible!"

A huge cheer went up as he held his hand out for calm.

"We have one last surprise for you," called out Jake with a grin. "Give a huge cheer for Mr Rich Santiago!"

As Rich loped out on stage, the whole room was screaming and cheering for all they were worth.

"Be gentle with him, folks," teased Jake as Rich moved into position beside Todd. "He's still a bit battered and broken. Mr Denby here is going to stay with us to help us out on Dragon Song!"

The resounding roar let Silver Lake know they were ready to have Rich back on stage.

All too soon Silver Lake were playing the end of Flyin' High and bidding their goodnights.

Alone in their hotel room a few hours later, Jake and Lori were curled up in bed, enjoying a late night meal of quesadillas that they'd ordered from room service. Much to Maddy's annoyance, they had shunned the plan for a band meal at a nearby restaurant. The band's manager had started to protest, but Lori had interrupted her tirade, stating firmly that she was exhausted and needed to get to bed. Remembering how tired she had felt during her pregnancy, Maddy had caved in, making them promise to be ready to leave by nine thirty next morning.

"Still tired, li'l lady?" teased Jake as she set her empty plate back on the trolley left by the hotel staff.

"Maddy was pretty angry, wasn't she?" giggled Lori as she snuggled back under the duvet beside her husband.

"Furious," admitted Jake, grinning. "She had gone to a lot of trouble earlier securing a table for us."

"There will be other meals."

"Plenty of them," agreed Jake with a yawn. "I'm just relieved you made it back today. I was getting worried you'd give up and head home instead."

"I was tempted," confessed Lori, wriggling closer to lay her head on his chest.

They lay wrapped in each other's arms, allowing themselves to relax and appreciate the silence. Gradually, Lori felt the stresses of the day ebb away as her breathing slowed and she was on the cusp of sleep. Inside, she could feel the baby wriggling, tiny ripples of activity washing through her swollen stomach. Reaching for Jake's hand, she laid it across her bump at the point where she'd last felt the baby.

"Feel anything?" she asked hopefully as she became aware of a fresh flurry of activity.

"Nothing," replied Jake, sounding a little disheartened.

"Must still be too soon. Sorry."

"Don't apologise, li'l lady. Plenty of time to feel that little Power Pack kicking."

"I guess so," sighed Lori sleepily.

Still wrapped in each other's arms, they both drifted off to sleep.

Silver Lake's tour continued to be blessed with sell out shows as the Silver Bullet took them from city to city. After Lori headed home, following the show in Kansas City, the boys headed back across the border to Canada for four shows. The injury to Rich's hand was still causing him a lot of pain, despite dosing himself with painkillers before the set. Eventually, he conceded defeat and Todd was drafted back in to share guitar duties. As the tour wound on, they fell into a natural routine whereby Rich played the first half of the set that was amended to eliminate any complex solos and Todd came out to join Jake and Ellen for Mysteries. Once the duet was over, Todd stayed on stage for the remainder of the show, filling in for Rich on the solos and more technically challenging numbers. It wasn't ideal, but the band all realised they had no other choice.

Plans for recording the final show of the tour for a live DVD release continued, as did the plan for a backup recording of the show in Detroit. When they arrived in the city, Rich was adamant that he could manage the whole set, but following sound check he agreed to a fresh compromise. Todd would still come out for Mysteries, stay for Vortex and Impossible then take his bow allowing Rich to finish the show. In the circumstances, it was the best solution. Next morning, when they watched a rough cut of the footage, they all agreed that it had worked out fine.

With the band away, life at the beach was quiet, allowing Lori time to focus on her art commissions. When she had returned from Kansas City, there had been a large envelope among the mail that was jammed into her large mailbox. Her name and address were written in flamboyant, almost Gothic script, arousing her curiosity as to who had sent it. She had left the envelope on her desk and forgotten about it until she sat down to work the following day. Carefully, Lori had slit it open with a knife, then she had slipped out the sheaf of paperwork from inside it. The letter was from Garrett and contained the proposals for the Weigh Station project, detailing the draft track listing and the list of confirmed artists. Seeing it all down on paper, Lori acknowledged that there was a lot of talent heading into JJL to play their part in the record.

There was a second set of paperwork in a buff coloured folder marked "strictly confidential." Inside it she found a note from Salazar for Jake attached to several sheets of music. The note said simply, "Mr Power, learn. Provide lyrics as you see fit. Expect you to join me for the week when you can. Sal."

Knowing that the contents of the folder may distract Jake from his Silver Lake duties, Lori decided not to mention it to him and left it to one side for him to discover when he returned home.

As the month wound on, the brutal winter weather continued, limiting her excursions outdoors. Howling, icy winds and torrential rainstorms were wreaking havoc up and down the coastline. There were several nights that Lori lay awake, unable to sleep due to the force of the wind buffeting the house, rattling every window and shingle. Trapped indoors, she quickly grew restless, however, she focussed her frustrations on her art. One of her commissions was for the cover work for a death metal band's debut EP. The aggressive, dark music mirrored the raw violence of the weather. Creating the storm influenced graphics proved cathartic for her.

Several times a day, her phone rang and Lori was able to enjoy short, snatched conversations with Jake. Still concerned about the toll the tour was taking on his voice, he was endeavouring to minimise the amount of talking he was doing during the day. His short phone calls were followed by numerous and often lengthy text messages.

Lori's twenty week hospital appointment was scheduled for the last Wednesday of February, four days before the end of the tour. She had asked to move it to the following week, but was advised against delaying it. When she had told Jake that he was going to miss the ultrasound scan, his disappointment was obvious but he understood. As she drove out to Beebe's maternity unit for her appointment, Lori too was feeling down about the fact he wasn't with her. It felt wrong to be "seeing" the baby without Jake by her side.

When the nurse called her into the room, she asked if Mr Power was joining them. It was the same nurse who had seen them back in January. Trying to keep her emotions in check, Lori explained that Jake was on tour and was actually in Detroit.

"Let me check something," said the nurse with an understanding smile. "There might be a compromise here, honey. I'll be back in a minute."

While Lori climbed up onto the exam table, she watched the nurse speaking to a colleague out in the hallway.

"Mrs Power," she began when she re-entered the room. "Would you be able to get your husband on the phone right now?"

"I can try," replied Lori.

"Do you use video messaging?" asked the nurse, passing Lori her bag.

"Yes," said Lori, rummaging through the bag in search of her cell phone. "But I'm not sure where Jake will be right now. He might not be able to Skype just now. Let me message him first. I don't want to call. He might be doing press interviews."

Quickly, she sent a message to Jake, asking if he was able to call her back.

While the nurse and the ultrasound technician prepared Lori for the scan, they waited for a reply from the touring father-to-be.

Nothing.

"Oh well, it was a nice thought," sighed Lori sadly as she checked again for a reply.

"Time for plan B," said the technician with a wink. "Dawn will hold your phone and video the monitor screen for you. That way, you can share the video with your husband later."

"Oh, thank you!" exclaimed Lori, her eyes filling with tears. "You've no idea how much I appreciate this."

"Lie back and relax, Mrs Power," said the technician. "Let's see if baby is ready to play movie star!"

"It certainly moves enough!" giggled Lori as she settled herself into position.

"Has your husband felt any kicks yet?"

"No," replied Lori, flinching slightly as the technician squirted cold gel onto her stomach.

"Won't be long," assured the nurse as she set Lori's phone to video. "Smile for your close up, Mrs Power."

Lori giggled and waved, then the nurse turned to focus the camera on the monitor screen. When the technician placed the probe on her stomach, Lori felt the baby wriggle in protest at the unexpected pressure. On the screen, she saw the outline of the baby clearly. It was lying on its back and its tiny arms and legs were flailing. Holding the sensor in place, the technician captured some information and measurements on the pc before returning her attention to Lori.

"Ok, for the benefit of your touring rock star daddy," she began. "Everything looks perfect. Baby is measuring as expected. We'll need to try to get them to turn over as I would like to get a good look at the spine. Mrs Power, can you please wriggle your hips a little to encourage baby to move round?"

No amount of hip shaking was getting the baby to turn over.

"Try lying on your side for a moment or two, then roll back over," suggested the nurse.

Lori did as she was asked and, when the technician placed the sensor back on her bump, the baby had finally rolled over and curled up with its back facing the camera.

"Perfect," declared the technician, zooming the screen in on the tiny spine. "Everything looks beautiful there. Nothing to worry about. Nice healthy, active baby."

"Relieved to hear it," said Lori, smiling at the image on the monitor screen. "How big is it now?"

"Full length is measuring seven and a half inches. Is your husband tall?"

"Six three," replied Lori.

"Explains it then. Baby is slightly longer than average at this stage. I'd estimate its weight is around twelve to fourteen ounces. Again, a little above average. It's early to be sure, but I'd guess this one could be a big baby."

"How big?" Lori almost squealed.

"Don't panic, Mrs Power. Under ten pounds. Possibly around the nine pound mark. Maybe a little over."

"Sounds huge!" exclaimed Lori. "My friend's twins were about six."

"Twins are usually a bit smaller," observed the nurse. "Don't fret though. I know you were concerned about the size and weight, but your orthopaedic consultant has assured us your pelvis is fine to cope with this."

"If you're sure," sighed Lori, looking and feeling less than convinced.

As the nurse handed her back her phone, the technician commented, "One very minor concern. Your placenta is lying a little low. I'd like to monitor it. Can you book another appointment for eight weeks time and we'll check if its moved up a bit?"

"Sure," agreed Lori.

"It's nothing to worry about at this stage so no need to fret," explained the technician. "Will Mr Power be back home by then?"

"Yes," said Lori smiling. "I'll make sure he comes with me."

"Perfect," stated the nurse with a wink as she wiped the sticky gel from Lori's taut skin.

"Here you go," interrupted the technician, handing her three photos of the scan. "More for the family album."

"Thank you."

When she got back out to the car, Lori sat and watched the short video of the scan, smiling with tears in her eyes as she saw her little Power Pack wriggling on the small screen. Even now that she could feel it moving, it still fascinated her that this tiny person was growing inside her. Still smiling, she mailed the video to Jake and sent him a separate message to say the next scan was scheduled for April 16th.

At last the rain had stopped lashing down and the sun was trying to fight its way through the black clouds. As she pulled out of the parking lot, the sky ahead of her was lit up by a beautiful rainbow. Surely a good omen.

Another rainbow blessed the sky as Lori's flight came into land at St Louis International airport late on Saturday morning. An early morning call from Jake while she had been in the departure lounge had been short and sweet, but he had told her that Grime would meet be at the airport to meet her. He had explained that Maddy and Jethro needed the band at the venue early to meet with the film crew and the media.

As she walked through the arrivals hall half an hour after landing, Lori scanned the area for the band's driver. Almost immediately, she spotted him standing discretely off to one side chatting on his phone.

"Good flight, Mrs Power?" he enquired as he stepped forward to take her suitcase.

"Hi, Grime. And its Lori not Mrs Power. Flight was fine. No delays. No issues," she replied with a smile. "How are things here?"

"Surprisingly calm," he remarked. "I'd expected fireworks by now, but it was all under control when I left."

As they stepped out of the terminal building, Grime signalled to a waiting limo to pull over. When he opened the rear door for her, Lori saw that there was already someone inside.

"Surprise, li'l lady," said Jake softly.

"Jake!" she gasped, eyes wide with amazement. "I never expected you to be here!"

"Thought I'd come and surprise you," he replied as she climbed into the spacious car beside him. "I told Jethro that I didn't want to do any press before sound check to rest my voice. Grime here managed to smuggle me out past Maddison."

"She's going to kill you when she finds out you escaped," giggled Lori, snuggling in beside him. Quietly, she added, "I've missed you."

"Not as much as I've missed you," said Jake, putting his arm around her shoulder. "Ever since you sent that video through, I've been counting the hours until right now."

"Last show of the tour. We couldn't miss it."

"And it's going to be awesome!" enthused Jake. "It's sold out!"

"Fantastic! Where do I get to watch from tonight?"

"There's a VIP box reserved up on the balcony. Annie flew in last night with Becky. Poor woman was a wreck by the time she arrived. She is really scared of flying! Linsey's here too. She joined us in Indianapolis."

"Silver Lake family gathering," joked Lori as the limo pulled away from the kerb. "Pity Kola has to work this week."

There was a queue of fans lined up outside the Pageant when the limo pulled up. Realising he couldn't sneak back into the venue unnoticed, Jake took a deep breath, smiled at Lori then opened the door. Before he was fully out of the car, Grime was by his side, ensuring that the fans didn't crowd him. Painting on his public smile, Jake went over to the waiting Silver Lake fans and patiently posed for photos and autographed everything they put in front of him, including one fan's shoulder. A few of the fans recognised Lori and she too calmly autographed a few CDs before Grime ushered them both into the theatre.

Hand in hand, Jake and Lori followed Grime upstairs to the dressing rooms. The bodyguard held up his hand and pointed to a door to their left, signalling that they should go that way. Quickly, Jake opened the door and guided Lori inside. They found themselves in a large store cupboard. As they both tried to stifle their giggles, they could hear Maddy's voice echoing shrilly in the hallway.

"Grime, have you seen Jake?"

"No, boss," replied Grime calmly.

"I've taken this place apart looking for him. He's nowhere to be found. Where the fuck can he be?"

"Is he in the venue? Or back in his dressing room? I just left Lori off in the venue."

"I'll check the dressing room again," she snapped. "If you find him before I do, tell him I need him on that stage right fucking now!"

Hugging each other as they attempted to smother their hysterical laughter, Jake and Lori listened to the sound of Maddy's stiletto heels click down the corridor. A few seconds later, Grime opened the door.

"You two better head into the venue. Boss has gone to the dressing rooms. She's none too happy, Mr Power."

"Thanks, buddy," said Jake with a mischievous smile. "I owe you a beer for that. Can we get to the stage through the back way?"

"Down those stairs to your right. Door at the bottom comes out beside the stage."

The door into the hall creaked loudly as Jake opened it. He held it for Lori as she hurried through behind him. They found themselves in the pit in front of the stage among a mass of cabling and camera equipment. Carefully, they threaded their way across and up the staircase at the far side of the stage.

"You better have a good excuse ready, Mr Power," warned Grey sternly. "Boss is mad at you."

"We heard," giggled Lori.

"What's the drama anyway?" asked Jake as he slipped off his leather jacket. "I thought we were done until sound check?"

"We were," replied Rich, coming over to hug Lori. "But sound check's been brought forward by an hour. The film crew want to run through the laser show for during Out Of The Shadows and Dragon Song."

"I hear you," nodded Jake, accepting his guitar from Todd. "Li'l lady, you might want to sit out front and watch this. See how it looks from out there."

"Fine by me," agreed Lori. "I'll sit far back out of sight until Maddy's calmed down. Where's Jethro?"

"He was on the phone back stage last I saw of him," said Rich. "If we see him, we'll send him out to you."

Jake watched as Lori carefully made her way off stage and walked across the wide empty general access area towards the seating at the rear. The lighting crew were testing one of the spots and, as the beam of light hit her, he noticed how much her baby bump had grown in the two weeks since he'd last seen her. Beside him, Grey noticed his smile as he watched her disappear into the shadows.

"Pregnancy suits her," commented the bass player. "She's looking fantastic."

"She is, isn't she? Positively glowing," agreed Jake quietly.

The remaining hours before show time disappeared in a flurry of activity and Lori soon found herself sitting in the VIP area beside Becky and Annie. Around them, the theatre was filling up rapidly and they could feel the excitement building in the air. None of the fans had been told in advance that the show was being filmed and they could hear voices from below commenting about the camera rigs.

"Will we be in the film?" Becky asked Lori hopefully.

"No, honey," replied Lori softly. "Not unless the camera films some shots of the crowd. I'm sure the boys have told them to steer clear of this area."

"I'd like to be in it," muttered the little girl, looking bitterly disappointed.

"Well, maybe if you sing loud enough during the show, we'll be able to hear you on the video," suggested Lori as a compromise.

"Don't encourage her, Lori," scolded Grey's mother, Annie. "Little Miss here has been singing all day!"

"I was just warming up, Grammy," stated Becky indignantly. "Just like Uncle Jake does!"

At exactly eight o'clock, the lights dimmed and After Life took the stage for their final support slot of the tour. To mark the occasion, Ellen had gone all out for a dark, sinister look. She appeared on stage in a dramatic, black, velvet cape with a large hood and a train. Keeping the hood up and cloak drawn about her, Ellen delivered the first two dark, demonic numbers of the set. As clouds of dry ice billowed out, she crouched down in the swirling mist, then shed the cloak, emerging from the mist a vision in black leather with a scarlet corset top. For the first time, Lori noticed that the young singer wasn't disguising her arm. The support band's performance was the best Lori had ever heard them play and the sell-out crowd were loving it. To end their short set, the two guitarists made a performance of helping Ellen back on with her cloak, then, at the end of their final number, there was a loud explosion, a flash of light and the songstress vanished from sight. A simple illusion that left the crowd begging for more.

"She scares me," whispered Becky as she snuggled into Lori, tears in her eyes.

"It's only make believe, honey," soothed Lori as she hugged the little girl. "You know Ellen. She's very sweet."

"I know," agreed Becky, resting her head on Lori's bump. "But when she's the witchy singer, she's scary."

"She's only pretending to be scary."

At that the baby gave a sharp kick and Becky sat bolt upright.

"Wow!" she exclaimed, all thoughts of being scared banished in an instant. "Your baby kicked me!"

Trying not to laugh, Lori rubbed her swollen belly feeling the baby kicking furiously. "I guess you weren't the only one Ellen scared. Don't tell Uncle Jake that the baby kicked you. He hasn't felt it yet."

"Ok. Our secret," promised Becky, tapping the end of her nose with her index finger and winking in a conspiratorial way.

In the wings, Silver Lake waited patiently for their cue to go out on stage. The house lights dipped again and the fans began the chant. "Silver Lake, Silver Lake, Silver Lake, Lake, Lake." All four musicians were fidgety, anxious to get the show started. At their feet, a camera man was trying and failing to film them discretely. As Maddy gave them the signal to move it on out, Paul crouched down in front of the camera and pretended to lick the lens, much to the surprise of the camera man.

As they opened the set for the final show of the tour, the crowd went wild. The powerful riff of set opener Engine Room was almost drowned out by the screaming fans. Silver Lake powered through the hard and heavy song, oblivious to the cameras surrounding them.

Three songs in and, as had become the standard routine, Jake stepped forward to address the crowd. "Good evening, St Louis!"

A wave of enthusiastic cheers hit him.

Shaking his head slowly, Jake said, "Folks, this show is being filmed for a future DVD release. Let's show the world what you've got. I said, good evening, St Louis!"

This time, the resulting roar almost deafened him.

"That's more like it," he declared with a grin. "We're three songs in so the next one's kind of obvious. This is Four!"

Laughter and cheers echoed round the theatre as Rich began the intro to the song.

All too soon it was time for the acoustic interlude. As ever, Jake sat perched on his high stool and played Stronger Within then followed it with Depths. He paused for a moment, took a deep breath, then began to speak straight from the heart to the fans, "Last summer we lost someone very close to us. There's not a night goes by that we don't miss him when we're out here. He's forever in the wings in our hearts. Gary, this one's for you. At The Beach, folks."

Delicately, Jake began to play the lilting French air intro to the instrumental number. It was the first time he had played the song acoustically in front of a live audience. When Rich and Grey had suggested adding it in, Jake had been hesitant. The song stirred up so many emotions in him that he still struggled with it, but he couldn't disagree that Gary would've loved to have been in The Pageant with them. The heavy, technically challenging midsection of the number sounded rounded and warm played on his acoustic guitar. At The Beach lost some if its raw edge and the rhythm became almost soothing. As the song returned to the closing section, a repeat of the French air beginning, Jake felt his band mates return to the stage behind him.

With the last notes floating out over the crowd, Jake bowed his head, breathing heavily. He could feel tears burning unshed in his eyes, but, somehow, he regained control over his emotions. As he raised his head, the crowd began to whistle and cheer loudly.

Two songs later, slightly further through the set than usual, Jake welcomed Ellen out on stage to duet with the band on Mysteries one last time. Instead of changing out of her After Life stage clothes, Ellen was still wearing her skin tight black leather jeans and scarlet corset. As the tour had wound its way through the country, her confidence had soared and this final duet was the best one yet. Both singers were note perfect and obviously enjoyed performing together. The crowd fed off their energy and were loving Mysteries.

"St Louis, give it up for the beautiful and talented Ellen one final time!" roared Rich at the end of the song. "And for the one and only Jake Power!"

When Silver Lake returned for their final encore, the fans sang their hearts out on Dragon Song. Before the cheers died away, Jake addressed the masses one final time.

"St Louis, you've been an amazing audience. Thank you!"

He stood back, grinning as they applauded and cheered with a renewed passion.

"We'd like to welcome out on stage now a special person who really saved our asses on this tour. St Louis, give a huge cheer for Mr Todd Denby!"

Looking nervous, the young guitarist stepped out on stage to join them.

"Vortex, ladies and gentlemen!"

Deliberately, Rich sat the song out, allowing Todd a final few moments in the spotlight in front of the Silver Lake fans. The grin on the young musician's face left the members of Silver Lake in no doubt that it had been the right decision to bring Todd back out for the last show. As he stood in a single beam of light for the guitar solo, Jake and Grey moved to flank him on either side, both in silent awe of the boy's skill. When the song drew to a close, Rich came forward again, clapped Todd on the shoulder, then joked with the crowd, "I'll need to watch my ass. This kid's fantastic! Give it up one more time for Todd!"

The crowd cheered and whistled as Silver Lake began the distinctive intro to Flyin' High. Despite his best efforts to retreat from the stage, neither Jake nor Rich would allow Todd to leave. It seemed fitting for him to remain out there to close the show.

"Till next time, St Louis!" roared Jake as the last notes faded away. "Stay safe."

The tour was over.

When Lori entered the dressing room a few minutes later the after show party was already beginning. The band and various invited guests were all gathered together talking animatedly. As she scanned the room, she couldn't see Jake. Beside her, Becky spotted her daddy and ran across the room, throwing herself into his arms. The weary bass player swept her up and hugged her tight, his joy at seeing her plain for all to see. In the corner, there was a camera man from the film company and he hadn't missed a second of the tender moment. With a smile, Lori thought that Becky might just get her wish about being in the film.

Spotting Jethro standing on his own, Lori went over to ask him where Jake was.

"He went to grab a shower and a change of clothes. He's down the corridor. Room on the left," replied the white haired, tour manager.

"Thanks, Jethro," said Lori, subconsciously running her hand down the left side of her bump.

"Baby Power enjoying the show?" asked Jethro, nodding towards her hand.

"Danced all night," revealed Lori with a giggle. "I'd better go and find my husband."

A knock at the dressing room door startled Jake. Fresh out of the shower, he had only just pulled on a clean pair of jeans. As he fastened the button on them, he stepped across to open the door. Out in the corridor, Lori stood leaning on her cane looking tired but radiant.

"You decent, rock star?" she teased softly.

"Just," replied Jake, stepping aside so she could enter the small dressing room.

Closing the door behind him, Jake reached out and drew her roughly into his embrace. Her cane fell to the floor with a clatter. He could feel her rounded stomach hard between them as he held her close. Breathing in her delicate floral perfume, Jake bent and nuzzled into her neck, gently licking the soft skin behind her ear. As he continued to explore her neck and throat, he heard her sigh deeply. Running his fingers along her jawline, Jake tilted her face up, then began to kiss her hard, hungry for the taste of her. He could feel the rest of his body responding to his need for her. Already his manhood was straining against the tight fabric of his jeans. Placing his hand on the small of her back, Jake pulled Lori closer to him.

Suddenly he felt a sharp movement against his erection. Before he could say anything, he felt the same sensation another twice.

"You felt that?" whispered Lori, gazing deep into his hazel eyes.

"I sure did, li'l lady," he replied, his voice thick with emotion. "I think our little Power Pack wants to play."

"Here?"

Reaching to lock the door, Jake replied, "Right here."

Glancing about the small room, Lori looked into his eyes a little anxiously, "Where?"

The dressing room was very sparsely furnished with only one small table and two chairs plus a low shelf below the mirror.

"Sh," said Jake, carefully sliding her black leggings down to reveal her black lace trimmed panties. He knelt in front of her, tugged off her short boots, then slipped her out of the skin tight soft trousers. Teasingly, he ran his tongue over her pregnant belly as he raised her tunic top up. While still tenderly licking her taut stomach, he reached down inside her panties to explore her feminine moistness. He was left in doubt that his wife was as ready for him as he was for her. Swiftly, he stood up and pulled her tunic off over her head. As she stood in front of him, in her black underwear, Jake thought she had never looked more beautiful.

Before he could stop her, Lori reached out and unfastened his jeans, sliding them and his boxer shorts down in one swift movement. His erect manhood sprang free. With a mischievous grin, Lori ran her well-manicured finger over its sensitive tip then teasingly down its length.

"Naughty, Mz Hyde," groaned Jake as he unfastened her bra, tossing it onto the floor.

Cupping her voluptuous breasts in his hands, Jake could feel his internal fire building as his wife continued to sensuously stroke his erection.

Roughly, he kicked off his jeans that had still been tangled around his ankles. He placed his hand inside her panties then slid them down over her still slender hips, barely noticing her omnipresent, faded scars.

Taking her by the hand, Jake led her over to one of the chairs and sat down. "Straddle me, li'l lady," he instructed, his voice husky with desire.

Carefully, she sat, legs spread across his well-muscled thighs and allowed him to lift her into position. Wriggling slightly to alter the angle of his back, Jake slowly lowered her down onto him. As soon as he felt himself rise inside her, he moaned softly. He had hoped to make love to her slowly and gently but he knew instinctively she was as hot and ready as he was for sex.

He thrust hard and fast, deep inside her. Around him, her body responded. As she rode him, he felt Lori arch her back, lean back her head and utter a low moan of pure pleasure.

Two more hard and fast strokes were all it took until they were consumed by their mutual climax.

Spent, he slid himself out from the warmth of her body and hugged her close.

"I love you, Mz Hyde."

"Love you too, rock star," she purred softly as he kissed her gently.

Her hard baby bump was pressed between them and, as she kissed him tenderly, Jake felt their baby kick again.

"Think we had an audience," he joked softly.

Giggling, Lori said, "I think we have but I think they've enjoyed this too."

"Hmm," said Jake, running his hand across her stomach. "Not sure how I feel about that, li'l lady."

Still giggling, Lori climbed slowly off his knee and reached down to retrieve her clothes.

"Well, let's see if this little Power Pack likes to party instead," she suggested. "We'd better get dressed before someone comes looking for us!"

Reluctantly, Jake got to his feet and reached for his boxers. As he watched Lori get dressed, he thought that the last few minutes had been the ultimate way to celebrate the end of the tour.

There were already signs of spring when Silver Lake returned to Rehoboth. After spending six weeks in each other's constant company, they had all agreed that they needed to take a break before reconvening to finish writing for the new record. Before they had left St Louis, Maddy and Jethro had called a short, formal band meeting to set the schedule for the coming weeks. It was quickly established that they were free of all band related commitments until March 24th, the date that they agreed on to meet up and resume writing in earnest for their third album. This plan left them three full weeks before they were committed to supporting the Weigh Station charity project at JJL. With the exact schedule for that still sketchy, the management team had taken the liberty of leasing the small rehearsal hall out at the studio to allow Silver Lake to work together when they weren't required by Mikey or Garrett. All four of them were happy with the flexibility this gave them. Jason had confirmed via email that they were booked to appear at three of the country's major rock festivals over three consecutive weekends in May. Each of their slots were late afternoon appearances on the Saturday, but they were all high profile shows guaranteed to draw large crowds and to help generate new interest in the band. The final item on the brief agenda was the recording schedule for the album. In the same email, Jason had confirmed that JJL was booked out for Silver Lake from June 2nd right through until August 29th. Extra time had been generously factored in to allow Jake some paternity leave in July. All of them were relieved that this allowed them to record with fewer time constraint pressures. Each of them had expressed their concern that the previous album recording had felt rushed. More importantly, it meant that Silver Lake were home all summer.

It was late when Jake and Lori finally arrived back at the beach house. Their flight from St Louis had been delayed, then there was a hold up in the baggage hall at Philadelphia. Tempers had started to fray among the road weary musicians, especially when Grey realised one of his guitar cases was missing. Having gathered up their luggage and Jake's guitars, Jake and Lori had slipped away quietly, leaving Jethro trying to pacify the irate bass player. Fortunately, the rest of the journey home was uneventful and they made good time on the empty stretches of highway.

While Jake unloaded the car, Lori crawled off to bed. She was exhausted after a hectic weekend and too many late nights. When Jake came down to the bedroom with their suitcases, he found her fast asleep. Setting the bags down, he decided that unpacking could wait until morning.

After weeks of late nights sleeping on the bus and in hotels, while longing for a night in his own bed with his own pillow, Jake couldn't sleep. He was beyond tired. Every inch of him felt like lead, but sleep refused to come. Beside him, Lori was curled on her side, her breathing deep and even as she slept soundly. Trying to be quiet, he slipped out of bed, pulled on a sweatshirt and wandered barefoot down to the kitchen.

"Time to resort to Mom's cure all," thought Jake as he lifted the milk jug from the refrigerator.

He filled a mug with milk and placed it in the microwave. Silently, he stood watching the timer count down, stopping it with one second to go before it "pinged" in case the noise disturbed his sleeping wife. With the mug in his hand, he wandered through towards the sunroom. A huge pile of mail sat on the dining room table. Putting the light on, but dimming the switch slightly, Jake sifted through six weeks' worth of mail, sorting it into piles- bills, junk, fan mail, business mail. At the bottom of the pile, he found the folder and note from Salazar Mendes. Inside the buff folder were a dozen sheets of music. Methodically, he scanned them, noting the perfection of Salazar's handwriting. A few of the songs had neat notes written in the margins, others had details of potential themes annotated along the top of the page. In total, there were ten full pieces of music in the folder, but none of them had any titles. Each of them was meticulously numbered. How was he to find time to write lyrics for all of these plus meet his Silver Lake commitments? Sipping his warm milk slowly, Jake read over each song again, hearing it in his head as he read the music. It was an honour to be trusted with these and the moment wasn't lost on him.

When he had re-joined the tour, Rich had told him about Garrett and Salazar's visit to Lori's apartment. His fellow musician had cautioned him to be careful around the reclusive bluesman, stating that he didn't feel entirely comfortable in his company. Jake had dismissed this as his friend being too cynical about people, but, as he read over the music in front of him, it was conjuring up some very dark imagery.

With a yawn, he put everything back into the folder and laid it to one side. Draining the last of the milk from the mug, Jake yawned again and decided that he was finally ready to sleep.

Bright sunshine flooding in through the window wakened Lori next morning. She listened to her husband's rhythmic breathing and smiled to herself. It was good to have him home again. The house felt so empty while he was out on the road.

Leaving him to sleep, she crept out of bed, spotting their unopened suitcases sitting in front of the closets. Taking care not to snap the catches open too loudly, Lori began to empty the bags, sorting the dirty laundry into plastic baskets. She was relieved that Maddy had arranged for all of the band's stage clothes to be taken away to be laundered separately. She smiled, though when she found a bulky laundry bag in Jake's smaller suitcase, stuffed full of underwear. He obviously didn't trust his boxers to a laundry service! Stifling a giggle, she dumped the contents of the bag into one basket. Soon she had the three suitcases more or less unpacked and had amassed five baskets of laundry. Carefully, she lifted the first basket and carried it down to the kitchen.

With the washing machine programmed, Lori went about her usual morning routine, then headed through to sit at her desk with her coffee. On her way through the dining room, she noticed that Jake had sorted his mail and that he'd found the folder from Salazar. As she sat drinking her coffee, Lori checked through her emails and her schedule for the next few weeks. Despite her best efforts to keep her workload light, Jason kept sending her through small commissions or add ons to the larger projects she already had in the pipeline. Once she had it all plotted out, her calendar was pretty full through until late-May. Lori added in the three festival dates, mindful that she had promised Jake that she would be there. The thought of two long overnight bus trips when she would be over thirty weeks pregnant concerned her a little, but she knew in her heart of hearts that nothing would stop her from being at those festivals.

It was mid-afternoon before Jake finally wandered through from the bedroom. His long hair was hanging round his shoulders in tangled strands as he rubbed the last remnants of sleep from his eyes.

"Good afternoon, rock star," said Lori, looking up from the drawing she was finalising.

"What time is it?" he mumbled, still half asleep.

"After three."

"Shit," muttered Jake stretching. "I had plans for this morning."

"Your body had other plans like sleep."

"I guess," he conceded with a sigh. "Think I'll head out for a run. Cleanse my soul with some ocean air."

A short while later, as he jogged gently across the soft sand down towards the harder packed wet stuff, an icy wind whipped round him. Pulling the zip up higher on his hooded sweat top, Jake began to run south down the beach. He could hear the waves crashing in on the shore over the music of his iPod as he pounded his way towards Dewey Beach. After weeks of being cooped up on the bus and snatching short treadmill sessions in hotel gyms, it felt good to be out in the fresh air again. He ran down the shore until he reached the boundary of Delaware Seashore State Park, then he turned for home.

On his way back to the house, Jake tried to ignore the tired ache that was spreading through his thighs and focussed his mind on Salazar's manuscript pages. Part of him wanted to call the eccentric musician to establish if he wanted lyrics for all ten pieces or if he was only to write accompanying words for some tracks. "Learn. Provide lyrics as you see fit" the note had said. Learning the music would be a start and, as the house finally came into view, Jake decided he would run through the songs after dinner.

Lori was in the kitchen unpacking grocery sacks when he came stumbling in the back door.

"Water," he gasped as he stood in the utility area bent over, hands resting on his burning thighs. "That was tough."

Passing him a glass of water, Lori asked, "How far did you go?

You've been gone a while."

"Right down to the state park and back," said Jake before draining the glass. "About ten miles all in."

"And is your soul feeling suitably cleansed?"

"Better than it was," he replied with a wink. "I'm going to jump in a shower, then do you want me to cook dinner?"

"Sure," agreed Lori, smiling at the contrast between the "on stage" Jake and the "at home" Jake.

"There's a cost, li'l lady."

"And that is?"

"I need your thoughts on some music I've to learn."

"Ah! You've read Sal's folder," she mused. "Of course, I'll listen."

Deciding that it was too cold down in the basement studio, Jake brought his practice amp up to the sunroom along with his resonator. His touring guitars were still piled in the lounge and, while Lori settled herself on the couch, he fetched his custom model and his treasured acoustic. The sheets of handwritten music sat on the footstool. As an afterthought, Jake grabbed his lyrics journal and a pen, just in case inspiration struck.

"Pick a number between one and ten, li'l lady," he said as he made himself comfortable on the footstool.

"Ten," replied Lori, watching as he shuffled the sheets of music until he found the one he was looking for.

Quickly, he scanned over the piece again, then picked up his electric guitar, plugged himself in, tweaked the tuning then began to play. The first run through didn't feel smooth and didn't flow. Unfamiliar with the piece, he faltered over a couple of sections. Salazar had given him both parts, lead and rhythm. With so little in the way of guidance, Jake surmised the he should learn both. By his third attempt, he'd found a feel for it and felt he could add a little more emotion to it. There was no doubt that it was a very dark and tortured blues tune. It created images of utter despair in his mind.

"That was intense," commented Lori when he was done. "Really added the blue to blues. So desperate."

"It's certainly not a cheerful start," agreed her husband as he reached for his journal. "It's conjuring up images of slavery to me. Badly treated slaves."

Over the next three hours, Jake worked his way through the remaining pieces of music, each time allowing Lori to select the piece by its number. Some of them felt instinctively right to him as he chopped and changed instruments, almost as though he had finally reached into Salazar's psyche and tapped into his creative flow of thoughts.

The final song to be selected was number two. It was the shortest but the music looked complex and fast paced. Selecting the vintage resonator, Jake began to play. Much to their surprise, the short, delta blues tune was bright and cheerful, playful almost.

"Must have been written on one of his better days," observed Jake as he prepared to play through it again.

"That's some contrast to the deep dark hole we've just been down," agreed Lori quietly. "These songs worry me."

"Why?"

"What frame of mind is Sal in? Does Garrett know the depths of this haunted despair? It's scaring me."

"I hear you," agreed Jake sadly. "Hearing these and hearing you and Rich say how odd he was when you met up with him in New York is worrying. But, we all know he's reclusive, eccentric and deeply troubled. More than a bit unstable."

"Hmmm," said Lori, getting to her feet. "It's how troubled that concerns me, Jake. Be careful around him. Don't get sucked in."

Over the next ten days both Lori and Jake immersed themselves in creativity, falling into an easy routine as the days passed. After breakfast together, they would work until early afternoon, share a late lunch, then take a walk if the weather was nice before returning to the house to work on until early evening. Whoever packed up first for the day cooked dinner. Both of them made steady progress with their respective projects. By the end of the week, Lori had finalised one of her major commissions plus add-ons and was able to take a few days out to work on the next LH jewellery collection.

Down in the basement, Jake had spent the first few days working on the ten Salazar Mendes songs. He wrote lyrics for four of them, but, after learning the others, he felt that the depth of the music spoke for itself. With a silent prayer, he emailed the lyrics to the bluesman for approval. Satisfied that he had taken the project as far as he could for now, he turned his attention to the Weigh

Station project. Progress with the planning was gathering pace and Mikey had sent through a final list of artists and songs to be split up and recorded. Emails flew backwards and forwards as, together with Garrett and Dr Marrs, they worked out a schedule based around who was playing what. The remaining members of Weigh Station formed the majority of the musicians involved in each track. It was agreed that Jake would sing Broken Bottle Empty Glass plus at least one duet but that his guitar skills would also be called upon for a few of the other tracks. With the schedule agreed, Jake decided he better refresh his memory of some of the older Weigh Station numbers he was expected to play on. Playing the anthems of his youth was fun and, alone in the basement, he felt like a teenager rehearsing in his bedroom. It was good therapy for him and, by the time he had rehearsed his Weigh Station commitments, Jake felt refreshed and more than ready to focus on the new Silver Lake record.

After their long, intense week, Jake and Lori decided to take Sunday off to spend the afternoon shopping for baby essentials. Having sought advice from Maddy on where to go in search of a crib, a bassinet and a stroller, they set off after lunch towards Lewes. The band's manager had recommended a small, family run business in preference to the selection on offer at the superstore out on the highway or the stores at the outlets.

A watery, early spring sun was shining as they headed out of town. In the passenger seat, Lori sat back, resting her hand on her growing baby bump while she listened to Jake sing along to the country rock song playing on the radio. She could feel the baby shifting restlessly.

"You ok, li'l lady?" asked Jake, noticing she was rubbing one spot on her swollen belly.

"I'm fine," replied Lori, smiling over at her husband. "This little Power Pack is just enjoying playtime in there. Feels like they're dancing to the music."

"It's mind blowing to think there's another human in there," marvelled Jake. "Two bonded souls."

"Pardon?"

"Sorry," he said quickly. "Just something I'd worked into some lyrics a few weeks back. Bonded Souls. Your soul and the baby's.

And, I guess, you could say my soul and yours make up a part of the baby's soul."

"Very philosophical, rock star," she teased as the baby gave a sharp kick.

Each day the movements were getting stronger; each day she felt as though her stomach was growing bigger.

When they entered the small store, both of them were surprised that, despite the narrow shopfront, it was huge inside. Slowly, they browsed the range of nursery furniture on display, debating choices of wood. Ever the practical one, Lori pointed out that the existing chest of drawers and bookcase in the spare bedroom that was to become the nursery were antique pine. She suggested firmly that they should stick with that finish.

"So, what do we need furniture wise?" asked Jake, gazing about.

"A crib, a nursing chair or a rocking chair. Maybe a changing table like Maddy has," replied Lori, spotting a range over to their right that looked to be the correct shade of wood.

They spent a few minutes deliberating between the different styles of crib before an assistant came over to offer them some help. Quickly, Lori explained what they were looking for and, under the guidance of the sales girl, had soon selected a traditional crib and a changing table. The range of nursing chairs was limited, so Lori decided to leave that key item for now.

A bassinet was next on the list and, shunning the overly ornate lacy styles, Lori selected a simple, white Broderie Anglaise covered wicker style.

"Safe choice, ma'am," commented the assistant warmly. "Especially if you don't know the sex of the baby."

"That was my thought," said Lori. "If this little one is a boy, I don't want him surrounded by lacy frills."

Behind her, Jake laughed and asked, "Do they not make these in denim and leather?"

"Jake!" scolded Lori with a giggle.

"Ok. Ok," he said, grinning. "It was only a thought, li'l lady. Now what's next on the list?"

"A travel system stroller."

Choosing their ideal stroller took longer. There were several styles to choose from and dozens of colours. Again, Lori opted to play safe with her colour choice, opting for a silver-grey travel system with contrasting turquoise trim. Silver Lake colours.

"It's a baby Silver Bullet," joked Jake as he checked the handle height could be adjusted on the model she had selected.

"I guess it is," giggled Lori as she checked the price tag. "Safe colours too."

"And lightweight," commented Jake, lifting the travel system. "Looks like we have ourselves a stroller."

On the way to the customer service desk, Lori picked up some sheets and blankets for the bassinet and the crib, sticking with white for now.

While she was arranging the delivery date for the items, Jake came over carrying a small, white, toy rabbit.

"He's coming with us too," he said with a wink as he sat the bunny down on the counter.

"He is?"

"Yes," stated Jake, running his fingers over the bunny's long soft ears. "I had one as a little kid. Every baby needs their bedtime bunny."

While they were both in the shopping mood, Lori suggested they take a run by the outlets on their way home so she could pick up a few basic baby clothes. Much to her surprise, Jake agreed, adding that he needed some new running shoes and some shorts. The traffic was heavier than they had anticipated, causing them to arrive later than planned. Deciding to divide and conquer, they went their separate ways, agreeing to meet up in an hour back at the car.

The sports outlet was crowded when Jake entered and he almost turned on his heel and left. He hated busy stores. He still struggled with being recognised off stage, especially if he was on his own and a crowded area was always high risk. Glancing round the store, he could feel his anxiety beginning to build. Taking a deep breath, Jake headed across to the footwear department. Scanning the shelves for his preferred brand of shoe, he tried to mentally block out his fellow shoppers. Eventually, he found the shoe he was searching for but couldn't find his size in the stack of boxes.

"Excuse me," he said politely to a nearby assistant. "Do you have these in a twelve?"

"Let me check, sir," replied the young male assistant. "Does it need to be in this colour combination?"

"Not especially," answered Jake. "It just has to be that model in a twelve."

"OK. Give me a moment, sir."

To keep himself occupied while he waited for the sales person to return, Jake browsed through a bargain bin of sports socks, choosing a few pairs to replace some of his well-worn favourites.

"Sir," began the boy as he returned carrying two large shoe boxes. "We only have these in your size in two colours at present. White or neon green."

Neither option was his colour of choice, however, Jake loved the fit of that model of shoe and really didn't want to have to find an alternative all for the sake of the colour.

"Can I try on the green, please? White isn't practical."

"Of course," said the boy, passing him the box.

Green they most certainly were when he saw them lying in the box.

"I'll not get lost running in the dark in these," joked Jake as he tried the lightweight shoe on for size. As expected, they were a perfect fit, even if they were a hell of a colour.

"Built in safety feature," commented the sales assistant. "Highly reflective when car lights shine on them."

"I don't pound many streets," said Jake, getting to his feet to confirm the shoes felt comfortable. "I tend to stick to the beach. Shortage of headlights down there."

"I guess. How do they feel?"

"Perfect, despite the colour. I'll take them."

"Do you have any other shopping to do in the store before paying for these, sir?"

"I do," replied Jake as he slipped his feet back into his boots. He handed the boy the box and the socks he'd picked up, then asked, "Can you leave them at the desk and I'll get them when I come over?"

"Of course. I'll put your name on the box."

Jake watched with surprise as the boy scrawled "Power" across the lid. He looked at the boy, raised one eyebrow and smiled, grateful that he hadn't drawn attention to him.

"Thank you," said Jake softly.

"Pleasure, sir," replied the boy, blushing slightly. "I remember reading that you don't like too much attention off stage. That your privacy is important to you. I respect that and your music."

"If only all folk did," replied Jake.

"Your shoes will be at the customer service desk for you when you're ready."

"Thank you," said Jake, noting that the boy's name was Mark.

It took him a while, but eventually Jake decided on two pairs of shorts and two new vests from the vast selection on display. As an afterthought, he picked up a new water bottle as he made his way back over to the customer service desk. Fortunately, there weren't many folk in line in front of him and no one gave him a second glance.

The girl at the cash register barely looked up as he handed over the bundle of clothing and said that some shoes and socks had been put aside for him.

"Name?" she said, her tone surly and tinged with boredom.

"Power."

"Cool name."

As Jake was signing the credit card receipt, the sales boy came over to check if he'd found everything he'd been looking for.

"Thanks, Mark. I did," replied Jake warmly. "And thanks again for your help. I'll be scaring the seabirds with these shoes!"

On his way back to the car, Jake detoured into one of the many clothing stores in search of a couple of shirts and some jeans. He was in the fitting room, trying on the jeans, when his phone began its R2D2 chime. Concerned it was Lori looking for him, he left the jeans unfastened and reached for the phone. The message wasn't from his wife. It was from Salazar. Short and to the point, it read, "Be at JJL tomorrow night at 9. Be prepared. Be available every night this week. Salazar."

"Yes, Meister. I'll be there. J," he typed quickly.

With trembling hands, Jake fastened the jeans, confirming they were a good fit, all the while his mind was racing. He was going into the studio for a week with Salazar Mendes!

Jake and Lori arrived back at the car at the same time, both of them clutching a handful of colourful shopping bags. Immediately, Lori noticed the smile on her husband's face.

"Not like you to look so happy about shopping," she commented as she placed her bags in the trunk.

"I got a message from Salazar while I was in the changing rooms."

"And?"

"I've to be at JJL every night this week with him."

"Ah, that explains the smile," laughed Lori. "I thought you had Silver Lake rehearsals this week?"

"No. We start on March 24th. This week I'd set aside for writing for the record. Guess I'll need to revisit my schedule."

"Well, remember to schedule in sleep, rock star," cautioned Lori softly. "Don't burn yourself out."

The outside of JJL was in pitch darkness as Jake climbed down from his truck shortly before nine on Monday evening. He had been determined not to be late for his appointment with Salazar, conscious that he didn't want to do anything that would risk upsetting the highly strung guitarist. To his right, he could see lights on in the house, including the porch light. It cast its shadow out across the lawn towards the old rocking chair that seemed to have become a permanent feature.

Swiftly, he gathered his guitar cases up and lifted his book bag. Almost as an afterthought, Jake had lifted his lyrics journal, deciding to err on the side of caution and bring it in case inspiration struck. Having locked the truck, he headed indoors out of the chill evening.

Inside the familiar studio, the lights were dimmed and the air was warm, A heady, unfamiliar aroma was wafting through the lounge. Sniffing the air, Jake concluded that it was church incense, reminding him of his grandmother's funeral. His maternal grandmother had died when he was eight years old and he recalled the funeral every time he smelled incense. It had been a traumatic experience for his eight year old self.

Strangely, the studio was silent. The refrigerator in the lounge hummed gently and he could hear the low buzz of the heating system. Apart from that, it was eerily quiet.

Pausing to lift a bottle of water from the fridge, Jake headed through to the live room. It too was dimly lit and appeared to be empty. Deducing that the lack of light had to be at Salazar's request, he resisted the temptation to reach for the light switch. Instead, he laid his bag and guitars down beside the old, leather couch, then pulled off his beanie, shaking his hair loose.

"Yin and Yang," commented a deep voice from behind him. "Light and dark."

Somewhat startled, Jake spun round and found himself face to face with Salazar. In the dim light, the tall, dark haired guitarist's skin was almost translucent, adding to the vampire image. Unusually, Sal wasn't dressed entirely in black. He was wearing a loose, blood red, silk shirt, open at the neck that revealed part of a tattoo along his collarbone.

"Ready to play, Mr Power?" he asked as Garrett appeared behind him.

"Sure," replied Jake, trying not to sound too eager.

In the control room the lights came on and Jake looked round in time to see Dr Marrs take his seat.

While Salazar settled himself on a stool with his trademark Fender Stratocaster, Jake brought out his Mz Hyde custom guitar and sat down opposite him.

"Open G," stated Sal softly.

"What are we starting with?" asked Jake as he adjusted the tuning to his guitar.

"Slavery," said the older musician. "You have lyrics for that one, don't you?"

"Yes, sir," replied Jake. "But I've not done any vocal warm up."

"Gentlemen," interrupted Dr Marrs firmly. "We've ten tracks on the board. We've five nights. Let's do guitar tracking tonight and see how far we get. Jake, vocals can wait until Thursday."

"Fine by me," called back Jake.

"Reverse order on the board," said Salazar, gazing intently across at the window of the control room. "No more interruptions, James."

Over in the corner, Garrett had brought out his own guitar and, pulling over a stool, came to join them.

"Sit this one out, Rett," said Sal, a tenderness in his tone. "I'll need you on six, seven and eight."

"Fine," agreed Garrett, laying his guitar down. "I'll wait in here, though, if you don't object."

Slowly, Salazar nodded, then bowed his head to play. Relieved that he had practiced this one earlier, Jake came in exactly on cue and, together, they created the musical imagery of the bleak depths of slavery in the past of the Deep South.

Over the next few hours, Jake fell under the older musician's spell. As before, they traded parts, playing each song through repeatedly until Salazar was satisfied with it. There was little in the way of conversation. After four hours, they had two out of the ten songs covered. The whole experience was a far cry from Jake's usual experience in the studio and he was finding the whole thing very intense. Playing in such extended periods of silence felt alien and he was relieved when Salazar declared, "Twenty minute break. Be back in here at two."

Without a backwards glance, the tall vampire-esque musician slipped out of the studio. Stifling a yawn, Jake followed him out into the lounge. Dr Marrs was already out there pouring two mugs of coffee. Handing one to Jake, he said, "You'll need this. I get the feeling we're in for a long night."

"Thanks, Jim. It's been an intense one so far."

"Different to your usual sessions in here?"

"Ever so slightly," declared Jake with a sleepy smile. "Where did he go?"

"Out back," replied the producer. "Garrett went with him."

"Smoke break?"

The producer nodded, "And I don't want to know what he's smoking."

When Jake re-entered the studio a minute or so after two, both Salazar and Garrett were sitting talking quietly. He could smell weed wafting about them both, but, if Dr Marrs could turn a blind eye to it, so could he in the circumstances. Taking a long drink from the red cup by his side, Salazar said, "We'll do track eight and then decide if we've time to do seven before dawn."

"Fine by me," agreed Jake, lifting his guitar from the stand.

"You'll play lead on this one," Sal stated. "Rett, you and I as we played it last night."

The seven o'clock breakfast news was on the radio as Jake parked the truck in its usual spot in the driveway. It had been a long time since he'd worked all night and he was dead on his feet. Dumping his gear in the lounge room, he practically crawled down the long, narrow hallway to the bedroom. He discarded his clothes on the floor and climbed into bed beside his sleeping wife. Almost the instant his head hit the pillow, he was asleep.

Feeling Jake climb into bed beside her, roused Lori from sleep. She had spent a restless night, worrying about how things were going out at JJL. Taking care not to disturb him, she rolled over onto her back and checked the time on the clock on the night stand. The movement was enough to waken the baby, who began to wriggle and stretch. Laying a hand on her growing bump, Lori watched her stomach twitch and lurch. After a few minutes, the baby settled and she decided it was time to get up and start her day.

Unsure of Jake's plans, Lori had decided to spend the day at her drawing board. Her current commission was taking shape slowly and, gauging that she had a few uninterrupted hours ahead of her, she seized the opportunity to try to break the back of the design challenge before her. The remit had requested a futuristic, industrial landscape and, initially, she had struggled for inspiration. Even the advance copy of the album wasn't helping her to visualise what the artist had requested. While Jake had been in the studio the night before, she had relaxed in front of the TV watching the sci-fi channel. One drama had inspired the scene she was now about to create.

The hours slipped by as she became engrossed in the depths of her fictitious skyline. Gradually, the design began to take shape as she outlined the entire piece in pencil. Having stopped for a quick snack for lunch, Lori returned to her desk, cleared her emails while she drank a coffee then returned her attention to the drawing board.

Footsteps approaching broke her concentration as Jake wandered into the study, wearing only his T-shirt and boxers.

"Afternoon," greeted Lori warmly. "You ok?"

"Still tired," replied Jake with a yawn. "I'm no good at working through the night. It was almost five thirty before we called it a night."

"What time are you due back at JJL?"

"Nine," he said with a groan as he stretched. "Think I'll go for a run before I jump in the shower."

"Don't be too long," cautioned Lori, checking the time. "I was kind of hoping we could have dinner together."

"I won't. I'll be no more than an hour."

A cold wind was blowing in off the ocean as Jake ran south down the beach. Waves were crashing in on the shore to his left, the noise of them breaking drowning out the music playing on his iPod. After being cooped up all night, it felt good to get some clean ocean air into his lungs. Knowing he had another long night ahead of him, he set a leisurely pace as he headed down towards the bath house and the state park. As he ran, Jake allowed himself to revise the next few tracks to be recorded in his mind. Before he had left JJL, Dr Marrs had said they needed to get tracks four through to seven done on Tuesday, leaving them Wednesday night for one, two and three. Jake could see at least another two long nights ahead of him. With a sigh, he turned and headed for home.

Once again, the studio was in virtual darkness when Jake arrived. It was also deserted. He could hear Dr Marrs' voice from behind the closed office door, but there was no sign of Salazar or Garrett. Deciding to make a start, Jake lifted his resonator out of its case and began to rehearse track seven as listed on the board. He was on his second run through it before Dr Marrs appeared behind the desk.

"Sorry, Jake," he apologised. "Important call about the Weigh Station project schedule. Can you start number seven again from the top?"

"Shouldn't we wait for Sal and Garrett?"

"No," stated the producer firmly. "Time isn't on our side here. Let's make a start."

Under the producer's guidance, Jake played through all parts for tracks seven and six. It was almost midnight and there was still no sign of Salazar.

"Let's break for ten minutes," suggested Dr Marrs. "Grab a drink and I'll try calling Garrett again."

By the time Jake came back into the studio with two cans of caffeine-loaded energy drinks, Dr Marrs had managed to speak with Garrett and promised Jake that the two musicians would be no more than ten minutes. There was a sleeve of solo cups lying on the couch and Jake emptied both cans of juice into one before returning to his seat and picking up his acoustic guitar. He began to play one of the songs he had been working on for the Silver Lake record.

"What's that?" called through Dr Marrs, his curiosity aroused.

"A work in progress," called back Jake with a grin. "Tentatively called Bonded Souls."

"You got lyrics for it?"

"Yes, sir, I do."

"Look forward to hearing it in June."

Before they could continue their conversation, the door opened and Salazar, closely followed by Garrett, walked in.

"A thousand apologies," declared Salazar theatrically. "Entirely my fault, Jake."

"No harm done. We made a start on tracks six and seven," replied Jake, setting his guitar back on the stand.

"Let's go back to seven," suggested Dr Marrs from the control room. "Sal, I have Jake's tracks recorded. You're up first."

Silently, the older man nodded, took his seat and accepted his guitar from Garrett. With a glance towards Dr Marrs and a nod to Jake, he bowed his head and began to play. Back to back, with barely a pause for breath, Salazar played through the various parts for both tracks six and seven then handed his guitar back to Garrett.

"I believe we've made up for lost ground," he said calmly.

"I believe you're right," agreed Dr Marrs with a smile. "Ready for track five?"

"I want to add a harmonica intro to it," stated Salazar. "A little improvisation piece."

"I like that," nodded the producer approvingly. "But who's going to play it?"

"Don't look at me!" declared Garrett, holding his hands up.

"Mr Power?" quizzed Dr Marrs. "Can you play harmonica?"

Grinning, Jake nodded before confessing, "It's been a while though. Do we have one?"

"Through in the back store room. There should be two or three brand new ones in a box on the top shelf on the right."

"Give me five minutes," said Jake, getting to his feet.

The large, walk-in music store was a veritable Aladdin's cave. Gazing round at the vast array of instruments and percussion items, Jake selected a harmonica from the box, then, deciding the store room was as good a practice space as any, began to play. He had learned to play harmonica as a child, even before he'd picked up a guitar. One of his father's air force colleagues had taught him. Over the years, he had played occasionally, back in the days when Silver Lake were still playing local bars. It had been almost three years since he'd picked one up.

It took him a few minutes to get the feel for it again and to feel confident enough to play in front of the others.

"Nothing ventured, nothing gained," thought Jake silently as he returned to the live room.

"You ready, Jake?" called out Dr Marrs.

"Give me a minute to adjust this mic," replied Jake. "I want to stand up to record this. Doesn't feel right sitting down."

"Take your time," purred Salazar, as he sipped his tea.

Before he stepped forward to play, Jake reached for his own juice cup and took a long mouthful of the energy drink. He wrinkled his nose at the taste, finding it surprisingly sour.

"Ok. Ready," he declared.

Over the next hour, the three musicians worked on the opening for track five. As well as Jake's harmonica part, Dr Marrs suggested adding a slow foot stomp to the start. Simple but effective and, after half a dozen takes, the producer declared he was happy. The clock had ticked past two o'clock before they began to track the guitars for track five. Despite the fact he had been in the studio for over five hours, Jake felt surprisingly alert and calm. While Salazar and Garrett recorded their parts for track five, he sat back on the couch, slowly finishing his juice.

"Track four," announced Dr Marrs at four a.m. "One run through then we're calling it a night."

"Let's go for a live version," suggested Jake. "Single take however it works out."

"Brave," commented Garrett, unsure how his perfectionist partner would react to Jake's proposal.

"A maverick solution to our time dilemma," acknowledged Salazar with a rare smile. "I approve. However, how about the best of three?"

"Safer bet," called through Dr Marrs. "Gives me something to play with if I need to mix the versions up."

"Best of three it is," agreed Jake.

Again, the seven o'clock news was on the radio as Jake pulled into the driveway, but he still felt fresh and awake. His head told him he should head indoors and try to grab some sleep, but his heart said otherwise. A riff had been revealing itself as he had driven home and he decided to forego sleep for a few more hours and head down to the basement to focus on his Silver Lake commitments.

By ten o'clock he had the new song more or less completed including lyrics. It had been a long time since he had felt this way. Despite his long night in the studio, Jake was still wide awake and keen to work on.

It was almost one before he shut down his laptop, switched off his amp and headed upstairs in search of some lunch. A loud rumbling from his stomach reminded him that he hadn't eaten since dinner the night before. When he stepped out into the house, he was greeted by silence. Wandering into the kitchen, he found a note from Lori saying, "Gone for lunch with Maddy and the meatballs. L x"

Having had two bacon sandwiches and some yogurt, Jake felt ready to sleep. Time was running away from him and he figured he'd be lucky to get five hours sleep before it was time to eat dinner and return to JJL. They had agreed to meet at eight that evening. Sun was streaming into the bedroom as Jake climbed into bed. The room was too light to encourage sleep and, having tossed and turned for half an hour, he finally pulled the pillow over his head to block out the sun. His sleep was troubled and nightmare filled. Visions of giant dragon-like creatures chasing him down dark, torch lit tunnels tormented him and, when the alarm rang at six o'clock, Jake wakened feeling more exhausted than he had when he went to bed. A thundery headache was hanging over him, threatening to develop into a migraine. A hot shower went some way to reviving him. He had found a bottle of Advil in the bathroom cabinet and swallowed two before his shower. Pulling on a clean pair of jeans, Jake could feel the painkillers beginning to dissipate the headache.

"Evening, sleepyhead," greeted Lori as he padded into the kitchen.

"Evening, li'l lady," he replied with a yawn.

"You still tired? How much sleep did you grab?" asked Lori her voice tinged with concern.

"About four or five hours. Was too fired up to sleep when I got home. Made good progress on my Silver Lake ideas," replied Jake, pouring himself a glass of OJ. "I'm tired now though. Guess it's going to be a long night. We've three tracks to do tonight."

"How many have you recorded?"

"Seven so far. Plan is to do the final three tonight. Vocals tomorrow night, then see what we need to fix come Friday," Jake explained. "It feels like Sal is on a finite amount of time here. No wiggle room."

"Has he been ok to work with so far?" asked Lori as she placed a bowl of spaghetti bolognese in front of him.

"So far so good. He was late last night, but he's been fine."

"Still drinking his tea?"

Jake nodded, "And taking regular smoke breaks for his preferred herbal cigarettes."

"Just be careful, rock star," whispered Lori as she set her own meal down.

"I'm just playing my guitar as instructed," replied Jake with a sleepy smile. "And a bit of harmonica."

JJL was lit up like a Christmas tree when Jake arrived. Every light in the building was on. The incense was still burning, leaving a sickly, sweet taste to the air, but the entire studio was bathed in bright light. In the live room, Salazar was already seated and playing. Gone was the vampire look, replaced with a white shirt, frayed, pale denim flares and bare feet. Jake noted that there were Native American symbols tattooed along the outer edges of the musician's long, slender feet.

"No Garrett tonight?" asked Jake as he took a seat opposite Salazar.

"He'll be in later. I asked him to stay away until midnight. Gives us time to work without him distracting me."

Feeling both brave and curious, Jake risked a personal question, "How long have you two been together?"

"Many lifetimes," replied Salazar with a smile. "In your terms though, Rett has been by my side for nigh on fifteen years." He paused, as if lost in a memory, then said, "Let's play, Mr Power."

With Dr Marrs silently watching from the control room, Salazar and Jake worked their way through the next track on the board. As they traded parts for track three, the producer halted them and asked if they would add an extra dimension to it. Both musicians listened as he suggested adding an acoustic track in among the electric blues. Lifting Jake's acoustic, Salazar began to play a contrasting blues piece. No one but Jake had ever played that acoustic and it was hard for him to bite his tongue and watch the elder statesman of blues play it.

"Perfect," declared Dr Marrs when Salazar was finished.

With a nod towards the control room window, Salazar handed the guitar back to Jake, "Your turn."

"Me?"

"Yes, Mr Power. You play it," instructed the older musician, a twinkle in his dark eyes. "If you can't remember it, improvise. Breathe the music. Feel it reverberate through your soul."

"I'll give it my best shot," promised Jake, running his hand over the body of his guitar.

Bowing his head so that his long hair fell over his face, shielding him from Salazar's intense stare, Jake tried to recall what he had heard played moments before. Try as he might, he couldn't replicate it. After a frustrating minute or two, Jake lifted his head and called through to the control room, "Jim, scrap that. Let me try something else."

Without looking at Sal, Jake began to play a very soft, slow blues influenced tune. He picked out the melody from the original tracking, but slowed it down subtly making it his own. To his ear, it fitted perfectly with the electric tracks they had just recorded, but he wasn't confident that the others would approve.

"Bravo!" complimented Salazar when he was finished. "You're a fast learner. I'm impressed."

"Awesome job, Jake," concurred Jim Marrs.

Blushing, Jake mumbled his thanks then excused himself and headed to the men's room.

When he returned to the studio with two cans of energy drink, he was surprised to find Garrett had arrived.

"Evening," said Jake warmly as he poured his juice into his plastic cup. The dregs of his earlier can covered the bottom of the cup. A voice in his head whispered that he'd drained the cup dry, but he dismissed it, surmising that he must have missed the last couple of mouthfuls.

"Evening," echoed Garrett. "We were debating whether to do track one and then finish on track two. What's your thought?"

"I'm easy either way," commented Jake calmly. "Track two would be a bit of fun to end on."

"Told you," muttered Salazar, flashing a dark look at his partner.

"Fine. Do what you feel works best for you," stated Garrett sourly. "Do you need me to play on track one?"

Before Jake could comment, Salazar snapped, "No. Not tonight."

"Then I'll go and keep Jim company back there."

Instantly, the relaxed Salazar was gone and the dark, haunted version of the blues musician reappeared. He drank deeply from his omnipresent solo cup, then picked up his battle scarred Stratocaster. For a few moments, he sat poised to play, then lifted his head, staring straight into Jake's soul. "You start this one."

"You sure?" questioned Jake. "We need an improv intro to it."

"I'm well aware of that. Play."

Pausing to take a deep breath, Jake settled himself on the stool, his brain racing as he tried to decide how to phrase the intro. Track one was one of his favourites to play and he'd tried several different intros in the safe confines of the basement at home. Now that he was in the studio, facing playing the intro for real, his mind went blank.

"In your own time, Jake," said Dr Marrs calmly. "Clock's ticking."

Trying not to focus on Salazar's presence, Jake began to play. Once he started, the notes seemed to fly off his fingers and dance on the strings. They hadn't discussed whether he was to stop playing after the introduction or just keep going. As he reached the point when the main body of the song was due to begin, he glanced up at Salazar. The older musician was already poised to come in but he nodded to Jake, indicating that he should keep playing.

Throughout the first attempt at the song, Salazar allowed Jake to shine, keeping his playing soft and subtle. As Jake let the final note ring out, the older musician tagged on a short improvisation to the end. With a grin, Jake recognised it as a section from his intro piece only played at double the speed.

"Perfect, gentlemen!" praised Dr Marrs from behind the glass. "Absolutely spot on."

"Thanks," called back Jake as he drank deeply from his juice cup.

"Take a break," instructed the producer. "Fifteen minutes, then we do track two. Let's be out of here for four. I need my beauty sleep."

While Salazar slipped outside to smoke, Jake remained in the studio, finishing off his juice. The smoky incense filled air was making him thirsty. Draining the cup, he went out to the lounge to fetch some water. When he re-entered the live room, Garrett came in at his heel.

"You ready for the last fandango?" asked Garrett as he flicked open the catches on a particularly battered looking guitar case.

"As I'll ever be," replied Jake, lifting his vintage resonator from its velvet lined surround. "It's been an incredible few nights. Will you guys be in tomorrow for the vocal tracking?"

"Sal wants to be here for a while," said Garrett. "But we'll see how tomorrow goes. It's getting harder and harder for him to come in here each night."

"He seemed quite chilled out when I arrived," observed Jake.

"It's taking more and more medication to keep him chilled," Garrett revealed. "This is harder for him than you will ever understand."

Their conversation was cut short by Salazar's arrival. His vintage resonator sat on a stand waiting for him. Once again, his mood seemed to have lightened.

"The final track," he said, almost sounding relieved. "Time to have some fun."

There had been a lengthy debate between Dr Marrs and Salazar over how they planned to approach this one. Seeking perfection, Dr Marrs had asked that they each record their track separately. Snorting in disgust, Salazar declared that they would play and record it live or not at all. There was a short, heated debate and a compromise was swiftly reached as they agreed to play three live versions, one with each of them leading.

When Jake had been presented with the folder of music, track two had quickly become his favourite of the ten songs to play. Sitting in between Salazar and Garrett, noting the relaxed smiles on their faces, he realised it was theirs too. Graciously, Salazar allowed his partner to lead first in an apparent attempt to make amends for being so dismissive earlier. Not for the first time, Jake felt somewhat star struck. Never in his wildest dreams could he have imagined the scenario he was now part of. Hearing the three resonators play in harmony was a beautiful sound. Much as he loved the rock music he usually played, Jake loved the Delta blues played on a resonator guitar.

"Mr Power," purred Salazar when they had finished the first version. "Your moment has come."

As Jake prepared to play, Salazar spoke. "Jim, can we change the plan? I want Jake to add a solo one minute in then I'll mirror it at the end. Rett, can you sit this one out?"

"How about we do this as an extra then go back to the original plan?" requested Dr Marrs, his exasperation at the constant changes evident in his tone.

"Fine. Fine," muttered Salazar, sounding equally frustrated.

"OK, but which are we playing first?" asked Jake.

"Go with the plan, then we'll record it my way," stated Sal bluntly. "If I'm not happy with any of it, we'll record a fifth version. Dr Marrs, that's my final offer. Accept it or I leave now."

"Fine by me, Sal," sighed the producer. "Do you need five minutes before we start?"

"No," snapped the vampiric musician coldly.

Calmly, Garrett handed him his cup and whispered something to him. With a nod, Salazar drained the cup, then announced that he was ready.

Their second and third runs through the track as a trio went smoothly, with Salazar opting to play a contrasting, slightly off-key version in the background. It added an extra element of fun, complimenting the performances of both Garrett and Jake. In the control room, Dr Marrs was looking pleased with what he was hearing.

Barely pausing for the final notes to fade out, Salazar said, "Time to shine, Mr Power."

For the next five and a half minutes, Jake played his heart out, pouring everything he had into the short sixty second solo, then allowing himself to get lost in the remainder of the song. The older musician's ability to replicate the improvised solo a couple of minutes later was incredible. He was note perfect from what Jake could recall. Together, they brought track two to an end.

As the final note rang out, Salazar handed his guitar to Garrett and left without a word.

Half an hour later, as Jake was preparing to leave, Dr Marrs came through to the live room. Garrett had left soon after Salazar, apologising for rushing off. Their guitars still sat on the stands where they'd left them. Several empty plastic cups lay scattered around the floor. Casually, the producer bent down and gathered them up. He sniffed at the dregs left in one, wrinkling his nose.

"Caffeine drinks at this hour?" he questioned, raising an eyebrow towards Jake.

"Less harmful than my esteemed friend's tea," countered Jake with a smile. Once again, he was buzzing despite the fact it was four fifteen in the morning. He could feel the after effects of the energy drinks coursing through his veins.

"Are you sure? You look almost as high as he did!" joked Dr Marrs, noting that Jake's pupils seemed very dilated.

"I'm just over tired, Jim, and all that incense is giving me a headache," replied Jake, running his hand through his hair. He noticed his hand was trembling slightly. "Can we lose the incense for tomorrow night? There's no way I can sing in this fog."

"Sure. I'm not even sure if Sal's coming in or not. I'll leave the AC running all night to clear the air for you. It'll be fine by tomorrow afternoon. What time do you want to make a start tomorrow?"

"Well, we've four vocal tracks to do," began Jake. "How about I aim to get here around six. Give me an hour to warm up. We should be good to start about seven."

"Fine by me, I'll be in here from lunchtime."

"See you tomorrow night, Jim."

"Drive safely."

The first light of dawn was streaking across the sky as Jake pulled into the driveway. A sudden feeling of nausea swept through him and he could feel his head starting to pound with an impending migraine. He grabbed his guitars and book bag and headed inside, feeling somewhat unsteady on his feet.

Lori was sound asleep when he slid into bed beside her. Seeing her curled up on her side, with her hand protectively resting on her baby bump, made Jake smile, despite the thunderstorm building in his head. He could see her stomach twitch slightly, but resisted the temptation to feel the baby's kicks, not wanting to risk wakening her. With a yawn, he lay down and closed his eyes. The world was spinning and he felt as though the bed was about to take off through the roof of the house. Deliberately, he focussed on his breathing in an effort to relax enough to allow sleep to come.

Several hours later, he was wakened by the sound of voices coming from the kitchen. He recognised Paul's voice, then, a few moments later, he heard Grey laughing. Rubbing the last remnants of sleep from his eyes, Jake sat up. As soon as he moved, his stomach heaved and he only just made it into the bathroom before he was violently sick. Sleep hadn't shifted his migraine and, having been sick a second time, he staggered to his feet. One look in the vanity mirror over the basin was enough to tell him he looked as rough as he felt. Jake searched through the bathroom cabinet until he found his migraine medication. He swallowed two of the pills, praying that they would shift the headache before he was due out at JJL.

Wearing only his T-shirt and boxers, Jake made his way down the hall to the kitchen.

"Afternoon, Mr Power," greeted Grey. "Jesus, you look like shit."

"Thanks," muttered Jake as he sat down at the table. "Migraine."

With a look of concern, Lori asked if he'd taken something for it. He nodded, then asked for a drink of juice.

"How's it been out at JJL with Salazar Mendes?" asked Paul, sitting down opposite his band mate. "Is he as hard to work with as you thought?"

"He's been great," replied Jake, forcing a smile. "He's an incredible musician. I've learned a lot from watching him. He's eccentric and unpredictable. It's been some week so far."

"What's left to do?" Grey asked as Lori handed him a mug of coffee.

"Vocals tonight, then a final wash up session tomorrow."

"Are you going to be alright to sing?" asked Lori softly.

"I'll need to be. It's only four tracks. Nothing that's too demanding. Well, one's a bit tricky, but I'll be ok," he paused to take a mouthful of juice. "What brings you guys out here anyway?"

"Fish," stated Paul with a grin. "We were out in my neighbour's boat first thing. Caught more than we can eat. Bass and flounder. Thought you guys could use some."

"And they even cleaned them first," added Lori with a relieved smile at the two musicians.

"Thanks," said Jake, feeling his stomach turn at the thought of food. "What time is it by the way?"

"Almost two thirty," answered Grey. "Shit! I better make a move. I need to collect Becky from school."

"When are we rehearsing?" quizzed Paul.

"Monday," replied Jake. "At least that's the current plan. Check with Rich though."

"Will do," said Paul, getting to his feet. "Hope that migraine shifts before tonight."

"So do I," sighed Jake, running his hand nervously through his hair. "I don't want to fuck this up at this stage."

"Take it easy," said Grey. "See you Monday."

When the time came for Jake to leave for the studio, his migraine had begun to lift. His head was still pounding, with the pain focussed above his left eye. Fortunately, the nausea had passed and he had even managed to eat some of the sea bass that Lori had broiled for dinner. Lifting his book bag, Jake said, "I'll leave my guitars in the lounge room. I promise I'll take them downstairs after tomorrow night. I shouldn't need them tonight though."

"When do you expect to be home?" asked Lori as the baby kicked restlessly, causing her to wriggle in her seat.

"No idea. Hopefully before two, but it depends how it goes. I'm not sure if Sal and Garrett are coming in to watch or not. Might be easier if they don't."

"And did you put your migraine meds in your bag?"

"Yes, li'l lady, I did. Stop fussing. I'll be fine," promised Jake, kissing her gently on the forehead. "Don't you stay up too late working."

"I won't. I'm almost done. Another couple of hours then I'll be finished."

"Right, I'm out of here," he declared as he picked up his truck keys. "Love you."

"Love you too, rock star."

When Jake stepped into JJL, he was relieved to note that the clouds of incense were gone. The air smelled clean and fresh, too clean and fresh in some respects. It reminded him of the clean bed linen aroma from his childhood. As he wandered through to the lounge to pick up some iced tea to take into the studio, he discovered the source of the smell. Two jar candles sat burning on the table, their flames flickering gently as the AC caught them.

"Evening, Jake," called out Dr Marrs warmly as he entered the live room.

"Evening, Jim," replied Jake, sounding weary.

"You OK?"

"Migraine," commented Jake. "I'll be fine. Though I'm blaming that fucking incense for it."

"It's been a bit pungent in here all week," admitted the producer. "However, it was Sal's orders and I didn't want to stress him out before we'd gotten started."

"Is he coming in tonight?" asked Jake, opening the iced tea and pouring it into a plastic cup.

Dr Marrs nodded, "He'll be here in an hour. Garrett's dropping him off."

"Guess I'd better get warmed up. Want me to go out back and spare you the pleasure of it?"

"You're fine where you are. I'm going over to the house for some dinner. I'll be back before seven."

Methodically, Jake began to work through his standard vocal warm up exercises. It had been a while since he'd recorded vocals and he wasn't prepared to take any risks. Although there were only four tracks, one of them was going to test his range to its highest limits and he didn't want to risk any unnecessary strains.

Just as he was beginning his final exercise, the door opened and Salazar slipped into the room. He nodded to Jake and wandered over to sit on the leather couch in the corner of the room. As he worked his way up and down the octaves of his range, Jake was acutely aware of the Sal's dark eyes boring into him.

"Impressive," commented the older man, his own voice sounding deeper and huskier than usual.

"Thanks," said Jake, suddenly feeling self-conscious in front of his idol. "Not sure how this is going to go tonight. I've felt like shit all day."

"Are you feeling well enough to sing?" enquired Salazar softly. "If you're sick, we can delay until tomorrow."

"I'll be fine. Migraine," explained Jake, before adding, "I think it was the incense. Strong, musky perfume can trigger it."

"Maybe," mused the vampiric maestro. "Smells like a laundry basket in here now."

"Reminds me of being a kid," began Jake. "That clean bed smell after my mom had picked up my room."

Their conversation was cut short as Dr Marrs entered the control room. Taking his seat behind the desk, he called through, "Jake, tracks ten, four, eight and three, In that order. No frills. Straight from the heart. Raw live performance."

"Can we switch four and ten round?"

"If you prefer."

Jake nodded as he headed into the booth to make a start. He placed the four lyrics sheets on the music stand in front of him then picked up the headphones. Pausing to read over the words for track four, Jake took several long, deep breaths in an effort to calm his nerves.

"Ready?" quizzed Dr Marrs' voice through the headphones.

"As I'll ever be."

Adjusting his position in the enclosed booth so that his back was to both Salazar and the control room, Jake began to sing. Recording blues vocals was a whole new experience for him and he quickly discovered it was one he enjoyed. Somehow it felt more soulful than some of the hard, heavy rock songs he was accustomed to. After he had delivered three renditions of the song, Salazar tapped the glass behind him.

"Jesus!" yelped Jake, his heart skipping a beat. "Don't creep up on me like that, please."

"Humble apologies," purred Salazar, bowing his head. "May I voice an observation?"

"Sure, now that you've scared the crap out of me."

"Come out into the room. Your voice is incredible but that booth is too clinical. Blues needs to breathe."

"Happy to give it a try," agreed Jake, lifting the lyrics sheets. "Jim, is that ok with you?"

"Fine," said the producer. "Give me a few minutes till I rig up a microphone in the room. Take five, Jake."

While the producer made the necessary adjustments to the microphones, Jake sat down on the couch, sipping on his iced tea. Nerves were beginning to flutter in the pit of his stomach as he allowed his mind to linger on the enormity of what he was about to undertake. He preferred to record vocals alone in the studio and having such an exalted audience in the room had unsettled him a little. As if sensing the younger man's nerves, Salazar said softly, "Forget I'm here, Jake. Relax and make this room your own. Own the words."

"I'll give it my best shot."

Free from the confines of the small booth, Jake poured his heart and soul into his next attempt at track four. The final piece of the puzzle clicked into place. Salazar had been right. It did feel more natural to sing these tracks in a more open space.

Half an hour later, Dr Marrs declared he was happy with what he had saved. Recording track ten ran smoothly. The dark tale of tortured slaves and clanking chains came straight from the heart and the extent of the emotion that Jake managed to convey in his performance surpassed everyone's expectations.

It was after midnight before they were finished the second song.

"Jim, can we do three next?" asked Jake as he took a long drink from his cup. "It's the biggest ask and I don't want to be too tired when we track it."

"Fine by me."

Track three was fast paced and the only one out of the four that took Jake to the limits of his upper register. His first two attempts ran smoothly enough, but he wasn't happy with the clarity of his performance. Halfway through his third through, Jake stopped.

"I need a minute here," he said, running his hands through his hair. "My head's pounding."

"You ok to keep going?" asked Dr Marrs, concerned about his health. "We can pick these up tomorrow."

"I'm going to grab some air for a minute," said Jake. "Can you dim the lights a bit? It's quite bright through here."

"Sure."

Five minutes later, Jake came back into JJL, feeling slightly better. The chill night air and a few long, slow, deep breaths had helped. Rummaging in his pocket, he searched for the migraine medication he'd brought with him. He popped the two pills from the strip and swallowed them. One of the pills caught in the back of his throat as he walked across the studio. He began to cough and choke. Instantly, Salazar was at his side with a drink. Gratefully, Jake swallowed some of the liquid, caught his breath, then took another long drink from the cup.

"Thanks," he said before clearing his throat again.

"You good to go, Jake?" asked Jim.

He nodded and resumed his position at the microphone. Licking his lips, Jake realised there was a bitter but familiar taste to the juice he'd just drunk.

It hadn't been his sweetened iced tea.

Salazar had given him his own cup of tea.

A feeling of fear and dread swept through Jake as he realised he had no idea what he had just swallowed. He had no idea what effect it was about to have on him. Taking a deep breath to steady his nerves, he stepped forward to the microphone and poured everything he had into the vocal track. He hit every note. Each one rang out crystal clear. Jake was word perfect throughout the seven-minute track. By the time, he was finished his heart was pounding and sweat was pouring from him.

Glancing round the studio, Jake could see things moving in the shadows, scuttling into the corners. Through the headphones, he could hear demonic voices hissing into his ears that they were coming to destroy his soul. His grasp on reality was slipping.

Angrily, Jake hauled off the headphones and threw them across the room.

"What the fuck is in that tea, Salazar?" he demanded fiercely. "What the fuck have you given me?"

"Just something herbal to relax you."

"I don't need that shit!" roared Jake, his face a mask of fury. "Jim, I need to go."

"Jake!" called out the producer as he watched him storm out of the studio. "Jake!"

Once outside, the cold, night air wrapped itself around Jake like a cloak. A battle was raging in his mind as the drugged tea coursed through his veins. He could feel it oozing through him; feel the drugs starting to seize control; feel old wounds opening up and welcoming them in like long lost friends. Climbing into the truck, he turned the key in the ignition and headed off down the driveway at high speed, swerving to avoid what looked like the Silver Lake imp as he reached the highway. Demonic creatures crawled over the hood of the truck, trying to claw their way in. He could see their long, skeletal, clawed fingers trying to prise open the windows of the cab. From behind him, he could hear one hissing, "There's no escape, Jacob. Welcome us back. We've missed your sweet soul."

Glancing in the mirror, he could see red glowing eyes staring at him.

He pressed his foot to the floor, trying to use speed to throw off the hallucinations.

Heading along E Lake Dr in the dark, small imps dropped onto the truck's roof from the overhanging branches. As he drove, Jake could hear their evil laughter, hear their taunts about devouring his soul.

After what felt like an eternity in hell, the house came into sight. Jake threw the truck into the driveway too fast and slammed straight into the tree. Steam immediately billowed up from the front of the truck. This brought visions of wraiths coming to join the other devils, who were tormenting him.

Heart pounding and with his entire body rigid with fear, Jake jumped down from the cab and fled indoors.

A moment of clarity shone through his trip and he knew he had to stay away from Lori; he had to keep her safe from these evil creatures.

Slamming the door behind him, Jake headed down into the basement. He didn't pause to put the light on. In the dark, he lost his footing on the steep stairs and went tumbling down the last few steps, his shoulder crashing through the wooden bannister spindles. Jake landed in a sprawled heap on the cold, concrete floor and found himself face to face with a large hooded creature with emerald green eyes. He scuttled to the side, ignoring the pain in his shoulder and grabbed the first thing he found. It was a guitar. Holding it by the neck, Jake staggered to his feet and took a swing at the hooded monster. The guitar flew straight through the creature with little resistance and smashed off the wall, instantly severing the neck of the instrument. Instinctively, feeling the need to protect himself, Jake reached for another.

A loud bang wakened Lori from slumber. Through her sleep haze, it had sounded as though it came from out the front. For a moment, she listened. She heard the front door open then slam shut, closely followed by Jake's footsteps rushing through the house. The distinctive screech of the basement door informed her he was in a hurry to get downstairs.

Hearing all hell break loose in the basement a few seconds later jolted her out of bed. From the bedroom, Lori could hear her husband yelling and hear the crash of things being thrown and smashed.

Without stopping to put on her robe or slippers, Lori limped out of the room and down the hall as fast as she could. Her sudden movement had disturbed the baby, who began to kick furiously at her ribs.

"Shh," she said softly, rubbing her firm round bump. "Let's see what's going on. Daddy sounds mad at something or someone."

Lori flicked on the lights to the basement, opened the door and started to make her way carefully down the steep stairs. At first, she couldn't see Jake. In front of her was a scene of total destruction. The cover had been torn off Paul's practice kit and the emerald green drums were scattered across the floor, two mangled guitars in their midst. Two more smashed guitars were buried in the band's practice speaker cabinets. In the corner, the desk had been overturned as had the couch.

As she reached the bottom step, a small movement to her right caught her eye. Jake was crouched down beside the staircase. His long hair was dishevelled, there was blood on his hands and his eyes were staring wildly at her. Instantly, she knew something was very wrong.

Before she could decide whether to turn and go back upstairs to phone for help or whether to approach him, Jake let out a blood curdling scream and launched himself towards her.

"Jake!" screamed Lori as his hands tangled in her hair and dragged her off balance. "Stop it! It's me! It's Lori!"

"Nice try, devil witch," he growled as he threw her roughly to the ground.

Up close now, Lori could see his eyes were bloodshot and his pupils almost fully dilated. He was dripping with sweat and trembling uncontrollably. He gazed down into her fear filled eyes. Panic began to build in her as Lori realised there was no recognition in those blood red, hazel eyes. Her husband's stare was cold and vacant. With a snort, he spat in her face and raised his hand, ready to strike her.

Putting a protective arm across her stomach, Lori tried to crawl out of his reach. He was too quick for her and was on top of her before she could move more than a few inches. He grabbed her by the shoulders and shook her like a rag doll, screaming, "Leave me the fuck alone, witch!"

"Jake," whimpered Lori through a veil of tears. "Jake, please stop. The baby. You'll hurt us both."

He tossed her back onto the floor. Her head thudded off the rug covered concrete, sending stars flashing before her eyes.

"Demon spawn!" he roared, reaching for the broken neck of a nearby guitar.

Fearing he was going to try to harm their unborn baby, Lori managed to roll over and curl herself into a ball to protect her stomach. The neck of the guitar came crashing down on her arm. She screamed in agony as she curled herself up tighter. Repeatedly, Jake lashed out with the piece of wood, hitting her ribs, back and shoulder with the headstock. Repeatedly, Lori screamed as the blows rained down on her. Despite her fear and the pain, she remained in an almost foetal position on the rug, knowing she had to protect her unborn child at all costs.

 Eventually, Jake aimed a blow at the side of her head.

The last thing Lori saw, before everything went black, was his tortured expression.

Breathing heavily, Jake got to his feet and stared down at the crumpled form of the demon witch, who lay at his feet. Angrily, he kicked her. A partially coherent thought flitted through his tortured mind as he reasoned that he had to get as far away from the house as he could to try to keep Lori and the baby safe. Glancing round to check for more evil creatures, he bounded back up the stairs and through the sunroom. He hauled open the patio doors, wrenching the door from its runners and fled across the deck down towards the beach. Once down on the sand, he began to run, heading away from the house towards town.

With a low groan of pain, Lori struggled to open her eyes. Her ear was ringing and her head was pounding. For a few moments, she lay still, not daring to move, unsure if Jake was still there; unsure if she was badly hurt or not. Apart from the buzzing noise in her head, the basement was silent.

"The baby," she thought anxiously.

Tentatively, she rubbed her swollen stomach, the slightest movement of her arm sending bolts of pain through her. When the baby responded and kicked restlessly, Lori felt her eyes fill with tears of relief. Gingerly, she dragged herself into a sitting position, the movement making her head spin. As she slowly began to move her battered limbs, she determined that nothing appeared to be broken. Eventually, Lori wriggled herself onto all fours and hauled herself onto her feet, using the upturned desk for support. She swayed unsteadily as she gazed round the basement. Only the two locked cabinets where Jake kept his more valuable guitars remained intact. Everything else lay broken and destroyed.

Still unable to make sense of what had happened, Lori slowly made her way over to the stairs and began to crawl up. Every movement sent splinters of pain through her. Once at the top of the staircase, she crawled over to the dining room table and dragged herself back to her feet. She stood leaning on the table for support for a few moments before stumbling her way through to the kitchen.

With shaking hands, Lori filled a glass with water and drank it slowly. Gradually, she was beginning to feel a little more in control of herself. She refilled the glass, then staggered over to sit at the kitchen table. A glance at the clock informed her it was just before six. She had lost at least four hours.

Around her, the house was silent and calm.

In her heart, Lori knew Jake wasn't there, but where was he? With a four-hour head start, he could be anywhere.

As she sipped the icy cold water, Lori deliberated on what she should do. A voice of reason in her head told her to call the police; a loving voice in her heart said she had to find Jake. With her throbbing head resting in her hands, Lori tried to fathom out where he would have run to.

A wave washing over his face roused Jake. He was face down in the wet sand. The ocean waves had soaked him through to his skin. The icy, cold, salt water nipped at his cut hands. As a second wave washed over his head, he dragged himself to his feet and gazed round. The boardwalk was up ahead and he realised he was only a block or so away from his old apartment. Glancing round in the dawn light, Jake reasoned that there were no demons following him. He would head for the apartment and call Lori from there. As far as he could remember, Scott was out of town so the place should be empty. Staggering unsteadily, with his heart still pounding, Jake made his way across the soft sand towards the boardwalk. As he lurched past one of the shop windows, he caught sight of his appearance. His hair was a tangled mess, his clothes were soaked in both blood and salt water. He'd lost a shoe somewhere. Keeping a look out for more evil creatures that might still be following him, he shambled his way up the deserted street to the familiar apartment block.

The spare key was still in its old hiding place, allowing him to let himself into the small apartment. Once indoors, everything began to spin and Jake felt nauseous again. He staggered through to the small galley kitchen to fetch a drink of water.

As he stood over the sink, sipping the cold water, his mind began to clear. He gazed down at his hands, marvelling at how they had come to be so badly cut and bruised. The remains of the drugged tea were still coursing through his veins. He could feel his old, addictive demons calling to him. They were almost purring as they whispered his name, luring him back into their drug addled depths. Their velvet voices promising him that "one hit will put everything right."

A memory from the past flashed into his mind. Before he had got himself clean, he and Paul had made a pact and stashed a small supply of drugs behind an air vent in the bathroom. One hit would be enough to calm him down; enough to let him sleep it all off.

Leaving the half-finished glass of water in the sink, Jake went through to the tiny bathroom. He knelt down beside the toilet bowl and prised the small, rectangular vent from the wall. Reaching inside, his fingers found the small, dusty, cloth bag.

He stuffed the vent back into place and returned to the living room. Blindly, he followed his old routine, one thought long since forgotten as he used the cigarette lighter to melt the resin in its foil package. Slowly, but expertly, Jake filled the hypodermic, then injected the contents into the first vein he could find in his left arm.

A familiar feeling of euphoria swept through him as he lay back on the couch and sighed. He had survived the demon attack. He was safe. Lori and the baby were safe.

A brief, lucid thought flooded his mind.

Lori!

That hadn't been a demon witch that he'd savagely attacked in the basement.

It had been Lori.

The effects of the drug took hold. He lay on the couch with tears flowing down his cheeks as his mind sailed off into the abyss of the drug's powers.

His last conscious thought before his world went black was, "What have I done?"

Back at the beach house, Lori slowly showered, allowing the hot water to cascade over her, washing away the worst of the pain from her bruises with its warmth. Feeling the baby moving normally helped to reassure her that it hadn't suffered any harm as a result of the events in the basement. Once she felt clean and a little calmer, Lori dried herself off, then dressed in yoga pants, a T-shirt and long sleeved hoodie. She slipped her feet into her favourite Converse then dragged the brush through her wet hair. Expertly, she wove it into one long, thick braid.

She sat staring at her reflection in the dressing table mirror as she tried to work out where Jake would've gone. The damaged truck was still in the driveway so he had left on foot. Her bruised reflection stared back at her. The left side of her face was purple and swollen. Her eye was black at the corner and there was a purple egg shaped lump on her forehead above it.

Rubbing her baby bump, Lori whispered softly, "Which way did your daddy go?"

Lifting her bag, Lori headed back down to the kitchen, took her car key from the hook then limped through to the sunroom. Noting the patio door hanging at an awkward angle, she sighed.

"Well, baby, at least we know how he left the house," she said softly as she stepped out onto the deck.

So early in the morning, the air was still bitterly cold. Lori stood unsteadily at the edge of the deck gazing across the beach. She looked straight out to the ocean, then dismissed that direction. In his frenzy, Jake had seemed scared of something. He would've fled the house seeking sanctuary from whatever demons were chasing him, she deduced. Gazing left towards town, she wondered if he'd gone to his old apartment. It seemed like as good a place as any to start.

Leaving the door hanging off its rail, Lori went round to the side of the house to her car. Seeing Jake's beloved truck smashed into the tree tugged at her heart. She also marvelled that the old tree had withstood the impact without crashing down through the roof of the house.

The roads into town were almost deserted as she headed instinctively towards Jake's apartment building on Laurel Street. While she had been driving, Lori had remembered that Scott was out of town and she wondered if Jake would've been able to get into the apartment. Parking her car at the side of the building, Lori slid out from behind the wheel. Every inch of her was hurting. Her entire left side was black and blue and her right hip was throbbing from where she'd landed hard on the concrete floor. Climbing the stairs to the apartment was agony, each step more painful than the one before it. When she finally reached the top, Lori held onto the bannister and paused to catch her breath.

Feeling light headed, she staggered over to the door of the apartment and tried the handle. The door opened.

"Jake!" she called out quietly. Her voice seemed to echo back at her. "Jake, are you here?"

A sour smell was wafting through the air. Slightly apprehensively, Lori opened the living room door. The first thing she saw was the foil and the discarded syringe lying on the coffee table. Her heart sank.

Jake was lying on the floor, face down in front of the couch beside a pool of fresh vomit.

"Jake!" cried Lori as she stumbled her way over to him. She was in too much pain to sit on the floor. Instead, she lowered herself down to sit on the edge of the coffee table. Stretching down to touch his shoulder, she called his name again.

He groaned but didn't move.

Reaching into her pocket for her phone, Lori knew she had no choice. She dialled 911, tearfully giving out the address and requesting urgent medical help. With tears blinding her, she called Maddy.

"Lori!" came her friend's brusque greeting. "You're up early."

"Oh, Maddy," sobbed Lori, her emotions finally crumbling. "It's Jake. He's taken something. I've called 911. He's unconscious."

"Calm down, honey," instructed the band's manager firmly. "Where are you?"

"At Jake's apartment. It's a long story."

"I'll send Paul straight over. Are you ok?"

"Not really," confessed Lori through her tears. "Jake attacked me."

Hearing herself say the words out loud suddenly made the events of the past few hours coldly real. While her friend was still talking, looking for answers, Lori ended the call and sat sobbing into her hands.

The paramedics and Paul arrived at the apartment at more or less the same time. While one of the paramedics went straight to Jake's side, the other began to question Lori about what had happened. Before she could begin to explain, Paul was beside her, suggesting the paramedic help Jake first and ask questions later.

"Sir, we're just trying to establish what Mr Power has taken," stated the uniformed medic firmly.

"From the foil on the table, I'd guess the last thing was heroin," commented Paul bluntly. "Old heroin at that. He's been clean for over six years, but that looks like the gear since before."

"What makes you say that, sir?"

"Because I remember us both agreeing to stash one emergency fix here in that cloth bag. I recognise it."

"Thank you," said the paramedic. "Mrs Power, I don't know who or what caused your injuries, but you need to get checked over too."

Tearfully, Lori nodded.

"I'll take her to the medical centre myself," said Paul firmly. "We'll follow you in."

On the floor, Jake began to struggle with the paramedic, growling incoherently. After a minute or two, they had him restrained and had administered some Ativan in an attempt to quieten him. With a protective arm around Lori's shoulder, Paul held her as they both watched the paramedics lift Jake onto the stretcher and fasten the straps over him.

"Mrs Power, we'll take your husband to the ER at Beebe."

"We'll be right behind you," promised Paul.

After the paramedics left, Paul held Lori in his arms while she sobbed. Soothingly, he rubbed her back and whispered quiet reassurances to her.

"What happened?" he asked softly as her sobs began to subside.

"I don't really know," she whispered, her voice hoarse from

crying. "Something must have happened out at JJL. He crashed the truck in the driveway. The bang wakened me. I heard him go down to the basement, then he began trashing the place. I went down to see what was going on. He started yelling at me about being a demon witch. He grabbed me by the hair and…"

Lori's emotions spiralled out of her control again as she sobbed inconsolably into Paul's shoulder.

"Is the baby ok?" whispered Paul, trying to remain calm for her sake. "Can you feel it moving?"

Soundlessly, Lori nodded.

"Let's go and get you checked out by a doctor. Come on," said the drummer, scooping her up into his arms. "I'll call Grey to come over and clean up this mess."

Lori sat silently in the passenger seat on the drive out to the medical centre, watching the world whiz by outside. She was vaguely aware of Paul calling Maddy then Grey then finally Dr Marrs. His conversations floated over her as she sat caressing her baby bump.

"Think you can walk in or do you want me to carry you again?" asked Paul with a warm smile as he stopped the car outside the emergency room entrance.

"I can manage," said Lori, forcing a weak smile.

While she took a seat in the waiting area, Paul went up to the desk to let them know she was there. The staff were expecting them, the paramedics having already advised them that they were on their way in. A male nurse brought a wheelchair over and helped Lori into it, then took her through to a cubicle to wait for the doctor. When Paul went to follow her, a nurse suggested he wait in the relatives' room until they had examined Lori. With memories of Silver Lake's car wreck haunting him anew, Paul did as he was told.

Through in the cubicle, a nurse helped Lori to undress and slip on a hospital gown, explaining that it would make it easier for the doctor to examine her. Without complaint, Lori complied. The nurse helped her up onto the gurney, then left, promising to return with the doctor shortly.

Lying back against the pillows, Lori listened to see if she could hear them working on Jake in a nearby curtain area. She couldn't. Fresh tears began to glide down her bruised cheeks.

A few minutes later, the curtain opened and a young female doctor entered, followed by the same nurse.

"Mrs Power," said the doctor warmly. "I'm Dr De Luca. How are you doing?"

"I'm sore. Scared," replied Lori quietly. "Where's Jake? Is he ok?"

"Your husband?"

Lori nodded.

"I believe he's still in resus. I'll get someone to check in a minute. Now, can you tell me what happened?"

Slowly and tearfully, Lori recounted her tale. Knowing it was pointless to hide anything, she told the doctor everything that had happened right up to the point where she dialled 911.

"You've had some night," sympathised the doctor. "Let's start with an ultrasound to check baby over. Lay those fears to rest first."

Almost the second that the probe connected with the layer of gel on Lori's swollen belly, the image of the baby appeared on the screen. Seeing the baby active, Lori sighed with relief. Methodically, the doctor checked the baby from every angle, nodding and smiling reassuringly at Lori.

"Active little one," she commented as the baby kicked hard again. "How many weeks are you?"

"Twenty four," replied Lori.

"Baby's slightly larger than average. I thought you were maybe further along," observed the doctor. "But perfectly healthy and looks none the worse of your ordeal."

"Thank you," sighed Lori, smiling weakly. "Jake's six three so I guess baby was never going to be small. Can you check on him now for me, please?"

"In a minute," promised the doctor firmly. "Let's take a look at these bruises first. Any areas particularly painful, Mrs Power?"

Lori shook her head, before confessing quietly, "They all hurt."

As she examined Lori's back and left shoulder, the doctor asked what she been struck with.

"The neck of a guitar. The head stock end," whispered Lori, fresh tears filling her eyes.

"Ah! Explains the small bruises that look like finger marks. Must be the machine heads," mused the doctor.

After giving Lori a thorough examination, Dr De Luca declared that nothing appeared to be broken.

"Can you check on Jake now, please?" pleaded Lori. "I need to know he's alright."

"Yes," said the doctor. "Wait here. I'll be right back."

When the doctor returned a few minutes later, she informed Lori that the police were waiting to question her. Eyes wide in horror, Lori declared firmly, "I didn't call the police. I've nothing to say to them at this moment, doctor."

"The paramedics called it in as a domestic violence incident."

"I don't give a damn," snapped Lori. "I am not talking to the police. This is a private matter. Now, do you have an update on my husband yet?"

"Mr Power is still in resus. They're working to stabilise his heart rate. It would be helpful if we knew what substances he has taken," explained the doctor. "Someone from his medical team will be in to talk with you shortly. What have I to tell the police officers?"

"That I have nothing to report and nothing to say," stated Lori bluntly. "Is Paul still here? Can he come in please?"

The doctor promised to check and, once again, left the cubicle, leaving Lori alone.

When the curtain opened next, it was Paul who stepped in.

"Hey, beautiful, how you doing?" he asked with his usual cheeky grin.

"Been better," admitted Lori. "Baby's fine. I'm just bruised. Nothing's broken. Apparently, the paramedics called the police though. I've refused to speak to them."

"I saw them arrive and called the boss," explained Paul, taking a seat beside the bed. "She'll sort this out. Don't worry."

"And what about Jake? They won't tell me much."

"I don't know much either. They've got him in resus as far as I know. I haven't seen him."

"Paul, I need to see him."

"Are you sure you want to?"

"Of course!" exclaimed Lori. "Why wouldn't I?"

"After what he did last night?"

"I know. I know. Paul, I need to understand why. I need to know what happened out at JJL. I need to know he's ok. I love him."

Fresh tears began to flood down her bruised face.

"Hey, no more tears, beautiful," soothed Paul as he stood up and put his arms around her. "I love him too. We'll figure this out. I promise."

"Paul, why now? What happened to him?"

"I'm not sure. I'm hoping Jim Marrs can shed some light on last night, but I can't get hold of him. I've left him a ton of messages."

The swish of the curtain interrupted their conversation as a tall, male doctor entered.

"Mrs Power?" he asked, glancing at the chart in his hands.

"Yes," replied Lori, roughly wiping her tears away. "Are you Jake's doctor? Is he ok?"

"I'm Dr Abel and, yes, I'm treating your husband. He's stabilised but he's not out of the woods yet. There's still drugs fighting with his body. We've sedated him to keep him calm. I'm hoping you can give me more of a clue as to what he's taken. I'm assuming this behaviour is out of character for him."

At that moment, Paul's cell phone rang and, excusing himself, he stepped out of the cubicle to take the call.

"It's completely out of character," began Lori, her voice trembling. "I've never seen him like that. He never touches drugs." She paused before whispering, "Jake had issues in the past. Six or seven years ago. He's been clean for a long time. He has a zero tolerance policy towards narcotics of any kind."

"Thank you. I had to ask," said Dr Abel, sitting on the edge of the gurney. "And how are you after your ordeal?"

"Sore. Confused. A bit scared," confessed Lori quietly, wiping away a fresh tear. "I just want to see him, Dr Abel. I love him."

"Let me clear it with Dr De Luca first," began Dr Abel with a reassuring smile. "Then I'll wheel you round to see him myself. He's heavily sedated so he probably won't know you're there."

"Thank you."

As the doctor rose to leave, Paul returned, stuffing his phone into his pocket.

"Dr, I think we know what he's taken."

"Was that, Jim?" asked Lori anxiously.

Paul nodded before continuing, "He drank Salazar's herbal tea. I don't know all the details. I've no idea what shit is in it, but Jim kept the dregs from the cup. He's on his way over with it. I figured you could test it or something."

"Thank you," said the doctor, scribbling some notes on the chart. "How long will it take him to get here?"

"About fifteen minutes," guessed Paul.

"If it's the same tea that Sal was drinking when I saw him in New York, I think its mushroom based," suggested Lori, glancing at Paul seeking reassurance.

Fifteen minutes later, Dr Abel returned with a wheelchair to fetch Lori. While he'd been gone, Paul had filled Lori in on his brief conversation with Dr Marrs. Hurriedly, he recounted Jim's tale of Jake's temper explosion and sudden, high speed departure from JJL. He added that Salazar had disappeared and that Jim hadn't been able to contact him or Garrett.

With her hands resting on her baby bump, Lori kept her head bowed as Dr Abel wheeled her down the hospital corridor.

"Lori!" shouted a familiar voice.

She lifted her head to see Dr Marrs rushing towards them, carrying a red solo cup with saran wrap sealing in the contents. When the producer saw her bruised appearance, he stopped dead in his tracks.

"Christ, Lori," he breathed, his face paling. "What's he done to you?"

"Doesn't matter," she muttered. "Is that Sal's tea?"

The producer nodded as he handed the cup to the doctor.

"Thanks, sir," said the doctor calmly. "I'll get this straight to the lab for analysis. Any idea what's in it?"

"No idea. Best guess would be mushrooms and a combination of other shit. Doesn't smell like any mushroom tea I've ever encountered," confessed the producer. "He always arrived with it in a bigger bottle and sipped it constantly while he worked."

"By he, do you mean Mr Power?"

"Hell, no! Salazar Mendes," stated Jim sharply. "He's been recording with Jake all week. It's only a hunch, but I think he's been slipping Jake some of this shit every night this week."

"Ok. Can you wait in the relatives' room with Mr Edwards, please?" suggested Dr Abel. "I'll see Mrs Power settled then come back with more questions."

There were four cubicles in the resus area, but only one had the curtains fully closed when the doctor wheeled Lori into the large room. A small Oriental nurse held the curtain aside as he manoeuvred her into position beside the bed. Jake lay slightly propped up, stripped to the waist with ECG electrodes stuck on his chest. An IV was pumping into a canula inserted into the back of his left hand. An oxygen mask covered most of his face.

"Oh, Jake," whispered Lori softly.

"I'll give you a few minutes with him," said Dr Abel quietly. "The nurse will be right outside the curtain if you need anything. Are you sure you'll be ok in here?"

Silently, Lori nodded.

Once alone with Jake, she edged the wheelchair closer to the bed, then reached up and lifted his hand, bringing it up against her cheek. For a few moments, she sat just holding his hand, watching him breathe. His breathing was still erratic and a glance at the monitor told her that his heart rate was still fluctuating. Every time it increased sharply, his eyelids flickered and occasionally his body twitched involuntarily. She guessed he was still hallucinating despite the sedation.

"Jake, it's going to be ok," she whispered, kissing his fingers. "We'll get you well. We'll get through this."

She paused, unsure what to say.

"Jim told me what Sal did. He's brought in some of that stuff for the hospital to test. Once they know what's in it, they'll have a better idea what to do next here to help."

Laying his hand down, Lori slowly stood up and stepped close to the bed. Tenderly, she ran her hand down his cheek, then felt the baby stirring restlessly. On impulse, she lifted Jake's hand again and held it to her bump, feeling the baby kicking hard.

"I don't know what was going through your head last night, but we're both ok. We've been checked out and we're going to be fine. Dr said baby's fine. Bigger than average but absolutely fine. Guess there's no hope of a neat, little, baby bump, rock star."

Exhaustion began to take its toll on her and Lori felt her legs begin to tremble beneath her. Slowly, she sank back down in the wheelchair, grimacing at the pain the movement caused her. Fighting back fresh tears, she sat silently holding Jake's hand, watching his tattooed chest rise and fall.

"Mrs Power," said Dr Abel as he stepped into the cubicle beside her. "The lab are running that sample through just now for us. We're going to admit Mr Power and take him upstairs now that he's stabilised. I've spoken to Dr De Luca. She wants to admit you for observation."

"No," said Lori firmly. "I want to stay with Jake."

"No disrespect, ma'am, but you're exhausted. You've been through a hell of an ordeal."

"No one is admitting me," stated Lori, staring at him.

"Very well, but I strongly recommend you get your friend to take you home for some rest. Mr Power will be kept under sedation for at least the next few hours. Once we have a clearer picture of what's in his system, we can work out a treatment plan. I'll call you personally if there's any change in his condition," promised the doctor warmly.

Reluctantly, Lori nodded.

When Paul pulled into the driveway at the beach house mid-afternoon, the first thing Lori noticed was that Jake's truck was gone and that her car was back in its usual spot. Grey's beaten up old Mustang was parked beside the Mercedes. Shunning Paul's offer of help, Lori slowly and painfully made her way indoors.

"Grey!" yelled Paul. "You here?"

"In the sunroom," called back the bass player. "Be with you in a minute."

Lori wandered through to the kitchen, poured herself a glass of water and sat down at the table. The short walk from the car had worn her out.

"When did you last eat anything?" asked Paul, his voice filled with concern.

"Last night," she confessed. "But I'm not hungry."

"But baby is. You need to eat, Lori. Let me fix you a sandwich at least."

Knowing it was pointless to argue, she forced a weak smile and said, "There should be some lunch meat in the refrigerator. Turkey. Bread's in the drawer below the coffee pot. Second drawer down."

A couple of minutes later, Grey came striding in carrying his tool box. He stopped in his tracks when he saw the bruising to Lori's pale face.

"Shit," he muttered, setting the metal box down on the floor.

"What the hell did he do to you?"

"Grey, they're only bruises."

"Lori, it looks like he was trying to kill you," stated the bass player bluntly.

"In his mind, he was trying to kill something. A demon witch, but not me," she whispered, her voice trembling.

"What was he hitting you with?"

"It doesn't matter."

"Lori," began Grey sternly as he knelt down in front of her. "What did he hit you with?"

Lowering her gaze, Lori whispered, "The neck and headstock from one of his guitars."

"Christ, he could've killed you and the baby!"

"I know," sighed Lori, tears welling up in her eyes. "But he didn't. He'd been drugged. Salazar did it to him."

"Have you spoken to the police?"

Bringing Lori's sandwich over, Paul said, "Grey, let her be. Maddy's dealt with the police. I'll fill you in later. Let's keep this between us. Keep it in the family. Jethro's on his way down from New York."

The dark, thunderous look that the drummer shot him was enough to quieten Grey down. He took a seat at the table and explained, "I've taken the truck into the shop where I used to work. Kola brought your car back here. I've fixed the sunroom door. I was about to make a start on the basement."

"Thanks, Grey. Leave the basement. It can wait," said Lori, nibbling on the soft Italian bread. "I'll need a full inventory for the insurance people. There's not much left intact down there."

Tears spilled down Lori's cheeks as she nibbled a little more of the sandwich then she sat the bread down on the plate with a weary sigh.

"Let's get you settled somewhere comfortable," suggested Paul tenderly. "Maddy's on her way over. When she gets here, Grey and I will make a start on that inventory."

"Thanks, guys."

As Lori lay curled up in bed, sleep refused to come. She had managed to eat half of the sandwich that Paul had prepared then excused herself, leaving the two members of Silver Lake staring after her as she shambled out of the room. Once down in the bedroom, she had carefully peeled off her clothes then slipped Jake's discarded Ramones T-shirt on. It still smelled of his deodorant, the familiar aroma making her heart ache. Despite everything that had happened, all she wanted was to be wrapped in his arms. The worn T-shirt was a poor substitute.

The baby was shifting about restlessly. Subconsciously, she gently rubbed her bump, feeling the sharp kicks under her fingertips. For the thousandth time, she offered up a prayer of thanks for the baby's safety. She had no idea how she had managed to protect them both, although the extensive bruising on her arm gave her a fair idea.

Gradually, exhaustion took control. Her eyes grew heavy. The baby began to settle. Together, they drifted off to sleep.

Feeling like a jackhammer was vibrating through his head, Jake slowly opened his eyes. He glanced round the unfamiliar room. The lights were down low, but it was obvious that he was in a hospital bed. The world was still spinning and his mouth felt as dry as a desert. Raising his left hand, he saw there was an IV attached. Looking down, he saw the electrodes stuck to his bare chest.

"And finally he awakes," said a familiar voice softly from the corner of the room.

"Jethro?" croaked Jake, struggling to sit up.

Crossing the room to take a seat beside the bed, the band's white haired manager asked, "How're you feeling, son?"

"Like shit."

"How much do you remember about last night?"

Images from the night before flashed through his mind, playing like a slideshow in front of his eyes. He recalled his erratic drive back from JJL, trying to dodge the evil creatures that had been attacking the truck; recalled the green eyed monster, lurking under a cloak in the basement, laying in wait for him. Visions of smashing his guitars into it crashed into mind. Then he remembered his frenzied attack on the witch, hearing her screams of pain echo in his mind.

The realisation of who had really been screaming in fear and agony hit him.

Raising his eyes towards the ceiling, Jake let out a blood curdling howl. Sobs wracked his body. At his side, the heart monitor's alarm triggered as his heart rate soared.

"Son, it's going to be ok," soothed Jethro, placing a hand on his shoulder. "You were drugged. You weren't in control."

"Lori?"

"Will be fine," promised Jethro calmly as two nurses charged into the room in response to the alarm.

Once the medical staff had settled Jake and were satisfied that he was calm, they left the room, one of them promising to return with a dinner tray for him.

"Jethro, is she really ok?" asked Jake, dreading hearing the answer.

"I'll not lie to you, son," began the older man. "You could've killed her, but you didn't. As far as I know, she's resting at home. Maddison is with her. I spoke to Grey about an hour ago."

"And the baby?"

"Is fine," assured Jethro warmly. "She was here earlier to see you while you were still in resus."

"She was?"

Jethro nodded, then said, "So, what do you remember?"

Running his hand through his tangled hair, Jake recalled, "I took some migraine pills out at JJL and choked on them. Salazar passed me a drink. I swallowed some to stop myself from choking. It left a bitter taste. It was that fucking tea of his. I'd drunk half the cup by then. I sang the vocal track and began to feel weird. Began to sweat and shake. I remember the shadows moving. I realised what he'd done to me. I think I threw my headphones at him. Then I left."

"Do you remember getting home?" prompted Jethro quietly.

"Not really. I was seeing evil black things swarming over the truck. They were dropping down out of the trees along the lake. The truck? I crashed my truck!"

"Grey's taking care of it. Don't panic."

"And the basement?" asked Jake, recalling vividly his rampage. "And Lori?"

Tears of fear and remorse glided down his cheeks.

"The boys are clearing up. They're all taking care of Lori too. I've not seen her yet, son, but it sounds like she's been beaten pretty badly."

"She was," confessed Jake, his voice barely above a whisper. "What happens now?"

"Well, you're going nowhere tonight," stated Jethro firmly. "If your heart rate remains stable overnight, you'll be discharged tomorrow. You're booked into rehab for an initial seven day plan. No arguments. No negotiation."

"Where?"

"Nowhere local. It's all arranged. The folks who run it are friends of mine. I'll drive you there myself. It's a nice facility. They do a great short programme for addicts who relapse."

"But I was drugged!" protested Jake, instantly angry at being called an addict.

"It wasn't Salazar that put that hypodermic in your hand and shot you full of heroin."

"What hypodermic? I've not touched that shit in over seven years, Jethro!"

"Until last night or early this morning."

Jake stared at the band's manager not entirely comprehending what he was saying.

"Jake," continued Jethro. "Lori found you unconscious, face down in a pool of vomit in your apartment. The needle, the foil and the lighter were on the table."

"The apartment? Lori found me?"

"Yes, she did. Paul has no idea how she managed to get herself there. It was Lori who called 911. She probably saved your life, Jacob."

Sun was spilling through the drapes and across the bed when Lori finally awoke. Before she even attempted to move, she knew it was going to hurt. From the angle of the light flooding into the room, she realised that she had slept all night and at least half of the day. Carefully, she sat up and swung her legs over the side of the bed.

"And where do you think you're going?" demanded a sharp voice from behind her.

It was Maddy's distinctive New York voice.

"Bathroom," replied Lori, without looking at her friend. "And don't even think about stopping me, Maddison!"

When she limped back into the bedroom, her friend was coming back through from the hallway, carrying a coffee and a toasted cinnamon raisin bagel.

"Thought you might be hungry, honey."

"Thanks," said Lori, sitting down on the bed.

"Back into bed. No arguments. You need to rest," instructed Maddy firmly.

"I can't stay in bed all day," protested Lori. "Besides, I need to see Jake."

"Back into bed, Lori."

Realising it was pointless to argue with her fiery, Goth friend, Lori slowly climbed back into bed. Once she was comfortably propped up on the pillows, Maddy handed her the mug and the plate.

"Honey, we need to talk," began Maddy. The caring friend voice was gone. It was the business-like Maddy who was sitting staring at her.

"I know," sighed Lori. "What time is it anyway?"

"It's about three, I think," answered her friend. "How're you feeling?"

"Stiff and sore. Still a bit shaken," Lori confessed before she took a small bite of the bagel.

"I'm not surprised."

"I'll be fine."

"And is the baby still moving about?"

"Yes. What is this? Twenty questions?"

"Lori, this is serious," said the band's manager plainly. "A lot's happened while you were asleep."

"Like what? Is Jake ok?" demanded Lori sharply. "I need to see him. Need to talk to him."

"Jake's going to be ok. Jethro's taken him away for a few days. They left before lunch so you can't see him until he gets back."

"Where's he taken him?"

"Rehab. He's been booked into a short-term relapse programme. If it all goes well, he'll complete the programme by next Sunday. If not, then his stay at the facility will be extended until he does."

"Where have you sent him, Maddison?"

"Somewhere where they will take good care of him."

"Where is he?"

"I'm not telling you, Lori, so stop asking," stated Maddy bluntly. "Now, the boys have cleaned up downstairs. I've left the full inventory on your desk, but I mailed it to David to start the insurance claim."

"You didn't tell him what happened, did you?"

"Not the whole story. I guessed you didn't need him rushing down here to fuss over you and lecture you," assured Maddy with a smile. "I passed it off as a band bust up. Fortunately, your husband didn't destroy anything too valuable and nothing irreplaceable."

"What about his truck?" asked Lori sadly.

"It's in bad shape. Grey can explain it better than me. Something about the engine. He didn't think it could be repaired."

"Jake loves that truck," sighed Lori softly.

"Grey will explain when you see him. He'll be over after dinner to stay with you tonight."

"I can stay by myself, Maddy," Lori protested indignantly. "What's happened with Salazar and Garrett? Any word from them?"

"That's another mess!" declared Maddy. "After Jake left JJL, it appears that Sal fled into the woods behind the studio. It took Garrett all night to find him, but he did. He's taken him back to New York and, as far as I know, was getting him assessed. Garrett called me last night to see if you were ok. He had heard via Dr Marrs about what Jake did when he left JJL. Anyway, Garrett says Sal confessed to slipping drugs into Jake's juice cup every night they were out there. Said Sal deliberately gave him his own cup when Jake choked on his migraine meds. As to why he did it, we don't know."

"What about the police? Is Jake going to be charged with possession because of what happened at his apartment?" asked Lori, trying to make sense of it all.

"Unlikely. Salazar on the other hand is in trouble with them."

"And the press? Have they got wind of this?"

"That's about the only stroke of luck we've had. We've managed to keep this under the radar so far," revealed Maddy. "You'll need to keep a low profile for a few days as a precaution."

"Anything else I should know?" asked Lori, before eating the final piece of the toasted bagel.

"I don't think so. Grey's coming over at six. He's bringing dinner. He'll stay with you tonight. Rich'll be over in the morning and I'll be back after lunch."

"No," stated Lori firmly. "I don't need babysitting. I'll be fine on my own."

"We'll see," replied Maddy, not wanting to antagonise her fragile friend.

"Can I call Jake if I can't see him?"

"No," said Maddy. "Not during the first seven days. If he

doesn't pass the programme, then he's allowed to call you for five minutes once during the second seven days."

The door to the room clicked shut. Jake sat down on the end of the bed and put his head in his hands, allowing his long hair to flow through his trembling fingers. In the space of forty eight hours, his entire world had unravelled and come crashing down around him. Alone for the first time since he'd left the hospital, he felt totally and utterly bereft. It had been dinner time when Jethro had pulled off the road and headed up a narrow, dirt track driveway. Eventually, almost a mile further on, he had stopped in front of a huge, old farmhouse. They had been welcomed in by a tall, slender, grey haired woman, who had announced that they were just in time for dinner. Declining politely, Jethro had explained he had a long drive ahead of him and couldn't stay. He fetched a holdall from the trunk of the car and a guitar case, saying this was all he had brought for Jake. With a hurried goodbye, Jethro had left him standing in the hallway, feeling like an unwanted orphan. The woman, who introduced herself as Ella, had ushered Jake through to the dining room. Around the table there had been five other adults of varying ages, all chatting about their day. He had sat quietly in their midst, picking at his meal. After the table had been cleared, they had sat together in the lounge room for what Ella said was "evening openness" time. Throughout the hour long group therapy session, Jake had sat in silence, watching and listening to three of the others open up about their relapses. With the session over, Ella had shown him upstairs to the attic bedroom.

With a sigh, Jake ran his hand through his hair and stood up, surveying the room. The guitar case was leaning against the wall and the holdall sat beside it. The room was a reasonable size, but the camp ceiling greatly reduced the head room over more than half the floor space. A chest of drawers sat with two drawers open and empty. Taking it as an invitation to unpack, Jake went over and opened the holdall. Inside, he found all new clothes, still with the tags on them. Obviously, Jethro hadn't gone back to the house, but had gone shopping instead. By the time the bag was empty, he had stowed seven plain white T-shirts, seven pairs of boxers, seven pairs of socks and three pairs of jeans in the drawers. He had also found two hooded zipper tops, one red and one black, plus a new pair of black hi-tops.

There was nothing familiar about any of it. Nothing personal. It felt and looked like a prison uniform.

In the end pocket, he found a wash bag with the essentials in it and, in the front pocket, two hardback notebooks and a packet of pens.

After they had left Rehoboth, Jethro hadn't returned his personal effects to him so he had no wallet, no money, no watch and no cell phone.

No means of escape.

Feeling the harsh reality of the world close in around him, Jake wandered over to the window. He had to duck to avoid hitting his head on the low angled ceiling. Outside, everything, as far as he could see, was pitch black. No sign of lights. No sign of life.

A folder lay on top of the chest of drawers with his name on it. Wearily, he picked it up and sat down on the floor beneath the window to read through it. Inside, he found a brief, handwritten welcome message from Ella and Frank, who he assumed was her husband. The itinerary for each of the next six days was mapped out for him. He was surprised to read that the schedule included more farm chores than therapy sessions. Each evening, there was an openness class. After lunch each day, there was an individual session slotted in for an hour. A few hour long slots before dinner had been left blank. It looked a far cry from the regimented out-patient rehab programme he had followed all those years ago.

With no watch and no clock in the room, Jake had lost all track of time. As he laid the folder to one side, he realised that he was exhausted. He stared over at the small bed with its patchwork counterpane and decided to turn in for the night.

When Lori wakened on Sunday morning, she awakened to the aroma of fresh coffee and bacon. She could hear voices coming from the kitchen, but they were too muffled for her to make them out. Still feeling stiff and bruised, she slowly slid out of bed and made her way into the bathroom. At Maddy's insistence, she had stayed in bed all of the day before and hadn't even showered. Standing under the jet of hot water, Lori felt some of the tension ease from her neck and shoulders. As she lathered her favourite perfumed shower gel over her baby bump, she felt the little one stir and begin to kick. Luxuriating in the safe confines of the shower, Lori took her time, but, as the water began to cool, she turned off the jet and stepped carefully out onto the mat.

Her whole body still felt battered and one glance in the mirror reminded her of why. Twisting slightly, Lori saw the extent of the bruising to her back and shoulder. She could clearly see the lines of small, dark bruises where the machine heads had hammered into her. With a shiver of lingering fear, she turned away from her reflection and went to get dressed.

As she hobbled down the hallway, Lori realised that the voices belonged to Rich and Jethro. Opening the door, she took a deep breath before stepping into the kitchen.

"Morning," she said softly as they both turned to stare at her.

"Shit, Lori!" exclaimed Rich when he saw the purple bruises on her face.

Without saying a word, Jethro stood up and came round the table to hug her. She buried her face in his chest , fresh tears tumbling down her cheeks. Tenderly, the older man held her while she cried, rubbing her back and whispering reassurances to her.

"I'm ok," she whispered eventually as the baby gave a sharp series of kicks to her ribs. "Nothing broken."

"Not even your heart, princess?" asked Jethro quietly.

"It's a bit battered and bruised too but not broken. I love him too much, Jethro. That crazed animal on Thursday night wasn't Jake."

"I could fucking kill him," growled Rich from behind her.

"Who? Jake?," asked Lori, stepping away from Jethro. Limping over to the refrigerator for some orange juice, she added, "Or Salazar?"

"Both of them!"

"Rich," she began calmly. "This wasn't entirely Jake's fault. Yes, I know he was out of control. I know he shouldn't have acted the way he did, but he was hallucinating through no fault of his own. If you need to be angry at anyone, be angry with Salazar not Jake."

"How could he have done this to you though?"

"It was dark. He was angry and scared. He obviously wasn't

263

seeing what was really there. I know in my heart that Jake didn't know it was me he was hurting."

"She's right," stated Jethro plainly. "Lori, honey, sit down and I'll fill you in on what he told me. Ricardo, make yourself useful and fetch this lady some breakfast."

Hearing Silver Lake's silver haired manager recount what Jake had told him brought fresh tears. Despite her pleas, he refused to reveal any details of where he had taken Jake. Calmly, he promised her that he was fine, that his heart rate had stabilised and that he had been released from Beebe without the need for any prescribed medication. She was relieved to hear that Jethro had taken the time to shop for emergency clothes for her husband and touched that he'd picked up a guitar from JJL for him to take into the rehab facility. His week would be tough enough without being denied access to his music as well.

As she drained the last mouthful from her coffee cup, Lori said, "Rich, can you do me a favour?"

"Anything," replied the guitarist without hesitation.

"When Grey was over last night he explained that Jake's truck is trashed. Something to do with the engine and something being all twisted up. Anyway, can you go out to the dealership and sort out a new truck?" she asked, resting her hand on her bump. "It doesn't have to be brand new. We passed that place last week and they had a black one, pre-owned, as their deal of the week. He was admiring it. See if it's still available. If it's not, do the best you can. It needs to be here by Friday, though."

"Lori, Jake loves his old truck. I'm not sure about this," began Rich, knowing just how much that the truck meant to his friend.

"I'm sure," stated Lori, forcing a smile. "I gave Grey instructions to repair the truck no matter the cost, but it's going to take a while. I'm not so sure Jake will feel the same about it when he gets back. Not after all that's happened."

"Ok," acknowledged Rich, checking the time. "I'll pick Linsey up. I'd arranged to take her to lunch, then we'll both head out there. I'll call you to talk numbers when I see what they've got."

"Thanks."

"Will you be alright here on your own for a few hours?" asked Jethro. "I've a meeting with Maddy at JJL then, I think, she said she was coming here to cook dinner."

"You know what, Jethro," sighed Lori. "I'd love a few hours on my own. I'll be fine."

"And you'll call one of us if you need anything?"

"Promise," she said warmly. "Now, off you go and leave me to enjoy my coffee in peace."

With the house to herself, Lori finally began to relax a little. For the first hour or so, she kept herself busy with some basic household chores, including laundry. As she sorted through the pile of clothes, splitting them into light and dark, she separated out three of Jake's T-shirts. Holding them close to her chest, Lori inhaled the fading smell of his deodorant mixed with sweat. For a few brief moments, she forgot the drama and the pain and simply lost herself in the aroma of "essence of Jake". Deciding against washing them just yet, she left them on the bed and took the rest down to the utility room.

At some point, Grey had brought Jake's personal items in from the truck and left them piled on a chair in the dining room. His battered book bag was among them. Just seeing it lying there tugged at her heart strings. Taking a deep breath, Lori picked it up and headed over to the door down to the basement then stopped.

Was she ready to face going back down there?

Dismissing the thought as nonsense, she switched on the light and opened the door. Slowly and painfully, Lori made her way down the steep stairs, noting that Grey, or someone, had repaired the broken bannister spindles and given them a coat of paint. With all of the broken gear cleared out, the place looked bare and lifeless. The desk had been righted as had the battered old couch. With her heart pounding with fear at the memories beginning to stir, Lori laid the book bag down on the desk. A small plastic bag fell out. Looking inside, she found Jake's wallet, his watch, his cell phone and a handful of picks. The phone was flat, disconnected from the world just like its owner.

Having been rostered on for barn work, Jake found himself mucking out four horse stalls shortly after dawn on Tuesday morning. The cold air was icy and his breath was coming in clouds as he worked. Unfamiliar with horses, he was careful to stay out of their way as he moved about the large stalls. By the third box, he was sweating and breathless. The bay mare, who occupied it, was watching his every move.

"It's ok, girl," he said softly. "I'm not going to hurt you."

The horse snorted as if to say "And you expect me to believe that, mister man?"

"Don't look at me like that," he complained as the horse continued to stare at him. "I know I hurt her. I know I hurt Lori. Could've killed her, but I'll never hurt anyone or anything again."

Eyes wide, the brown horse blew through her nose, shook her head, then continued to stare at him, listening to his every word.

"How am I going to make amends?" he asked, reaching over to clap the horse on the shoulder. "Will she even want me back after what happened?"

As he raked up the old straw, Jake continued, "You know, old girl, I've really fucked this up. Before last week, life looked so good. Lots of work lined up. Writing new material for Silver Lake. A few shows lined up for May. Recording a new album over the summer. A whole summer at home. Now, that's a luxury! Then there's the baby."

He paused, leaning on the rake, "God, I hope Lori and the baby are ok. If I've..."

His emotions spiralled out of control as his throat closed over and tears fell unbidden from his eyes.

"Christ, what have I done?" he yelled to the world around him. "What has he done to me? Salazar and that fucking tea of his! Why did he force it on me? Why did he want to do that to me?"

The horse continued to stare at him, shifting restlessly in the stall.

"Everyone warned me to be careful round him. I thought I was being careful and look where it got me," sighed Jake, running his hand through his hair. "How do I make this mess right?"

Before he could say anything else, the horse shuffled round, nudging him, then kicked out, catching Jake just below his butt. The force of the kick was enough to send him sprawling face first into the pile of soiled straw. He lay there in the stinking pile for a few moments, then began to laugh.

"A kick in the ass? Is that what you think I need, old girl?" he said as he scrambled to his feet. Dusting himself down, he wrinkled his nose at the smell of manure. "And I'd already worked out that

I'm in the shit, thank you."

When he re-entered the farmhouse a while later, he chose to go in via the back door to avoid trailing muck through the house. He had expected the kitchen to be empty and was surprised to find Ella standing at the sink.

"Morning," he said shyly.

The older woman turned to face him and, noting his dishevelled, stinking state, she began to laugh, "Dear Lord, what happened to you, Jake?"

"A little equine therapy advice," replied Jake, stripping off his soiled T-shirt.

"Ah, Molly therapy," laughed Ella, trying not to stare at his tattooed body. "Are you hurt?"

"I'm good. My butt hurts like hell, but I'll live," he said with a smile. "Might've been the kick in the ass I deserved."

"That's the first time you've smiled all week," observed Ella quietly.

"Not been much to smile about," sighed Jake. "Guess my horse therapy has restored my sense of humour to an extent."

"Go and get cleaned up, then meet me on the back porch," instructed Ella. "It's time you got some Ella therapy too, son."

Stepping out onto the back porch, Jake found Ella sitting at a small table, breakfast laid out in front of her. For a moment, he stood admiring the view of the farm landscape that stretched for miles in front of him.

"Not quite the beach," observed Jake as he sat down. "But that's pretty. Tranquil."

"It's a good place to reflect and think," commented Ella as she poured him a coffee. "The others left last night. You're my only guest for the rest of the week."

"Guest? Is that what I am?"

"I'd like to think that's what you are," she replied, passing him a mug of strong black coffee. "Did you know that Jethro was a guest here a few years back? He stayed for three months."

"Three months?" exclaimed Jake sharply. "Will I need to stay for that long?"

"Only if you want to. He could've left after about six weeks, but

Coral McCallum

he chose to stay."

They sat in silence for a few minutes, then Ella said, "Why don't you tell me a bit about yourself? How did an international rock star come to be getting kicked in the butt by my horse?"

"It's not a pretty tale and not one I'm proud of," began Jake solemnly. "But, if you want to hear it, then I've nothing better to do right now."

At his own pace, Ella allowed him to talk. She listened as he told her how he'd originally met Lori down on the beach, told her all about Silver Lake, the wedding, the baby. While he talked, the older woman sat back and listened quietly. Mid-morning, Frank appeared in the doorway, announcing that it was time for Jake's therapy session, but Ella shooed him back indoors, saying it could wait. With a laugh, Ella declared, "He doesn't like it when I change his routine. Now, where were we? I think we'd reached last Thursday night, hadn't we?"

Jake nodded. Beginning with his arrival at JJL, he recounted the events that led up to the erratic drive home. As he began to describe the events that unfolded in the basement, he felt his emotions begin to slip out of his control. As tears filled his hazel eyes, Ella stopped him and said this chapter of his story needed a fresh pot of coffee and some donuts.

When she returned a few minutes later, Jake had regained some control over his frayed feelings and was able to continue. It tore at his very soul as he described how scared and threatened the presence of the "demon witch" had made him feel. As he spoke, pictures filled his mind, only this time he saw it all clearly. Saw Lori curled protectively in a ball on the floor. Saw his hand bring the headstock down repeatedly on her arm, ribs, shoulder and back. Saw himself strike her on the side of the head with it. Saw himself kick her as she lay unconscious on the floor. His voice trembling and barely audible, Jake recalled fleeing from the house and running along the beach until there was no air left in his lungs. Tasting salt water in his mouth, he explained about wakening face down on the sand with waves washing over him. Feeling a wave of revulsion crush him, he confessed to digging out the old stash of heroin and injecting it into his veins to escape the torment. His face a mask of self-hatred, Jake concluded, "The next thing I remember was waking up in the hospital."

"So, what happens when you leave here?" asked Ella softly.

"Lord knows," sighed Jake. "I need to see my wife. I need to see Lori. Need to talk to her. I just hope she wants to see me."

"And your music? What about it?"

"If Lori doesn't want me then none of it matters. She's my priority. I need to make this mess right somehow."

"And if someone else offers you a fix? Or a drink?"

"They can go to hell," stated Jake without hesitation. "Ella, I know you don't believe me, but I'm not an addict. I was drugged without my knowledge. I've no real idea why I dug out that old stash. Shit, it wasn't even mine. It was Paul's. I was never into injecting myself. Yeah, I'd done it a few times but it wasn't my vice. It was Paul's. The only thing that gets injected into me now is ink."

"And you've plenty of that from what I saw earlier," mused Ella with a smile. "Is there a story behind them?"

"Yup," nodded Jake, glancing down at the music tattooed on his forearm. "Each of them is about a chapter in my life."

"And what about this chapter?"

Remembering the kick in the butt he'd taken earlier, Jake smiled, before adding, "I've an idea what'll represent it."

"Ever ridden a horse?" asked Ella.

"Once or twice a long time ago."

"Let's go for a ride. You can tell me all about those tattoos."

By Friday afternoon, Lori was feeling like a caged lion. She hadn't been out of the house for a week and the walls were steadily closing in on her. Gradually, as the days had gone by, her physical aches had eased and the bruises had begun to fade out into a rainbow of colours. The dark purple bruising to her face was beginning to fade out to various shades of green at the edges. As she stood at the patio doors in the sunroom, gazing out on a clear, crisp Spring afternoon, Lori decided, bruises or no bruises, she needed fresh air.

With the hood up on her hoodie and a pair of sunglasses on, in an attempt to hide her bruises from the world, Lori set off slowly along the beach. Erring on the side of caution, she had taken both of her canes with her. The last thing she needed was a fall on the sand. As she slid the patio door over behind her, she sent Maddy a quick message, "Gone for a walk south along the beach. Sunroom door open if you arrive before I get back. Don't worry. I'm fine. Just needed air. L x."

There was an icy, cold wind blowing in off the ocean from the north. Beside her, the waves crashed in, sending foam swarming up the beach towards her feet. Not caring whether her feet got wet or not, Lori allowed the scummy water to swirl round her boots, the odd bit of seaweed tangling round her canes. She took her time and slowly meandered down the coast, lost in her own thoughts. Above her, the gulls were screeching and swooping. Pausing for a moment, she watched them soaring on the air currents.

She was totally alone down on the sand, not another soul in sight.

Earlier on, a delivery truck had pulled up in front of the house and she had stood back and watched as two young men carried the replacement equipment down to the basement. As she had signed for the delivery, Lori had felt a fresh stab of pain in her already tender heart. Like the rest of her, it was beaten and bruised. As the week had wound on, she had tried to focus on happier times, but during the nights, her sleep was tormented by nightmares. They weren't nightmares of Jake but instead of a dark, hooded ghoul following her every move. Her dreams were so vivid that she could almost feel its icy touch and smell its rotting breath. She was still sleeping in Jake's worn shirts and wakening to the faded smell of him was the only thing keeping her sane.

As she walked, Lori ran over the imaginary conversation she needed to have with her husband. It was a dialogue she had visualised repeatedly throughout the week. A dialogue that never reached its end. The motion as she wandered along the sand disturbed the baby, triggering a series of sharp kicks to her tender ribs. With tears stinging her eyes, Lori began to fret about what the future held for her and the baby. Would Jake want to come home? What torment was going through his head? Was therapy going to help lay his ghosts to rest?

The fact that no one could give her any answers or any indication of how long he'd be in rehab for was driving her insane. Mentally, Lori had been scoring off the days and reasoned that the next day was the seventh full day in whatever facility he was at. If Jethro was correct, then, at the very least, she could hope for one brief and precious phone call over the weekend. It was enough of a lifeline to keep her going.

Stamping sand off her feet on the deck a while later, Lori spotted the twins on a play mat in the sunroom. Through the closed doors, she could hear Maddy's muffled voice. Knowing she wasn't arriving home to an empty house made her smile.

Hearing the patio door open, little Wren looked up from the blocks she was playing with. She squealed with delight when she saw Lori and came crawling over towards her.

"Hi, Wren," said Lori with a smile. "Where's your Mommy?"

A serious look on her face, Wren pointed into the house, "Mama. Mama."

"That's right, honey. I can hear her talking on the phone," replied Lori as she unzipped her jacket.

"Ake?" quizzed the little girl, looking round. "Ake?"

"Oh, honey, Uncle Jake's not here," sighed Lori, fresh tears filling her eyes. "Soon, Wren. He'll be home soon."

After enjoying a delicious evening meal on Saturday evening,

Jake offered to help Ella clear the table and wash up. He was still the only "guest" at the farmhouse, but Frank had let slip over dinner that they were expecting three new arrivals over the next couple of days.

"Leave Ella be, son," instructed Frank gruffly. "You and I need to have a talk."

"Another openness session?" asked Jake, his stomach churning at the thought of another hour of soul searching. The one on one sessions had been uncomfortably intense over the past few days.

Frank shook his head, "No, son. A real talk. Come on through to my study."

Slightly apprehensively, Jake followed the older man. Despite the fact that he towered over Frank by a good six inches, there was something about the weather beaten old farmer that made him feel as though he was a little boy about to get a lecture or a punishment. He hadn't been in the study before and was surprised that it was lined down two walls with books. Framed photos covered the remaining two walls. There was no window. Furniture was sparse too.

"Take a seat, son," suggested Frank, pointing to an old wooden kitchen chair.

Dutifully, Jake sat on the chair, hearing it creak as it took his weight. The older man sat on a well-worn, leather captain's chair at the desk and began to sort through a folder of paperwork. Silence filled the room. For almost fifteen minutes they sat like this before Frank closed the folder over and placed a sheet of paper on top of it. He turned in his chair and sat silently staring at Jake for a few more minutes.

Eventually, after what felt like an eternity to Jake, Frank smiled and said, "When Jethro called me and asked me to take you in, I almost said no. This isn't a place for rock stars. It's for real people. Normal, everyday folks who fall off the path, but he talked me round. Said you were different. Explained the circumstances. Told me I'd like you."

He paused for a moment, then continued, "We've had famous folks here before. Prima Donnas expecting hotel service. No interest in therapy sessions. No openness about them. Obviously here because they were told to come. At first, I thought you'd be the same. I thought wrong of you, son, and I owe you an apology for that."

"Thank you, sir," said Jake quietly, unsure where the conversation was going.

"You're alright, Jake," commented Frank with a smile. "Right from the get go, you opened up, didn't try to deny what you'd done to your wife. Didn't make excuses for your behaviour. Didn't expect any special rock star treatment. You're harder on you than I could ever be. You've surprised me. You've left an impression on me. There's not many folks manage that nowadays."

"Is that a good thing?"

"In your case, it is," acknowledged Frank, picking up a pen. "I called Jethro before dinner to bring him up to speed on how this week's gone."

"And?" interrupted Jake anxiously.

"Patience, son," cautioned the older man warmly. "Spoke to him for almost an hour. Assuming you're agreeable to it, he's going to be your "rehab buddy" when you leave here. For the first month, you'll need to check in with him every day. Once a week, you'll have a face to face meeting with him. If that goes well, then you can phase the meetings out or keep them going. That'll be between you and that old silver haired fox. If you break the deal, miss an arranged meeting or stray off the straight and narrow, you'll be back here within twenty four hours and be here for a month minimum. Do I make myself clear, Jacob?"

Flinching at the use of his full name, Jake nodded.

"This is only the start of your journey. You need to figure the rest out for yourself. You need to find the right words when you see your wife. You need to pray that she still loves you after what you put her through. Jethro's filled me in on that too."

"Is Lori ok?" asked Jake with a worried look towards the old man.

"Far as I hear it, she's doing ok."

With a sigh of relief, Jake bent forward, burying his face in his hands.

"You'll be able to ask her yourself tomorrow, hopefully," said Frank calmly. "If she'll listen to you, that is. I can't help you with that one, son."

"As long as she's ok," whispered Jake, his voice thick with emotion. "As long as the baby's ok too."

He looked up into the older man's face and confessed, "I've no idea what I'm going to say to her. No idea how we begin to recover from this. No idea if we can recover from this."

"Well, you better start figuring it out," said Frank. "Jethro will be here after breakfast to collect you."

"I can leave?"

"If you feel ready to."

"Thank you," said Jake with more than a hint of nerves in his voice. "I guess this place has been the kick in the ass I needed."

"Yes," chuckled Frank. "I heard about your "Molly therapy". Maybe we should offer it to everyone who comes here."

"It's certainly left its mark," admitted Jake, visualising the huge bruise on his butt.

"Now, I've a favour to ask of you, son," began Frank with a smile. "Hard to believe, but Ella was too shy to ask you herself. We've heard you playing that guitar up in the attic in the middle of the night most nights. How about you bring it down to the kitchen and play it properly for us?"

"And you won't think I'm being a prima donna if I do?" joked Jake with a hint of mischief.

"No, son, we won't."

"Give me five minutes," said Jake, getting to his feet.

"Will you sing too?" asked Frank hopefully. "Jethro told Ella that she'd love your voice."

"No pressure then. If Ella wants me to sing, then I'd be honoured to sing for her."

"Call it your final openness session," said Frank with a wink.

Sitting in the farmhouse kitchen a short while later, Jake felt nervous and self-conscious as he began to play for his hosts. Guessing that they weren't rock fans, he played a couple of well-known country ballads, a couple of Lynyrd Skynyrd classics, then asked Ella what she would like him to play for her. Blushing, she asked if he'd play Stairway To Heaven. Flashing her a smile, he obliged then Frank requested that he play something he'd written, rather than hiding behind cover versions. Feeling himself relax, comfortable with the guitar in his hands, Jake played the acoustic version of Depths for the older couple.

"That's quite something," said Frank, nodding approvingly.

"Is that the song that's tattooed on your arm?" asked Ella, her curiosity getting the better of her.

"No, ma'am. That's a song called Stronger Within. The first song I wrote for and about my wife. For Lori," explained Jake softly, sensing what was coming next.

"Will you play it?"

The question hung in the air. In his mind, Jake could visualise the very first time he'd played it to Lori in the sunroom; remembered, with a smile, how proud he'd felt playing it for her at Atlantic City. Before his emotions seized control, he nodded.

Keeping his head bowed, he began to pick the familiar, gentle melody. At the first attempt nerves took hold and he missed his cue to come in on vocals.

"Let's try that again," he apologised quietly.

At the second time of asking, his timing was perfect. Whether it was by design or due to the growing feeling of fear, his voice was huskier than usual, making the vocal all the more haunting. With every word, he saw images of Lori flash before his closed eyes. Out of all the songs he'd ever written or performed, playing Stronger Within in the remote farmhouse kitchen was perhaps the toughest gig ever. His audience were hanging on his every note and, when the song was done, he sat for a moment, head bowed over the guitar, trying to compose himself. He was aware of a movement beside him. It was Ella. Placing her hand on his shoulder, she smoothed his hair with her other hand, reminding him for a moment of his mom, "That was beautiful, Jake. Your wife must be a very special person. Now, you've a long day ahead of you tomorrow. It's a long drive home from here. Time for bed."

Overnight a storm had blown in off the ocean, lashing the Delaware coast with torrential rain and gale force winds. Much to Lori's surprise, no one had made any arrangements to check up on her for the day. It was the first day since her world had been turned upside down that she'd awakened to an empty house. The silence was soothing as she lay in bed listening to the storm raging outside.

By late morning, she was tired of resting in bed. Her book wasn't holding her attention. The baby had wriggled to one side and was pressing on a nerve, meaning, no matter which way she lay, she couldn't get comfortable. Eventually, she surrendered, deciding that a soak in the tub might be in order.

Lying back in the bubble filled bathtub, Lori finally felt the baby somersault and move from the nerve it had been pressing on. The relief was immediate, even if it meant that her bump was even more prominent to the front. Running her hand over her rounded stomach, Lori tried to figure out what way up the baby was lying. She could feel it stirring, then noticed a sharp rounded bit protruding low down on her right.

Rubbing it gently, she mused, "Is that your foot, little one?"

The small, hard bump disappeared, tucked back inside once more.

Giggling to herself, Lori scooped up some fragranced bubbles, drizzling them on top of her swollen belly.

When the water began to feel cool, Lori spun the dial to drain the tub then carefully climbed out. As she reached for the fluffy bath sheet, she caught sight of her reflection in the full length mirror. Her bump was decidedly larger since the baby had changed position; her bruises were slowly fading from red to green, some of the smaller ones already turning yellow. The bruising on her face and arm was still unsightly. Turning away from the mirror, Lori wrapped herself in the warm towel.

In the passenger seat of Jethro's car, Jake sat silently staring out of the window as mile after mile of bleak, rain soaked highway slipped by. Mentally, he was torn in two. Half of him was delighted to be heading home; half of him was terrified of going home. Would it even still be home?

Occasionally, the band's manager would try to engage him in conversation, but, after the first hour, the older man surrendered, leaving Jake to his thoughts.

As they passed Dover Downs several hours later, Jethro said, "I should call Lori. Let her know we'll be there soon."

"Don't," said Jake instantly, shuddering at the memory of a similar situation. "I made the same call about here the day we lost Gary. Wait a bit before you call her."

"Alright," agreed Jethro, sensing how emotionally fragile his passenger was. "How about I call her when we reach the outskirts of town? I could ask if she wants me to bring in something for dinner."

"Are you coming in for dinner?" asked Jake hopefully.

"No, but you both need to eat. Maddison is expecting me for dinner. I'll take you home, then leave you both to sort things out. You need your privacy to do this, son. You don't need this old man getting in the way. However, if you need me, just call and I'll be right over."

"What am I going to say to her?"

"I don't know, Jake," sighed Jethro, keeping his eyes on the road. "But you've about an hour to figure it out."

For the first time in over a week, Lori had settled down to do some work on her current commission. The deadline was looming large on the horizon and she was still far from finished it. While she had been concentrating on her drawing board, the afternoon had disappeared. It felt good to have something to focus her attention on after all the drama of the previous few days and, for a few short hours, Lori had been able to blot out the pain of the real world. As the last of the day's grey light began to fade, her phone rang on the desk beside her.

"Jethro," she greeted warmly. "Hi."

"Hi, princess," came the older man's familiar voice. "You ok today?"

"Getting there. I've been working. It's keeping my mind off

everything," replied Lori, rubbing the base of her back where it was beginning to ache from sitting.

"Have you planned dinner?"

"Not yet."

"Good. Don't," he said. "I'll be there in thirty minutes. I'll bring something in. What do you feel like?"

"Pizza," answered Lori, without hesitation. "Pepperoni with cheese fries."

"Your wish is my command, princess."

With her iPod playing quietly in the background, Lori set two places at the dining room table. As she carried the container of apple juice through from the kitchen, she heard Jethro's car pull up in the driveway. Returning to the kitchen for two glasses, she heard the door slam shut. With her back to the back door, Lori was reaching into the cupboard beside the sink when she heard the door open and felt the rush of icy ocean air swirl in around her ankles.

"Hi," she greeted as she turned around with the two glasses in her hands.

Jake stood in the doorway.

"Jake!" gasped Lori, letting go of both of the glasses.

They smashed on the floor at her feet, shards of blue glass splintering across the tiled floor.

"Hi," said Jake, his voice husky. "I brought your pizza," he added, indicating the box that was in his hand.

Tears welled up in her eyes as Lori stood staring at him. As they started to spill down her cheeks, she took a step towards him.

Noticing that she was in her bare feet, Jake said, "Don't move. You'll cut your feet."

Swiftly, he stepped into the kitchen, set down the pizza box and the carton of cheese fries, then fetched the broom from the hall cupboard. In a few seconds, he had the glass swept into a pile. All the while Lori had stood silently watching him, tears gliding down her cheeks.

"I'll put that out in the trash later," said Jake, resting the broom against the wall. "We'd better eat that pizza before it goes cold."

"Where's Jethro?" asked Lori, glancing at the back door.

"He's gone to Maddy's for dinner."

"Oh!"

"Look, if you want me to go, that's ok," began Jake, trying not to stare at the fading bruises, a fresh wave of guilt threatening to engulf him.

"No," she said, stepping forward. "I don't want you to go anywhere."

"You sure, li'l lady?" he asked nervously.

Wrapping her arms around his waist, Lori nodded, blinded by her tears. Slowly and a little tentatively, Jake reached out to hold her. As he felt her lean her bruised cheek against his chest, his own grasp on his emotions began to crumble. Holding her tenderly, he breathed in the familiar floral scent of her shampoo, smelled her favourite perfume. Neither of them were able to speak. Snuggling closer to him, Lori whispered, "I love you."

Those three little words shattered Jake's remaining hold over his emotions. Pulling her close, he wept as he held her. Over and over, he repeated how sorry he was; how sorry he was for hurting her; how sorry he was for scaring her; how sorry he was for letting her down.

Suddenly, the baby gave a sharp kick, strong enough that they both felt the jolt. It was enough to bring Jake back to reality. Letting go of Lori, he dropped to his knees in front of her, placing his hands on either side of her rounded baby bump.

"And I'm sorry for scaring you too, little Power Pack. Sorrier than you can ever believe for hurting your mommy. I promise nothing like that will ever happen again. I'll never scare you, little one. Never scare your mommy either."

Gently, he kissed Lori's belly, then rested his forehead on its hard, rounded surface. Again, the baby stirred and kicked hard.

"Guess you asked for that," said Lori with a little nervous giggle.

When Jake looked up, she was smiling down at him.

"Oh, Lori, I'm so sorry," he repeated for the hundredth time.

"Sh, rock star," she said warmly. "Let's eat. I'm starving and that pizza's growing cold over there."

The empty pizza box sat on the table in front of them, as did the empty carton of cheese fries. Pouring them both another glass of apple juice, Jake sighed. As they'd eaten, neither of them had said very much.

As she picked the remains of the cheese whizz from the box, Lori asked, "Did you see the truck out front?"

"I did," said Jake with a small smile. "Isn't that the one I was admiring when we drove past the dealership?"

"It is," replied Lori. "Don't panic. Grey has the other truck, but it's in bad shape. He can explain better than me. Something about cracked engine mounts and something else was all twisted up. He's arranging to get it repaired."

"Guess I drove into the tree pretty hard," he conceded, shuddering at the memory of the black imps showering down from the tree onto the truck and the sharp jolt of the impact.

"I'm just relieved the tree survived," observed Lori. "If it had come down, it would've destroyed the roof. It's a big, old oak."

"It sure is," agreed Jake. "Maybe you should get someone out to take a look at it."

"One step ahead of you," she replied with a mischievous smile. "The tree guy's coming tomorrow after lunch to inspect it."

"I'd better finish sweeping up that glass," said Jake, getting to his feet.

Lori put out a hand to stop him, "Leave it just now. Maybe we better talk about the last few days. It's hanging like a noose over us."

Sitting back down, Jake took her hand, running his finger over her engagement ring, "Where do you want me to start?"

"With what happened in the studio?" suggested Lori, half of her not really wanting to hear what he had to say, but the other half knowing that she had to hear him out.

Slowly, Jake began to tell her his version of events. He paused several times to compose himself as the tale unfolded. At some points, his voice was so quiet that Lori struggled to hear him. When he reached the part in the story where he was in the basement, his emotions spiralled out of control once more. Talking about the visions he had believed to be real and describing his attack on them, his attack on her, tore him apart. Trying to explain to Lori that, in his head, he'd been trying to protect her when he could see how bruised she still was broke his heart.

His memory of fleeing along the beach and ultimately reaching his apartment was patchy. The hallucinations had continued to torment him and he confessed to resorting to Paul's old stash of heroin in a last ditch attempt to escape from them. Fear had driven him to it, mixed with a half realisation of what had actually happened in the basement.

"If you want me to leave. Want me to move out. I can be gone in a few minutes," he said quietly. "I wouldn't blame you if never wanted to see me ever again."

"You're not going anywhere," stated Lori firmly. "Your turn to listen."

Holding Jake's hand, Lori recalled how she had wakened with the bang of the truck hitting the tree. Choosing her words carefully, she described her version of the events in the basement. Explained about coming to on the basement floor, then about her fear and panic as she tried to work out where he would have run to. There were fresh tears in Jake's eyes when she told him of her struggle to get up to his apartment and of her fears when she found him unconscious on the floor. With tears in her own eyes, Lori told him how embarrassed and scared she had been at the medical centre and about how hard it had been to leave him there alone.

"Oh, Lori, I'm sorry," he repeated yet again. "And you're sure you want me to stay?"

"For the last time, yes," she said with a smile. A glance at her watch told her it was after ten o'clock. Her back was aching from sitting on the hard, dining room chair for so long. "Can we continue this in the sunroom? I'm sore sitting here."

"Sure," agreed Jake, coming round to help her to her feet. It didn't escape his notice that she flinched when he touched her bruised arm. "You go on through. I'll clear up that glass and bring you through some juice."

"Thanks. There's a bag of chips on the counter. Bring those too," she said as she hobbled slowly towards the sunroom.

Alone in the kitchen, Jake stood leaning on the edge of the sink, staring out the window into the dark. Suddenly, he felt mentally and physically drained. Even after hearing Lori's repeated reassurances, he couldn't quite comprehend that she wanted him home. Seeing the fading bruises on the side of her face had frightened him. Knowing that, drugged or not, he'd been capable of inflicting them tore at his very soul. He remembered all too clearly now bringing the headstock down on her back and shoulder repeatedly and shuddered to think how badly bruised they still were. With trembling hands, Jake brushed the shards of glass into the empty pizza box then made the familiar trip out to the trash can. After his week of rehab out at the remote farmhouse, the normality of the chore wasn't lost on him.

When he entered the sunroom a few minutes later, carrying two glasses of juice, Jake smiled to himself as he caught sight of Lori lying on the couch. She was propped up on a pile of pillows and her eyes were closed.

"You asleep, li'l lady?" he asked softly as he set the glasses down on the occasional table beside the couch.

"Not quite," she replied with a sleepy smile. "Come and sit down. Tell me about where you've been for the past week. No one would tell me where you were."

"Honest answer," confessed Jake, sitting cross-legged on the floor in front of her. "I'm not entirely sure."

Lori giggled.

"When Jethro took me out of the hospital, I didn't care where we went," admitted Jake slowly, running his hand nervously through his hair. "I didn't take note of where he took me. We drove for hours. Five, maybe six hours. Somewhere in northern Pennsylvania. Out in the middle of nowhere. It was more like a retreat than rehab. An old farmhouse run by an amazing couple. Ella and her husband, Frank. You'd have liked them."

"So, what did you have to do all week?"

With a sigh, Jake said, "A bit of everything. For the first half of the week there were three other folk staying. We attended lectures, some group sessions where we were encouraged to open up about stuff. There was a lot of one on one sessions. CBT kind of approach to reaffirm coping mechanisms. And a shit load of farm chores."

"Farm chores?" echoed Lori curiously. "You don't look like a farm hand to me."

"They had some cattle. Ella kept chickens and horses. My morning chore was to muck out the horse stalls. All very menial tasks aimed to bring you back to basics."

"Did it help?"

Jake nodded, then said with a grin, "Was just the kick in the ass I needed."

"Pardon?"

"Ella's mare, Molly, kicked me square on the butt one morning.

Sent me sprawling headlong into a pile of shitty straw. It was the sharp reminder that I needed at the time. Left one hell of a bruise," he explained, still aware of the tender spot below his butt cheek. Realising he had no right to complain about bruises, he bowed his head feeling embarrassed.

Smiling at the mental picture of Jake face down in a horse stall, Lori reached out to touch his shoulder, "It's going to be alright, isn't it?"

"Lori," he began, placing his hand on top of hers. "I hope so, but I don't know. It's up to you. Do you want it to be ok? Want us to be ok? To be together?"

"Of course!" she declared emphatically. "What Salazar did was despicable! The consequences have put us both through hell but we'll get through this. Get through it together."

"After what I did to you, how can you lie there and say that?" asked Jake quietly. "How can you even bear to look at me?"

"Because that monster in the basement wasn't really you. From what you've said and what Jethro and the doctor told me, you were as scared as I was. Maybe more so. The only monster in all of this is Salazar Mendes."

Jake flinched at the mention of his fallen idol's name. Staring down at the floor, he finally asked, "What happened after I left JJL?"

"I'm not too sure," began Lori slowly. "Salazar ran off. Garrett spent all night searching the woods out the back for him. Eventually, he found him and took him back to New York. I've not spoken to Garrett. I've not really spoken to anyone. I did hear from Jim that Salazar's been checked into a secure facility. The Delaware police are waiting to get authority to speak to him."

"Did you have to speak to them?"

"Who? The police?"

Jake nodded, dreading the answer.

"I refused," whispered Lori. "Paul was with me at the hospital. He called Maddy and, as far as I know, she dealt with it all."

"Is Paul in trouble over the drugs at the apartment?"

Lori shook her head. "I'm not sure the ins and outs of it all. No one's been telling me much. I know he was interviewed, but he wasn't charged with anything due to lack of evidence."

"But the foil and the needle?"

"Apparently were never found," replied Lori. "As I said, no one's told me anything. They've closed ranks to protect me. Kola brought my car back here. If I had to guess, I'd say you have her to thank."

"Kola?"

Lori nodded, "While Paul was with me at Beebe, Grey and Kola began the tidy up. Grey cleared up here and, I'm guessing, Kola cleaned up the apartment."

"And the basement?" asked Jake, feeling his stomach lurch at the memories of trashing the rehearsal space.

"More or less as good as new," revealed Lori. "The band's gear has all been replaced. Insurance is taking care of that. Bannister's been fixed." She paused, then added, "I've only been down there once since."

"Sorry," whispered Jake, his emotions tumbling into a fresh cycle of turmoil.

"Wasn't easy," confessed Lori with a weak smile. "But there's nothing to see. No obvious reminders."

"Guess I need to cross that bridge myself," sighed Jake, dreading the very thought.

"Yes, but not tonight," replied Lori with a yawn. "It's late. Baby and I are tired. It's time for bed."

"You sure about this?"

"Yes," she stated firmly as she levered herself into a sitting position. "It's been a long day for both of us. Bedtime, rock star."

"I'll be down in a minute," promised Jake, stalling for time.

After Lori left the sunroom, Jake sat on alone for a few minutes. He could hear the familiar noises of the house. The creak as Lori opened the en suite door. The clanking of the pipes as she ran the water. Beautiful, comforting sounds to his ears. Sitting on the oriental rug, he reflected on the past few hours. Countless times during the week, he'd tried to imagine how things would be when he came back to the beach house. Nothing had come close to the reality of it all. The reality had been better than he could ever have dared to believe.

Stifling a yawn, he got stiffly to his feet, switched off the lamp and wandered slowly through the house. He paused beside the door to the basement, a chill running through him. For a split second, he contemplated opening the door, but the fear of facing it again stopped him. There was plenty time to overcome that hurdle.

When he entered the bedroom, Lori was just coming out of the bathroom. She had changed into her pyjamas, the short sleeves of the top revealing the bruises on her arms. Seeing her arms still so discoloured, Jake paled visibly.

"Oh, Lori," he breathed, his voice filled with remorse. "Your arm…"

"Jake, stop," she said firmly. "They're only bruises. Fading bruises. I'm fine."

"But they're bruises I caused."

Realising there was only one way to get everything out in the open once and for all, Lori slipped the T-shirt top over her head, tossing it onto the bed. Next, she lowered the soft waistband of her yoga pants. Moving to stand directly in front of him, she said calmly, "Look at me, Jake."

Staring at his feet, he replied, "I can't."

"Yes, you can," stated Lori, reaching out to touch his arm. "And once you have, then that's it. Nothing else to see. Nothing else to come between us."

With his heart pounding in his chest, Jake raised his head to look at his beautiful, bruised, pregnant wife. She had turned so that she was side on to him, confronting him with the full extent of the fading injuries. Reaching out with a trembling hand, Jake traced the outline of the bruises on her arm, her shoulder, across her back and down her ribs. He expected her to flinch at his touch; she didn't. Tentatively, he stepped forward and kissed the vivid bruise on her cheek. Wrapping her in his arms, he buried his face in her neck, fresh tears mingling with her golden blonde hair.

"It's going to be alright," promised Lori softly as she welcomed his arms around her.

"How can you ever forgive me for this? I can still see the…"

"Sh."

"But, Lori," began Jake.

"No buts," cautioned Lori. "No secrets. No hiding from what happened. No running from what we've both been through. We need to be totally honest with each other. Yes, you hurt me. Yes, you scared the crap out of me. Twice."

"Twice?" echoed Jake, stepping back to look her in the eye.

"Yes, twice. The first time in the basement and the second time in your apartment," revealed Lori, reaching for her discarded top. She pulled it roughly over her head, then added, "I thought you were dead."

"I'm guessing round about then I was wishing I was," sighed Jake wearily.

During the night, the storm picked up again. Jake lay awake listening to the wind swirling round the house. He could hear things being blown about outside. Beside him, Lori lay curled on her side, snoring softly, her hair spread over the pillow. Despite having felt so tired when they had gone to bed, Jake was wide awake. He had no idea what time it was. In the dark, he couldn't see Lori's old fashioned alarm clock and he still didn't have either his watch or his phone. It dawned on him that he still had no idea where they were. He assumed Jethro must have them. Fingering a strand of Lori's silky, soft hair, he smiled. For the first time since his world had been turned upside down, he allowed himself to believe that everything was going to be alright. In his heart, he knew some wounds were going to take time. There were still many hurdles to overcome, including seeing his band mates. He had little or no idea how they were going to treat him. With a wry smile, Jake could hear the dressing down Maddy was likely to give him. On the drive back to the beach, Jethro had already warned him that she was furious with him. Then there was the unfinished work out at JJL. What was to happen with it?

As the first light of dawn streaked across the sky, Jake was still lying wide awake. At his side, Lori remained sound asleep, with her hand protectively over her baby bump. During the night, as he'd lain watching her, she had been restless, twitching as though bad dreams were tormenting her sleep. Taking care not to make any noise, Jake slowly got up out of bed, fetched his running gear and tiptoed out of the room.

Dressed in his long running tights and winter zip through top, Jake pulled on his beanie, guessing it would be cold down on the beach. Almost as an afterthought, he left a note on the kitchen table for Lori saying when he had left, the direction he was heading and when he expected to be back. The last thing he needed was for her to waken, find him gone and panic that he'd left during the night.

The storm had blown piles of seaweed and ocean debris up onto the shore. In the early morning light, seabirds were picking through the seaweed, oblivious to Jake running past them. He loped along the wet sand at a leisurely pace, intending it to be a long, easy run down to the state park boundary. It felt good to have his lungs filled with sea air again. With each long, easy stride, Jake felt some of the weight of his world lift from him.

A fresh pot of coffee and a glass of water were waiting for him when he returned to the house. On the kitchen table sat his wallet, watch and cell phone. From the depths of the house, he could hear Lori in the shower. Hauling off his beanie, Jake laid it on the table beside his phone. He tested the small, black handset and, as expected, discovered its battery was flat. Wondering where his charger was, Jake turned his attention to the glass of water. Once he'd refilled it and downed a second glass, he poured himself a coffee. Reaching into the refrigerator for the half and half, he spotted a phone charger on top of the refrigerator.

Within a few moments, he was sitting at the table with his coffee, listening to his phone buzz itself senseless with an endless stream of messages rattling into it.

"Morning," said Lori as she appeared in the kitchen behind him. "Found your phone I hear."

"Yeah. Where was it?"

"Basement," she replied. "I fetched it for you before I jumped in the shower. Thought that might make things a bit easier. I brought your book bag up too. It's in the sunroom."

"Thank you," said Jake with a relieved sigh. "Don't know if I can face going down there yet."

"One step at a time."

"What's the next step?" he asked as she poured herself a coffee.

"A shower. You smell bad!" laughed Lori as she wrinkled her nose. "Then you can make breakfast."

"Sounds like an easy start."

When Jake padded down the hallway towards the kitchen, he could hear Lori talking on the phone. She smiled at him as entered the room and mouthed "Maddy", whilst pointing at the phone. Nodding, he busied himself at the stove making pancakes and bacon. Eventually, Lori managed to end the call, promising faithfully to call her friend the following day.

"Is the boss still mad at me?" asked Jake as he set a plate of food down in front of her.

"Not as a mad as she was," admitted Lori, reaching for the maple syrup. "Jethro's set her straight on a few points. He's told her to give you some space for a day or two."

"How long till she gets here?" he joked, only half in jest.

"You're safe for today," promised Lori. "However, she did ask me to remind you that the Silver Lake rehearsals are due to start this week."

Without replying, Jake turned back to the stove.

"Jake," began Lori softly. "One step at a time remember. You've plenty of time on that one."

"I guess," he sighed, pouring more pancake batter into the pan.

"Can I make a suggestion?"

"Go for it."

"I've a couple of hours work to do this morning. Why don't you go for a drive? Try out the new truck. See where the mood takes you."

"Maybe," nodded Jake, half of him not wanting to leave the house and face the world.

"You could pick up some groceries too," suggested Lori hopefully. "I'd go myself, but I'm under strict orders from Maddy and Jethro to lay low for a few more days."

"Write me a list and I'll see what I can do," said Jake. "No promises though."

"One step at a time. Go to the store over in Lewes or head up to Milford if it's easier."

"Perhaps."

Climbing into the cab of the truck, the first thing to strike Jake was the smell of leather. His old truck hadn't had leather upholstery. Adjusting the seat and the mirrors to the correct angle, Jake noted that it was a lot more luxurious than its predecessor. The stereo was an upgraded model and it had built in satellite navigation. A far cry from the old dog-eared copy of the AAA map book that had lived in the glove compartment in his old truck. With a smile, he noted it was an automatic. Lori never had got to grips with the stick shift gearbox.

Driving slowly past the lake towards town, Jake could already feel himself falling in love with his new ride. He'd had his previous truck for a long time, driven almost two hundred thousand miles in it over the years and hoped that it could be fixed but he acknowledged that a new truck was a new start. No demons or ghosts in this one.

On his way back from the Giant, Jake decided, on a whim, to head into Rehoboth and pick up some steak sandwiches for lunch. As he approached Danny's tattoo parlour, he spotted a parking space and, on a second whim, decided to pull over.

Hearing the gentle tinkling of the wind chime above the door, Danny stepped out from the store room cum office.

"Good morning! My favourite celebrity client come to call!" he declared theatrically.

"Cut the crap, Dan," said Jake with a grin as he stuffed his truck keys in his pocket. "How's business?"

"Quiet today. I had a full sleeve scheduled, but the darling girl cancelled first thing."

"Looking for something to ink to pass the time?"

"I've always got time to ink you, Jake," replied the small man, his eyes gleaming mischievously.

"Well, today's your lucky day," stated Jake. "I'm after something simple."

"What?"

"A horseshoe."

"Should I ask why?" enquired Danny, somewhat surprised by the request.

"Best not to," replied Jake quietly.

"OK. Step this way and I'll show you the selection I've done before. Unless you've brought a design with you?"

"No," said Jake, shaking his head. "Bit of a spur of the moment decision."

Jake browsed through more images of horseshoes than he could ever have imagined before settling on a simple, slightly geometric, three-dimensional design.

"Nice," complimented the ink artist. "Should only take a couple of hours. Do you want anything else added to it?"

"No," said Jake calmly. "Just the horseshoe."

"And where may I ask is it to go?"

"You're going to fucking love this," muttered Jake before saying, "Right butt cheek. But be careful, Dan. It's still bruised around there."

"Ah, my day is made!" laughed Danny, reaching for a pair of latex gloves. "Go and make yourself comfortable in the cubicle."

"And before you ask," said Jake, "Absolutely fuck all chance of photographing this one!"

When the tattoo artist entered the cubicle, he suggested to Jake that he stand and bend over rather than lie on the table.

"That's some bruise," commented Danny as he swabbed the area with witch hazel. "You sure about this? It'll hurt."

"I'm sure."

"How'd you even get a bruise like that? Looks nasty."

"A horse kicked me," explained Jake. "Now, no more questions, please, Dan."

For almost two hours, the diminutive artist worked silently, the only noise in the tattoo parlour being the buzz of his gun. Despite the bruising, he skilfully shaded the design and kept the lines precise. Having wiped it down with a hot towel, he held the mirror for Jake to approve the design.

"Perfect as ever, Dan. Thanks."

"I never dreamed that you'd allow me the privilege of inking your posterior," teased Danny as he carefully taped a dressing over the fresh design.

"That makes two of us," commented Jake wryly, pulling his jeans back on slowly over the new tattoo.

With Jake out of the house, Lori struggled to concentrate on the design in front of her. Had it been too soon to suggest he go out? Had she been too firm with him? Was he ok? Her anxiety was picked up by the baby who decided to kick and squirm relentlessly. After half an hour, Lori gave in and got up to fetch a glass of juice, hoping that if she moved about the baby would settle. When she returned to her drawing board, she reconnected with the design and was soon absorbed in the detail of it. The project was due to be submitted at the end of the week, but meeting the deadline was going to be tight. Deciding to err on the side of caution, she paused to email Jason to request an extension of a further week. Knowing what a stickler for scheduling and deadlines that the Englishman was, she expected him to immediately decline her request. A few minutes later, a soft ping from her laptop alerted her to a reply. Much to her amazement, Jason had agreed to the extension. As she read his brief message, Lori felt a weight lift off her shoulders.

A glance at her phone told her it was after one thirty and still no sign of Jake returning. His phone was still charging in the kitchen and she had no idea where he was and no way to contact him. She began to panic that something had happened to him. He'd been gone for over three hours.

Suddenly, she heard the truck pull up outside and the cab door slam.

"Lori!" came the familiar call from the kitchen a few seconds later. "Lunch!"

As quickly as she could, Lori hurried through from the study.

"Hi. I was getting worried about you," she called as she limped in.

"Sorry," he apologised sheepishly. "Will a steak sandwich make up for it?"

"Depends on what you are making amends for," she teased as she sat at the table. Wrinkling her nose at a familiar smell of witch hazel, she added, "Do you have a fresh sin to confess, rock star?"

"Pardon?" asked Jake, looking at her anxiously. "Why?"

"Relax," said Lori warmly, noting the worried look in his eyes. "I'm playing with you. Did you drop in on Danny when you were out?"

Passing her a sandwich, Jake nodded.

"And?" she prompted.

"And I made his day," confessed Jake, finally smiling and melting the worried look.

"You did? How?"

"Let him ink my butt cheek."

Giggling helplessly, Lori agreed that that would've made the tattoo artist's day, maybe even his year. When she'd composed herself, Lori asked what he'd had done.

"A reminder of the last ten days," Jake replied softly. "A reminder of the kick in the ass that I got. I asked him to ink a horseshoe over the bruise where the horse kicked me."

"You can show me later," said Lori with a smile. "Don't want you getting caught with your pants down. The tree guy's due any minute."

As they ate their lunch, Lori filled Jake in on her morning and the progress that she'd made. When she explained about getting an extension on her deadline without any challenges, Jake commented, "Guess Jason's someone else I need to face sooner or later. How much does he know?"

"I've no idea. I've not spoken to him. Not told him anything. Ask Jethro or Maddy," replied Lori. "Did you check your messages yet? Your phone buzzed a few times while you were out."

"Not yet," murmured Jake, gazing down onto his empty plate. "Maybe later."

"Well, Jethro messaged me. Says he needs to talk to you. He'll be over for dinner later," announced Lori quietly.

With a sigh, Jake said, "He's the one person I can't hide from. One of the post rehab conditions is that I check in with him daily for the first month. I need to meet with him face to face weekly too. If I miss a meeting, I need to go back there for at least a month. No arguments. And I've no intentions of going back."

"Jake, you don't need to hide from anyone," whispered Lori, reaching out to take his hand. "Everyone understands. They know what happened. Maybe it would be better to see them all?"

"Not yet," answered Jake instantly. "I need to get my head round being back here. Need the time with you. I just need a few days."

"Ok, but the longer you wait, the harder it will get."

"I know. I know."

After the tree surgeon left, giving the old, oak tree a clean bill of health, Jake lifted his cell phone and wandered down to the bedroom to listen to and read the various messages that had piled up over the past week or so. Lori had returned to work on her commission and he didn't want to disturb her. Part of him needed to be alone when he checked the phone, unsure of how he would react to what he might find on it. For a brief second he had contemplated going down to the basement. He had got as far as putting his hand on the door handle, then immediately changed his mind. Those ghosts could wait a while longer.

Lying down on the bed, Jake opted to listen to his voicemails first. There weren't as many of them as he'd thought there might be. As he'd expected, several were from Dr Marrs and Garrett from the Thursday night, then there were a couple from Lori obviously from the Friday morning at some point. There were no more until Sunday when Paul had left a few messages asking him to call when he could. The last one was from less than an hour before. It was Garrett asking him to call him as soon as he got the message. Without a second thought, Jake deleted them all.

He scanned through the text messages until he reached one that made his blood run cold. It was from Salazar. "Sorry will never be enough. Finish the record. I'm finished. Sal."

It took Jake all of his will power not to smash the phone into a million pieces. With a deep breath, he deleted all the messages and switched his phone off.

With his anger at Salazar's message still coursing through him, Jake lay back, staring up at the ceiling. Finish the record! Could he? Should he? Why should he? Even through his fury, Jake conceded it was a great record that deserved to be heard someday. There was only that one vocal track left to record….

The thought hung in the air.

The next thing Jake knew, he was wakening with a start. He had dozed off as he had relaxed on the bed, then fallen into a nightmare filled sleep. As he woke, the last thing he recalled was being in a studio to record vocals but couldn't sing. Whenever he tried to start the song, a small, croaky squeak came out. A cold sweat washed over him as he shivered at the memory. Around him the bedroom was in darkness. Having lost all track of time, Jake reached for his phone and switched it on. The screen lit up and read "6:15". In his hand, the phone buzzed to alert him to a fresh text message. It was from Jethro. "Will be with you at 6. Therapy meeting, then dinner. No debate. Jethro."

Rubbing his eyes, Jake sat up with a yawn, stuffed his phone into his pocket and padded down the hall towards the kitchen.

"Good evening, Jake," greeted Jethro warmly as he stepped into the brightly lit kitchen. "You're late. Meeting was scheduled for six."

"No change there," joked Jake with a sleepy smile. "Sorry. I must've fallen asleep."

"And you probably needed it," agreed the older man wisely. "As I hear it, you didn't sleep too well last week."

"I didn't," conceded Jake.

Over at the stove, Lori, who was stirring a pot of Bolognese added, "And you never slept last night either."

"How long until we eat, princess?" asked Jethro, getting up from his seat at the table.

"How long do you need? I can slow this down if you need some time."

"Give us an hour if you can," suggested Jethro with a glance at Jake. "I've some formalities to go through so this might take longer than your usual weekly session will. It's up to you really how long each meeting lasts."

"Have you done this before?" asked Jake, fetching himself a glass of water.

"Many times over the past few years," revealed the band's manager. "While I stayed longer at the farm than most, Frank took me through some counselling training. I took a few classes after that. Frank was my meeting buddy while I focussed on staying sober for the first three years."

"Guess we all need someone," sighed Jake, running his fingers nervously through his hair.

"That we do, son," agreed Jethro with a smile. "Let's head downstairs. Keep ourselves out of your lovely wife's way."

"What about the sunroom?" suggested Jake, feeling a wave of panic welling up inside him. "Or the lounge room?"

"No, Jake," said the older man calmly. "Call it lesson one. We're going downstairs."

Before Jake could argue, Jethro had walked through and opened the door to the basement.

"After you, Jake," he said, stepping aside.

"Jethro," began the trembling musician as he reached the top step, "I can't. I can't go down there."

"Yes, you can, son," countered Jethro firmly. "All the lights are on. I'm right behind you. Now, head down those steps."

Slowly, his legs trembling beneath him, Jake descended the steep staircase. When he reached the bottom step, he stopped and gazed round the basement. Everything was back in its correct positions. In fact, the basement rehearsal space had never looked more clean and organised. Gone were the remnants of Paul's green, practice kit. Instead a brand new black kit sat in its place. The guitar stands were occupied with identical instruments and despite himself, Jake tried to figure out which ones were the originals and which ones were new.

He closed his eyes. Instantaneously, memories of the attack on the green eyed, cloaked demon then on the witch came flooding back. Blow by blow, he relived the entire scene in his mind. His knees buckled, forcing him to sit down hard on the wooden step, burying his face in his hands.

"You ok, son?" asked Jethro, taking a seat a couple of steps above him. "Take your time. Breathe."

"I could've killed her," said Jake, his voice cracking with the fresh, raw emotions he was experiencing. "You've seen her. I've no idea how she's survived. No idea how she can even bear the sight of me."

"She loves you. Your wife is a tough cookie. Perhaps, subconsciously, you knew it was a hallucination in front of you. Maybe you didn't attack Lori with as much force as your mind's telling you that you did."

"Jethro, I hit her hard," confessed Jake. "She's still got the impression of the machine heads all down her back. Row after row of them."

Upstairs in the kitchen, Lori kept herself busy while the guys were down in the basement. When Jethro had arrived, she'd explained to him that Jake hadn't been able to face going back down there. She knew he had chosen to force Jake's hand, but she now felt guilty about it. Her husband had looked so scared as he'd left the kitchen. Having laid the table, Lori turned the heat off below the pot of Bolognese and headed through to the sunroom to catch up on the TV news until it was time to resume cooking dinner.

Stretching out on the couch, she realised just how sore and tired she was. After sitting at her drawing board for so long, her back was aching, as was her pelvis. Mentally, she felt drained. Once she was comfortable and relaxed, the baby decided it was playtime, beginning to wriggle and kick. Gently, Lori rubbed her swollen belly, wincing occasionally as a sharp kick assaulted her tender ribcage.

The news programme had finished and there was still no sign of the basement door opening. Half-heartedly, Lori skipped through the channels, finally settling on one of the music channels, who were showing a documentary about the history of Hollywood's Sunset Strip and its infamous night clubs. In the past, she had visited them all and soon found herself smiling at the memories the old footage evoked. Just as she was getting caught up in the nostalgia trip, Lori heard the creak of the basement door opening.

"Lori," called Jake as he closed the door over.

"In the sunroom," she called back.

"Want me to finish off dinner?" he offered.

"No, it's ok," she assured him as she switched off the TV. "It's all under control. Give me five minutes to boil the noodles. Where's Jethro?"

"Making an urgent call," explained Jake.

"You ok after being down there?" asked Lori softly, reaching out to hug him.

"Yes and no," he replied, wrapping his arms around her. "Flashbacks were more vivid. A few more memories came crashing back in. I've worked some of them through with Jethro. I can't shift some of the images. It's like they're imprinted on the inside of my brain."

"It's just going to take time," she soothed as she snuggled into his chest. Through his T-shirt she could hear his heart pounding. "Maybe you should try working it out through your music. Write about it a bit."

"That's what Jethro suggested," admitted Jake with a heavy sigh. "I made a start on that while I was at the farm. Not much, but a start."

"One step at a time," reminded Lori, hugging him tight.

Dinner was ready to be served by the time Silver Lake's manager emerged from the depths of the basement. From the serious look on his face, Lori gauged that his call hadn't gone smoothly. Conversation over their meal centred on the documentary that Lori said she had been watching. After some coaxing from Jethro, she joined him in reminiscing about some of the parties they had attended. The band's manager regaled them with stories about some of the bands that he had managed on the West Coast in the dim and distant past. It warmed Lori's heart to see her husband gradually relax and join in with their laughter. By the time their plates were empty, the atmosphere felt normal as though nothing untoward had happened.

"Coffee, Jethro?" suggested Lori as she rose to clear away the plates.

"No, thank you, princess. I need to get back out to JJL. I'm staying with Jim for a while, but we have some business to discuss tonight," he replied, helping her to gather the plates.

"Will there be room in the JJL house for you when the Weigh Station guys arrive?" asked Lori, remembering that recording for the charity album was due to start within a couple of weeks.

"No," he said as they entered the kitchen. "I'll de-camp to Maddison's or a hotel."

"You're more than welcome here," Lori offered warmly.

"Thank you, but you have enough on your plate without me in your guest room," he assured her then very quietly added, "I need a word where Jake won't hear us."

Nodding, Lori said," Can you do me a favour and help me out with the trash?"

"Of course," he replied, picking up on her lead.

Closing the back door behind them, Lori led the way round the side of the house to the trash cans, safely out of range of Jake's hearing.

"What's wrong?" asked Lori, dumping the plastic bag into the trash can.

"I spoke to Garrett before dinner. There's no easy way to say this," began the older man solemnly. "The police interviewed Salazar yesterday afternoon about the incident at JJL. His psychiatrist terminated the interview before he was formally charged with anything."

"And?" interrupted Lori anxiously.

"And he was found dead this morning. He hanged himself," revealed Jethro calmly. "I didn't want to be the one to tell Jake. I'm not sure the boy's ready to handle that."

"You're right. He's not. I'll tell him," offered Lori. "Though Lord knows how. Poor Garrett. He must be a mess."

"He is. Said he'd tried to reach Jake earlier. Wanted to know if he'd heard from Salazar."

"If he has then he hasn't told me."

"Are you sure you're alright to deal with this?" checked Jethro, his voice filled with concern for her. "You've been through hell recently too."

"I'd rather be the one to tell him, but I might wait a day or so. I'll play it by ear."

"As long as you're sure," said Jethro. He paused, then declared, "I'd better get going. Jim wants to talk about the record that Sal and Jake were working on. Garrett wants it finished and released."

"Is there much left to do to finish it?"

"There's one vocal track left to record according to Jim," revealed Jethro. "Let me talk to him though before you mention that to the boy. I'll call you tomorrow."

"Ok. If you speak to Garrett, please pass on my sympathies. I'll call him if I can," said Lori, turning to go back indoors.

"Lori," called Jethro softly. "Look after him. He's fragile, but he'll be fine. He just needs time and you."

With a wave, Lori headed back inside.

Stepping back into the warmth of the kitchen, she could hear Jake playing his acoustic guitar through in the lounge. It was the first music she'd heard him play since he came home. There was an air of melancholy about the melody that was filtering through the house. It wasn't a song she was familiar with but, as she stood in the kitchen listening, she was slowly falling in love with it. Suddenly, Jake stopped playing, then began the song again from the beginning, only this time he began to sing a sad vocal track, almost mournful but honest. Listening to the words. Lori became aware of the lump filling her throat. With unshed tears glistening in her eyes, she heard Jake pour his heart into the song, pour his feelings of regret and fear into the lyrics. He sang a surprisingly catchy, slow chorus about "Mister Man having a hand in the game. Mister Man staking his claim." Not wanting to interrupt, Lori waited in the kitchen until Jake stopped and moved on to a different melody, again one unfamiliar to her. Realising that she couldn't stay there all night, Lori wandered through to the lounge to join him.

"Hey, rock star," she said as she sat on the cream leather couch. "Don't recognise that one."

"Something new," replied Jake as he continued to pick out the melody on his favourite acoustic guitar. "Has Jethro left?"

"Yes. He was in a hurry to get back out to JJL," said Lori, wriggling as she tried to get herself into a comfortable position.

"You ok?" asked Jake, picking up on her discomfort.

"I'll be fine once this little Power Pack moves over a bit," she admitted as the baby kicked her sharply. Rubbing the side of her bump, she looked at Jake and asked simply, "Will you play for me? I've missed hearing your music."

Closing his eyes, Jake began to play the tormented tragic melody that she had listened to from the kitchen. His voice wavered and faltered on some of the lines, but, determined to retain control over his emotions, Jake made it through to the end of the song.

"Well?" he asked when the song was over.

"That's a powerful one," replied Lori, smiling over at him proudly. "Very emotional. Will it become a Silver Lake song or stay a Jake song?"

"I don't know," he said, shrugging his shoulders. "That depends on the rest of them. Depends on if they still want me around after all that's happened."

"Does it have a name?"

"Mister Man," revealed Jake quietly. "I wrote the lyrics the night after the horse kicked me in the ass. Wrote it from her disapproving stance."

"Well, I don't disapprove of it."

"Thanks," he whispered, flashing her a sad smile. "I'm still working on lyrics for the second one. Have a listen and see what this conjures up to you."

Gradually, as Jake played for her, another piece of the puzzle fell back into place; another step towards restoring normality between them. The second melody was more upbeat and distinctly more positive than Mister Man but neither of them could connect with its theme. The lyrics remained hidden.

"They'll come in their own good time," said Lori, trying to stifle a yawn. "Time for bed, rock star."

"I'll be through in a minute," promised Jake as he laid his guitar back in its case. "Let me take this gear downstairs first."

Without a second thought, Jake lifted the guitar cases that had been left in the lounge and took them down to the basement. Flicking on the lights, he walked down the stairs, feeling his heart pounding hard in his chest. During his meeting with Jethro, the older man had said that he had to try to resume his normal life and not dwell on the "what ifs" and not to relive the trauma of it all repeatedly. He suggested that he move forward one step at a time, but that being able to go down into the basement was a focus for the next week. Once he could come and go without too much anxiety, he was to work at building up the length of time he could spend down there. Focussing on keeping his breathing calm and trying to shut out the memories screaming in his head, Jake carefully put the guitars back in their rightful places. When the last one was back on the rack, he turned on his heel and bounded back upstairs, relieved to be back in the warmth of the house.

Deciding that an early morning run might help to clear his mind after yet another restless night, Jake headed out shortly after seven on Wednesday morning. A bitterly, cold wind was blowing down the beach. He could still feel the effects of his ten mile run in his legs so he set off at a slower pace, opting to head towards Rehoboth for a change. Maintaining a leisurely pace, he ran up as far as the bath house to the north of the town, then turned for home. The icy wind was blowing straight in his face, catching his breath as he pounded along the sand.

The chill was certainly clearing his mind. In an effort to shut out the biting cold, Jake ran over the melody line for the song with no lyrics, trying to connect in his mind with the song's story. As he drew level with the end of Rehoboth Avenue, he was re-writing the music in his mind, adding an edge of darkness to it. With a more menacing feel to the music, lyrics about the demons from his hallucination began to emerge.

The fronts of his thighs were screaming in agony when he eventually reached the house. Desperate for a hot shower, Jake stamped the sand off his feet on the doorstep and entered the house through the back door. Immediately, a wave of warmth engulfed him; immediately, he heard voices in the kitchen. Grey was sitting at the table having breakfast.

"Good morning, Mr Power," he called out warmly.

"Morning," said Jake, still gasping for breath. Pouring himself a glass of water, he added, "It's fucking freezing out there. Arctic blast coming in off the ocean."

"Jump in the shower and I'll make you some breakfast," suggested Lori caringly.

"Can I get seconds?" asked Grey with a grin. "You make the best scrambled eggs ever."

"Flatterer," teased Lori with a giggle.

"Give me ten minutes," said Jake, pulling off his beanie and hauling the ponytail band from his long, tangled hair. "I need to

302

thaw out first."

As he emerged from the bedroom, wet hair hanging around his shoulders, Jake inhaled the aroma of bacon mixed with freshly brewed coffee. He paused part way down the hall as a realisation hit him. For the first time in almost two weeks, he felt calm and relaxed.

Setting a plate of bacon and scrambled eggs down in front of each of the musicians, Lori said, "I hope you left me some hot water, rock star."

"Should be plenty," said Jake, smiling at her.

"There better be," she cautioned playfully. "Baby and I don't like cold showers."

The two members of Silver Lake sat eating for a few minutes before Jake finally broke the deafening silence, "Go on. Yell at me. Get it over and done with."

"I wasn't planning on it," commented Grey between mouthfuls. "You weren't?"

"No," said the bass player. "I can't speak for Rich. He was pretty mad at you when I spoke to him on Sunday. Paul and I had a long talk with Jethro. I'm not mad at you. I was. When I saw the mess you'd made of Lori, I could've killed you. She spoke to me too. Calmed me down."

"No one regrets it more than me," confessed Jake, staring down at his plate. "I never want to put her or anyone else through that hell. I never want to go back there."

"Why did you run for your apartment?" asked Grey, curiosity getting the better of him. "Were you looking for the drugs?"

"No," replied Jake, shaking his head. "I wanted to steer the demons away from here. Wanted to keep Lori safe. I didn't want them to hurt her..."

"And the smack?"

"I needed to end the hallucination. I needed to be free of the demons. I wasn't thinking straight. I was fucked up before I shot it up. I don't really remember taking it. I just knew the demons shrank back into the shadows. It all went dark. Next thing I remember is waking up in the hospital with Jethro there."

Nodding, Grey acknowledged, "That's more or less what Jethro said. He lectured us all while you were away. Told us to go easy on you. Said you weren't entirely to blame. Explained what that bastard Mendes did to you. Hope he rots in hell."

"Part of me wants him to tell me why," sighed Jake, running his hand through his damp hair. "Hear him explain it to me. He'd apparently been slipping me that shit all week."

"Well, you'll never hear now."

"Why?"

"Jake, the bastard's dead. Hanged himself. Didn't you know?" revealed Grey, genuinely surprised.

"No. I didn't know," admitted Jake quietly. "Let me guess, Jethro told Lori when he was here the other night. She's tried to protect me from it until she thought I was ready." He paused, feeling his emotions beginning to slip into an abyss. Closing his eyes, he took half a dozen long, slow, deep breaths, regrouped his thoughts as he'd been taught during the rehab sessions then continued, "I always knew she was incredible. Knew she was stronger than she appears. I have no idea how she's made it through the last couple of weeks. The very fact she protected the baby from me. Grey, I nearly killed her. I could've lost her forever because of him….."

Seeing that his friend was struggling to remain composed, Grey said, "But you didn't and you haven't."

"How do we move on from this fuck up?" asked Jake, praying that his friend had the answers.

"We do what we do best, Mr Power," stated Grey with a reassuring smile. "We stick together. We play music. We've a record to write, remember?"

"Is it really that easy?"

"It's worth a shot," said the bass player, then changing tack added, "And about your truck. It's pretty much fucked. I know Lori said to repair it at any cost, but what do you want to do with it?"

"There's a lot of Silver Lake history in that truck," declared Jake wistfully. "But, if I'm being brutally honest, after everything that's happened, I don't want to see it ever again. It's twenty years old almost. Junk it."

"You sure?"

Jake nodded.

"If you're sure. Think about it until the weekend. If you still want to junk it, then we can tow it out to the wrecker's yard in Lincoln."

"Ok, I'll think about it."

"Now, what about band rehearsal?" asked Grey calmly. "You feeling up to playing?"

The question hung in the air.

"When?"

"How about Friday? Give you another couple of days to sort things out in your head," suggested Grey hopefully.

"Friday sounds good. Where? Here?"

"It'll need to be. JJL is booked out this week. Both studios," said Grey. "I already checked."

"Alright. Here on Friday," agreed Jake, his stomach already churning. "But I'm not giving any guarantees about how long I can be downstairs for. There's a lot of ghosts and shit still haunting me down there."

"I hear you. We'll go at your pace. No pressure. Let's just collect our thoughts with where we're at for the new record and take it from there."

"Works for me."

"Right I'd better make tracks. I've to take a run out to JJL to help Kola. She called first thing. Something loose on her bike."

"See you Friday then."

After Grey left, Jake went back down to the bedroom in search of Lori. He'd meant it when he said that he understood why she hadn't told him about Salazar's death, but he needed her to know he knew. When he walked into the bedroom, Lori was pulling her T-shirt on over her head. She had her back to him. He could still see the yellow bruises lining her back and large marks on her arms. The bruising to her face was more or less gone. Hearing his footsteps, she turned to face him. For a moment, Jake saw her perfectly silhouetted and marvelled at the perfection of her pregnant body. With her rapidly growing belly, she looked radiant.

"Have I told you how beautiful you are, li'l lady?" he said softly as he wrapped his arms around her. "Pregnancy suits you. You're beautiful."

"You need to get your eyes checked," giggled Lori. "I'm going to be huge before this little one arrives. I'm scared to think how big

I'll be by the time he or she arrives."

"When do you next go to the hospital for a check-up?" he asked, placing a hand on her firm baby bump.

"Two weeks today," she replied. "They've scheduled a scan for twenty eight weeks. I had one in the emergency room when they checked me over. The doctor commented then that this little one isn't so little."

"I'm just relieved that I never hurt our baby," whispered Jake hoarsely. Pulling her close, he buried his face in her neck, kissing her gently. "Grey told me about Salazar."

"Oh!"

"It's ok. I know you knew. I get why you never said."

"I just couldn't find the right time or the right words. I'm sorry," she apologised quietly.

"I understand. I'm not sure how I feel about it all. I was hoping for some answers from him when I felt ready to hear them. Guess I'll never know, unless Garrett can fill me in."

"Did Grey mention the record?"

"Silver Lake's new record?"

Shaking her head, Lori said, "No. Garrett wants the record that you were working on with Salazar finished and released. Jim's been stalling him. I suspect it's his way of coping. They were together for a long time."

"He's left me a few messages," confessed Jake. "I never replied to them."

"Do you think you can finish it?"

"Maybe. It's only one vocal track to be done, but not now. I don't feel ready for that. I need to get my Silver Lake commitments in order and there's Dan's record to do. We're due to start that on the 14th."

"No one expects you to rush straight back in, Jake," said Lori softly. "Take all the time you need."

"I'll take it slowly. At least at first. Grey and I agreed to a rehearsal on Friday. Let's see how that works out first."

By Friday morning, Jake was regretting agreeing to the Silver Lake rehearsal. They had arranged to meet up at ten thirty and, as the clock ticked closer, he could feel nerves and panic starting to seize control. Twice over the past two days he had tried to spend more than a few minutes down in the basement. He had attempted to practice the songs he had stockpiled for the record, but, after twenty minutes, he could feel the walls closing in and a blanket of fear begin to engulf him. A tense phone call with Maddy hadn't helped his fragile emotional state. She had called him from Paul's cell phone on Wednesday afternoon, tricking him into answering. There were half a dozen unanswered messages on his phone from her, but she had guessed correctly that he wouldn't ignore a call he thought was from Paul. For fifteen minutes, she had berated him for attacking Lori, for using drugs and, generally, for risking everything. He had listened to the lecture, then hung up the call without saying a word. When she called back an hour later, Maddy apologised for losing her temper. They had talked and, after almost an hour on the phone, peace and harmony were more or less restored. It had all served to unsettle his delicate emotional state. Following the guidance he'd received in rehab, Jake reached out to Jethro, explaining all that had happened. His "rehab buddy" spent almost two hours talking to him, reassuring him and reinforcing the coping techniques he had been taught.

At the sound of a car in the driveway, his stomach lurched, leaving him feeling physically sick with fear. The first to arrive was Rich. He knocked on the back door, then let himself in.

"Morning," called Lori brightly, as she stood in the kitchen folding some laundry that she'd taken out of the dryer.

"Morning, Lori," greeted Rich. "You're looking a lot better than you were the other day. You ok?"

"I'm fine," she assured him with a smile.

"Where is he?" asked the guitarist, an angry edge to his question.

"Behind you," said Jake quietly as he entered the kitchen.

Before he could brace himself, Jake saw his friend raise his fist ready to throw a punch. The blow caught him square on the jaw, rattling his teeth and sending him reeling back into the wall.

"Rich!" screamed Lori sharply. "Enough!"

"You ever hurt her again, Jake, I'll fucking kill you!" growled Rich, his face a mask of fury.

Rubbing his jaw, Jake gazed at Rich then at Lori then returned his gaze to Rich, "Ok, I guess I deserved that."

"And a hell of lot more!"

"Rich!" snapped Lori angrily. "That's enough. Now both of you sort this out right now! I will not tolerate that kind of behaviour in my home! Do I make myself clear?"

"Sorry, Lori," apologised Rich, without taking his eyes off Jake.

"And Jake's apology?" she prompted sharply.

"Leave it, Lori," intervened Jake. Calmly, he turned to his band mate, "Are you done? Did punching me make you feel better?"

"Harrumph," muttered Rich, stuffing his hands into his pockets. Eventually, he sighed and said, "Sorry, but when I saw the mess you'd made of Lori….."

"Rich, no one regrets that more than I do," interrupted Jake, struggling to retain his composure. He knew only too well how hot-headed his fellow musician could be and had half expected the reaction. "Now, do you feel the need to take another swing at me or can we talk and move on?"

At that moment, the back door opened and both Grey and Paul came clattering into the house. Immediately, both of them realised that they'd walked in on an incident. One look at the fiery red mark on Jake's jaw informed them both of what had happened.

Stepping in between them, Grey said, "This stops here now, Rich! We agreed, remember?"

"I know, but…" began Rich.

"No buts," stepped in Paul, from the other side. "We're family. We stick together. We support each other not throw punches. And, Rich, for the record, that was no way to behave in front of Lori. Don't you think there's been enough violence in her life over the past few weeks?"

"I'm sorry, Lori," said Rich contritely.

"Apology accepted, but only once you apologise sincerely to my husband."

"Sorry, buddy," said Rich, extending his hand towards Jake.

Taking his hand, Jake shook it, then pulled him into an awkward embrace. "I'll send you the bill for the dental work. Think you've loosened a few teeth with that blow."

That was enough to break the ice.

Armed with mugs of coffee and a box of donuts that Grey had brought with him, Silver Lake trooped down to the basement, closing the door behind them. Taking a seat on the bottom step, Jake sat quietly drinking his coffee while the others settled themselves down. The space suddenly felt crowded and cramped. A wave of anxiety was building and he could feel his heart beginning to pound. From his seat behind his new drum kit, Paul recognised the nervous look on Jake's face and suggested they make a start.

"OK, what have we got for this record so far?" asked Grey, helping himself to a second donut. "Anything?"

"I've a few bits and pieces," replied Jake. "And there's that blues song we worked out a few weeks back too."

"I've a couple," began Rich. "I've got some lyrics looking for some music too."

As the four of them began to bounce their ideas around, they began to lose track of what they had that they could build on.

"Jake, run up and get some large sheets of paper from Lori. We need a makeshift board down here," instructed Rich firmly, his former school teacher voice commanding authority. "And a couple of marker pens."

When Jake returned with three sheets of poster paper and a packet of pens, Rich wrote up the various song ideas they had amassed. Scanning the list, Grey asked Jake if he had any more gems hidden.

"I might have two, possibly three," he said quietly, remembering the dark theme that had emerged for his latest effort. "One of them still needs lyrics and they all need work."

"Can you have them ready for us to rehearse next week?" asked the bass player hopefully. "I'd feel happier about this shit if we were better prepared before we lose time with the Weigh Station charity thing."

"I'll do my best to have them ready for you to run through by Monday," promised Jake, his stomach heaving at the thought of committing to spending time in the basement.

"Are we steering this in a particular direction?" asked Paul, twirling his drumsticks through his fingers. "Is there an underlying theme emerging here?"

They all exchanged glances before Jake said, "I'd like to keep it on the heavy side if we can. The heavier stuff from Impossible went down really well with the fans when we played it live. I don't want to fill this record with ballads."

"Hard and heavy suits me," agreed Grey with an approving

nod. "Engine Room and Vortex were great to play live. Fans loved them, but they still love a ballad or a softer song or two."

"And they'll get them," promised Jake. "I just don't want to see us produce a twelve or fourteen track record with eight or ten ballads on it."

"Totally agree," stated Rich bluntly.

"Right, so what do we have then?" asked Paul, squinting to read Rich's writing on the makeshift board. "Five? Four?"

"Five definites and possibly three or four more," replied Rich quickly adding it all up. "Not enough yet, but it's a solid start."

"Suggestion," began Jake, running his hand through his hair. "Let's run through the five we think we've got then go our separate ways until Monday."

"You trying to get rid of us already?" joked Paul with a cheeky grin.

"No!" stated Jake defensively. "I just need a couple of days to tidy up those three songs."

"You sure?" pushed Paul, watching his friend's reaction.

"Ok, I'm struggling a bit here," confessed Jake, getting up from his seat on the step. "I need a bit of time. There's still too many ghosts in my head when I'm down here."

His three band mates stared at him, each of them unsure of what to say or how to react. For a second, they each thought that Jake was going to turn round and go back upstairs. Instead, he walked across the room, lifted his Mz Hyde custom model, plugged in the lead and said simply, "Let's play."

After his fellow band members left, Jake fetched a glass of water, then returned to the basement. A few half-formed ideas were running through his mind. Again, he lifted his Mz Hyde guitar and sat down to work out a riff that was slowly coming to life. For the next two hours, he focused on his music, forgetting the rest of the world. Gradually, he built up the piece of music. A memory of an intro section that he'd composed months before filtered through and he scoured the files on his laptop until he found it. Smiling to himself, he continued to build the song, even coming up with a heavy bass riff. Having messed about with the tempo and tuning of the various sections, he came up with an almost death metal style track.

"Well, they wanted hard and heavy," thought Jake as he played back what he had recorded so far on his laptop.

One of Grey's bass guitars sat on a stand. Laying his own instrument aside, Jake picked up the heavy, unfamiliar guitar and slowly worked out the bass line for the new song. His bass playing was clunky, almost staccato, but he got the gist of what he was after.

Before he called it a day, Jake ran through the track one final time. The new track still needed a drum track and lyrics, but, overall, he was satisfied with his progress.

When he emerged from the basement, Jake was surprised to find the house in almost complete darkness. In the kitchen, the two small night lights were on and he found a note on the table from Lori saying she'd gone out to fetch dinner. The two night lights were creating an intimate atmosphere in the empty room. Unsure how long his wife would be, Jake set two places at the table, then lit a couple of small, fragranced votive candles, placing them in the centre. As he set them down, he heard the scrunch of tyres on the gravel outside.

"Ah, romantic Chinese for two," joked Lori when she came in carrying the bag of food.

"Something like that," replied Jake with a smile. "What did you get?"

"I picked you up some Singapore shrimp and noodles," answered Lori, lifting the cartons from the bag. "I just went for some Hong Kong style chicken and rice. Hope that's ok?"

"Sounds great, li'l lady. I'm starving. I hadn't realised it was so late."

"Productive day?"

"Eventually. Was a bit awkward and strained," replied Jake as he sat down opposite her at the table. "One song began to come together after the boys left."

"I noticed," she said with a giggle. "When did you start to play bass, rock star?"

Blushing, Jake replied, "I was only trying to get the basic bass riff recorded for it to help with the rest of the structure. I'm shit at playing bass. Really shit."

"Perhaps Grey will give you some lessons," teased Lori, her blue eyes twinkling with mischief in the candlelight.

"I'll get him to fix that bass line next week," muttered Jake, looking embarrassed, then changing the subject, asked how her day had been.

"Great. I got quite bit done," answered Lori, rising to fetch them both a drink. "It's getting uncomfortable to sit for too long though. This little Power Pack has been restless all afternoon."

"Distracting you?"

"Very much so," admitted Lori, sounding more than a little frustrated. "I'm trying to focus on the roulette wheel design in front of me and its rocking out in there to your new death metal riff."

"Sorry," apologised Jake, visualising the baby head banging to Silver Lake.

"It's fine," assured Lori, resting her hand on her growing bump. "It was worth it to hear the house filled with music again. It's been too quiet around here. I think baby's worn out. I'm sure he or she is asleep. There's not been much movement for an hour or so."

"Baby Power's not the only one worn out," sighed Jake, suddenly feeling mentally drained. "It's been a long day."

"You've made a few big leaps forward though," observed Lori, choosing her words carefully.

"I guess," he agreed quietly, rubbing his jaw where Rich had punched him that morning.

"Do you want to check in with Jethro or do you want to talk it over with me?"

"Both," replied Jake. "I feel better having seen everyone. It felt good, really good, to be working again. Playing with the band is what I do best. It all felt right, but I still struggle being down in the basement. It'll get easier, but there's still shadows in every corner."

"But you managed to stay down there on your own after they left for about three hours," countered Lori with a reassuring smile. "Our wounds are still healing, Jake. Don't be so hard on yourself. One step at a time remember."

"I know. You made a big step forward too," he observed. "Wasn't that your first venture out for a few days?"

Lori nodded, "First time since I came home from the emergency room, apart from a walk along the shore the other day."

"I hate to ask," began Jake awkwardly. "I've put you through so much. I don't have a right to ask…"

"Spit it out, rock star."

"I need to draw a line under all this shit. Get closure on it as

Frank advised before I came back. There's two things I need to do to achieve that," began Jake, his tone suddenly serious. "Since I can't get closure with Salazar, I need to talk to Garrett." Even saying his former idol's name burned in his throat. He paused, then continued, "I'll call him tonight. The second thing is where I need your support. I need to record that last vocal track. I need to finish the record. That means going back to JJL."

"And you want me to come back with you?"

Jake nodded, "And stay in the studio with me the whole time."

"When do you want to go out there?"

"I was going to call Jim. See if he's free tomorrow or Sunday," revealed Jake.

"Just let me know when I need to be ready. I'll go with you," replied Lori without hesitation. "Don't rush this though if you're not ready."

"I'm as ready as I'll ever be. I need to do it."

"I understand."

When their meal was over, Lori declared that she was going for a bubble bath to see if it would ease her aching back. Leaving Jake to tidy up the kitchen and to make his calls in private, she limped slowly down the hall. Every step was causing her pain, something she didn't want to confess to Jake, knowing it would only add to his worries. Her balance didn't feel as steady as it usually did and she was beginning to worry about falling.

As she lay back in the hot, foaming water, she was aware of Jake's voice in the background as he talked on the phone. With a contented sigh, Lori felt herself relax. Closing her eyes, she smiled as she rubbed her baby bump. For the first time since their world had been turned upside down, she felt as though everything really was going to be alright.

Having the house filled with the sound of Silver Lake again had been a beautiful thing. Seeing Jake gradually relax back into normality was warming her heart. It had scared her that their world had been thrown into such turmoil through little fault of their own. Both of them were going to bear the scars of it for a long time to come.

As the water began to grow cold, Lori eased herself back up into a sitting position and twisted the dial to release the water. Just as she was about to get out of the tub, there was a soft knock at the door.

"May I come in?" asked Jake tentatively. His awkwardness tugged at her heartstrings.

"Perfect timing, rock star," she replied with a smile. "You can help me out."

Needing no second invitation, Jake stepped into the hot, steamy room and offered her his hands. Once she was standing up in the tub, he reached round for the large, fluffy, bath sheet. Smiling, Jake wrapped the warm towel around her, then scooped her up into his arms. Unsure as to how she would react, he kissed her on the forehead, then carefully set her down on her feet.

"Thank you," whispered Lori softly, inwardly wishing he hadn't put her down.

They faced each other like two awkward teenage virgins, both of them knowing what they wanted, but neither of them wanting to make the first move.

"Dry me," instructed Lori quietly, a mischievous smile half-formed on her lips.

"Your wish is my command," agreed Jake theatrically.

Slowly and ever so gently, Jake unwrapped her, using the towel to dry her soft, damp skin. He dried her shoulders and arms, her back then the backs of her legs. Kneeling on the hard, tiled floor, he dried her slender feet, teasing her by drying each toe individually. Having dried the fronts of her legs, Jake nestled the towel round the swell of her stomach, kissing her firm bump gently. Lori giggled at the gesture.

"What's so funny, li'l lady?" he enquired from his lowly position.

"I think you just kissed the baby's ass," revealed Lori, filling the bathroom with her musical laughter.

It was the first time she had really laughed since he'd returned home. Hearing that wonderful sound again made Jake tingle with pleasure. Feeling more confident, he cupped her breasts in his hands, feeling them heavier than he expected. Tenderly, he kissed each of them in turn, then looked up into her blue eyes.

Running her hand through his hair, Lori whispered, "Make love to me."

"Here?"

"Well, maybe not right here," she giggled nervously.

Discarding the towel on the floor, Jake swept her up into his arms and carried her through to the bedroom. Treating her as if she were made of crystal, he very gently laid her down in the centre of their large bed. Without a word, Jake stepped back and swiftly removed his clothes. He could feel Lori's bright blue eyes following his every move. Naked, he lay down beside her, running his hand over her stomach and down the front of her thigh.

"You sure about this?" he asked nervously. "If you're not, I understand."

"Sh," she scolded softly, then, seeing the concerned look in his eyes, added, "Yes, I'm sure."

Feeling his pulse racing, Jake leant over to kiss her. At the touch of his lips to hers, he felt them part and the tip of her tongue brush along the edge of his. He moved his hand round to the soft inner flesh of her thigh and gently worked his way up towards her. Beside him, Lori meowed quietly as his long, slender fingers caressed her, finding her moist and ready for him. With part of him terrified of hurting her, Jake entered her slowly, then began to rhythmically move inside her, his strokes long and teasing. Despite the awkwardness of her growing belly, Lori responded to him, moving in perfect harmony beneath him. Unable to restrain himself any longer, Jake's strokes quickened as the fire built within him. With three long, hard, deep movements he climaxed. Lori too had reached the peak of her orgasm and moaned contentedly before making a small sound like a cat purring.

Lying beside her a few minutes later, with his hand resting on her baby bump, Jake whispered huskily, "I love you. Both of you. I must be the luckiest guy alive right now."

"We love you too," responded Lori as the baby obligingly kicked. "We've missed making love to you."

"I've missed everything about you."

"What was it you said a while back? Bonded souls?" mused Lori smiling at him. "That we are. Bonded forever."

As Jake pulled off the highway into JJL on Sunday afternoon, the studio was bathed in bright sunshine. Instead of heading for his usual parking space, he halted the truck in front of the building. Already he could feel nerves beginning to stir in the pit of his stomach.

"You sure this is a good idea?" asked Lori quietly as she unfastened her seat belt.

"No," admitted Jake, forcing an anxious smile. "But I need to do it. The longer I wait, the harder it gets. I don't want to mess up the Weigh Station project in a couple of weeks. It's now or never."

As they entered the studio building, both of them heard music. Instantly, Jake recognised it as the guitar track from the song he was due to complete. Hearing his late fallen idol's music, along with his own contribution, sent chills rattling down his spine.

"Show time," he said, taking Lori's hand.

When they entered the control room, they found Dr Marrs at the desk, focussed on the tracking details on the screen in front of him. Behind him, Kola was sitting cross-legged on a chair with her laptop balanced on her knees. Both of them looked up at the soft sound of the door closing.

"Afternoon," welcomed Dr Marrs brightly.

"Hi," replied Jake, feeling suddenly shy and embarrassed to be there.

"Grab a coffee," suggested the producer. "You're early. I need another half hour here."

"Early?" laughed Jake, breaking the ice. "That's a first for me!"

"Well, it had to happen sometime," joked Dr Marrs, returning his focus to the task in hand. "Half an hour, Jake."

"I'll go and warm up," suggested Jake. "Call me through when you're ready."

Instead of retreating to the small practice room beside the main office, Jake began his vocal warm up routine in the lounge. Having Lori there, watching from her seat on the leather settee, was easing his nerves somewhat. As methodically as ever, he began to work his way through his standard, reduced warm up routine.

After about forty five minutes, Kola came through from the control room, When she heard the racket of Jake's operatic vocal scales, she screwed her face into a frown before commenting, "And that's what warms the pipes up? Sounds hellish."

"Sure does," said Jake with a smile. "Keeps it all sounding sweet."

"Rock stars," muttered Kola as she poured herself a mug of strong, black coffee.

Pausing his routine, Jake said, "I believe I owe you a huge thank you."

"What for?"

"For clearing up the apartment. For bringing Lori's car back safely," replied Jake, keeping his tone warm and friendly but even, unsure as to how the sound engineer would react. "And for.... you know."

Turning to stare at him with her large, dark brown eyes, Kola smiled. "No need. If that evil bastard hadn't taken the easy route out, I'd have killed him for what he did. That man may have been a musical genius, but he was one scary, twisted son of a bitch."

Surprised by the coldness in her voice, Jake glanced at Lori, before agreeing, "He was certainly fucked up in the head."

"Well, as long as he's not fucked yours up," stated Kola bluntly. "Dr Marrs is ready for you. You're good to go."

"Give me ten minutes to finish up here and we'll be in."

Instead of heading into the live room, Jake took Lori by the hand and entered the control room.

"Jake," said Dr Marrs, swivelling his chair round to face him. "Sorry I kept you. How're you doing?"

"No problem. I'm ok. Getting there," replied Jake quietly.

"And Lori," began the producer, relieved to see her looking less bruised. "How's that baby belly coming along?"

"Swell," joked Lori with a giggle. "We're fine. Getting fatter every day!"

"You're looking fantastic," complimented the producer warmly.

Blushing, Lori smiled, "Thank you."

"What's the plan for the day?" asked Jake, keen to get started before his nerves gave out.

"Well, I hate to do this to you, but there's an issue with part of the guitar tracking for track two. Do you feel up to playing as well as singing for me?"

"What's wrong with it?"

"Salazar missed a section. I've messed about with what I've got taped, but nothing's filling in that gap. Here, listen and you'll hear it yourself," explained Dr Marrs.

The producer played the number through twice for them and Jake had to admit there was a part of the bridge missing. He also picked up that the solo had been cut short.

"Jim," he began. "I'll play it as best as I can but it'll be my way not his."

"I can't ask any more of you than that. Your guitar's still set up through there for you. Glad we did that one last. Meant nothing's been touched."

"Bridge and solo? That's all you need?" checked Jake.

The producer nodded.

"Show time, li'l lady," declared Jake, squeezing Lori's hand.

Sitting on the familiar stool in the studio, facing the control room and safe in the knowledge that Lori was only a few feet away, Jake began to run through the short bridge section of the song. Focussing on the instrument in front of him, Jake breathed slowly and deeply in an effort to remain calm. After another run through, he gave the producer the nod that he was good to go on the next run through.

It took them three takes but eventually Jake was given the thumbs up from both Dr Marrs and Kola.

"Let's go live with the solo," suggested Jake as he refined the guitar's tuning. "It might sound more emotional if it's less rehearsed."

"Perhaps," mused Dr Marrs, conscious that it had to fit in with what he had already recorded. "What the hell! Go for it. Just play. I'll record it all and see what we get."

"I'm going to grab a juice," said Lori, wriggling forward and heaving herself to her feet. Leaning heavily on her cane, she asked, "You want anything?"

"Water, please," replied Jake before adding, "Don't open it though."

With an understanding nod, Lori limped awkwardly out of the studio.

When she returned a couple of minutes later, Jake had changed guitars and was running through a few practice riffs. With a smile, he thanked her for the water as he opened the bottle. He took a long drag on it, then screwed the lid back on tightly.

"Let's do this."

For the next hour, Jake played through the solo. Initially, he stuck as closely as he could recall to the original then he heard a ghost in his head whisper, "Take this. Make it your own, Mr Power."

Even allowing himself to think of Salazar stirred an anger in Jake that he channelled into his performance. He poured all his reserves into the solo and delivered it as best he could.

"Jim, I'm done," he sighed, laying the guitar down. "You get what you need?"

"And then some!" declared Dr Marrs enthusiastically. "I don't know where that came from but that was incredible!"

"Thanks."

"Right. Take a break, then we'll get that vocal done," suggested Dr Marrs with a glance at the clock.

"I'm fine," said Jake, taking another drink from his water bottle. "I'll run through it and warm up again a bit. Give me fifteen minutes."

"Fine. I'll be back in here in fifteen."

The lyrics sheets were stacked in the vocal booth when Jake went over to it. He sifted through them until he found the one he was searching for. He started to sing then stopped midway through the first verse.

"You ok?" called over Lori from her seat on the settee.

"Yeah," muttered Jake, running his hands through his hair. "No."

Leaving the booth, he wandered across the room to sit beside her.

"I can see him. Hear him in every corner of this room," confessed Jake softly. "Christ, I can even smell that fucking incense of his!"

"You know you can stop anytime you want," reminded Lori,

placing her hand on his knee. "You've been brilliant all afternoon. Jim'll understand if it's been enough for one day. We can come back another day to do the vocals."

"It's now or never," stated Jake bluntly. "Time to close this chapter of fucking disaster."

Without another word, Jake walked back to the booth, put on the headphones and began to run through the song once more.

By the time Dr Marrs and Kola returned to their seats behind the desk, Jake was ready to go. He ran over a few test lines for the producer, swallowed another mouthful of water, offered up a silent prayer then began to sing. Under normal circumstances singing the fast paced, sleazy blues song would've been his guilty musical pleasure. This song, however, no longer held any pleasure for him. In his heart, Jake knew he had one shot at this. One chance to nail it before the demons began to tug at his memory. He poured his heart and soul into the song, minorly fluffed one line, but kept going, powering his way through to the last long, lingering, high note.

"I'm done," he stated when the song was over.

"Yes, you are!" agreed Jim Marrs. "That was fucking awesome. Where did you pull that performance from, Mr Power?"

"I knew I only had one crack at it," revealed Jake, hanging his headphones up. "I just gave it my all. Gave it the remains of my soul."

"You sure did," nodded the producer with a grin.

"We're out of here," declared Jake, feeling his anxieties beginning to push their way towards the surface. "Li'l lady wife, are you buying me dinner on the way home?"

"I guess I am," acknowledged Lori with a warm smile. Lifting her cane and her bag, she allowed Jake to help her to her feet before adding, "Since you sang so beautifully for your supper."

"Don't forget your guitars," called through Dr Marrs. "I think you've three through there."

Guitar cases in hand, plus one in a soft case over his shoulder, Jake bade everyone goodnight.

Fog was blanketing the area on Monday morning. As Lori stood at the sink, gazing out of the window at the swirls of grey mist, she heard a car in the driveway then the slam of its door closing. A few moments later, the back door opened beside her and Grey stepped into the kitchen.

"Morning, beautiful," he called out cheerfully. "Gorgeous morning out there!"

"It is?" laughed Lori.

"Well, it might be. Can't see a fucking thing out there," admitted the bass player with a mischievous grin. "But you look fabulous."

"You're delusional!" she declared. "I'm a mess this morning. And I'm feeling fat not fabulous."

"Well, you're positively glowing to me," said Grey warmly. "That strained look has finally vanished. I was getting worried about you, young lady."

"Thanks, Grey," replied Lori softly, feeling her cheeks turn red.

"Where's Jake?"

"He's gone out for a run," explained Lori as she poured them both a coffee. "Said he needed to clear his head. You know he went back out to JJL yesterday?"

"No. He never said."

"He went back. Well, we both went out there so he could finish the record. I think it was preying on his mind."

"And how did it go?" enquired Grey, genuinely surprised to hear that his friend had completed the recording so soon.

"He was sensational!"

"Who's sensational?" asked Jake as he clattered in through the back door. His face was flushed and beads of sweat were lined up along his eyebrows.

"You, rock star," answered Lori, smiling at him. "I was telling Grey about yesterday."

"Had to be done," stated Jake awkwardly. "Jim needed it wrapped up too. Garrett's been pushing him for it. Closure all round."

"And is it closed?" asked Grey directly.

"Mostly," admitted Jake as he fetched himself a glass of water. "I don't know if it'll ever be closed. No one can give me the answers I need. No one can explain why he would deliberately do that to me. That lack of closure is eating at me, if I'm being totally honest."

"Have you spoken to Garrett?" asked Grey. "Maybe he's got some answers."

"I've left him a couple of voicemails," replied Jake, draining his glass. "Right, I need a shower, then I need your help before the others get here."

"You do?"

Lori giggled before agreeing, "Oh, he definitely does! You'll love this!"

Raising one eyebrow, Grey said, "Confess all, Mr Power. Were you playing bass again?"

"It wasn't so bad!" protested Jake.

"I've heard you play bass!" laughed his friend. "Becky plays better bass than you do!"

"Harrumph," muttered Jake. "I need a shower."

By the time Rich and Paul had arrived to rehearse, Grey had "fixed" the bass track to Jake's new song. They played it through for their fellow band members to seek their approval. On the second run through, Rich joined in with a solo that he had that was still looking for a song. Having heard it a few times, Paul promised to work on a drum track for it. Over the weekend, both Rich and Paul had been busy writing new material. The guitarist brought two completed new songs to the table while Paul had two partially completed. Once they had added in the songs Jake had come up with, they agreed that they had ten songs towards the album, eleven if Jake could come up with lyrics for the new one.

Eventually, hunger drove the four members of Silver Lake up from the basement. As they clattered up the stairs and into the kitchen to make lunch, Jake called through to Lori, "You eaten?"

"Not yet," she called back from her seat at her drawing board.

"Grilled cheese ok?"

"Perfect."

As Lori padded through from the study, she smiled at the scene unfolding in her kitchen. The four rock stars were working together to prepare the simple meal.

"If their fans could see them now," she thought as she watched Rich lay the table.

A few minutes later, all five of them were enjoying a leisurely lunch around the kitchen table.

"I forgot to share my mom's news," began Grey between mouthfuls. "She slipped off to Atlantic City for the weekend. She came back late last night with her winnings. Twenty thousand dollars worth of winnings!"

"Go, Annie," said Paul with a grin.

"Love it!" giggled Lori. "How on earth do you keep her away from Las Vegas?"

"That's easy. She's shit scared of flying. She will only get on a plane as a last resort," revealed Grey. "Good job! Can you imagine the damage she could do there?"

As he listened to the conversation, an upbeat melody began to run through Jake's mind. Visions of Annie sitting at the gaming tables made him smile as he worked the music through in his head.

"Right, boys," said Rich, in true school teacher fashion. "Back to work."

"I need to head at three," stated Grey. "I need to fetch Becky from school."

While the band trooped back downstairs, Lori tidied up the kitchen, loaded the dishwasher, then returned to her drawing board. Her latest project sat half-finished on the angled board in front of her. Picking up where she'd left off before lunch, she worked steadily while being serenaded by Silver Lake's rehearsal.

The normal rhythm of life around the beach house had finally been restored.

Reflecting back on lunch, Lori was concerned that Jake was still quieter and more withdrawn than usual around the band. She understood it was early days and that the whole Salazar debacle had left a lasting imprint on his soul but she was still concerned. Only that morning when Maddy had called to remind her about the twins' birthday party, she too had voiced her concerns. Lori had promised that they would both be there, but she had caveated it by saying how long they stayed depended on how Jake was feeling. Both of them had chatted and agreed that they needed to be patient with Jake and give him the space he needed to put the incident behind him. Maddy also added that Lori needed time too.

Shortly after three, Grey came running upstairs, calling out his goodbyes as he rushed off to collect his daughter. A short while later, Paul and Rich left too, leaving Jake alone downstairs.

Lori waited with bated breath to see if he too would come rushing back up into the sanctuary of the house. There was silence for a few long minutes, then she heard him begin to play an unfamiliar song.

Alone in the basement, Jake deliberated over which guitar to use to capture the melody that had been running through his head since lunch. He reached for his Mz Hyde signature model, altered the tuning and began to play. The fresh melody sounded even better than he had dared to hope and, as he played, he expanded it, enjoying playing something that felt like a bit of fun and less intense than some of the material Silver Lake has been focussing on earlier in the day. As he played, a chorus started to form in his mind, then the lyrics began to reveal themselves. Quickly, Jake grabbed his leather bound journal and scrawled the lyrics across the first blank page.

Next morning, when the band reconvened, Jake played them the new song he'd written. He smiled to himself as he watched Rich's toe begin to tap and Paul began to drum along to it on his knees. Only Grey remained motionless and quiet. When the song ended, Jake looked round the room, anticipating a reaction or feedback from his fellow band members. Tension hung in the air until Grey threw his head back and laughed.

"I fucking love it, but my mom will be after your blood when she hears it, Mr Power," he declared.

"You think?"

"We know!" stated Rich and Paul in unison.

"It's fucking awesome!" chortled Grey. "Play it again."

Over the next couple of hours, "Lady Gambler" took shape and, by lunchtime, Silver Lake had added it to their makeshift board, bringing the grand total of songs to twelve.

"What's the plan for the rest of the week?" asked Paul as they wound up their rehearsal late afternoon. "I'm tied up with family stuff for the next few days."

"I really should work on some of the Weigh Station tracks," acknowledged Jake half-heartedly. "The project kicks off on Monday."

"Are you ready for it?" quizzed Grey, concerned that it was too high a profile project too soon.

Running his fingers through his hair, the standard signal that he was anxious, Jake sighed, "I don't honestly know. I've not spoken to Garrett yet. The Weigh Station guys fly in on Friday. When I was out at JJL, I spoke to Jim. Said to him that I wasn't doing the press launch. There's a few gaps in the schedule that need filled."

"How many tracks are you playing on?" asked Rich curiously. "I know we've all got one each."

"Four, I think," replied Jake. "I've to duet with Tori on Battle Scars and with Ellen on Miles From Home. I've to play on Wreckless. The big question's hanging over Broken Bottle Empty Glass. Salazar was to duet with me on it."

"Could Mikey play or Garrett?" suggested Rich, in an effort to be helpful.

"I guess so. Not my call though."

"Could you do it as a solo tribute to Dan?" proposed Grey.

"Perhaps," mused Jake quietly. " I'll find out next week."

"I guess our rehearsals are on hold for a couple of weeks then," observed Paul.

"We've still to work out the set for those three festivals in May too," reminded Rich, consulting the calendar on his cell phone. "We're playing Rockville on May 3rd then Carolina Rebellion on May 11th and Rock on the Range on May 17th."

"Don't remind me," muttered Jake, for the first time truly dreading the thought of appearing in front of such large crowds. "Roll on June."

"Let's have a think and try to grab a few minutes to work out a schedule on Sunday at the meatballs' party," suggested Paul, sensing that Jake needed the pressure lifted for a few days.

"Works for me," agreed Grey. "I need to run. I'll see you all Sunday."

Alone again in the basement, Jake sat staring at the makeshift board with the twelve working titles listed on it. Three of them still needed lyrics. The two hard and heavy tracks both felt dark and slightly evil. The first one was the song he had been contemplating while he'd been out for his run a couple of days before. Then the lyrics that had emerged reflected the story of the demons from the drug induced hallucination. At the time, he had dismissed them as too painful to commit to paper. Now, though, he was reconsidering.

His lyrics journal lay open on the desk beside him. Writing about the demonic creatures from his nightmares was going to be a challenge. To write about them and risk setting them free again within the confines of the basement was a step too far. With the pen trembling in his hand, Jake closed the journal over, grabbed it and headed upstairs.

As he passed through the study, heading for the sunroom, he called out to Lori, "I'm going down to the beach for a bit. I won't be long."

The beach in front of the house was deserted, not even a bird in sight. A warm, spring sun was shining down, heating the sand. Even the wind had dropped, leaving the ocean a sea of calm in front of him. Folding his long legs with ease, Jake sat cross-legged on the soft sand, safely out of reach of the gentle waves that were teasingly lapping at the shore. With his hand still trembling nervously, he bowed his head over the notebook and began to set the demonic lyrics free.

Back at the house, Lori was engrossed in her roulette wheel design, while trying to ignore the frantic kicking going on inside her. The design was taking shape and she was secretly pleased with the overall effect. Instead of numbers, the design called for the band in question's name to be detailed in the black and red segments. The album's title was incorporated into the dice. Reaching for some scrap paper, Lori began to draft out her drawing of the dice, trying to determine the best angle for them.

Her concentration was disturbed by the sound of a car stopping in the driveway outside. She listened closely, hearing the door clang shut, then the click of footsteps approaching up the front steps. Leaning heavily on her cane, Lori was half way to the front door when the bell finally rang. Through the frosted glass panels, she could see a man standing on the top step with his back to her. Immediately, she recognised it as Garrett Court.

As she opened the door, he turned to face her, forcing a weak, strained smile. Instantly, Lori noticed his pale, gaunt expression and the dark shadows under his eyes. He wore his grief like a mask.

"Garrett," she greeted warmly. "Come in."

"If this is a bad time....I didn't know whether to call first," he began nervously.

"You're always welcome here," assured Lori, moving aside to let him step into the hallway. "Come on through to the sunroom."

"Is Jake here?" enquired the older musician as he followed her through the lounge towards the sunroom.

"He's down on the beach," replied Lori. "He promised he wouldn't be gone too long."

"How is he?" asked Garrett, his voice filled with concern. "And, how are you? I am so sorry you had to suffer because of this mess. I feel so guilty about everything. Wish I could turn the clock back. Do something."

Taking a seat on the smaller of the two couches and indicating that her visitor should do the same, Lori replied, "I'm fine, Garrett. Still a few bruises and aches, but I'm ok."

"And the baby?"

"Is perfectly fine too," she promised him. "As for Jake, he's getting there. He's still struggling to get his head round it all. Jethro's been a huge support to him since he came home. He's trying to come to terms with things and the fact that he'll never really know why. He needs answers he can never get."

"None of us will," sighed Garrett quietly.

"And, how are you? Are you alright?" asked Lori, unable to bring herself to say she was sorry about Salazar's death.

"I don't know," admitted Garrett wearily. "I'm just taking it day by day. There's been so much to do. So much red tape. So many formalities. I came down here a few days early to clear up some loose ends at the rental house."

"It can't be easy," sympathised Lori, feeling his pain.

"We were together a long time, Lori," he began, his voice husky with emotion. "And despite the evil thing that he did to Jake, I still loved him. Still love him."

"Have you any idea why he drugged Jake?" asked Lori softly, dreading the answer.

"I have a couple of theories but I don't know for sure. He had been really unstable for months. Worse than I'd ever seen him. I tried to get him to delay the record until he felt stronger, but he refused."

"Are you going to share these theories with Jake?" interrupted Lori.

"If he asks me to," said Garrett. "I owe him as much of an explanation as I can give. I'll be honest with him. I'm not sure I have the answers that he needs to hear though."

"Why don't you go down onto the beach and find him?" suggested Lori softly. "Might be easier for you both if you talk down there."

"Thanks, Lori. I truly wish I could turn the clock back."

Once he started to write the lyrics around the demons that continued to haunt him, Jake's pen flew across the pages. He poured the tormented tale straight from his heart. In less than an hour, he had written four potential verses and the chorus. Writing it all down had been cathartic. With his haunted memories heavy in heart, Jake set the book aside and sat gazing out at the ocean. Watching the gentle swell rise and fall in front of him calmed his racing heart. Breathing slowly and deeply, he felt his sense of equilibrium return to normal.

He was due to meet Jethro next morning for his weekly check in. As he sat on the sand, Jake began to run over in his mind what he planned to say to his "rehab buddy". Opening up about his feelings seldom came naturally to him, but the band's manager knew him well enough to sense when he was holding something back. He'd have to be totally honest about everything that continued to prey on his sanity.

"Jake," called a familiar voice from behind him. "Mind if I join you?"

"Garrett!" exclaimed Jake, spinning round quickly, sending sand spraying across his leather bound journal.

"Sorry, didn't mean to startle you," apologised the older man humbly. "May I sit down?"

"Sure," agreed Jake, his heart suddenly pounding in his chest as his anxieties threatened to flood through him. "I didn't think you'd be down here until next week."

"I had a few loose ends to tie up before we hit the studio," explained Garrett, sitting down on the sand beside him.

"Am I one of those loose ends?" joked Jake feebly, in an effort to mask his fear.

"Kind of," admitted Garrett warmly. "We've played voicemail tag long enough. I thought I'd drop by. Check you and Lori were ok. See if I can do anything to right the wrong."

"Can you wind back the clock three weeks?"

"I wish I could," Garrett sighed heavily. "Christ, how I wish I could."

"Listen, none of this fuck up is your fault," said Jake, keeping his gaze fixed firmly on the ocean in front of him.

"I feel like it is," confessed the older man. "If I'd stopped him going into the studio. If I'd got him more professional help. If I'd been firmer with him. Jake, he's been a loose cannon for months."

"Did you get to say goodbye?" asked Jake calmly.

"No," whispered Garrett. He cleared his throat then continued, "I only saw him once at the hospital. We parted on bad terms. I gave him hell for what he did to you. Despite what the doctors said about keeping the truth away from him until he was stable, I told him everything. Blamed him for everything. Yelled at him for putting you and Lori in such danger. Christ, the last thing I said to him was that I didn't think I could still love a monster like him. I helped tip him over that final edge."

"I'm sorry," said Jake softly, genuinely feeling his friend's pain and guilt. "But why me? Why did he want to do that to me?"

"Control," stated Garrett, his voice thick with emotion. "Possessiveness. Obsession."

"I don't get it."

"Do I need to spell it out?" said Garrett sharply, his eyes boring into Jake. "He was in love with you!"

"What?"

"You were all he's talked about since New Year. He was totally obsessed with you. Wanted to mould you to be like him. Wanted you to be his. Wanted you to want him," revealed Garrett. "Christ, you got him out of New York City! You inspired him to write and play. Lord, you even got him into a studio to record! You brought out the very best and the very worst in him!"

"I never suspected...." began Jake awkwardly.

"Why would you?" sighed Garrett, his wounds of grief re-opened once again. "I don't know what happened inside his head that last week. He was barely talking to me. I think he realised that you could never be his and that he had to try to gain control over you some other way."

"So, he began lacing my drinks with that concoction of his? Did he think getting me high was the solution?" accused Jake angrily. "Garrett, I've been drug free for over six years! I went through a real struggle cleaning my act up. Everyone who knows me knows I don't touch drugs. I don't even smoke dope! His mad plan sent me spiralling back into hell! Almost killed Lori and the baby. Could've destroyed my world!"

"I know and I can't say how sorry I am about everything that you and Lori have been through."

Side by side the two musicians sat in silence, both of them staring out across the vast expanse of ocean.

Jake's mind was in turmoil after hearing Garrett's revelations. Not even for a moment had he suspected that Salazar was sexually attracted to him. He'd innocently assumed it was his musical talent that was the attraction. A feeling of revulsion washed through him as he recalled the number of late night hours they'd spent together at JJL. Inwardly, Jake pondered on whether Dr Marrs had known then dismissed the thought. Glancing over at Garrett, he realised the full extent of the older musician's pain and grief, knew he was going through his own hell with everything that had happened. As his anger abated, Jake realised how rejected and alone the older man must be feeling.

"Garrett," he began calmly. "Neither of us are ever going to know what was going on in his fucked up head, but I don't want it to screw up our friendship. Maybe we should be helping each other through this? Help each other get through the Weigh Station project too?"

"You mean that?"

Jake nodded, "I wasn't planning on telling those Weigh Station boys all about this. Maddison and Jethro have gone to great lengths to keep this under the radar. Folk have even hidden evidence for me to save my ass here. Jim won't breathe a word either."

"If you're sure," began Garrett.

"I'm sure," said Jake firmly

"You're being more generous here than I deserve."

"That's bullshit," said Jake. "You were as innocent in all of this as me. But just for the record, I'm a happily married, heterosexual male!"

Smiling for the first time, Garrett winked at him, "Don't worry. You're not my type,"

"Thank fuck for that!" laughed Jake.

With the awkwardness over and done with, the two musicians sat chatting through the plan for the immediate future. When Jake revealed he'd backed out of the press launch for the Weigh Station project, Garrett begged him to reconsider, claiming that if he was absent that may draw more attention to him than if he went through with it. On reflection, Jake had to concede that he might be right and promised to reconsider. As they talked their way through the track list that Mikey had drawn up, Jake voiced his concerns about Broken Bottle Empty Glass. Garrett suggested that he do it as a solo performance, pointing out that he'd owned the song latterly on the stage in London. Again, Jake conceded that he might be right, but agreed to leave the final decision up to Dr Marrs. Confident in the producer's judgement, Jake confirmed he would go with whatever worked best for the record.

Since they were talking about recording, Garrett thanked him for finding the strength to finish off the blues album. Together, they discussed it and Jake listened attentively to Garrett's plans to release it in the Fall.

While they talked, a breeze began to blow in from the ocean and soon both of them were getting cold sitting on the sand.

"Will you stay for dinner?" invited Jake as the two men walked back to the house.

"I'm not sure," began Garrett, not wanting to impose on them.

"Lori will be mad at me if you don't," cautioned Jake warmly. "Might do us all some good too."

"Thanks," said Garrett with a sad smile. "I'd love to."

It was approaching midnight before Garrett finally said goodnight to Jake and Lori. When the two musicians had arrived back at the house, Lori already had the table set for dinner and was busy in the kitchen preparing one of Jake's favourites, chicken parmesan. Over dinner, they had reminisced about Dan and Weigh Station, then Garrett started to tell tales about Jethro when he had been based in England. The relaxed atmosphere did all three of them the world of good. Each of them was mindful not to mention Salazar but, occasionally, it was impossible to ignore his involvement in the tale being spun. While Jake walked Garrett back out to his car, Lori headed down the hallway to bed.

All evening the baby had been restless, kicking and wriggling incessantly. As she slipped on her pyjamas, Lori rubbed her belly, whispering, "Time to settle down, little one. Its bed time."

She smiled as she felt the baby push back against the palm of her hand.

When Jake finally joined her in the bedroom, she was curled up on her side reading her book.

"You ok, li'l lady?" he asked as he pulled off his T-shirt. "You look worn out."

"I'm fine. Just tired and a bit uncomfortable," replied Lori with a sleepy smile. "This little Power Pack has been rocking out all night to those old stories. My ribs are black and blue."

"Oh, I'm sorry," said Jake warmly. "Those old stories were therapeutic. It was good to just shoot the breeze for a while."

"It was nice to see both of you laughing and relaxed," she acknowledged, closing her book and laying it to one side.

As Jake lay down beside her, she wriggled towards him, laying her head on his chest and allowing her baby bump to rest against him. With a smile, Jake put his arm around her and drew her closer to him, then kissed her lightly on the top of the head.

"Thanks for tonight."

"Did you get the answers you need?" asked Lori, running her finger along the outline of the dragon tattoo on his shoulder.

"Most of them," answered Jake as he laid his hand on her swollen belly. He paused as he felt the baby move under his hand. "According to Garrett, Salazar was obsessed with me. In love with me. He wanted to control me and thought that by getting me hooked on his mushroom tea he could win me over. In a fucked up way, it kinda makes sense."

"It does?" queried Lori, gazing up into his troubled hazel eyes.

"Yeah," sighed Jake, kissing her forehead. "Doesn't make it any easier for Garrett. He's lost, but at least he has this Weigh Station record to focus on. We kind of agreed to help each other through it."

"Are you going to be ok to go through with it? There's bound to be a lot of media attention out at JJL for a while."

"I have to be," stated Jake quietly. "Time to put my big boy pants on and step back out there."

"I prefer you with no pants, rock star," she teased with a girlish giggle.

"Naughty, Mz Hyde, very naughty."

As Jake turned the truck off Wolf Necke Road into the farmhouse's driveway, he was surprised to see so many cars there. A few of them he recognised, but not all of them. Realising that the twins' birthday party was a bigger affair than he had expected, Jake felt a wave of panic building inside him. Since his return to Rehoboth, he'd steered clear of large groups of people and wasn't sure he felt ready to face so many now.

Sensing his anxiety, Lori reached out to touch his thigh, "It'll be ok. We don't need to stay long. Maddy and Paul will understand."

"I'll be fine," said Jake, sounding less than convincing as he parked the truck under the shade of an oak tree in the front yard. "I see Jethro's car back there and Grey's truck. A few friendly faces'll help."

"And don't forget your number one fan will be looking for her Uncle Jake," teased Lori in an effort to lighten the mood.

As they walked round to the rear of the farmhouse, following the party noise, Jake noticed that Lori had brought both of her canes. He watched as she walked very deliberately along the uneven path, but resisted the urge to comment or offer help. The party guests were spread out across the yard and the large deck at the back of the house. One of the first people Jake spotted was Jethro, who was sitting in an old rocking chair with Hayden on his knee.

"Jake! Lori!" cried Maddy from the deck. "You finally made it!"

"Sorry, Maddy, are we late?" asked Lori as she climbed the three steps up onto the deck.

"A little," admitted her friend.

"My fault," apologised Jake, flashing her a smile. "I kept us late in leaving."

"Delighted you made it," said Maddy, hugging him with one arm. Little Wren was wriggling in her mother's other arm. "Glad to see you looking so well too."

Reaching her chubby arms out, the little girl cried, "Ake! Ake!"

"Hello, princess," said Jake, kissing her cheek. "How's my favourite big girl?"

"Show Uncle Jake your party trick, honey," said Maddy as she set her tiny daughter down on her feet.

Giggling, the little girl took half a dozen tottering steps, then grabbed Jake's leg.

Swooping her up into his arms, he declared, "Who's a clever girl then?"

Staring at him with her big brown eyes, she said seriously, "Wren."

Everyone laughed, giving the little girl a fright. She buried her face in Jake's hair.

"It's ok, princess," he soothed, hugging her tight. "No one's laughing at you. You're a very clever girl."

"Lori, you ok?" asked Maddy, noting, with concern, her friend's canes.

"I'm fine. Just a bit unsteady on my feet with this growing bump," assured Lori warmly. "My centre of gravity is all over the place."

"All out front from the looks of it," teased Paul, appearing from inside the house. "But you look fabulous."

"Thanks."

From across the sun deck, Mikey from Weigh Station called out, "Good afternoon, Mr Power."

"Hi," replied Jake, shifting Wren's weight onto his hip and rescuing his hair from her tiny, firm grasp. "When did you guys arrive?"

"Friday," replied the English guitarist. "We drove down here yesterday."

"Are you staying out at JJL?" asked Lori as she took a seat beside him.

"That we are."

"Fabulous house," declared Phil, the band's drummer.

"Short commute to work," joked Steve, the bass player, with an impish grin.

"You ready for the press launch tomorrow, Jake?" asked Mikey as he took a sip of his drink. "Garrett said you'd decided to join us after all."

"Ready as I'll ever be," said Jake, forcing a smile. "Where is

Garrett? I thought he'd be here."

"So did I," admitted Maddy, glancing at her watch. "Time to light the BBQ."

"I'll go and help Paul with it," offered Jake, anxious to be away from the scrutiny of the members of Weigh Station.

As he walked across the yard with Wren snuggled into his shoulder, Jake breathed a sigh of relief. Spotting the anxious look on his face, Jethro called him over.

"You ok, son?" he asked as Jake sat down on the grass at his feet.

"Not really," confessed Jake, settling Wren on his knees. "I feel like I'm lying to everyone. Feel like a fraud."

"With the boys from Weigh Station?"

Jake nodded.

"You could always trust them with the truth," suggested the older man calmly. "They've seen enough dramas in their time to know when to keep quiet. They'll understand. It might make it easier on Garrett too."

"Perhaps," mused Jake. "I can't tell them what I did, though."

"Ok, I get that, but you can tell them what Salazar did to you."

"Maybe. Let me speak to Garrett first."

"Jake," began Jethro wisely, "Don't make this road any harder to travel than it already is."

"I won't," promised Jake sincerely. "I just don't want to say anything that contradicts what Garrett might have already said. I don't want him to look a fool here."

"Fair point, son," agreed Jethro, wrestling with a fractious Hayden. "Now, did I hear Maddison mention BBQ?"

"Yes, sir, you did. I was on my way to tell Paul to light the coals."

Dusk was settling over the farmhouse when they heard the rumble of another car in the driveway. A few minutes later, Garrett came striding round the side of the house carrying two large gift wrapped boxes.

"Sorry I'm so late, Maddison," he apologised. "I had to drive back up to New York last night to sign more paperwork. So many loose ends. So much red tape. I've only just arrived back down here."

"It's fine, Garrett. No need to apologise," purred Maddy. "I'm delighted you made it. There's still plenty food left if you're hungry."

"No thanks. I grabbed a sandwich on my way down when I stopped for gas."

"Well, find a seat and I'll fetch you a drink," suggested their hostess.

Spying an empty seat beside Lori, Garrett walked over to join her.

"Hi," he greeted quietly. "You're looking radiant this evening."

"Thanks," giggled Lori, smoothing her loose tunic down over her bump. "I'm not feeling it. I'm exhausted."

"Long day?"

"Yes," she admitted, with a yawn. "If you're looking for Jake, he's over at the grill with Paul and Mikey."

"How is he?"

"Better since you were over the other night."

"Glad one of us is," sighed the older man wearily. "I need to talk to him about something, but maybe I better wait a few days."

"If it's likely to distress him, please wait," suggested Lori.

"It's ok. It can wait for now. We've a tough enough week ahead."

Their conversation was interrupted by Jake's arrival on the sun deck. As there were no empty seats, he sat down at Lori's feet.

"You ok?" she checked quietly, putting a hand on his shoulder.

"Just," he whispered. "Give me a few more minutes, then do you mind if we head home?"

"Not at all," she agreed, getting awkwardly to her feet. "Here, take my seat. I'm going to have a word with Maddy before we leave."

"Thanks," said Jake, watching closely as she steadied herself, then gripped her canes tightly. "Ten minutes, li'l lady."

Inside, the farmhouse was warm and quiet. Slowly, Lori made her way through the house towards the kitchen in search of her friend. She found her preparing a tray of drinks to take back out to her guests.

"Hi," said Lori, trying to disguise her fatigue. "We're going to head home in a few minutes."

"Oh!" exclaimed Maddy. "You ok?"

"I'm fine. Tired but fine," assured Lori. "Jake's struggling a bit. He wants to get home. Think he just needs some space before tomorrow's press launch."

"How is he? He's not really said much to me all day."

"He's ok, but he's still fragile around people. Garrett was over the other night and they talked so that helped him sort through some stuff. Jethro's been fantastic with him."

"And are you and him ok?" asked Maddy, her voice overflowing with concern. "I've been trying to give you both some space."

"We'll be fine, Maddy. It's all just going to take time. Healing is a slow process."

"I guess. How's the Power Pack coming along? I can't believe how big you've got. You're all baby!"

"Don't I know it!" laughed Lori as the baby kicked sharply. "I'm beginning to understand how you felt. I'm seeing John on Wednesday to check my pelvis out. Everything feels a bit unstable. A bit loose. I've also got an ultrasound appointment. I'm pretty sure I'm still measuring ahead going by the size of this bump."

"Big is beautiful!" declared Maddy, giving her a hug. "And you look fabulous, honey."

"Thanks. I'll let you know how the appointments go. Thanks for today. It's been good to get away from the house for a while."

It was raining heavily as Jake drove out to JJL on Monday morning. The press conference was scheduled for midday but he'd promised Garrett and Mikey that he'd be there by eleven. True to form, he was running late. As he turned off the highway, it was almost eleven thirty. Already the front of the studio was crammed with cars and media personnel. Slowly, he drove round to the rear of the building, finding a space beside Kola's Harley Davidson. A wave of anxiety was beginning to build in his stomach and Jake wished he'd brought Lori with him for moral support. Deciding that he couldn't face the crowd of journalists at the front of the studio, he called Dr Marrs and asked if they could let him in the back door. The producer agreed, advising him to knock twice when he was outside. Stuffing his phone back into his pocket, Jake grabbed his guitars and his book bag then hurried over to the door. He had barely knocked it a second time when Kola opened it.

"You're late," she stated bluntly. "That crazy Scotsman is looking for you."

"Thanks for the warning," said Jake as he stepped past her.

When he walked through to the lounge, Jake was surprised to see it had been re-arranged and that extra chairs had been brought in. Both of the long, leather couches had been lined up at one end and there were several rows of seats facing them.

"All very formal," commented Jake as Mikey came through from the live room.

"Too fucking formal," muttered the Englishman. "Blame Laughlan. It's all his idea."

"Well, well, if it isn't the gorgeous Jake Power!" exclaimed a familiar voice from behind him. It was Tori, the lead singer from Molton.

"Good morning," he said almost shyly, feeling his cheeks redden. "I wasn't expecting to see you here today."

"I was passing by, more or less. I've a show in Baltimore tonight, so thought I'd stop by."

"We need all the moral support we can get," joked Jake.

"Feel like joining the press conference?" invited Mikey. "Add a little glamour to the event?"

"If it helps you boys out, I'd be glad to," purred Tori with a wink to Jake.

Shortly before noon, Weigh Station's manager rounded up all the assembled musicians in the lounge, instructing them to make themselves comfortable on the couches. In his gruff Glasgow accent, he cautioned them all about revealing too many details, adding that if they weren't sure if they could divulge the information then they should remain silent. Once he was sure they were all settled, he requested that the media personnel be allowed to enter.

Sitting between Mikey and Dr Marrs, Jake began to fidget. He could feel a trickle of sweat running down his back as he regretted agreeing to this for the hundredth time. If he was asked any questions about Salazar, he didn't know if he would be able to answer them.

The initial questions were directed at Mikey, Garrett and Dr Marrs as the three of them explained the background to the project. They then quizzed Tori about her involvement with the late Dan Crow. She revealed that he had mentored her on her first European tour, teaching her how to care for her voice.

"Speaking of voices, Jake," began one of the journalists. "How many tracks are you singing on?"

"That's still to be finalised," replied Jake. "Two, maybe three."

"And are you and Tori duetting on any?"

"You'll have to wait and see," he said with a smile.

"You fronted the band at their twenty fifth anniversary show. How did it feel to lead the band out that night?"

"It was an incredible honour," began Jake with a glance over at Mikey. "It was a fantastic show. I was flattered to be asked to do the vocal chores. Obviously, I wish circumstances had been different. Wish Dan had been there."

"Dan left instructions that you were to front the band going forward, didn't he?"

"Yes, he did," acknowledged Jake.

"And is there any truth to the rumours flying round that Weigh Station, fronted by you, are the mystery guests for the Sunday night at Rock on the Range next month?"

The question brought Jake up short.

No one had mentioned any live Weigh Station shows to him. With an anxious glance towards Laughlan, he took a moment then replied, "I'm committed to my Silver Lake duties that weekend."

For a further fifteen minutes, the questions continued, but very few of them were directed towards Jake. His heart went out to Garrett when one journalist offered his condolences over Salazar's death. The grieving musician mumbled his thanks then sat staring down into his lap, lost in his own thoughts.

"Final question!" called out Laughlan brusquely.

"When will the record be released?"

"Well, if you'd let us get started," joked Dr Marrs playfully. "No, seriously. We hope to have it out in the Fall. October most likely."

With the media presence gone, the various musicians debated the plan for the afternoon session with Dr Marrs. He had two boards gridded out in the live room. One was the standard track listing and the other was the planned recording schedule. Scanning down it, Jake noted he wasn't needed again until Thursday, when he was due to duet with Tori. His duet with Ellen was scheduled for the following Thursday. Broken Bottle Empty Glass was still listed among the tracks, but Jake couldn't work out when he was scheduled to record it.

"You ready to make some music?" asked Mikey, appearing beside him.

"Guess so," replied Jake, forcing a smile.

"Listen, kid, are you ok? You were quiet at Maddison's yesterday and you don't seem yourself today," observed the older musician quietly.

"Yes and no," admitted Jake, then deciding to take Mikey into his confidence as Jethro had suggested, added, "Can I have a quiet word for a minute?"

"Sure. Is something wrong? Is it your wife or the baby?"

"Nothing like that," said Jake, leading the way out of the live room.

JJL was still a hive of activity so Mikey suggested they take a walk across to the house to find a quiet space. The last of the journalists were just leaving as they crossed the driveway, heading towards the front porch of the studio house. There were two rocking chairs and a swing set on the large shaded porch. Pointing to the swing and indicating he should sit down, Mikey made himself comfortable in one of the wooden rockers.

"Alright, tell Uncle Michael what's eating at you?"

"What's Garrett told you about Salazar's death?" asked Jake, stalling for time.

"Not a lot," admitted the Englishman. "He hinted at an incident in the studio down here. Some kind of breakdown that led to his hospitalisation. Said he hanged himself."

"Yeah, well, it's that incident that's eating at me. Killing me slowly," began Jake, keeping his eyes downcast. "Salazar drugged me."

"What?"

"He deliberately gave me that fucking drug mix he drank. He'd been slipping it into my juice all that week, but on the Thursday night, I choked on two migraine pills. He deliberately gave me his cup of shit to drink instead of my own. I'd swallowed half of it before I realised," revealed Jake, his voice barely above a whisper. "It sent me on a really bad trip. I did some stuff I'm not proud of, including other drugs. Lori found me unconscious at my old apartment the next day. Called 911. Probably saved my life. Jethro got me into a rehab facility somewhere in northern Pennsylvania. I spent a week there sorting myself out."

"Shit, Jake. I never knew. Never guessed. Why though?"

"He wanted to control me. According to Garrett, he was obsessed with me. Perhaps even in love with me in his own warped way."

"Christ, that's pretty fucked up," said Mikey, barely believing what he was hearing. "Are you ok to go through with this project? If you need more time….."

Jake interrupted him, "I'll be fine. I just need a little space. It's still all really raw. Being in JJL is hard. Too many shadows in corners."

"Can we make it any easier for you?"

"Just bear with me," said Jake, feeling a sense of relief at having more or less the truth out in the open.

"Sure. Take all the time you need."

"Thanks. And can we keep this between us? Dr Marrs and Kola know the whole story, but I don't need anyone else knowing. I need to focus on putting it behind me."

"I hear you and I appreciate you confiding in me. If there's anything I can do to help, let me know. Just ask."

"Thanks. Appreciate that."

"So, are you ok to play this afternoon for an hour or so? We thought we'd jam a few of the tracks by way of a rehearsal. Phil's staying back tonight to do his drum tracks. He likes to work after dark."

"I'll hang about for a couple of hours, then I need to get back to the house. I've a rehab buddy meeting after dinner tonight," Jake explained. "And after all this, I need to spend time with Lori."

"She must have got a hell of a fright when she found you," commented Mikey.

"Mikey, if I tell you the rest of this mess, it goes no further, right? Promise me?" said Jake, his eyes fixed on the Weigh Station guitarist.

"You have my word."

Slowly and painfully, Jake told the older man the full horrific extent of his trip thanks to Salazar's tea. When the tale was told, he sat trembling with his head in his hands.

"Christ, Jake, you've both been to hell and back there. I don't know what to say to you."

"It's been a tough few weeks, but we're getting there. Lori's been incredible. So forgiving. More understanding than I deserved."

"She's a wonderful girl," agreed Mikey warmly. They sat in silence for a few minutes, then Mikey stood up. "Mr Power, if you're ready, let's head back over and do what we both do best."

"Sounds like a plan."

All day Lori had struggled to concentrate on her roulette wheel design. Every few minutes, she kept checking her phone to see if there were any messages from Jake. Despite his best acting efforts, her husband had failed to disguise his anxiety before he had left for JJL. Mid-afternoon, she abandoned her commission, fearful that she was about to make a mistake and ruin hours of work.

Having made herself a coffee, Lori settled down on the couch in the sunroom with her laptop, deciding to check her emails. As usual her inbox was crammed full of junk. Yet again, she made adjustments to her spam filters, cleared out the trash emails, then turned her attention to the few that were left. One caught her eye. It was from Garrett and the subject was "In Chains." Curious, Lori opened it first. Over the years, she had had a few emails from Garrett and their formality always made her smile. This one was no exception. In his own eloquent way, Garrett was asking if she could find time in her pre-maternity schedule to complete the cover artwork for the record that Salazar had recorded with Jake. He revealed that the album was to be titled "In Chains" and that he'd found notes among his late partner's effects, suggesting that he had envisaged old style, slavery chains and a red rose for the artwork.

Immediately, a vision of shackles and a wilting, blood red rose filled her head. The image was so clear that she could almost smell the heady perfume of the flower. Despite her full schedule for the coming weeks, Lori typed up a reply to Garrett accepting the commission.

With her imagination all fired up, Lori scoured the internet for photos of various styles of slavery chains. She hadn't appreciated the extent of the variety of shackles used to restrain slaves in the past. Quickly though, she selected a straight forward design of traditional ankle shackles. Laying her laptop to one side, she levered herself off the couch and limped through to the study to fetch her sketchpad and pencils.

Reclined on the couch with her sketchbook resting against her baby bump, Lori was soon engrossed in creating the links of the chains.

As he pulled into the driveway, Jake carefully parked the truck in his usual spot, trying not to look at the damage to the tree's bark. The tree bore wounds almost as deep as his own. Much as he had loved his old truck, he had quickly fallen in love with the new one. Maybe it was because there were no bad memories associated with it; perhaps it was the leather upholstery and top of the range gadgets. Glancing at the clock, he wondered if he had time for a run before Jethro arrived. Having been cooped up all day, his body was crying out for some fresh air. Gathering up his guitars and book bag, he locked up the truck and dashed round the side of the house.

He deposited his gear at the door to the basement, noting that Lori wasn't at her desk. Jake wandered through to the sunroom in search of her. Spotting his wife reclined on the couch engrossed in her work, he stood in the doorway watching her for a moment or two. He couldn't make out what she was drawing, but could tell from the way she was so focused on it and by the speed with which she was sketching that her creative juices were flowing freely.

"Having fun, li'l lady?" he asked as he crept up and knelt down beside her. Admiring the links of chain on the page, he commented, "Nice. Very nice."

"Thanks, and yes, I'm having fun," said Lori as she wriggled to sit up a bit.

"New commission or fun?"

"Call it a favour for a friend," she replied cryptically.

"I thought your schedule was full?"

"It is but I couldn't refuse to help Garrett. It's for the record you did out at JJL," explained Lori softly. "It's an easy, simple design. Slave chains and a red rose. Shouldn't take too long."

"As long as you're sure you're not taking on too much, li'l lady," he cautioned with concern.

"Don't fuss. I've worked out where I can fit this in. I'm pregnant not ill," countered Lori. "This one will take me three days. Four at the most."

"Slave chains and a rose?" mused Jake thoughtfully. "What's he calling it?"

"In Chains."

"I like that. Fits," said Jake with a smile. "What time are we expecting Jethro to get here?"

"Before five," replied Lori, closing her sketchbook over. "He called earlier and insisted that he wants to take us out for dinner after he's caught up with you."

"Did he say where?"

"No. Sorry."

"Ok, I guess I don't have time for a run before he gets here," sighed Jake getting to his feet. "I'd better take my gear downstairs."

"How did it go out at JJL?"

"So so," admitted Jake. "Press stuff was awkward. Apparently, there's rumours of a Weigh Station set at Rock on the Range. It was news to me!" he paused, then added, "I took Jethro's advice. I spoke to Mikey. Explained about what happened. All of it."

"I'm sure he understood."

"He was great. Kept a fatherly eye on me all afternoon. I couldn't settle in the studio with so many folks about. I need to talk to Jethro about that. Need to find a way to work through it."

"One step at a time," reminded Lori as she allowed him to help her up.

"I know. I know," muttered Jake, his frustration with himself evident.

It was almost six before Jethro arrived at the beach house. Apologising profusely for being late, he suggested that they go to dinner first and that he could have his meeting with Jake afterwards. Silver Lake's manager said he'd taken the liberty of booking a table at a new restaurant in Lewes.

When they arrived, the restaurant was packed. As they waited to be shown to their table, Jake held Lori's hand, squeezing it tight. After what felt like an eternity to him, but was in fact only a couple of minutes, their hostess showed them to a quiet, corner table, largely shielded from view by a large plant.

"Perfect, thank you," said Jethro.

"How did you hear about this place?" asked Lori as they sat browsing the menu.

"Dr Marrs brought me out here last week," he replied. "I can recommend the crab cakes. Jim said the beef was good too."

Conversation over dinner centred on the activity out at JJL and the Silver Lake schedule for the coming weeks. Travel arrangements for the band's three festival appearances were still to be finalised.

"Are you coming to all three, Lori?" asked Jethro, checking the draft schedule on his cell phone.

"As long as I'm cleared to travel," she replied, noting Jake's look of relief. "I see the doctor on Wednesday, so I'll confirm it to you then. It's only the one that we need to fly to, isn't it?"

"Yeah," said Jake. "Rockville. The others we're going to on the Silver Bullet. It's a long haul out to Ohio for you though. Make sure you tell them that, li'l lady."

"I will," promised Lori.

"How many weeks until the baby's due by the time we head to

Ohio?" asked Jethro, sharing Jake's concerns about her well-being.

"Seven," stated Lori, then sensing their concerns, added, "It's Ohio we're going to. It's not a third world country. What's the worst that can happen?"

"You go into labour while I'm on stage," replied Jake with a grin.

"Don't even joke, Mr Power," laughed Jethro. "There's nothing in the schedule about delivering babies in the lounge of the Silver Bullet!"

"Heaven forbid!" giggled Lori, feeling the baby stir. "And believe me, I've no intentions of giving birth anywhere other than a hospital!"

The waiting room at the maternity unit was crowded when Jake and Lori arrived on Wednesday morning. As she looked round at the other expectant mothers, Lori wondered how many weeks along they were as she compared the size of her growing bump to theirs. There was one young girl sitting to her left who looked hugely pregnant and exceedingly uncomfortable.

"Has to be twins," whispered Jake, spotting who she was watching.

"I hope so!" whispered back Lori with a nervous giggle. "Suddenly I feel tiny."

"Mrs Power!" called the nurse. "Through to room three. Second door on the left."

When they entered the room, Lori noted it was yet another different midwife waiting to greet them.

"Good morning," greeted the midwife with a broad smile. "How are you, Mrs Power?"

"It's Lori," corrected Lori, instantly warming to the middle-aged woman. "I'm fine. I feel huge and a bit sore but otherwise ok."

"You're looking fantastic, honey. Now let's check you over, take your bloods then we'll do the ultrasound. I see from your history that you're twenty eight weeks, but that you've been measuring ahead."

"Yes, and at my last scheduled scan they were concerned the placenta was lying low," replied Lori.

As the nurse drew the blood samples from Lori's arm a few minutes later, Jake flinched. Seeing the hypodermic needle sent shivers through him. Suddenly, he was hit by a flashback of injecting himself in the arm in his apartment. His face must have paled considerably as the nurse asked, "Are you ok, Mr Power? You're not going to pass out on me, are you?"

"Not a fan of needles," he mumbled, running his hand nervously through his hair.

"Jake," said Lori softly. "You sure you're ok?"

She offered him her other hand, sensing his growing anxiety.

"I'm fine, li'l lady," he said. "I'll explain later."

"All done," declared the nurse as she put a Band-Aid over the spot on Lori's arm where the needle had been seconds before. "Now, is Baby Power ready to smile for us, do you think?"

"I hope so," said Lori, squeezing Jake's hand. "Daddy here missed the last look at our little Power Pack."

With a little help from the nurse, Lori climbed onto the exam table, slid her leggings down a little and pulled up her tunic top. Expertly, the midwife spread a liberal amount of gel over her bump, then pressed down firmly with the probe. Almost instantly the pressure triggered a flurry of frenzied kicks from the baby. The computer screen showed the image of the baby's legs kicking furiously.

"Don't think baby liked that," commented the midwife with a laugh. Gently, she rubbed the side of Lori's bump. "Sorry, little one, I just need to check you out and let mommy and daddy see how big you've grown."

Standing beside the exam table, Jake stared incredulously at the baby on the screen. He could feel emotional tears stinging at his eyes as he marvelled at how perfect the baby looked. Swallowing hard, he asked hoarsely, "Is everything ok? Nothing's too low?"

"Everything looks perfect, Mr Power," assured the midwife. "Baby's very active. As you can see, the head's not engaged yet. First babies tend to turn early, but there's still plenty of time. Placenta is fine too. Now, give me a moment to grab some measurements, then I'll capture a couple of photos for you."

"Thanks," said Lori, unable to take her eyes off the computer screen. "Is it still a big baby?"

"Yes, but not too big, honey."

After another few minutes of probing with the sensor, the nurse declared she was done. While the printer churned away in the background, she wiped the gel from Lori's stomach, then helped her to sit up.

"Everything's looking great. Assuming your dates are correct, which I think they are, baby's about three pounds, give or take a few ounces. I measured them at seventeen and a half inches. Still slightly above average, but daddy here's quite tall, so it's understandable. I think because of your history, we'll schedule a final scan for thirty six weeks."

"Is that normal?" asked Jake anxiously.

"Yes, Mr Power. It's going to be a big baby for your wife to deliver. If we scan again at thirty six weeks, we'll have a clearer idea of the final weight and size estimate and can finalize the birth plan," explained the midwife calmly. "I see from your notes that you've had pelvic surgery. Have you seen your orthopaedic consultant recently?"

"That's our next stop," replied Lori, smoothing out her top. "I've been feeling a little unsteady on my feet. Balance is a little off."

"Perfect. I'll email round the scan details to Dr Brent and let him assess you. Do you have any more questions before you head round there?"

"Am I ok to fly in two weeks?" asked Lori. "We're going to Florida for the weekend then we've two bus trips the following two weekends."

"As long as it meets the airlines rules, then you're good to go. Make sure you don't sit for too long on the flight. Keep moving every half hour or so. Otherwise, have a great trip. You going to Disney?"

"No, to Jacksonville for Rockville," answered Jake. "It's a work thing."

"Work? Are you a musician?"

"Yes, ma'am," said Jake, flashing her one of his Power smiles. "The band are playing on Saturday."

"My son lives in Orlando. I believe he's heading to that festival. Who do you play with?"

"Silver Lake," revealed Jake almost shyly. "Tell him to come and say hi. Main stage around six."

"Will do."

In contrast to the crowded ante-natal clinic. Dr Brent's waiting room was more or less empty. There were only two other patients waiting- a young man with his arm in a cast and a teenage girl with her knee in a brace. Having told the receptionist that she was there, Lori took a seat in the corner beside Jake. He was sitting gazing down at the three scan pictures that they'd been given. In one you could see the baby's face clearly. It was this one he was staring at.

"You satisfied now that he or she is ok?" whispered Lori,

placing her hand on his thigh. "Everything's looking good."

"I've been so scared that they'd find something wrong. Discover an injury or a problem that they missed in the emergency room," confessed Jake softly, keeping his eyes on the photo. "Our little Power Pack's perfect."

"It is, isn't it," said Lori proudly. "Twelve weeks and we get to meet him or her."

"I'm sure it's a her," stated Jake with a smile.

"That's funny," giggled Lori, resting her hand on her bump. "I'm positive it's a boy."

"Well, one of us has to be right!"

Their conversation was interrupted by the receptionist calling Lori's name. Slowly, she got to her feet, lifted her canes and steadied herself. Behind her, she felt Jake move to follow her.

"I'm a big girl, rock star. You wait here. If I need you, I'll come and fetch you," she said calmly.

As she entered John Brent's office, he was standing by the window talking on his cell phone. Smiling, Lori noted that he looked to have recovered from his own leg injury as there was no sign of a brace or a cane. With a wave, the doctor indicated she should take a seat. He watched Lori carefully as she lowered herself onto the chair beside his desk.

Putting his phone in his pocket, John apologised for keeping her waiting.

"It's fine," said Lori with a warm smile. "Nice to see you've fully recovered."

"Thanks. I was lucky," admitted the doctor. "Nice clean break and it's healed really well."

"Glad to hear one of us was lucky," she said wistfully.

"And, how are you? You're looking radiant, Mrs Power," he complimented as he sat down at the desk.

"I'm fine. All baby bump and a bit unsteady on my feet. My pelvis and my back don't feel quite as they usually do."

"Something concerned me when I was reading over your notes, Lori," began the doctor, his tone more serious than normal. "Want to tell me about your visit to the ER?"

"What do the notes tell you?" asked Lori quietly, as she tried to determine how much to tell the doctor.

"That you were badly beaten. Badly bruised. That you refused to be admitted for observation."

"That's about the size of it," agreed Lori. She paused, then continued, "Someone slipped Jake some drugged tea. He reacted badly to it. He was in the ER too. In his hallucination, he thought I was someone else. Thought I was a witch trying to harm the real me."

"Jake beat you?"

Lori nodded, then explained as briefly as she could what had happened and how she had eventually found her husband unconscious. The doctor listened without interrupting her. Struggling to hold back her tears, Lori explained about Jake's time in rehab.

"And how are things now?" asked John, passing her a Kleenex.

"We're fine. We're healing together," she replied with a small smile. "Jake's still working through the trauma of it all and the guilt, but he's got a strong rehab buddy helping him."

"And he's got you," added John warmly. "You've got each other. You've both been through hell, haven't you?"

"It's been tough," she conceded. "But we've got this little Power Pack to focus on now. I can't believe there's only twelve weeks to go."

"Little?" laughed John, noting her large belly. "I'm not so sure about that, Lori!"

Giggling, she had to agree.

"Ok, let's check out your pelvis and make sure it's still intact. It's natural that you'll begin to feel it move more as the ligaments soften ready for the birth. The internal fixation to your pelvis won't be affected by that as it was away from the joints. Your metalwork's on the iliac crest and the ilium. Nowhere near the pubis," explained the doctor calmly. "Are you ok to get up on the exam table?"

"Yes, thanks," said Lori as she got to her feet.

Once she was settled on the table, John Brent checked out her range of movement thoroughly. As he assessed her, he spotted how often her stomach twitched as the baby lurched under the taut skin.

"Active little bundle," he observed as he saw the pointed bump of a foot protruding at her side.

"Yes!" laughed Lori, rubbing her stomach. "Lord help me as he or she gets bigger!"

Helping her to sit up and to stand down from the exam table,

John said, "Everything feels fine. If you're feeling unsteady though, I'd strongly advise reverting to using your crutches for the last trimester. They'll give you a bit of added stability."

Sighing, Lori nodded, "I expected you to suggest that. It feels like a backwards step."

"Not at all. It's common for expectant mothers to need additional pelvic support and to use crutches. I don't think you'd benefit from a support band. Try one if you think it might help with the weight of the baby, but I think the crutches are the answer for you."

"Makes sense, I guess," she agreed reluctantly.

"Try to get plenty of rest too. Don't be working long hours. Don't be standing for hours at the side of a stage either," cautioned the doctor. "Listen to your body. Don't push it too hard here."

Lori nodded.

"Give the crutches a try for a few weeks. If you've any concerns, call me or book another appointment. Are you to have another scan before the baby's due?"

"Yes. I've to get one on June 9th when I reach thirty six weeks. They want to check that the baby's not grown too big for me to deliver."

"Why not make another appointment with me that day too? Won't do any harm," suggested the doctor, bringing his schedule up on the screen. He slotted her in for eleven thirty, having left plenty of time for her ante-natal appointment before it.

"Any other questions?" he asked as she added the appointment to the calendar in her cell phone.

"No, I'm good," said Lori, preparing to leave. "Now to give Jake the good news that the crutches are back for a while."

"Is he with you?"

"He's in the waiting room. He's probably a wreck by now," she replied with more than a hint of concern in her voice. "He's overthinking a lot of stuff these days. And he's very protective."

"Don't let him smother you. You're pregnant, not ill," cautioned John.

"Exactly! See you on June 9th, John. Thanks again."

"Take care, Lori."

It was early afternoon when they arrived back at the beach

house. The sun was shining and, while they had been at the medical centre, it had developed into a warm day.

"Do you feel up to a walk along the beach?" asked Jake as he watched Lori search in the hall closet for her red crutches.

"As long as we don't go too far," she called back. "Gives me a chance to remember how to use crutches again."

"It won't be for long, li'l lady," said Jake softly, understanding how much she detested using her elbow crutches. "It'll all be worth it in the end."

"I know. I know."

"Come on. Some ocean air will make you feel better."

Taking things at Lori's pace, they walked slowly down the beach on the hard packed, wet sand, taking care to stay out of reach of the waves. As they walked, they chatted through everything the midwife had said and then Lori had explained again everything that John had said. Talking it all through reminded them just how short a space of time twelve weeks was. By the time they had compared schedules and commitments, Lori realised she was going to have to work until mid-June to meet all of hers. There were only eight weeks until Silver Lake were due in the studio to start work on their third album. With a weary sigh, Jake admitted their track list was still a few songs light.

As they turned and headed back home, their conversation turned to the potential ideas Jake had for the missing songs. He confided that he had a few rough ideas, but was concerned about using them. When Lori asked why, he explained that he'd written a few songs about what had happened and his time in rehab, but that they were too personal and the emotions still too raw to share.

"What happened back at the medical centre when they were doing my bloods?" asked Lori, suddenly remembering how pale he'd gone.

"Flashback," stated Jake simply, staring straight ahead along the beach. "It just hit me. It was the first time I've remembered actually putting that needle in my arm and easing the plunger home."

"Ah, I see," she said softly. "You looked like you'd seen a ghost."

"Guess I had. Not one I ever want to see again."

"I hadn't realised that heroin was a ghost from your past. From what you'd said before, I thought you had been more into coke and pills," observed Lori, not wanting to push him too far but also feeling she needed to probe a little deeper.

"I did it on occasion. It was Paul's vice. I never liked it. Never got a taste for it, thank God! He had a hard time getting clean. Relapsed a couple of times before he made it."

"And you?"

"That was my first and last relapse in over six years," he confessed honestly. "Lori, I'm scared to even swallow an Advil or Tylenol now. I've not touched a drop of alcohol since. I'm terrified to take anything that will alter my consciousness. I trust you to pour me a drink, but I can't even relax to let anyone else pour me a coffee!"

His confession came tumbling out. He stopped and turned to face the ocean, not wanting her to see the tears in his eyes.

"Lori, I'm scared every time I'm out of your sight. Being out at JJL with all those people the other day scared the crap out of me. Jethro suggested talking to a doctor and getting something prescribed to take the edge off it all but that's only going to compound the problem. I've no idea how I'm going to manage to record this Weigh Station record!"

"But you were ok when we were out there last week?"

"Yes, but it was only you and me in there. The thought of all those other artists dropping in and of doing the two duets with the girls is terrifying me. I don't know if I can do it."

"Would it help if I was there?" offered Lori, unsure of what else to suggest.

"Maybe. I honestly don't know," sighed Jake, turning back to face her. "I need to find a way through this. Work out a coping mechanism."

"We'll get through this," promised Lori. "Whatever it takes, we'll work this out. And remember, I love you, rock star."

Hugging her tightly, Jake buried his face in her hair to hide his tears. He held her for a few minutes, feeling her bump pressing against him, then cupped her face in his hands. Slowly, he kissed her.

"I love you too, li'l lady," he said, his voice husky, filled with emotion. "I've no idea how I'd have got through the last few weeks without you. I can't begin to understand how you've coped. I can't comprehend why you can still trust me. That you still love me. But I'm eternally grateful that you do. I couldn't do this on my own."

"Do you remember what Grey said at our wedding?" asked Lori quietly as she gazed up into Jake's troubled, hazel eyes. "He said "when frustration, difficulties and fear assail your relationship as they threaten all relationships at one time or another, remember to focus on what is right between you, not only the part which seems wrong. In this way, you can ride out the storms when clouds hide the face of the sun in your lives, remembering that even if you lose sight of it for a moment, the sun is still there." We'll weather this storm together, rock star."

"One step at a time as you keep reminding me," he said with a weak smile.

As they walked up the path from the beach to the deck, they could hear voices. Much to their surprise, they found Grey and Becky sitting on the deck waiting for them. When she saw her Uncle Jake, the little girl came hurtling towards him. Unable to resist her, Jake swept her up into his arms, holding her high above him for a moment before sitting her on his shoulders.

"I can see for miles!" she declared, gazing about her.

"Hold on tight, princess," cautioned Jake. "I don't want to drop you."

"What can you see from up there?" asked Lori, smiling up at the little girl.

"I can see Grammy in Atlantic City!" stated Becky, pointing up the beach.

The three adults started to laugh.

"Has your mom escaped again?" asked Jake, setting Becky down.

The bass player nodded, "We dropped her at the bus a couple of hours ago. She's there till Sunday."

"Another church group outing?" giggled Lori as she opened the patio doors.

"According to her it is," laughed Grey. "We thought we'd drop by to see you guys before we headed home."

"I've not seen Uncle Jake for weeks!" complained Becky dramatically.

"Did you miss me, honey?" asked Jake, following her into the sunroom.

"Yes!"

"I've missed you too," replied Jake, realising that he had missed the little girl.

"Do you guys want to stay for dinner?" invited Lori.

"If you're sure it's no trouble," said Grey, knowing his daughter would protest if he said no. "We can't stay late. Becky has school tomorrow and Kola promised to be over after work tonight. She's due at our place around eight."

"It's no trouble. We're not having anything fancy. I've still to go food shopping so it's mac'n'cheese or take out," replied Lori.

"Mac'n'cheese!" cried Becky enthusiastically.

"Fine by me," added Grey grinning.

"Come on, Becky," said Lori. "You can help me cook dinner while the boys do boy things."

With the girls out of earshot, Grey asked how things had gone out at JJL at the start of the week, adding that he was scheduled to do his bass tracks on Friday. He explained that he'd had a call from Jim Marrs asking if he would play on two tracks instead of just the original one.

"I'm back out there tomorrow to do vocals," revealed Jake. "Duet with Tori."

"And is this going to result in three days of silence over the weekend like last time?" joked Grey, remembering Jake's first duet with the Molton star.

"Not if I can help it!" laughed Jake. "Battle Scars isn't as high pitched, thank God!"

"What's the plan with the Silver Lake rehearsals?" asked Grey, opening his schedule on his phone. "Paul's in the studio on the 21st and Rich is out there the 23rd."

"I'm back there on the 24th," said Jake. "Duet with Witchy Woo. I'm not sure what song we're doing though. I've still to get a slot to do Broken Bottle too. Guess I need to check up on that one."

"Well, we need to rehearse and pull a set together for these festivals," stated Grey bluntly. "I don't want us falling on our asses out there."

"The boss booked out the small rehearsal room out back for us, didn't she? We could use it. Four days should be enough for us," suggested Jake.

"I'll message the boss to check. Rings a bell. That would work out ok though," agreed Grey, beginning to type a message to Maddison.

"We could hopefully work out the last few songs for the album too," added Jake. "By my reckoning, we're at least four songs light."

"You got any more gems hidden up your sleeve, Mr Power?"

"Maybe. A few ideas. A couple of quite dark lyrics floating about," admitted Jake. "I'll do my best to come up with something."

"Well, if you need a bass line, call me," warned Grey. "No trying to play them yourself!"

Laughing, Jake agreed.

When Jake walked into JJL next morning, the place was deserted. As a precaution, he'd brought along a couple of guitars, just in case Dr Marrs asked him to stay back to record Broken Bottle. They'd exchanged a few emails the night before and the current idea was that Jake would record it as a solo performance to close the record. It seemed like a fitting tribute to the late Dan Crow.

As Jake reached the live room, he could hear someone singing behind the closed doors. The voice wasn't one he was familiar with but the song was familiar. It was one of Weigh Station's earliest ballads, Angel Wings. A glance through the glass panel of the door revealed the identity of the mystery chanteuse.

It was Kola.

Waiting out of sight until she reached the last line, Jake listened closely. Despite all the time he'd spent with her in the studio, she'd never confessed to being able to sing. The voice he was hearing was one of the best female rock voices he'd ever heard. As she nailed the last note, he opened the door and stepped into the room.

Instantly, the shy sound engineer whirled round, her face a mask of panic, "Jake!"

"Morning," greeted Jake warmly. "That sounded incredible. I'd forgotten how good that song was."

"How long were you listening?" gasped Kola, flushing scarlet at having been overheard.

"Long enough to know you are hiding one of the best voices I've heard for a long while," answered Jake as he set his guitar cases down on the floor. "Will you humour me and sing it again? I've not played that song for years. I used to play it for my mom. She loved it.

"I'm not sure," began Kola, looking like a rabbit caught in the headlights.

"Please," begged Jake with a smile. "There's no one else here. It's just you and me. Who's going to know?"

"Ok," she relented. "But, if anyone comes in, we stop."

"Deal," agreed Jake, lifting his beloved acoustic guitar out of its case. "Just give me a minute."

Discretely, he propped his cell phone up on the open lid of the velvet lined case and set it to record. Sitting down on the couch, he quickly checked the tuning of his guitar, then gave Kola the nod, "On three."

"One, two, one, two, three," he counted steadily as he began to play the song.

It had been over ten years since he'd last played Angel Wings and Jake silently prayed that he didn't ruin Kola's performance. Deliberately, he kept his playing soft and gentle as he listened to the young sound engineer pour her heart and soul into the vocals. Kola's voice was warm and husky, adding an extra loving element to the ballad. The lyrics spun a sad tale of the pain of losing a loved one unexpectedly and of watching them spread their angel wings.

As before, she nailed the last long, high note, then collapsed on the floor in a fit of girlish giggles.

"That was intense!" she declared with a giant smile. "Thanks, Jake. That was fun."

"Thank you," he said as he casually got up to lay his guitar back in its case and to stop the recording. "I haven't played that in a long time. Glad I remembered it all. I used to sit in our kitchen at home and play that for my mom when it was just her and I in the house. My brothers and my dad always gave me a hard time about my music. Only my mom believed in me."

"Mom's are like that," said Kola softly.

In the background, they heard Tori's voice out in the lounge. Immediately, Kola got to her feet and headed for the door. She paused as she reached it, turning back to look at Jake. Playfully, she blew him a kiss, then disappeared out into the hallway.

With a smile, Jake slipped his phone back into his pocket. He hoped that his basic recording was half as good as the performance had been. In his heart, he knew that Angel Wings deserved to be the closing track on the record. Now he had to find a way to convince Garrett, Mikey and Dr Marrs of this fact and to sweet talk Kola into a proper recording of it.

Before he could get too carried away with the idea, the door opened and Tori swept in carrying two cups of coffee.

"Morning!" she called brightly. "Latte? Two sugars?"

"Morning," replied Jake. "Thanks for the coffee."

"Pleasure. You ready to sing your heart out with me?"

"As I'll ever be," he said, lifting the lid off the coffee cup. Tentatively, he sniffed the coffee before taking a sip. "Be gentle with me. Our last duet didn't end well."

"Didn't it?" quizzed Tori, looking confused.

"Not for me. Strained my voice. Had three days of total vocal rest. Silence. Couldn't sing for a week," confessed Jake, remembering how scary and miserable his three silent days had been.

"Lord, I never knew!" gasped Tori, genuinely looking shocked at what she was hearing. "Today'll be different. It's you and me, not you and Molton."

"Is there a difference?"

"Oh, yes!" laughed Tori, kicking off her trademark spiked heel boots. "We're going to have some fun!"

From the control room, Dr Marrs called through, "When you're quite finished, are you ready to make a start?"

"Yes, darling," purred Tori with a mischievous wink at Jake. "Let's run through it a few ways, then agree the best split."

"Fine by me," agreed Jake, putting the lid back on his latte. "Ladies first."

For more than an hour, they worked on how best to split up the Weigh Station anthem. There were three verses and three choruses. Initially, they worked their way through it with Tori singing the first verse, then they repeated it with Jake starting things off. They played about with the chorus, trading lines, then trading choruses. Much to Jake's surprise, Tori's screamer "metal queen" vocals were gone. In their place, she sang with a warm, rich, bluesy tone that sat much lower in her range. It complimented his mid-range beautifully, making the duet easier to master regardless of who sang first.

After an hour and a half, Dr Marrs said, "Take a fifteen minute break, guys. I want to listen to some of this then make a decision. Clock's ticking here. Go grab a coffee."

Needing no second invitation to take a break, the two vocalists made their way through to the lounge. While Jake poured them both a coffee, Tori flopped down on the couch and let out a long sigh.

"You ok, sunshine? Voice still intact?" she asked as he handed her a cup.

"I'm fine. You ok?"

"Couldn't be better. Battle Scars is one of my favourites. I duetted it with Dan himself a long time ago," she declared with a wistful smile.

"What was the split, then?" asked Jake, taking a seat at the table.

"He did the first verse, I did the first chorus, we both sang the second verse and chorus. I took the last verse and we did the final chorus together. Worked like a charm."

"Then, regardless of what Dr Marrs says, that's how we are splitting it," said Jake. "If it was Dan's way, then it's the right way for this one."

"Totally agree."

"Can I ask you something?"

"Anything, darling. Anytime."

"Why don't you usually sing the way you were performing in there? You've a fantastic voice for that style of vocals."

"I'd love to," confessed Tori quietly. "But Molton's record company and the management beg to differ. They want the distinctive Molton sound. I've been recording some solo stuff. Its more blues based rock with a hint of country. It's fun to do something a bit different now and then. Keeps it all fresh."

While they drank their coffee, they chatted over their own musical preferences, discovering more in common than Jake had bargained for. Without an audience, the "real" Tori emerged and he found himself warming to her, feeling less intimidated than he usually felt in her presence.

"Guys," called out Dr Marrs from the far side of the lounge. "Can you step back in here for a minute?"

Once in the control room, the producer explained the way he wanted Battle Scars to be split up. Both Jake and Tori listened to him then put forward Tori's suggestion. The producer considered their proposal, then made a counter suggestion.

"Let's do it both ways," he suggested, checking the time. "Then I want a full run through from each of you."

"Jim, I need to be out of here by three," said Tori firmly. "I've a show tonight in Philadelphia. I need to make it in time for sound check at five. Five thirty at the outside."

"Well, let's get started then."

With a few minutes to spare, Jake and Tori completed all four versions of the song to Dr Marrs' satisfaction. He had wanted as close to a live sound as he could get and both vocalists obliged by delivering storming performances. When they asked which duet worked better, the producer conceded that Dan's way had sounded more natural and that lyrically it made more sense. A "toot" of a horn alerted Tori to the arrival of her driver. Quickly, she hugged Jake then dashed out of the live room without a backwards glance.

"How are you holding up, Jake?" called through Dr Marrs. "You feel up to tracking some guitars for me?"

"I could so with some air for a few minutes," confessed Jake, running his fingers through his hair and feeling them catch on some knots. "Give me a half hour then I'm all yours for another couple of hours."

"Great but only if you're sure."

"Jim, I'm ok," promised Jake with a smile. "Just let me clear my head. Call Lori and just switch off for a bit."

"Take your time. We'll be ready and waiting when you are."

Helping himself to a bottle of juice from the refrigerated cabinet in the lounge, Jake wandered through the studio and outside. Dragging an empty plastic crate round to the rear of the building, he sat down and stretched out his long, denim clad legs, basking in the warm, spring sunshine. He closed his eyes and listened to the birds in the trees beyond the rehearsal studio. A blue jay was screeching loudly, distressed by some unseen danger.

Satisfied that he was alone, Jake listened to the playback of the recording he'd made earlier. It sounded better than he had hoped. His guitar was gentle enough not to drown Kola's straight from the heart vocals. The fit of giggles at the end added a little *je ne sais quoi* to the song. His next challenge was letting Dr Marrs hear it without Kola discovering that he'd surreptitiously recorded her.

After a while, a chill breeze got up and Jake began to feel cold. Draining the last of his juice, he got to his feet and headed back inside for another couple of hours.

"Ok, Jim," he called as he re-entered the live room. "What's the plan? Broken Bottle?"

"No, Mr Power. I need a lead guitar for Battle Scars. One of our guests dropped out on us. Scheduling conflict," explained the producer.

"Drop D?" checked Jake as he opened his guitar case and lifted out his Mz Hyde custom.

"Sure is."

"Let me run through it a couple of times. Check my way fits with what you've got," Jake proposed as he plugged the lead into his guitar.

"All I've got is bass and drums," laughed the producer, "Plus your vocals. Free rein with the guitar track."

"Lead and rhythm?"

"If you've time. Mikey can pick one up tomorrow if need be."

"Let's see how this goes," said Jake with a smile. "Battle Scars is fun to play. Love it!"

Darkness had fallen by the time Jake left the studio. Alone and undistracted, he'd finally relaxed in the live room, under the watchful eyes of Dr Marrs and Kola. They had played around with a few variations before settling for something a little different to the original, but more in keeping with the duet. With the lead guitar track and solo safely recorded, Jake had agreed to lay down a couple of rhythm tracks before calling a halt for the day.

As he'd left, he'd said to Jim Marrs that he had a new song to run past him but that he'd mail it to him. Engrossed in his production duties, Dr Marrs had nodded and said he'd watch out for it.

With his gear stowed in the back of the truck, Jake called home to check what the plans for dinner were. Lori confessed that she had been working all afternoon and hadn't thought about cooking. Resisting the urge to give her a lecture about sitting for too long at her drawing board, Jake offered to stop off in town and pick up something from his favourite fish restaurant.

He was surprised, half an hour later, to get a parking spot right outside the door of the restaurant. As he stepped down from the cab, he spotted two familiar faces coming out carrying a bag of food. It was Scott and Ellen.

"Jake!" called out Scott cheerfully. "How you doing?"

"I'm good, thanks," replied Jake before adding a little sheepishly, "Apologies about that..eh.."

"Don't worry about it," interrupted the young photographer. "As long as you're ok."

"I'm fine," assured Jake calmly before turning his attention to Ellen, "This is a surprise. I didn't know you were in town already."

"I flew in a few days early," she said shyly. "Wanted some time with Scott before After Life head over to the west coast. We've a support slot. Six shows. Ten days on the west coast."

"Great stuff," nodded Jake, genuinely pleased to hear that the young band had picked up another tour. "Are you still ok to work on our duet next week?"

"Looking forward to it," admitted Ellen, blushing slightly. "I'll need to work on the song a bit this week."

"Me too," confessed Jake with a wink. "Come over to the house one afternoon. We can have a run through there in peace if you want. I'm sure Lori will be glad to see you too."

"Sounds like a smart idea," agreed Ellen. "I'll call you on Monday to work something out. We're away this weekend."

"Where you off to?"

"New Orleans," revealed Scott. "We're vampire hunting."

"I've seen enough of them," muttered Jake under his breath before adding. "Great city. Very pretty. Have a fun weekend."

"We'll try," promised Ellen shyly.

After Jake had called, Lori had finished off the section she was working on then tidied up her desk. Having placed two plates in the oven to heat, she set the table in the kitchen. She had only just lit the candle in the centre of the table when she heard Jake's truck in the driveway. Rubbing her baby bump, she said, "Daddy's home, honey."

Opening the back door with a clatter, Jake stumbled into the house weighed down with his guitars, book bag and the bag containing their dinner.

"Evening, li'l lady," he said, brushing a kiss on her cheek as he passed. "You look fabulous."

"Thanks," said Lori relieved to see her husband home looking relaxed and happy. "Good day?"

"Actually, you know something, it was," admitted Jake grinning. "Revelationary too."

"Oh! Do tell?" giggled Lori, curious to know what had managed to restore Jake's relaxed good humour.

"Sit down and I'll explain over dinner," he said. "I met Scott and Ellen when I stopped to pick up dinner."

"I didn't know he was back in town."

"Neither did I," agreed Jake as he dished up their meal. "Ellen's going to call on Monday about rehearsing here before we do our duet out at JJL next week."

"Inviting a strange woman down into the basement?" teased Lori with a mischievous smile. "Tut tut, Mr Power."

"She seemed nervous about the duet."

"I'm teasing you, rock star," giggled Lori. "Now tell me about these revelations."

"I'll tell you about one, then reveal the other after dinner."

While they ate, Jake explained about the different, softer side to Tori that he'd seen. His passion for the duet shone through in his every word. It warmed Lori's heart to see his creative fire reignited.

"So, what's the second revelation?" asked Lori when he'd finished talking about recording Battle Scars.

"I've a mystery recording to play for you after dinner," answered Jake cryptically. "But, if I can make it happen, it's going to be the last track on the Weigh Station record. It's perfect."

"Now I'm intrigued."

"Patience, li'l lady," he cautioned softly. "Your turn to tell me about your day."

While Lori stretched out on the couch, Jake sat on the floor in front of her and fished his cell phone out of his pocket. He found the recording of Angel Wings then sat back to gauge his wife's reaction to the song. Hearing the recording for a second time still sent excited chills tingling up and down his spine. Yet again, he marvelled at the fact that Kola was deliberately hiding her vocal talents.

When the song was over and they'd both laughed at the natural giggles that ended it, Lori asked, "Who was that? It's fantastic!"

"Guess," teased Jake, slipping the phone back into his pocket.

"I've no idea," said Lori, trying to think who the mystery chanteuse could be. "I've definitely not heard that voice before. I'd remember if I had."

"Kola," revealed Jake.

"Kola?" echoed Lori instantly. "Wow!"

"Sure is," said Jake, before going on to explain about arriving out at JJL and finding her in the live room.

"Do you think you can convince her to record it for the album?"

"I hope so," sighed Jake, trying hard to stifle a yawn. "I'll mail this over to Jim and, hopefully, between us we can convince her. On the other hand, he might agree to go with the version we've got and use it as an Easter egg."

"Maybe Grey can help you to persuade her," Lori suggested.

"If he knows she can sing."

Life over the next few days slipped into a leisurely routine. They both slept late, worked for a few hours, lunched together and took a short walk along the beach before returning to the house to work on for another few hours. Each evening, while Lori cooked dinner, Jake would check in with Jethro, sticking rigidly to his rehab plan. As the days wore on, the shadow of the incident with Salazar Mendes finally began to recede and there was more of the "old" Jake and less of the anxious one. The nightly calls with Jethro helped, as did their weekly meeting on the Tuesday afternoon. Instead of meeting at the house, they'd met in town, at the café where Jake had taken Lori on their first date two years before. When he confessed this to Silver Lake's manager, Jethro prompted him to open up a bit more about Lori and the effect the whole thing had had on them. They had talked for over an hour before the older man was convinced that they really had put it firmly behind them. He did, however, make one observation. Calmly, he pointed out that Jake and Lori had both avoided being in the basement together and suggested that they might want to change that before the baby arrived.

While Jake had been working on new material for the Silver Lake record, Lori had completed her roulette wheel design and begun work on the Weigh Station project's cover. An email from Mikey revealing the name of the album had given her the inspiration that she needed. He had said they'd settled on Chequered Past as the track listing spanned their entire twenty five year back catalogue. He also invited Lori to attend a media day out at JJL, stating that she was to be interviewed about her involvement in the band's artwork and the current project. A second email asked if she could possibly pull together a draft design by then.

Time wasn't on Lori's side, but she had replied that she would agree to the interview and try to have a sample ready for the cover design. After a bit of thought, she decided to create a chequerboard type cover and grid it into sixteen small images. She still had the drawings for the album covers that she had produced for Weigh Station over the years and opted to use pieces from them to fill some of the sixteen squares. Once she had pulled that together, she was left with four panels that required a new drawing. She also needed to link them somehow. The link had to tie in with the late Dan Crow too. Patiently, Lori scoured her photo files seeking inspiration from images of the late Weigh Station front man. Eventually, she spotted that he always wore the same bracelet on stage. It resembled a bike chain, but was the only theme she could find to link up his whole career.

When Jake came up from the basement late on Wednesday afternoon, he found Lori sitting out on the sun deck surrounded by sketches of pieces of chain. Picking one up, he said, "You having fun, li'l lady?"

"Yes and no," confessed Lori, pausing, pencil still poised over the page. "I've found the pattern to link the design panels, but I'm having a fight with the angles of it. It's not sitting well for the corners."

"What is it? Looks kind of familiar."

"It's Dan's chain bracelet that he wore on stage," explained Lori, showing him the photo she had printed off as a sample. "It's the only thing I could find to link it all together."

"Looks perfect," Jake agreed, nodding approvingly. "Are you going to have a rough copy ready for tomorrow?"

"No," sighed Lori wearily, "But I will have a section of it done, if I can get the right turn worked out. I can draw it bending to the left, but the right isn't flowing smoothly yet."

"Take your time, li'l lady. Don't rush it," cautioned Jake, concerned that she was working too hard and not resting enough.

"I've almost figured it out. I just need another couple of hours," she replied. "I need to make the most of the time while this little Power Pack is settled. I think they're asleep."

"Well, don't work too hard," said Jake warmly. "I'm going to run out to see Paul for an hour or so. Want me to bring dinner in on my way back?"

"Please," said Lori. "Steak sandwiches would be good and some cheese fries."

"I'll see what I can do," promised Jake. "I'll be back about six thirty. Seven at the latest."

Gently, he kissed her on the top of the head, then headed round the side of the house to the truck.

There was no sign of Paul's car in the driveway when Jake arrived at the farmhouse. Unusually, the house seemed quiet. Hooking his sunglasses into the neck of his T-shirt, Jake loped up the steps onto the porch and rang the bell. A few seconds later Maddy opened the door.

"Afternoon," she greeted brightly.

"Hi, Maddison," said Jake, flashing her a smile. "Is Paul about?"

"He's taken the meatballs to the food store. He should be back in a few minutes. Come on through. Want a coffee or a juice?"

"Coffee would be good," replied Jake, feeling his anxiety about accepting a drink from someone fluttering in his stomach.

As if sensing his apprehension, Maddy said, "Can you go through and fetch it while I finish off an email and shut down my laptop?"

"Sure," said Jake, hoping his relief wasn't too obvious.

"There's clean cups in the dishwasher," added Maddy. "I'll literally be two minutes."

When she joined him in the farmhouse's kitchen, she apologised for abandoning him.

"I had to get a reply off to Laughlan," she explained. "Looks like you are in demand for Rock on the Range, darling."

"So, the Weigh Station set's happening?"

Silver Lake's Goth manager nodded, "An hour long set about seven o'clock on the main stage on the Sunday. You ok with that?"

"Do I have a choice?" countered Jake quietly as he stirred his coffee.

"Not really," admitted Maddy bluntly.

"It'll be fine," sighed Jake, running his hand through his hair. "I'll just paint the Disney Power smile on as Lori would say."

"And how is Lori today?" asked Maddy, changing the subject. "I hope she's resting enough. She looked worn out at the meatballs' party."

"I left her working on the Weigh Station cover," said Jake. "She's pushing herself too hard, but I think it's her way of coping with everything that's happened. This, plus Garrett's design, are the last she's to finish before the baby arrives."

"Garrett's design?"

Jake nodded, "He wants to release Salazar's last record. Asked Lori to do the cover for it. In the circumstances, she couldn't refuse him. It's one design."

"And how do you feel about it being released?" asked Maddy, her tone no longer business-like but softer and caring.

"I'm ok with it," murmured Jake, staring down into the mug of milky liquid. "It's closure for Garrett. It's a great record. Despite all that happened, I'm proud of the work I put in on it."

"You won't need to do any promotion for it, will you?"

"Garrett's not asked. If he does, the answer will be no," stated Jake firmly. "I need to keep that shit behind me once and for all."

"How's putting it behind you going? Jethro's impressed with how far you've come, but he's concerned about you too."

"I've got my head round the big things," revealed Jake without looking up. "I'm ok down in the basement again. I'm getting there with being at JJL. Still jittery if the room's busy. It's all the little things that are harder to work on."

"Like what?" pushed Maddy softly, sharing her fellow manager's concern for the musician.

"Trust," began Jake. "I don't trust anyone to pour me a drink of anything. I can't drink out of a red solo cup. I'm scared to take any pills or to touch alcohol. I don't want to take anything that might alter my consciousness."

"And when you get another migraine?"

"I'll suffer it," he said, staring at her with a deadly serious look in his hazel eyes. "I'm not risking behaving like that ever again."

"Oh, Jake," she sighed. "I wish I could help you through this."

"Just make sure it specifies blue cups on our rider for the shows. And no caffeine energy drinks. I can't stomach them either anymore."

"That's easy. How do you feel though about going out on stage at Rockville? Will you be ok with that? It's a huge crowd for your first show."

"I'll find out May 3rd," laughed Jake nervously. "It'll be ok. As long as my water bottles aren't opened and are clearly marked as mine."

Their heart to heart was interrupted by Paul's arrival back from the store. Leaving the conversation unfinished, Jake and Paul disappeared through to Paul's music room to work on a track for the Silver Lake album. The drummer had called him to help out with a song he'd written. When he heard the rough recording of the track, Jake nodded approvingly, then asked if Paul had any lyrics for it. There was a sad edge to the music, an almost desperate feel to it. Without saying anything, the Silver Lake drummer passed Jake a notebook open at a page of neatly written lyrics. Silently, Jake read them over then re-read them.

"Did you write these?" he asked finally.

"Grey helped a bit," revealed Paul. "We were shooting the breeze when we were out fishing the other day. You know, talking about all the shit that's happened and then this song that we'd been playing with. The lyrics just kind of came to both of us."

Reading them over again, Jake felt a tug at his heart. His two band mates had written about their personal fears for a friend going through hell; their concern that they had been lured down a dark trail; their love for the person; their hope that they could be brought back from an all-consuming darkness. Feeling a lump in his throat, Jake realised that they had written it about him.

"There's one possible problem," he said as he handed the notebook back to his friend.

"What?" asked Paul anxiously.

"I don't know if I can sing those," explained Jake. "They're fucking fantastic, but so personal. I love them but…"

"We thought of that," began Paul, reaching over to his laptop. "Grey's going to do the honours. Listen."

For the next four minutes, Jake listened to a second rough recording of the song. The bass player's voice was perfect for the emotional lyrical content. There was a roughness to it that added an honest dimension to the song.

"Well, I'll be damned," said Jake when the song ended. "The boy can sing."

"That he can," acknowledged Paul. "Said someone's been coaching him. Wouldn't say who though."

Thinking back to the recording he'd made of Kola singing Angel Wings, Jake smiled to himself.

"I love that song," said Jake quietly. "Appreciate the effort you guys have gone to with it. Appreciate the love. Does it have a title yet?"

"Dark Trails."

"It's on the board when we hit JJL next month. Has Rich heard it yet?"

"Yup. He's working on a solo for it."

"As long as he's ok with it," said Jake. "He's still keeping his distance a little after what happened."

"He'll come round," assured Paul. "Grey will convince him."

"I hope so," sighed Jake, getting to his feet. "Right, I need to head home. Big press day tomorrow at JJL. Dreading it, but I've my duet with Ellen when it's over to look forward to."

"Say hi to Witchy Woo for me," said Paul, trying to keep the mood light. "Tell her to be gentle with you."

"I will. See you out at JJL next week."

Next morning, it was Lori who was anxious as they drove up the highway towards JJL. She had taken extra care with her appearance, trying to dress to minimise the size of her baby bump. Despite having been emailed the questions for the interview, she was more nervous than Jake had ever seen her. It distracted him from his own anxieties as he watched her fidgeting in the passenger seat of the truck.

"If it's making you this stressed, li'l lady," he began softly. "You don't need to do it. Mikey and the others will understand."

"I bet Dan's having a good laugh at this," she muttered as the baby kicked her sharply in the ribs. "It's the media seeing me so heavily pregnant and on crutches that's bothering me."

"Why?"

"I don't know," said Lori, rubbing her twitching, swollen belly. "I guess I don't want to be photographed and filmed hobbling about looking like I've swallowed a basketball!"

"You're not that big yet," assured Jake as he turned off the highway. "You're beautifully expectant. Plus, you've ten more weeks growing to do."

"And is that supposed to make me feel better, rock star?" she challenged sharply.

The driveway was already crowded with vehicles, including the film crew's large mobile studio truck. Slowly, Jake drove around to the rear of the building, noting that Garrett's old wreck of a car was blocking the back door. Once he'd parked, he hurried round to help Lori down from the cab, hovering anxiously beside her until she had steadied herself on her red crutches.

"Show time, li'l lady," he whispered, kissing her playfully on the tip of her nose.

Almost the instant that they appeared round the side of the studio complex, half a dozen photographers buzzed around them. Forcing a smile, Lori focussed her attention on walking to the front door without stumbling. Beside her, Jake was laden down by three guitars and his book bag plus his wife's folio folder. Cries of "When's the baby due?" followed them as they entered the building.

"You ok?" asked Jake, once they were in the lounge.

"I am now," sighed Lori with a relieved smile. "I was so scared I'd fall out there in front of them all."

"Relax. They'll be gone before you need to go back out there," promised Jake.

"I know, but they'll be laying in wait for us at the three outdoor festivals."

"True. What happened to the Disney Hyde smile?"

"I'm too hormonal for that," stated Lori bluntly.

Behind them, the office door opened and Dr Marrs wandered out into the lounge with Jen, the journalist who had interviewed Lori in Atlantic City the year before. A third person stepped out at their back. It was Jason Russell.

"Jake!" he called out in his "stiff upper lip", English accent. "How are you? And Lori, you're looking marvellous. Positively blooming!"

"Morning, Jason," said Jake, placing a protective arm around Lori's shoulder. "We're both good. You?"

"Jet lagged," confessed the Englishman. "Last minute visit. I only arrived last night."

"How long are you here for?" asked Lori.

"Ten days," he replied. "Thought I'd fly down to Florida to experience Rockville for myself. Lend a bit of moral support to Silver Lake."

"The more the merrier," agreed Lori, feeling Jake's grip tighten on her shoulder.

"Lori," interrupted Jen, glancing down at the sheaf of papers in her hand. "I thought we'd do the interview in the control room. We're all set up and ready whenever you are."

"Thanks, Jen. Give me a minute to freshen up and I'll be through."

"Jake," said Dr Marrs, "They're waiting for you in the live room. Photo shoot."

"On my way," he replied, sounding less than enthusiastic. "Lori, I'll see you back out here later."

"Disney smiles all round," whispered Lori as he bent to kiss her forehead.

As Jen followed Lori into the control room, she asked when the baby was due.

"End of June," replied Lori, lowering herself into the seat normally occupied by Dr Marrs.

"Exciting," said Jen, taking a seat opposite her. "My sister's due in August. It's her third."

"Not sure I could do this three times," joked Lori. "Ask me again in July or August."

"You're looking fabulous," complimented the journalist. "Lou's twice as big as you already."

"Thanks. I feel huge."

While the cameraman finished setting up, the two women chatted through the plan for the interview. Lori's folio folder lay open on the mixing desk and she talked Jen through the various parts of the artwork that she'd brought with her.

Eventually, the cameraman said he was ready and the two women assumed their formal positions. Still feeling self-conscious about her baby bump, Lori smoothed down her black tunic, then rested her hand on top of her swollen belly.

Jen delivered her introductory spiel to the camera, concluding with, "And I've been joined now by the radiant and talented Mz Lori Hyde or should I say Power?"

"Still Mz Hyde for professional purposes," said Lori, forcing a nervous smile.

"And soon to be a mommy too," continued Jen. "Congratulations to you and Jake."

"Thanks," blushed Lori. "We're both excited to meet this baby."

"So, is the cover art for this charity record your last project before the baby arrives?"

"Not quite," revealed Lori. "I've a small, private commission to finish too before I stop work at the start of June."

"Now, recording is well underway for the record in memory of Dan Crow. When did you become involved with the project?"

And so commenced the hour of questioning. As she delivered her answers, Lori began to relax and to actually enjoy chatting with the journalist. She was careful not to reveal too many personal details of the project, dodging queries about which tracks Jake was due to appear on. When the conversation moved on to the album title and artwork, Lori talked through the parts of the design that she'd brought along.

As the hour drew to a conclusion, Jen asked one final question, "Dr Marrs let slip that the final track on the record is to be Broken Bottle Empty Glass. Any idea who is going to star on it along with Jake? Prior to his untimely death, it had been widely rumoured that Salazar Mendes was going to come out of retirement for this project."

Pausing for a moment as she tried desperately not to react to the mention of Salazar's name, Lori said, "I believe that had been discussed at the start of the year. Jake's not recorded that track yet, as far as I know, so they may have amended the track list."

"Could he do it as a solo track? As a final tribute to Dan's legacy?"

"Perhaps. We'll have to wait and see when the record comes out," answered Lori warmly.

"Thanks, Lori. We'll leave it there," announced Jen with a nod to the cameraman, indicating that he should stop filming. "It's been a pleasure to chat to you. Thank you."

After an hour of posing for the photo shoot, Jake's patience had worn thin. He suspected that had the photographer been Scott, he may have been more tolerant, but, as the clock ticked round to midday, he declared he needed a break and left the live room. The lounge was empty as he marched through it. A wave of disappointment hit him. He'd hoped Lori would've been there.

Once outside, he was relieved to discover the place was quiet. All the remaining media personnel were in the building. As he turned the corner, heading for the upturned crate he'd sat on the week before, Jake thought he heard music coming from the small rehearsal studio at the rear of the property.

Curious to know who was rehearsing, he made his way over, entering the long, low building as quietly as he could. Through the porthole window in the door, he could see Ellen rehearsing the Weigh Station song they were due to duet after lunch. As he peered into the room, he spotted the ends of Lori's scarlet crutches over to the side. It was all the invitation he needed to enter.

Hearing the creak of the door, Ellen stopped instantly.

"Hi," called out Jake with a warm smile. "Mind if I join you, ladies?"

Lori was sitting on the edge of the low practice stage, sipping on a bottle of water.

"The more the merrier," she called over. "Is your photo shoot finished?"

"Not quite," confessed Jake "I escaped for some air. Needed a break." He paused, then turned to Ellen, "You should've come into the studio. Joined in the fun."

"No thank you," she replied abruptly. "I've had enough of the press this week."

"How come?"

"Jake," cautioned Lori softly. "Leave it."

"Lori, it's ok," began Ellen with a heavy sigh. "Someone leaked photos of me to the British press. Photos that were used in court in Thailand after the night club explosion. Let's just say they're not pretty."

"Shit," said Jake. "Who would do that? And why?"

"No idea," replied the young, British songstress sadly. "The band's lawyers are all over it, but it's too late. The images are all over the internet. I've had some pretty vile messages too from folk who've seen them.""

"You ok to be here today? We can reschedule," said Jake, at a loss as to what was the right thing to say.

"I'll be fine as long as it's just us. No press. No cameras."

"Guess we've both got our ghosts with us today," acknowledged Jake, giving her a brotherly hug. "I'll get you through this, if you get me through it."

"Deal," replied Ellen, smiling up at him.

"Guys," said Lori, getting slowly to her feet. "I'll leave you to rehearse."

"Lori," called out Jake. "Can you tell Jim we're here? Call me when the press circus has left."

"Will do," promised Lori as she made her way to the door.

It was late afternoon before Jake's phone vibrated in his pocket. As he'd expected, it was a message from Lori, declaring that the coast was clear for them to come back over to JJL.

"You ready to do this?" he asked as Ellen collected her bag and jacket from the stage.

"As ready as you are," she replied.

Her subtle observation made Jake laugh. "We're a damaged, screwed up pair today, aren't we?"

"That we are," giggled Ellen shyly. "If it was anyone other than you, I'd have cancelled today."

"I'm flattered," said Jake, feeling his cheeks flush red. "Show time, Witchy Woo."

The two vocalists were still giggling like teenagers when they entered the deserted live room. From the control room, Dr Marrs called through, "Care to share the joke?"

"It's a long story," called back Jake. "Another time."

"Whatever," muttered the producer not even attempting to hide his exasperation. "OK, guys, time's short here, thanks to the all day, two hour press convention!"

"How long have we got?" asked Jake, picking up his headphones.

"Couple of hours tops."

With a glance over at Ellen, Jake called back, "If you're happy to go with what we've rehearsed, we'll be done in one."

"Let me hear it, folks."

Exactly as they'd rehearsed it, Jake and Ellen performed Miles From Home. The huskiness of Ellen's vocal was complimented by the warmth of Jake's. They had slowed the song down a bit, but still kept it in line with the tracking that had already been laid down. At the producer's request, they sang it through twice more, then Dr Marrs asked them to perform it at the original tempo.

Duetting again with Ellen helped Jake to relax in the studio. Playing Mysteries with her on the last Silver Lake tour had always been one of the highlights of the set and he began to wonder if they should invite her to guest on their new record.

"Jake!" yelled the producer sharply, shattering his day dream. "On your own from the top. Ellen, you'll be up next."

Pausing only to swallow a mouthful of water, Jake stepped up to the mic and, on the producer's cue, began to sing Miles From Home from the top. Acting on instinct, he altered his tone, singing with a more raw but lonesome style. Standing with his eyes closed on the world around him, he immersed himself in the song's lyrics about the loneliness of being out on the road and missing home.

"Perfect!" declared Dr Marrs when the last note faded out. "Ellen, match that, then I think we might need a final duet."

Rising to the challenge, Ellen sang her version in a melancholy tone. As he sat on the couch sipping his water, Jake watched her every move. Behind her tinted glasses, he could see she had her good eye focussed on him, as if she were drawing strength from his presence.

"Excellent, Ellen," complimented the producer warmly. "Now combine those. Keep your vocals exactly as you just delivered and I think we'll be home and dry."

As the two vocalists prepared to sing, Lori slipped into the control room. Standing in the shadows at the back of the dimly lit room, she watched as Jake poured his heart and soul into the song. Beside him, Ellen was channelling all the hurt and pain of recent days into her haunted vocals. Together they were creating a tragic vision of the loneliness of a homesick rock star's tour existence.

When they finished, Dr Marrs declared, "That's the one! Well done, guys."

"And they beat your two hour deadline," commented Lori quietly. "They sound great together."

"That they do," agreed the producer. "It's nice to see the old Jake through there too."

"He's slowly coming back to me," she said with a smile. "There's a little bit more of him every day."

"Think he'll come back out tomorrow to do Broken Bottle for me?"

"If it's just him on his own, then I'm pretty sure he will," replied Lori, watching her husband gathering up his belongings through in the live room.

"Don't want to push him too hard here," commented the

producer. "But I've a record to get finished and we're almost out of time."

Out in the lounge, Jake and Ellen were both relaxing on the leather couches with well-earned bottles of water when Lori came through with Dr Marrs. Now that the pressure was off, she could see how tired her husband looked.

"You ready to drive me home, rock star?"

"Yeah," replied Jake as he tried to stifle a yawn. "What do you want to do about dinner?"

"We can pick something up on the way," suggested Lori.

"Jake," called out Dr Marrs, "You free any time tomorrow? Say after four?"

"Can be," agreed Jake as he stood up.

"Feel up to coming in and doing Broken Bottle for me?"

"Just me?"

"Just you," promised the producer.

Nodding, Jake said, "I'll be here."

"Thanks. Appreciate it."

The air over JJL was silent as Jake climbed out of the truck next evening. As the afternoon had worn on, Jake had felt his anxieties beginning to gather like storm clouds. A phone call from Dr Marrs asking him to hold off arriving until after seven, hadn't helped. Suddenly, it all felt like that last fateful night with Salazar. Fears and flashback memories were weighing heavily on him as he entered the building. Instantly, a familiar aroma engulfed him and his stomach heaved. It was the smell of fresh laundry.

As he walked nervously across lounge, he spotted that the two jar candles were lit, their flames dancing.

Another reminder that he didn't need.

Trying to ignore the wave of nausea threatening to engulf him, Jake replaced the lids on the jars, snuffing out the vibrant flames.

"Jake," said a familiar voice behind him. "Have you got a minute?"

It was Garrett Court. The older man looked tired and even more haggard than before. On the floor at his feet sat two battered guitar cases.

"Garrett!" Jake exclaimed. "Sure. You ok?"

The older man nodded, then suggested they take a seat.

"I wanted to talk to you about this when I came out to the house, but I bottled it," he confessed quietly as he sat staring down at his trembling hands. "Then Jim suggested I waited until the record was done. I'm driving back home tonight so it's now or never."

"What is?" asked Jake, struggling to comprehend where the conversation was heading.

"These are yours now," said Garrett, pushing the two guitar cases towards him. "Apparently, he wanted you to have them."

Suddenly, Jake realised what was in the two battered hard cases. The cases contained Salazar's trademark Stratocaster and his vintage resonator.

"Garrett, I can't," began Jake, his own voice wavering. "They should be yours."

Garrett shook his head, "Sal wanted you to have them. He had planned to gift them to you when you finished making the record. He'd already decided it would be his last."

"I don't know what to say," stuttered Jake, feeling all the mental wounds beginning to tear open. "I don't know if…."

"They're yours. Keep them. Sell them. Play them. Decision is yours."

Before Jake could reply, Garrett got to his feet, "Give me a call next time you're in New York. We can do dinner or something."

Silently, Jake watched his idol leave the studio, shoulders hunched under the weight of his grief.

He was still sitting in the lounge, with his head in his hands, when Dr Marrs arrived half an hour later.

"You ok, Jake?" asked the producer as he poured himself a coffee. "Sorry. I got caught up saying goodbye to the Weigh Station guys. They're heading down to Florida for a few days."

Looking round and sniffing the air, the producer asked, "Who blew out Kola's candles?"

"I did," stated Jake, looking up. "The smell stirred up some ghosts. Then Garrett arrived bringing more."

"Eh?"

"Garrett dropped by," said Jake quietly. "He left me a parting gift. Well, gifts actually. Gifts from Salazar."

He nodded towards the two guitar cases.

"Shit," muttered Dr Marrs under his breath. "Are they what I think they are?"

"Yup," said Jake, standing up. "I'm not sure I can even touch them."

"That's understandable," acknowledged the producer. "Want me to store them here for now?"

Jake nodded, "I sure as hell don't want them in the house!"

"Leave them with me," said Jim, lifting the two cases. "I'll put them in the store for you. If you decide you want them, then you know where they are."

"Thanks, Jim," sighed Jake, feeling some of the weight lift off his shoulders. "I'll head in and get set up."

"You sure you're ok to do this tonight?"

"I'll be fine," replied Jake, sounding more confident than he felt. "Besides, you need this wrapped up, don't you?"

"I do," admitted the producer. "But I listened to that recording of Angel Wings you sent me. We need to use it."

"Have you told Kola you've heard it?"

"Yeah, and she's mad at you for being devious and recording it," admitted Dr Marrs with a grin. "However, I think I've talked her round."

"You have?"

"We'll find out in a couple of hours," he said. "If she shows up here, are you ok to play it?"

"Sure," agreed Jake. "It's the perfect way to end the record."

"Couldn't agree more. Now, go and get set up. I'll be through in a minute."

After a bit of debate about how to approach recording Broken Bottle Empty Glass, Jake convinced Dr Marrs to go with a live acoustic version. As time was of the essence, the producer conceded that it made sense. During the first few runs through, nerves threatened to take control, but, eventually, Jake got his head into the zone in the live room and totally focussed on the song. Drawing on every last ounce of emotion, he performed the perfect rendition shortly before ten o'clock. The husky vocals had left his throat dry and sore. As he reached for his water bottle, the live room door creaked open and Kola stepped in.

"Evening," said Jake with a welcoming smile. "Pleased to see you."

"I can't believe I've been talked into this," she muttered, fixing an intense stare on him.

"It's not too late to change your mind, if that's what you prefer," said Jake softly, aware that his voice was a little huskier than usual. "And, I'm sorry about recording you the other day without your permission."

"I've been convinced to forgive you for that transgression," she replied with a glare towards the control room window. "If my father finds out about this, my life will be hell."

"And who's going to tell him?" called through Dr Marrs. "I've already promised you that we won't credit you. The track will be an Easter egg. Not even listed."

Sensing the sound engineer's nerves, Jake felt himself reverting to school teacher mode. Calmly, he said, "I've a suggestion. Let's just have a bit of fun in here. Nothing formal. Let Jim record everything live. The beauty of the first version was that it was raw and natural. Let's try to recapture some of that."

"How?"

"Let's jam for an hour. We can play anything. You choose one then I'll choose one. When we both feel ready, we'll try Angel Wings."

"Ok," she agreed nervously. "What do you want to start with?"

"Lady's choice," offered Jake as he picked up his acoustic guitar.

"My mind's gone blank," whispered Kola shyly.

"Do you know the words to Stairway To Heaven?"

"Who doesn't?"

"Fine. Let's start there," proposed Jake, flashing her a smile. "Jim, keep everything off for now."

Patiently, Jake coaxed the nervous sound engineer through a handful of classic rock songs. After forty five minutes, he suggested they pause for a break then try Angel Wings. As he'd anticipated, she declined to join him in the lounge, electing to stay in the studio. Promising to be back shortly, Jake nodded to Dr Marrs, indicating that he should start recording as he left the room.

Out in the lounge, the producer met Jake beside the coffee machine.

"I hope you know what you're doing, Mr Power," stated Dr Marrs bluntly. "Are you sure she's going to deliver?"

"Positive," replied Jake confidently. "I've tried this approach with students before. I give it another thirty seconds and our little songbird will start to sing. She'll want to reassure herself that she can do it in front of us."

As the producer opened his mouth to reply, they both heard Kola begin to sing. After a faltering start, she paused and began again.

"Well, I'll be damned!"

"Told you," said Jake with a smile. "Now we let her run through it two or three times before I go back in."

"And let me guess, you'll play it a few times so I capture the guitar track, but I'll be using one of these vocal tracks?"

Jake nodded, "And if she doesn't do that dirty giggle at the end, you can use the original laughter."

"Mr Power, you're devious!" laughed Dr Marrs. "But I love it!"

When Kola finished her third run through of Angel Wings, Jake re-entered the live room, acting as casually as possible. Handing her a bottle of water, he asked if she was ready to record the Weigh Station song. Begging her patience, he ran through the guitar part twice on his own, paused for a sip of water then said he was ready. Together, they performed Angel Wings straight through twice by way of a rehearsal, then Jake called out to Dr Marrs, who was still recording, "Let's go for it with this one."

"I hear you," called back the producer.

Much to Jake's amazement, Kola's performance was breath taking. Gone were her nerves and insecurities as she sang her heart out. There was a renewed richness to her tone, giving her voice an air of confidence that had previously been absent. Praying he wouldn't mess up, Jake kept his playing delicate to compliment her vocal. As the last notes faded away, he flashed her one of his "Power" smiles and winked. It was all that was needed to make her giggle helplessly.

"That was fun!" she declared once she'd stopped laughing.

"Sure was," agreed Jake. "Jim, did you get what you needed?"

"Yup, sure did. Thanks, boys and girls. Time to wrap it up for the night."

As they stepped out into the chilly, midnight air, Jake thanked Kola for agreeing to come in and sing for them. Pulling on her motorbike helmet, she smiled and said, "You're welcome. I enjoyed it. Just don't ever tell my dad I did that."

"My lips are sealed," promised Jake sincerely. "Ride safe. Tell Grey I'll see him out here first thing on Monday."

"Will do," said Kola. "Have a good weekend!"

The familiar pre-tour routine took over at the beach house over the next few days. For most of the time, Jake and Lori's schedules seemed to slip past each other. He'd waken early and head off for a run before showering and heading off to JJL. During the day, Lori paced herself carefully, but managed to make progress with the Weigh Station cover and merchandise designs. She was conscious that she couldn't sit at her drawing board for much longer than an hour at a time, so she split her day into sections, making sure she scheduled some time for a walk on the beach. Silver Lake's rehearsals usually wound up late afternoon, so Jake was home in time to help with dinner.

They were due to leave for Rockville on the Friday afternoon. As had become another pre-tour ritual, the band gathered at the beach house on Thursday evening for dinner. The weather had been warm, so Lori suggested to Jake that he fire up the grill and BBQ, even if it was too chilly to eat outdoors. By six thirty, everyone had arrived, including Todd, who was to resume his guitar tech duties for the three festival appearances.

All of Lori's house rules about eating in the sunroom went out the window as the band sprawled all over the house. Maddy had brought two booster seats for the twins that she had strapped onto two of the wooden kitchen chairs, meaning the meatballs could sit at the kitchen table to enjoy their dinner. While Maddy fed them, Lori busied herself preparing drinks for everyone.

"This place gets more like The Waltons every time we meet up!" giggled Lori as she poured some apple juice into sippy cups for the twins.

"More like the Clampits on tour!" joked Maddy as she spooned fruit puree into Hayden's open mouth.

"It's nice to hear the house full of life," admitted Lori, passing one of the cups to Wren. "This could be one of the last "family" gatherings before this little Power Pack puts in an appearance."

"Less than ten weeks to go," commented her friend. "And you're looking fantastic. Such a perfect baby bump."

"Huge more like!"

"Ok, admittedly it's not the smallest baby belly," laughed Maddy. "But it's so beautifully rounded. From behind, you'd never guess you were pregnant. You've still got a waist!"

"Just," said Lori as the baby kicked sharply. "I just hope I'm ok on the flight. We're cutting this fine."

"You've still a few weeks before the airline veto flying. Stop worrying. You'll be home on Sunday night. It'll be a breeze."

"As long as the show goes smoothly," sighed Lori.

"Is Jake wound up about it?"

Lori nodded, "He's still a bit fragile around crowds. Once he's out on stage, he'll be fine."

"We've kept his press appearances to the bare minimum," explained the band's manager. "The Silver Bullet will meet us at the airport and, if he so desires, he can stay on the bus until sound check time on Saturday. His main press commitment is scheduled for after Silver Lake's set."

"That should make it easier for him."

"Should make what easier for who?" asked Jake, suddenly appearing in the kitchen beside the two girls.

"We were talking about Saturday's schedule," explained Maddy as she unstrapped Wren from the booster seat. Handing her daughter to Jake, she added, "I was explaining to your beautiful wife that your only press commitment for the weekend is after the set."

Hugging the little girl tightly, Jake smiled, "Thanks for that, boss. I'll be fine. You ladies are worrying too much."

"Are we?" asked Lori, sensing an air of bravado in her husband's voice.

Throughout the two hour flight to Jacksonville, Jake sat quietly listening to his iPod. Beside him, Lori was engrossed in her book, her own earbuds nestled in her ears. He was grateful to her for leaving him to travel in virtual silence, lost in his own thoughts. Calmly, he had talked himself through some of the visualisation and meditation techniques that he'd been taught in rehab. Centring his thoughts on his breathing, Jake had stilled the initial wave of panic. Behind him, he was aware of Rich and Grey chatting through the plans for the new album. In front, Maddy was trying to keep Paul calm. No matter how many flights they took, Silver Lake's drummer still hadn't conquered his fear of flying. With a smile, Jake thought perhaps he should teach Paul some of his coping techniques.

As the plane began to descend, Jake glanced out at the clear, pitch black, Florida night. Below them, the city lights were twinkling brightly. Gazing down, he wondered if they'd flown over the showground. The Friday night headliners would be on stage below them somewhere. Less than twenty four hours until Silver Lake would step out onto that main stage. In his heart, Jake was looking forward to performing live in front of the Silver Lakers, as their fans liked to be known as. The thought of his post-set interview sent shivers rattling down his spine. He was to be interviewed for a local rock radio station. It would be his first solo press appearance since the whole sorry Salazar incident.

His train of thought was interrupted by the captain's announcement to the passengers that they would shortly be coming in to land and that all electronic devices should be switched off until they were inside the terminal building. With a sigh, Jake stopped his music and removed his earphones.

In her usual efficient manner, Maddy had the band organised, the luggage collected and everyone through to the arrivals lounge before half of their fellow passengers had found their suitcases. The Silver Bullet was waiting outside for them, a familiar face standing on the sidewalk beside it. Grime smiled and waved as he saw them approach.

"Evening," greeted Jake as they reached the band's minder. "Didn't expect to see you."

"Boss' orders, Mr Power," replied the burly Texan. "Mrs Power, you're looking fabulous. How long until the baby's due?"

"Ten weeks," said Lori almost shyly as she allowed Grime to help her to climb aboard the band's tour bus and temporary home.

It was a short half hour ride out to Metropolitan Park where the festival was being held. During the journey, Maddy issued the band with their schedules for Saturday, checking and double checking that everything was in order. As they entered the showground, there was a brief hold up at security before they were directed to their parking bay for the weekend.

"Right, guys," instructed Maddy, her tone sharp and business-like. "You're free until ten o'clock tomorrow morning. Be sensible. Keep the noise down. Get some sleep. I'm going to check in with the organisers then I'll be back."

Paul and Rich rose to go with her while Grey reached into the refrigerator for some beers.

"Want one?" he said, offering a can to Jake.

Shaking his head, Jake said, "Not tonight. Maybe tomorrow."

"Mr Power," said Jethro calmly, "Do we need to grab a few minutes?"

"No, I'm good for now," promised Jake as he settled back on the couch, draping his arm around Lori's shoulders. "Maybe after breakfast."

"Ok. Just give me the nod," said the band's elder statesman. "I'm going to turn in. I'll see you lovely people for breakfast. First up, make some coffee."

"Night, Jethro," called Lori, her voice sounding sleepy.

"You tired, li'l lady?" asked Jake, hugging her close.

"A bit," she replied with a yawn. "Think I'll head down to my bunk too. Try to make myself comfortable."

"Maddison said she'd put some extra pillows in yours," said Grey, opening his beer. "If you need any more they're in the footlocker below my bunk."

"Thanks," said Lori, levering herself to her feet. "I'll see you both in the morning."

"I'll come down and say goodnight in a few minutes," said Jake as he watched his wife carefully make her way through the bus.

Alone in the lounge area, Jake and Grey stretched out on the long couches to watch some TV. Grey had found a ball game for them. The two musicians watched the game quietly for a while, then, as he cracked open a second beer, Grey asked, "How you feeling about playing tomorrow?"

"Ok," replied Jake. "This all feels normal so far. None of this links to what happened. I'll be fine. It's the interview afterwards that'll freak me out a bit. Maddy says she's approved the question list, but you know those folks seldom stick to it."

"You'll sail through it. You'll still be buzzing from the set."

"Hope so," sighed Jake.

The mercury levels were still reading in the low eighties Fahrenheit as Silver Lake gathered at the side of the main stage. They were on the Righty Stage shortly before six. All day, Jake had kept a low profile, spending most of his time on the bus with Lori. They had ventured out early afternoon to watch After Life open proceedings for the day on the Lefty Stage. A huge crowd was already assembled in front of the two prime stages, but its size didn't appear to phase Ellen. She played her witch role with her usual perfection and soon had the Florida crowd in the palm of her hand. When After Life's set ended with their standard explosion and disappearing trick, the fans had gone berserk. Seeing Ellen and her boys enjoy a solid set had helped to ease Jake's own nerves.

While the crew completed their final checks on stage, Jake paced anxiously back and forwards. The capacity crowd were growing restless and the chant of "Silver Lake, Silver Lake, Silver Lake, Lake, Lake" was echoing round.

"Show time, boys," declared Maddy.

Paul was the first to run out on stage, closely followed by Rich and Grey as the cheers threatened to engulf them. With a final glance over at Lori, Jake followed the others out onto the sun drenched stage. The thunderous cheers from the Rockville crowd drowned out the first few bars of Engine Room as Silver Lake powered their way into their set. Once he was halfway through the opening number, Jake felt his nerves begin to melt as he gazed out at the endless sea of bodies in front of them. They followed Engine Room with Dragon Song, which the assembled fans enthusiastically sang along to, then went straight into Four.

"Hello, Jacksonville!" bellowed Jake at the end of Four.

As expected, a huge cheer came surging back at him.

"Can't hear you!" he screamed. "I said, hello, Jacksonville!"

The resulting, deafening roar from over seventy thousand rock fans made him smile.

"More like it. Thank you," said Jake grinning. "Fuck, it's hot out here! Appropriately, this is Out Of The Shadows!"

Silver Lake were in full control of the huge stage. Even Grey moved to the front and played a little with the fans during Impossible. Mid-set, Todd brought out Jake's acoustic guitar and, accepting it from his protégé with a wink, Jake shunned the stool that had been brought out for him. Instead, he headed towards the side of the stage and down the steps to the lower runway.

"Literally bringing it down a bit here, folks," he joked as he sat on the edge.

With his head bowed, he played the intro to Lady Gambler, then winked at the fans in the front row. "That'll be on our new record later this year. If you know the words to this one, please sing along. This is Stronger Within."

As ever, the acoustic ballad proved to be a firm favourite with the Silver Lakers. In awe of the Florida choir, Jake turned the second chorus and third verse over to them before bringing things back to the stage for a final chorus.

"Thank you!" he called out as he got to his feet. "You guys are fucking awesome!"

Behind him, the rest of the band began to play the long intro to Far Reaches to allow him time to get back up and to switch guitars. This time, it was Rich who ventured down to the lower runway for his solo.

Their one hour set was almost over before they realised. As they began the distinctive intro to Flyin' High, to bring their things to an end, Jake leaned over to Rich and said, "Keep it going during your solo. I'm going down there."

Two verses in, Jake gave Rich and Grey the nod, then bounded across the stage and down to the lower level. He swung his guitar round his back as Rich began the extended solo and jumped down into the pit. While Rich stood centre stage above him, Jake ran along the front rail, shaking hands with the diehard fans, the Silver Lakers, only just making it back up onto the stage in time for the final verse and chorus.

"Rockville, you've been fucking fantastic!" yelled Jake. "Till next time!"

In the wings, Lori was ready to greet her husband as he came off stage. Seeing her standing there, Jake rushed over and almost lifted her off her feet as he swept her up in a huge bear hug. Her large baby bump was firm between them as his enthusiastic embrace was rewarded with a series of firm kicks from the baby. Keeping a supportive arm around Lori's waist, Jake bent down and kissed her stomach.

"Goofball," giggled Lori, noting that several photographers had obviously captured their intimate moment.

"Did our little Power Pack enjoy the show?" asked Jake as he picked up her discarded crutches.

"Almost as much as I did," declared Lori, adjusting her grip on her red sticks. "The only time baby settled down was during Stronger Within."

Grinning, Jake admitted, "That felt good out there. Put the ghosts back into the past. Was great to be back in front of a crowd."

"Well, you get to do it all over again next weekend, rock star," she teased as they began to follow the others back stage. "I just hope it's not as hot in North Carolina."

Both of them looked up in time to see Maddy striding towards them, her spike heels click clacking on the floor.

"Mr Power, you've five minutes until your interview," reminded the band's manager sharply.

"Duty calls," sighed Jake, kissing Lori tenderly. "Wish you could come with me, li'l lady."

"I'll meet you back at the Silver Bullet," promised Lori before kissing him back. "Then we can come back here to watch the headliners."

"It's a date. I'll be about an hour."

The radio station's mobile studio was set up across the showground, near the giant Ferris wheel. A small crowd was already gathered outside, patiently waiting for Jake to arrive. Silver Lake's Out Of The Shadows was playing loudly through the PA speakers either side of the open fronted tent as Jake loped towards it.

"Glad you made it," greeted Kaitlyn, the DJ for the evening rock show.

"Sorry I'm late," apologised Jake with a nervous smile. "Took me longer to get over here than I thought."

Out Of The Shadows faded out and the DJ began the interview, "Slightly out of breath and still oh so hot and sweaty from Silver Lake's set, we'd like to welcome Jake Power to the show."

"Thank you," said Jake blushing. "It was quite a sprint to get over here."

"How was your set? Sounded great from way over here. Crowd seemed to love it."

"It was awesome. Fans were fantastic. It's been way too long since we played live. Loved every minute of it," gushed Jake passionately.

"Silver Lake wound up the Impossible Depths tour earlier this year. So, what have you been up to since then?" asked Kaitlyn.

"We've been working. Writing. We go into the studio next month to record the new album," revealed Jake as he helped himself to a bottle of water from the centre of the table.

"And you gave the fans a little taste of that out there, didn't you?"

"Just a little piece of one of the songs we plan to record," explained Jake, sounding a little coy.

"You've got two other projects on the go too, haven't you?"

continued Kaitlyn. "If my research is correct, the charity record in memory of the late Dan Crow is more or less complete and you also spent time in the studio with the late, great Salazar Mendes shortly before his untimely death, didn't you?"

Pausing momentarily to collect his thoughts, Jake gave the DJ a detailed update on the Weigh Station project, letting slip that he'd recorded two duets for the album. Deliberately, he refrained from answering her point about Salazar, hoping that she'd let it drop. Kaitlyn didn't.

"It must have been an incredible experience to record with Salazar Mendes too," she pressed. "When can the fans expect that album to be released?"

"Working with Salazar was an intense experience," replied Jake evasively. His palms were beginning to sweat through nerves. "I'm not sure when the record will be ready. I finished recording the last bits and pieces after his death. It's all done. Now, I guess it's in the hands of the record company and his estate."

"Does it have a title?"

"In Chains," revealed Jake, before taking a long drink from his water bottle. "My wife, Mz Hyde, is doing the artwork for it."

The mention of Lori's name was enough to divert Kaitlyn's line of questioning away from Salazar. Instead, she quizzed him about the Weigh Station artwork, then said, "I guess it's fair to say you and Mz Hyde have another project on the go too. I saw her earlier on when After Life were on stage. When's the baby due?"

"End of June," said Jake, smiling warmly. "I guess there's no hiding that project now!"

"Do you know what you're expecting?"

Jake shook his head. "A healthy baby hopefully. We didn't want to spoil the surprise. We're both a little old fashioned that way."

"So, is there some paternity leave in that hectic schedule of yours?"

"There's a couple of weeks pencilled in. We're recording close to home so that makes the logistics easier. I'm hoping we can record around the baby's arrival so I can get some time at home."

Conversation returned to the Silver Lake plans for the summer before Kaitlyn wound the interview up by wishing Jake and Lori all the best with their new arrival then she played Stronger Within to close things out.

When Jake stepped out of the tent, several fans approached him for photos and autographs. Painting on his Disney Power smile, Jake patiently posed and signed for almost twenty minutes. Spying Jethro standing to one side, tapping his watch, Jake apologised that he had to go and headed over to meet his rehab buddy.

"You ok, son?" asked Jethro warmly.

"I'm good," replied Jake, before adding, "In fact, I'm really good. Today's been incredible."

"You boys were fantastic out there," agreed the older man as they headed back towards the bus. "Hope next week's as big a success."

Heat certainly wasn't an issue the following weekend when the Silver Bullet pulled into the showground at the annual Carolina Rebellion festival. Torrential rain was heaving down and the forecasters were predicting thunderstorms for the entire weekend. The band's journey had taken two hours longer than scheduled, with the result that they'd already missed one press appointment. As the driver manoeuvred the tour bus into their allotted parking bay, Maddy and Jethro were both instantly on their phones, attempting to reschedule the band's media commitments. Through the rain streaked windows, all of them could see that outside the site was slowly turning into a swamp.

"This is going to get messy," grumbled Grey as the first flash of fork lightning lit up the dark skies.

"As long as they don't cancel us," commented Rich. "I don't mind getting wet out there but I'm not playing in a thunderstorm."

"Forecast's for the storm to pass through by four," said Jake, checking the weather app on his phone. "We'll be fine. We're not due out there till after six."

By the time Silver Lake were ready to venture off the bus, the storm was right overhead. On the stages, the festival had been suspended on safety grounds, but the tens of thousands of sodden rock fans were still milling about in the mud, praying for the weather to clear. Event staff were scurrying around in the performers' enclosure, endeavouring to keep all the bands informed of the revised scheduling times. With their shoulders hunched and their heads bowed, Silver Lake sprinted across the backstage area to the huge hospitality marquee where they were scheduled to give a series of short interviews before heading out for their slot in the record label's "signing tent" to meet and greet their fans.

Back on the bus, Lori found herself alone. With a smile, she realised it was the first time that she had ever had the bus completely to herself. She had declined to venture out in the storm for fear of slipping in the mud. With an hour or so of peace and quiet ahead of her, she fetched a can of juice, then settled down on the couch with her book. As she stretched out, Lori felt her lower back relax, the weight temporarily re-distributed. With her growing baby belly swelling in front of her, she could now relate to the discomfort Maddy had been so vocal about while she was carrying the twins. There were still eight weeks to go until "B-day" but Lori was growing quietly concerned about how much bigger and more awkward she was going to get. Her bump was still all to the front and beautifully rounded, but her most recent midwife appointment had revealed she was now measuring four weeks ahead.

With her book propped up on the baby, Lori was soon engrossed in the story and oblivious to the rain lashing the windows. Every now and again, the baby shifted restlessly but apart from that, all was still and peaceful.

As forecast, the storm had blown through by the time Silver Lake clattered back on board the bus. It was still raining heavily, but the festival had recommenced. Out on the Rebellion stage, the nearest one to the Silver Bullet, Time March were starting their set half an hour later than billed. Their thunderous death metal was reverberating across the showground.

"Hey, li'l lady," greeted Jake, coming to sit beside her. "You ok?"

"Ugh! You're dripping!" squealed Lori as several large drops of water rained on her and her book.

"Sorry," he apologised with a mischievous grin. "It's still coming down hard out there. You feel up to coming out to grab something to eat?"

"Guess I'd better," said Lori, levering herself into a more upright position with a groan. "How slippery is it out there?"

"It's not so bad. The organisers have laid some sheeting down to create a few walkways. You'll be fine."

A few minutes later, Lori stepped rather nervously down from the bus, with Jake close by, watching her every move. His fellow musicians had gone on ahead, all three of them declaring that they were starving. Slowly and carefully, Jake and Lori made their way across to the nearest catering tent.

"What do you want to eat?" asked Jake as they joined the rest of Silver Lake at one end of a long trestle table.

"Surprise me," said Lori, taking a seat on the bench beside Grey. "Something with chicken would be good."

"Don't take too long, son," cautioned Jethro from further down the table. "You're due to start your warm up in fifteen minutes."

"Plenty of time."

Jake returned to the table carrying a tray with two plates of chicken salad and a bowl of fries. Conscious of time, he wolfed down his light meal, then disappeared with Jethro to find a quiet corner to complete his warm up routine. The rest of the Silver Lake party were able to enjoy their meal at a more leisurely pace.

"Molton are due out on the Rebellion stage in a few minutes," commented Rich, reading the revised running order off a nearby noticeboard. "I fancy watching some of their set."

"Me too," said Lori as she finished the last of her salad.

"I'm heading back to the bus," said Grey as he got up from the table. "Going to call home. This is the first weekend Becky has stayed home with Kola in charge. I want to check my girls are ok."

"Paul, what about you? You coming with us?" asked Rich, helping Lori to her feet.

"No, I'm going to check on my kit," replied Silver Lake's drummer. "Want to speak to my guy about making a few changes. I'll catch you up."

A makeshift shelter had been rigged up beside the main stage using a large plastic sheet. When Rich and Lori arrived stage side, Molton were huddled together under it, waiting for their cue to go on. Out on stage, two members of their stage crew were brushing the water off the front of it.

"Be careful out there," cautioned Rich as Molton headed out.

Undeterred by the abysmal weather, Tori commanded the huge stage with her usual flamboyance and soon had the crowd dancing in the mud. Fifteen minutes into their set, Rich tapped Lori on the shoulder, signalling that he needed to head back to find the rest of Silver Lake. After he darted off, Lori was joined by Zack, the drummer from Time March, and, together, they huddled under the blue shelter watching Molton's every move."

As Tori announced their final number to the crowd, Silver Lake arrived stage side. Their crew were standing on the opposite side of the stage ready to complete a swift turnaround. From her vantage point, Lori could see Todd checking through the cabinet that housed the band's guitars, making sure everything was in place.

As Molton left the stage to deafening cheers from their fans, Tori paused beside Silver Lake, "Watch your feet, boys. There's a real slippery patch near the front. There's an oily sheen off it. You'll spot it."

"Thanks for the warning," said Jake, making a mental note to take extra care.

Slightly later than billed, Silver Lake took to the stage to a colossal roar from the huge crowd. They launched straight into Engine Room to open their hour long set as the rain continued to lash down. At the front of the crowd, Jake could see the rail was lined with Silver Lake fans. At the end of Dragon Song, he stepped forward, noting the wet, oily patch to his right that Tori had warned them about.

"Good evening!" he roared into the mic.

A loud cheer echoed back towards the stage.

"I said good evening!" bellowed Jake for a second time, grinning as he surveyed the sea of sodden people in front of him. "You all ok out there?"

The group of Silver Lakers right down at the front went wild.

"This is Depths," announced Jake as he adjusted the weight of his guitar on his shoulder. The cool, damp weather was causing his weaker shoulder to ache.

Half an hour later, with the band soaked through to their skin, they reached the acoustic interlude. As Jake settled himself on the tall stool centre stage, Paul dashed back out with a huge umbrella to shelter him. The drummer's kind gesture raised a huge cheer from the drenched fans.

"I wish this was big enough to cover you all," commented Jake with a smile. "We really appreciate you coming out to see us in the shitty weather. I dedicate this to each and every one of you. This is Stronger Within."

No amount of rain could dampen the Silver Lakers spirits and they sang along in perfect harmony with him. Their passion and enthusiasm never ceased to amaze him. Jake turned the last verse over to the crowd and grinned at Paul as they sang it back to him.

"That was beautiful. Thank you!" praised Jake as he stepped down from his perch on the stool.

Quickly he changed guitars while Paul loped back to his drum kit. Rich moved into position to Jake's left, but Grey was still out of sight. With an anxious glance to his right, Jake stepped forward to the microphone, "Folks, this next one is Vortex!"

Out of the corner of his eye, he saw Grey sprint back on stage. As they began the intro, the bass player came rushing to his side to take up his position. His foot hit the oily slick and, arms flailing, the bass player's feet slid from under him. He crashed down onto the stage, landing flat on his back. His head hit the hard surface with an audible crack.

Instantly, the band stopped playing. The crowd gasped, then stood in stunned silence.

With his bass lying across his chest, Grey lay still on the wet stage, out cold.

"Someone get some help out here!" yelled Rich as he rushed across the stage.

Jake knelt beside his friend, instinctively checking for a pulse. He breathed a sigh of relief as he felt it throb under his fingers.

"Is he ok?" asked Rich as he knelt on the wet stage beside them.

"He's out cold," said Jake shakily.

Beside them, the bass player let out a low moan as his eyelids flickered.

Two first aid responders came running out onto the stage, closely followed by Jethro. Paul too appeared beside them.

"Boys," began Jethro calmly. "One of you apologise that the show's over for today. The paramedics are on their way over."

Nodding, Jake got to his feet as the first aid personnel began to check Grey out.

His hands were trembling as he gripped the microphone.

"Apologies, folks, but we won't be continuing our set," he began, lost for more appropriate words. "Grey needs medical attention. We'll update you all as soon as we can. Thank you."

As the paramedics arrived with a stretcher, Grey was starting to come round. Carefully, they fitted the bass player with a neck brace as a precaution. Someone had already moved his bass out of the way. It lay discarded to one side, its strap curled in the oily slick that had caused his fall. As the medical team slowly lifted him onto the stretcher, Grey groaned and swore loudly.

"You ok there?" asked Jake, appearing at his friend's side.

"Hurts like fuck," mumbled Grey, without opening his eyes.

One of the medics said, "We've given you some pain relief. It'll begin to ease things in a few minutes. Hang in there, sir."

As they wheeled Grey from the stage on the gurney, Silver Lake followed them to a sympathetic cheer from the fans. At the side of the stage, Jethro and Maddy gathered the band together.

"One of us needs to go with him," protested Rich anxiously.

"I'm going with Grey," stated Jethro firmly. "The rest of you go back to the bus with Maddison. No argument. When I know what's going on, I'll call her."

Before any of them could comment, he turned and walked briskly after the paramedics.

"Now what?" asked Jake as Lori stepped over to join them.

"We wait," stated Maddy calmly. "Come on, guys, back to the Silver Bullet."

Two hours had passed and there was still no word from Jethro. The mood on the Silver Bullet was sombre as they all sat silently waiting for news. Outside, they could hear the headliners beginning their set. Growing restless, Jake began to pace up and down, anxiously running his hands through his hair. In the corner, Rich was sitting with his head in his hands, staring at his feet. Paul had vanished. All of their phones lay on the low table.

Eventually, Maddy's lit up as it began to vibrate.

"Jethro!" she greeted abruptly.

Paul reappeared within seconds from the sleeping quarters.

All of them strained to hear what was being said. As she listened to her co-manager, Maddy smiled at the others and mouthed, "He's ok." When she finally got a word in, she said, "Thank Christ for that! And you're sure you're ok to stay there with him?"

A few seconds later, Maddison said her farewells and laid her cell phone back down on the table. "Grey's ok. No serious damage."

"Thank God," sighed Rich. "I was getting worried."

"We all were," confirmed Jake. "So, what's the story, boss?"

"They want to keep him there overnight for observation because he was knocked out," explained Maddy. "He's damaged his tail bone, but there's nothing they can do for that other than give him pain meds. He'll be really sore for a couple of weeks, but he'll be ok. Jethro's going to stay with him tonight, then hire a car and drive home tomorrow. We pull out of here at eleven as planned."

Both Jake and Rich started to protest, but the fiery Goth cut them short, "No arguments. We leave as planned."

"Can't we at least go and see him for a few minutes?" asked Jake, anxious to see Grey to reassure himself that his friend really was alright.

"Not tonight, Mr Power," stated Maddy bluntly. "You can see him tomorrow when he gets home."

"I guess," relented Jake, knowing when he heard that tone in her voice that it was pointless debating any further.

It was breakfast time next morning when the Silver Bullet pulled off the Coastal Highway into JJL. The band had left their cars there and had agreed that most of their stage gear should be returned to the rehearsal room in preparation for the pre-production sessions. As they all stepped wearily off the bus into the bright, early morning sunshine, Dr Marrs was waiting for them.

"Good morning!" he called out cheerfully.

"Morning," called back Jake, as he helped Lori down the steps. "Any chance of some breakfast?"

"And coffee?" added Lori, adjusting her grip on her crutches.

"Bacon, pancakes and coffee coming up," replied the producer. "Table's already set."

"Jim, I think I love you," declared Jake as the band followed him towards the studio house.

Soon, they were all seated in the large kitchen enjoying Dr Marrs' freshly made pancakes with maple syrup. Both Rich and Paul had wanted eggs with their bacon. The drummer and the producer worked side by side preparing scrambled eggs while Jake made another bowl of pancake batter.

At the table, Maddy and Lori exchanged smiles as they watched their respective rock stars hard at work.

As Jake finished mixing the batter, he felt his phone begin to vibrate in his pocket. He reached for it, catching the call just before it went to voice mail, "Grey, good morning."

"Not much good about it," grumbled the bass player. "Thought

I'd better call and let you know we're about to head home."

"You ok?"

"As long as I don't want to move," replied Grey. "Sitting hurts like hell. My head's pounding and I'm walking like John fucking Wayne."

"You're in for a long day, buddy," observed Jake. "It's at least an eight hour ride home."

"I know," sighed his friend. "We should get back about seven tonight."

"Do you need us to take Becky overnight?" offered Jake.

"No, it's ok. Kola's going to stay with us for a day or so. Thanks for the offer though."

"Any time. Let me know you get back safely. I'll take a run out to see you tomorrow."

"Will do. Need to go. Doc's here to sign me out."

The baby was shifting restlessly as Lori relaxed on the sun lounger, enjoying the mid-afternoon sunshine. In contrast to the miserable weather they had left in Charlotte, the Delaware Riviera was bathed in clear skies with temperatures in the mid-seventies. Its warmth was easing off all the kinks in her muscles after an uncomfortable, sleepless night in the bunk on the bus. Slowly, Lori ran her hand over her baby belly, feeling the baby lurch and kick firmly. A small smile crept across her lips as she marvelled yet again at the fact that their baby was growing inside her.

Music was echoing up from the basement. Almost as soon as they had arrived home, Jake had disappeared downstairs, closing the door tightly behind him. It struck Lori that that was the first time he'd closed the door while he was downstairs alone since before the whole Salazar incident. It marked another step towards putting it all behind them. Over the past couple of hours, she had been treated to various Weigh Station classics, then Jake had moved on to the tracks he had been writing for the next Silver Lake record. It warmed her heart to hear him playing and occasionally singing in the heart of the house.

Late afternoon, Jake emerged from the basement in need of some fresh air. A headache was beginning to build, a combination of the thundery North Carolina weather from the day before and a lack of sleep on the bus ride home. His solo rehearsal had gone some way to soothing his frayed nerves. Over the next few weeks his schedule was packed and he could feel a wave of panic starting to gather momentum. His double appearance at Rock on the Rage was also weighing heavy on him, assuming that was, that Grey was fit to play. The latest email he had received from Laughlan had confirmed that Weigh Station would play a one hour set on the Sunday night, just before the headliners took to the stage to close the festival. Two shows in two days with two different bands was a daunting prospect.

As he stepped out onto the deck, Jake found Lori asleep on the sun lounger. Even asleep, she looked radiant. Pregnancy was most definitely suiting her. She was wearing her black bikini top with her sarong tied loosely around her hips below the swell of the baby. Quietly, Jake knelt down on the warm deck and laid his hand on her firm rounded stomach. At first, he felt no movement, then he felt a little flutter under his fingertips. A ripple of movement was suddenly apparent on the other side of Lori's stomach as the baby kicked sharply. Its acrobatics were enough to disturb her. Sleepily, she opened her eyes, blinking at the bright sunlight.

"Afternoon, li'l lady," said Jake, his voice soft and slightly husky after singing downstairs.

"Hi," she whispered. "Guess I dozed off."

Jake nodded with a smile, "Do you feel up to a walk?"

"As long as we don't go too far," replied Lori, wriggling to sit up. "I could do with stretching my legs for a bit, but my back's sore after sleeping on the bus last night."

"Let's head along the beach for a bit," suggested Jake, helping his wife to her feet.

"Give me a minute to grab a shirt and visit the loo."

It was quiet down on the sand. This early in the season, there were very few tourists midweek. Only a handful of fishermen were stationed along the water's edge. Keeping clear of their lines, Jake and Lori walked slowly south down the beach. With Jake by her side, Lori had only brought one crutch for support. As they wandered on, Jake kept a supportive arm around her waist, taking care to set a leisurely pace. They meandered along in virtual silence for about ten minutes. Lori stopped suddenly and pointed out to the ocean. Both of them stood watching the pod of dolphins making their way down the coast. Letting out a long sigh, Jake ran his hands through his hair.

"You ok?" checked Lori softly.

"Yeah. Just tired. Bit of a migraine," he confessed, sounding weary. "I was checking my schedule before we came out. Busy few weeks coming up."

"But, at least you're at home for them," countered Lori, conscious that he had a lot of commitments to juggle and mindful that he was still fragile at times.

"True," conceded Jake with a smile. "I'm not planning on straying too far until after the baby's here."

"Eight weeks or so to go."

"Not long," he acknowledged. "We'll need to start getting more organised. And then there's a name to agree on."

"We've got all the big things ordered," reminded Lori. "Names? Now, there's a debate waiting to be had! Did you have any in mind?"

She had been compiling a mental list for a while but was aware that they hadn't discussed names much at all.

"A couple. You?"

"Some. I've more for a boy than a girl," replied Lori, subconsciously resting her hand on her bump. "I kind of wish we knew who was in there."

"My money's on a little princess," stated Jake, laying his hand over hers.

"No, it's a little prince. I have a feeling about it."

"Time will tell. So, what do you want to call our little Power Pack if he's a boy?"

"We could name him after my dad?" suggested Lori.

"Let's stay away from family names. And no biblical one's either."

"Jacob wasn't on the list. Don't panic," teased Lori, knowing only too well how much her husband detested his given name. "And it's kind of hard to totally avoid biblical names."

"What about Jesse?"

"Hm," mused Lori. "Wasn't on my list, but it's a possibility."

Hand in hand, they walked on, trading boy names back and forth. When they turned to head for home, they switched to girl names. Both of them laughed and joked about names that were definitely off the list. Names they associated with their pasts. As they walked up the path to the house, they were no closer to reaching agreement than when they'd started.

Next afternoon, leaving Lori working in her study, Jake drove across town to visit Grey. It had been a while since he had been out that direction and, as he parked the truck outside the bass player's house, Jake noted that his driveway was still full of old cars. Kola's Harley Davidson was parked in front of the house, looking pristine in comparison to some of Grey's treasured wrecks.

"Hi, Jake," greeted Kola as she opened the front door. "Come to laugh at the patient?"

"Hi, Kola. Is he behaving himself?"

"No," she declared bluntly. "He's meant to be resting, but you try telling him."

"You try resting when your ass hurts like hell," growled Grey from the lounge room behind her.

Walking into the small living room, Jake spotted his friend lying on the settee, flat on his back with his knees bent.

"Afternoon," said Jake, taking a seat. "How's the back?"

"Agony if I move. Not so bad if I don't move"

"You going to be ok for Saturday?" enquired Jake, concerned that they were going to have to cancel a second set.

"Yeah. I'll be ok. Standing is easier than sitting. Just don't be expecting any fancy moves from me," assured Grey, rolling onto his side slowly, then very gingerly sitting up. "Want a beer?"

"No, thanks. Coffee would be good though," said Jake as Kola reappeared in the room.

"I'm going to fetch Becky from school," she said, as she lifted Grey's car keys. "Won't be long."

"Drive safe, angel."

"I will," promised Kola with a smile. "We'll go food shopping on the way back. Jake, are you staying for dinner?"

"No thanks, Kola. I promised Lori that we'd go out to the steakhouse tonight."

"Ok. Keep an eye on him until I get back."

Jake could almost feel his friend's pain as he watched Grey struggle to his feet, then only just managed to stifle a laugh as he watched him walk stiffly into the kitchen.

"Something funny, Mr Power?" quizzed Grey as he set up the coffee pot.

"Not at all," replied Jake, his hazel eyes twinkling with suppressed laughter.

"Feels like I'm walking like a toddler with a full diaper," muttered the bass player as he brought two mugs out of the cupboard. "At least my head's clearer. I've a lump on the back of it where I cracked it off that fucking stage."

"You certainly went down with a bang," agreed Jake, remembering the sickening noise all too clearly. "You sure you'll be ok to play by the end of the week?"

"Yeah," promised Grey. "I've some strong pain meds I can take to ease things off. I'll probably spend the bus ride out there in my bunk though. Don't fancy sitting around in the back lounge for nine hours or more like this."

"Whatever works for you. I know Lori's anxious about the ride too. She's struggling to get comfortable anywhere right now."

"How long to go?"

"About eight weeks. Her lower back and her pelvis are giving her trouble. She doesn't say much, but I can see the signs," replied Jake.

"I can sympathise with her."

The two friends chatted about the plans for the weekend as they drank their coffee. Jake confessed to feeling nervous about leading Weigh Station out for their set.

"Big weekend for you," acknowledged Grey, empathising with his friend's anxiety. "We'll hang about to watch. I've not seen you front those boys yet."

"This is the first show where I will front them. The anniversary show in London was still really a guest spot. This is the real deal. Not sure I can pull it off."

"Of course you can."

"Time will tell," muttered Jake, gazing down into the dregs of his coffee.

Back at the beach house, Lori had made a start on her final version of the artwork for In Chains. She had exchanged a few emails with Garrett, clarifying the design requirements and the deadline date. After a brief email debate, they agreed the rose should be deep, blood red in colour. Lori suggested, almost as an afterthought, that it be in full bloom, just at the point of wilting, with one fallen petal in the foreground. Garrett immediately loved the idea. They agreed on a deadline of 15th June.

As she began to sketch out the shackles, Lori suddenly felt totally comfortable and at ease. It was the first time for days that she had felt that she was both physically and mentally relaxed. The baby stirred gently but soon settled and she assumed it was asleep. Gradually, the image took shape in front of her. She took great care to get the angle and the shading of the chain's links just perfect, so that in time, the stem of the rose would slot perfectly through them.

To give it a little more authenticity, Lori decided to add some rust spots to the chain.

Resting her hand on her bump, she surveyed the first couple of links and smiled. It was the first commission that she had undertaken for a few months that actually felt like fun. Sketching the chain links was therapeutic. Playing a little with the detail, she added in a little crack to one link.

She was so engrossed in the detail that she never heard Jake arrive home.

"Lori?" he called out from the kitchen.

"In the study," she replied, the sound of her voice disturbing the baby, causing it to shift restlessly. "How's Grey?"

"Stiff and sore. Walking like a cowboy," laughed Jake as he wandered through the dining room to join her. "Says he'll be fine for Rock on the Range on the weekend. Not too sure I believe him."

"He has to be sore," sympathised Lori. "Don't be too hard on him."

"We won't," promised Jake with a mischievous wink.

"What's your schedule for the rest of the week looking like?" asked Lori. "Does Grey have time to recover for a few days before you guys get together?"

"He's got tomorrow and Wednesday," replied Jake. "I'm rehearsing with Weigh Station for the next two days. There's a half day Silver Lake rehearsal on Thursday then we travel on Friday."

"No press commitments?"

"Not until we reach Ohio," sighed Jake. "I'll be glad when Sunday's over. It's going to be a tough weekend."

"Nothing you can't handle, rock star," said Lori confidently. "Now, did you not promise to take me to dinner?"

"I sure did."

The two days of Weigh Station rehearsals ran on late into the evenings. All of them knew that time was tight and that the eyes of the music world would be on them. They recognised that the fans and the media would be focussing on their every move, their every song choice and on Jake's performance in particular. As they compiled the set list for their sixty minute appearance, there were several heated moments as the three original members of the band debated which tracks to include and which needed to be omitted.

Eventually, they agreed on a ten song set list and rehearsal was able to commence. With each song, Jake felt the pressure on him increase. He knew it was inevitable that folk would compare him to the late Dan Crow no matter what he pulled out of the bag. In his heart, he wanted to stamp his own identity on the vocals and not risk appearing on stage as a "karaoke" version of the band's late singer. He tried to keep as closely as possible to the original arrangements, but, by the middle of Tuesday afternoon, he knew something wasn't working.

"Can we break for half an hour?" asked Jake at the end of the second run through of Battle Scars.

"Sure," agreed Mikey sharply. "Back in here at four, guys."

Without a backwards glance, Jake left the rehearsal studio and headed over to the main JJL building in search of some coffee. He could hear voices in the lounge as he entered the studio and soon found Dr Marrs and Laughlan, the Weigh Station manager, chatting with Jethro.

"Afternoon," said Jake casually as he headed over to the coffee machine.

"You got a set ready for me?" asked Laughlan, his Scottish accent sounding more aggressive than he intended his question to be.

"Yes, sir," replied Jake, adding half 'n' half to his coffee. "We're working our way through it."

"And?" said Jethro. "Am I sensing a but here?"

"Not really," began Jake, reluctant to appear negative about their progress. "I guess I'm just anxious that I don't sound as though I'm trying to copy Dan. I want to put my own mark on this, but I don't want to bruise any egos."

"I hear you, son," said Laughlan with a nod to Jethro. "We'll sit in on the next session. Toss our tuppence worth in."

"Can't do any harm."

With the two managers standing to the side, Weigh Station started the set from the top again after the break. The first two songs went smoothly, then, as they began Midnight Raiders, Laughlan intervened.

"Mikey!" he yelled brusquely. "A moment of your precious time."

Rehearsal was paused while the large Scot took the Weigh Station guitarist out of earshot. Five minutes later, they returned and Mikey clambered back up onto the low stage.

"Let's start again, guys," he said calmly. "Jake, lets freshen these old songs up a bit."

With a nod, Jake reached for the microphone, ready to begin Midnight Raiders for the third time.

When they reconvened on Wednesday for their final rehearsal, things ran like clockwork. Weigh Station was like an old, well-oiled machine and, now that Jake had settled somewhat into his new role, things flowed smoothly. With a few runs through under their belt, all of them felt happier with the set. As they were packing up, Mikey threw a question to Jake that brought him up short. "How are you going to make Weigh Station Jake different from Silver Lake Jake?"

"I don't follow you," commented Jake, looking confused.

"You need to develop a different stage persona. Wear different clothes. Tie that hair back. Wear shades. I don't fucking know, but there needs to be a differentiation."

"I guess," acknowledged Jake. "I'll have a think. Go through my stage clothes. See what I can come up with."

"You need to establish a trademark Weigh Station look even if it means you go out there stripped to the waist!"

"No way!" declared Jake with a grin. "I can do the occasional song like that, but not an entire show. Too damn cold out in Ohio for a start!"

"Give it a thought. Fans would love it!"

"I'll work something out," promised Jake, lifting his jacket and his book bag. "I'll even go shopping if it comes to it."

"Get that beautiful wife of yours on the case," suggested Mikey with a wink. "Now, get out of here. We'll see you in Ohio!"

"See you Sunday."

"Saturday," corrected the older musician. "We're all coming to see your Silver Lake set."

"Till Saturday then."

During the drive back into town, Jake tried to come up with a "look" for his Weigh Station persona. He drew the conclusion that Mikey was right and that he would need to do something different to separate the two bands. But what to wear? Fashion and image was a whole new dilemma for him. Having parked the truck in the driveway, Jake pulled out his cell and typed a message to Maddy, explaining the dilemma and pleading for urgent assistance.

"Twenty bucks in the pot!" growled Grey as Jake arrived almost an hour late for Silver Lake's rehearsal on Thursday morning.

"Sorry," said Jake, handing a crumpled twenty dollar bill to the bass player. "No excuses. I over slept."

"Hmph," muttered Grey, pocketing the cash. "Are you warmed up and good to go?"

"Sure am," Jake replied, lifting his black Gibson from the rack. "What are we starting with?"

"Engine Room," stated Rich. "Full set run through. Same as Carolina Rebellion, then we can decide if we need to change anything for John Wayne in the corner there!"

"Very funny," grumbled Grey as he limped awkwardly across the room.

By lunchtime, they had run through their one hour set twice. All of them had surreptitiously kept half an eye on their injured bass player to see if he appeared to be struggling with any of the songs. Miraculously, Grey seemed to be fine as long as he stood more or less in one position.

"What's the plan for this afternoon?" asked Paul as they trooped across to the main building for lunch.

"Can we run through Vortex again?" asked Rich, opening the door to JJL.

"I've a suggestion," began Jake as they entered the lounge. "How do you feel about swapping Depths to the acoustic version? Gives Grey a few minutes rest. Rich and I can carry it."

"I'd appreciate that," admitted Grey as he took a seat at the table, lowering himself onto the chair gingerly. He failed to disguise the agony that the movement caused him.

"Fine by me. Let's try it out after lunch," agreed Rich, reaching for a sandwich from the selection on the table. "How did the Weigh Station rehearsals go?"

"Good, thanks," said Jake. "Still all feels surreal. They're coming to watch us on Saturday."

"And we're staying to watch you on Sunday," revealed Paul

411

with a mouth full of pastrami on rye. "Make sure you don't fuck it up out there."

"Thanks," muttered Jake, feeling the nerves twitch in his stomach.

As Silver Lake were packing up for the day, the studio door opened and Maddy came in with the twins in their stroller. When she saw Jake, Wren squealed with delight.

"My number one fan," laughed Jake, kneeling down beside her. "And how's my favourite baby girl today?"

The little girl squealed again and reached out to grab his hair.

"Your number one fan is tired and cranky," stated Maddy sharply. "She won't take a nap. I've not had a minute to think all day with her!"

"Demanding just like her mommy," joked Paul from the safety of the far side of the room.

"What brings you out here, boss?" asked Jake, getting to his feet. "Jethro's already been in and run over the schedule for tomorrow."

"I've brought a couple of outfits for you for Sunday," Maddy revealed as she lifted a garment carrier from the handle of the stroller.

"Oh, fashion parade, boys!" quipped Paul from his corner.

Glaring at her partner, Maddy said, "No need to model these here. Take the gear home. Try it on. See what feels comfortable. Ask Lori's opinion too."

"Thanks, boss," said Jake, flashing her a "Power" smile. "I'll try these on tonight."

"I didn't include footwear. I was assuming you could work that bit out for yourself."

"Converse it will be," stated Jake. "They've not failed me yet."

"Boots. Work boots might be better," suggested Maddy. "Take Lori's advice."

Jake nodded.

Glancing round, Maddy checked, "You guys all set for Saturday? Grey, you going to be fit to play?"

"Don't fret, Maddison. I'll be fine," promised Grey, forcing a pained smile. "Just don't expect any fancy footwork."

"Take it easy," replied the band's manager in a rare show of warmth. "We really don't need any more trips to the emergency room."

Standing in the bedroom, with a towel tied around his slender hips, Jake unzipped the garment bag and inspected the outfits Maddison had pulled together. When he had arrived home from the studio, he had headed straight out for a run, conscious that it would be his last chance to stretch his legs for a few days. Pounding out the miles down the beach and back had helped to clear his head, but had done little to calm the growing nerves lurking in the pit of his stomach. Two shows in two days with two bands..... the whole idea was scaring him to his very core.

Inside the garment carrier, he found two stage outfits. One was a pair of black trousers, a black silk shirt and a long, scarlet silk scarf. The other was a pair of skin tight, blue jeans, a white vest that was extra low cut under the arms and a worn, biker style, leather jacket. Both subtly different from his Silver Lake stage clothes.

He hung both outfits up on the outside of the closet door, then stood back to stare at them. Before he could decide which one to try on first, he heard Lori coming down the hallway.

"Hey, rock star, what you up to?" she asked as she entered the room, balancing a basket of clean folded laundry under one arm.

"You shouldn't be carrying that," scolded Jake, immediately taking the basket from her.

"Stop fussing. I'm fine."

"I beg to differ," stated Jake bluntly as he set the basket down on the bed. "You told me the hospital said not to lift anything heavy."

"That's not what I class as heavy," retorted Lori sharply, knowing in her heart he was right.

"Hmph," snorted Jake. "Anyway, while you're here, you can help me make a decision."

"What about?"

"My Weigh Station look."

Surveying the two options hanging in front of the closet, Lori commented, "I'm not sure about the scarf. Try the all black on first though."

A short while later, Jake stood in front of the cheval mirror, gazing at his reflection. The black leather biker look was one he'd steered clear of in the past, but, now that he could see it, it wasn't so bad. From her seat on the bed, Lori nodded approvingly.

"Love it!" she declared. "Much more you than the silky shirt look."

"I didn't feel right in that shirt," admitted Jake. "The pants felt ok though."

"I'd go with that if I were you," advised Lori, rubbing her swollen stomach. "The jacket looks great on you."

"You sure?"

"Positive," she stated as she got awkwardly to her feet. "Different to Dan. Different to the Silver Lake you. It looks great."

"If you say so, li'l lady."

"I do. Now, take it all off and pack it in the bag with the rest of your things. We've an early start tomorrow."

The Silver Bullet was parked in front of JJL when Jake and Lori arrived next morning. As he drove round to the rear of the studio, Jake saw that everyone else's cars were already there. He parked the truck in his usual spot, then hurried round to help Lori down.

"You're late, Jake!" yelled Maddy from behind him. "We're due to pull out in ten minutes."

"Plenty of time, Maddison," he called back as he lifted their holdalls out of the back of the truck. "We're travelling light."

"Just get your ass over here!" yelled the band's manager as she turned on her heel to go back on board the Silver Bullet.

Giggling beside him, Lori commented, "We'd better hurry, rock star. I know that Maddy look."

"Oh, so do I!" he sighed. "Right, let's go. I'll come back over for my guitars in a minute."

When they boarded the bus, Jake stowed their holdalls in their lockers, then ran back to the truck to fetch his book bag and guitars. Most of his guitars had been left out at JJL but he had taken two home to work on some new songs. He had only just re-boarded the bus when he heard the driver start the engine.

"Cutting it fine, Mr Power," commented Grey from his reclined position on the couch. The injured bass player was lying flat on his back, his knees bent and his head resting in Kola's lap, "Boss is in a foul mood today."

"I am not in a foul mood," snapped Maddy as she joined them in the lounge.

"If you say so, boss," replied Jake, taking a seat by the window.

They felt the bus lurch into motion and pull out onto the highway, all of them safe in the knowledge that they were in for a long ride.

It was some twelve hours later before the Silver Bullet parked up in the band's allotted spot for the weekend. After a couple of hours, Grey had muttered his apologies and limped off to his bunk for the remainder of the journey. Having promptly followed him, Kola returned to the lounge, explaining that the vibration from the road was sending knives of agony through him. Looking a little concerned, she added that he'd taken some pretty heavy duty pain medication and was going to try to sleep for a few hours.

The rest of them had whiled away their time watching DVD's and reading. Jake had excused himself and headed down to the smaller lounger to work on some new material. It didn't escape Lori's attention that he had taken his Weigh Station lyrics book with him. All of them could sense his growing nerves. Eventually, Jethro excused himself and headed down the bus to check on him, using the excuse that that they were long overdue a buddy to buddy catch up.

Twelve hours on the bus didn't take as much of a toll on Lori as she had feared. With Maddy's help and a few pillows from the bunks, she had managed to make herself comfortable, even managing to doze off for a couple of hours during one of the superhero films the band had voted to watch. The rhythmic vibration from the road seemed to soothe the baby, sparing her ribcage its daily assault for a few blissful hours.

When the bus door finally opened, they could hear the roar of the crowd from inside the stadium. Judging by the noise and the time, the Friday night headliners, Never Enough, had just taken to the main stage.

"I'd hoped to see those guys," commented Rich as he recognised the Canadian band's opening number. "Boss, you got the access passes there? I might run over and catch that set."

"Right here," replied Maddy, passing him the lanyard with the various laminated access passes attached. "Don't get lost out there!"

"We'll catch up with you," called out Jake as he helped Lori to her feet. "Fancy catching them myself."

As the Silver Lake guitarist disappeared off into the crowd and the dark, the remaining members of the band went in search of the nearest catering facilities. They were stopped a few times by fellow musicians and VIP fans, but finally found themselves somewhere to grab a late dinner.

Leaving Grey and Lori sitting at the table, the others went to fetch their meals, promising not to be long.

"You ok?" asked Lori as she watched the band's bass player grimace in pain.

"I'll live," he said, adjusting his position. "I saw the doc yesterday. He said I've trapped a nerve. The pain down the back of my leg is excruciating if I move the wrong way. How're you holding up?"

"I'm good," said Lori, gazing down at her large baby bump. "Carrying this little Power Pack is taking its toll on me, but there's not long to go now."

"How many weeks left?"

"Just over six. Maybe seven," she replied. "It's not long when you factor in all the commitments we have over the next few weeks."

"Sandy was four weeks early when we had Becky," commented Grey with a wink. "So, don't bank on having too much time."

"Thanks for the warning," giggled Lori as Jake approached them carrying a tray piled high with food.

As soon as their meal was over, Jake led Lori through the backstage maze towards the main stage. The headline act had been taking the music world by storm recently and both of them were curious to hear first hand what all the fuss was about. From what they could hear, as they made their way to the side of the stage, Never Enough's live show was far heavier than their album had alluded to. The side of the stage was crowded, but, using her charm, Lori managed to squeeze through to where Rich was standing with Zack, the drummer from Time March.

With his arm draped across Lori's shoulder, Jake focussed his attention on the high energy Canadians out on stage. The five piece band were putting on an energetic display, barely pausing for breath between songs. Within seconds, his toe was tapping and his head was nodding in time. The fans lining the rail were all headbanging and, for the first time in a long time, Jake found himself wishing he was down there among them. To his right, he could see the band's set was having the same effect on Rich. When Never Enough ended the night with an almighty explosion of air cannons along the front of the stage, Jake and Rich were both nodding approvingly.

"Fucking awesome!" Jake proclaimed. "Absolutely fucking

insane show!"

"Our little Power Pack certainly rocked out," confessed Lori, rubbing the right hand side of her large belly.

"Just proves they've got great taste in music already," teased Jake, laying a hand on her bump. Immediately, he could feel the baby kicking furiously.

"Or they were scared half to death," laughed Lori. "Those guys were loud!"

"They sure were," agreed Jake, nodding in agreement "Ok, time to head back to the bus. I'm beat."

In the wee small hours, sleep was eluding Jake as he lay in his bunk. His mind was alive with lyrics. The more he tried to calm it, the more the lyrics became jumbled together. Weigh Station and Silver Lake songs morphed into one giant medley in his mind. He rolled over onto his back and stared up at the ceiling above him. As had become his personal tradition, he had a photo of Lori taped to the ceiling. Seeing her smiling down on him usually soothed his nerves. As the clock ticked slowly on, not even her smile could calm him enough to induce sleep. Knowing she was asleep in the bunk below helped a little. Having her with him, especially after all he'd put them through, meant the world to him. Her very presence was helping to keep his anxieties in check.

He allowed his mind to wander over thoughts about the baby and the coming weeks. For the millionth time, he wondered if their little Power Pack was a boy or a girl. A vision of the three of them down on the beach in front of the house having a picnic began to form in his mind. Dreaming of holding the baby while watching the waves wash in soothed him and, eventually, sleep came.

In the lower bunk, sleep was eluding Lori. The small, claustrophobic space was closing in on her. She had brought in some extra pillows and positioned one under her bump in an attempt to get comfortable. Another one she had placed between her knees as she lay on her side. After rocking out to Never Enough, the baby had been calm for an hour or so, but the minute that Lori was on the cusp of drifting off to sleep, it began to stir restlessly. After a few uncomfortable minutes, Lori was forced to roll over onto her back. She could feel the unborn baby arch its back, then turn itself round, causing her skin to lurch and move in a most disconcerting manner. For a few minutes, her bump looked decidedly off centre then the baby wriggled and squirmed and kicked some more before finally settling into its new position. Suddenly, Lori was aware that she could breathe easier and that there was less pressure on her lungs. Gently, she rubbed her tender belly as she rolled back over onto her side.

Much as the thought of giving birth in a few short weeks scared here, she was looking forward to family life with Jake and their little Power Pack. A vision of the three of them out on the deck in the early evening formed in her mind's eye. She could imagine herself sitting on the lounger, nursing the baby while Jake sat playing his guitar. The image and gentle melody line were still on her mind as she finally drifted off to sleep.

Next day dawned clear and fine as the festival site came to life not long after sunrise. The Silver Lake camp were a little more leisurely with their start to the day. Both of the band's managers were up and dressed first, closely followed by Rich. Leaving Maddy to sort out the coffee pot, Jethro and Rich headed off in search of breakfast for the band.

The aroma of freshly brewed coffee wakened Lori, that and the urge to pee. As quickly as she could, she clambered out of her bunk and scurried into the small toilet. When she emerged, she felt her bump heavier than it had been the day before.

"Morning!" called Maddy brightly. "Going to be the perfect day for a rock festival."

"You think?"

"Sun's shining. Forecast's good," began her friend then she paused. "Oh! Your bump's dropped!"

Smiling, Lori nodded. "Feels like it. Baby was struggling to turn around last night after I went to bed. Thought I was going to burst! However, I can breathe again. I just hope it's not a sign of imminent labour. I can't remember what the book said."

"Don't panic," replied Maddy warmly. "I believe first babies drop into position early and stay there for a few weeks. One of the twins was really low for about a month."

"I'm not panicking," giggled Lori. "In fact, I feel great. I'm ready to rock!"

"Well, maybe don't rock it out too much," cautioned Jake from behind her. "I've enough on my mind this weekend without you deciding that Ohio is a good place to give birth."

Their conversation was halted as Jethro and Rich returned with a box of pancakes and waffles and a carton containing some bacon. Within a few moments, the smell of food had enticed Grey and Kola from their bunks and, finally, Paul too lumbered through to join them, more asleep than awake. Once everyone was seated with some breakfast, Maddy reverted to business mode and gave them the rundown of the day's itinerary. Each of the band members had press commitments spread throughout the day and across the site. In an effort to preserve Jake's voice, his interviews were all scheduled to be completed by one thirty. The band were set to do a quick sound check around two thirty and were due out on the main stage around six fifteen.

"What's your plans for the day, li'l lady?" asked Jake as he read over the printed itinerary.

"I thought I'd catch After Life's set this afternoon. They're on around three on the main stage," said Lori, stifling a yawn. "I've been asked to appear at one of the signing tents for half an hour. I think I'm there just before you and Rich."

"I meant to speak to you about that, princess," interrupted Jethro, looking a little sheepish. "Laughlan and I set up an interview for you and Jake while you're there. It's more of a Weigh Station interview than a Silver Lake one. Just a few questions about the story behind the album art."

"I suppose I can oblige," replied Lori with a smile. "Am I doing the same tomorrow?"

"Not quite," said the band's older manager. "Tomorrow's a half hour TV slot with Jake and Mikey."

"TV?" quizzed Lori, her voice rising in surprise. "Looking like this? I don't think so!"

"Sorry, but it's all arranged. The TV crew will meet you on board Weigh Station's bus at midday."

"Well, I'll see how I feel in the morning," stated Lori bluntly, her tone firmer than she perhaps intended. "I don't recall agreeing to any TV, Jethro!"

Before either of them could continue the debate, Jake suggested that they finish getting ready then go for a walk around the site before his first interview at eleven.

Sun was already beating down on the stadium, sending the temperatures soaring. Slowly, Lori walked through the VIP area with Jake by her side. Fans were spilling into the site anxious to secure that precious front row spot. Several of them stopped Jake for a photo and an autograph. Painting on his Disney Power smile, he obliged then slowly altered their route towards the press area. As they approached the location of Jake's first interview, they spotted Maddy coming towards them with Grey limping along a few paces behind her.

"You ready, Mr Power?" she asked as soon as she was in earshot.

"As I'll ever be, Maddison," he replied. "Grey, you ok to be walking around?"

"I'm fine. Don't fuss. Rich has got caught up so we've swapped slots," answered Grey. "One more after this then I'm done until sound check."

"Boys," interrupted Lori softly. "I'm going to go back to the bus for an hour or so. Jake, I'll meet you at the signing tent at one fifteen."

"Be careful, li'l lady," said Jake, suddenly anxious at the thought of her walking around the festival on her own.

"I'm always careful."

When Lori approached the signing tent, there was a small crowd already gathered, most of them wearing Silver Lake or Weigh Station shirts. She could see Jake's blonde head just inside the tent and smiled to herself at the realisation that he was early for their appearance.

"Sorry, am I late?" she apologised when she reached the tent.

"Not at all, Mz Hyde," assured the journalist who was due to interview them both. "Congratulations. I didn't realise you were pregnant."

"Thank you," said Lori, feeling herself blush.

"Do you want me to find you a seat?" offered the journalist.

"I'm fine standing," said Lori as Jake appeared at her side.

He put a protective arm around her shoulders and suggested that they get started.

The interview was brief and focussed on Lori's involvement with Weigh Station's art work, Jake's involvement with the band then finally the journalist began to ask about the forthcoming Dan Crow tribute record.

"How many tracks do you appear on?"

"A few," replied Jake cryptically. "I sing on some and play on others."

"Is there any truth to the rumour that you had to fill in for the late Salazar Mendes on a couple of them?"

With a nervous glance at Lori, Jake replied, "He had been scheduled to record a couple of tracks one the record but the producer re-arranged those following his death."

"And did you do the honours?"

"No," answered Jake, shaking his head. "That task fell to Garrett Court. Worked out pretty cool in the end."

"And Lori, you've done the artwork for this one too, haven't you?"

"Yes," she replied warmly. "It was fun pulling it together. Adding in little pieces from the past covers and coming up with some new sections."

"Is this your last commission before the baby arrives?"

"No," admitted Lori, slightly embarrassed to be talking about the baby. "I've one other cover to finalise, then a jewellery collection to pull together. I've another three or four weeks to work."

"I believe Silver Lake are due to start recording soon. Is that correct, Jake?"

"Yes. We head into the studio at the start of June and start recording on June 10th. There's still some pre-production to finish off, but the record's mostly written."

"So, you won't be far from home when the baby arrives?"

"That's the plan," said Jake, taking Lori's hand in his. "That is, unless my beautiful wife decides to go into labour this weekend."

"That's not going to happen," giggled Lori. "I've still more than six weeks to go."

"Well, we wish you all the best when the baby arrives and we look forward to hearing both the Dan Crow record and the Silver Lake one when the time comes. Thanks for joining us today, folks."

"Pleasure," said Jake, shaking the journalist's hand. He then turned to the waiting fans, "Now, I believe some of you are waiting to get your stuff signed. Is that right?"

Patiently, Jake and Lori autographed all the memorabilia and items presented to them. After a while, they could see Jethro hovering to one side, indicating that they needed to watch the time. With the last CD insert signed, Jake and Lori prepared to leave the signing tent.

"Cutting it fine, folks," commented Jethro when they reached him. "Have you both eaten lunch?"

"No," said Jake. "We can grab something on the way over to sound check. I'm still pretty full after those pancakes this morning."

"Speak for yourself!" stated Lori. "Baby and I are starving!"

"Well, we can't have that," said Jethro with fatherly concern. "There's a good outlet on the way to sound check. I ate from it earlier. Great vegetarian selection."

"No offence, Jethro," giggled Lori. "But I want some meat."

"They serve that too, princess."

"Great. Lunch, then I'm going to watch After Life," she stated firmly.

"You'll need to watch the time. They're due on stage in about twenty minutes," observed Jake, checking the time. "You might want to take your lunch round to the stage with you."

A slight delay in proceedings worked in Lori's favour, meaning she had time to eat her burger before taking up a position at the side of the main stage. After Life's manager, Rocky, offered to fetch her a chair, but she declined, saying it was actually easier to stand.

Beside her, After Life were pacing, anxious to be out on stage. In full witch garb, Ellen led the band out to a loud roar from the growing crowd. She used her witch's cloak to dramatic effect through the first three numbers, then shed it from her shoulders, revealing a new sexier look. The young songstress was wearing a skin tight pair of leather jeans, thigh length, spike heeled boots and a purple corset top. From her vantage point at the side of the stage, Lori noted that she had a flesh coloured top on under it that hid the worst of the scarring on the stump of her arm. It was quite a contrast to the shy singer, she'd first encountered in London eight months before.

A couple of songs before the end of the set, Jake appeared beside Lori and, together, they watched the closing segment of After Life's show, including Ellen's usual disappearing trick. The crowd went wild as the remaining members of the band waved and took a final bow.

"Those guys are a band to watch," commented Jake. "Great performers."

"They put on a good show," agreed Lori, rubbing her swollen belly. "Now, I hate to admit it, but I need to sit down and I need to pee again."

"Let's get you back to the bus for a rest," suggested Jake, concerned that his wife was overdoing things.

As they made their way back across to the bus, Jake noted that Lori was walking slower than usual. Her face was pale and drawn by the time they reached the Silver Bullet.

"You ok, li'l lady?" he asked as she paused for a moment before climbing the steps.

"Yes," she replied. "Just a little more uncomfortable walking since the baby changed position. It feels heavier now that it's lower."

"You're not getting any twinges? You're not in pain?"

"Relax, rock star! No twinges. No pain. No contractions. I'm just very pregnant. This little Power Pack still has six weeks to go before they're cooked."

"And you're sure this is all normal?"

"Perfectly normal," promised Lori as she hauled herself up the steps and into the bus.

After a couple of hours rest, Lori felt refreshed and more than ready to watch Silver Lake play. She had dozed for a while and, when she awoke, discovered that the band had already changed into their stage clothes and were ready to head back over to the stadium.

As Lori reached the side of the stage, she found the three members of Weigh Station already there. While the Silver Lake crew made the final preparations out on stage, Lori and Mikey chatted about the bands they had seen so far and those that they wanted to see on Sunday. Lori confessed to wanting to see the last two acts due out after Silver Lake but conceded she might not have the stamina to last until the bitter end.

Behind them, Silver Lake were going through their final pre-show rituals. Out of the corner of her eye, Lori spotted Grey swallowing two painkillers. The injured bass player was putting a brave face on things, but she guessed from the look in his eyes that he was currently in agony.

"Show time, boys!" declared Maddy sharply. "Let's do this!"

As the Silver Lake intro tape played, Paul led the band out onto the huge stage in front of a capacity stadium crowd. Rich followed him out, then Grey slowly followed. As Rich and Grey began the intro to Engine Room, Jake loped out to join them. The crowd erupted at the sight of his blonde head bent forward over his guitar. When he came in on vocals, Jake spotted several "We love you, Jake," signs along the rail. He could feel his cheeks redden as one of the fans blew him a kiss.

They had agreed to mix the set up a bit to keep it as easy for Grey as possible so Engine Room led into Dragon Song then Jake stepped forward.

"Good evening, Ohio!" he roared.

The fans screamed back at him.

"I can't hear you!" bellowed Jake with a grin. Playing with the audience was one of the highlights of a show. "Good evening, Ohio!"

The wall of noise that surged towards the stage was impressive and he nodded approvingly.

"You folks look beautiful," complimented Jake. "Feel free to help us out on this next one if you know the words. This is Out Of The Shadows!"

The festival fans lapped up Silver Lake's performance, drinking in Jake's every word. When they reached the end of Out Of The Shadows, Jake looked over at Rich and the two musicians exchanged conspiratorial glances. Knowing what number was next on the set, Grey was slowly shuffling his way forwards and into position.

"Folks, we began to play this next one last weekend at Carolina Rebellion. It didn't end so well for Mr Grey Cooper here on bass. Please give a huge cheer for him. He's in agony with a back injury," announced Jake as a spotlight was trained on Grey.

As the crowd cheered wildly, Grey stepped forward, still walking like John Wayne. Beside him, Rich and Jake began to play the theme tune to the classic TV series Rawhide. Instantly, the crowd picked up on the joke, singing along to the first verse and chorus while Grey stood there smiling at being the butt of his band mates' prank.

"Thank you for the sympathy," said Grey, addressing the fans via Jake's mic. "I think these jokers really meant to play Vortex!"

Despite his injuries, Grey managed to maintain his usual stance beside them as they played the hard and heavy number. His fellow band members could sense his pain, but saw from the steely look in his eyes that he wasn't about to be beaten by it.

"Almost there," whispered Jake to him as they finished the lengthy song.

While the rest of the band stepped off stage, Todd dashed out with Jake's acoustic guitar. As he'd done on occasion before, Jake shunned the stool, choosing instead to sit down on the edge of the stage. He smiled out at the sea of faces in front of him, then began to play a short section from one of the new as yet unrecorded Silver Lake songs. He played a little snatch of Bonded Souls, glancing over at Lori, who was standing at the side of the stage.

"You'll hear more of that one later this year," teased Jake. "The next song has a special place in my heart and its inspiration is here with me today. Lori, this is for you!"

With a quick glance over at his wife, Jake bowed his head and began the gentle intro to Stronger Within. An enormous cheer echoed round the stadium as the fans recognised what was coming When he began the vocal, the crowd were right there with him, singing their hearts out. Their passion for the song made him smile.

"Over to you," called out Jake at the start of the final verse.

Word perfect, the huge crowd carried the song through to the final chorus when, still grinning, Jake joined them.

"Beautiful, folks. Thank you," he said warmly. He paused to gaze out across the stadium, then continued. "Folks, some of you might know this one better as one of the heavier tracks from Impossible Depths. Personally, I prefer it like this. This is Depths."

Judging from the roar from the fans at the end of the acoustic version of the song, they enjoyed it too. Quickly, Jake scrambled to his feet, then darted across the stage to exchange guitars.

He was mildly surprised when Todd handed him his Mz Hyde custom but slung it on swiftly, trusting that it was tuned for the next two songs. A subtle check as he plugged it into his radio pack confirmed it was.

"Ohio, this is Fear Of The Sun."

Two songs later, with the end of the set in sight, Jake addressed the Silver Lakers once more, "We'd like to welcome a very special friend out on stage to perform with us now. Please give a huge Ohio cheer for our favourite Witchy Woo! Ellen, from After Life!"

With a shy wave to the capacity crowd, Ellen ran on stage to join Silver Lake. Gone were the witch robes from her earlier set, replaced instead with skin tight jeans, purple top and a black frock coat. She had swapped her usual dark glasses for more rounded, purple tinted ones, creating a whole new look.

"This is Mysteries!" roared Jake.

Standing either side of Rich, Jake and Ellen both kept their heads bowed while the guitarist played the slow, eerie intro section. Keeping his head bent, Jake delivered the first spoken section of the song with a husky, menacing edge to his voice. As his voice drifted out across the hushed crowd, Grey and Paul stormed in with the song's thundering, powerful rhythm. Stepping forward, Ellen led the vocals, keeping her voice warm and husky for the first verse. Jake joined her for the chorus and their voices rang out in perfect harmony to the delight of the fans. During Rich's mesmerising solo, Jake and Ellen moved to opposite sides of the stage in preparation for trading lines in the final verse. This time, Jake stepped back to allow Ellen to perform the closing segment. Dropping to her knees, crouching like a demonic creature, the young vocalist spoke the final rhyme in a hissed, dark, evil tone, sending shivers down Jake's spine. His mind was flooded instantly with a flashback to the night in the basement, seeing again the "hooded demon" taunting him. A wave of fear threatened to engulf him and he could feel himself begin to tremble.

The fans' hysterical wild applause bought him just enough time to attempt to clear his mind and re-focus. Sweat was pouring from him as he embraced Ellen, calling out to the audience, "Give it up for the beautiful and talented Witchy Woo, Ellen!"

Two songs later and Silver Lake were closing their set with Flyin' High. Just as he had done at Rockville, during the solo, Jake jumped down from the stage and ran along the rail shaking hands with the Silver Lakers who lined it. He paused briefly beside the girls with the "We love you, Jake" signs to allow them to take a couple of photos and to steal a few kisses before making his way back on stage for the final verse and chorus.

"Thank you, Ohio! Till next time!" bellowed Jake, tossing some picks out into the sea of fans. "You've been fucking fantastic!"

Jake stepped offstage straight into Lori's arms, holding her tight. Immediately, she noted the haunted anxious look in his eyes.

"You ok, rock star?" she asked softly as he buried his face in her hair, kissing her neck.

"Yes. No. I've no idea," he muttered. "I had a flashback out there. Shook me up a bit."

Before he could explain further, the Weigh Station guys crowded round, congratulating him, then Jethro was herding them all away from the side of the stage. Grey was being supported by Rich and Paul as he limped slowly behind Jake and Weigh Station. With a worried look on her face, Kola was hovering around them.

Eventually, they found a quiet corner to gather in. Ignoring the stares from those around him, Grey lay down on the ground, flat on his back with his knees bent up, in an effort to get relief from the pain shooting through his lower back. While Maddy and Kola fussed over him, the others helped themselves to bottles of water. Looking pale and anxious, Jake stood off to one side, slowly sipping his water.

"Tell me about what happened out there," prompted Lori softly as she appeared by his side.

"I don't really know," he began. "It was during Mysteries. Right near the end when Ellen started that last section. The way she was crouched down. The way her coat was draped about her. That hiss in her voice. She was brilliant. Incredible. Instantly, all I could see was the basement though. It only lasted a few seconds, but it was so real."

Wrapping her arms around him, Lori rested her head on his chest. She could hear his heart still pounding.

"Talk to Jethro," she suggested warmly. "The main thing is that you held it together. You knew it wasn't real. You were able to see beyond it. Able to go on."

"I guess," he sighed, rubbing her back. Her baby bump made their embrace awkward, but Jake was comforted by the warmth of her pressed against him. He was aware of the baby stirring in her stomach and moved one hand to gently massage her large, rounded belly. "Hope the show didn't scare our little Power Pack here."

"Baby loved hearing their daddy out there," replied Lori, smiling up at him. "Mommy loved when you played the acoustic stuff because baby stopped dancing for a few minutes."

"You holding up ok, li'l lady?" asked Jake, conscious that he hadn't given her wellbeing much thought all afternoon.

"I'm fine," she assured him. "A little tired, but fine."

"You still wanting to hang around back here for the rest of the show?"

Lori nodded, "Let's grab something to eat first though. We can catch what's left of Evil Nation's set, then watch Molton."

"Fine by me," agreed Jake. "I'll try to grab a few minutes with Jethro after dinner."

As the band finished their meal an hour or so later, Jake got up from his seat and walked down to the end of the long, trestle table to where Jethro was sitting. The band's manager was deep in conversation with Mikey when Jake laid a hand on his shoulder.

"Got a minute?" he asked, trying to keep his tone calm.

Throughout the meal, Jake had replayed the moment on stage over and over in his mind. He had stirred his food around the plate, barely managing to eat half of it.

"Sure, son," replied Jethro, picking up on the anxiety in the younger man.

"Let's walk back to the Silver Bullet. I need to pick something up anyway."

Having promised to meet Lori back at the main stage, Jake followed the smaller, silver haired man across the site to the enclosure where the buses were parked. Weigh Station's bus was now parked beside theirs and, as they passed it, they could hear Laughlan's dulcet tones echoing out from inside.

Once on board the Silver Bullet, Jethro fetched them both an iced tea from the refrigerator then asked what was wrong.

"Flashback," stated Jake. "Hit me out on stage when Ellen was finishing up Mysteries. All of a sudden, I was back in the basement. Back in front of those fucking demons. The fear was real again. Took me all my time to finish the set. Guess I went onto autopilot for a few minutes. I just can't shake it. It's like those demons are still inside. Still trying to claw their way to the surface."

"I was watching you out there. I thought something had happened. And before you panic, your performance was flawless. It's just I saw this look cross your face for a moment or two. Saw you wrestle with it," said Jethro. "You coped with it. You knew it wasn't real. You kept control."

"Barely," muttered Jake, running his hand through his hair. "How long is this likely to last? I feel like I'm being haunted. Tormented. It's driving me insane."

"I wish I could tell you, son," soothed the older man. "The mind's a very complex thing. It plays tricks on you. What you have to remember is that you went through a major trauma that night and over the following ten days. It wasn't a minor thing that can just be brushed off."

"I suppose."

"Remember how long it took you to put Gary's death behind you," continued Jethro, his tone fatherly and filled with concern. "It took months. This, in a lot of ways, is just as big, if not a bigger deal. It's going to take time. You've made huge steps forward. Today's a prime example. You coped. You held it together. You stayed out there and did what you do best. No one watching would have known. I bet even Ellen didn't notice."

"I know you're right," sighed Jake, running his hands through his hair. "It scares the shit out of me. In a lot of ways this has been tougher than losing Gary. There's so many reminders. So many fears. Christ, I still can't do a simple thing like go for a drink at a bar!"

"All in good time, son," soothed Jethro. "You need to focus on your beautiful wife, the baby and, much as it pains me to say it, holding it together tomorrow night out there."

Jake nodded. "I'm having nightmares about forgetting the lyrics. They keep merging into Silver Lake/Weigh Station mixes! I don't want to let those guys down. They need this to work as much as I do."

"It's a high pressure set. No denying that," agreed Jethro. "You want to catch up around lunchtime tomorrow? I'll talk you through a few techniques you can use to stay calm and focussed."

Again, Jake nodded, "I'd appreciate that. Thank you."

"Ok, I'll find you between press commitments," promised his mentor. "Now, if you're ready, let's go and find your lovely wife. I don't like leaving her wandering round here on her own, just in case she goes into labour."

"Me neither," admitted Jake. "Sometimes she's too damn stubborn for her own good. I can tell she's starting to really struggle with this pregnancy."

"Well, after tomorrow night, you can take her home and make sure she rests."

"I intend to."

When Jake finally joined Lori at the side of the stage, Evil Nation were nearing the end of their set. Someone had fetched her a seat and she sat surrounded by the guys from Weigh Station plus Rich and Paul. Maddy was off to one side, talking animatedly with Evil Nation's manager. Standing behind his wife, Jake put his hand on her shoulder, then bent forward to kiss the top of her head. She turned to smile up at him, squeezing his hand as if to reassure him that she was fine.

As Evil Nation began their final song, Molton appeared at the side of the stage. Dressed in a revealing, short, leather dress that left little to the imagination, Tori strutted over to talk to Jake and Lori.

"Fancy a duet, Mr Power?" she suggested, leaning in close and ruffling his hair.

"Perhaps another time," said Jake, flashing her a smile. "Need to save my voice for tomorrow night."

"Pity. I thought we could do Battle Scars. A sort of teaser for the record and your spot tomorrow night. We could get Mikey out too," coaxed Tori, her tone honeyed and persuasive.

"Maybe," replied Jake, his resolve crumbling a little. "What the hell! If Mikey's up for it, let's do it!"

The Molton songstress kissed him on the cheek, then glided over to where Mikey was standing with Rich. Jake watched as she draped her arms around him and turned on the charm. A few seconds later, she brushed Mikey's cheek with a kiss, then swept over to join the rest of Molton.

Shaking his head disbelievingly, Mikey came over to Jake.

"Looks like we're on after they play Demon In Her Heart," he said. "Remind me how we got talked into this?"

Turning to face them, Lori surmised, "It's one of two reasons, gentlemen. Either you both fell for her feminine wiles or you're both scared to say no to her."

Laughing, Jake conceded that Tori did still intimidate him somewhat.

"Listen, I'm not taking any chances here, folks," began Jake. "I'm going to go and run through some basic warm up exercises. I don't want to risk messing up my voice for tomorrow. I'll be back in half an hour."

As they watched Jake disappear out of sight, Mikey asked Lori if he was alright.

"He will be," she replied softly. "It's a big weekend for him. Plus, he's terrified I go into labour before we get home."

"I guess he's got a lot on his shoulders," agreed the English musician. "After all that's happened, I'm just glad he's here."

"Me too," admitted Lori, quietly. "Me too."

Molton were four songs into their ninety minute set before Jake returned to the side of the stage. As he approached, Lori was relieved to see her husband was smiling and looking relaxed. He knelt down beside her, resting his hand on her baby bump, grinning as he felt the baby kicking furiously. Lori placed her hand over his and smiled.

"Ohio!" screamed Tori out on stage as Demon In Her Heart ended. "I'd like you to give to give a huge Rock on the Range welcome to two very special friends of mine."

The capacity crowd roared back.

"Folks, we're being joined by Mikey and Jake from Weigh Station for this next one!"

As the fans screamed and cheered, Jake and Mikey ran out on stage.

"This is Battle Scars!" roared Tori as Jake took up his position beside her.

Following the same split of the Weigh Station anthem as they had recorded back at JJL, Tori and Jake traded verses. The sea of fans in front of them initially looked surprised by the change in vocal style from their beloved rock goddess, the queen of scream, but they were easily won over to the lower range, blues influenced rock voice.

On stage, Jake's earlier fears seemed to have been laid to rest as he thundered his way through his share of the performance. Battle

Scars had been one of his personal favourite rock songs since his teens and to be playing it in front of a sell out crowd with Mikey and Molton was another "pinch me, is this real?" moment for his inner rock fan.

All too soon, he was standing with his arm around Tori's shoulder as they sang, head to head, through the final chorus. To their left, Mikey was back to back with Molton's guitarist, playing as if his life depended on it.

"Ladies and gentlemen, give it up for Jake and Mikey from the mighty Weigh Station!" screamed Tori, reverting to type the second the final note was played.

With the rapturous cheers of the Molton fans ringing in their ears, Jake and Mikey stepped off stage.

Less than twenty four hours later, Weigh Station were back at the side of the stage, waiting impatiently for their cue to go on. Throughout the early part of the day, Jake and Lori had kept a low profile. After the TV interview on board the Weigh Station bus, they had melted into the crowd for a few hours, sitting anonymously out in the tiered seating at the far end of the stadium. To any casual onlooker, they were just another couple of rock fans among thousands. No one gave them a second glance. As arranged, they had made their way back to the Silver Bullet for five o'clock. They detoured through the vendor village, the lure of the various stalls too much for Lori to resist. She bought a few pieces of merchandise for Jake to add to his stage wardrobe while Jake treated himself to a couple of new belt buckles and a new belt, complete with free key chain.

They had arrived back at the Silver Bullet ten minutes early, much to Maddy's amazement, shared a light, early dinner with the rest of Silver Lake then, while Lori took a nap, Jake went to warm up with the Weigh Station camp.

As the clock ticked closer to eight o'clock, Jake paced restlessly around the side of the stage. He felt uneasy in the unfamiliar stage clothes. Instead of the white, vest t-shirt that he had intended to wear, he had switched it at the last minute for one of the vests Lori had picked up that afternoon. The label at the neck was scratching him, adding to his discomfort. Crouching down to tighten the laces on his tattered, black Converse, Jake felt something rip. His jeans had split across the back of his thigh, just below his bum cheek.

"Fuck," he muttered to himself, realising it was too late to change. "Dan, I bet you're loving this."

"Mr Power," interrupted Mikey. "Talking to yourself?"

"Yeah," confessed Jake as he stood up. "Just ripped the ass out of my jeans."

The older musician roared with laughter.

"As long as you're wearing underwear!"

"Always," acknowledged Jake, seeing the humour in it. "And before you ask, I'm not taking my pants off out there!"

Before their relaxed banter could continue, Laughlan called the band together.

Two extra special guests had joined Lori and the members of Silver Lake in the wings. Dan's daughters, Melissa and Jenny, had arrived just as Laughlan summoned the band. Both girls had greeted Lori warmly; both congratulated her on the baby, declaring she looked marvellous. Having been seated all day, Lori had declined to sit through the Weigh Station set. Leaning heavily on her crutches, she shifted her weight a bit as the baby kicked sharply.

"You ok, princess?" checked Grey, who was standing behind her. "Not about to give birth?"

"I'm fine," she replied, turning to smile at the bass player. "You holding up ok?"

He nodded, but the pain etched in his face told a different story.

"Move it out of here, boys," ordered Laughlan gruffly as the stage lights flickered.

Weigh Station's intro tape began to play as the fans erupted into a thunderous, cheering mass. The three original members of the band ran out first to a huge welcome cheer, then, a few moments later, as Steve and Phil began to play their set opener, Wreckless, Jake loped out to join them.

The tidal wave of screams and whistles almost blew him away. He hadn't anticipated such a huge, warm welcome from the diehard Weigh Station fans.

The hard and heavy Weigh Station anthem swiftly whipped the crowd into a frenzy. As the spotlights swept around the stadium, Jake spotted two large circle pits in the centre, safely out of the reach of the security personnel. The sight made him smile and he felt his nerves begin to subside.

With the opening number under his belt, Jake fully immersed himself in the role of front man during Download and Midnight Raiders. Judging from their smiles, Steve and Mikey were enjoying playing live again.

"Ohio!" roared Jake to the crowd at the end of Midnight Raiders. "You look beautiful tonight!"

The fans roared back appreciatively at him.

"Sing along if you know this one. This is Arizona Fire."

By the end of the fast and furious fourth number, sweat was pouring from Jake. The heat from the lights, plus the warm evening air, was making wearing the leather jacket unbearable. Snatching a moment between songs, Jake slipped it off, tossing it safely to the side of the stage. It landed at Melissa's feet. When he saw her, he flashed her a smile, then turned his attention back to the set.

Accepting his guitar from Todd, Jake plugged himself in as he stepped forward to the mic.

"Folks, this is one of the first songs I ever played with these guys. Seems a lifetime ago since we played this in Ireland. This is Sunset After The Storm."

A hush fell over the stadium as Jake began the intro in a soft light, but haunting, voice before launching into the fast, frenzied verses that followed. His guitar part was easy, allowing him to focus on the complexities of the lyrics. During Mikey's solo, Jake stepped back to the rear of the stage to stand with Steve, leaving the spotlight trained on the band's lead guitarist.

"Dan's girls are loving this," commented the bass player towards the end of the song.

With a quick glance into the wings, Jake saw the two girls dancing and clapping in time.

After a rousing rendition of Brain Fried, a song from the band's very first record, Jake paused for a moment to catch his breath. Beside him, Mikey was switching to an acoustic guitar. As the older musician checked the tuning, Jake turned his attention back to the fans.

"Time to slow it down a bit. We've rearranged this one just for tonight, folks. This is Broken Bottle Empty Glass."

Leaving Mikey in the spotlight on stage, Jake headed down to the lower level at the front, choosing to sing his vocal from there. The warm, throaty lyrical style was a stark contrast to the rest of the set. Along the barrier, the ever loyal Weigh Station fans were in full voice as Jake prowled across the width of the stage. Leaving the crowd to sing the third chorus, he rushed back up to re-join Mikey in time for the final verse and chorus. Judging by the fans' reaction, the acoustic version had been an instant hit.

"Thank you," called out Jake as the remaining members of Weigh Station returned to the stage. "We've a couple more songs left. This one's appropriate! It was a twelve hour bus ride to get here this weekend. This is Long Travelled Roads!"

Sweat was dripping from all of them by the time Weigh Station reached their final number. With his vest shirt sticking to him, Jake ran his hands through his hair, wiping the sweat away from his eyes.

"Ohio, you've been fucking awesome!" roared Jake. "We're going to leave you with Rock It Out On Fire! Rock this one out with us!"

The fans needed no second invitation as Weigh Station powered their way through their standard set closer. As the spotlights swept dramatically over the stadium, all Jake could make out was a sea of writhing bodies. Down at the front, security had their hands full as several crowd surfers passed overhead from the darkness beyond the reach of the lights.

As the final chords faded out into the night, Jake bade the fans goodnight and Weigh Station left the stage accompanied by a triumphant roar from their fans.

Pausing to grab a towel from a stage hand, Jake headed straight into Lori's arms.

"That was sensational!" she squealed as he held her tight. "You were amazing out there."

"It felt good. Different but good."

"Jake, you were fucking fantastic!" declared Mikey, draping his sweaty arms around them both.

"You guys made it easy for me," replied Jake humbly. "I'm just the hired voice."

"Bull shit!" stated the Weigh Station elder statesman. "You're one of us."

"Move it on out, boys and girls," shouted Laughlan loudly. "Come on. These guys need space. Move your butts!"

As Jake walked slowly away from the main stage beside Lori, they were joined by Dan's daughters.

"That was an amazing show," enthused Jenny. "Thanks for keeping Miles From Home in there."

"Thank you," replied Jake, smiling over at her. "It's one of my favourites too."

"Dad would've loved that," added Melissa. "He always loved to play a huge festival crowd. One of my earliest memories is of him carrying me out on stage at Donnington at the end of a headline show. I was about four and was wearing my Disney princess pjs."

"Glad you came better dressed tonight, Miss Crow," teased Jake, flashing her one of his Power smiles. "I hope our little Power Pack grows up with fond memories like that."

When they returned to the buses, Maddy had dinner for both bands arranged. A veritable banquet had been set out on a long, trestle table between the two buses. Screens had been erected at either end to give the bands a little privacy from the media and VIP guests who were milling about. Once they were all seated, it felt more like a family feast. Plates of chicken, corn on the cob and bowls of potato salad and coleslaw were passed up and down the table. Laughlan and Jethro sat at either end, like two father figures keeping a watchful eye over their families. Both Dan's daughters had joined them and were soon relaxed and laughing in the midst of the two bands.

Rich passed Jake an unopened bottle of beer across the table, "You've earned that."

For a moment Jake paused, then accepted the bottle from his band mate. He twisted the top off it, then raised it in a toast, "To friends and family."

"To you," acknowledged Rich, clinking their bottles together.

Blushing, Jake took a long chug on the bottle. His first beer in almost twelve weeks.

He felt a hand on his thigh as Lori leaned over and whispered, "Another big step forward, rock star."

Slowly, he kissed her then downed the rest of the bottle of beer.

Two hours later, as the fireworks to close the festival lit up the night sky, the joint Weigh Station/Silver Lake dinner was winding down. Both bands were scheduled to leave the site before midnight. Dan's daughters had said their farewells after they'd eaten, excusing themselves, saying that they wanted to catch the end of the headline band's set. As they had disappeared into the night, Rich has passed Jake a second beer.

This time he had sipped it slowly, still anxious at the thought of drinking alcohol. He had draped his arm around Lori's shoulder, drawing her close to him. In response, she had snuggled in closer, resting her head on his chest.

"Right, boys," declared Laughlan, suddenly lumbering to his feet, "Time to get this show on the road. Say your goodbyes and get your asses onto that bus. You've ten minutes till we pull out."

There were a few chaotic emotional moments as they all said their goodbyes. Whether by accident or design, Jake and Mikey were the last to say farewell to each other.

"Take care of yourself, young man," said the older English musician. "You put on a hell of a show tonight. I was proud to be out there beside you."

"Thanks," replied Jake, giving him a hug. "And thanks for all the support over the last few weeks."

"You've had it rough, son," agreed Mikey, keeping his voice quiet. "But you've survived. Now take that beautiful wife of yours home to have that baby. We'll see all three of you in September when we launch Chequered Past. Be thinking about a London launch party."

"Sounds like a plan."

"And give some thought to making a new Weigh Station record next year," added Mikey with a wink. "There's life in these old dogs yet."

With a laugh, Jake clapped him on the back and wished him a safe journey home.

The skies were cloudless and the sun was shining as Jake drove them back down the highway towards Rehoboth. Their overnight bus journey had passed uneventfully. Worn out after two long days, both Jake and Lori had slept soundly for the majority of the twelve hour ride. They had stopped about three hours out of town for breakfast at a Bob Evans before finally arriving back at JJL around lunchtime.

Maddy had had the foresight to phone ahead and ask Dr Marrs to have lunch waiting for them. All of them had been anxious to get home, but hunger got the better of them and they enjoyed a relaxed picnic lunch on the porch of the studio house. With promises to catch up during the week, Silver Lake had then all gone their separate ways.

As Jake turned off the highway, he noted that Lori had dozed off again in the passenger seat. He smiled as he stole a glance at her.

It had been a long weekend for both of them. He was aware how weary he still felt and fretted that it had all been too much for his heavily pregnant wife. Despite all the hours of travel, hours spent at the side of the stage and being interviewed and photographed at every turn, Lori hadn't uttered one word of complaint. Stoically, she had taken it all in her stride.

The band had agreed to take the rest of the week off before meeting up to continue pre-production work on the record. While they had been eating lunch, Dr Marrs had reminded them that they had the rehearsal studio booked out, prompting a debate about continuing to work on their new material. Eventually, they had agreed to meet there on Monday, giving them two weeks before recording was due to commence.

Turning the truck into E Lake Dr, Jake was conscious that they were still a few songs light. He had hoped that they could have had about eighteen to choose from. At the last count, he was till four or five short.

As he bumped the truck into the driveway, Lori stirred beside him.

"Home sweet home, li'l lady," he announced as he turned off the engine.

"Thank God," sighed Lori wearily. "I'm exhausted. I think I could sleep for a week."

"Well, I'm not stopping you," replied Jake, his voice filled with concern. "You need to slow down until our little Power Pack arrives. You're worn out, Lori."

"I'm not going to argue with you," she conceded. "I'm just glad to finally be home."

"Let's get you inside."

Leaving Jake to empty the truck, Lori wandered through to the sunroom and opened the patio doors, filling the place with fresh ocean air. After being shut up for a few days, the house smelled stale. She paused in the doorway to take a few deep breaths, filling her lungs with the clean, salt tinged air. Resting her hand on her bump, she gazed out across the deck to the beach beyond. Half of her yearned to go for a long stroll along the sand; half of her just wanted to crawl into bed. The baby stirred, jamming its feet into her already tender rib cage.

"Ok, little one," she said, rubbing the hard bulge in her bump. "Let's go soak in the tub and see if that eases off my back."

As she limped slowly back through the house, she passed Jake in the hallway and informed him she was going for a bath. He kissed her gently and said he would finish unloading the truck then run out to the food store. With a nod, Lori continued on down the long, narrow hallway towards their bedroom.

Unloading the truck took Jake longer than he'd expected. Knowing he had a few days at home, he'd brought most of his guitars back to the house. By the time he'd carried them all down to the basement and stowed them away, it was after three. Wearily, he brought their holdalls into the kitchen and sorted through the clothes to retrieve the dirty laundry. Having loaded the washing machine, he finally headed out to the food store. After all the support Lori had given him over the last three weekends, the least he could do was to pick up the chores and cook dinner.

As he pushed the cart up and down the aisles in the store, picking up the essentials, Jake smiled to himself. It was the same every time he returned from a tour or a festival. As he debated with himself over which pieces of chicken to buy, it struck him that the day before he'd been more focussed on sound check and set lists. Putting the chicken breasts into the cart, he smiled. Normality had resumed.

The house was quiet when he arrived home. He stowed the groceries away, then tiptoed down to the bedroom to check on Lori. It didn't surprise Jake when he found her asleep on top of the bed. She'd braided her long, damp hair, dressed in a baggy T-shirt and yoga pants, but had obviously then lain down for a nap. Her breathing was deep and even, indicating that she was sleeping soundly. Silently, Jake stood beside the bed, watching her for a few minutes. He felt a lump in his throat as he reflected how lucky he was to be married to her; how lucky he was that she had found it in her heart to forgive him for all that he had put her through. A movement at her stomach caught his eye and he watched in wonder as the baby kicked sharply. Jake could see the perfect outline of a tiny foot through the thin cotton of his wife's T-shirt. The kick had disturbed Lori, who stirred in her sleep, but never wakened. Not wanting to disturb her, Jake tiptoed back out of the bedroom. Once back in the kitchen, he closed over the door to the hallway and busied himself sorting through the rest of their laundry until it was time to start dinner.

A rumbling in her stomach and the delicious smell of food cooking roused Lori from her nap. For a few moments, she lay where she was, then a pressing feeling on her bladder alerted her to the fact she needed to pee urgently. Cautiously, she rolled over then got stiffly to her feet. Taking extra care, she made her way into the bathroom without using her crutches.

When she returned to the bedroom, she could hear Jake singing down in the kitchen. The nap had done her the world of good and she felt rested. The ache in her lower back was gone. Even the pressure on her pelvis felt less, almost as though her body had finally resigned itself to her current state of advanced pregnancy. As she lifted her crutches from the corner, Lori spotted her reflection in the full length mirror. It was the first time she'd seen herself since her baby bump had dropped. Seeing her round, ripe belly swollen in front of her made her smile. She was going to be a mommy soon!

"Not long now, little one," she whispered as the baby stirred inside her. "Let's go and see what your daddy has cooked for dinner."

As she pushed open the kitchen door, Lori caught Jake mid-song. He spun round as the door squeaked, but continued to sing along to the Guns N Roses classic playing on the radio.

"Smells good," said Lori as she sat down at the kitchen table. "I hadn't realised I was so hungry until I smelled food."

"It'll be ready in five minutes," promised Jake, flashing her a smile. "I've just to boil the noodles."

"Can I help you with anything?"

"No, li'l lady," he said. "You rest up. I have this under control."

Within five minutes, Jake was dishing up his favourite chicken parmesan dish and had poured them both a glass of apple juice.

"Thanks," said Lori quietly. "Looks delicious."

"It was the least I could do. You looked wiped out when we got back. I was worried about you."

"I'm fine, rock star," she assured him. "Yes, I was tired when we got back, but that's normal. You try carrying this not so little

Power Pack around 24/7. Since it moved, I feel heavier. I feel like I'm really waddling. I saw myself in the mirror when I got up. If I get much bigger, I think I'll explode."

"You're still beautiful," said Jake softly, reaching out across the table to touch her hand. "Still hot."

"This shape?" laughed Lori. "You're delusional! I'm huge!"

"No, you're heavily pregnant and extremely sexy with it."

Lori blushed scarlet.

To spare her blushes, Jake asked about her plans for the next few weeks, anxious to establish how much longer she intended to work for.

"I've still to finish off the In Chains cover for Garrett. There's a few tweaks to be made to the Chequered Past cover. All of that should take me four or five days, allowing for the fact I can't sit for long these days," she explained, flinching as the baby assaulted her with a furious frenzy of kicks. "Then I hope to pull together another LH collection for Lin."

"And then you'll take a break?"

Lori nodded, "The only project I'm taking between now and the end of the year is the Silver Lake one. My diary is closed until next year. Promise."

"Relieved to hear it," admitted Jake. "When does the baby stroller and furniture arrive? I really need to work on the nursery before we hit the studio."

"The furniture's arriving on Friday."

"Guess I'm decorating this week instead of song writing," declared Jake, secretly pleased at the thought of some manual labour for a few days. "What colour are we going with?"

"Lemon," replied Lori without hesitation. "Nice and neutral. We can add a frieze once we know who's coming to live with us."

"Ok. I'll head out to Lowes in the morning and pick up some paint."

"Only if you let me help," stated Lori firmly.

"We'll see about that."

By lunchtime the following day, Jake had been to the hardware to pick up the paint, had cleared all the furniture out of the room, shifting most of it up to the attic, and spread dust sheets ready to start work. After grabbing a sandwich for lunch, he set to work, leaving Lori sitting at her drawing board making the final changes to the artwork for Chequered Past.

They had decided the nursery would be the bedroom next to theirs as it was the smaller of the two spare bedrooms. With the furniture gone and the drapes removed, it looked far from small. It was a corner room and, as a result, had two windows – one looking out across the driveway and the other offering an oblique view of the beach.

It had been several years since Jake had tackled any decorating and, with a wry smile, he realised the last room he had painted had been the sunroom when he had worked for the construction company. Deftly, he masked the edges of the windows and door frames, followed by the baseboards, then began the thankless task of painting the woodwork. The fumes from the paint began to tickle his throat so Jake opened both windows, allowing the gentle ocean breeze to waft through, then returned to work.

"Jake!" called Lori from the hallway. "Dinner!"

Dinner? He'd been so engrossed in the simple task of glossing the woodwork that he had lost all track of time.

"Give me ten minutes," he yelled back. "Only a little bit to go and I'm done."

When he entered the kitchen, Lori began to giggle.

"What's so funny, li'l lady?" he asked as he sat down at the table.

"You've white paint streaked through your hair!" she giggled.

"I have?"

Lori nodded, "I'm guessing you ran your hand through your hair at some point. The evidence is all over your hand."

"Yeah, I might have," conceded Jake with a grin. "I'll wash it out after dinner. That's the baseboards and windows done. I'll do the door after dinner then we can do the walls tomorrow. I reckon it'll need two coats of paint though."

"And how many coats do you need?" teased Lori as she dished up their meal.

"Very funny, li'l lady. How was your day?"

"Productive. Baby behaved so I was able to concentrate for a few hours. The last bits of Chequered Past are done and mailed off for approval. Garrett and Mikey both want some merchandise designs, but I can pull that together by cutting up the album cover.

I'll do that tomorrow or Thursday. Won't take long. I've set Friday aside to work on In Chains."

"I thought you were going to slow things down?"

"I promise I'll take regular breaks and not overdo it," assured Lori calmly. "But, pregnant or not, I need to get it done. I've still got deadlines to meet here. Contractual obligations."

"I guess," agreed Jake a little reluctantly. "Once I've painted that door, I'm going downstairs to work on some songs for the record."

"Pots and kettles, rock star!"

Painting the door didn't take Jake long and by eight thirty, after a hot shower to remove the paint from himself, he was ready to head down to the basement. A quick glance into the sunroom reassured him that Lori was finally resting. She was curled up on the couch, engrossed in a movie. A rare but welcome sight.

The air down in the basement studio was cool compared to the rest of the house. Hurriedly, Jake switched all the lights on, then lifted his cherry red Gibson from its stand and began to practice a few chord progressions. Allowing his mind to empty, he sat and played, giving no thought to what he was actually playing. Gradually, Jake became aware that he was repeating the same melody line. A spark of an idea began to flicker.

Time lost all meaning as Jake expanded on the simple melody. Oblivious to the world out with the basement, he recorded the melody, then developed a solo from part of its construction. The bridge flowed naturally from there. In his head, he could hear a potential bass line and drum track, but recognised that he should leave those well alone for now. There was a vibrancy to the music. It felt fresh and new. His mind began to think about lyrics to accompany it. He mentally trawled through a few themes, but drew a blank. Just as he was about to call it a night, he remembered watching Lori sleeping the day before; recalled the clear outline of the baby's foot that he'd seen. The memory was enough to trigger the idea of something vulnerable fighting for survival; fighting for their beliefs. Sluggishly at first, the words began to trickle from his pen onto the blank page of his journal, gathering speed as he wrote. Three verses and a chorus tumbled onto the lined page. With a yawn, Jake closed the leather bound journal over, deciding to call it a night.

There was still a light on in the bedroom when he entered, but he wasn't surprised to find his wife sound asleep with her book propped up on her stomach. Carefully, he lifted the book, slipping her discarded bookmark into her place. He smiled when he saw that she was using her VIP pass from the last Silver Lake tour as a bookmark. As quietly as he could, he undressed then slipped under the thin summer duvet to lie beside her.

Seeing Lori lying there sleeping so peacefully filled his heart with love. After spending time in the basement, memories of the attack were still preying on his mind. If he'd killed her or killed their baby, Jake knew that he couldn't have lived with himself. It still scared him to think that the baby could still have suffered some, so far, undetected harm. He knew in his heart that that fear wouldn't be laid to rest until he held his son or daughter in his arms.

Lori's belly twitched, a small flurry of movement, and Jake smiled. Reaching over under the bedcovers, he rested his hand over the spot where the baby was moving. It was low down, just above Lori's hips and Jake guessed it was tiny punches he was witnessing. The baby continued to move under his outstretched palm while Lori slept on.

Jake's last thoughts as he drifted off to sleep were of how lucky he was to have married such a wonderful woman.

When Jake awoke next morning, Lori was already awake and lying on her side watching him. She was running her finger over the tattoo of the Silver Lake knot that adorned his chest. Her light touch was tickling him.

"Mornin'," said Jake, his voice husky with sleep,

"Morning, rock star," she purred softly. With a smile, she moved her hand and began to trace her fingers round the outline of the Celtic guitar that was inked down his ribcage. Her hand strayed down to the lower edge of the design, pausing just above his hip bone.

"Are you trying to turn me on, Mz Hyde?"

"Might be," she teased with a wink.

"You sure it's ok?" quizzed Jake, fearful that if he made love to her that he'd harm the baby or bring on an early labour.

"Perfectly safe," whispered Lori, running her hand down his inner thigh. With a glance at her hugely, swollen stomach, she added, "Although we may need to…"

Laughing, Jake pulled her towards him, "I'll figure it out, li'l lady."

Cupping her heavy breast, he ran his tongue around the dark areola of her nipple. A bead of milk formed on the tip of the erect nipple. He expertly licked it off, then traced down the curve of her breast, gliding his tongue down over the swell of her stomach. Sensually, he ran his tongue over the top of her bump and down towards her blonde, pubic hair line. Under his erotic caress, Lori moaned softly, rolled onto her back and parted her legs, ready to welcome him. Slipping his fingers between her thighs, Jake found her moist and eager for him.

"We're going to have to improvise here, li'l lady wife," he observed before sliding down the bed to kneel on the floor.

Lovingly, he helped her to slip down to the bottom edge of the mattress, folding the duvet over the wooden bed frame to cushion it a little. For a moment, Lori looked uncomfortable until Jake positioned a pillow under the base of her back and two more under her shoulders.

Displaying a tenderness that she had never seen, Jake massaged her small, slightly swollen feet and ankles then positioned them around his waist. Slowly, terrified that he'd hurt her, Jake moved forward and entered her dark, wet, feminine warmth. Taking care not to thrust too deeply, he moved in a slow, gentle rhythm, feeling her respond to his caresses. Digging her heels into his buttocks, Lori urged him on. Needing little invitation, Jake came hard and fast, penetrating deep inside her, praying inwardly that his desires weren't causing any harm. He climaxed a second or two before Lori's orgasm surged through her.

With a low moan of satisfaction, she sank back onto the pillows as Jake gently withdrew from her.

"Love you," he whispered, resting a hand on her stomach. "Both of you."

He felt her stomach tighten for a few seconds, then relax under his hand. A moment or so later it tightened again. Eyes wide with fear, he asked, "Is that normal? Have I hurt you?"

"Braxton Hicks," stated Lori, wriggling awkwardly into a sitting position.

"Pardon me?"

"Practice contractions," explained Lori with a smile. "And, no, I'm not about to go into labour. No need for panic."

"Guess I should read more of that baby book that Maddy gave you," acknowledged Jake, looking slightly sheepish. "I'm a few weeks behind in the development stages."

"Somehow, I don't think this will go by the book," giggled Lori, struggling to her feet. "When did you or I ever do anything by the book?"

"True," laughed Jake. "Just hope our little Power Pack doesn't take its timekeeping from me."

"God, if they do, I'll still be pregnant on Labor Day!"

After lunch, Jake relented and allowed Lori to help him roller the lemon eggshell paint onto the nursery walls. He'd already painted two walls before lunch while she had worked on the merchandise designs for Chequered Past for a couple of hours. Together, they worked away, chatting about the future and wondering how many sleepless nights they were in for. By late afternoon, the room had had its first coat and was beginning to look more like a nursery.

Stretching her back, Lori let out a groan.

"You ok?"

"Just a bit sore," she confessed. "Can you clear up while I go and lie down for a while?"

"Sure," replied Jake. "It's a nice afternoon. You could lie out on the deck for a while. I'm going to head out for a run when I'm done here. I'll cook dinner later if you want."

"Works for me," agreed Lori, forcing a smile.

Half an hour later, as Jake stepped out on the sun deck, ready to go for his run, he found Lori sound asleep on the sun lounger. Once again, her book lay discarded on her stomach. Smiling, he again slipped her VIP pass in at the correct page, then set off down the path.

There were still a few families down on the sand and a few lone fishermen scattered along the shoreline as he ran south towards the bath house, heading for the lifeguard station. After the stresses and strains of the weekend, it felt good to feel the ocean spray on his face and the wind in his hair. No one gave him a second glance as he ran along the damp, hard packed sand. It felt good to be anonymous, lost in his own thoughts. After he'd made the turn, Jake allowed his mind to wander back to the Silver Lake record. Methodically, he ran through each of the songs that they had lined up to work on, including the one he had written the night before. He was genuinely pleased with what they had compiled so far, but he couldn't shake the feeling that they needed more. In his heart, Jake knew if he tried to force a song, it wouldn't work, wouldn't flow. His only hope of coming up with a few more was that inspiration would strike once they regrouped in the rehearsal room at JJL.

"Twenty bucks in the pot, Mr Power!" growled Grey as Jake walked into the rehearsal room almost an hour late on Monday morning.

"Sorry," muttered Jake, handing him two crumpled ten dollar bills. "I was busy."

"Doing what?" demanded the bass player sourly as he stuffed the money into his pocket.

"Assembling the crib," confessed Jake as he opened his guitar case.

"Need me to check its safe for Baby Power?" offered Paul from behind his drum kit. "I know how great you are at furniture assembly. I remember that table you bought from IKEA for the apartment. Collapsed the second I put my beer down on it!"

"No need. Lori has checked it over."

"And how is the mommy-to-be?" asked Grey. "She looked exhausted out in Ohio."

"She was," agreed Jake. "She's ok though. Been resting more and slowing down a bit. I guess she's not got much choice these days."

"How long to go now?" asked Rich.

"About five weeks, give or take."

"If it's got your time keeping talents, poor Lori will still be pregnant on Labor Day!" joked Grey.

"That's the second time I've heard that joke!" muttered Jake, feigning anger. "If I'm honest, I think the baby will take after their mommy and arrive politely early."

"Time will tell," stated Grey. "Now let's get to work before you go on paternity leave!"

"Anyone brought anything new with them?" enquired Rich as he surveyed the makeshift board that had been drawn up.

"I might have one," replied Jake as he slung his guitar strap over his head. "Give me a minute to change tuning and I'll let you hear it."

After the second run through of the new song, Paul began to work out a drum track. His beat inspired Grey, who picked out a heavy rhythm. The four of them messed about with different options for a couple of hours, then just before they stopped for lunch, they ran through it from the start. When they finished playing it, all four of them were nodding.

"Ok, it's in," stated Rich bluntly, lifting a marker pen. "Track sixteen. Does it have a working title yet?"

"Not really," began Jake. "Something like Worth Fighting For."

"That'll do for now," agreed Rich, scrawling the title on the board. "After lunch, let's run through the board top to bottom. See where we get to by six. I need to wrap it up then. I'm picking up Linsey."

By five thirty they were at track ten, tentatively called Witchcraft. With a long sigh, Jake shook his head.

"Let's call it a day," he said quietly. "I'm not singing that one tonight."

"You ok?" asked Rich, concern echoing through his voice.

"Yeah," replied Jake just a little too swiftly.

"Jake," said Grey softly. "We know you, buddy. What's up?"

"There's a lot of ghosts in that one," he revealed quietly. "I need to be in the right frame of mind to tackle it. To be honest, it might need to be scrubbed."

"We hear you," sympathised Grey. "However, it's one of the best fucking songs on the board."

"I know," sighed Jake, exasperated by his own weakness. "Let me sleep on it. We can try it in the morning when I'm fresh."

"Can we do anything to make this any easier on you?" asked Paul, stepping out from behind his kit.

Jake shook his head. "Not that I can think of. Turn back time, maybe? Fuck knows!"

Laying his guitar carefully back in its case, Jake picked up his book bag and prepared to leave. At the door, he paused and turned round, "Let me call Jethro. Sort a few things out in my head. See if it looks better in the morning."

"If it's that tough, we can forget about it," offered Rich. "We can come up with an alternative."

Shaking his head, Jake disagreed, "Grey's right. It's an awesome song. One of the best we've got and the fans will love it. I'm just not feeling it right now. Bear with me for a day or so."

Without a backwards glance, he opened the door and left.

When he arrived back at the house, Jake found Lori sitting at her desk working on the In Chains cover. Dropping his bag on the dining room table, he called out that he was going down to the basement for a couple of hours. Barely looking up from the design in front of her, Lori mumbled something about dinner being late. He never replied.

Warily, he walked down the steep stairs into the rehearsal space. Ghosts of the attack smothered him before he reached the bottom step. Trembling uncontrollably, Jake half sat, half collapsed onto the bottom step, burying his head in his hands. From out of nowhere, waves of anxiety swept over him. He could feel his sense of control spiralling into a dark abyss. Tears welled up in his eyes as flashback memories filled his head; memories he'd not recalled before. Visions of Lori lying in a crumpled, battered heap only a few feet from where he sat, sent shivers of fear into his very core.

Jake let out a primal scream that reverberated through the house.

"Jake?" called a soft voice from somewhere behind him.

It was Lori.

Without raising his head from his hands, Jake listened to her slow, unsteady footsteps as she made her way down the stairs. He was barely aware of the soft groan she tried to disguise as she lowered herself down to sit on the step above him. The soft touch of her hands on his shoulders made him flinch.

"Talk to me, Jake," she suggested calmly. "What's happened? Did something happen at JJL? Did one of the boys say something?"

Still shaking, Jake shook his head.

"Jake, talk to me."

"I think I'm losing it," he whispered, his voice thick with emotion.

"Want to try and tell me about it?" coaxed Lori, running her hand through his hair. "Or do you need me to call Jethro?"

"I have no fucking idea what I need," admitted Jake, turning to rest his head on her knees.

Comfortingly, Lori continued to run her hand through his hair. Her light touch was soothing. Gradually, his breathing slowed and became more even. The trembling stopped. In silence, Lori continued to smooth her hand over his head and down his shoulder. Seeing her strong rock star husband looking so fragile and vulnerable was scaring her.

"I'm sorry," whispered Jake, his voice thick and choked.

"Sh," she said softly. "Just relax. Clear your mind. Let it all go."

"You sound like Jethro," commented Jake with a weak smile. "I'm trying to let it go. Trying to put it all behind us. Focussing on the future. On the baby. Christ, it's hard! I thought I was winning too, until this afternoon."

"You are winning," assured Lori, still rubbing his shoulder

gently. "This isn't easy. I get that. We all do. It's ok to have an off day."

"All over a stupid, fucking song! One that I fucking wrote!" muttered Jake. "When will this ever end?"

"I wish I knew," she sighed. "What song triggered all of this? One of the new ones?"

Sitting up, Jake nodded and explained the approach that Silver Lake had taken to their rehearsal, ending with his wave of panic at being faced with having to sing Witchcraft. "So, now I know it's first on the list for tomorrow," he concluded.

"I think deep down you know what you need to do," said Lori, smiling at him. "Play it for me. Play it right here. Right now."

"I don't know…"

"Try," encouraged Lori warmly. "There's only you, me and our little Power Pack here."

"I guess," relented Jake, forcing an anxious smile.

Hesitantly, he got to his feet, headed across to the guitar rack and lifted down one of his plain finished custom models. His heart was pounding. His hands felt sweaty. A knot of fear was twisting in his gut. Taking a deep breath, Jake began the dark, haunted intro to the song. When he started to sing the first verse, he connected with some previously hidden inner reserve of strength. His voice rang clear and pure around the basement as he sang of the demons and the witch; he sang about the imps "swarming his car and his soul"; about the illusion "shattering his heart and melting his mind". The lyrics had he had penned that day down on the beach tore him to the very core, but Jake knew they rang true; knew the song was something a little bit special. As he reached the final chorus, he risked a glance over at Lori. There were tears on her cheeks, but she was smiling.

The last note faded out into the empty, dark corners of the room.

"Well, li'l lady?" he asked, sounding like a little boy seeking his class teacher's approval.

Without saying a word, Lori heaved herself to her feet, making her way down the last couple of steps and over to her husband. She reached out to hold him, ignoring the awkwardness of her baby belly.

"That song is incredible," she said sincerely as she looked up into Jake's haunted, hazel eyes. "I completely understand why it's so hard on you. I know it's tearing you apart inside, but it's brilliant." She paused as the baby kicked sharply at her ribs. Jake felt the movement and placed his hand on her stomach, rubbing the spot where the tiny foot had lashed out. "Jake, if you can sing that with such emotion down here for me and stay in control, you can sing that song anywhere."

"You reckon?"

"I reckon."

Next morning, Jake was the first to arrive for rehearsal. With the studio to himself, he sat on the edge of the low practice stage and began to play the solo from one of the new songs that they had mischievously titled Battle To The Death. There was a guitar duel planned for it and both Jake and Rich were already battling to outdo one another with the complexity of their respective solos. With his fingers suitably loosened up, Jake ran through his guitar part for Witchcraft.

"Sounding sweet!" called out Grey as he arrived carrying a tray of coffees and a box of donuts.

"Morning," replied Jake, laying his guitar down. "One of those for me?"

"Yup. Your name's on it," said Grey, setting the cardboard tray down. "You ok this morning?"

Jake nodded. "How's your back?"

"A lot easier. Doc gave me a shot in it on Monday when we got home. Really eased things off. I've to go back June 9th for another one," explained Grey, tearing open the box of donuts.

"Same date as our last baby scan," observed Jake with a smile.

"Then recording our music baby starts next day," joked the bass player.

"Unless our Power Pack decides to arrive early!"

A few minutes later, Rich and Paul arrived together, apologising for being late and trying to blame Maddy for delaying them.

"Twenty bucks each!" growled Grey. "And an extra twenty for trying to pass the buck and blame the boss!"

"Fine. Fine," grumbled Rich, pulling two crisp twenty dollar bills from his wallet. "Jake, you good to go on Witchcraft?"

"As I'll ever be," sighed Jake, feeling his stomach tighten at the thought.

It took them almost half an hour to get themselves organised. Just as they were about to start, the door opened and Jethro walked in with Jason on his heel.

"Morning!" called out the Englishman. "I was in the area and thought I'd drop by to see how pre-production was going."

"We're getting there," replied Rich.

"Seventeen songs on the board," added Grey. "Hoping to add a couple more before recording starts."

"And you, Jake?" asked Jason warmly, turning his attention to Silver Lake's vocalist.

"All good," he replied, sounding calmer than he felt. "We were just about to make a start for the day."

"Perfect. What are you starting with?"

"Track nine," called out Paul, mindful of Jake's reaction to the thought of playing track ten.

"No, we were up to ten," countered Jake. "Witchcraft."

"You good to go on it?" asked Grey, staring intently at Jake in an effort to gauge his emotions.

Jake nodded, "From the top."

If Jason or Jethro picked up on the air of tension in the room, neither of them said. Taking a deep breath and mentally endeavouring to clear his head, Jake began to play the gentle intro, keeping his touch light and haunting, hinting at the air of evil to come. Closing his eyes, he reached inside himself and delivered the lyrics with the same clean, pure tone that he'd found the night before in the basement. He knew his bandmates were playing their respective parts, but a part of him had zoned them out, allowing him to focus on the lyrics.

As the song ended, Jake stood with his head bowed and his chest heaving. He'd poured everything into the song and it had drained him physically as well as mentally.

"That, boys, was quite something," complimented Jason, nodding approvingly. "Dark though. Menacing. Heavy."

"We're exploring a few different levels on this record," explained Rich. "That's about as dark as it gets."

"Drawing on recent events?" quizzed the Englishman, without really thinking of the impact of his observation.

Jake's face darkened. Instead of replying, he excused himself and left the room.

"Subtle, Mr Russell," muttered Jethro, feeling Jake's pain. "Really subtle!"

Outside, it was already developing into a hot, late spring day. Seeking the sun's warmth, Jake wandered down the path and across to the main JJL building and the sanctuary of the plastic crate he had sat on so many times before. The anticipated anxiety at singing Witchcraft hadn't materialised, however Jason's throwaway line had stirred up the ghosts. With a sigh, he sat down on the crate, stretched his long, denim clad legs out in front of him and rested his head back against the building. He could feel the heat of the sun chasing the ghosts back into the shadows.

"Jake," said Jethro quietly sometime later. "You ok?"

"Actually, you know what," began Jake without moving. "I think I am."

"Lori called me earlier. Told me you were struggling a bit yesterday. Said you might need a buddy."

"She worries too much," replied Jake softly. "But she's right. I could do with a meeting. See if we can lay these ghosts to rest a bit better. Yesterday out here was tough. Last night at home was tough, but Lori talked me through it. This morning was fine until Jason opened his fucking mouth."

"He didn't think, son," apologised the band's white haired manager. "He doesn't mean anything by it."

"It's fine," assured Jake with a smile. "I realised, as I came out here, it's really ok. Yes, I've drawn on recent events for some of the songs on this record. It's been therapeutic. I needed to do it. I can see that now."

"Any of the rest of those new songs going to send your stress levels sky high?"

"Just one," confessed Jake with a grin. "Lady Gambler. When Grey's mom hears it, I'm dead meat!"

Back at the beach house, Lori was trying to get comfortable to work on the In Chains design. No matter what angle she sat at, either her large baby bump got in the way or the position was uncomfortable and her back protested. There was still a few days' work required to finish the project off. When they'd returned from

Ohio, she had received an email from Garrett asking for two T-shirt designs as well as the album cover, then a second email asking for a potential single cover. Knowing time was against her, Lori had emailed back a compromise, she would do a second design for the single, but the two covers would need to double up as T-shirts. Garrett had agreed, explaining that the single he had chosen was track ten, In Chains, but that he wanted a different shackled imagery for it.

Having tried every possible position, Lori decided there was only one option left. She would need to set up her trusty easel and stand. It stood folded in the corner beside the window. Carefully, she set it up and positioned the pad of paper on it.

Standing to sketch or paint always reminded her of being in college. As she sketched the outline of the shackled feet she intended to draw, memories of her college days flitted through her mind, raising a few wistful smiles. Soon, she was immersed in the detail of the design and almost oblivious to the gentle movements of the baby.

After a couple of hours, Lori began to tire. While it was more comfortable to work standing at the easel, it was more exhausting than sitting.

"OK little one," she said, rubbing her bump. "Let's eat lunch then head out to the deck for a while."

Hot sunshine was bathing the deck when she finally stepped outdoors. It was too hot for the top and trousers she was wearing so Lori returned to the bedroom to change. Guessing that Jake wouldn't be home until nearer dinner time, Lori decided to put her bikini on. She was self-conscious about her heavily pregnant body but she also wanted to be comfortable out in the sun. Lifting one of Jake's cotton shirts to use as a cover up, Lori limped back through the house and out onto the deck.

She sank back onto the cushioned mattress of the lounger and sighed. Every bit of her ached and she now fully understood why Maddy had been so grouchy during the final weeks of her pregnancy. Rubbing her swollen stomach, Lori smiled as she visualised being out here in a few weeks with the baby in her arms. The thought of actually going through labour and giving birth scared her, but she was desperate to meet their little Power Pack.

The sun's warmth made her drowsy and, with lists of baby names scrolling through her mind, Lori drifted off to sleep.

It was after five before Jake turned the truck into E Lake Drive and the temperatures were still in the high seventies. Having been cooped up in the studio all day, he was desperately in need of some fresh air and decided that he felt like going for a swim.

As he walked round the side of the house, Jake wasn't surprised to find his wife asleep on the sun deck. He was mildly surprised to find her sound asleep wearing only her bikini. Smiling to himself, Jake thought how beautiful she looked. So relaxed. So natural. His eyes barely registered the scars on her thigh. Instead, he was drawn to the swell of her ripe breasts and the curves of her belly. "Soon," he thought to himself. "Soon we'll be a family."

Deciding against disturbing her, he slipped into the house. Once changed into his favourite orange neon shorts, Jake crept back out and across the deck. The soft sand was hot under his feet as he jogged towards the water's edge. Without a thought to the fact that the water would still be cold, Jake ran out into the surf for a few yards before diving into an incoming wave. The chill of the water caught his breath and he emerged gasping. Feeling the cold, salty ocean rinse away the stresses and strains of the day, Jake swam out from the shore for about fifty yards, then began to swim south, parallel to the beach for a few minutes before turning to swim home.

A coastguard cutter went past, disturbing the relatively calm ocean. Like an overgrown teenager, he played in the swell of the waves it left in its wake, body surfing them expertly. He was beginning to feel chilled, despite the warmth of the late afternoon sun. Reluctantly, Jake body surfed into the shore on the last of the big waves.

"Hey, rock star!" cried a voice from further up the beach.

Still on his hands and knees in the shallows, Jake looked up to see Lori carefully making her way across the sand, carrying a towel for him. Spying that she was only using one crutch, Jake held his breath, silently praying that she wouldn't stumble.

"How'd you know I was down here?" called out Jake once she was closer to him.

"Powers of deduction. I found a pile of clothes on the floor in the bedroom. Your running shoes were still in the utility so I guessed you'd gone for a swim. I spotted those orange shorts of yours from the deck!"

"You should come in," suggested Jake, smiling up at her. She'd slipped one of his shirts on over her bikini, its tail only just covering her thigh.

"Isn't it cold?"

"Not too cold," he said, scrambling to his feet. "Dip your toes in. It might help those puffy ankles you were complaining about."

Dropping the towel and laying her crutch down, Lori stepped tentatively towards Jake, taking his outstretched, wet hand to steady her. Slowly, he led her out into the shallows where gentle waves lapped over their ankles. A few steps further and the water was up to Lori's knees.

"You ok, li'l lady?" checked Jake, still holding her hand.

"I'm fine," she replied, smiling. "I was thinking about the first day you talked me into coming into the water with you. The day you saw my scars."

"Seems like a lifetime ago," mused Jake. "Feel like going out a bit deeper? See how our Power Pack reacts to feeling water round them?"

"I'm not sure."

"It'll be fine. I'll hold onto you," he promised, stepping forward to encourage her.

"And you won't let me fall?"

"No, I won't."

Step by step, they waded out a little deeper until the water was tugging at Lori's shirt. A few steps further on, it was lapping at the underside of her swollen stomach. Clutching Jake's strong hands tightly, Lori allowed him to lead her out until the water was just below her breasts. The ocean was supporting the weight of the baby and for the first time in months she felt "light."

"Want to swim a little?" suggested Jake with an impish grin.

"I don't know…" she began, feeling the baby kick and squirm inside.

"It'll help ease your back."

"Just for a minute or two. Baby isn't too happy. They're kicking like crazy."

Taking leisurely strokes, they swam side by side down the

beach for about five minutes, then turned and swam back towards home. For those few moments, Lori enjoyed having the salt water support the weight of the growing baby, relishing the freedom of movement she felt.

Taking her hand, Jake helped his wife back into the shallows. The wet shirt clung to her, accentuating her baby bump. In the late afternoon sun, Jake thought she'd never looked more beautiful.

When they reached the spot where she had left the towel, Jake bent down to pick it and her crutch up, shaking sand over both of them.

"Let's BBQ," he suggested with a lazy smile. "I feel like some burgers and a few beers while we watch the sun go down."

"Sounds like heaven to me, rock star."

For the next ten days, life around the beach house slipped easily into a relaxed routine. Each morning Jake rose early, went for a run along the beach before heading out to JJL to rehearse. While her husband was at the studio, Lori would start her day leisurely, work for a few hours from late-morning through to mid-afternoon, then retire to the sun lounger out on the deck. Most evenings, Jake made a point of being home for six, giving them time for a leisurely stroll or a swim before dinner.

Rehearsals out at JJL ran like clockwork as Silver Lake worked on the new songs on the board. A few new riffs and melodies came to life, but they decided amongst themselves to stick with the seventeen songs already noted. They had a conference call with their management, Jason and various other key players in the process and, after some debate around time frames, agreed to release the new album in early October with fourteen tracks, with a follow up plan to release a deluxe edition in December containing the three remaining songs. Tentatively, they agreed to tour the US in October followed by a trip to Europe through mid-November until Christmas. The very thought of being separated from Lori and their little Power Pack tore at Jake's heartstrings but business was business.

By the end of the first week in June, Lori had finalised her designs for Garrett and submitted them for his approval. She had played a little with the single cover despite her original remit. The album cover would still have the shackles with the rose intertwined in the chain; the single cover depicted dusty, shackled feet with fallen rose petals scattered around them. Both of the designs were very powerful and, even though she was biased, Lori felt they ranked among her best work.

From the comfort of the sun lounger, she made a start on the jewellery designs for the next LH collection. Perhaps it was the early summer sun or the clean ocean air, but this time she opted for an ocean theme to the designs. During their late afternoon strolls

along the sand, Lori kept her eyes peeled for unusual shells, asking
Jake to pick them up for her when she spied one. He teased her
relentlessly about being too lazy to bend down to reach them
herself, knowing full well that it was practically a physical
impossibility for her. During these final weeks of her pregnancy,
her already cumbersome baby belly was expanding daily and
growing heavier by the hour. Her nerves about the actual birth
were beginning to grow and there were several nights, when she
was able to sleep, that her slumber was disturbed by nightmares
about delivering the baby.

When Jake helped her out of the car at the maternity unit for her
final ultrasound appointment, Lori groaned as he pulled her to her
feet.

"I'm going to have to rent a better car for a few weeks," she
muttered as she adjusted her grip on her crutches. "This one's too
damn low!"

Raising an eyebrow, Jake said, "I've a better idea, li'l lady. Hang
up your car keys until the baby arrives. I'm worried about you
driving these days."

"You might be right," she conceded wearily as they made their
way across the parking lot.

The waiting room was empty when they arrived and, before
Lori had time to sit down, they were called through by the nurse.
As they entered the room, Lori was relieved that it was the same
welcoming midwife that she'd seen at her previous appointment.

"Wow!" she exclaimed with a twinkling smile. "Someone's
blossomed beautifully!"

"That's one way to put it," said Lori, forcing a smile. "I feel like
I'm about to pop any second."

"That's only natural, honey," assured the older woman, helping
her to sit down. "How are you feeling? Any specific problems?"

"Apart from feeling like a whale?"

"Any pains? Pins and needles? Swelling?" prompted the
midwife. "Headaches? Nausea?"

Lori shook her head. "My feet get a little puffy by the end of the
day. I've had plenty Braxton Hicks contractions. I tire easily."

"All perfectly normal at this stage. Your body's telling you to
slow down."

"You try telling her that!" stated Jake bluntly from where he was standing near the door.

"Ah," mused the midwife with a nod. "Been over doing things, Lori?"

"A bit, I guess," admitted Lori reluctantly. "I had a deadline to meet on a work commission. It's done. I'm officially on maternity leave now."

"Sounds good to me. Now, let's check your blood pressure then draw some bloods. I'll need a urine sample too, honey."

It took a few minutes to complete all the routine checks then the midwife invited Lori to make herself comfortable on the exam table.

As she squirted the cold gel into Lori's large baby bump, she explained that she hoped to get a more accurate estimate of the baby's weight and a final check on its position. Pressing down firmly on the transducer, she moved it over Lori's stomach. At first, neither Lori nor Jake could make out the image displayed on the monitor screen, then they both spotted a foot kicking out.

"Someone doesn't like this," commented the midwife. "Let me take the measurements I need, then I'll talk you through what we're seeing."

She moved the sensor over all aspects of Lori's stomach, searching a little lower down than on previous visits. All the while, the baby shifted restlessly, punching and kicking.

"Still a very active baby," she observed as she typed a few details into the PC. "Ok, so where are we at? Thirty six weeks, according to your notes. You've measured ahead since early on and you're still measuring ahead. Baby looks long. I make it about twenty, maybe twenty one inches. Weight wise baby is around eight pounds so no wonder you're feeling heavy and tired, honey."

"How much bigger will this little one get?" asked Lori a little anxiously.

"Hard to say. I'd expect baby to be nearer ten pounds in four weeks if you go that long," replied the midwife. "The head's fully engaged. It's lying well down into your pelvis. Right now, baby is in the perfect position for labour, but there's still time for him or her to move. If they try to turn, you'll really feel it!"

"Oh, I know!" exclaimed Lori, recalling the last time the baby had lurched itself round. "Do you think I'll make it to my due date?"

"Impossible to say. From the way things look right now, you could go into labour any day or you could still be waiting in five weeks' time. We won't let you go much beyond forty weeks so no need to panic."

"Will Lori need to plan a C-section?" asked Jake, concerned by what he was hearing about the baby being larger than average.

"I don't think so, Mr Power. I'm sure Lori's pelvis is wide enough to deliver this little one naturally."

"How will she know when she's in labour?" asked Jake. "And how long will it last?"

"Generally speaking, first babies take longer to come into the world, Mr Power. On average, the first phase of labour lasts twelve to fourteen hours. The second phase, when Lori will want and need to push usually take around an hour maybe a bit longer. Every labour is different. Some last longer and others are a lot quicker. Quick first labours are quite rare, so you'll have plenty of time to get here once the contractions are established."

"Established?" quizzed Jake, not fully understanding the terminology.

"Once they are coming about every four or five minutes and lasting for up to a minute. That's the time to head in here. Lori, if your waters break first, give us a call and we'll advise you if you need to come straight in," explained the older woman calmly. "Now, I'll schedule weekly appointments for you so we can check your blood pressure is stable. All perfectly normal at this late stage."

During the drive home, Lori was quieter than normal. Her silence worried Jake a little. After they'd left the antenatal clinic, she had had a quick appointment with John Brent, who had done his best to reassure her that her leg was coping with the extra weight and that the fixation to her pelvis was secure and could not harm the baby. Like the midwife, he advised plenty of rest and, to Jake's relief, advised her not to drive until after the birth.

"Want to stop and grab some lunch before we go home?" asked Jake as they approached the outskirts of town.

"No, thanks," she said quietly.

"Li'l lady, what's eating at you?"

"It all seems so imminent. I feel like a ticking time bomb," replied Lori, her voice trembling a little. "What if my waters break in a public place? What if you're in the studio and can't get home on time? What if I can't cope with the actual birth?"

"I can be home in thirty minutes, forty tops," promised Jake, understanding her fears. "The nurse said it would take hours so I've time to get home from New York never mind JJL."

"New York! You're not planning to go to New York are you?"

"No, I'm not. I'll be as close to home for as long as I can. Promise. I'll have my phone in my pocket at all times. You will be absolutely fine." Jake hoped his tone was more reassuring than he really felt. He was sharing Lori's nerves, but did not want her to know he too was worried and more than a little scared.

"Promise?"

"I promise," he said sincerely. "I've no plans to go further than JJL until after the baby arrives. The guys have a meeting in Philly on June 30th but I've already said I'm not going."

"Don't you have to be there?"

"Yes, but they can call me if they need my input. It's with the legal guys and the accountants. Not my scene, li'l lady. That's Rich's forte."

"No further away than JJL?"

"No further away than JJL. Promise."

June 10th dawned cool and misty and, for the third year in succession, Jake headed into the studio with Silver Lake. It seemed a lifetime ago that they'd arrived nervously at the studio in Manhattan, handed the opportunity of a lifetime on a plate. Although she had never confessed, Jake was sure that the "free sessions" had been paid for by Lori. As he drove up the highway, he reminisced to himself about that first trip to New York; reminisced about celebrating Lori's 30th birthday. Birthday! He had completely forgotten that there were only six days until her birthday.

By the time he pulled off the highway into JJL, Jake was stressing about what to buy his wife for her birthday.

"Twenty bucks, Mr Power," called out Grey as Jake entered the live room.

"Whatever," muttered Jake, pulling a crumpled wad of notes from his pocket. "Why did no one remind me about Lori's birthday?"

"She's your wife!" laughed Rich from his seat on the couch. "You shouldn't need reminding!"

"Harrumph," grumbled Jake. "I suppose you've all got her a gift?"

"Linsey picked something up a couple of weeks back at a craft fair."

"Kola and Becky went shopping the other night," added Grey with a wink.

"Maddy's been organised for weeks," threw in Paul.

"Great!"

A voice from the control room called through, "And my gift's been bought and wrapped for a week!"

"Thanks, Jim," acknowledged Jake sourly. "Guess I'll think of something before Monday."

"Gentlemen, time to get this party started," stated Dr Marrs firmly. "You know the drill. Write up the board. Break for coffee, then we'll run through it track by track before deciding who needs to be in when."

"We've seventeen songs to go up there," commented Rich, getting to his feet. "Might take today and tomorrow to play through it."

"It will if you don't get started!"

Reverting to school teacher mode, Rich took control of writing up the working titles of the seventeen new Silver Lake songs. They debated changing the running order and the names of a few, but Jim overruled them, declaring bluntly, "Just write the damn things up there, Ricardo!"

Over coffee, they answered the producer's endless questions about the various tracks and their own thoughts as to the theme or undercurrent of the record.

"Grey's got a lead vocal to do this time out," revealed Jake as he drained his cup. "Track six. Dark Trails."

"Interesting," nodded the producer. "Any other surprises lined up for me?"

"Track nine. Lady Gambler is a bit tongue in cheek," said Grey. "Jake's taking a crack at my mom with his lyrics. She's going to be after his ass when she hears it."

The producer laughed at the thought of an irate Annie Cooper chasing Jake, then firmly declared that their coffee break was over and that it was time to start work.

After the weeks and months of writing and rehearsing, it felt good to be back in the studio to actually record. Silver Lake had played through the first five songs before Kola interrupted their progress by saying lunch was ready. As they all trooped out into the lounge to eat, Jake decided that the sound engineer knew them too well and that they were all creatures of habit. Everyone's favourite sandwich and drink sat on the table waiting for them. Studio life had resumed.

Maternity leave and relaxation didn't come easy to Lori. With Jake out of the house at JJL and her car keys confiscated, she felt restless and more than a little trapped. After a while, she found herself wandering aimlessly through the house searching for something to occupy her. Inevitably, she found herself in the newly decorated nursery. Much as she loved the sunroom, this quiet corner room was rapidly becoming her favourite part of the house. The pine nursery furniture was all set up ready for the baby's arrival. The crib was made up with neutral white and lemon bed linen. On a stand beside it stood the bassinet, all wicker and white broderie anglaise. It too was made up with soft, white bedcovers. The stroller was stowed away in the corner closet. Absent-mindedly, Lori opened the top two small, deep drawers of the dresser. Tiny bodysuits and all-in-ones were neatly folded, again all in neutral colours. Tiny white socks and a white sun hat lay among them. In one corner, Lori's hospital bag sat packed in readiness as it had done for a week.

"All that's missing is you, little one," said Lori, resting her hand on her large firm belly.

The walls of the nursery were bare she noted as she glanced round. A spark of inspiration ignited inside her and Lori headed through to the study in search of her sketchpad and pencils. As she was searching in her desk drawer, the phone rang.

"Hello," she said, noting the out of area message on the caller ID.

"Hi Lori! It's Lucy," greeted her sister-in-law brightly. "How are you?"

"Still pregnant," replied Lori a little sourly. "Fat. Hot and tired."

"Awh, I remember it well," sympathised Jake's sister warmly. "Not long to go now though."

"I hope not," sighed Lori as the baby delivered another sharp kick to her tender rib cage. "How're you and the boys?"

"All good. The boys are getting big and bad," giggled Lucy. "That's kind of why I called. Are you guys at home this weekend?"

"Yes," replied Lori. "Jake might be working, but I'll be here. Are you coming down?"

"Just for the day. I want to bring your birthday present down, if that's ok?"

"Why not come down for the weekend? Come down on Friday night. Stay till Sunday," suggested Lori hopefully. "It would be good to have some company."

"Well, Robb's away this weekend," began Lucy a little hesitantly.

"Please, Lucy," begged Lori.

"Oh, why not!" laughed her sister-in-law. "The boys would love a weekend at the shore."

"Great. We'll see you all on Friday."

"I'll leave after school so we should be with you by seven."

"Don't eat dinner on the way down," Lori cautioned. "We can eat together when you get here. Who knows, we might be able to talk Jake into picking up a pizza."

"Perfect. See you both Friday."

Out at JJL, progress on the new Silver Lake record was slow and steady. Once they had played all seventeen songs through for Dr Marrs, he asked them to start again but play their top fourteen, forcing them to earmark those destined for the deluxe edition. This triggered a heated debate among the members of Silver Lake but, eventually, they agreed that tracks two, four and twelve would be held back. With that agreed, they worked out the schedule for the next few days.

"Jake," called out the producer late on Thursday evening as they were packing up. "I don't need you out here until Tuesday, but can you re-work the solo for track three over the weekend?"

"Sure," agreed Jake. "Anything else?"

"Take another look at track eight. It could be heavier. A bit darker."

"I'll see what I can do. My sister's coming down for the weekend so I might not have a lot of free time till Monday."

"Make time," stated Dr Marrs bluntly.

"I didn't know Lucy was visiting," commented Grey as they left the studio. "Can I bring Becky over? She'd love to see the boys."

"Sure. Come over on Saturday. We can BBQ," suggested Jake, before turning to Rich and Paul. "You guys are welcome too."

"I'll check with the boss," said Paul. "But it should be fine."

"What do you need us to bring?" asked Rich. "I could get Linsey to make her seafood salad."

"Perfect," nodded Jake. "Last pre-baby BBQ."

"You could make it an early birthday party for Lori," prompted Grey. "I assume you've got her gift sorted?"

"Not exactly," admitted Jake a little sheepishly. "I need to sort that out tomorrow morning. I just need to go and pick it up, then sneak it into the house over the weekend."

An early heatwave was forecast for the Delaware shore for the weekend and, by late on Friday afternoon, the mercury levels were still in the high eighties. Both Jake and Lori had spent most of the day indoors. Jake had closeted himself down in the basement to work on the solo for track three while Lori had spent most of the day lying on the couch with the air conditioning set low in an effort to keep comfortable. Propped up on a pile of cushions, she had spent the morning sketching. She had designed a small, cute, dark blue dragon, a baby dragon, and had been working on various designs on and off all week. Originally, she had planned to draw just a couple as artwork for the nursery, but her imagination had run riot and she now had a dozen small dragon drawings. Her plans were now evolving into either a frieze or a mural for the nursery. Sketching was keeping her mind off how uncomfortable she was feeling. Lucy had called just after lunch to say they were setting off earlier than planned and should be in Rehoboth for about four o'clock.

Shortly before three, Jake emerged from the basement looking tired.

"I'm heading out for a run before Lucy arrives," he called through to Lori in the sunroom. "I need to clear my head."

"Don't be too long. She should be here in an hour."

"I'll be back before then," promised Jake as he went to get changed.

As he pounded his way along the sand, Jake realised that he hadn't actually seen his young sister since February; he hadn't seen her since his visit to rehab. They had barely talked on the phone as neither of them seemed to have time to chat when the other one was free. He was looking forward to seeing her and his two nephews.

He had run north up the beach towards town, aiming to reach the first of the two WW II look out towers before turning for home. On the way back to the house, he allowed his mind to wander back to the record and to the songs he needed to work on. He had made progress with the solo, but he couldn't see how to make track eight heavier or darker. As he ran, Jake went over the lyrics in his head, searching for inspiration.

The house came into sight almost before he noticed that he was so near to home. His two nephews were playing on the sand in front of the white, picket fence, passing a football to one another.

"Here!" called out Jake, signalling that he wanted the ball.

Josh threw it. Jake caught it, then sprinted off, hugging the ball to his chest. The two small boys came flying after him, screaming his name shrilly. He slowed enough to let them catch and tackle him to the ground.

"Josh! Sam!" scolded Lucy from the end of the path. "Enough!"

Scrambling to his feet, covered in sand, Jake called back, "It's fine, Lucy. I started it."

"You're worse than them!"

Mischievously, Jake rushed towards her, pretending that he was going to grab her.

"Get away!" she squealed. "You're all sweat and sand!"

"Chill. I'm not that cruel," he said, flashing her a smile. "Or brave!"

Lucy laughed and, ignoring his sand covered state, hugged him tight. "It's good to see you. I've been worried about you after.....you know..." Her voice tailed off.

"I'm fine," he said softly, keeping his voice almost a whisper so the boys wouldn't over hear. "We can talk about it later."

"Only if you're up to it," whispered Lucy before adding. "Lori looks fantastic! I can't believe the baby's almost here."

"Me neither," admitted Jake. "She's coped so well with everything but she's struggling now. It's a big baby."

"So she told me!" exclaimed Lucy, remembering the births of her own two boys, who had both been small babies. "Poor Lori!"

"Uncle Jake! Uncle Jake!" shouted Josh. "Mom said we can get pizza tonight. Pizza from the place where you used to work!"

"Oh, she did, did she?" said Jake, staring quizzically at his little sister.

"I did," she confessed with a giggle. "And for my second sin, I said you'd show them where you used to work."

"Thanks," he said plainly before turning to his nephews. "Let me grab a shower then we can go and see what pizza you guys want for dinner."

While Jake and the boys went into town to fetch dinner, Lucy and Lori set the table out on the deck and lit the citronella lanterns.

"No red cups," cautioned Lori as Lucy brought some plastic cups from the house. "There's blue ones on the attic step. I meant to throw the red ones in the trash."

"Why? They're new," quizzed Lucy, looking confused.

"Take them home with you if you can use them," said Lori, rubbing the side of her bump where the baby was kicking restlessly. Quietly, she added, "When Jake was poisoned, the drugged tea was in a red solo cup. He can't drink from them anymore."

"Oh!"

"There's a few ghosts from that still lurking around," explained Lori. "Don't pour him a drink. Let him do it himself. Don't open the bottle for him. Let him do it himself. It's a trust thing."

"Anything else?"

"That's the main two," said Lori quietly. "He'll tell you about the others in his own good time. He's still not good at talking about it all."

"And what about you?" asked Lucy warmly, her voice filled with concern. "He could've killed you and the baby. Are you ok? Really ok?"

"We're fine. We have to be," dismissed Lori with a smile. "I think I hear the truck."

The girls had just sat down at the table when the boys appeared round the side of the house carrying three large pizza boxes and a box of cheese fries. Like a small plague of locusts, the two boys descended on the pizza.

"Did they recognise you in the restaurant?" asked Lori, helping herself to a large slice of pepperoni.

"They offered Uncle Jake his old job back," giggled Sam, his mouth covered in tomato sauce.

The two girls laughed as Jake quipped, "My first shift's on Monday!"

Once the pizza was finished, Jake took his nephews back down onto the beach to throw the ball about while the sun set. He enjoyed spending time with them and playing the role of the "cool uncle". Eventually, Josh said he was tired and Sam, feeling brave, asked his uncle if he'd play his guitar for him.

"I'll make a deal with you," bartered Jake. "You guys run on up to the house, get your pjs on and brush your teeth, then I'll play for a bit."

The two boys scampered up the beach at full speed, while Jake wandered back to the house at a more leisurely pace.

"What lit the fire under the boys?" asked Lori as he reappeared on the deck.

"I made a deal with them," replied Jake cryptically with a wink at his sister.

"Should I be concerned?" asked Lucy.

Jake shook his head and laughed, "No need to panic. Sam asked if I'd play my guitar for them. I said I would if they both got ready for bed first. Josh's dead on his feet."

"I need to bring them here more often," declared Lucy. "Bedtime at home is a battleground these days."

"I'd better fetch something to play," commented Jake, laying the ball down on the table. "I'm going to grab a beer. Want one?"

"I'll get them," offered Lucy getting up. "Lori, do you want anything?"

From her reclined position on the lounger, Lori said, "Actually, I'd love a beer. One won't hurt, right?"

"I'm sure it won't do any harm," replied Jake warmly. "As long as it's only one."

"Might give the baby hiccups," teased Lucy as she headed indoors.

Within five minutes, the two boys were back outside, in their pjs with their teeth brushed. Josh had brought his bedraggled, bedtime bear with him and clambered up onto his mom's knee. When Jake came back up from the basement, he sat down on the deck, leaning against the railing, and began to tune the guitar that he'd brought out with him. Lori recognised it as the one he'd been presented with on TV on the west coast. She smiled when Sam chose to sit beside him, mirroring his body position. Patiently, Jake explained how to tune the guitar to his young nephew then showed him a couple of chords. The little boy's hands were too small for the neck of the guitar, but he stretched his fingers round as best he could.

"Ok, so what do you want me to play?" asked Jake, once he was satisfied the guitar was in tune.

"You know I love when you play me Maggie May," said Lucy shyly.

With a nod, Jake began the Rod Stewart classic, remembering how his little sister used to beg him to play it when they were both kids.

"Guess I'd better play Lori's favourite next," teased Jake as he began the intro to Simple Man.

Before the song was done, Sam was sound asleep on Lucy's knee, contentedly hugging his bear and sucking his thumb. The gentle, acoustic music and the soothing sound of Jake's voice had settled the baby and Lori was convinced that their little Power Pack was also asleep.

Taking a chug on his beer, Jake turned to Sam and said, "Your turn to choose one."

"Do you have any new songs?" asked Sam hopefully.

"I might have," teased Jake mischievously. "I'm not sure though that I'm allowed to play them. Maddy might yell at me if she found out."

"She's scary!" stated Sam instantly, causing the three adults to laugh at the seriousness of his expression.

"If I play some new songs, it has to be a secret," said Jake firmly. "That goes for you too, Lucy Lou."

"Our lips are sealed," promised his sister, anxious to hear anything new from her brother.

"Promise?"

"Promise," agreed Sam.

With a nod, Jake bowed his head and began to play a gentle but sad melody. When he began to sing, he kept his voice soft and a little mournful. His sister and nephew sat enchanted by the song, both smiling when he sang the slow but infectious chorus, "Mister Man having a hand in the game. Mister Man stating his claim." From her seat, Lori thought back to the first time she'd heard Jake play the song.

"Wow!" exclaimed Sam when the song was done.

"Like it?"

"It's sad but yes," replied the boy. "Will that be on your new album?"

"Sure will," revealed Jake, smiling down at his nephew.

"Can you play anymore new ones?" quizzed Sam hopefully.

"One more then it's bedtime," said Lucy firmly. "You'll wear Uncle Jake out."

"This one's a bit of fun," said Jake. "See if you can work it out, Lucy."

Winking over at Lori, Jake began to play the catchy intro to Lady Gambler. Halfway through the song, Lucy's toe was tapping and she was trying hard not to laugh.

"Oh, that has to be about Annie!" she declared with a giggle. "Has she heard it yet?"

"Not yet," replied Lori with a smile. "She'll skin him when she hears it."

"Maybe," admitted Jake grinning. "But she loves me deep down."

"Right, Sam, bedtime," said Lucy, struggling to get to her feet without waking the sleeping Josh. "Say goodnight to everyone."

"Night," said Sam with a yawn.

"Night," said Jake as he continued to strum a gentle country style melody.

"I'm going to bed too," announced Lori, levering herself to her feet. "I'll soak in the tub first, then call it a night."

"You ok, li'l lady?" asked Jake, a look of concern in his eyes.

"I'm fine," she assured him. "Tomorrow's going to be a long day with everyone coming over. I just want to get an early night."

"I'll be in soon," promised Jake softly.

"No rush," answered Lori. "Stay out here and chat to Lucy over another beer or two. She's been worried about you. Think she needs big brother time."

Understanding what Lori wasn't saying, Jake nodded and kept on playing.

The sun had set before Lucy came back outside carrying two open bottles of beer. She handed one over to Jake then said, "Sorry. I forgot and opened it for you."

"Relax," said Jake, accepting the cold beer from her. "It's fine."

"Is everything fine, Jake?" she asked, coming to sit on the deck beside him. "I've been worried about you. You've not really told me much. When I heard what happened, I was scared."

"Most things are fine," began Jake softly. "Don't panic. I've not touched drugs since. Christ, this is only the fourth or fifth beer I've had since March. I'm clean."

"Want to tell me what really happened that night?"

Haltingly, Jake told his sister all that he could remember about drinking the drugged tea, driving home, the hallucinations, attacking Lori then fleeing along the beach. With tears in his eyes, he told her about wakening up in the hospital with Jethro watching over him and about being whisked off to the farm for his week in rehab. Silently, with tears gliding down her own cheeks, Lucy listened. When he finished his tale, Jake sat bent over his guitar with his head in his hands.

"Oh, Jake, I'm so sorry," whispered Lucy, placing a hand on his thigh. "So, so sorry that he put you and Lori through all that."

"It's done. It's over," muttered Jake without looking up. Rubbing away his tears, he raised his head and forced a smile, "Lori's been incredible. So strong. So forgiving. I don't deserve her."

"Yes, you do," said his sister firmly. "You two need each other."

"I owe my life to her," confessed Jake. "If Lori hadn't found me. Hadn't dialled 911…."

"Sh," interrupted Lucy. "Don't think like that."

Jake nodded. "I'll feel happier when the baby's here and I can see for myself that everything's really ok. I'm terrified I hurt our little one. Did some damage that all the scans have missed."

"You'll find out soon enough," soothed his sister. "My guess is that Lori's going to go into labour any day. Her bump's so low. She looks so uncomfortable and tired too."

"She's been fantastic!" enthused Jake, smiling. "So strong through these last few weeks. Even out in Ohio three weeks ago, she was at the side of the stage all night."

"That poor baby will be born with its little ears ringing," teased Lucy.

"Probably," conceded Jake with a grin. "Those shows were pretty loud."

From the sun deck, Lori could hear the squeals of the children down on the beach where they were playing with the four members of Silver Lake. Happy to leave the boys in charge for a while, the girls were all relaxing in the sun with "mocktails". Kola and Grey had arrived an hour earlier with two coolers filled with all the ingredients to make a variety of non-alcoholic cocktails. Immediately, Maddy, Linsey and Lucy had agreed to join Lori in a non-alcoholic, pre-birthday celebration. Conversation had initially surrounded the potential ingredients for the ideal "mocktail", but had inevitably moved onto baby talk. Soon, they were all trying to guess when the baby would arrive, what sex it would be and what weight. Business-like as ever, Maddy took charge, producing a notebook and pen from her capacious purse.

"Lucy, give me your guess first," instructed the Goth firmly. "Date, sex, weight and name."

Studying her sister-in-law, Lucy said, "June 22nd, boy, nine pounds three and Jesse."

"Linsey?"

"June 30th, girl, nine pounds six and Bethany."

"Kola?" prompted Maddy.

"I've no idea," began the shy sound engineer before softly suggesting. "June 28th, girl, nine pounds nine ounces and….. Isabella."

"I'll guess a boy on July 4th, ten pounds four called Luke."

"Lord, I hope they're here before July 4th!" exclaimed Lori with a nervous giggle. "And that they weigh less than ten pounds anything!"

"Well, if baby takes its timekeeping skills from Jake…." began Maddy.

"I know! I'll still be pregnant on Labor Day!" laughed Lori as the baby kicked her sharply under her ribs.

"Can we do gifts now?" asked Lucy hopefully.

"Let's wait until the boys come back up from the beach," suggested Lori. "And you girls didn't need to get me anything."

"Nonsense," stated Maddy bluntly. "You deserve a little spoiling."

Their light hearted, girly chat continued until Jake and Grey returned to light the BBQ. As ever, Wren had attached herself to Jake. The little girl clung tightly to her "Silver Lake Uncle" as he asked Grey to do the honours with the coals. By the time the coals had heated, the others were gathered back on the sun deck. The older children had headed straight into the sunroom, immediately sprawling across the rug in front of the TV and the cartoon channel.

"Now, can we do presents?" pleaded Lucy, as Jake laid the first of the burgers on the grill.

"Now's as good a time as any," called over Jake.

While Lucy ran indoors to fetch her gift, Linsey passed Lori a small gift bag. Inside, Lori found a beautifully hand carved, wooden trinket box. The Silver Lake knot was carved into the round lid.

"That's gorgeous! Thank you!" she exclaimed. "Just what I need for storing my earrings."

Kola produced a large turquoise box with a silver ribbon from behind the cool box. Smiling shyly, she said, "I hope this is the right stuff. Becky chose it. She was adamant that you'd love it."

Carefully, Lori undid the bow, lifted the lid and found her favourite fragrance, shower gel, bath oil and body butter nestled in tissue paper inside.

"Perfect! Thank you," she said, smiling. "Becky was right. This is my absolute favourite perfume. I'm impressed she remembered."

"Me next!" squealed Lucy, who had returned to the deck carrying a large, flat, rectangular parcel.

Trying not to tear the pretty butterfly paper, Lori peeled back the tape and opened her gift. Inside lay a beautiful cross-stitch showing the two hares from "Guess How Much I Love You?" and the phrase "I love you right up to the moon and back."

"Oh, Lucy, did you stitch this?" gasped Lori, instantly falling in love with the picture.

"Yes," replied her sister-in-law modestly. "As soon as I saw the kit in Michael's, I knew I had to stitch it for you."

"I love it," said Lori, her eyes twinkling with delight. "Thank you. It must have taken you hours!"

"A few," confessed Lucy, blushing red.

"Not sure I can follow that," said Maddy, producing a small, black gift bag with a silver ribbon on it. "Happy birthday for Monday, darling."

Opening the tiny, shiny bag, Lori found a small tissue paper packet and inside that a small, silver bracelet with three round disc charms attached. Each of them had the Silver Lake knot engraved on one side. Two of them had letters engraved on the reverse- a J and an L. The third charm was blank on the reverse.

"Oh, I love it, Maddy!" she declared.

"Plenty of space to add more charms if you decide to have any more little Power Packs," teased her friend. "There's a new artisan jewellers opened in Lewes. I had her make it for you. She'll engrave the baby's initial when you're ready. She loved the knot design and can't wait to meet you."

"Let me see how things go with this baby before you go planning for us to have any more!" laughed Lori.

From over at the grill, Jake called out, "You'll need to wait until Monday for your gift from me, li'l lady."

"Haven't you been shopping yet, Mr Power?" teased Grey and Maddy in unison.

"I have but the birthday girl will have to be patient until Monday," he replied firmly.

As the sun set and, with everyone fed, Paul and Maddy were the first to prepare to leave. Both of the twins were growing tired and Hayden was beginning to whine annoyingly.

"Let's agree to do this again for the 4th July," suggested Lori. "We can celebrate this little Power Pack's arrival."

"Confident that they'll be here by then?" joked Paul with a grin.

Lori nodded as she felt another painful kick stabbing at her ribs.

"Sounds like a plan," agreed Maddy, scooping Hayden up into her arms. "Let me know if you want to go shopping or for lunch next week. I'm free Wednesday through till Friday."

"We'll see," sighed Lori. "I don't think I want to stray too far from home for the next few days. I'm too uncomfortable and the heat isn't helping."

"Shops have AC," countered Maddy. "I'll call you on Monday anyways."

With a chorus of goodbyes, Paul and Maddy headed off round the side of the house. A short while later, Rich and Linsey made their excuses, explaining that they were meeting Scott in the Greene Turtle. It was after ten before Grey said he had better take his girls home.

"Have you moved in together yet?" asked Lori, finally voicing the question that no one had dared to ask.

"More or less," revealed Kola shyly, with a glance over at Grey. "I've a few things to pick up from my brother's place tomorrow, then I'm there, I guess."

"That's fantastic," said Lori warmly.

"About time there was a woman about to keep Grey in check," joked Jake, hugging Kola awkwardly. "If you need a hand moving anything, just ask."

"Thanks."

With all of their guests gone and Lucy busy putting the boys to bed, Jake moved over to sit beside his wife. As he sat on the deck beside the lounger, he thought she looked tired.

"Have you enjoyed your day?" he asked, laying a hand on the swell of her stomach. "Did this little Power Pack behave?"

"I've had a lovely day," she sighed, laying her hand over his. "But I'm beat. The baby's been restless all afternoon. My ribcage feels like it's about to explode."

"Not long now, li'l lady. You'll soon be lying there cradling this little one in your arms."

"Lord, I hope so!"

There was no long lie in or breakfast in bed for Lori on her birthday as she had an antenatal appointment at nine. Despite having rested all day the day before, she was still worn out when she saw the nurse. Her fatigued state earned her a sharp dressing down and she was ordered to take things easy until the baby arrived. When he heard this, Jake said she was to spend the rest of the day on the couch or lying on the lounger out on the sun deck. Knowing it was pointless to argue, Lori agreed on the grounds that they went out for dinner.

"Where do you fancy eating tonight, birthday girl?" asked Jake as they drove home.

"Well, this is likely to be our last meal out as a couple for a while," mused Lori, fidgeting in her seat as the baby continued their onslaught on her tender rib cage. "Why don't we go back to where we had our first meal out together? Back out to the steakhouse on the highway?"

"You sure?"

"Positive," she replied. "I feel like a rib eye steak."

Jake laughed, "Very funny, li'l lady. I thought ribs were literally a sore point?"

"They are but I really feel like a good steak."

"Fine. Steakhouse it is tonight."

When they arrived back at the house, Jake apologised that he still had some work to finish off before going out to JJL the next day. With a weary smile, Lori said that was fine and that she felt like taking a nap. Instead of heading for the sunroom, Jake was surprised to see her limp back down towards the bedroom. Why had no one warned them that the last few days of pregnancy were so hard to endure? It scared him to see her so worn out and he prayed silently that the baby would arrive sooner rather than later.

It was quiet and cool down in the basement. Not wanting to disturb Lori, Jake decided to work on track eight and to try to find that extra dark edge using an acoustic guitar. He played it over a few times to himself but was still at a loss as to what to add. Nothing was working. Suddenly, something lying on the desk caught his eye. It was the Ebow that he'd been gifted a while back by Dr Marrs. He had experimented with the device for a few days before laying it aside. Picking the small gadget up, Jake wondered how it would sound. Immediately, he changed guitars, opting for his Mz Hyde custom model. After a few trial runs, he decided it sounded quite nice. The Ebow effect didn't add a darker tone to the song, but it created an almost flute-like, haunted edge to it. Satisfied that he'd stumbled across the missing element, Jake quickly recorded the revised version of the track and mailed it off to Dr Marrs. A glance at the time on his laptop informed him it was after two and they hadn't had lunch. He also realised that he hadn't given Lori her birthday presents either.

When he wandered into the bedroom, Jake wasn't surprised to find his wife sound asleep, her large baby belly snuggled in a nest of pillows. Gently, he laid a hand on her shoulder and brushed a kiss across her cheek.

"Lunchtime, birthday girl," he whispered. "And gift time."

"Mm," murmured Lori sleepily. "Wha' time is it?"

"Gone two," replied Jake, kissing her again. "I've prepared a salad for lunch. Nothing heavy. Don't want to spoil your appetite for that steak later."

"Help me up," said Lori, rubbing sleep from her eyes.

"You ok?"

Nodding, she replied, "Yes. I needed that nap. I feel a bit more human. Now, did you mention something about a gift?"

"Yes. There's three of them," revealed Jake, helping her to her feet. "But you're only getting one just now. The other two can wait until dinner."

"But it's my birthday!" protested Lori, pretending to be upset at having to wait.

"Patience, li'l lady," he said warmly as he put a protective arm around her waist. "Follow me."

"Where are we going?"

"The nursery," revealed Jake as they crossed the hallway.

Pushing the door open, he stepped aside to allow Lori to enter the room first. In the corner, under one of the windows, sat a glider-style, rocking chair, complete with matching gliding footstool. The wooden frame matched the furniture perfectly and the lemon gingham fabric toned in with the rest of the room. A large plump cushion was propped up on the chair. It was a midnight blue colour with the nursery rhyme "Twinkle, Twinkle Little Star" embroidered on it in silver thread.

"Oh, Jake!" gasped Lori. "I love it! That's the chair we were looking at in Lewes. You remembered!"

Hugging her tight, Jake kissed her slowly but tenderly, feeling the baby twitch between them, "Happy birthday, li'l lady wife."

"Can I try it out?"

"Of course," said Jake. "Make yourself comfortable."

"Comfortable?" giggled Lori. "I'll tell the jokes!"

A few seconds later, she was seated on the rocking chair with her feet resting on the stool. As she gently glided back and forth, Lori had to confess that she felt comfortable.

"Well, you can rock to your heart's content all afternoon," said Jake with a wink. "I need to do a little more work for the record before tomorrow. But first, lunch."

While Jake disappeared back down to the basement, Lori fetched her book and returned to the nursery, settling herself on the new rocking chair. As she gently glided back and forth, she rubbed her bump, feeling the baby stir under her hands. For the first time, it dawned on her that in a few days these little intimate moments would be gone. Despite the discomfort and the awkwardness of pregnancy, Lori silently admitted to herself that she was going to miss feeling the baby move inside her. Deliberately, she tried to keep her mind away from thoughts of being in labour and of the actual birth. At the hospital that morning, the midwife had advised her to read up on what to expect when the time came, what signs to watch out for. She had quizzed Lori about her own mother's experience of giving birth and about whether there had been any complications. Feeling a little embarrassed, Lori had had to answer that she didn't know what her own mother had gone through. It wasn't something that her mom had ever talked about. It had always been a taboo topic of conversation. Lori explained that she was an only child but that she remembered her father saying that they had hoped for more children, only Lori's mother had vetoed their plans. The conversation had left her wondering what her own mother had experienced that had deterred her from having any more babies.

A light drizzle was falling as they drove out to the steakhouse on the Coastal Highway. As they passed the outlets, Lori looked longingly at the "Sale" signs and "up to 70% off" posters and sighed. There were still a few bits and pieces she wanted to pick up before the baby arrived, but she knew Jake was scheduled to be out at JJL every day for the next two weeks. Realising that she would need someone to take her out to Beebe for the next antenatal appointment, Lori decided to ask Maddy if she could drive her then they could go shopping for an hour or so and maybe even grab some lunch.

"Penny for them, li'l lady?" enquired Jake.

"I was just thinking about next week's appointment at Beebe. If I get Maddy to drive me out there, then we could go shopping afterwards."

"Ah, the lure of your favourite signs!" laughed Jake. "If you're sure you'll feel up to it, then it's a great idea. Dr Marrs has me blocked out most of each day up until June 27th. If I don't get everything done by then, I'll be in the studio that weekend too."

"And if I go into labour before then?"

"I'll be there in a half hour," promised Jake, pulling off the highway and into the small parking lot in front of the steakhouse.

With a smile, Lori realised that he'd parked the Mercedes in the same spot that he'd parked in the first night they had dined there. In a parallel of that night, Jake came round to help her out of the car, hovering round her until she had steadied herself on her crutches.

"I'll be so glad to be rid of these again," muttered Lori as they entered the restaurant.

"Hi," said Jake to the young hostess, who was waiting to greet them. "I've a reservation for Power."

"Good evening. Your table's ready, sir," she replied, lifting two menus and a wine list from under the counter. "If you could follow me please."

Slowly, they followed her to a corner table at the window. The same table as they had shared that first night. A bouquet of red roses sat on the table.

"Am I sensing a conspiracy?" enquired Lori as she sat down.

"Perhaps," agreed Jake, sitting down opposite her.

Lori smiled, then said, "Well, if we're keeping with traditions, you best order the 16oz prime rib, rock star."

"Not sure I could eat a steak that size tonight," he confessed. "Are you having the fillet mignon?"

Lori shook her head. "No. I promised myself a ribeye steak, fries and onion rings."

"Think I might have the same."

Once they'd placed their order, Jake reached across the table and took her hand. "Don't you want your birthday gifts, li'l lady?"

"Oh! I thought the rocking chair was my gift."

Jake reached into his jeans pocket and brought out a small blue satin pouch with a silver ribbon round it and an odd looking poker chip.

"Happy birthday."

Lori opened the pouch and lifted out a silver Celtic Triskelion pendant. The curves of its three legs reminded her of cresting ocean waves.

"It's beautiful," she breathed, smiling over at her husband. "So simple, but so pretty."

"There's a lot of legends around its true meaning," explained Jake quietly. "One meaning is father, mother, child. It suggests family. It can also mean past, present, future."

"I love it!" said Lori, her voice husky with emotion. She lifted the poker chip, examining it closely. It was a $250 chip, according to the writing on one side. When she flipped it over, Lori saw that it was from Danny's tattoo parlour.

"I thought maybe you'd like to get the knot inked somewhere to symbolise family after our little Power Pack arrives," explained Jake. "The poker chips are Danny's new style of gift certificate."

"Ah!" she exclaimed. "I see. Neat idea."

"No rush to use it. You just need to let him know where and when or, if you prefer, you can cash it in."

"And are you planning new ink when you become a daddy?" teased Lori, slipping the poker chip and the necklace into the satin pouch."

Jake nodded. "Don't ask what or where. I have it all planned, li'l lady. You'll see in good time."

Over the next ten days, life around the beach house was both a hive of activity and inactivity. The heat wave returned, making being outdoors almost unbearable for Lori. Much as she loved the heat of summer, at thirty eight weeks pregnant, she was wishing it was October. Confined to the air-conditioned house for the greater part of each day, she spent much of her time in the nursery, relaxing in her rocking chair with her book and her iPod. When she felt up to it, she would stand at her easel to work on the series of dragon drawings that she'd commenced. The little, blue dragon was developing a personality through the series of drawings and, ever the businesswoman, Lori began toying with the idea of marketing him. She would have loved to have the energy to make a start on the mural she had in mind for the nursery, but the weight and awkwardness of her baby bump put paid to that.

As the days dragged on, Lori found if she sat for too long her back and pelvis began to ache; if she stood for too long her leg throbbed; if she lay down she was plagued by heartburn. On the evenings when Jake made it home before dark, they would stroll slowly along the beach. Walking seemed to help, as long as she took it slowly and didn't venture too far. Having observed her greatly compromised gait, Jake teased her about walking like a little penguin, declaring her "mommy waddle" to be cute.

Out at JJL, things were progressing at a pace as Dr Marrs guided Silver Lake through the recording of their third album. After a conference call with Jason Russell and the record label, the band were asked to fully complete two of the seventeen tracks as soon as possible. Knowing that Jake planned to take some family time after the baby arrived, the record company wanted a single ready for an early release. When Jake protested that it would need promoting and that would mean media commitments, Maddy and Jethro intervened, reminding him that there were three other members of the band who could pick those up. This decision changed Dr Marrs' structured schedule somewhat, almost tipping the producer's stress levels over the edge. A more relaxed band meeting, over tacos in the kitchen of the JJL house, remapped the schedule and saw the band agree that Lady Gambler and Baby Eyed Blues, the first song they'd written for the record, would be the two songs to be recorded first.

By the last Friday in June, Silver Lake had completed the two songs in their entirety, plus recorded drums and bass tracks for another six. Both Grey and Paul were granted a few days leave to go fishing while Rich and Jake made a start on the guitar tracks for the six songs. Knowing that each day brought them closer to the birth of the baby, Jim Marrs worked Jake hard, pushing him just a little bit further than he did Rich. When Jake challenged him about this, the producer said bluntly, "You need to earn your paternity leave, Mr Power."

The plan, while Jake was on leave, was for Grey and Paul to finish the other nine bass and drum tracks and for Rich to track his guitar parts. Allowing a few down days for all of them, Dr Marrs said he hoped Jake would consider coming in for a few hours a day from mid-July. Much to the producer's relief, Jake had agreed but qualified his agreement with one condition – it all hinged on how Lori was after the birth of the baby and how much she needed his help.

The closer it got to Lori's due date, the more Jake's anxiety grew. At home, he tried his best to disguise his fears and to remain calm in front of his wife, but, at the studio, everyone could see how nervous he was becoming. He grew quieter and quieter as the time passed. Whenever the producer said to stop or to take a break, Jake instantly reached for his phone to check for messages from Lori. If time allowed, he would retreat to the upturned plastic crate out the back and phone home.

As Rich began to pack up late on the Friday afternoon, Jake went to follow suit.

"Mr Power," called through Dr Marrs from the control room. "Can you spare me another few hours?"

Jake sighed, then checked the time before replying, "I want to be home for ten, Jim."

"I'll have you home for nine thirty."

Clapping him on the back, Rich wished him luck on being home before midnight and escaped out the door, looking forward to two days off.

Wearily, Jake turned back to face the window, "What's the plan?"

"I need two more from you, I'm afraid."

"Two?"

The producer nodded. "Can we do track eight then see how far we get with track ten?"

"Let me grab a coffee and a bottle of water first," sighed Jake, fearing that Rich's observation may have been correct.

When he returned to the live room, Jake asked, "Electric or acoustic track first for Exodus West?"

"Let's do the Ebow section first."

Nodding, Jake went to rummage in his book bag for the device, guessing that Dr Marrs might try to squeeze a little more time from him.

It was almost nine before the producer was happy with the guitar track for track eight.

"Can we re-negotiate the deal?" asked Jim optimistically. "How early can you come in tomorrow? I'd really like track ten done before Monday."

Running his hands through his hair, Jake yawned. He had hoped to go for a run in the morning, but fully understood where the producer was coming from. If he set his alarm for five, he could still put in a few miles and be out at JJL for just after eight.

"You drive a hard bargain," muttered Jake. "OK, if you provide breakfast, I'll be here about eight, but I'm leaving at twelve. No argument."

"Jake, you're a star. Pancakes or waffles?"

"Pancakes," replied Jake with a grin. "And bacon."

"I'll see you here for breakfast at eight then."

An overnight storm had broken the heat wave and, as Jake left the house to head north up the beach, a cool breeze was blowing in off the ocean. The storm had thrown some debris up on the beach, but, as he ran along the hard packed sand, the beach tractors were already out clearing it away and raking the sand in readiness for the day's visitors. A few early morning joggers and fishermen were out but, for the most part, the seabirds were his only companions. After so long cooped up in the studio, it felt good to get out in the early morning air to stretch his legs. Initially, Jake had intended to turn at the WW II towers, but instead he kept going until he reached Herring Point.

On the return leg of his run, Jake's mind wandered to the studio session ahead of him. Track ten was Witchcraft, the song about his hallucination and battle with the imaginary demons. Mentally, he played it over as he pounded along the sand, trying to ignore the wave of fear building inside him. He conceded that Dr Marrs was right to get that one in the can sooner rather than later. Despite his best efforts, Jake still struggled with that song. He prayed that in time it would get easier to perform as the fans were bound to love it when they heard the album.

When he arrived back at the house, Jake was surprised to find Lori in the kitchen. She was standing by the sink swallowing something down with a glass of water.

"Morning. You ok?" he asked breathlessly.

Lori nodded. "Just taking something for the pain in my back and my leg."

"What did you take?"

"Just the one Vicodin," she replied quietly. "I checked. It's safe. If it doesn't help, I'll take another later."

"Be careful with that stuff, li'l lady," he cautioned softly.

"I will. Promise," she said, forcing a smile. "I'm going to soak in the tub for a bit."

"Don't use all the hot water! I need a shower. I'm due out at JJL in less than an hour."

"Ok. You shower first, then I'll take a bath."

"Thanks," said Jake, giving her a sweaty hug. "I'll be back by lunchtime. If it's not too hot, we could go for a walk. Might help to ease your back."

"Sounds good," agreed Lori. "I might take a nap before you get home. I didn't sleep much with the storm last night."

"Yeah, it was a good one," commented Jake, remembering the huge peals of thunder just after midnight.

Once Jake left for the studio, Lori filled the tub , adding some of the bubble bath that Becky had chosen for her birthday, deciding that even if she felt fat and sore and ready to pop at any minute, she could still smell nice. The combination of the painkillers and the warmth of the water helped to soothe the ache that was radiating across the base of her back. The dull throbbing in her leg began to melt away too. For the first time in several hours she was more or less pain free. The heat from the water seemed to have calmed the baby too, as it moved gently, causing the twitch of her stomach to send ripples across the surface of the water.

"OK, little one," she whispered, rubbing her hugely pregnant belly. "When daddy comes home later he has almost three days free. This weekend would be a good time to come out and meet us."

Getting out of the tub proved to be difficult, but eventually Lori hauled herself out, wrapping herself in a huge, green, fluffy bath sheet. She sat on the low stool that Jake had moved into the bathroom for her to get dried off, then dressed in a loose, vest tunic and her maternity, Capri cut jeans. The broad, soft, elasticated waistband of the jeans offered some support to her back and helped a little with the weight of her bump. As she made her way back through to the bedroom, Lori caught sight of herself in the mirror. Could she possibly get any bigger?

Her cell phone was lying on the bed and with a mischievous giggle, she whispered to the baby, "Let's take a bump photo and send it to daddy, little one. Suggest that today might be a good day to be born."

Still giggling, Lori took the photo, then forwarded it onto Jake. As she slipped the phone into her pocket, she thought, "Who am I kidding? You're not due for nearly another week and, if you take your time keeping skills from your daddy, it could be closer to two!"

Instead of taking her nap indoors, Lori headed out onto the sun deck. The cushion on the lounger was still damp after the storm so she pushed it off onto the deck to dry, then retrieved the old one from the plastic storage crate. It was a bit stale smelling so she fetched two beach towels from the bathroom and lay them over the top before she lay down. With the sun swathing the deck in warmth and with a gentle breeze blowing in off the ocean, Lori soon drifted off to sleep.

As promised, Dr Marrs had a plate of pancakes and syrup, with maple cured, crispy bacon on the side, waiting for Jake in the lounge at JJL when he arrived.

"Smells fucking amazing," declared Jake, taking a seat at the table. "I'm starving."

"Well, eat up, Mr Power. Clock's ticking," said the producer as he poured him a mug of coffee. "Hopefully this'll help put some of those demons to rest and let you get this one recorded."

"I hope so," sighed Jake between mouthfuls. "This really is delicious."

"Eat!" commanded Dr Marrs with a fatherly smile. "I'll see you through there."

The sounds of R2D2 echoed out of Jake's pocket as he entered the live room. It was a message from Lori. When he opened it, Jake was relieved to see it was a photo and not an announcement that she was in labour. He smiled at the image of his heavily pregnant wife on the small screen. She looked remarkably relaxed and radiantly healthy. Still smiling, he text back, "You're beautiful. Love you. See you soon, J x"

Recording his parts for the guitar track on Witchcraft didn't prove to be as challenging as Jake had feared. One part was a little more technical than the others, but, fuelled by pancakes and bacon laced with maple syrup, Jake's fingers flew over the frets and the music soared.

"Jake!" interrupted Dr Marrs. "Do you still have that Ebow with you?"

"Yeah. It's in my bag."

"Try that part again using it," instructed the producer firmly.

"We might be onto something here."

"If you say so, sir."

It took them until just after midday but eventually both Dr Marrs and Jake were happy with what they'd recorded.

"Thanks for that, Jake," said Jim as they prepared to leave. "Appreciate you coming in today. Now, assuming Baby Power doesn't put in an appearance, can you be back out here on Tuesday?"

"Sure," agreed Jake, lifting his book bag.

"Plan is to record your part for tracks eleven and twelve. It'll be just you. The guys don't come back down from Philly until Tuesday afternoon."

"I'll see you bright and early," agreed Jake then with a wink added, "And you can provide breakfast again."

"Eight o'clock sharp!"

A run of Braxton Hicks' contractions wakened Lori from her nap not long after midday. As soon as she moved, she knew she needed to pee. Leaning heavily on her crutches, she made her way indoors and down the hall to the bathroom. The pain had returned to her back and felt even worse than it had a few hours earlier. Silently cursing the old lounger pad for being unsupportive, she went back to the kitchen to find her pain medication. She swallowed down two Vicodin, then sighed wearily, rubbing her back as the baby kicked out sharply. Guessing that Jake wouldn't be too far away, she prepared some pastrami and salad sandwiches for lunch. She had just put the jar of mayonnaise back in the refrigerator when she heard his truck pull into the driveway.

"Hi," called out Jake as he clattered in the back door beside her.

"Hi yourself, rock star," she replied brightly. "Perfect timing. I just fixed lunch."

"Thanks. I'm starving," declared Jake, picking up the two plates of sandwiches. "Want to take these outside?"

Lori nodded and led the way back out to the sundeck. While she sat down at the table, Jake went back indoors to fetch them some juice.

"Did you take a nap?" he asked as he sat down opposite her.

"Yes," replied Lori. "I've been out here all morning. Think I slept for a couple of hours. I had to put the old mattress pad on the lounger. The storm had soaked the new one through. That old one is so thin and lumpy! My back was agony again when I woke up."

"Did you take more pills?"

"Just one," she lied, not wanting a lecture on the addictive effects of Vicodin. "It's easing off a little. A walk should help too."

"As long as you feel up to it," said Jake softly, his eyes filled with concern for her.

"I feel fine today. Baby's been restless for the last half hour. Really pressing down on everything. It all feels so heavy now."

"The midwife said that was natural, didn't she?"

"All perfectly normal," assured Lori calmly.

"And you're not too tired to go for a walk?"

"No," stated Lori. "I probably need the exercise. My leg's playing up a bit. I could do with stretching it out for a while."

"Fine. I'll get changed once we've had lunch, then we can see where the mood takes us," said Jake, before taking another bite out of his sandwich.

Taking things slowly, Jake and Lori walked south down the beach, away from the crowds filling the beach nearer town. The breeze was still blowing in gently off the ocean, keeping the temperature below eighty. After lunch, Jake had changed out of his jeans into his cut off shorts and had decided to walk barefoot along the beach. Lori too had left her sandals on the deck and was enjoying feeling the cool, damp sand between her hot, puffy toes. Every now and then, they stopped to gaze out across the water, scanning the ocean swell for dolphins.

As they meandered, Lori asked Jake how his morning had gone out at JJL and about the progress on the record. Patiently, she listened as he told her about the changes Dr Marrs had suggested for Witchcraft then voiced his fears about singing the vocals for it. They were so lost in conversation that they had almost reached the bath house before either of them noticed how far they had walked.

"Do you want to sit down for a few minutes?" suggested Jake, fretting that they had come too far for Lori. "Let you catch your breath a bit?"

Lori paused, then let out a sharp gasp as she clutched her stomach.

"Lori?"

"My waters just broke," she gasped as she stared down at the wet patch of sand around her feet and at the fluid trickling down her legs.

"Stay calm!" said Jake, looking far from calm. "The midwife said there would be hours to go after your waters broke. Are you ok to walk back?"

Lori nodded, afraid to speak in case Jake realised how scared she was.

They'd only been walking for a few minutes when the first contraction gripped Lori. Its strength caught her breath as the pain cinched in a tight band round her. She felt her legs begin to tremble. Remembering to pant, she attempted to breathe through the pain.

"Wow!" she spluttered as the crushing wave of pain subsided. "If that's only the start, I'm not looking forward to this."

"I'd better call Beebe," said Jake, fishing in his pocket for his phone. "Fuck! Fuck! Fuck!"

"What's wrong?"

"No cell. I left it at the house. Give me yours, li'l lady?"

"It's in the kitchen," confessed Lori, feeling a wave of panic beginning to rise inside her.

"Can you keep walking?" asked Jake anxiously.

"For now," answered Lori, with a nod.

Suddenly, as they both glanced up and down the beach, they realised that there was no one else in sight. No tourists. No fishermen. No one.

Trying to hurry as best she could, Lori kept walking towards home with Jake right by her elbow.

Less than two minutes later, another strong contraction gripped her. Biting down on her bottom lip, Lori bent forward and leaned down on her crutches until she felt the pressure ease.

Breathing heavily, she nodded to Jake and they set off again.

A few moments later, Jake broke the silence between them.

"Lori," he began, "I could run on ahead. Call the hospital and come back for you."

"No!" she stated sharply. "Don't leave me! Don't leave me alone out here, Jake! I'm scared."

Her fragile control over her emotions crumbled and tears began to flow down her strained face.

"Sh, li'l lady," soothed Jake softly as he put his arm around her.

"I'll not leave you. We'll be home soon. Let's just take this slowly. There's plenty of time."

"How long did we take to get here?" she asked as she felt another contraction building.

"About half an hour. Maybe a little more."

Nodding, Lori kept walking until the strength of the contraction forced her to stop. As she panted her way through the pain, Jake stood rubbing her back. Again, the crushing pain ebbed away.

"Let's keep going."

Reaching the house seemed to take an eternity. With every step, Lori felt the dragging pressure on her cervix building. Each contraction came stronger and faster and lasted longer than its predecessor. She began to feel as though her body was trying to rip itself apart.

This was all happening too fast!

Beside her, Jake had gone quiet and kept running his hands through his hair, helpless to help her. She could see from the expression on his face that her husband was as frightened as she was.

Just as they began to make their way up onto the soft sand in front of the house, a brutally, strong contraction seized her. This time, her knees gave way and she collapsed onto the sand, landing on all fours.

"Lori!" cried Jake as he dropped to his knees beside her, sending sand spraying over her. "You ok?"

The contraction had her firmly in its grasp and she could only grunt a primal response. The tight, crushing pain seemed to last an eternity before it began to subside a little.

"Have you hurt yourself?" asked Jake when she finally looked up at him.

Lori could only shake her head to indicate "no".

Taking care not to cause her anymore pain, Jake helped her to her feet. She was only just steady on her crutches when another contraction ripped through her with equal force. This time, Jake stood in front of her, holding her weight as she bent over in obvious agony.

Three more contractions punctuated their short walk across the hot, soft sand to the low, white, picket fence.

Another two crushed through Lori as they made their way up the sandy path.

"Lounger," panted Lori as they stepped onto the deck.

"You want to sit there?" quizzed Jake stupidly.

"Yes!" she snapped angrily. "This fucking hurts!"

Calmly, Jake helped her to lie down on the lounger then ran indoors to grab the phone. With trembling hands, he brought up the maternity unit's number.

"Help!" he cried when someone finally answered. "My wife's gone into labour on the beach. We made it home, but I don't think there's time to get to you. This baby's coming fast!"

"Stay calm, sir," said the voice on the end of the phone. "What's your wife's name?"

"Lori Power," answered Jake as he rushed through the house back out onto the deck. "Hurry, please!"

"How far apart are the contractions, Mr Power?"

"About every minute or so. She's in agony here. We need help!" yelled Jake, panic ringing in his voice.

"Stay calm, Mr Power. I need you to listen and check a few things for me. Can you do that?"

"Yes," replied Jake, taking a deep breath.

"Ok. The paramedics are on their way. There will be a midwife with them. It'll take them about twenty minutes to reach you."

"Thank you," sighed Jake, taking some relief from the fact that help was on the way.

"Can I speak to your wife, please?"

"Give her a minute," said Jake as he watched Lori pant her way through another fierce contraction. As the pressure slackened, she lay back and gazed up at him, her blue eyes filled with fear and tears. Forcing a smile, Jake passed her the phone.

"Hi," said Lori breathlessly.

"Hi, Lori. Your midwife is on her way to you," explained the calm voice on the phone. "How are you coping?"

"Barely," gasped Lori, choking back her tears. "I need to push."

"Not yet, honey," cautioned the calm voice.

"No! I do!" yelled Lori shrilly. "I need to push right fucking now!"

"Stay calm, honey."

"You try staying calm!" she screamed back sharply. "Oh, here's another one coming...."

Lori dropped the phone as the pain of the contraction tore through her. This time she let out a roar of agony as it reached its peak.

Patiently, the nurse on the phone talked Jake through removing Lori's sodden jeans and underwear. She advised him to get Lori to kneel on the lounger on all fours. Despite the pain, Lori tried to adopt the position, gripping the back rest of the wooden lounger tightly. Next, the nurse asked Jake if he could see the baby's head.

"Yes," he said as he looked incredulously at the crown of the baby's head in front of him. "Fuck! It's coming!"

Before he could receive any further instructions, another contraction gripped Lori. Pressing her knees down into the thin mattress and digging her elbows into the backrest, Lori gave in to the urge to push, pushing as hard as she could. Jake watched wide-eyed as the baby's head moved and emerged a little further.

"It's coming," he heard himself say into the phone. "It's coming right fucking now!"

"Mr Power! Jake!" said the nurse sharply. "You need to stay calm for me. Stay with me. Can the phone be put on speaker mode?"

"Yes," replied Jake, pressing the button on the handset.

"Good. Now, both of you listen to me," instructed the nurse firmly, taking control of the situation as best she could in the circumstances. "Jake, fetch some towels quickly. You'll need something to wrap the baby in. And something to use to clamp the cord. Be quick!"

While Jake ran into the house, another fearsome contraction engulfed Lori. Again, she screamed in pain, bearing down hard as she gripped the back of the lounger.

"You're doing great, Lori," praised the nurse. "Keep breathing. Pant through the pain. Sounds as though you're nearly there, honey."

"I'm scared," whispered Lori tearfully. "It's not meant to be like this. I'm meant to be there with you."

"I know, honey, but baby has other ideas. Won't be much longer. You're doing brilliantly."

Jake returned with an armful of towels from the bathroom and two large bulldog clips from Lori's drawing board. As he laid them down beside the lounger, another contraction seized Lori.

Grunting loudly, she pushed hard, hearing the nurse's voice encouraging her to keep pushing. As the contraction wore off, she slumped forward, her legs and arms shaking with the effort. In the distance, Lori could hear Jake telling the nurse that the baby's head was nearly out. She barely registered the instructions Jake was being given as another contraction began to build. Gripping the lounger with all of her strength, Lori pushed as hard and for as long as she could, hearing herself groan and swear loudly as she did so.

"The head's out!" exclaimed Jake as he gazed down on the baby's tiny, red, screwed up face for the first time.

"Lori!" called out the nurse. "A couple of big pushes and baby'll be here. Breathe deeply till the next contraction, then push hard and steady for as long as you can, honey."

"This hurts like fuck!" yelled Lori into the lounger mattress. Another contraction began to crush her and she screamed as she pushed again with all her might.

"Baby's here!" gasped Jake, holding the mucus and blood covered baby in his arms. "Shit, I've delivered a baby! The baby's here! I'm holding a baby!"

In the distance, they could both hear the approaching siren of the ambulance.

Sobbing and shaking violently, Lori sank to her knees as the aftershock of giving birth set in.

"Jake," stated the nurse, still the voice of calm. "Clamp the cord with the clips you brought out. Is the baby breathing? Clear baby's mouth with your finger gently, then rub them down with one of the towels. Wrap baby up nice and snugly."

Having placed the two clips around the blue, lumpy umbilical cord, Jake rubbed the baby with one of the towels, taking care to clear the blood and mucus from their tiny nose and mouth. As he wrapped the towel around the baby, it began to cry, quietly at first, but building swiftly to loud, shrill wails.

"Sh, little one," he soothed. "You're safe. Daddy's got you."

At that moment, two paramedics came rushing round the side of the house, closely followed by one of the midwife's that Jake recognised from the clinic. Immediately, the medical team assessed the situation and assumed control. One of the paramedics accepted the baby from him while his colleague and the midwife attended to

Lori.

"Sir, do you want to cut the cord?" asked the younger of the two paramedics, offering him a pair of surgical shears.

Numbly, Jake nodded and, with shaking hands, took two or three attempts to cut through the tough umbilical cord.

The midwife had helped Lori into a more comfortable position and was rubbing her stomach to encourage another contraction to allow her to deliver the placenta.

The next few minutes were a blur to both Jake and Lori, both of them in shock at what had just happened. Trembling, Jake knelt beside his wife and took her hand. She was pale and shivering, tears still flowing down her cheeks.

"You were incredible, li'l lady. So strong," he whispered, kissing her hand. "I'm so proud of you."

Gazing up at him, Lori whispered, "Is the baby ok?"

"Baby's fine," promised Jake, smiling down at her. "Absolutely perfect."

"Is it a boy or a girl?"

Jake looked round at the midwife. In all the chaos of the baby's dramatic arrival, he hadn't checked.

Holding the baby, clean and neatly wrapped in a fresh towel in her arms, the midwife passed the baby to Lori.

"You have a beautiful, baby girl, honey. She's absolutely perfect."

"A girl?" echoed Lori, eyes wide and tear-filled. For the first time, she looked down at her baby daughter as fresh tears flowed freely down her cheeks. "Hello, angel."

"A little girl?" repeated Jake, tears brimming in his own eyes. "My two perfect li'l ladies."

As she cradled the baby, Lori felt another wave of tight cramping clutching at her. A look of panic crossed her worn out face.

"Sh," said the midwife, pressing firmly on Lori's stomach. "Give me one more push, honey."

Exhausted as she was, Lori obliged then let out a long sigh.

"Good job, honey," complimented the midwife. "Placenta's out. That's you all done."

"Thank God for that," sighed Lori wearily.

Politely, the midwife suggested Jake hold the baby while she examined Lori.

Cradling his tiny daughter in his arms, Jake wandered over to sit at the picnic table. The baby was staring up at him with bright eyes and an intense gaze. Gently, he ran his hand over her downy, blonde head. The baby gave a little cry and began to open and close her tiny rosebud mouth.

"Is she ok?" Jake asked one of the paramedics.

"She's fine. I guess though, she's hungry," he replied.

"I can't believe she's really here," sighed Jake, not taking his eyes off his baby girl. "She's so tiny. So beautiful."

"Not so tiny!" laughed the paramedic. "She weighed in at nine pounds and nine ounces."

"Wow!" gasped Jake. "And I delivered her."

"You did a great job. A really great job," complimented the medic. "Stayed reasonably calm. Didn't panic. Kept in control."

"Thanks. I just did what the lady on the phone said to do. Lori did all the hard work."

"She's a superstar," agreed the medic, nodding. "That's not been an easy delivery. That's been a tough experience for all of you. Not what you'd planned for your afternoon?"

"Not exactly."

An hour later, Lori had been thoroughly examined and given a clean bill of health. She'd suffered a couple of minor tears, but nothing that wouldn't heal naturally. Once the midwife had checked her over and was satisfied that everything was alright, she had helped Lori to her feet and escorted her into the house to get cleaned up. In a motherly fashion, she assisted Lori to shower, washing away the remnants of the afterbirth and blood stained mucus, then helped her into some clean clothes. Her calm demeanour and casual chatter helped soothe Lori and, by the time she lay down on the bed, she felt calmer and more in control of her emotions.

"Were you planning to breastfeed or to give your little angel a bottle?" asked the midwife softly as she placed another pillow behind Lori's shoulders.

"Breastfeed," answered Lori quietly then confessed, "But I don't know how to."

"Let me fetch your little girl and we'll give it a go. Don't fret. I'll show you what to do and how to encourage her to latch on. It might take her a while, but let's see how she goes."

While the midwife had been attending to Lori and teaching her the basics of breastfeeding, the two male paramedics had helped Jake clear up the sun deck. Once the soiled mattress pad and towels have been disposed of, one of them subtly suggested to Jake that he might want to get cleaned up. Suddenly realising he was covered in dried blood and mucus, Jake had headed indoors for a shower. Not wanting to disturb Lori and the midwife, he'd darted into the bedroom to grab a change of clothes then retreated to the main bathroom to shower.

When he emerged, long hair dripping down the back of his white, cotton shirt, the medical team were preparing to leave. The midwife promised to return in the morning, but advised Jake, if they had any questions or concerns, to phone the maternity unit straight away. Nodding, Jake thanked them all then waved them goodbye as the ambulance pulled out of the driveway.

Quietly, he tiptoed down to the bedroom. When he entered the room, Lori was still propped up on the bed with their tiny daughter in her arms.

"Hi, li'l ladies," said Jake almost shyly.

"Hey, angel, it's daddy," whispered Lori with a tired smile.

Jake was relieved to see the pain and fear had faded from her eyes.

Climbing onto the bed, he lay down on his side beside them. Watching their baby daughter, he breathed, "She's perfect."

"She is, isn't she?" agreed Lori. "I can't believe she's here."

"You were amazing," praised Jake, his voice husky with emotion. "I've no idea how you coped back there. No idea how you've coped these past few weeks."

"Sh," interrupted Lori, reaching out to touch his arm. "You were the hero earlier. If you hadn't been here…what if I'd gone into labour like that and you'd been at JJL?"

"I don't even want to think about that," confessed Jake. "Wasn't quite the way we'd planned things, was it?"

"Not quite," admitted Lori with a little anxious giggle. "But all ends well. She's just perfect."

"She is," marvelled Jake, mesmerised by his baby daughter. "And, how are you? You ok?"

"Sore. Tired," confessed Lori, before adding, "I'll be fine. Just trying to get my head round how fast it all happened."

"Yeah," nodded Jake with a lazy grin. "So much for their estimated fourteen to sixteen hours! I don't think you lasted much more than one."

"Confession," said Lori, her cheeks flushing red. "The midwife gave me into trouble. Apparently, I read the signs wrong this morning. She said my back ache was most likely the early stages of labour. Mild contractions. She agreed it was still a dangerously quick delivery and a very fast active phase of labour."

"I'm just glad you're both ok."

"So, what are we going to call our little angel?" asked Lori, gazing down at their sleeping daughter. "Any ideas?

"I'm not sure," began Jake hesitantly.

"Melody," suggested Lori with a smile. "Melody Hyde Power."

"Melody?" echoed Jake softly. "I hadn't thought on that. Melody Hyde Power?"

Lori nodded.

"I like it," he said. "Melody Power."

Sitting up, he reached over and gently lifted the baby from her mother's arms and nestled her into the crook of his own arm. "Melody."

The baby opened her eyes briefly, then went back to sleep.

"You should get some sleep too," suggested Jake as he watched Lori yawn.

"I should. I'm beat. Will you be ok with her?"

"We'll be fine," assured Jake warmly. "You grab a nap and I'll take our baby girl on a tour of her house."

"Wake me if she cries," said Lori as she snuggled down on the bed. "She might still be hungry."

"Sleep, Lori," instructed Jake firmly. "We'll be fine together."

Closing the bedroom door over, Jake walked across the hallway to the nursery. Whispering softly to his daughter, he showed her where she would sleep when she was a little bigger, then carried her down the hallway into the kitchen, through to the dining room, pointing out the door to the basement and daddy's workspace, the lounge room and her mommy's workspace. Together, they wandered into the sunroom then back out onto the deck.

Outside it was still warm, the early evening sun just starting to glow red. Everything on the sun deck was back in its normal place. No sign of the dramas of a few hours earlier. The only sound now was the rhythmic thud of the waves crashing in and the occasional cry of a seabird.

Gazing out over the ocean, Jake smiled. As he looked down at the sleeping baby girl in her arms, all the trauma, all the pain, the fear, the nightmares from the past few months finally melted away. No matter how hard he had tried, Jake had still been terrified that in his drugged state he'd harmed the baby. Holding her now, those fears evaporated.

On a whim, Jake headed down the path onto the beach. The soft sand was still warm under his feet as he carried the baby towards the water's edge. He allowed the small waves to flood in over his bare feet and to soak the bottom of his jeans. Carefully, he loosened the blanket from around his little girl's tiny feet, marvelling again at the absolute perfection of them and at her tiny curled up toes. Bending down, he dipped his hand in the crystal, clear ocean water, then ran his wet hand over his daughter's feet.

"The ocean and the beach are in your soul," he whispered as he covered her up again. "Never forget that, Miss Melody."

He stood for a few minutes watching the sunset then slowly made his way back to the house, now a family home.

By July 4th, Rehoboth was in the grip of another heatwave, with the mercury levels having topped a hundred degrees for four days straight. News of the baby's swift arrival had spread through the extended Silver Lake family within hours of her birth, but Jake and Lori had politely asked everyone to give them a few days to recover. Only Maddy had ignored her friend's request, arriving on the Sunday afternoon to check for herself that Lori really was alright after her ordeal. She hadn't stayed long, just long enough to be sure the new mother was fine and coping. As he'd walked the band's manager back out to her car, Jake had promised that the BBQ was still on for 4th July as planned.

The new family had taken life slowly all week. At the midwife's insistence, Lori and Melody had gone out to Beebe on the Monday for a thorough check up. Both of them were given a clean bill of health by the post-natal team. As a precaution, Lori had called John Brent to explain what had happened. Understanding her concerns, he had promised that he would see her straight after she was done at the maternity unit. When Lori had walked into his office, using only one cane, the doctor had smiled, complimenting her on how well she looked, all things considered. He had arranged for a series of X-rays to be done and, having reviewed the images, assured Lori that both her pelvis and leg were fine. As she rose to leave his office, John suggested that next time she might want to plan a C-section. Laughing, Lori said, "Who says there will be a next time?"

There was little in the way of routine in the Power household by the end of the week as Lori focussed on getting used to feeding and caring for her baby daughter. Following the advice Maddy had given her, she napped when Melody slept. By Thursday, Jake had declared, "This schedule is crazier than being on tour!" Lori couldn't disagree.

After breakfast on Friday, Jake called through the house to her that he was heading into town for a couple of hours, saying he had to pick up some last minute supplies for the BBQ. Once in the truck, he headed straight into town for a pre-arranged appointment with Danny.

It was almost one before Jake returned to the house, feeling a little guilty at having been away longer than planned. His visit to the tattoo parlour had taken almost an hour longer than he had bargained for, then he had run out to the food store, remembering at the last minute that they needed some extra bags of ice.

As he carried the grocery sacks into the kitchen, Lori was standing at the counter, putting the finishing touches to a bowl of potato salad.

"Sorry, li'l lady," apologised Jake, dumping the bags on the floor. "I got held up."

"At Danny's?" she quizzed, noting the dressing on her husband's right forearm.

Jake nodded, "Let me get the ice and the beers in the cooler and I'll show you."

"You'd better hurry," cautioned Lori, sealing the bowl in front of her with saran wrap. "Maddy called to say they were on their way. They'll be here in a half hour."

"Where's Miss Melody?"

"Asleep in the lounge room in her stroller," said Lori, smiling. "I fed her a little while ago. We should be ok for a couple of hours at least."

"I'll go check on her," said Jake, desperate to see his daughter after being away from her all morning.

Smiling and shaking her head, Lori began to prepare them both a sandwich for lunch. Just as she set the plates down on the table, Jake came back through.

"Still sleeping," he announced with a proud smile. "I could watch her all day."

"Me too," confessed Lori, taking a seat. "Now, about this new ink, rock star?"

Carefully, Jake peeled back the tape to reveal the new design on his forearm. He had asked Danny to tattoo the Triskelion knot on the inside of his wrist. At the last minute, he'd changed the design of the knot in favour of a more intricate 3D one with more Celtic detailing. Above the knot, Jake had had two tiny footprints inked.

"How did you....?" began Lori, immediately realising that the footprints were an imprint of Melody's tiny feet.

"I sent Dan a few photos to work from," confessed Jake. "Then took a photo of the imprints the hospital took. Like it?"

"It's perfect," said Lori with a smile. "Love it."

By mid-afternoon, the entire Silver Lake family were gathered at the beach house. The large umbrella had been erected over the sun deck, providing at least some shade from the intense sun. From the deck, Lori could hear Rich and Paul playing with Becky and the twins down on the sand. Over at the grill, Jake had lit the coals and, with Grey's help, was preparing to cook the first batch of food. The girls were all gathered under the shade of the umbrella with Melody snuggled into Lori's shoulder.

"So, who guessed the correct date and weight?" asked Linsey. "I can't remember who guessed what."

"Kola was closest," revealed Maddy, after checking her notebook. "The only thing she missed was the name."

The shy sound engineer blushed slightly, then confessed, "I knew the name but didn't want to jinx things. It's a knack I've inherited from my grandmother. A Native American trait. She's a Hopi shaman."

"Wow!" gasped Maddy, eyes wide. "I never knew. Is this your mom's mom?"

"No, my dad's," revealed Kola quietly. "He was always embarrassed by his Hopi heritage. I'm fascinated by it."

Their conversation was interrupted by the arrival of Scott, along with Ellen and, at their back, Todd appeared hand in hand with Kate. At Jake's request and with Lori's consent, Scott had brought his camera bag with him.

While he set up his gear, Lori excused herself and headed indoors to feed and change her daughter before her first photo shoot. She knew she'd been lucky. The baby had taken to breast feeding easily. Lori, on the other hand, was struggling a little with the demands of it, but was determined to persevere for at least the first six weeks.

With the baby fed and dressed in a little white, cotton sundress, Lori re-joined the party. Leaving their guests to chat quietly, Jake, Lori and Melody posed for some family shots for Scot indoors then again outside. The star of the show slept through it. Having taken some shots of mother and daughter, Scott asked Jake to pose for him.

"Take your shirt off for me," requested the photographer. "I want a few skin contact shots."

In Jake's strong, bare, tattooed arms, the baby girl looked tiny. While the photographer was still at work, Melody opened her eyes, allowing him to capture some beautiful shots of her awake. There was just time for a few photos with the others before the baby's patience wore out and she began to wail. Expertly, Jake scooped her out of Kola's arms, settling her on his shoulder as he whispered soothingly to her. She whimpered for a few moments, then settled back down to sleep.

"Lori, will I put her in the stroller?" suggested Jake. The stroller sat on the deck in the corner under the shade of its own parasol and the giant umbrella.

"Yes," agreed Lori from her seat on the bench between Maddy and Ellen. "Let her nap in peace while we eat. Is the food nearly ready?"

"Almost," called over Grey from his position at the grill.

There followed the usual frenzy of activity as they all gathered round the table, fixing themselves plates of food. Everyone had mucked in to help with the BBQ by bringing along a salad or a dessert. No one stood on ceremony. No egos. The wine and beer flowed as freely as their conversation.

"It's a far cry from the first BBQ we had out here," commented Paul, gazing round. "We've grown in numbers somewhat!"

"We've come a long way too," added Grey, reflecting on the past couple of years. "Been through a lot together."

A subdued hush fell over the party as each of them thought back on the highs and lows that the band had been through. Before the mood grew too sombre, Grey cleared his throat and said, "I guess now is as good a time as any to make an announcement."

All eyes were on him as he laid his hand on Kola's thigh.

"This beautiful girl has agreed to be my wife," said the bass player with a proud smile. "We're getting married!"

"Congratulations!" declared Jake, delighted to see his friend looking so happy.

"Oh, another wedding to look forward to!" squealed Maddy excitedly. "Congratulations!"

"Thank you," said Grey with a glance over at his fiancée. "We're still working on the wedding plans. No sense in rushing these things."

"It'll be perfect whenever you decide to tie the knot," said Lori, remembering her own wedding day fondly. "Congratulations to you both."

As the sun began to sink lower in the sky, Lori found herself needing a moment alone. So much had happened over the past week that she hadn't had much time to herself. Discretely, she checked that the baby was still sleeping, then wandered down the path to the beach. She'd left her cane lying in the house so she took extra care as she made her way across the soft sand, still feeling a little unsteady on her feet. The damp, hard packed sand felt cold under her feet as she stood gazing out across the ocean. Scanning the waves, watching for dolphins, she breathed deeply, feeling her body relax a little. With each deep breath, the tension melted a little more from her shoulders. A rogue wave washed in further than the others, sending a flood of foaming water over her bare feet. As she allowed the water to swirl around her, Lori reflected on how she had felt when she'd first returned to the beach house after her accident.

She recalled standing a few hundred yards further along looking out at the ocean on the day that she'd met Jake. Memories of their early dates, of Jake moving in, of his proposal at the high school Christmas social, of the lows of the car wreck to the highs of their wedding, of the trauma of the whole incident with Salazar to the dramas of Melody's arrival into the world. All of it swam through her mind.

"Penny for them, li'l lady," said Jake softly as he appeared at her shoulder with Melody in his arms.

"Hi," whispered Lori with a wistful smile. "I just needed a minute. I was thinking back to the day I met you. Thinking about everything we've been through. All the highs. All the lows."

"More highs than lows, I hope," said Jake warmly. "It's been some journey so far."

Glancing down at their baby daughter, he added, "But one that's just beginning a new chapter."

Lovingly, Jake put his arm around Lori, pulling her into his embrace. With their daughter between them, Jake kissed Lori slowly and tenderly. He breathed in the familiar scent of her perfume and sighed, "I love you, li'l lady."

"Love you too, rock star," she purred contentedly.

"What was it Paul said at our wedding?" asked Jake, kissing her on the forehead.

"Now you are two persons, but there is only one life before you."

"Bonded Souls," said Jake, kissing her again. "Let's go home, li'l lady. We've family waiting."

To be continued......

Also by Coral McCallum

Stronger Within
Impossible Depths

Coral McCallum lives in Gourock, a small town on the West coast of Scotland with her husband, two teenage children and her beloved cats.

https://coralmccallum.wordpress.com

https://www.facebook.com/pages/Coral-McCallum

https://twitter.com/CoralMcCallum

12593314R00300

Printed in Great Britain
by Amazon